W9-CLA-426

"For a long time the DeVoto *Portable* was the handiest single-volume collection for the general reader. This one is even better. It's an indispensable anthology of America's indispensable author."
—Justin Kaplan

"If this isn't the thoughtfulest and usefulest hand-tooled gilt-edged one-volume Twain, I am a horned toad."
—Frederick Crews

"Bernard DeVoto would have agreed loudest of all that it's time to redo *The Portable Mark Twain*, time for a fresh look at basic materials and for building in new materials that have turned up since 1946. Though a tough judge of literary critics, he would also have agreed, I feel, that Tom Quirk was the best choice to put state-of-the art wheels, styling, and accessories on this pacesetter for Mark Twain anthologies."
—Louis J. Budd, James B. Duke Professor of English (Emeritus), Duke University, author of *Our Mark Twain*

"Mark Twain is back amongst us (and not a moment too soon), trailing rainbows and thunderbolts of the American language that he invented, mostly. His escort and great good friend on this visit, Tom Quirk, offers an introduction that reminds us why Twain will never not be necessary to a true understanding of our country. And Mark takes it—and us—from there."
—Ron Powers, author of *Dangerous Water: A Biography of the Boy Who Became Mark Twain*

"Trying to put your arms around Mark Twain is like trying to embrace the Mississippi. He is endless. This *Portable*, however, should open his richness to the new reader and remind the older ones of the wealth they may have forgotten. Reading him again is like biting into fresh bread."
—Arthur Miller

PENGUIN CLASSICS

THE PORTABLE MARK TWAIN

SAMUEL LANGHORNE CLEMENS was born on November 30, 1835, in Florida, Missouri, about forty miles southwest of Hannibal, the Mississippi River town Clemens was to celebrate as Mark Twain. He left home in 1853, earning a living as an itinerant typesetter, and four years later became an apprentice pilot on the Mississippi, a career cut short by the outbreak of the Civil War. For five years, as a prospector and a journalist, Clemens lived in Nevada and California. In February, 1863, he first used the pseudonym "Mark Twain" as the signature to a humorous travel letter; and a trip to Europe and the Holy Land in 1867 became the basis of his first major book, *The Innocents Abroad* (1869). *Roughing It* (1872), his account of experiences in the West, was followed by a satirical novel, *The Gilded Age* (1873), *Tom Sawyer* (1876), *A Tramp Abroad* (1880), *Life on the Mississippi* (1883), and his masterpiece, *Adventures of Huckleberry Finn* (1885). Following the publication of *A Connecticut Yankee in King Arthur's Court* (1889) and *Pudd'nhead Wilson* (1894), Twain was compelled by debts to move his family abroad. By 1900 he had completed a round-the-world lecture tour, and, his fortunes mended, he returned to America. He was as celebrated for his white suit and his mane of white hair as he was for his uncompromising stands against injustice and imperialism and for his invariably quoted comments on any subject under the sun. Samuel Clemens died on April 21, 1910.

TOM QUIRK is professor of English at the University of Missouri–Columbia. He is the editor of the Penguin Classics editions of Mark Twain's *Tales, Speeches, Essays, and Sketches* (1994) and *The Innocents Abroad* (2002), and Ambrose Bierce's *Tales of Soldiers and Civilians and Other Stories* (2000), and coeditor of *The Portable American Realism Reader* (1997). His books include *Coming to Grips with Huckleberry Finn* (1993), *Mark Twain: A Study of the Short Fiction* (1997), and *Nothing Abstract: Investigations in the American Literary Imagination* (2001).

The Portable Mark Twain

Edited with an Introduction by
TOM QUIRK

PENGUIN BOOKS

PENGUIN BOOKS
Published by the Penguin Group
Penguin Group (USA) Inc., 375 Hudson Street, New York, New York 10014, U.S.A.
Penguin Group (Canada), 10 Alcorn Avenue, Toronto,
Ontario, Canada M4V 3B2 (a division of Pearson Penguin Canada Inc.)
Penguin Books Ltd, 80 Strand, London WC2R 0RL, England
Penguin Ireland, 25 St Stephen's Green, Dublin 2, Ireland (a division of Penguin Books Ltd)
Penguin Group (Australia), 250 Camberwell Road, Camberwell,
Victoria 3124, Australia (a division of Pearson Australia Group Pty Ltd)
Penguin Books India Pvt Ltd, 11 Community Centre, Panchsheel Park, New Delhi – 110 017, India
Penguin Group (NZ), cnr Airborne and Rosedale Roads, Albany,
Auckland 1310, New Zealand (a division of Pearson New Zealand Ltd)
Penguin Books (South Africa) (Pty) Ltd, 24 Sturdee Avenue, Rosebank, Johannesburg 2196, South Africa

Penguin Books Ltd, Registered Offices:
80 Strand, London WC2R 0RL, England

This edition first published in Penguin Books 2004

1 3 5 7 9 10 8 6 4 2

Copyright © Penguin Group (USA) Inc., 2004
All rights reserved

Grateful acknowledgment is made for permission to reprint "Corn-Pone Opinions" from *Europe and Elsewhere* by Mark Twain, edited by Albert Bigelow Paine. Copyright 1923 by Mark Twain Company, renewed 1951 by Mark Twain Company. Reprinted by permission of HarperCollins Publishers Inc.

LIBRARY OF CONGRESS CATALOGING IN PUBLICATION DATA
Twain, Mark, 1835–1910.
The portable Mark Twain / edited with an introduction by Tom Quirk.
p. cm.
Includes bibliographical references (p.).
ISBN 0-14-243775-1
1. Humorous stories, American. 2. Twain, Mark, 1835–1910—Correspondence.
3. Authors, American—19th century—Correspondence. I. Quirk, Tom, 1946– II. Title.
PS1302.Q56 2004
818'.409—dc22 2004057341

Printed in the United States of America
Set in Sabon

Except in the United States of America, this book is sold subject to the condition that it shall not, by way of trade or otherwise, be lent, resold, hired out, or otherwise circulated without the publisher's prior consent in any form of binding or cover other than that in which it is published and without a similar condition including this condition being imposed on the subsequent purchaser.

The scanning, uploading, and distribution of this book via the Internet or via any other means without the permission of the publisher is illegal and punishable by law. Please purchase only authorized electronic editions, and do not participate in or encourage electronic piracy of copyrighted materials. Your support of the author's rights is appreciated.

Contents

Introduction

I

During his last decade, Samuel Clemens was writing, or rather dictating, his "Autobiography." It was a work that only death could complete and would be published, if at all, long after he was gone. Clemens embraced the premise, for it meant that he might speak, so he liked to believe, without reserve or constraint; speak with the bluntness only a dead man might enjoy. In casual yet systematic fashion, he committed himself to narrating his life according to whim and random recollection. The publication in 1906 of a bastardized version of his earlier anthology, *Mark Twain's Library of Humor* (1888), at once incited his fury and provoked a certain introspection and became a subject for one morning's dictation. Perusing the contents, "Mark Twain" reflected in his "Autobiography" on the fate of nineteenth-century humorists. For the forty years "wherein I have been playing professional humorist before the public," he observed, a host of literary comedians have come and gone. "Why have they perished? Because they were merely humorists. Humorists of the 'mere' sort cannot survive. Humor is only a fragrance, a decoration." And *Why* (he implicitly asks) *have I lasted?* Because (he implicitly answers) *I am a moralist, and they were not.* "Humor must not professedly teach and it must not professedly preach," he continued, "but it must do both if it would last forever. By forever, I mean thirty years. With all its preaching it is not likely to outlive so long a term as that."

Already, Twain is indulging in fuzzy math. The fame of the mere humorist is extinguished in a few years, but even the humorous moralist cannot expect more than thirty years. However, Twain himself has just observed that he has been a professional humorist for forty years, a full decade beyond "forever." But he is not through with his calculations:

> I have always preached. That is the reason that I have lasted thirty years. If the humor came of its own accord and uninvited I have allowed it a place in my sermon, but I was not writing the sermon for the sake of the humor. I should have written the sermon just the same, whether any humor applied for admission or not. I am saying these vain things in this frank way because I am a dead person speaking from the grave. Even I would be too modest to say them in life. I think we never become really and genuinely our entire and honest selves until we are dead—and not then until we have been dead years and years. People ought to start dead and then they would be honest so much earlier.

In order to be absolutely honest with his readers, Clemens imagines speaking from beyond the grave, bound by neither time nor occasion. The presupposition, of course, is that he is being beforehand with a world not yet born, and he adopts the position of a ghost in the narrative machine of his own making. But behind the undertaking there is also the presumption that Mark Twain will be of continuing interest for generations to come, far longer than the thirty (or perhaps forty) years allotted to him or any other humorist. And, his protestations notwithstanding, Twain remains a humorist to the last. The mysteriously complicated, even irreconcilable, carbon dating of his lasting fame is finally a sly prologue to the punch line—"People ought to start dead."

The vaunted boast of this self-assessment (at once retrospective and predictive) is in stark contrast to the confession he made to his brother Orion, in an 1865 letter: "I have had a 'call' to literature, of a low order—i.e., humorous. It is nothing to be proud of, but it is my strongest suit, & if I were to listen to that maxim of stern duty which says that to do right you must multiply the one or the two or the three talents which the Almighty trusts to our keeping, I would long ago have ceased to meddle with the things for which I was by nature unfitted &

turned my attention to seriously scribbling to excite the laughter of God's creatures. Poor, pitiful business!" When he made this declaration, Clemens was thirty years old, high time for a man to have settled into an occupation, however lowly. It is true that he had turned his hand to other work from an early age. It is probably true that he would have been content to have remained a riverboat pilot, had not the Civil War effectively ended that career; at least he made that claim more than once. It is unfortunately true as well that he did not cease to meddle in things beyond his peculiar ken—as entrepreneur and businessman, publisher and self-appointed philosopher, inventor and investor—and much of this meddling cost him hard coin and caused him grief.

In any event, these two statements, made approximately forty years apart, will serve well enough to bracket the career of Mark Twain. Those same four decades provide a vast reservoir of writings from which to gather up representative features of Twain's art and genius—secular sermons and tall tales; vicious wisecracks and tender comedy; testaments of political outrage and deep compassion; antic, and sometimes merely silly, comic indulgence. *The Portable Mark Twain* means to give as complete a picture as possible of Twain's art and comedy. But the complete corpus of Twain's prodigious output is anything but "portable." When one lumps together, in addition to the writings published in his lifetime, the approximately 12,000 extant letters, the voluminous notebooks, the speeches, the unpublished and (in his mind) unpublishable writings, the unfinished manuscripts, not to mention the "Autobiography" itself, some 2,500 pages in typescript, one is tempted to conclude something that is manifestly untrue: Here was a man who had no life apart from writing. But, in fact, for good or ill, he gave over a great deal of time to his business concerns, to his friends and family, to his search for one sort of health cure or another, to his cockamamie schemes for world betterment and personal profit (ranging from food additives to an ingenious bed clamp to keep the baby's covers on), and to his vast and diverse reading. Add to this the hundreds of thousands of hours of talk, acres and acres of the stuff—spontaneous after-dinner monologues, hundreds of newspaper interviews, peripatetic chatter with comrades, or improvised bedtime stories for the children—and one soon enough recognizes that Twain's writings formed only a part, and perhaps not the best part, of the man.

Still, as a matter of simple "coverage" of his written work, this anthology casts a wide enough net to catch the flavor and inexhaustible variety of the man at nearly every stage of his life. At the very least, his salient qualities are here. Those qualities are several, and all their possible combinations make them virtually unnumbered. William Dean Howells, in a review of *Mark Twain's Sketches, New and Old* (1875), named the characteristic traits of the humorist. Twain is a master of "burlesque," though, Howells adds, in its special tendency to double back on itself, his travesty acquires a novel subtlety and suppleness. He has a "fine, forecasting humor," by which I think Howells meant that the author has an ambulatory style that, on the promise of some joke as yet unspotted, engenders in his readers an eager willingness to follow wherever he might lead. Twain is finely "American" in his boisterous "extravagance of statement"; he is reassuringly trustworthy and amiable in his "incorruptible right-mindedness"; and his delightful "dryness," his apparent oblivion to his own comedy, permits readers, under the spell of his crafty art, to feel smarter than perhaps they should.

More important than all these, Howells detected a "growing seriousness of meaning in the apparently unmoralized drolling." In California, Twain had sometimes been called the "Moralist of the Main," and several of his journalistic pieces left his indignant seriousness in little doubt. However, Eastern readers knew Twain as the literary comedian and not much more. Howells was doing the humorist a service in pointing out this other dimension of the man. In fact, Howells singled out "A True Story" as much the best piece in the collection and a sketch generally misunderstood by critics who, expecting a joke and not wanting to be left out, altogether missed the "rugged truth" of this moving story of slave life. This is a reasonably complete list of Twain's gifts, and I would add only Louis J. Budd's identification of a "quintessentially Twainian quality"—"an emotional-intellectual drive, an integrative, pleasure-sharing ability to soar above or outside of commonly accepted experience." That flight from ordinary experience at times may have been mere escape from trials and tribulations, but as often, as Budd observes, it provided the author a special pleasure that one might justifiably call "ecstasy."

For several decades, it has been fashionable to think of Clemens as having been cooped up and hemmed in (whether he was restrained by the inheritance of a Calvinist conscience, the pressures of a pervasive Victorian gentility, or some perverse inner check hardly matters). He sometimes complained that the world at large valued him only as a funny man, incapable of deep conviction and firm principle, but that may or may not mean he was disposed to be secretly subversive of the prevailing order. Of course Twain himself invites such psychoanalytical second-guessing when he confesses to his frustration with the occupation of humorist, as he did, for example, in an 1875 letter to Howells, by complaining his customary audience required him to "paint himself stripèd and stand on his head every fifteen minutes." When Clemens first adopted the pen name "Mark Twain" in 1863, he likely felt some liberation in the persona. Mark Twain appears in a variety of guises (as the tenderfoot, the dandy, the muggins, and so forth) but always in ways that are far less complicated than was the author himself. Still, in disguise, Clemens could speak more forthrightly than he might in his own person. Eventually, however, he began to complain that the public had not got him "focused" right and thought of him as perpetually jolly and decidedly unserious. Humor was his bread and butter, but often it was a bitter portion to swallow. This dilemma must have eventually contributed something to the deterministic philosophy he adopted in later years.

Twain's late philosophic meditations, expressed in "Corn-Pone Opinions" (1901), *What Is Man?* (1906), and elsewhere, merely added quasi-intellectual support to a long-standing conviction that conduct and thought are imposed from without. The average man or woman desires above all else, he argued, a sense of self-approval that can only be had by gaining the approval of others. Similarly, the approval of the public required Twain to perform antics of one sort or another that, in their turn, became a humiliation to himself and his family. Small wonder that he should complain that truthful and frank expression is all but impossible. Still, it is at least thinkable that the author's levity stemmed not simply from a desire to please or to be evasive or to subvert, but because he couldn't help himself. Perhaps he was addicted to the ecstatic privilege that such flights above and beyond earth-bound decorum and right thinking might afford.

What is more certain, at any rate, is that he was good at it. At a dinner honoring Andrew Carnegie in 1907, for example, Twain gave a speech and found his comic opportunity in Carnegie's promotion of simplified spelling. "He's got us all so we can't spell anything," Twain fumes. Any rational reformer would address the root of the problem—the alphabet:

> There's not a vowel in it with a definite value, and not a consonant that you can hitch anything to. Look at the "h's" distributed all around. There's "gherkin." What are you going to do with the "h" in gherkin, I'd like to know. . . . Why, there isn't a man who doesn't have to throw out about fifteen hundred words a day when he writes his letters because he can't spell them! It's like trying to do a St. Vitus's dance with wooden legs. . . .
>
> It's a rotten alphabet. I appoint Mr. Carnegie to get after it, and leave simplified spelling alone. Simplified spelling brought about sunspots, the San Francisco earthquake, and the recent business depression, which we would never have had if spelling had been left all alone. . . . Simplified spelling is all right, but, like chastity, you can carry it too far.

Who, in the history of humankind, ever *tried* to do a St. Vitus's dance? And did the person who put the "h" in "gherkin" do it as a prank, or was it an act of malice prepense, purposely designed to bring about sunspots? And now that the problem has at last been properly diagnosed, who else but Mark Twain would have the nerve to sic the great Andrew Carnegie on it?

II

Early and late, Twain was capable of such antic comedy. As often as not, it supports rather than contests prevailing moral opinion. In a speech called "Advice to Youth" (1882) Twain advises young boys and girls not to "meddle with old unloaded firearms; they are the most deadly and unerring things that have ever been created." He continues: "You don't have to take aim even. No, you just pick out a relative and bang away, and you are sure to get him. A youth who can't hit a cathedral at thirty yards with a Gatling gun in three-quarters of an hour, can take up an old empty musket and bag his mother every time, at a hundred." Here, Twain is having it both ways. He is outrageous in expression. How did the youth come by a Gatling gun and why on earth does he want to fire on a cathedral? But he is very conventional in his outlook. After all, what could be more agreeable and proper to his Victorian audience than to warn children away from guns? Twain has at once satisfied his audience that he is the master humorist of the age and bolstered his image as a moral sage, but one free of any familiar finger-wagging or fustian rhetoric.

The material for humor seemed to be constantly available to him. There is of course the comedy of situation. His notebook germ for *A Connecticut Yankee in King Arthur's Court* (1889) is an inventory of comic possibilities:

> Dream of being a knight errant in armor in the Middle Ages. Have the notions and habits of thought of the present day mixed with the necessities of that. No pockets in the armor. No way to manage certain requirements of nature. Can't scratch. Cold in the head—can't blow—can't get at handkerchief, can't use iron sleeve. Iron gets red hot in the sun—leaks in the rain, gets white with frost & freezes me solid in winter. Suffer from lice & fleas. Make disagreeable clatter when I enter a church. Can't dress or

> undress myself. Always getting struck by lightning. Fall down and can't get up.

The humorous situation was only one of many weapons in his comic arsenal.

There was also the comedy of animals—of moulting cows, asthmatic horses, insomniac clams, and swearing blue jays. There was the comedy of customs—of burials (of the stalwart Buck Fanshaw or the unlucky William Wheeler, who got nipped by the machinery of a carpet factory and had to be buried "just so"); and of sentimental grief (expressed in the morbidly bad poetry of Emmeline Grangerford, alas). There was the comedy of vegetables (of Simon Erickson's fanatic desire to grow turnips as a vine or Pudd'nhead Wilson's acute adage: "Training is everything. The peach was once a bitter almond; cauliflower is nothing but cabbage with a college education."). There was comedy in holidays and hospitality, in sacred places and in slang; there was comedy in apprenticeship and penmanship, in clothes, furniture, and scripture, in undertakers and editors. Amazingly, with such imaginative power at his disposal, Twain never really pressed his advantage. He did not condescend to his created characters, no matter how mean their condition or amusing their idiom. Nearly always, Twain refused to play the humorist as bully; he preferred to pick on someone or something his own size or at times much bigger. Two notable exceptions are to be found in his treatment of the particularly vulnerable states of Arkansas and New Jersey, however.

As a purely chronological matter, this collection includes diverse specimens of his writing, beginning in 1865 with the publication of the famous jumping frog story and continuing throughout his writing career to his last years. And if *The Portable Mark Twain* does not exhaustively survey the author's professional life, it at least touches upon nearly every important phase of it. In a letter to an unidentified correspondent, Twain confessed that he confined himself in his writings to "familiar" experience. That experience was diverse, he reported, and included stints as jour printer, pilot, soldier, prospector, journalist, publisher, lecturer, and the like. The inventory ends with this revealing disclosure: "I have been an author for 20 years and an ass for 55." Ass or no, Clemens nevertheless dramatized his recollected experience with an exquisite attention to detail and mood. There are in "Early Days" (1907) delicious memories of the time spent on his uncle John Quarles's farm close to his birthplace in Florida, Missouri. In "Old Times on the Mississippi" (1875) Clemens vividly recalls his childhood ambitions in Hannibal and his awkward apprenticeship under the seasoned riverboat pilot, Horace Bixby. There are comic pictures of "the boys" in Nevada Territory, of Twain himself tearfully grieving at the tomb of Adam or puzzling over the vast canvasses of the Old Masters. There are the biting satires of colonial endeavor and the decimation of native populations, and the almost but not quite reverential description of the Sea of Galilee seen by starlight.

In matters of geography, too, this volume is reasonably comprehensive. The great Mississippi River valley receives the greatest space, and this is as it should be, if for no other reason than it is the setting of his masterpiece, *Adventures of Huckleberry Finn.* There are also specimens from his actual travels in the Holy Land and in Germany and Italy and his round-the-world tour made in 1895–96, as well as the wholly fantastic journeys to Camelot and the Garden of Eden (magically transported to Niagara Falls). Twain had Pudd'nhead Wilson say in one of his maxims, I have "traveled more than any one else and I have noticed that even the angels speak English with an accent." This is arrant nonsense, of course. If David Wilson, attorney at law, a.k.a. the "pudd'nhead," had had a lick of sense or an ounce of self-respect, he would have left Dawson's Landing instantly. Instead, he perversely lingered most of his life fashioning maxims for his "Calendar," collecting fingerprints, and living among people who had decided from the moment he stepped off the boat that he was a "lummox," a "labrick" and many other unflattering things.

Twain, on the other hand, had indeed traveled more than most people, enough to know that, the effects of British colonialism notwithstanding, the English language and the Anglo-

Saxon point of view were not the only games being played in the world. In fact, by the end, Clemens had circumnavigated the globe and gone nearly everywhere except the place he set out for in 1857, the Amazon. But he got diverted into riverboating and did not look back. Twain later transferred the childhood ambition to get to South America to Huckleberry Finn, but Huck never made it either.

Twain (and Clemens, too, for that matter) had also traveled up and down the social ladder in remarkable ways. In his San Francisco days, it was oysters and champagne one day, unemployment and despair the next. In the mid-1880s he owned his own publishing house that had just published the monumentally successful memoirs of Ulysses S. Grant, and he had high hopes for his investments; ten years later he was trying to find his way out of debt. These swings in personal fortune probably made him that much more alert to thwarted ambition and to matters of class distinction and the spurious lines that divide human creatures from one another. Clemens knew firsthand the profligacy of ambition and the meagerness of destiny, but in this, as in most matters, he was on both sides of the question. He could have Pudd'nhead Wilson sardonically remark, "There isn't a Parallel of Latitude but thinks it would have been the Equator if it had had its rights." Yet in "Extract from Captain Stormfield's Visit to Heaven" (1909) he could picture true "heavenly justice"; the hereafter was a place where one was judged and rewarded according to an inward greatness that, on earth, often never had the opportunity to develop.

As a rule, Twain recognized the markers of supposed merit for what they are, patent absurdities. In his day they might be pretentious titles, epaulets, or bad French; in our own they might be stretch limos, buns of steel, or bad French. He typically satirized such inequity and pretense with an eager glee. In *The Innocents Abroad* (1869), for example, Twain meets the Czar of Russia and marvels at the terrible yet whimsical authority he wields: "If I could have, I would have stolen his coat. When I meet a man like that, I want something to remember him by." However, the author himself was not exempt from like affectation. Clemens had a love/hate relation with the

English and more than once satirized their aristocratic ways. Nevertheless, he sometimes strutted around in the scarlet robes he had worn when he received an honorary degree from Oxford—there was no other red that could compare with it, he thought, "outside the arteries of an archangel." He once bragged, "An Oxford decoration is a loftier distinction than is conferrable by any other university on either side of the ocean." And, in the persona of Mark Twain, Clemens could become the ultimate name-dropper. He recounts in *Following the Equator* (1897) a visit by a Mohammedan "god." A direct descendant of the Prophet and worshipped accordingly, this walking deity wants to discuss the "philosophy of Huck Finn." Twain's reaction is predictable: "It would be false modesty to pretend that I was not inordinately pleased. I was. I was much more pleased than I should have been with a compliment from a man."

These sorts of encounters between social unequals can make for great comedy, and Twain applied the attendant mechanisms of social adjustment (envy and flattery, obsequiousness and exasperation, indifference and condescension) in a variety of ways and to diverse effects. "The Celebrated Jumping Frog of Calaveras County" (1865) begins with a letter addressed to Artemus Ward. Twain, in this instance cast in the role of a dandified gentleman, expresses his "lurking suspicion" that he has been set up. In urging him to search for the edifying company of Rev. Leonidas W. Smiley, Ward has deliberately thrown Twain in the way of Simon Wheeler and a reminiscence of the notorious Jim Smiley. What follows, of course, is a rambling and hilarious narrative about a "fifteen minute nag," a bull pup named "Andrew Jackson," and the precocious jumping frog "Dan'l Webster." If Twain had been less impatient with Wheeler, we might have heard the tale of a "yaller one-eyed cow" as well, but he storms off in a huff and his readers necessarily must follow. In "An Encounter with an Interviewer" (1874), a "peart" young reporter from the *Daily Thunderstorm* seeks an interview with the estimable Mr. Twain. The persona here is simpleminded and afflicted with an "irregular" memory, and Twain leads the interviewer on a wild goose chase for even the most basic information. The young man—having learned that Twain is 180 years old, attended Aaron Burr's funeral, and many other curious things—leaves exasperated and befuddled. Twain regrets the departure: "He was pleasant company, and I was sorry to see him go."

In "The Story of the Old Ram" (1872) Twain the tenderfoot is tricked by "the boys" into mouth-watering anticipation to hear Jim Blaine's inebriated tale. The storyteller meanders about, getting further and further from the announced subject, and it is not until the raconteur falls asleep mid-sentence that Twain perceives that he has been "sold." There are many other instances of unlikely pairings of character—those emissaries from the "grand divisions of society" in Virginia City, Nevada, Scotty Briggs and the Parson; or Twain the self-satisfied and ignorant substitute editor for an agricultural journal (who advises among other things that "clams will lie quiet if music be played to them") and the outraged editor who rebukes him; or Hank Morgan, the practical, hardheaded, nineteenth-century Yankee, and Sandy, the good-hearted, innocent, sixth-century jabberer.

Some of Twain's encounters were not humorous, however, nor were they intended to be. In "A True Story, Repeated Word for Word as I Heard It" (1874) the former slave and now a servant, Aunt Rachel, literally and figuratively towers above the author, clearly his moral superior. For once, Clemens did not hide behind the camouflage of an adopted persona but is known simply as "Misto C—" and as such bears the full weight of an unwanted recognition: namely, that his judgment of Aunt Rachel's character borders on criminal stupidity and callousness. Similarly, in one of the most affecting episodes in *Huckleberry Finn,* after playing yet another joke on Jim, Huck receives such a tongue lashing from the fugitive slave that he mulls over his deserved upbraiding and finally "humbles" himself to a black man. "The Private History of a Campaign That Failed" (1885) was published in the company of other Civil War memoirs in the *Century* magazine. Clemens had spent a very brief time in the pro-Confederate Marion Rangers before removing to the Nevada Territory, and he freely admits that perhaps he "ought not be allowed much space among better people." For the most part his description of the campaign is pure burlesque at the author's expense, but a sudden revulsion of moral feelings brought about by the shooting of an innocent man decides him on quitting the business of war "while I could save some remnant of my self-respect." It is almost a certainty that this killing was pure fabrication, introduced to provide the author with a moral dilemma he might respond to with the sort of sensitivity he had attributed to Huckleberry Finn, whose narrative he had completed only a few months before writing this memoir. Clemens is extenuating his conduct during the war, but he is also expressing a value. The ultimate worth and dignity of a man or woman cut across class lines and unmistakably declare themselves, if only by appealing to one's moral sympathies and wounded sense of justice.

III

Despite the orthodox language of Clemens's confession to his brother that he was answering to the inner promptings of the Lord's will in becoming a humorist, it is more likely that he was following the path of least resistance. Comedy came naturally to him. It was apparently irresistible and, for the most part, something more than mere "fragrance" or "decoration." Far from doing God's work, at least as early as 1865 and probably before, he seemed motivated to offer up the comforts of laughter as relief from a world that, depending on his mood, he had decided was an annoyance, a trial, an affliction, or a tragedy; a world that, if it could not be redeemed, might at least be made more tolerable. At any rate, in the same letter to Orion he confided a less than reverential regard for the workings of providence: "I have a religion—but you will call it blasphemy. It is that there is a God for the rich man but none for the poor."

The poor was not his cause, but it was, from time to time, his affiliation. There was not much young Clemens inherited from his father that he could not disavow or outgrow, but he did seem to be permanently affected by the idea that prosperity was just around the corner. In the 1820s, John Marshall

Clemens had purchased at least 70,000 acres in Tennessee, and he held fast to the conviction that it would one day make the family rich. It didn't. To the contrary, it engendered in the children false hopes. As Clemens recalled late in life, "It put our energies to sleep and made visionaries of us—dreamers and indolent. . . . It is good to begin life poor; it is good to begin life rich—these are wholesome; but to begin it prospectively rich! The man who has not experienced it cannot imagine the curse of it."

It was a curse that Sam Clemens could never quite shake. No doubt that prospective fortune grew in proportion to the degree the family felt the pinch of necessity. John Clemens died in 1847, but even before that his debts had mounted; the family auctioned off property, sold their furniture, and took in boarders. Young Sam Clemens never experienced the penury of Tom Blankenship (the impoverished and neglected Hannibal boy who apparently served as the model for Huck Finn), but at times he must have felt something of a child of misfortune himself. Still, the visionary in him persisted throughout his life, as even only a few items from the large inventory of his enthusiasms will attest. In the Nevada Territory in the 1860s, Clemens thought he would strike it rich by trading in mining stocks. He didn't. As the owner of his own publishing house, he enthusiastically believed every Catholic family in the world would purchase the authorized biography *Life of Pope Leo XIII* (1887). They didn't. He was right to believe that an automatic typesetter would make a fortune; he was wrong to believe the inventor James W. Paige, an inveterate tinkerer and perfectionist, would ever produce a commercially viable product. He was wrong, too, in investing around a quarter of a million dollars in the project and as a consequence leaving his own publishing concern undercapitalized. In 1894, Clemens entered into voluntary bankruptcy; by 1898, largely through the success of his around-the-world lecture tour, he was able to repay his debts in full. One would think Clemens might have learned the wisdom of Pudd'nhead Wilson's maxim published in *Following the Equator:* "There are two times in a man's life when he should not speculate: when he can't afford it and when he can." However, in 1900 Clemens began investing in a food supplement called Plasmon and eventually lost around $50,000.

These are merely instances, but they indicate, in Clemens, a tendency that was abroad in the land. Get-rich-quick schemes, grand aspirations, exploitation, and corporate and government corruption abounded after the Civil War. Twain dramatized the passion for instant wealth in such tales as "The Facts in the Case of the Great Beef Contract" (1870), "The £1,000,000 Bank Note" (1893), "The Man That Corrupted Hadleyburg" (1899), and "The $30,000 Bequest" (1904). Twain and Charles Dudley Warner wrote a novel naming the era *The Gilded Age* (1873), but the literary historian Vernon Parrington might have come closer to the spirit of the times when he called it "The Great Barbecue": "A huge barbecue was spread to which all presumably were invited. Not quite all, to be sure; inconspicuous persons, those who were at home on the farm or at work in the mills and offices, were overlooked; a good many indeed out of the total number of the American people. But all the important persons, leading bankers and promoters and business men, received invitations. There wasn't room for everybody and these were presumed to represent the whole. It was a splendid feast."

The Gilded Age is political and social satire, but the character of Colonel Beriah Sellers outshines the invective and is finally more interesting than the convoluted plot of the novel. He is, at any rate, something more than a mere satirical device and better illustrates the impulses behind the venality of a certain kind of American than do Twain's tales and sketches that explore this theme. Sellers is an altogether memorable creation—part visionary and part windbag; at once calculating and naïve. He is a quixotic braggart, but capable of quickly improvising explanations for events that might permit him some scrap of dignity. He is compromised in his material condition but rich in the affection of his wife and children. "Good gracious, it's the country to pile up wealth!" he proudly exclaims, but he dines on turnips and water and heats the room with a tallow candle. Sellers is a major stockholder in the soap bubbles of his effervescent imagination and charitably disposed to let others in on the ground floor of his next big deal. There is something majestically helpless about the man that simultaneously commands our sympathy and provokes our laughter.

Clemens based the character of Colonel Sellers on the personality of his mother's cousin, James Lampton, but there was a portion of himself in the figure as well. Clemens's imagination, when it was functioning well, was at once projective and assimilative, which is to say it was a compound of keen observation (of mannerisms, colloquial idiom, gesture, and the like) and a genuine identification with the created character. In his "Autobiography," he emphasized only half of this equation: "Every man is in his own person the whole human race, with not a detail lacking. I am the whole human race without a detail lacking; I have studied the human race with diligence and strong interest all these years in my own person; in myself I find in big or little proportion every quality and every defect that is findable in the mass of the race." Samuel Clemens, unique in himself, acknowledged that he was representative, too—representative of material ambition and the desire to be accepted into a social order he had some doubts about, but also of a certain native social and cultural uncertainty vying with an equally native pride and vernacular boisterousness.

It was audacious, and risky, to announce, as he did in the Preface to *The Innocents Abroad* (1869), that the purpose of his book was "to suggest to the reader how he would see Europe and the East if he looked at them with his own eyes instead of the eyes of those who traveled in those countries before him. I make small pretence of showing any one how he ought to look at objects of interest beyond the sea—other books do that, and therefore, even if I were competent to do it, there is no need." The author proposes no cultural authority to report on his journey to the Old World and the Holy Land; what he does propose, on the other hand, is more extraordinary—that he can see, feel, and speak for a vast cross-section of the American public and serve as their surrogate abroad. There is, potentially, obnoxious presumption in this claim, but in point of fact, the public embraced the book. The publishers advertised Twain as "The People's Author," and if sales figures are any indication, they were right. Almost instantly *The Innocents Abroad* became a best-seller and remains one of his most popular books.

What is more, in the course of writing *The Innocents Abroad*, the "Mark Twain" persona gradually, perhaps imperceptibly, began to become something more than an ad hoc impersonation, outfitted for the purposes of comic vision alone. His original plan was to give a comic account of his voyage with fellow travelers he eventually came to call "pilgrims." As such, he was playing the part of irreverent journalist, whose imagination was stimulated by direct observation and recent experience. When the terms of his contract required him to produce a book manuscript much longer than he had anticipated, his notes and published "letters" to newspapers had to be supplemented by recollection. One result was that he abandoned the present-mindedness of the reporter for the broader purposes of the imaginative raconteur. He was becoming, almost in spite of himself, a "literary person."

This is oversimplification, of course. But the fact remains that much of Twain's best writing is the work of remembrance. *Roughing It* (1872) recounted experiences several years old; when "Old Times on the Mississippi" (1875) was written, Clemens had been away from the river more than a decade; and *The Adventures of Tom Sawyer* (1876) was a "hymn" to childhood precisely because it consisted of spontaneously youthful adventures recollected in maturity. *Tom Sawyer*, particularly, is nostalgic in the root sense of the word. There was likely a certain "homesickness" in Twain that motivated him to cast an eye backward to a simpler and mischievously happier time and to picture for the adult reader youth as it is remembered, perhaps at times even as it had been lived. Tom's free play of his romantic imagination inflicted on his comrades, his successfully conducted pranks or his childish transgressions (followed swiftly by the expected punishment and the equally expected affectionate forgiveness), and his adventures in puppy love were gratifying to the writer and the reader alike.

There are in *Tom Sawyer*, of course, sinister elements lurking about the edges of the novel. But what is finally more disturbing than the grotesqueness and the violence in the book is the apparent fact that Tom, for all his puckish defiance of the adult powers that be, is clearly and inevitably becoming neither wise nor mature but merely becoming a grown-up. In that sense, he is an embedded reporter from antebellum St. Petersburg who disturbs but never really challenges the prevailing social order. What is more, in the final chapters he uses his persuasive influence to bring the pariah Huckleberry Finn into the fold. Huck had meandered into the novel swinging a dead cat and having definite thoughts about how to cure warts and was conceived as one more comrade for Tom. To associate with Huck at all is in the eyes of the town an act of insubordination, and as a consequence Tom revels in his company. Nevertheless, Tom envies Huck's aimless freedom, ignorantly supposing that sleeping in a hogshead and living hand to mouth is blissful relief from constraint. On the other hand, there is no reason to doubt Tom's sincerity when, after the boys return to town to attend their own funeral, he grabs the hand of a shyly retreating Huck and exclaims, "Aunt Polly, it ain't fair. Somebody's got to be glad to see Huck."

Perhaps it was at that moment that Twain recognized Huckleberry Finn was a fundamentally interesting creation. Originally, Twain wrote a concluding chapter for *Tom Sawyer* describing Huck's cramped life at the Widow Douglas's but eventually removed it from the manuscript. The opening chapter of *Huckleberry Finn* may in fact be a rewriting of that chapter told from Huck's point of view. What is more certain, at any rate, is that at some time Twain saw that Huck had his own story to tell and that only he could tell it. In the summer of 1876, apparently as an idle amusement ("more to be at work than anything else," he claimed), he began to write what he called in a letter to Howells "Huck Finn's Autobiography." He wrote several hundred manuscript pages that summer but abruptly stopped midway through Chapter 18. "I like it only tolerably well, as far as I have got," he reported, "and may possibly pigeonhole or burn the MS when it is done." He did pigeonhole the work from time to time, only to return to it periodically and to increase the number and significance of

Huck's adventures. By 1883 Twain was personally proud of the result but uncertain of public reception: "I expect to complete it in a month or six weeks or two months more," he told Howells. "And I shall like it, whether anybody else does or not."

When Twain adopted Huck's point of view, he created a lens through which to view life along the river in the antebellum South, to survey its manners and customs, recreate its superstitions, sentimentality, and vainglorious gestures, its sloth, venality, and violence. Because Huck was not, and did not care to be, part of the social world he so effectively renders in his own distinctive and ungrammatical idiom, he perforce became the author's satirical instrument. But Huck is a great deal more as well. He admires, or attempts to admire, all manner of affectation, from chalk fruit to Tom Sawyer's "style" to "The Ode to Stephen Dowling Bots, Dec'd," because he automatically assumes the existing order is somehow incontestably right. And precisely to the degree that he is excluded from that world, his earnest but failed attempts to appreciate or understand it create in the adult reader a solid contempt for sham, deception, pretense, and the like.

Adventures of Huckleberry Finn was an experimental novel, but with a difference. It is an improvisational affair, full of narrative inconsistencies or improbabilities; and a glance at Twain's working notes for the novel indicate that the selection of episodes to dramatize was almost an arbitrary consideration for him. In that sense, his prefatory "Notice" for the book, that "persons attempting to find a plot in it will be shot," might be taken seriously. In any event, *Huckleberry Finn* is a masterpiece almost in spite of itself. Far from being motivated by a Melvillean devotion to the "great Art of Telling the Truth" or a Jamesean artistic ambition to face the "beautiful difficulty" of dramatic rendering, or even a Poundian desire to "Make It New," Twain seems to have begun the book as a sport. In the end, Twain did indeed tell a great many truths ("covertly and by snatches," as Melville said Shakespeare did), and he exhibited a technical mastery over his material that, were he ever disposed to do so, even Henry James might admire. And the book was new in the way Ezra Pound thought modern literature should be. The testimony of a host of American and English writers (Somerset Maugham, H. L. Mencken, Willa Cather, Sherwood Anderson, Sinclair Lewis, Robert Louis Stevenson, George Bernard Shaw, John Barth, and many, many more) bears witness to the significance of a book that, despite its obvious faults, achieves greatness. Ernest Hemingway's praise of *Huckleberry Finn* is the most familiar, but it is also typical: It is "the best book we've had. All American writing comes from that. There was nothing before. There has been nothing as good since."

Evidently conceived as the product of idle leisure, *Huckleberry Finn* often expressed the author's personal longings. Twain could envy Huck's unpestered freedom and identify with his rejection of the torments of "sivilisation," though life at the Widow's required only minor concessions of him—mumbling over his victuals, wearing shoes and starched collars, going to school; in a word, behaving. Soon enough, however, the author recognized that Huck's sensibility and the world he inhabited were far from idyllic. This is no "hymn" to youth; an accurate body count of the dead folks in the book might indicate it is something of a dirge instead. The mounting seriousness of the story begins to come into focus with the introduction of the abusive Pap and continues throughout (in the form of slave catchers, lynch mobs, casual bigots, cruel loafers, aristocratic murderers, mindless feuding families, conniving con men). Still, as vividly drawn as these contemptible characters are, there are no out and out villains in the book; they are not evildoers, but they have rather blandly been disloyal to their own humanity. Huck sometimes is implicated in the disturbing events of the narrative but as often serves as perplexed witness to them, and in neither case does he reveal a damning moral judgment, merely a confused child-like sympathy. T. S. Eliot astutely observed that Huck really has no imagination but he does have "vision." Huck "sees the real world; and he does not judge it—he allows it to judge itself." Condemnation (moral, social, or political) is left for the adult reader; Huck is too busy getting out of one scrape after another.

His adventures are intermittently punctuated with rare comedy, of course, but at times with unnecessary burlesque as well. It would be a mistake to forget that *Huckleberry Finn* is a very humorous novel, but at its heart is a troubling moral dilemma. Everything the boy has been taught upholds slavery as a sacred institution and views the slaves themselves as subhuman objects of toil or amusement. So far as he is aware, his decision, or his several decisions really, to help Jim to freedom is in the eyes of the church and the state a sin and a crime. Huck's diverse encounters with all manner of people along the river are interesting in themselves, but the book simply would not cohere without the presence of the fugitive slave Jim.

Excepting perhaps Don Quixote and Sancho Panza, whose exploits Twain knew well, there is no more unlikely fictional pair than Huck and Jim. One is a child; the other, a grown man. One is white; the other, black. One is an unwanted outcast; the other is valuable property, by his own reckoning worth eight hundred dollars. Huck wants to go south, eventually to the Amazon, to get shed of a cruel father, on the one hand, and a superintending guardian, on the other. Jim wants to go north to Canada, work for wages, and buy his family out of slavery. Huck wants to be free from constraint and responsibility; Jim wants the liberty to be a participant in the social order. Huck and Jim have little in common, but together they form, in Twain's words, a "community of misfortune." Unable to cultivate what is best in them or to express their freedom except by slipping the knot of necessity, they are collateral damage in the experiment of democracy.

The characters seem blind to their misfortune, however. If they do not openly question society's estimation of them, neither are they filled with self-loathing. When they grieve it is not for themselves but for others. Their occasional happiness is nearly always mingled with gratitude. Often their sympathies are misplaced, but they are genuine. Huck, for example, is truly anxious for the safety of the supposedly drunken circus rider, and when Jim learns that the boy "dolphin," rightful heir to the French throne, was locked up in a cell to die, his heartfelt response is "Po' little chap." These are comic mistakes in judgment because Huck and Jim take fictions for fact, but in their own fashion the reactions are as revealing of their fundamental decency as, say, Jim's self-recrimination for hurting his deaf daughter or Huck's regret for his cruel deception of Jim after they were separated in the fog. Together, the two know as much about the constitutional machinery of the republic or the failed promises of democracy as they do about British aristocracy or the French language, but their mixed-up exploits nevertheless constitute, in Ralph Ellison's phrase, a "great drama of interracial fraternity." As such, they provide, at once, an image of the nation's possibilities and serve as an emblem of its largely self-inflicted limitations.

IV

To say that most everything Twain wrote after *Huckleberry Finn* is a falling off and that a decline in creative energy corresponded to a darkening pessimism in the man is to repeat a commonplace. It is also to speak a half-truth. To be sure, in his last years Clemens was often skeptical and cynical. By 1894 he had lost his publishing house and had declared bankruptcy. He was humiliated, but he had other worries as well. His wife, Olivia, had always been frail, but her health was more and more uncertain; and Clemens himself had suffered from various ailments for years. He had embarked on a round-the-world lecture tour in 1895, in order to repair his fortunes and, by paying off his debts, to restore his good name. Clemens and his wife were still out of the country when their oldest daughter, Susy, died of spinal meningitis in 1896. After a prolonged illness, Olivia died in 1904; Jean, the youngest daughter, died from an epileptic seizure in December, 1909. In addition, Clemens had become disgusted and angry over his country's chauvinistic swagger and its imperialistic policies, attitudes expressed most powerfully in "To the Person Sitting in Darkness" (1901), and he believed that the nation had forsaken worthier objectives to satisfy a rapacious greed. In a word, if Twain had turned pessimist, he had his reasons.

What is more, these subtractions from his life were complemented by a personal determinist philosophy that had been latent in his thinking since the 1870s but came more and more to the fore as an explanatory principle for human conduct and as a means to puncture the balloon of human vanity. The salient features of Clemens's determinism are these: that thought is merely the mechanical putting together of sense impressions; that human beings are ruled by an interior master, or conscience, which commands us to gratify it; that originality is a myth and all our ideas derive from heredity and temperament or environment and training, and that instinct is merely "petrified thought" passed down from one generation to another. The author thought his "philosophy" quite scandalous and took some measures to disclose it without damaging his public image. In point of fact, however, much of what he had to say comported well enough with the conclusions of nineteenth-century science and psychology and there was little, if anything, that was very shocking about it.

There was a curious discrepancy in his system, however, since, in contradiction of his own mechanical and materialistic assumptions, Twain retained a belief that the mind, or "me," existed apart from its own mental machinery. That "me" took many forms, apparently. After his daughter Susy's death, Clemens complained to his friend Howells that he had become a "dead" man, a mere "mud image, & it puzzles me to know what it is in me that writes, & that has comedy-fancies & finds pleasure in phrasing them. . . . the thing in me forgets the presence of the mud image & goes its own way wholly unconscious of it & apparently of no kinship with it." In *A Connecticut Yankee*, he has Hank Morgan proclaim man's duty in this "sad pilgrimage, this pathetic drift between the eternities, is to look out and humbly live a pure and high and blameless life, and save that one microscopic atom in me that is truly *me*." Elsewhere, he describes this self as a "vagrant thought," "wandering among the empty eternities." In a letter to his sister-in-law, Susan Crane (reprinted in this volume), he muses that his whole life might have been a dream and that he has no certain way to prove it otherwise. These are not the musings of an out-and-out materialist who believes human beings are machines and nothing more.

In any event, his system served him well enough in the creation of such short fiction as "The Man That Corrupted Hadleyburg" (1899), *What Is Man?* (1906), "Little Bessie" (ca. 1908), and *Letters from the Earth* (ca. 1909); and in parts (but only in parts) of *Pudd'nhead Wilson* (1894) and *A Connecticut Yankee*. Twain might even explain the physical organization of microorganisms as a form of social hierarchy governed chiefly by pride and envy, as he did in "Three Thousand Years among the Microbes" (1905). He would reaffirm his philosophy in essays such as "Corn-Pone Opinions" (1901) and "The Turning Point of My Life" (1910) and in several of his letters. In one of his more amusing philosophic outbursts in a letter to Joseph Twichell (reprinted in this volume), he describes his experience of reading the Puritan Jonathan Edwards on the will as resembling "having been on a three days' tear with a drunken lunatic." In a word, however dark this philosophic vision may have been, it did not harness the sheer audacity of his humor or the sting of his wit. Nor did it impinge upon his social and political convictions or restrain his fiery denunciation of tyranny, imperialism, and demogoguery.

On the other hand, Twain was continually driving beyond the limits of his own philosophy, without regard to logic, system, or continuity. In Chapter 31 of the novel, Huckleberry Finn is tortured by his guilty conscience for depriving Miss Watson of her rightful property by helping Jim to freedom. However improbable his decision is (and given his upbringing it is improbable indeed), he is heroic in choosing to go to hell rather than betray his companion. Twain himself later described Huck's conduct as the triumph of a "sound heart" over a "deformed conscience." Hank Morgan believes that "training is everything" and foolishly attempts to transform King Arthur's England by introducing nineteenth-century ideas of political and religious liberty and the conveniences provided by industrial progress and technological efficiency. The conjunction of these two worlds makes for wonderful comedy, of course. However, in the end the dying Morgan believes his own modern world is the product of delirium and dream and reaches out, across thirteen centuries, for everything that is dear to him—his wife, his child, his friends, his antique life.

Ultimately, Twain's determinism is not very interesting in itself, not as philosophy and not as an existential position he fashioned out of his own disappointments. Ironically perhaps, it was useful because it permitted him certain antic freedoms that were more in his line than synthetic explanations of human behavior. And his philosophizing does seem to have supplied him with a rationalized defense post from which he might launch repeated attacks on human vanity or, alternately, on a God that equipped human nature with a "moral sense" but without the necessary means to lead, except passively, the moral life. Twain might ridicule human conceit in several ways: by locating his species as a mere speck in the infinite vastness of space or by treating the human creature as the assembled concatenation of infinitesimally small but overproud particles or as the product of millions of years of evolutionary process leisurely fumbling its way toward some undisclosed end. It was the very absurdity of the human condition, regarded through the lens of incongruous frames of reference, that inevitably summoned humorous remark. "It is easy to find fault if one has that disposition," Pudd'nhead Wilson records. "There once was a man who, not being able to find any other fault with his coal, complained that there were too many prehistoric toads in it."

In 1896, Twain remarked, "The mysterious and the fabulous can get no fine effects without the help of remoteness; and there are no remotenesses any more." That was a dilemma he might easily remedy. By locating the human comedy in the distant reaches of space or in a cholera germ in the bloodstream of a tramp, or by reaching back into prehistory, all the way back to the Garden of Eden, Twain found there remained plenty of fine effects to be had. He might observe human foibles in himself and others and dramatize them under such alien conditions and thereby construct a different sort of comedy, one that applied broadly to universal human nature and could teach the lessons of humility and a common destiny. Humility is a social virtue and laughter is its companion. Humiliation, by contrast, is a stigma, alienating and corrosive. However cynical Twain became in his later years, his comedy never degenerated into the merely derisive or spiteful. He remained to the end the reader's genial companion and ally.

Despite his insistence that originality was impossible, Twain often enough transcended the terms of his own intellectual system and explored literary territory that was at least fresh and often unexampled. He did this in his "Autobiography" by ransacking his recollection vaults, creating a life out of fickle remembrance, and offering it to an indefinite future. He did it as well in his comedies of first and final things. His Captain Stormfield, who sailed for heaven but arrived at the wrong port, is sympathetically ridiculous because he has brought with him the baggage of wrongheaded but conventional expectation about the hereafter. Stormfield learns that planet Earth is pretty insignificant in the grand scheme of things; it is referred to locally as the "Wart." He tries his hand at plucking a harp (he knows only one tune) and using his wings (he collides with a Bishop, and they exchange sharp words), only to find out that these customs are not required. When Stormfield drops his prepossessions about paradise and his final reward, he begins to see things anew and more clearly, and we do too. We also begin to suspect why he is there and not the other place.

Twain also wrote often about beginnings, most extensively about the experiences of Adam and Eve in the Garden and after. By doing so, he was willfully depriving himself of his constituted gospel of training and inherited ideas. Eve characterizes the pair's situation in their innocent state: "Interests were abundant; for we were children, and ignorant; ignorant beyond the conception of the present day. We knew *nothing*—nothing whatever. We were starting at the very bottom of things—at the very beginning; we had to learn the a b c of things." Twain did not conceive of the pair, nor do they really conceive of themselves, as children—obedient or otherwise. They are self-appointed "scientists," who through repeated observation and experimentation are trying to get the hang of the place called Paradise. It is Adam's assigned task to name things, but Eve beats him to the punch every time, simply because she *knows* the right name for every beast and bird. She also knows that Sunday is a day of rest, whereas Adam thought every day was. Thereafter, his diary for Sunday is always the same: "Pulled through." Eve puts up signs everywhere—"Keep off the grass." "This way to the Whirlpool."—and believes Eden would make a swell summer resort.

Adam and Eve are evicted from the Garden, but not for eating of the apple. The forbidden fruit, it turns out, is the "chestnut." Adam partook of this fruit in the form of a hackneyed joke he told, as old as creation, and he compounded the felony by laughing himself silly over it. Many years earlier, in *The Innocents Abroad,* Twain stood at the Tomb of Adam and tearfully lamented that the old man had not lived to see him, "his child." In "Extracts from Adam's Diary" Twain re-imagines his ancestor as one who has discovered a hairless and toothless creature he can't quite identify. Eve has instinctively named it Abel. Adam supposes it might be a fish and throws it in the water. Eve retrieves it. It might be a frog, a bird, or a snake; but it isn't. He decides it is "either an enigma or some kind of bug." He becomes so convinced that it is a kangaroo that he names it "*Kangaroorum Adamiensis.*" He rejects that hypothesis and concludes it must be a "zoological freak," either that or a tailless bear. Adam wears himself out looking for another specimen of the species; meanwhile Eve has caught another one and named it Cain.

There is preposterous and affecting comedy in these, our first parents, trying to discover where babies come from and establishing themselves, without benefit of consultation or clergy, as the first family. Driven from the Garden, Adam and Eve discover in a new and apparently unsponsored world the lasting pleasures of one another's company. "After all these years," says Adam, "I see that I was mistaken about Eve in the beginning; it is better to live outside the Garden with her than inside it without her. . . . Blessed be the chestnut that brought us near together and taught me to know the goodness of her heart and the sweetness of her spirit." If an old joke brought about the Fall, it appears that Adam and Eve have had the last (and the first) laugh.

In his old age, Twain's once hopeful optimism may have reached the end of its tether, but, for forty years and more, the imaginative reach of his humor had traveled far and wide—from the Nevada Territory to the Black Forest, from Plymouth Rock to the Rock of Gibraltar, from the outer reaches of the universe to the inner life of microbes, from the creation to the hereafter. Through it all, in multiple personae and in unequal doses to be sure, his antic geniality, his irascible sympathy and self-righteous indignation, his zany irreverence, and ridiculous solemnity traveled with him. The ebullient humor and amiable presence of Twain can be felt on nearly every page of his best work and remain, perhaps, his most important and durable features. Those qualities are good companions, and portable indeed.

Suggestions for Further Reading

The sheer volume of criticism and scholarship concerning Mark Twain's life and writings is immense. The bibliography below is meant to list resources for reliable information about the author and his work, identify certain collections or editions of Twain's writings that may be of interest but not generally known, and to indicate the range of interpretive approaches to his work, particularly *Adventures of Huckleberry Finn.* Under the general editorship of Robert Hirst, The Mark Twain Project has prepared and continues to prepare authoritative texts of Twain's notebooks, travel narratives, short fiction, novels, letters, and unpublished writings. These texts are published by the University of California Press and the historical introduction, notes, and annotations are an unusually rich resource of accurate and pertinent information about Twain and his writing. Readers with a specialized interest in Twain scholarship will find these volumes especially rewarding. The items listed below were selected as particularly appropriate for a general audience.

REFERENCE

Camfield, Gregg, *The Oxford Companion to Mark Twain* (New York, 2003)

LeMaster, J. R., and James D. Wilson, eds., *The Mark Twain Encyclopedia* (New York, 1993)

Long, E. Hudson, and J. R. LeMaster, *The New Mark Twain Handbook* (New York, 1985)

Rasmussen, R. Kent, *Mark Twain A to Z: The Essential Reference to His Life and Writings* (New York, 1995)

Tenney, Thomas Asa, *Mark Twain: A Reference Guide* (Boston, 1977). Annual supplements to this reference guide have been published in *American Literary Realism* (1977–1983) and the *Mark Twain Circular* (1984–present)

EDITIONS

Baetzhold, Howard G., and Joseph B. McCullough, eds., *The Bible According to Mark Twain: Writings on Heaven, Eden, and the Flood* (New York, 1996)

Budd, Louis J., ed., *Mark Twain: Collected Tales, Sketches, Speeches, and Essays*, 2 vols. (New York, 1992)

Fatout, Paul, ed., *Mark Twain Speaking* (Iowa City, Iowa, 1976)

Kiskis, Michael, ed., *Mark Twain's Own Autobiography* (Madison, Wis., 1990)

Zwick, Jim, ed., *Mark Twain's Weapons of Satire: Anti-Imperialist Writings on the Philippine-American War* (Syracuse, N.Y., 1992)

BIOGRAPHY

Andrews, Kenneth R., *Nook Farm: Mark Twain's Hartford Circle* (Cambridge, Mass., 1950)

Baetzhold, Howard G., *Mark Twain and John Bull: The British Connection* (Bloomington, Ind., 1970)

Fatout, Paul, *Mark Twain on the Lecture Circuit* (Bloomington, Ind., 1960)

Dolmetsch, Carl, *"Our Famous Guest": Mark Twain in Vienna* (Athens, Ga. 1992)

Emerson, Everett, *Mark Twain, a Literary Life* (Philadelphia, 2000)

Ferguson, Delancey, *Mark Twain: Man and Legend* (New York, 1943)

Harris, Susan K., *The Courtship of Olivia Langdon and Mark Twain* (New York, 1996)

Hill, Hamlin, *Mark Twain: God's Fool* (New York, 1973)
Kaplan, Fred, *The Singular Mark Twain: A Biography* (New York, 2003)
Kaplan, Justin, *Mr. Clemens and Mark Twain, a Biography* (New York, 1966)
Meltzer, Milton, *Mark Twain Himself: A Pictorial Biography* (Columbia, Mo., 2002)
Paine, Albert Bigelow, *Mark Twain: A Biography*, 3 vols. (New York, 1912)
Powers, Ron, *Dangerous Water: A Biography of the Boy Who Became Mark Twain* (New York, 1999)
Skandera-Trombley, Laura, *Mark Twain in the Company of Women* (Philadelphia, 1994)
Steinbrink, Jeffrey, *Getting to Be Mark Twain* (Berkeley and Los Angeles, 1991)
Ward, Geoffrey C., and Dayton Duncan, with a preface by Ken Burns, *Mark Twain* (New York, 2001)
Wecter, Dixon, *Sam Clemens of Hannibal* (Boston, 1952)

CRITICISM

Bellamy, Gladys, *Mark Twain as a Literary Artist* (Norman, Okla., 1950)
Branch, Edgard M., *The Literary Apprenticeship of Mark Twain* (Urbana, Ill., 1950)
Bridgman, Richard, *Traveling in Mark Twain* (Berkeley and Los Angeles, 1987)
Budd, Louis J., *Mark Twain: Social Philosopher*, rev. ed. (Columbia, Mo., 2001)
———, *Our Mark Twain: The Making of His Public Personality* (Philadelphia, 1983)
Covici, Pascal, Jr., *Mark Twain's Humor: The Image of a World* (Dallas, Tex., 1962)
Cox, James M., *Mark Twain: The Fate of Humor* (Columbia, Mo., 2002)
DeVoto, Bernard, *Mark Twain's America* (Boston, 1932)
Gerber, John, *Mark Twain* (New York, 1988)

Gibson, William M., *The Art of Mark Twain* (New York, 1976)
Gillman, Susan, *Dark Twins: Imposture and Identity in Mark Twain's America* (Chicago, 1980)
Howells, William Dean, *My Mark Twain* (New York, 1910)
Krauth, Leland, *Proper Mark Twain* (Athens, Ga., 1999)
Lynn, Kenneth S., *Mark Twain and Southwestern Humor* (Boston, 1970)
Melton, Jeffrey Alan, *Mark Twain, Travel Books, and Tourism: The Tide of a Great Popular Movement* (Tuscaloosa, Ala., 2002)
Messent, Peter, *Mark Twain* (New York, 1997)
Michelson, Bruce, *Mark Twain on the Loose: A Comic Writer and the American Self* (Amherst, Mass., 1955)
Quirk, Tom, *Mark Twain: A Study of the Short Fiction* (New York, 1997)
Rogers, Franklin R., *Mark Twain's Burlesque Patterns as Seen in the Novels and Narratives, 1855–1885*, (Dallas, Tex., 1955)
Sloane, David E. E., *Mark Twain as a Literary Comedian* (Baton Rouge, La., 1979)
Smith, Henry Nash, *Mark Twain: The Development of a Writer* (Cambridge, Mass., 1962)

CRITICISM ON *ADVENTURES OF HUCKLEBERRY FINN*

Arac, Jonathan, *Huckleberry Finn as Idol and Target: The Functions of Criticism in Our Time* (Madison, Wis., 1997)
Blair, Walter, *Mark Twain and Huck Finn* (Berkeley and Los Angeles, 1960)
Chadwick-Joshua, Jocelyn, *The Jim Dilemma: Reading Race in* Huckleberry Finn (Jackson, Miss., 1998)
Doyno, Victor A., *Writing "Huck Finn": Mark Twain's Creative Process* (Philadelphia, 1992)
Fishkin, Shelley Fisher, *Was Huck Black?: Mark Twain and African-American Voices* (New York, 1993)

Inge, M. Thomas, *Huck Finn among the Critics: A Centennial Selection* (Frederick, Md., 1985)
Mensh, Elaine, and Harry Mensh, *Black, White, and Huckleberry Finn: Re-Imagining the American Dream* (Tuscaloosa, Ala., 2000)
Quirk, Tom, *Coming to Grips with Huckleberry Finn* (Columbia, Mo., 1993)
Sattelmeyer, Robert, and J. Donald Crowley, eds., *One Hundred Years of "Huckleberry Finn"* (Columbia, Mo., 1985)
Twain, Mark, *The Annotated Huckleberry Finn,* edited by Michael Patrick Hearn (New York, 2001)
Wieck, Carl, *Refiguring Huckleberry Finn* (Athens, Ga., 2000)

Note on Texts

In some instances, I have supplied titles for excerpted pieces because the chapter title or running head was not especially descriptive of the text at hand. Whenever possible, the texts used are taken from the first American book publication of the text in question.

The text for "The Celebrated Jumping Frog of Calaveras County" is taken from *The Celebrated Jumping Frog of Calaveras County and Other Sketches* (New York: C. H. Webb Publisher, 1867). "How I Edited an Agricultural Journal Once" was first published in the *Galaxy* for July, 1870, the source for the text printed here. "An Encounter with an Interviewer" first appeared in the volume *Lotus Leaves,* edited by John Brougham and John Elderkin (Boston: William F. Gill and Co., 1875), the source for the text printed here. "A True Story, Repeated Word for Word as I Heard It" first appeared in *Atlantic Monthly* for November, 1874, the source of the text printed here.

The texts for the following selections were derived from the first American edition published by The American Publishing Company of Hartford, Connecticut: "The Sea of Galilee" and "At the Tomb of Adam" are from *The Innocents Abroad* (1869). The texts for "The Story of the Old Ram," "Buck Fanshaw's Funeral," and "Letters from Greeley" are from *Roughing It* (1872). The text for "Colonel Sellers Entertains Washington Hawkins" is from *The Gilded Age* (1873) which was jointly written with Charles Dudley Warner. The texts for "Jim Baker's Blue-Jay Yarn" and "The Hair Trunk" are taken from *A Tramp Abroad* (1880). The text for "Pudd'nhead Wilson's Calendar" is from *The Tragedy of Pudd'nhead Wilson and the Comedy Those Extraordinary Twins* (1894). The texts for "Pudd'nhead Wilson's New Calendar" and "Decimating the Savages" are from the first American edition of *Following the Equator* (1897).

"A Boy's Ambition," "Perplexing Lessons," and "Continued Perplexities" first appeared in "Old Times on the Mississippi," serialized in the *Atlantic Monthly* from January to August, 1875; they were later included as Chapters 4, 8, and 9 of *Life on the Mississippi.* The texts for these selections, along with "The River and Its History," "Sunrise on the River," and "The House Beautiful," are taken from the first American edition of *Life on the Mississippi* (Boston: James R. Osgood and Company, 1883).

The text for *Adventures of Huckleberry Finn,* with one notable exception, derives from the first American edition of the novel (New York: Charles L. Webster & Company, 1885). Following the example of Bernard DeVoto's *Portable Mark Twain,* the "raftsmen episode," first published in Chapter 3 of *Life on the Mississippi,* but originally intended as part of the novel, has been restored as part of Chapter 16 of *Huckleberry Finn.*

"The Private History of a Campaign That Failed" was first published in the *Century Magazine,* December, 1885 and is the source for this text. The texts for "The Yankee in Search of Adventure" and "The Holy Fountain" are from the first American edition of *A Connecticut Yankee in King Arthur's Court* (New York: Charles L. Webster & Company, 1889).

Mark Twain wrote "Extracts from Adam's Diary" in 1892 and asked his business manager, Fred Hall, to place it in either *Cosmopolitan* or *Century* magazine. Hall was unsuccessful in placing the manuscript, but Iriving S. Underhill, wishing to promote Niagara Falls as a tourist attraction, asked Twain for a contribution for *The Niagara Book.* Twain revised "Adam's Diary," making Niagara Falls Park the scene for the work, instead of the Garden of Eden. The text printed here is from *The Niagara Book. A Complete Souvenir of Niagara Falls Containing Sketches . . . by W. D. Howells, Mark Twain . . . and Others* (Buffalo: Underhill & Nichols, 1893).

"To the Person Sitting in Darkness" was published in the *North American Review,* February, 1901, and is the source for this text. "Corn-Pone Opinions" was written in 1901 but was first published in *Europe and Elsewhere,* Albert Bigelow Paine, ed. (New York: Harper and Brothers Publishers, 1923), the source of the present text. A chapter from Twain's ongoing "Autobiography," "Early Days" was published in the *North American Review,* March, 1907, and is the source for this text.

The texts for "Plymouth Rock and the Pilgrims," "Education and Citizenship," and "The Alphabet and Simplified Spelling" are from the first American edition of *Mark Twain's Speeches* (New York: Harper and Brothers Publishers, 1910). "Advice to Youth" and "Farewell Banquet for Bayard Taylor" are from *Mark Twain Speaking,* Paul Fatout, ed. (Iowa City: University of Iowa Press, 1976).

The letter to Frank Nichols (3/1885) was published in the Boston *Daily Advertiser* on April 2, 1885. The letter to Susan Crane (3/19/1893) is reprinted with permission from the Hartford House, Hartford, Connecticut. The remaining letters are from the two-volume *Mark Twain's Letters,* arranged with comment by Albert Bigelow Paine (New York: Harper and Brothers Publishers, 1917).

Chronology

1835 Samuel L. Clemens is born in Florida, Missouri.

1839 The Clemens family moves to Hannibal, Missouri, on the Mississippi River.

1847 His father, John Marshall Clemens, dies March 24.

1849–1851 Apprentices with Joseph Ament, printer; sets type for the Hannibal *Courier.*

1853 Leaves Hannibal for St. Louis; spends August in New York City; visits Philadelphia.

1857 Meets Horace Bixby, the riverboat pilot, who agrees to take him as an apprentice.

1858–1859 Apprentices as a "cub" pilot; receives his license April 9, 1859.

1861 In June, joins the Marion Rangers, a group of volunteers sympathetic to the Confederate cause. The unit disbands after two weeks.

In July, travels with his brother Orion to the Nevada Territory.

1862 Joins staff of the Virginia City, Nevada, *Territorial Enterprise.*

1863 In three "Letters from Carson," he first uses the pen name "Mark Twain."

1864 Moves to San Francisco and works as a reporter for the *Morning Call.* Publishes sketches in the *Golden Era* and the *Californian.*

1865 "Jim Smiley and His Jumping Frog" is published in the New York *Saturday Press* and is widely reprinted throughout the country.

1867 In June, sails on the *Quaker City* for Europe and the Holy Land as a correspondent for the *Alta California* and the New York *Tribune.*

Contracts with the American Publishing Company to make letters from voyage into a book.

Meets Olivia Langdon.

1869 Becomes engaged to Olivia Langdon.

The Innocents Abroad is published.

1870 Marries February 2; moves to Buffalo, New York.

Son Langdon is born; dies 18 months later.

1872 *Roughing It* is published.

Daughter Olivia Susan (Susy) is born.

1873 *The Gilded Age* (coauthored with Charles Dudley Warner) is published.

1874 Daughter Clara is born.

The Clemenses move into their still uncompleted house in Hartford, Connecticut, in the fall.

In November, publishes "A True Story" in the *Atlantic Monthly,* Twain's first attempt to tell a serious story in African-American dialect.

Begins writing articles about his years as a Mississippi riverboat apprentice.

1875 In January, the first installment of "Old Times on the Mississippi" appears in the *Atlantic Monthly.*

In September, *Mark Twain's Sketches New and Old* is published.

1876 In the summer begins writing "Huck Finn's Autobiography" at Quarry Farm, overlooking Elmira, New York.

Publishes *The Adventures of Tom Sawyer.*

1877 In December, delivers the "Whittier Birthday Speech" in Boston. Many, including Clemens's friend William Dean Howells, are shocked by the burlesque that features tramps impersonating Longfellow, Holmes, and Emerson.

1878 In April, the Clemens family travels to Germany and makes excursions throughout Switzerland and Italy. They return home September, 1879.

1880 In March, *A Tramp Abroad* is published.

Daughter Jane Lampton (Jean) is born.

1881 In December, *The Prince and the Pauper* is published.

1882 In preparation of expanding the "Old Times on the Mississippi" articles into a book, travels to St. Louis and takes a riverboat down to New Orleans and then back north, stopping off at his hometown, Hannibal.

1883 In May, *Life on the Mississippi* is published.

1884 In May, he and Charles L. Webster start their own publishing company.

In July, begins writing "Huck Finn and Tom Sawyer Among the Indians."

In November, begins a four-month lecture tour with George Washington Cable.

In December, the English edition of *Adventures of Huckleberry Finn* is published.

1885 His own publishing house, Charles L. Webster & Company, issues the first American edition of *Adventures of Huckleberry Finn,* on February 18.

"The Private History of a Campaign That Failed," is published in the December issue of *Century.*

Begins investing in the Paige typesetting machine.

1889 *A Connecticut Yankee in King Arthur's Court* is published by Charles L. Webster & Company.

Optimistic about the prospects for the Paige typesetter and that he will be able to retire from writing and live off the profits.

1890 His mother, Jane Lampton Clemens, dies.

1891 With the publishing house deeply in debt, he stops his payments for the support of the Paige typesetting project.

Unable to afford the maintenance of their Hartford house, the family moves to Europe.

1893 "Extracts from Adam's Diary" is published in *Niagara Book.*

1894 Clemens declares voluntary bankruptcy.

The Tragedy of Pudd'nhead Wilson and the Comedy of Those Extraordinary Twins is published by the American Publishing Company.

1895 Begins his round-the-world lecture tour in order to pay creditors.

1896 His daughter Susy dies.

1898 Remaining debts paid in full.

1901 "To the Person Sitting in Darkness" is published in the *North American Review* and as a pamphlet by the Anti-Imperialist League.

The family moves to Riverdale-on-the-Hudson in New York.

Writes "Corn-Pone Opinions"; published posthumously.

1902 Visits Hannibal and St. Louis for the last time.

Receives an honorary Doctor of Laws degree from the University of Missouri–Columbia.

1903 Settles in Italy for Olivia's health.

1904 Olivia Clemens dies June 5.

1905 Writes "Eve's Diary," published in *Harper's Magazine.*

A seventieth birthday party in his honor is given at Delmonico's; 172 people attend.

1906 *What Is Man?* is published anonymously by DeVinne Press.

Begins to publish "Chapters from My Autobiography" in the *North American Review.*

1907 Receives an honorary Litt.D. degree from Oxford.

Publishes "Extract from Captain Stormfield's Visit to Heaven" in *Harper's Magazine* (Dec. 1907–Jan. 1908).

1908 Conceives the idea of forming a club called the "Aquarium," whose members would be schoolgirls between ten and sixteen years old called "angelfish."

Moves into new house in Redding, Connecticut, and at daughter Clara's suggestion calls it "Stormfield."

1909 Daughter Jean dies December 24.

1910 Travels to Bermuda; begins to have chest pains.

Returns to Stormfield; dies April 21.

TALES AND SKETCHES

Twain's genius was constitutionally eruptive, and for that reason much of his best work is to be found in his short fiction where the spontaneity of his imagination, combined as it almost always was with meticulous revision, could be given free rein. The writer was naturally adept at most short forms—the tall tale, the sketch, the burlesque and parody, the fable—but he was also disposed to ring some changes on narrative conventions. "The Celebrated Jumping Frog of Calaveras County" is a case in point. Clemens had heard a man named Ben Coon tell the story in a mining camp in the California foothills and made brief notes for a tale to be written at some future date. When Artemus Ward requested a humorous tale of him for a collection of such stories, Twain had his opportunity, and he chose the familiar form of the frame tale to structure the narrative. A frame tale typically begins with a genteel narrator (educated, correct, and a bit stodgy) who comes in contact with a vernacular character (unrefined and ungrammatical) who, in his turn, spins a humorous yarn. The genteel character returns at the end to round things off. Because this sort of humor was popular in Eastern periodicals, there was a temptation for the writer to condescend to the frontier ruffian and to make him a figure of fun in order to please an audience generally perceived to be above and apart from such types. Twain, on the other hand, more often than not makes the teller (in this case Simon Wheeler) and the principal character (here, Jim Smiley) amusing and certainly limited in understanding and opportunities, but they are sympathetic too. And within Wheeler's frame of reference, Smiley and the mysterious stranger who bests him are men of "transcendent genius." The Twain persona, on the other hand, is blind to the humor of the story and only belatedly recognizes that he has been, from the beginning, the butt of a joke concocted by Artemus Ward. "The Story of the Old Ram" is another frame tale, and once again, Twain, in the role of tenderfoot in the Nevada Territory, realizes that he has been set up by the "boys." In believing that he has the privilege of hearing the notorious story of the old ram, told by a man who must be "symmetrically" drunk to tell it, Twain perceives, by the end, that he has been "sold." Jim Blaine, on the other hand, is unaware that anything he has said is funny, and, instead of concluding a tale that really has never gotten started, he falls asleep midsentence.

"How I Edited an Agricultural Journal Once," "Buck Fanshaw's Funeral," "Letters from Greeley," and "An Encounter with an Interviewer" do not depend on the device of the frame tale as a form, but they do participate in the humor of encounters between and among characters of different backgrounds and experience. Two of them benefit from Twain's journalistic experience—he wrote "How I Edited an Agricultural Journal Once" at a time when he was one-third owner of a Buffalo newspaper and was involved in making editorial decisions of his own; as a journalist and, later as something of a celebrity himself, Twain had been on both sides of the reporter's notepad and knew something about the latent comedy in any encounter with an interviewer. His days in the West had thoroughly acquainted him with the slang and argot of the mining camps, and with men such as Buck Fanshaw, a "bully boy with a glass-eye" and who never "shook his mother." "Letters from Greeley," on the other hand, is founded on two widely known facts—that Greeley was an amateur farmer who published his views on agriculture and that his handwriting was notoriously illegible. All of these tales depend on some form of miscommunication for their humor, but beyond and above that common foundation, Twain's humorous imagination might soar to unexplored territory. Everyone has had trouble deciphering another's handwriting, but who else but Twain could read into the scrawl: "Bolivia extemporizes mackeral." Everyone in a temper has improvised some sort of profanity, but who else but Twain could unleash these ripe expletives upon the regular editor of an agricultural journal: "you cornstalk, you cabbage, you son of a cauliflower . . . You turnip! . . . Yam! . . . Pieplant!"

In dramatic contrast to Twain's tall tales and humorous sketches, "A True Story, Repeated Word for Word as I Heard It" is a morally serious story. Nevertheless, Clemens enlisted the devices of humor and modified them to his purpose. The Aunt Rachel of this tale was, in fact, Mary Cord, the servant of Clemens's sister-in-law, Susan Crane, at Quarry Farm, which overlooks the town of Elmira, New York. Clemens had more than once boasted that, because he had grown up around slaves in Missouri, he was better acquainted with the temperament of blacks than New Yorkers. Susan Crane was not convinced, and urged Clemens to ask Mary Cord to tell her own story. Clemens was reluctant, but one evening he did ask the woman about herself, and the result was the inspiration for one of his finest short works. By the end of her story, Clemens must have known that he had been set up by Susan Crane and that the effect of Mary Cord's tale was transforming. Once again, Sam Clemens had been "sold," but in an entirely serious way. "A True Story" is not merely a transcript of what he heard, however. He shaped the narrative, giving it a coherent beginning, middle, and end; and through the artful management of gesture, what Twain sometimes called "stage directions," he made Aunt Rachel a dignified and powerful moral presence. Twain submitted the story to the *Atlantic* magazine and—somewhat to his surprise—the editor, William Dean Howells, was pleased to publish it. It was the first time Twain had had anything accepted by that prestigious magazine. And it was probably the first time, as well, that he recognized that he could tell a genuinely "literary" tale with a serious moral purpose entirely in dialect. This recognition would later prove important when he began to write *Huckleberry Finn.*

"The Celebrated Jumping Frog of Calaveras County" (1865)

In compliance with the request of a friend of mine, who wrote me from the East, I called on good-natured, garrulous old Simon Wheeler, and inquired after my friend's friend, *Leonidas W.* Smiley, as requested to do, and I hereunto append the result. I have a lurking suspicion that *Leonidas W.* Smiley is a myth; that my friend never knew such a personage; and that he only conjectured that, if I asked old Wheeler about him, it would remind him of his infamous *Jim* Smiley, and he would go to work and bore me nearly to death with some infernal reminiscence of him as long and tedious as it should be useless to me. If that was the design, it certainly succeeded.

I found Simon Wheeler dozing comfortably by the bar-room stove of the old, dilapidated tavern in the ancient mining camp of Angel's, and I noticed that he was fat and bald-headed, and had an expression of winning gentleness and simplicity upon his tranquil countenance. He roused and gave me good-day. I told him a friend of mine had commissioned me to make some inquiries about a cherished companion of his boyhood named *Leonidas* W. Smiley—*Rev. Leonidas* W. Smiley—a young minister of the Gospel, who he had heard was at one time a resident of Angel's Camp. I added that, if Mr. Wheeler could tell me any thing about this Rev. Leonidas W. Smiley, I would feel under many obligations to him.

Simon Wheeler backed me into a corner and blockaded me there with his chair, and then sat me down and reeled off the monotonous narrative which follows this paragraph. He never smiled, he never frowned, he never changed his voice from the gentle-flowing key to which he tuned the initial sentence, he never betrayed the slightest suspicion of enthusiasm; but all through the interminable narrative there ran a vein of impressive earnestness and sincerity, which showed me plainly that, so far from his imagining that there was any thing ridiculous or funny about his story, he regarded it as a really important matter, and admired its two heroes as men of transcendent genius in *finesse*. To me, the spectacle of a man drifting serenely along through such a queer yarn without ever smiling, was exquisitely absurd. As I said before, I asked him to tell me what he knew of Rev. Leonidas W. Smiley, and he replied as follows. I let him go on in his own way, and never interrupted him once:

There was a feller here once by the name of *Jim* Smiley, in the winter of '49—or may be it was the spring of '50—I don't recollect exactly, somehow, though what makes me think it was one or the other is because I remember the big flume wasn't finished when he first came to the camp; but any way, he was the curiosest man about always betting on any thing that turned up you ever see, if he could get any body to bet on the other side; and if he couldn't, he'd change sides. Any way that suited the other man would suit him—any way just so's he got a bet, *he* was satisfied. But still he was lucky, uncommon lucky; he most always come out winner. He was always ready and laying for a chance; there couldn't be no solitry thing mentioned but that feller'd offer to bet on it, and take any side you please, as I was just telling you. If there was a horse-race, you'd find him flush, or you'd find him busted at the end of it; if there was a dog-fight, he'd bet on it; if there was a cat-fight, he'd bet on it; if there was a chicken-fight, he'd bet on it; why, if there were two birds setting on a fence, he would bet you which one would fly first; or if there was a camp-meeting, he would be there reg'lar, to bet on Parson Walker, which he judged to be the best exhorter about here, and so he was, too, and a good man. If he even seen a straddle-bug start to go anywheres, he would bet you how long it would take him to get wherever he was going to, and if you took him up, he would foller that straddle-bug to Mexico but what he would find out where he was bound for and how long he was on the road. Lots of the boys here has seen that Smiley, and can tell you about him. Why, it never made no difference to *him*—he would bet on *any* thing—the dangdest feller. Parson Walker's wife laid very sick once, for a good while, and it seemed as if they warn't going to save her; but one morning he come in, and Smiley asked how she was, and he said she was considerably better—thank the Lord for his inf'nit mercy—and coming on so smart that, with the blessing of Prov'dence, she'd get well yet; and Smiley, before he thought, says, "Well, I'll risk two-and-a-half that she don't, any way."

Thish-yer Smiley had a mare—the boys called her the fifteen-minute nag, but that was only in fun, you know, because, of course, she was faster than that—and he used to win money on that horse, for all she was so slow and always had the asthma, or the distemper, or the consumption, or something of that kind. They used to give her two or three hundred yards start, and then pass her under way; but always at the fag-end of the race she'd get excited and desperate-like, and come cavorting and straddling up, and scattering her legs around limber, sometimes in the air, and sometimes out to one side amongst the fences, and kicking up m-o-r-e dust, and raising m-o-r-e racket with her coughing and sneezing and blowing her nose—and always fetch up at the stand just about a neck ahead, as near as you could cipher it down.

And he had a little small bull pup, that to look at him you'd think he wan't worth a cent, but to set around and look ornery, and lay for a chance to steal something. But as soon as money was up on him, he was a different dog; his under-jaw'd begin to stick out like the fo'castle of a steamboat, and his teeth would uncover, and shine savage like the furnaces. And a dog might tackle him, and bully-rag him, and bite him, and throw him over his shoulder two or three times, and Andrew Jackson—which was the name of the pup—Andrew Jackson would never let on but what *he* was satisfied, and hadn't expected nothing else—and the bets being doubled and doubled on the other side all the time, till the money was all up; and then all of a sudden he would grab that other dog jest by the j'int of his hind leg and freeze to it—not chaw, you understand, but only jest grip and hang on till they throwed up the sponge, if it was a year. Smiley always come out winner on that pup, till he harnessed a dog once that didn't have no hind legs, because they'd been sawed off by a circular saw, and when the thing had gone along far enough, and the money was all up, and he come to make a snatch for his pet holt, he saw in a minute how he'd been imposed on, and how the other dog had him in the door, so to speak, and he 'peared surprised, and then he looked sorter discouraged-like, and didn't try no more to win the fight, and so he got shucked out bad. He give Smiley a look, as much as to say his heart was broke, and it was *his* fault, for putting up a dog that hadn't no hind legs for him to take holt of, which was his main dependence in a fight, and then he limped off a piece and laid down and died. It was a good pup, was that Andrew Jackson, and would have made a name for hisself if he'd lived, for the stuff was in him, and he had genius—I know it, because he hadn't had no opportunities to speak of, and it don't stand to reason that a dog could make such a fight as he could under them circumstances, if he hadn't no talent. It always makes me feel sorry when I think of that last fight of his'n, and the way it turned out.

Well, thish-yer Smiley had rat-tarriers, and chicken cocks, and tom-cats, and all them kind of things, till you couldn't rest, and you couldn't fetch nothing for him to bet on but he'd match you. He ketched a frog one day, and took him home, and said he cal'klated to edercate him; and so he never done nothing for three months but set in his back yard and learn that frog to jump. And you bet you he *did* learn him, too. He'd give him a little punch behind, and the next minute you'd see that frog whirling in the air like a doughnut—see him turn one summerset, or may be a couple, if he got a good start, and come down flat-footed and all right, like a cat. He got him up so in the matter of catching flies, and kept him in practice so constant, that he'd nail a fly every time as far as he could see him. Smiley said all a frog wanted was education, and he could do most any thing—and I believe him. Why, I've seen him set Dan'l Webster down here on this floor—Dan'l Webster was the name of the frog—and sing out, "Flies, Dan'l, flies!" and quicker'n you could wink, he'd spring straight up, and snake a fly off'n the counter there, and flop down on the floor again as solid as a gob of mud, and fall to scratching the side of his head with his hind foot as indifferent as if he hadn't no idea he'd been doin' any more'n any frog might do. You never see a frog so modest and straightfor'ard as he was, for all he was so gifted. And when it come to fair and square jumping on a dead level, he could get over more ground at one straddle than any animal of his breed you ever see. Jumping on a dead level was his strong suit, you understand; and when it come to that, Smiley would ante up money on him as long as he had a red. Smiley was monstrous proud of his frog, and well he might be, for fellers that had traveled and been everywheres, all said he laid over any frog that ever *they* see.

Well, Smiley kept the beast in a little lattice box, and he used to fetch him down town sometimes and lay for a bet. One day a feller—a stranger in the camp, he was—come across him with his box, and says:

"What might it be that you've got in the box?"

And Smiley says, sorter indifferent like, "It might be a parrot, or it might be a canary, may be, but it an't—it's only just a frog."

And the feller took it, and looked at it careful, and turned it round this way and that, and says, "H'm—so 'tis. Well, what's *he* good for?"

"Well," Smiley says, easy and careless. "He's good enough for *one* thing, I should judge—he can outjump ary frog in Calaveras county."

The feller took the box again, and took another long, particular look, and give it back to Smiley, and says, very deliberate, "Well, I don't see no p'ints about that frog that's any better'n any other frog."

"May be you don't," Smiley says. "May be you understand frogs, and may be you don't understand 'em; may be you've had experience, and may be you an't only a amature, as it were. Anyways, I've got *my* opinion, and I'll risk forty dollars that he can outjump any frog in Calaveras county."

And the feller studied a minute, and then says, kinder sad

like, "Well, I'm only a stranger here, and I an't got no frog; but if I had a frog, I'd bet you."

And then Smiley says, "That's all right—that's all right—if you'll hold my box a minute, I'll go and get you a frog." And so the feller took the box, and put up his forty dollars along with Smiley's, and set down to wait.

So he set there a good while thinking and thinking to hisself, and then he got the frog out and prized his mouth open and took a teaspoon and filled him full of quail shot—filled him pretty near up to his chin—and set him on the floor. Smiley he went to the swamp and slopped around in the mud for a long time, and finally he ketched a frog, and fetched him in, and give him to this feller, and says:

"Now, if you're ready, set him alongside of Dan'l, with his fore-paws just even with Dan'l, and I'll give the word." Then he says, "One—two—three—jump!" and him and the feller touched up the frogs from behind, and the new frog hopped off, but Dan'l give a heave, and hysted up his shoulders—so—like a Frenchman, but it wan't no use—he couldn't budge; he was planted as solid as an anvil, and he couldn't no more stir than if he was anchored out. Smiley was a good deal surprised, and he was disgusted too, but he didn't have no idea what the matter was, of course.

The feller took the money and started away; and when he was going out at the door, he sorta jerked his thumb over his shoulders—this way—at Dan'l, and says again, very deliberate, "Well, *I* don't see no p'ints about that frog that's any better'n any other frog."

Smiley he stood scratching his head and looking down at Dan'l a long time, and at last he says, "I do wonder what in the nation that frog throw'd off for—I wonder if there an't something the matter with him—he 'pears to look mighty baggy, somehow." And he ketched Dan'l by the nap of the neck, and lifted him up and says, "Why, blame my cats, if he don't weigh five pound!" and turned him upside down, and he belched out a double handful of shot. And then he see how it was, and he was the maddest man—he set the frog down and took out after that feller, but he never ketched him. And——

[Here Simon Wheeler heard his name called from the front yard, and got up to see what was wanted.] And turning to me as he moved away, he said: "Just set where you are, stranger, and rest easy—I an't going to be gone a second."

But, by your leave, I did not think that a continuation of the history of the enterprising vagabond *Jim* Smiley would be likely to afford me much information concerning the Rev. *Leonidas W.* Smiley, and so I started away.

At the door I met the sociable Wheeler returning, and he buttonholed me and recommended:

"Well, thish-yer Smiley had a yaller one-eyed cow that didn't have no tail, only jest a short stump like a bannanner, and——"

"Oh! hang Smiley and his afflicted cow!" I muttered, good-naturedly, and bidding the old gentleman good-day, I departed.

"How I Edited an Agricultural Journal Once" (1870)

I did not take the temporary editorship of an agricultural paper without misgivings. Neither would a landsman take command of a ship without misgivings. But I was in circumstances that made the salary an object. The regular editor of the paper was going off for a holiday, and I accepted the terms he offered, and took his place.

The sensation of being at work again was luxurious, and I wrought all the week with unflagging pleasure. We went to press, and I waited a day with some solicitude to see whether my effort was going to attract any notice. As I left the office, toward sundown, a group of men and boys at the foot of the stairs dispersed with one impulse, and gave me passage-way, and I heard one of them say: "That's him!" I was naturally pleased by this incident. The next morning I found a similar group at the foot of the stairs, and scattering couples and individuals standing here and there in the street, and over the way, watching me with interest. The group separated and fell back as I approached and I heard a man say; "Look at his eye!" I pretended not to observe the notice I was attracting, but secretly I was pleased with it, and was purposing to write an account of it to my aunt. I went up the short flight of stairs, and heard cheery voices and a ringing laugh as I drew near the door, which I opened, and caught a glimpse of two young, rural-looking men, whose faces blanched and lengthened when they saw me, and then they both plunged through the window, with a great crash. I was surprised.

In about half an hour an old gentleman, with a flowing beard and a fine but rather austere face, entered, and sat down at my invitation. He seemed to have something on his mind. He took off his hat and set it on the floor, and got out of it a red silk handkerchief and a copy of our paper. He put the paper on his lap, and, while he polished his spectacles with his handkerchief, he said:

"Are you the new editor?"

I said I was.

"Have you ever edited an agricultural paper before?"

"No," I said; "this is my first attempt."

"Very likely. Have you had any experience in agriculture, practically?"

"No, I believe I have not."

"Some instinct told me so," said the old gentleman, putting on his spectacles and looking over them at me with asperity, while he folded his paper into a convenient shape. "I wish to read you what must have made me have that instinct. It was this editorial. Listen, and see if it was you that wrote it:

> "Turnips should never be pulled—it injures them. It is much better to send a boy up and let him shake the tree."

"Now, what do you think of that?—for I really suppose you wrote it?"

"Think of it? Why, I think it is good. I think it is sense. I have no doubt that, every year, millions and millions of bushels of turnips are spoiled in this township alone by being pulled in a half-ripe condition, when, if they had sent a boy up to shake the tree—"

"Shake your grandmother! Turnips don't grow on trees!"

"Oh, they don't, don't they? Well, who said they did? The language was intended to be figurative, wholly figurative. Anybody, that knows anything, will know that I meant that the boy should shake the vine."

Then this old person got up and tore his paper all into small shreds, and stamped on them, and broke several things with his cane, and said I did not know as much as a cow; and then went out, and banged the door after him, and, in short, acted in such a way that I fancied he was displeased about something. But, not knowing what the trouble was, I could not be any help to him.

Pretty soon after this a long, cadaverous creature, with lanky locks hanging down to his shoulders and a week's stubble bristling from the hills and valleys of his face, darted within the door, and halted, motionless, with finger on lip, and head and body bent in listening attitude. No sound was heard. Still he listened. No sound. Then he turned the key in the door, and came elaborately tip-toeing toward me, till he was within long reaching distance of me, when he stopped, and, after scanning my face with intense interest for a while, drew a folded copy of our paper from his bosom, and said:

"There—you wrote that. Read it to me, quick! Relieve me—I suffer."

I read as follows—and as the sentences fell from my lips I could see the relief come—I could see the drawn muscles relax, and the anxiety go out of the face, and rest and peace steal over the features like the merciful moonlight over a desolate landscape:

> "The guano is a fine bird, but great care is necessary in rearing it. It should not be imported earlier than June nor later than September. In the Winter it should be kept in a warm place, where it can hatch out its young.
>
> "It is evident that we are to have a backward season for grain. Therefore, it will be well for the farmer to begin setting out his corn stalks and planting his buckwheat cakes in July instead of August.
>
> "Concerning the Pumpkin—This berry is a favorite with the natives of the interior of New England, who prefer it to the gooseberry for the making of fruit cake, and who likewise give it the preference over the raspberry for feeding cows, as being more filling and fully as satisfying. The pumpkin is the only esculent of the orange family that will thrive in the North, except the gourd and one or two varieties of the squash. But this custom of planting it in the front yard with the shrubbery is fast going out of vogue, for it is now generally conceded that the pumpkin, as a shade tree, is a failure.

"Now, as the warm weather approaches, and the ganders begin to spawn—"

The excited listener sprang toward me to shake hands, and said:

"There, there—that will do! I am all right now, because you have read it just as I did, word for word. But, stranger, when I first read it this morning I said to myself, I never, never believed it before, notwithstanding my friends kept me under watch so strict, but now I believe I *am* crazy; and with that I fetched a howl that you might have heard two miles, and started out to kill somebody—because, you know, I knew it would come to that sooner or later, and so I might as well begin. I read one of them paragraphs over again, so as to be certain, and then I burned my house down and started. I have crippled several people, and have got one fellow up a tree, where I can get him if I want him. But I thought I would call in here as I passed along, and make the thing perfectly certain; and now it *is* certain, and I tell you it is lucky for the chap that is in the tree. I should have killed him, sure, as I went back. Good-by, sir, good-by—you have taken a great load off my mind. My reason has stood the strain of one of your agricultural articles, and I know that nothing can ever unseat it now. *Good*-by, sir."

I felt a little uncomfortable about the cripplings and arsons this person had been entertaining himself with, for I could not help feeling remotely accessory to them; but these thoughts were quickly banished, for the regular editor walked in! [I thought to myself, Now if you had gone to Egypt, as I recommended you to, I might have had a chance to get my hand in; but you wouldn't do it, and here you are. I sort of expected you.]

The editor was looking sad and perplexed, and dejected. He surveyed the wreck which that old rioter and these two young farmers had made, and then said:

"This is a sad business—a very sad business. There is the mucilage bottle broken, and six panes of glass, and a spittoon, and two candlesticks. But that is not the worst. The reputation of the paper is injured, and permanently, I fear. True, there never was such a call for the paper before, and it never sold such a large edition or soared to such celebrity; but does one want to be famous for lunacy, and prosper upon the infirmities of his mind? My friend, as I am an honest man, the street out here is full of people, and others are roosting on the fences, waiting to get a glimpse of you, because they think you are crazy. And well they might, after reading your editorials. They are a disgrace to journalism. Why, what put it into your head that you could edit a paper of this nature? You do not seem to know the first rudiments of agriculture. You speak of a furrow and a harrow as being the same thing; you talk of the moulting season for cows; and you recommend the domestication of the pole-cat on account of its playfulness and its excellence as a ratter. Your remark that clams will lie quiet if music be played to them, was superfluous—entirely superfluous. Nothing disturbs clams. Clams *always* lie quiet. Clams care nothing whatever about music. Ah, heavens and earth, friend, if you had made the acquiring of ignorance the study of your life, you could not have graduated with higher honor than you could to-day. I never saw anything like it. Your observation that the horse-chestnut, as an article of commerce, is steadily gaining favor, is simply calculated to destroy this journal. I want you to throw up your situation and go. I want no more holiday—I could not enjoy it if I had it. Certainly not with you in my chair. I would always stand in dread of what you might be going to recommend next. It makes me lose all patience every time I think of your discussing oyster beds under the head of 'Landscape Gardening.' I want you to go. Nothing on earth could persuade me to take another holiday. Oh, why didn't you *tell* me you didn't know anything about agriculture?"

"*Tell* you, you cornstalk, you cabbage, you son of a cauliflower! It's the first time I ever heard such an unfeeling remark. I tell you I have been in the editorial business going on fourteen years, and it's the first time I ever heard of a man's having to know anything in order to edit a newspaper. You turnip! Who write the dramatic critiques for the second-rate papers? Why, a parcel of promoted shoemakers and apprentice apothecaries, who know just as much about good acting as I do about good farming, and no more. Who review the books? People who never wrote one. Who do up the heavy leaders on finance? Parties who have had the largest opportunities for knowing nothing about it. Who criticise the Indian campaigns? Gentlemen who do not know a war-whoop from a wigwam, and who never have had to run a foot race with a tomahawk or pluck arrows out of the several members of their families to build the evening camp-fire with. Who write the temperance appeals and clamor about the flowing bowl? Folks who will never draw another sober breath till they do it in the grave. Who edit the agricultural papers, you—yam? Men, as a general thing, who fail in the poetry line, yellow-covered novel line, sensation-drama line, city-editor line, and finally fall back on agriculture as temporary reprieve from the poor-house. *You* try to tell *me* anything about the newspaper business! Sir, I have been through it from Alpha to Omaha, and I tell you that the less a man knows the bigger noise he makes and higher the salary he commands. Heaven knows if I had been ignorant instead of cultivated, and impudent instead of diffident, I could have made a name for myself in this cold, selfish world. I take my leave, sir. Since I have been treated as you have treated me, I am perfectly willing to go. But I have done my duty. I have fulfilled my contract, as far as I was permitted to do it. I said I could make your paper of interest to all classes, and I have. I said I could run your circulation up to twenty thousand copies, and if I had two more weeks I'd have done it. And I'd have given you the best class of readers that ever an agricultural paper had—not a farmer in it, nor a solitary individual who could tell a watermelon from a peach-vine to save his life. *You* are the loser by this rupture, not me, Pie-plant. Adios."

I then left.

FROM

Roughing It (1872)

"THE STORY OF THE OLD RAM"

Every now and then, in these days, the boys used to tell me I ought to get one Jim Blaine to tell me the stirring story of his grandfather's old ram—but they always added that I must not mention the matter unless Jim was drunk at the time—just comfortably and sociably drunk. They kept this up until my curiosity was on the rack to hear the story. I got to haunting Blaine; but it was of no use, the boys always found fault with his condition; he was often moderately but never satisfactorily drunk. I never watched a man's condition with such absorbing interest, such anxious solicitude; I never so pined to see a man uncompromisingly drunk before. At last, one evening I hurried to his cabin, for I learned that this time his situation was such that even the most fastidious could find no fault with it—he was tranquilly, serenely, symmetrically drunk—not a hiccup to mar his voice, not a cloud upon his brain thick enough to obscure his memory. As I entered, he was sitting upon an empty powder-keg, with a clay pipe in one hand and the other raised to command silence. His face was round, red, and very serious; his throat was bare and his hair tumbled; in general appearance and costume he was a stalwart miner of the period. On the pine table stood a candle, and its dim light revealed "the boys" sitting here and there on bunks, candle-boxes, powder-kegs, etc. They said:

"Sh—! Don't speak—he's going to commence."

I found a seat at once, and Blaine said:

"I don't reckon them times will ever come again. There never was a more bullier old ram than what he was. Grandfather fetched him from Illinois—got him of a man by the name of Yates—Bill Yates—maybe you might have heard of him; his father was a deacon—Baptist—and he was a rustler, too; a man had to get up ruther early to get the start of old Thankful Yates; it was him that put the Greens up to jining teams with my grandfather when he moved west. Seth Green was prob'ly the pick of the flock; he married a Wilkerson—Sarah Wilkerson—good cretur, she was—one of the likeliest heifers that was ever raised in old Stoddard, everybody said that knowed her. She could heft a bar'l of flour as easy as I can flirt a flapjack. And spin? Don't mention it! Independent? Humph! When Sile Hawkins come a browsing around her, she let him know that for all his tin he couldn't trot in harness alongside of *her.* You see, Sile Hawkins was—no, it warn't Sile Hawkins, after all—it was a galoot by the name of Filkins—I disremember his first name; but he *was* a stump—come into pra'r meeting drunk, one night, horraying for Nixon, becuz he thought it was a primary; and old deacon Ferguson up and scooted him through the window and he lit on old Miss Jefferson's head, poor old filly. She was a good soul—had a glass eye and used to lend it to old Miss Wagner, that hadn't any, to receive company in; it warn't big enough, and when Miss Wagner warn't noticing, it would get twisted around in the socket, and look up, maybe, or out to one side, and every which way, while t' other one was looking as straight ahead as a spy-glass. Grown people didn't mind it, but it most always made the children cry, it was so sort of scary. She tried packing it in raw cotton, but it wouldn't work somehow—the cotton would get loose and stick out and look so kind of awful that the children couldn't stand it no way. She was always dropping it out, and turning up her old dead-light on the company empty, and making them oncomfortable, becuz *she* never could tell when it hopped out, being blind on that side, you see. So somebody would have to hunch her and say, "Your game eye has fetched loose, Miss Wagner dear"—and then all of them would have to sit and wait till she jammed it in again—wrong side before, as a general thing, and green as a bird's egg, being a bashful cretur and easy sot back before company. But being wrong side before warn't much difference, anyway, becuz her own eye was sky-blue and the glass one was yaller on the front side, so whichever way she turned it it didn't match nohow. Old Miss Wagner was considerable on the borrow, she was. When she had a quilting, or Dorcas S'iety at her house she gen'ally borrowed Miss Higgins's wooden leg to stump around on; it was considerable shorter than her other pin, but much *she* minded that. She said she couldn't abide crutches when she had company, becuz they were so slow; said when she had company and things had to be done, she wanted to get up and hump herself. She was as bald as a jug, and so she used to borrow Miss Jacops's wig—Miss Jacops was the coffin-peddler's wife—a ratty old buzzard, he was, that used to go roosting around where people was sick; waiting for 'em; and there that old rip would sit all day, in the shade, on a coffin that he judged would fit the can'idate; and if it was a slow customer and kind of uncertain, he'd fetch his rations and a blanket along and sleep in the coffin nights. He was anchored out that way, in frosty weather, for about three weeks, once, before old Robbins's place, waiting for him; and after that, for as much as two years, Jacops was not on speaking terms with the old man, on account of his disapp'inting him. He got one of his feet froze, and lost money, too, becuz old Robbins took a favorable turn and got well. The next time Robbins got sick, Jacops tried to make up with him, and varnished up the same old coffin and fetched it along; but old Robbins was too many for him; he had him in, and 'peared to be powerful weak; he bought the coffin for ten dollars and Jacops was to pay it back and twenty-five more besides if Robbins didn't like the coffin after he'd tried it. And then Robbins died, and at the funeral he bursted off the lid and riz up in his shroud and told the parson to let up on the performances, becuz he could *not* stand such a coffin as that. You see he had been in a trance once before, when he was young, and he took the chances on another, cal'lating that if he made the trip it was money in his pocket, and if he missed fire he couldn't lose a cent. And by George he sued Jacops for the rhino and got jedgment; and he set up the coffin in his back parlor and said he 'lowed to take his time, now. It was always an aggravation to Jacops, the way that miserable old thing acted. He moved back to Indiany pretty soon—went to Wellsville—Wellsville was the place the Hogadorns was from. Mighty fine family. Old Maryland stock. Old Squire Hogadorn could carry around more mixed licker, and cuss better than most any man I ever see. His second wife was the widder Billings—she that was Becky Martin; her dam was deacon Dunlap's first wife. Her oldest child, Maria, married a missionary and died in grace—et up by the savages. They et *him*, too, poor feller—biled him. It warn't the custom, so they say, but they explained to friends of his'n that went down there to bring away his things, that they'd tried missionaries every other way and never could get any good out of 'em—and so it annoyed all his relations to find out that that man's life was fooled away, just out of a dern'd experiment, so to speak. But mind you, there ain't anything ever reely lost; everything that people can't understand and don't see the reason of does good if you only hold on and give it a fair shake; Prov'dence don't fire no blank ca'tridges, boys. That there missionary's substance, unbeknowns to himself, actu'ly converted every last one of them heathens that took a chance at the barbacue. Nothing ever fetched them but that. Don't tell *me* it was an accident that he was biled. There ain't no such a thing as an accident. When my uncle Lem was leaning up agin a scaffolding once, sick, or drunk, or suthin, an Irishman with a hod full of bricks fell on him out of the third story and broke the old man's back in two places. People said it was an accident. Much accident there was about that. He didn't know what he was there for, but he was there for a good object. If he hadn't been there the Irishman would have been killed. Nobody can ever make me believe anything different from that. Uncle Lem's dog was there. Why didn't the Irishman fall on the dog? Becuz the dog would a seen him a coming and stood from under. That's the reason the dog warn't appinted. A dog can't be depended on to carry out a special providence. Mark my words it was a put-up thing. Accidents don't happen, boys. Uncle Lem's dog—I wish you could a seen that dog. He was a regular shepherd—or rather he was part bull and part shepherd—splendid animal; belonged to parson Hagar before Uncle Lem got him. Parson Hagar belonged to the Western Reserve Hagars; prime family; his mother was a Watson; one of his sisters married a Wheeler; they settled in Morgan county, and he got nipped by the machinery in a carpet factory and went through in less than a quarter of a minute; his widder bought the piece of carpet that had his remains wove in, and people come a hundred mile to 'tend the funeral. There was fourteen yards in the piece. She wouldn't let them roll him up, but planted him just so—full length. The church was middling small where they preached the funeral, and they had to let one end of the coffin stick out of the window. They didn't bury him—they planted one end, and let him stand up, same as a monument. And they nailed a sign on it and put—put on—put on it—sacred to—the m-e-m-o-r-y—of fourteen y-a-r-d-s—of three-ply—car - - - pet—containing all that was—m-o-r-t-a-l—of—of—W-i-l-l-i-a-m—W-h-e—"

Jim Blaine had been growing gradually drowsy and drowsier—his head nodded, once, twice, three times—dropped peacefully upon his breast, and he fell tranquilly asleep. The tears were running down the boys' cheeks—they were suffocating with suppressed laughter—and had been from the start, though I had never noticed it. I perceived that I was "sold." I learned then that Jim Blaine's peculiarity was that whenever he reached a certain stage of intoxication, no human power could keep him from setting out, with impressive unction, to tell about a wonderful adventure which he had once had with his grandfather's old ram—and the mention of the ram in the first sentence was as far as any man had ever heard him get, concerning it. He always maundered off, interminably, from one thing to another, till his whisky got the best of him and he fell asleep. What the thing was that happened to him and his grandfather's old ram is a dark mystery to this day, for nobody has ever yet found out.

"BUCK FANSHAW'S FUNERAL"

Somebody has said that in order to know a community, one must observe the style of its funerals and know what manner of men they bury with most ceremony. I cannot say which class we buried with most eclat in our "flush times," the distinguished public benefactor or the distinguished rough—possibly the two chief grades or grand divisions of society honored their illustrious dead about equally; and hence, no doubt the philosopher I have quoted from would have needed to see two representative funerals in Virginia before forming his estimate of the people.

There was a grand time over Buck Fanshaw when he died. He was a representative citizen. He had "killed his man"—not in his own quarrel, it is true, but in defence of a stranger unfairly beset by numbers. He had kept a sumptuous saloon. He had been the proprietor of a dashing helpmeet whom he could have discarded without the formality of a divorce. He had held a high position in the fire department and been a very Warwick in politics. When he died there was great lamentation throughout the town, but especially in the vast bottom-stratum of society.

On the inquest it was shown that Buck Fanshaw, in the delirium of a wasting typhoid fever, had taken arsenic, shot himself through the body, cut his throat, and jumped out of a four-story window and broken his neck—and after due deliberation, the jury, sad and tearful, but with intelligence unblinded by its sorrow, brought in a verdict of death "by the visitation of God." What could the world do without juries?

Prodigious preparations were made for the funeral. All the vehicles in town were hired, all the saloons put in mourning, all the municipal and fire-company flags hung at half-mast, and all the firemen ordered to muster in uniform and bring their machines duly draped in black. Now—let us remark in parenthesis—as all the peoples of the earth had representative adventurers in the Silverland, and as each adventurer had brought the slang of his nation or his locality with him, the combination made the slang of Nevada the richest and the most infinitely varied and copious that had ever existed anywhere in the world, perhaps, except in the mines of California in the "early days." Slang was the language of Nevada. It was hard to preach a sermon without it, and be understood. Such phrases as "You bet!" "Oh, no, I reckon not!" "No Irish need apply," and a hundred others, became so common as to fall from the lips of a speaker unconsciously—and very often when they did not touch the subject under discussion and consequently failed to mean anything.

After Buck Fanshaw's inquest, a meeting of the short-haired brotherhood was held, for nothing can be done on the Pacific coast without a public meeting and an expression of sentiment. Regretful resolutions were passed and various committees appointed; among others, a committee of one was deputed to call on the minister, a fragile, gentle, spirituel new fledgling from an Eastern theological seminary, and as yet unacquainted with the ways of the mines. The committeeman, "Scotty" Briggs, made his visit; and in after days it was worth something to hear the minister tell about it. Scotty was a stalwart rough, whose customary suit, when on weighty official business, like committee work, was a fire helmet, flaming red flannel shirt, patent leather belt with spanner and revolver attached, coat hung over arm, and pants stuffed into boot tops. He formed something of a contrast to the pale theological student. It is fair to say of Scotty, however, in passing, that he had a warm heart, and a strong love for his friends, and never entered into a quarrel when he could reasonably keep out of it. Indeed, it was commonly said that whenever one of Scotty's fights was investigated, it always turned out that it had originally been no affair of his, but that out of native goodheartedness he had dropped in of his own accord to help the man who was getting the worst of it. He and Buck Fanshaw were bosom friends, for years, and had often taken adventurous "pot-luck" together. On one occasion, they had thrown off their coats and taken the weaker side in a fight among strangers, and after gaining a hard-earned victory, turned and found that the men they were helping had deserted early, and not only that, but had stolen their coats and made off with them! But to return to Scotty's visit to the minister. He was on a sorrowful mission, now, and his face was the picture of woe. Being admitted to the presence he sat down before the clergyman, placed his fire-hat on an unfinished manuscript sermon under the minister's nose, took from it a red silk handkerchief, wiped his brow and heaved a sigh of dismal impressiveness, explanatory of his business. He choked, and even shed tears; but with an effort he mastered his voice and said in lugubrious tones:

"Are you the duck that runs the gospel-mill next door?"

"Am I the—pardon me, I believe I do not understand?"

With another sigh and a half-sob, Scotty rejoined:

"Why you see we are in a bit of trouble, and the boys thought maybe you would give us a lift, if we'd tackle you—that is, if I've got the rights of it and you are the head clerk of the doxology-works next door."

"I am the shepherd in charge of the flock whose fold is next door."

"The which?"

"The spiritual adviser of the little company of believers whose sanctuary adjoins these premises."

Scotty scratched his head, reflected a moment, and then said:

"You ruther hold over me, pard. I reckon I can't call that hand. Ante and pass the buck."

"How? I beg pardon. What did I understand you to say?"

"Well, you've ruther got the bulge on me. Or maybe we've both got the bulge, somehow. You don't smoke me and I don't smoke you. You see, one of the boys has passed in his checks and we want to give him a good send-off, and so the thing I'm on now is to roust out somebody to jerk a little chin-music for us and waltz him through handsome."

"My friend, I seem to grow more and more bewildered. Your observations are wholly incomprehensible to me. Cannot you simplify them in some way? At first I thought perhaps I understood you, but I grope now. Would it not expedite matters if you restricted yourself to categorical statements of fact unencumbered with obstructing accumulations of metaphor and allegory?"

Another pause, and more reflection. Then, said Scotty:

"I'll have to pass, I judge."

"How?"

"You've raised me out, pard."

"I still fail to catch your meaning."

"Why, that last lead of yourn is too many for me—that's the idea. I can't neither trump nor follow suit."

The clergyman sank back in his chair perplexed. Scotty leaned his head on his hand and gave himself up to thought. Presently his face came up, sorrowful but confident.

"I've got it now, so's you can savvy," he said. "What we want is a gospel-sharp. See?"

"A what?"

"Gospel-sharp. Parson."

"Oh! Why did you not say so before? I am a clergyman—a parson."

"Now you talk! You see my blind and straddle it like a man. Put it there!"—extending a brawny paw, which closed over the minister's small hand and gave it a shake indicative of fraternal sympathy and fervent gratification.

"Now we're all right, pard. Let's start fresh. Don't you mind my snuffling a little—becuz we're in a power of trouble. You see, one of the boys has gone up the flume—"

"Gone where?"

"Up the flume—throwed up the sponge, you understand."

"Thrown up the sponge?"

"Yes—kicked the bucket—"

"Ah—has departed to that mysterious country from whose bourne no traveler returns."

"Return! I reckon not. Why pard, he's *dead!*"

"Yes, I understand."

"Oh, you do? Well I thought maybe you might be getting tangled some more. Yes, you see he's dead again—"

"*Again?* Why, has he ever been dead before?"

"Dead before? No! Do you reckon a man has got as many lives as a cat! But you bet you he's awful dead now, poor old boy, and I wish I'd never seen this day. I don't want no better friend than Buck Fanshaw. I knowed him by the back; and when I know a man and like him, I freeze to him—you hear *me*. Take him all round, pard, there never was a bullier man in the mines. No man ever knowed Buck Fanshaw to go back on a friend. But it's all up, you know, it's all up. It ain't no use. They've scooped him."

"Scooped him?"

"Yes—death has. Well, well, well, we've got to give him up. Yes indeed. It's a kind of hard world, after all, *ain't* it? But pard, he was a rustler! You ought to seen him get started once. He was a bully boy with a glass eye! Just spit in his face and give him room according to his strength, and it was just beautiful to see him peel and go in. He was the worst son of a thief that ever drawed breath. Pard, he was *on* it! He was on it bigger than an Injun!"

"On it? On what?"

"On the shoot. On the shoulder. On the fight, you understand. *He* didn't give a continental for *any*body. *Beg* your pardon, friend, for coming so near saying a cuss-word—but you see I'm on an awful strain, in this palaver, on account of having to cramp down and draw everything so mild. But we've got to give him up. There ain't any getting around that, I don't reckon. Now if we can get you to help plant him—"

"Preach the funeral discourse? Assist at the obsequies?"

"Obs'quies is good. Yes. That's it—that's our little game. We are going to get the thing up regardless, you know. He was always nifty himself, and so you bet you his funeral ain't going to be no slouch—solid silver door-plate on his coffin, six plumes on the hearse, and a nigger on the box in a biled shirt and a plug hat—how's that for high? And we'll take care of *you*, pard. We'll fix you all right. There'll be a kerridge for you; and whatever you want, you just 'scape out and we'll 'tend to it. We've got a shebang fixed up for you to stand behind, in No. 1's house, and don't you be afraid. Just go in and toot your horn, if you don't sell a clam. Put Buck through as bully as you can, pard, for anybody that knowed him will tell you that he was one of the whitest men that was ever in the mines. You can't draw it too strong. He never could stand it to see things going wrong. He's done more to make this town quiet and peaceable than any man in it. I've seen him lick four Greasers in eleven minutes, myself. If a thing wanted regulating, *he* warn't a man to go browsing around after somebody to do it, but he would prance in and regulate it himself. He warn't a Catholic. Scasely. He was down on 'em. His word was, 'No Irish need apply!' But it didn't make no difference about that when it came down to what a man's rights was—and so, when some roughs jumped the Catholic bone-yard and started in to stake out town-lots in it he *went* for 'em! And he *cleaned* 'em, too! I was there, pard, and I seen it myself."

"That was very well indeed—at least the impulse was—whether the act was strictly defensible or not. Had deceased any religious convictions? That is to say, did he feel a dependence upon, or acknowledge allegiance to a higher power?"

More reflection.

"I reckon you've stumped me again, pard. Could you say it over once more, and say it slow?"

"Well, to simplify it somewhat, was he, or rather had he ever been connected with any organization sequestered from secular concerns and devoted to self-sacrifice in the interests of morality?"

"All down but nine—set 'em up on the other alley, pard"

"What did I understand you to say?"

"Why, you're most too many for me, you know. When you get in with your left I hunt grass every time. Every time you draw, you fill; but I don't seem to have any luck. Lets have a new deal."

"How? Begin again?"

"That's it."

"Very well. Was he a good man, and—"

"There—I see that; don't put up another chip till I look at my hand. A good man, says you? Pard, it ain't no name for it. He was the best man that ever—pard, you would have doted on that man. He could lam any galoot of his inches in America. It was him that put down the riot last election before it got a start; and everybody said he was the only man that could have done it. He waltzed in with a spanner in one hand and a trumpet in the other, and sent fourteen men home on a shutter in less than three minutes. He had that riot all broke up and prevented nice before anybody ever got a chance to strike a blow. He was always for peace, and he would *have* peace—he could not stand disturbances. Pard, he was a great loss to this town. It would please the boys if you could chip in something like that and do him justice. Here once when the Micks got to throwing stones through the Methodis' Sunday school windows, Buck Fanshaw, all of his own notion, shut up his saloon and took a couple of six-shooters and mounted guard over the Sunday school. Says he, 'No Irish need apply!' And they didn't. He was the bulliest man in the mountains, pard! He could run faster, jump higher, hit harder, and hold more tangle-foot whisky without spilling it than any man in seventeen counties. Put that in, pard—it'll please the boys more than anything you could say. And you can say, pard, that he never shook his mother."

"Never shook his mother?"

"That's it—any of the boys will tell you so."

"Well, but why *should* he shake her?"

"That's what *I* say—but some people does."

"Not people of any repute?"

"Well, some that averages pretty so-so."

"In my opinion the man that would offer personal violence to his own mother, ought to—"

"Cheese it, pard; you've banked your ball clean outside the string. What I was a drivin' at, was, that he never *throwed off* on his mother—don't you see? No indeedy. He give her a house to live in, and town lots, and plenty of money; and he looked after her and took care of her all the time; and when she was down with the small-pox I'm d—d if he didn't set up nights and nuss her himself! *Beg* your pardon for saying it, but it hopped out too quick for yours truly. You've treated me like a gentleman, pard, and I ain't the man to hurt your feelings intentional. I think you're white. I think you're a square man, pard. I like you, and I'll lick any man that don't. I'll lick him till he can't tell himself from a last year's corpse! Put it *there!*" [Another fraternal handshake—and exit.]

The obsequies were all that "the boys" could desire. Such a

marvel of funeral pomp had never been seen in Virginia. The plumed hearse, the dirge-breathing brass bands, the closed marts of business, the flags drooping at half mast, the long, plodding procession of uniformed secret societies, military battalions and fire companies, draped engines, carriages of officials, and citizens in vehicles and on foot, attracted multitudes of spectators to the sidewalks, roofs and windows; and for years afterward, the degree of grandeur attained by any civic display in Virginia was determined by comparison with Buck Fanshaw's funeral.

Scotty Briggs, as a pall-bearer and a mourner, occupied a prominent place at the funeral, and when the sermon was finished and the last sentence of the prayer for the dead man's soul ascended, he responded, in a low voice, but with feeling:

"AMEN. No Irish need apply."

As the bulk of the response was without apparent relevancy, it was probably nothing more than a humble tribute to the memory of the friend that was gone; for, as Scotty had once said, it was "his word."

Scotty Briggs, in after days, achieved the distinction of becoming the only convert to religion that was ever gathered from the Virginia roughs; and it transpired that the man who had it in him to espouse the quarrel of the weak out of inborn nobility of spirit was no mean timber whereof to construct a Christian. The making him one did not warp his generosity or diminish his courage; on the contrary it gave intelligent direction to the one and a broader field to the other. If his Sunday-school class progressed faster than the other classes, was it matter for wonder? I think not. He talked to his pioneer small-fry in a language they understood! It was my large privilege, a month before he died, to hear him tell the beautiful story of Joseph and his brethren to his class "without looking at the book." I leave it to the reader to fancy what it was like, as it fell, riddled with slang, from the lips of that grave, earnest teacher, and was listened to by his little learners with a consuming interest that showed that they were as unconscious as he was that any violence was being done to the sacred proprieties!

"LETTERS FROM GREELEY"

We stopped some time at one of the plantations, to rest ourselves and refresh the horses. We had a chatty conversation with several gentlemen present; but there was one person, a middle aged man, with an absent look in his face, who simply glanced up, gave us good-day and lapsed again into the meditations which our coming had interrupted. The planters whispered us not to mind him—crazy. They said he was in the Islands for his health; was a preacher; his home, Michigan. They said that if he woke up presently and fell to talking about a correspondence which he had some time held with Mr. Greeley about a trifle of some kind, we must humor him and listen with interest; and we must humor his fancy that this correspondence was the talk of the world.

It was easy to see that he was a gentle creature and that his madness had nothing vicious in it. He looked pale, and a little worn, as if with perplexing thought and anxiety of mind. He sat a long time, looking at the floor, and at intervals muttering to himself and nodding his head acquiescingly or shaking it in mild protest. He was lost in his thought, or in his memories. We continued our talk with the planters, branching from subject to subject. But at last the word "circumstance," casually dropped, in the course of conversation, attracted his attention and brought an eager look into his countenance. He faced about in his chair and said:

"Circumstance? What circumstance? An, I know—I know too well. So you have heard of it too." [With a sigh.] "Well, no matter—all the world has heard of it. All the world. The whole world. It is a large world, too, for a thing to travel so far in—now isn't it? Yes, yes—the Greeley correspondence with Erickson has created the saddest and bitterest controversy on both sides of the ocean—and still they keep it up! It makes us famous, but at what a sorrowful sacrifice! I was so sorry when I heard that it had caused that bloody and distressful war over there in Italy. It was little comfort to me, after so much bloodshed, to know that the victors sided with me, and the vanquished with Greeley.—It is little comfort to know that Horace Greeley is responsible for the battle of Sadowa, and not me. Queen Victoria wrote me that she felt just as I did about it—she said that as much as she was opposed to Greeley and the spirit he showed in the correspondence with me, she would not have had Sadowa happen for hundreds of dollars. I can show you her letter, if you would like to see it. But gentlemen, much as you may think you know about that unhappy correspondence, you cannot know the *straight* of it till you hear it from my lips. It has always been garbled in the journals, and even in history. Yes, even in history—think of it! Let me—*please* let me, give you the matter, exactly as it occurred. I truly will not abuse your confidence."

Then he leaned forward, all interest, all earnestness, and told his story—and told it appealingly, too, and yet in the simplest and most unpretentious way; indeed, in such a way as to suggest to one, all the time, that this was a faithful, honorable witness, giving evidence in the sacred interest of justice, and under oath. He said:

"Mrs. Beazeley—Mrs. Jackson Beazeley, widow, of the village of Campbellton, Kansas,—wrote me about a matter which was near her heart—a matter which many might think trivial, but to her it was a thing of deep concern. I was living in Michigan, then—serving in the ministry. She was, and is, an estimable woman—a woman to whom poverty and hardship have proven incentives to industry, in place of discouragements. Her only treasure was her son William, a youth just verging upon manhood; religious, amiable, and sincerely attached to agriculture. He was the widow's comfort and her pride. And so, moved by her love for him, she wrote me about a matter, as I have said before, which lay near her heart—because it lay near her boy's. She desired me to confer with Mr. Greeley about turnips. Turnips were the dram of her child's young ambition. While other youths were frittering away in frivolous amusements the precious years of budding vigor which God had given them for useful preparation, this boy was patiently enriching his mind with information concerning turnips. The sentiment which he felt toward the turnip was akin to adoration. He could not think of the turnip without emotion; he could not speak of it calmly; he could not contemplate it without exaltation. He could not eat it without shedding tears. All the poetry in his sensitive nature was in sympathy with the gracious vegetable. With the earliest pipe of dawn he sought his patch, and when the curtaining night drove him from it he shut himself up with his books and garnered statistics till sleep overcame him. On rainy days he sat and talked hours together with his mother about turnips. When company came, he made it his loving duty to put aside everything else and converse with them all the day long of his great joy in the turnip. And yet, was this joy rounded and complete? Was there no secret alloy of unhappiness in it? Alas, there was. There was a canker gnawing at his heart; the noblest inspiration of his soul eluded his endeavor—viz: he could not make of the turnip a climbing vine. Months went by; the bloom forsook his cheek, the fire faded out of his eye; sighings and abstraction usurped the place of smiles and cheerful converse. But a watchful eye noted these things and in time a motherly sympathy unscaled the secret. Hence the letter to me. She pleaded for attention—she said her boy was dying by inches.

"I was a stranger to Mr. Greeley, but what of that? The matter was urgent. I wrote and begged him to solve the difficult problem if possible and save the student's life. My interest grew, until it partook of the anxiety of the mother. I waited in much suspense.—At last the answer came.

"I found that I could not read it readily, the handwriting being unfamiliar and my emotions somewhat wrought up. It seemed to refer in part to the boy's case, but chiefly to other and irrelevant matters—such as paving-stones, electricity, oysters, and something which I took to be 'absolution' or 'agrarianism,' I could not be certain which; still, these appeared to be simply casual mentions, nothing more; friendly in spirit, without doubt, but lacking the connection or coherence necessary to make them useful.—I judged that my understanding was affected by my feelings, and so laid the letter away till morning.

"In the morning I read it again, but with difficulty and uncertainty still, for I had lost some little rest and my mental vision seemed clouded. The note was more connected, now, but did not meet the emergency it was expected to meet. It was too discursive. It appeared to read as follows, though I was not certain of some of the words:

> 'Polygamy dissembles majesty; extracts redeem polarity; causes hitherto exist. Ovations pursue wisdom, or warts inherit and condemn. Boston, botany, cakes, folony undertakes, but who shall allay? We fear not. Yrxwly,
>
> HEVACE EVEELOJ.'

"But there did not seem to be a word about turnips. There seemed to be no suggestion as to how they might be made to grow like vines. There was not even a reference to the Beazeleys. I slept upon the matter; I ate no supper, neither any breakfast next morning. So I resumed my work with a brain refreshed, and was very hopeful. *Now* the letter took a different aspect—all save the signature, which latter I judged to be only a harmless affectation of Hebrew. The epistle was necessarily from Mr. Greeley, for it bore the printed heading of *The Tribune,* and I had written to no one else there. The letter, I say, had taken a different aspect, but still its language was eccentric and avoided the issue. It now appeared to say:

> 'Bolivia extemporaizes mackerel; borax esteems polygamy; sausages wither in the east. Creation perdu, is done; for woes inherent one can damn. Buttons, buttons, corks, geology underrates but we shall allay. My beer's out. Yrxwly,
>
> HEVACE EVEELOJ.'

"I was evidently overworked. My comprehension was impaired. Therefore I gave two days to recreation, and then returned to my task greatly refreshed. The letter now took this form:

> 'Poultices do sometimes choke swine; tulips reduco posterity; causes leather to resist. Our notions empower wisdom, her let's

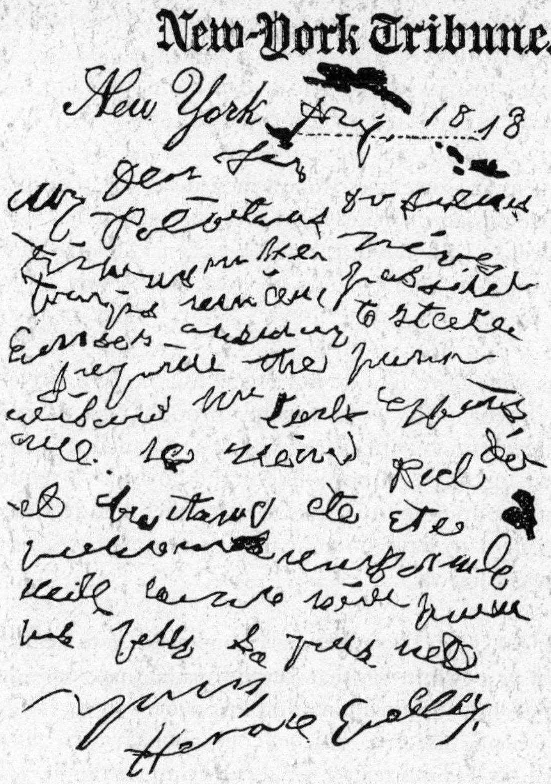
New-York Tribune.

afford while we can. Butter but any cakes, fill any undertaker, we'll wean him from his filly. We feel hot. Yrxwly,

HEVACE EVEELOJ.'

"I was still not satisfied. These generalities did not meet the question. They were crisp, and vigorous, and delivered with a confidence that almost compelled conviction; but at such a time as this, with a human life at stake, they seemed inappropriate, worldly, and in bad taste. At any other time I would have been not only glad, but proud, to receive from a man like Mr. Greeley a letter of this kind, and would have studied it earnestly and tried to improve myself all I could; but now, with that poor boy in his far home languishing for relief, I had no heart for learning.

"Three days passed by, and I read the note again. Again its tenor had changed. It now appeared to say:

> 'Potations do sometimes wake wines; turnips restrain passion; causes necessary to state. Infest the poor widow; her lord's effects will be void. But dirt, bathing, etc., etc., followed unfairly, will worm him from his folly—to swear not. Yrxwly,
>
> HEVACE EVEELOJ.'

"This was more like it. But I was unable to proceed. I was too much worn. The word 'turnips' brought temporary joy and encouragement, but my strength was so much impaired, and the delay might be so perilous for the boy, that I relinquished the idea of pursuing the translation further, and resolved to do what I ought to have done at first. I sat down and wrote Mr. Greeley as follows:

> "DEAR SIR: I fear I do not entirely comprehend your kind note. It cannot be possible, Sir, that 'turnips restrain passion'—at least the study or contemplation of turnips cannot—for it is this very employment that has scorched our poor friend's mind and sapped his bodily strength.—But if they *do* restrain it, will you bear with us a little further and explain how they should be prepared? I observe that you say 'causes necessary to state,' but you have omitted to state them.
>
> "Under a misapprehension, you seem to attribute to me interested motives in this matter—to call it by no harsher term. But I assure you, dear sir, that if I seem to be 'infesting the widow,' it is all *seeming* and void of reality. It is from no seeking of mine that I am in this position. She asked me, herself, to write you. I never have infested her—indeed I scarcely know her. I do not infest anybody. I try to go along, in my humble way, doing as near right as I can, never harming anybody, and never *throwing out insinuations*. As for 'her lord and his effects,' they are of no interest to me. I trust I have effects enough of my own—shall en-

deavor to get along with them, at any rate, and not go mousing around to get hold of somebody's that are 'void.' But do you not see?—this woman is a *widow*—she has no 'lord.' He is dead—or pretended to be, when they buried him. Therefore, no amount of 'dirt, bathing,' etc., etc., howsoever 'unfairly followed' will be likely to 'worm him from his folly'—if being dead and a ghost is 'folly.' Your closing remark is as unkind as it was uncalled for; and if report says true you might have applied it to yourself, sir, with more point and less impropriety.

Very Truly Yours, SIMON ERICKSON.

"In the course of a few days, Mr. Greeley did what would have saved a world of trouble, and much mental and bodily suffering and misunderstanding, if he had done it sooner. To-wit, he sent an intelligible rescript or translation of his original note, made in a plain hand by his clerk. Then the mystery cleared, and I saw that his heart had been right, all the time. I will recite the note in its clarified form:

[Translation]

'Potatoes do sometimes make vines; turnips remain passive: cause unnecessary to state. Inform the poor widow her lad's efforts will be vain. But diet, bathing, etc. etc., followed uniformly, will wean him from his folly—so fear not.

Yours, HORACE GREELEY.'

"But alas, it was too late, gentlemen—too late. The criminal delay had done its work—young Beazely was no more. His spirit had taken its flight to a land where all anxieties shall be charmed away, all desires gratified, all ambitions realized. Poor lad, they laid him to his rest with a turnip in each hand."

So ended Erickson, and lapsed again into nodding, mumbling, and abstraction. The company broke up, and left him so. . . . But they did not say what drove him crazy. In the momentary confusion, I forgot to ask.

"An Encounter with an Interviewer" (1874)

The nervous, dapper, "peart" young man took the chair I offered him, and said he was connected with the *Daily Thunderstorm,* and added,—

"Hoping it's no harm, I've come to interview you."

"Come to what?"

"*Interview* you."

"Ah! I see. Yes,—yes. Um! Yes,—yes."

I was not feeling bright that morning. Indeed, my powers seemed a bit under a cloud. However, I went to the bookcase, and when I had been looking six or seven minutes, I found I was obliged to refer to the young man. I said,—

"How do you spell it?"

"Spell what?"

"Interview."

"O my goodness! What do you want to spell it for?"

"I don't want to spell it; I want to see what it means."

"Well, this is astonishing, I must say. *I* can tell you what it means, if you—if you—"

"O, all right! That will answer, and much obliged to you, too."

"I n, *in,* t e r, *ter, in*ter—"

"Then you spell it with an *I?*"

"Why, certainly!"

"Oh, that is what took me so long."

"Why, my *dear* sir, what did *you* propose to spell it with?"

"Well, I—I—I hardly know. I had the Unabridged, and I was ciphering around in the back end, hoping I might tree her among the pictures. But it's a very old edition."

"Why, my friend, they wouldn't have a *picture* of it in even the latest e— My dear sir, I beg your pardon, I mean no harm in the world, but you do not look as—as—intelligent as I had expected you would. No harm,—I mean no harm at all."

"O, don't mention it! It has often been said, and by people who would not flatter and who could have no inducement to flatter, that I am quite remarkable in that way. Yes,—yes; they always speak of it with rapture."

"I can easily imagine it. But how about this interview. You know it is the custom, now, to interview any man who has become notorious."

"Indeed! I had not heard of it before. It must be very interesting. What do you do it with?"

"Ah, well,—well,—well,—this is disheartening. It *ought* to be done with a club in some cases; but customarily it consists in the interviewer asking questions and the interviewed answering them. It is all the rage now. Will you let me ask you certain questions calculated to bring out the salient points of your public and private history?"

"O, with pleasure,—with pleasure. I have a very bad memory, but I hope you will not mind that. That is to say, it is an irregular memory,—singularly irregular. Sometimes it goes in a gallop, and then again it will be as much as a fortnight passing a given point. This is a great grief to me."

"O, it is no matter, so you will try to do the best you can."

"I will. I will put my whole mind on it."

"Thanks. Are you ready to begin?"

"Ready."

Q. How old are you?

A. Nineteen, in June.

Q. Indeed! I would have taken you to be thirty-five or six. Where were you born?

A. In Missouri.

Q. When did you begin to write?

A. In 1836.

Q. Why, how could that be, if you are only nineteen now?

A. I don't know. It does seem curious, somehow.

Q. It does, indeed. Who do you consider the most remarkable man you ever met?

A. Aaron Burr.

Q. But you never could have met Aaron Burr, if you are only nineteen years—

A. Now, if you know more about me than I do, what do you ask me for?

Q. Well, it was only a suggestion; nothing more. How did you happen to meet Burr?

A. Well, I happened to be at his funeral one day, and he asked me to make less noise, and—

Q. But, good heavens! If you were at his funeral, he must have been dead; and if he was dead, how could he care whether you made a noise or not?

A. I don't know. He was always a particular kind of a man that way.

Q. Still, I don't understand it at all. You say he spoke to you and that he was dead.

A. I didn't say he was dead.

Q. But wasn't he dead?

A. Well, some said he was, some said he wasn't.

Q. What did you think?

A. O, it was none of my business! It wasn't any of my funeral.

Q. Did you— However, we can never get this matter straight. Let me ask about something else. What was the date of your birth?

A. Monday, October 31, 1693.

Q. What! Impossible! That would make you a hundred and eighty years old. How do you account for that?

A. I don't account for it at all.

Q. But you said at first you were only nineteen, and now you make yourself out to be one hundred and eighty. It is an awful discrepancy.

A. Why, have you noticed that? *(Shaking hands.)* Many a time it has seemed to me like a discrepancy, but somehow I couldn't make up my mind. How quick you notice a thing!

Q. Thank you for the compliment, as far as it goes. Had you, or have you, any brothers or sisters?

A. Eh! I—I—I think so,—yes,—but I don't remember.

Q. Well, that is the most extraordinary statement I ever heard!

A. Why, what makes you think that?

Q. How could I think otherwise? Why, look here! who is this a picture of on the wall? Isn't that a brother of yours?

A. Oh! yes, yes, yes! Now you remind me of it, that *was* a brother of mine. That's William,—*Bill* we called him. Poor old Bill!

Q. Why? Is he dead, then?

A. Ah, well, I suppose so. We never could tell. There was a great mystery about it.

Q. That is sad, very sad. He disappeared, then?

A. Well, yes, in a sort of general way. We buried him.

Q. *Buried* him! *Buried* him without knowing whether he was dead or not?

A. O no! Not that. He was dead enough.

Q. Well, I confess that I can't understand this. If you buried him and you know he was dead—

A. No! no! we only thought he was.

Q. O, I see! He came to life again?

A. I bet he didn't.

Q. Well, I never heard anything like this. *Somebody* was dead. *Somebody* was buried. Now, where was the mystery?

A. Ah, that's just it! That's it exactly. You see we were twins,—defunct and I,—and we got mixed in the bath-tub when we were only two weeks old, and one of us was drowned. But we didn't know which. Some think it was Bill, some think it was me.

Q. Well, that *is* remarkable. What do *you* think?

A. Goodness knows! I would give whole worlds to know. This solemn, this awful mystery has cast a gloom over my whole life. But I will tell you a secret now, which I never have revealed to any creature before. One of us had a peculiar mark, a large mole on the back of his left hand,—that was *me*. *That child was the one that was drowned.*

Q. Very well, then, I don't see that there is any mystery about it, after all.

A. You don't? Well, *I* do. Anyway I don't see how they could ever have been such a blundering lot as to go and bury the wrong child. But, 'sh!—don't mention it where the family can hear of it. Heaven knows they have heart-breaking troubles enough without adding this.

Q. Well, I believe I have got material enough for the present, and I am very much obliged to you for the pains you have taken. But I was a good deal interested in that account of Aaron Burr's funeral. Would you mind telling me what particular circumstance it was that made you think Burr was such a remarkable man?

A. O, it was a mere trifle! Not one man in fifty would have noticed it at all. When the sermon was over, and the procession all ready to start for the cemetery, and the body all arranged nice in the hearse, he said he wanted to take a last look at the scenery, and so he *got up and rode with the driver.*

Then the young man reverently withdrew. He was very pleasant company, and I was sorry to see him go.

"A True Story, Repeated Word for Word as I Heard It" (1874)

It was summer time, and twilight. We were sitting on the porch of the farm-house, on the summit of the hill, and "Aunt Rachel" was sitting respectfully below our level, on the steps,—for she was our servant, and colored. She was of mighty frame and stature; she was sixty years old, but her eye was undimmed and her strength unabated. She was a cheerful, hearty soul, and it was no more trouble for her to laugh than it is for a bird to sing. She was under fire, now, as usual when the day was done. That is to say, she was being chaffed without mercy, and was enjoying it. She would let off peal after peal of laughter, and then sit with her face in her hands and shake with throes of enjoyment which she could no longer get breath enough to express. At such a moment as this a thought occurred to me, and I said:—

"Aunt Rachel, how is it that you've lived sixty years and never had any trouble?"

She stopped quaking. She paused, and there was a moment of silence. She turned her face over her shoulder toward me, and said, without even a smile in her voice:—

"Misto C—, is you in 'arnest?"

It surprised me a good deal; and it sobered my manner and my speech, too. I said:—

"Why, I thought—that is, I meant—why, you *can't* have had any trouble. I've never heard you sigh, and never seen your eye when there wasn't a laugh in it."

She faced fairly around, now, and was full of earnestness.

"Has I had any trouble? Misto C—, I's gwyne to tell you, den I leave it to you. I was bawn down 'mongst de slaves; I knows all 'bout slavery, 'case I ben one of 'em my own se'f. Well, sah, my ole man—dat's my husban'—he was lovin' an' kind to me, jist as kind as you is to yo' own wife. An' we had chil'en—seven chil'en—an' we loved dem chil'en jist de same as you loves you' chil'en. Dey was black, but de Lord can't make no chil'en so black but what dey mother loves 'em an' wouldn't give 'em up, no, not for anything dat's in dis whole world.

"Well, sah, I was raised in ole Fo'ginny, but my mother she was raised in Maryland; an' my *souls!* she was turrible when she'd git started! My *lan'!* but she'd make de fur fly! When she'd git into dem tantrums, she always had one word dat she said. She'd straighten herse'f up an' put her fists in her hips an' say, 'I want you to understan' dat I wa'n't bawn in de mash to be fool' by trash! I's one o' de ole Blue Hen's Chickens, *I* is!' 'Ca'se, you see, dat's what folks dat's bawn in Maryland calls deyselves, an' dey's proud of it. Well, dat was her word. I don't ever forgit it, beca'se she said it so much, an' beca'se she said it one day when my little Henry tore his wris' awful, an' most busted his head, right up at de top of his forehead, an' de niggers didn't fly aroun' fas' enough to 'tend to him. An' when dey talk' back at her, she up an' says, 'Look-a-heah!' she says, 'I want you niggers to understan' dat I wa'n't bawn in de mash to be fool' by trash! I's one o' de ole Blue Hen's Chickens, *I* is!' an' den she clar' dat kitchen an' bandage' up de chile herse'f. So I says dat word, too, when I's riled.

"Well, bymeby my ole mistis say she's broke, an' she got to sell all de niggers on de place. An' when I heah dat dey gwyne to sell us all off at oction in Richmon', oh de good gracious! I know what dat mean!"

Aunt Rachel had gradually risen, while she warmed to her subject, and now she towered above us, black against the stars.

"Dey put chains on us an' put us on a stan' as high as dis po'ch,—twenty foot high,—an' all de people stood aroun', crowds an' crowds. An' dey 'd come up dah an' look at us all roun', an' squeeze our arm, an' make us git up an' walk, an' den say, 'Dis one too ole,' or 'Dis one lame,' or 'Dis one don't 'mount to much.' An' dey sole my ole man, an' took him away, an' dey begin to sell my chil'en an' take *dem* away, an' I begin to cry; an' de man say, 'Shet up yo' dam blubberin',' an' hit me on de mouf wid his han'. An' when de las' one was gone but my little Henry, I grab' *him* clost up to my breas' so, an' I ris up an' says, 'You shan't take him away,' I says; 'I'll kill de man dat tetches him!' I says. But my little Henry whisper an' say, 'I gwyne to run away, an' den I work an' buy yo' freedom.' Oh, bless de chile, he always so good! But dey got him—dey got him, de men did; but I took and tear de clo'es mos' off of 'em, an' beat 'em over de head wid my chain; an' *dey* give it to *me*, too, but I didn't mine dat.

"Well, dah was my ole man gone, an' all my chil'en, all my seven chil'en—an' six of 'em I hain't set eyes on ag'in to dis day, an' dat's twenty-two years ago las' Easter. De man dat bought me b'long' in Newbern, an' he took me dah. Well, bymeby de years roll on an' de waw come. My marster he was a Confedrit colonel, an' I was his family's cook. So when de Unions took dat town, dey all run away an' lef' me all by myse'f wid de other niggers in dat mons'us big house. So de big Union officers move in dah, an' dey ask me would I cook for *dem*. 'Lord bless you,' says I, 'dat's what I's *for.*'

"Dey wa'n't no small-fry officers, mine you, dey was de biggest dey *is;* an' de way dey made dem sojers mosey roun'! De Gen'l he tole me to boss dat kitchen; an' he say, 'If anybody come meddlin' wid you, you jist make 'em walk chalk; don't you be afeard,' he say; 'you's 'mong frens, now.'

"Well, I thinks to myse'f, if my little Henry ever got a chance to run away, he'd make to de Norf, o' course. So one day I comes in dah whah de big officers was, in de parlor, an' I drops a kurtchy, so, an' I up an' tole 'em 'bout my Henry, dey a-listenin' to my troubles jist de same as if I was white folks; an' I says, 'What I come for is beca'se if he got away and got up Norf whah you gemmen comes from, you might 'a' seen him, maybe, an' could tell me so as I could fine him ag'in; he was very little, an' he had a sk-yar on his lef' wris', an' at de top of his forehead.' Den dey look mournful, an' de Gen'l say, 'How long sence you los' him?' an' I say, 'Thirteen year.' Den de Gen'l say, 'He wouldn't be little no mo', now—he's a man!'

"I never thought o' dat befo'! He was only dat little feller to *me,* yit. I never thought 'bout him growin' up an' bein' big. But I see it den. None o' de gemmen had run acrost him, so dey couldn't do nothin' for me. But all dat time, do' *I* didn't know it, my Henry *was* run off to de Norf, years an' years, an' he was a barber, too, an' worked for hisse'f. An' bymeby, when de waw come, he ups an' he says, 'I's done barberin',' he says; 'I's gwyne to fine my ole mammy, less'n she's dead.' So he sole out an' went to whah dey was recrutin', an' hired hisse'f out to de colonel for his servant; an' den he went all froo de battles everywhah, huntin' for his ole mammy; yes indeedy, he'd hire to fust one officer an' den another, tell he'd ransacked de whole Souf; but you see *I* didn't know nuffin 'bout *dis.* How was *I* gwyne to know it?

"Well, one night we had a big sojer ball; de sojers dah at Newbern was always havin' balls an' carryin' on. Dey had 'em in my kitchen, heaps o' times, 'ca'se it was so big. Mine you, I was *down* on sich doin's; beca'se my place was wid de officers, an' it rasp' me to have dem common sojers cavortin' roun' my kitchen like dat. But I alway' stood aroun' an' kep' things straight, I did; an' sometimes dey'd git my dander up, an' den I'd make 'em clar dat kitchen, mine I *tell* you!

"Well, one night—it was a Friday night—dey comes a whole plattoon f'm a *nigger* ridgment dat was on gurad at de house,—de house was head-quarters, you know,—an' den I was jist a-*bilin'!* Mad? I was jist a-*boomin'!* I swelled aroun', an' swelled aroun'; I jist was a-itchin' for 'em to do somefin for to start me. *An'* dey was a-waltzin' an a-dancin'! *my!* but dey was havin' a time! an' I jist a-swellin' an' a-swellin' up! Pooty soon, 'long comes *sich* a spruce young nigger a-sailin' down de room wid a yaller wench roun' de wais'; an' roun' an' roun' an' roun' dey went, enough to make a body drunk to look at 'em; an' when dey got abreas' o' me, dey went to kin' o' balancin' aroun', fust on one leg an' den on t'other, an' similin' at my big red turban, an' makin' fun, an' I ups an' says, '*Git* along wid you!—rubbage!' De young man's face kin o' changed, all of a sudden, for 'bout a second, but den he went to smilin' ag'in, same as he was befo'. Well, 'bout dis time, in comes some niggers dat played music an' b'long' to de ban', an' dey *never* could git along widout puttin' on airs. An' de very fust air dey put on dat night, I lit into 'em! Dey laughed, an' dat made me wuss. De res' o' de niggers got to laughin', an' den my soul *alive* but I was hot! My eye was jist a-blazin'! I jist straightened myself up, so,—jist as I is now, plum to de ceilin', mos',—an' I digs my fists into my hips, an' I says, 'Look-a-heah!' I says, 'I want you niggers to understan' dat I wa' n't bawn in de mash to be fool' by trash! I's one o' de ole Blue Hen's Chickens, *I* is!' an' den I see dat young man stan' a-starin' an' stiff, lookin' kin' o' up at de ceilin' like he fo'got somefin, an' couldn't 'member it no mo'. Well, I jist march' on dem niggers,—so, lookin' like a gen'l,—an' dey jist cave' away befo' me an' out at de do'. An' as dis young man was a-goin' out, I heah him say to another nigger, 'Jim,' he says, 'you go 'long an' tell de cap'n I be on han' 'bout eight o'-clock in de mawnin'; dey's somefin on my mine,' he says; 'I don't sleep no mo' dis night. You go 'long,' he says, 'an' leave me by my own se'f.'

"Dis was 'bout one o'clock in de mawnin'. Well, 'bout seven, I was up an' on han', gittin' de officers' breakfast. I was a-stoopin' down by de stove,—jist so, same as if yo' foot was de stove,—an' I opened de stove do' wid my right han',—so, pushin' it back, jist as I pushes yo' foot,—an' I'd jist got de pan o' hot biscuits in my han' an' was 'bout to raise up, when I see a black face come aroun' under mine, an' de eyes a-lookin' up into mine, jist as I's a-lookin' up clost under yo' face now; an' I jist stopped *right dah,* an' never budged! jist gazed, an' gazed, so; an' de pan begin to tremble, an' all of a sudden I *knowed!* De pan drop' on de flo' an' I grab his lef' han' an' shove back his sleeve,—jist so, as I's doin' to you,— an' den I goes for his forehead an' push de hair back, so, an' 'Boy!' I says, 'if you an't my Henry, what is you doin' wid dis welt on yo' wris' an' dat sky-yar on yo' forehead? De Lord God ob heaven be praise', I got my own ag'in!'

"Oh, no, Misto C—, *I* hain't had no trouble. An' no *joy!*"

FROM *THE INNOCENTS ABROAD* (1869)

The Innocents Abroad was Twain's first successful book and remains one of his funniest. It is the comic record of Twain's travels in Europe and the Holy Land in the company of Americans, most of whom he found so proper and self-righteous that he came to call them "pilgrims." Part of the satirical purpose of the book is to expose sacred sites as bleak and uninviting and the travelers' giddy and reverential regard of them as overblown and sentimental. His simpleminded weeping over the tomb of his dead relative, Adam, is a case in point. There are moments, however, when Twain drops his role as comic iconoclast and antic realist and offers solemn and presumably sincere descriptions of places and people that are admiring, most notably the place of the Crucifixion and the Sphinx. His description of the Sea of Galilee belongs in this latter group.

"The Sea of Galilee"

The celebrated Sea of Galilee is not so large a sea as Lake Tahoe* by a good deal—it is just about two-thirds as large. And when we come to speak of beauty, this sea is no more to be compared to Tahoe than a meridian of longitude is to a rainbow. The dim waters of this pool can not suggest the limpid brilliancy of Tahoe; these low, shaven, yellow hillocks of rocks and sand, so devoid of perspective, can not suggest the grand peaks that compass Tahoe like a wall, and whose ribbed and chasmed fronts are clad with stately pines that seem to grow small and smaller as they climb, till one might fancy them reduced to weeds and shrubs far upward, where they join the everlasting snows. Silence and solitude brook over Tahoe; and silence and solitude brood also over this lake of Genessaret. But the solitude of the one is as cheerful and fascinating as the solitude of the other is dismal and repellant.

In the early morning one watches the silent battle of dawn and darkness upon the waters of Tahoe with a placid interest; but when the shadows sulk away and one by one the hidden beauties of the shore unfold themselves in the full splendor of noon; when the still surface is belted like a rainbow with broad bars of blue and green and white, half the distance from circumference to centre; when, in the lazy summer afternoon, he lies in a boat, far out to where the dead blue of the deep water

*I measure all lakes by Tahoe, partly because I am far more familiar with it than with any other, and partly because I have such a high admiration for it and such a world of pleasant recollections of it, that it is very nearly impossible for me to speak of lakes and not mention it.

begins, and smokes the pipe of peace and idly winks at the distant crags and patches of snow from under his cap-brim; when the boat drifts shoreward to the white water, and he lolls over the gunwale and gazes by the hour down through the crystal depths and notes the colors of the pebbles and reviews the finny armies gliding in procession a hundred feet below; when at night he sees moon and stars, mountain ridges feathered with pines, jutting white capes, bold promontories, grand sweeps of rugged scenery topped with bald, glimmering peaks, all magnificently pictured in the polished mirror of the lake, in richest, softest detail, the tranquil interest that was born with the morning deepens and deepens, by sure degrees, till it culminates at last in resistless fascination!

It is solitude, for birds and squirrels on the shore and fishes in the water are all the creatures that are near to make it otherwise, but it is not the sort of solitude to make one dreary. Come to Galilee for that. If these unpeopled deserts, these rusty mounds of barrenness, that never, never, never do shake the glare from their harsh outlines, and fade and faint into vague perspective; that melancholy ruin of Capernaum; this stupid village of Tiberias, slumbering under its six funereal plumes of palms; yonder desolate declivity where the swine of the miracle ran down into the sea, and doubtless thought it was better to swallow a devil or two and get drowned into the bargain than have to live longer in such a place; this cloudless, blistering sky; this solemn, sailless, tintless lake, reposing within its rim of yellow hills and low, steep banks, and looking just as expressionless and unpoetical (when we leave its sublime history out of the question,) as any metropolitan reservoir in Christendom—if these things are not food for rock me to sleep, mother, none exist, I think.

But I should not offer the evidence for the prosecution and leave the defense unheard. Wm. C. Grimes deposes as follows:

> We had taken ship to go over to the other side. The sea was not more than six miles wide. Of the beauty of the scene, however, I can not say enough, nor can I imagine where those travelers carried their eyes who have described the scenery of the lake as tame

> or uninteresting. The first great characteristic of it is the deep basin in which it lies. This is from three to four hundred feet deep on all sides except at the lower end, and the sharp slope of the banks, which are all of the richest green, is broken and diversified by the wâdys and water-courses which work their way down through the sides of the basin, forming dark chasms or light sunny valleys. Near Tiberias these banks are rocky, and ancient sepulchres open in them, with their doors toward the water. They selected grand spots, as did the Egyptians of old, for burial places, as if they designed that when the voice of God should reach the sleepers, they should walk forth and open their eyes on scenes of glorious beauty. On the east, the wild and desolate mountains contrast finely with the deep blue lake; and toward the north, sublime and majestic, Hermon looks down on the sea, lifting his white crown to heaven with the pride of a hill that has seen the departing footsteps of a hundred generations. On the north-east shore of the sea was a single tree, and this is the only tree of any size visible from the water of the lake, except a few lonely palms in the city of Tiberias, and by its solitary position attracts more attention than would a forest. The whole appearance of the scene is precisely what we would expect and desire the scenery of Genessaret to be, grand beauty, but quite calm. The very mountains are calm.

It is an ingeniously written description, and well calculated to deceive. But if the paint and the ribbons and the flowers be stripped from it, a skeleton will be found beneath.

So stripped, there remains a lake six miles wide and neutral in color; with steep green banks, unrelieved by shrubbery; at one end bare, unsightly rocks, with (almost invisible) holes in them of no consequence to the picture; eastward, "wild and desolate mountains"; (low, desolate hills, he should have said;) in the north, a mountain called Hermon, with snow on it; peculiarity of the picture, "calmness"; its prominent feature, one tree.

No ingenuity could make such a picture beautiful—to one's actual vision.

I claim the right to correct misstatements, and have so corrected the color of the water in the above recapitulation. The waters of Genessaret are of an exceedingly mild blue, even from a high elevation and a distance of five miles. Close at hand (the witness was sailing on the lake,) it is hardly proper to call them blue at all, much less "deep" blue. I wish to state, also, not as a correction, but as matter of opinion, that Mount Hermon is not a striking or picturesque mountain by any means, being too near the height of its immediate neighbors to be so. That is all. I do not object to the witness dragging a mountain forty-five miles to help the scenery under consideration, because it is entirely proper to do it, and besides, the picture needs it.

"C. W. E.," (of "Life in the Holy Land,") deposes as follows:

> A beautiful sea lies unbosomed among the Galilean hills, in the midst of that land once possessed by Zebulon and Naphtali, Asher and Dan. The azure of the sky penetrates the depths of the lake, and the waters are sweet and cool. On the west, stretch broad fertile plains; on the north the rocky shores rise step by step until in the far distance tower the snowy heights of Hermon; on the east through a misty veil are seen the high plains of Perea, which stretch away in rugged mountains leading the mind by varied paths toward Jerusalem the Holy. Flowers bloom in this terrestrial paradise, once beautiful and verdant with waving trees; singing birds enchant the ear; the turtle-dove soothes with its soft note; the crested lark sends up its song toward heaven, and the grave and stately stork inspires the mind with thought, and leads it on to meditation and repose. Life here was once idyllic, charming; here were once no rich, no poor, no high, no low. It was a world of ease, simplicity, and beauty; now it is a scene of desolation and misery.

This is not an ingenious picture. It is the worst I ever saw. It describes in elaborate detail what it terms a "terrestrial paradise," and closes with the startling information that this paradise is "a scene of *desolation and misery.*"

I have given two fair, average specimens of the character of the testimony offered by the majority of the writers who visit this region. One says, "Of the beauty of the scene I can not say enough," and then proceeds to cover up with a woof of glittering sentences a thing which, when stripped for inspection, proves to be only an unobtrusive basin of water, some mountainous desolation, and one tree. The other, after a conscientious effort to build a terrestrial paradise out of the same materials, with the addition of a "grave and stately stork," spoils it all by blundering upon the ghastly truth at the last.

Nearly every book concerning Galilee and its lake describes the scenery as beautiful. No—not always so straightforward as that. Sometimes the *impression* intentionally conveyed is that it is beautiful, at the same time that the author is careful not to *say* that it is, in plain Saxon. But a careful analysis of these descriptions will show that the materials of which they are formed are not individually beautiful and can not be wrought into combinations that are beautiful. The veneration and the affection which some of these men felt for the scenes they were speaking of, heated their fancies and biased their judgment; but the pleasant falsities they wrote were full of honest sincerity, at any rate. Others wrote as they did, because they feared it would be unpopular to write otherwise. Others were hypocrites and deliberately meant to deceive. Any of them would say in a moment, if asked, that it was *always* right and always *best* to tell the truth. They would say that, at any rate, if they did not perceive the drift of the question.

But why should not the truth be spoken of this region? Is the truth harmful? Has it ever needed to hide its face? God made the Sea of Galilee and its surroundings as they are. Is it the province of Mr. Grimes to improve upon the work?

I am sure, from the tenor of books I have read, that many who have visited this land in years gone by, were Presbyterians, and came seeking evidences in support of their particular creed; they found a Presbyterian Palestine, and they had already made up their minds to find no other, though possibly they did not know it, being blinded by their zeal. Others were Baptists, seeking Baptist evidences and a Baptist Palestine. Others were Catholics, Methodists, Episcopalians, seeking evidences indorsing their several creeds, and a Catholic, a Methodist, an Episcopalian Palestine. Honest as these men's intentions may have been, they were full of partialities and prejudices, they entered the country with their verdicts already prepared, and they could no more write dispassionately and impartially about it than they could about their own wives and children. Our pilgrims have brought *their* verdicts with them. They have shown it in their conversation ever since we left Beirout. I can almost tell, in set phrase, what they will say when they see Tabor, Nazareth, Jericho and Jerusalem—*because I have the books they will "smouch" their ideas from.* These authors write pictures and frame rhapsodies, and lesser men follow and see with the author's eyes instead of their own, and speak with his tongue. What the pilgrims said at Cesarea Philippi surprised me with its wisdom. I found it afterwards in Robinson. What they said when Genessaret burst upon their vision, charmed me with its grace. I find it in Mr. Thompson's "Land and the Book." They have spoken often, in happily worded language which never varied, of how they mean to lay their weary heads upon a stone at Bethel, as Jacob did, and close their dim eyes, and dream, perchance, of angels descending out of heaven on a ladder. It was very pretty. But I have recognized the weary head and the dim eyes, finally. They borrowed the idea—and the words—and the construction—and the punctuation—from Grimes. The pilgrims will tell of Palestine, when they get home, not as it appeared to *them,* but as it appeared to Thompson and Robinson and Grimes—with the tints varied to suit each pilgrim's creed.

Pilgrims, sinners and Arabs are all abed, now, and the camp is still. Labor in loneliness is irksome. Since I made my last few notes, I have been sitting outside the tent for half an hour. Night is the time to see Galilee. Genessaret under these lustrous stars, has nothing repulsive about it. Genessaret with the glittering reflections of the constellations flecking its surface, almost makes me regret that I ever saw the rude glare of the day upon it. Its history and its associations are its chiefest charm, in any eyes, and the spells they weave are feeble in the searching light of the sun. *Then,* we scarcely feel the fetters. Our thoughts wander constantly to the practical concerns of life, and refuse to dwell upon things that seem vague and unreal. But when the day is done, even the most unimpressible must yield to the dreamy influences of this tranquil starlight. The old traditions of the place steal upon his memory and haunt his reveries, and then his fancy clothes all sights and sounds with the supernatural. In the lapping of the waves upon the beach, he hears the dip of ghostly oars; in the secret noises of the night he hears spirit voices; in the soft sweep of the breeze, the rush of invisible wings. Phantom ships are on the sea, the dead of twenty centuries come forth from the tombs, and in the dirges of the night wind the songs of old forgotten ages find utterance again.

In the starlight, Galilee has no boundaries but the broad compass of the heavens, and is a theatre meet for great events; meet for the birth of a religion able to save a world; and meet for the stately Figure appointed to stand upon its stage and proclaim its high decrees. But in the sunlight, one says: Is it for the deeds which were done and the words which were spoken in this little acre of rocks and sand eighteen centuries gone, that the bells are ringing to-day in the remote islands of the sea and far and wide over continents that clasp the circumference of the huge globe?

One can comprehend it only when night has hidden all incongruities and created a theatre proper for so grand a drama.

"At the Tomb of Adam"

The Greek Chapel is the most roomy, the richest and the showiest chapel in the Church of the Holy Sepulchre. Its altar, like that of all the Greek churches, is a lofty screen that extends clear across the chapel, and is gorgeous with gilding and pictures. The numerous lamps that hang before it are of gold and silver, and cost great sums.

But the feature of the place is a short column that rises from the middle of the marble pavement of the chapel, and marks the exact *centre of the earth*. The most reliable traditions tell us that this was known to be the earth's centre, ages ago, and that when Christ was upon earth he set all doubts upon the subject at rest forever, by stating with his own lips that the tradition was correct. Remember, He said that that particular column stood upon the centre of the world. If the centre of the world changes, the column changes its position accordingly. This column has moved three different times, of its own accord. This is because, in great convulsions of nature, at three different times, masses of the earth—whole ranges of mountains, probably—have flown off into space, thus lessening the diameter of the earth, and changing the exact locality of its centre by a point or two. This is a very curious and interesting circumstance, and is a withering rebuke to those philosophers who would make us believe that it is not possible for any portion of the earth to fly off into space.

To satisfy himself that this spot was really the centre of the earth, a sceptic once paid well for the privilege of ascending to the dome of the church to see if the sun gave him a shadow at noon. He came down perfectly convinced. The day was very cloudy and the sun threw no shadows at all; but the man was satisfied that if the sun had come out and made shadows it could not have made any for him. Proofs like these are not to be set aside by the idle tongues of cavilers. To such as are not bigoted, and are willing to be convinced, they carry a conviction that nothing can ever shake.

If even greater proofs than those I have mentioned are wanted, to satisfy the headstrong and the foolish that this is the genuine centre of the earth, they are here. The greatest of them lies in the fact that from under this very column was taken the *dust from which Adam was made.* This can surely be regarded in the light of a settler. It is not likely that the original first man would have been made from an inferior quality of earth when it was entirely convenient to get first quality from the world's centre. This will strike any reflecting mind forcibly. That Adam was formed of dirt procured in this very spot is simply proven by the fact that in six thousand years no man has ever been able to prove that the dirt was *not* procured here whereof he was made.

It is a singular circumstance that right under the roof of this same great church, and not far away from that illustrious column, Adam himself, the father of the human race, lies buried. There is no question that he is actually buried in the grave which is pointed out as his—there can be none—because it has never yet been proven that that grave is not the grave in which he is buried.

The tomb of Adam! How touching it was, here in a land of strangers, far away from home, and friends, and all who cared for me, thus to discover the grave of a blood relation. True, a distant one, but still a relation. The unerring instinct of nature thrilled its recognition. The fountain of my filial affection was stirred to its profoundest depths, and I gave way to tumultuous emotion. I leaned upon a pillar and burst into tears. I deem it no shame to have wept over the grave of my poor dead relative. Let him who would sneer at my emotion close this volume here, for he will find little to his taste in my journeyings through Holy Land. Noble old man—he did not live to see me—he did not live to see his child. And I—I—alas, I did not live to see *him*. Weighed down by sorrow and disappointment, he died before I was born—six thousand brief summers before I was born. But let us try to bear it with fortitude. Let us trust that he is better off, where he is. Let us take comfort in the thought that his loss is our eternal gain.

FROM
THE GILDED AGE
(1873)

The Gilded Age was a jointly written novel. Clemens and his neighbor in Hartford, Connecticut, Charles Dudley Warner, decided to try their hands at a political novel, and for the most part they wrote independently, fusing the chapters together in sometimes strained ways. The most memorable character in the book was Twain's creation—Colonel Sellers was patterned after his mother's cousin, James Lampton, a visionary who was always just this side of prosperity. In the chapters below, Sellers is entertaining the son of a friend and former business associate. Washington Hawkins is the son of Silas Hawkins, a figure modeled to some extent on Clemens's father. Silas has long believed that his 75,000 acres of Tennessee land will make him prosperous but has just recently missed an opportunity to sell it. Hawkins and Colonel Sellers had once been in business together; both had made and lost one or two fortunes and now live in relative poverty. Several of the Hawkins children have left home in order to help the family out of its financial predicament. Much like Samuel Clemens's brother Orion, Washington is a dreamer and therefore particularly susceptible to Sellers's grandiose dreams of wealth. In the opening of the following chapter, Washington has traveled to Hawkeye, Missouri, where he believes Sellers will start him on the path to riches.

"Colonel Sellers Entertains Washington Hawkins"

Bearing Washington Hawkins and his fortunes, the stage-coach tore out of Swansea at a fearful gait, with horn tooting gaily and half the town admiring from doors and windows. But it did not tear any more after it got to the outskirts; it dragged along stupidly enough, then—till it came in sight of the next hamlet; and then the bugle tooted gaily again and again the vehicle went tearing by the houses. This sort of conduct marked every entry to a station and every exit from it; and so in those days children grew up with the idea that stage-coaches always tore and always tooted; but they also grew up with the idea that pirates went into action in their Sunday clothes, carrying the black flag in one hand and pistolling people with the other; merely because they were so represented in the pictures—but these illusions vanished when later years brought their disenchanting wisdom. They learned then that the stage-coach is but a poor, plodding, vulgar thing, in the solitudes of the highway; and that the pirate is only a seedy, unfantastic "rough," when he is out of the pictures.

Toward evening, the stage-coach came thundering into Hawkeye with a perfectly triumphant ostentation—which was natural and proper, for Hawkeye was a pretty large town for interior Missouri. Washington, very stiff and tired and hungry, climbed out, and wondered how he was to proceed now. But his difficulty was quickly solved. Col. Sellers came down the street on a run and arrived panting for breath. He said:

"Lord bless you—I'm glad to see you, Washington—perfectly delighted to see you, my boy! I got your message. Been on the look-out for you. Heard the stage horn, but had a party

I couldn't shake off—man that's got an enormous thing on hand—wants me to put some capital into it—and I tell you, my boy, I could do worse, I could do a deal worse. No, now, let that luggage alone; I'll fix that. Here, Jerry, got anything to do? All right—shoulder this plunder and follow me. Come along, Washington. Lord I'm glad to see you! Wife and the children are just perishing to look at you. Bless you, they won't know you, you've grown so. Folks all well, I suppose? That's good—glad to hear that. We're always going to run down and see them, but I'm into so many operations, and they're not things a man feels like trusting to other people, and so somehow we keep putting it off. Fortunes in them! Good gracious, it's the country to pile up wealth in! Here we are—here's where the Sellers dynasty hangs out. Dump it on the door-step, Jerry—the blackest niggro in the State, Washington, but got a good heart—mighty likely boy, is Jerry. And now I suppose you've got to have ten cents, Jerry. That's all right—when a man works for me—when a man—in the other pocket, I reckon—when a man—why, where the mischief *is* that portmonnaie!—when a—well now that's odd—Oh, now I remember, must have left it at the bank; and b'George I've left my check-book, too—Polly says I ought to have a nurse—well, no matter. Let me have a dime, Washington, if you've got—ah, thanks. Now clear out, Jerry, your complexion has brought on the twilight half an hour ahead of time. Pretty fair joke—pretty fair. Here he is, Polly! Washington's come, children!—come now, don't eat him up—finish him in the house. Welcome, my boy, to a mansion that is proud to shelter the son of the best man that walks on the ground. Si Hawkins has been a good friend to me, and I believe I can say that whenever I've had a chance to put him into a good thing I've done it, and done it pretty cheerfully, too. I put him into that sugar speculation—what a grand thing that was, if we hadn't held on too long!"

True enough; but holding on too long had utterly ruined both of them; and the saddest part of it was, that they never had had so much money to lose before, for Sellers's sale of their mule crop that year in New Orleans had been a great financial success. If he had kept out of sugar and gone back home content to stick to mules it would have been a happy wisdom. As it was, he managed to kill two birds with one stone—that is to say, he killed the sugar speculation by holding for high rates till he had to sell at the bottom figure, and that calamity killed the mule that laid the golden egg—which is but a figurative expression and will be so understood. Sellers had returned home cheerful but empty-handed, and the mule business lapsed into other hands. The sale of the Hawkins property by the Sheriff had followed, and the Hawkins hearts been torn to see Uncle Dan'l and his wife pass from the auction-block into the hands of a negro trader and depart for the remote South to be seen no more by the family. It had seemed like seeing their own flesh and blood sold into banishment.

Washington was greatly pleased with the Sellers mansion. It was a two-story-and-a-half brick, and much more stylish than any of its neighbors. He was borne to the family sitting room in triumph by the swarm of little Sellerses, the parents following with their arms about each other's waists.

The whole family were poorly and cheaply dressed; and the clothing, although neat and clean, showed many evidences of having seen long service. The Colonel's "stovepipe" hat was napless and shiny with much polishing, but nevertheless it had an almost convincing expression about it of having been just purchased new. The rest of his clothing was napless and shiny, too, but it had the air of being entirely satisfied with itself and blandly sorry for other people's clothes. It was growing rather dark in the house, and the evening air was chilly, too. Sellers said:

"Lay off your overcoat, Washington, and draw up to the stove and make yourself at home—just consider yourself under your own shingles my boy—I'll have a fire going, in a jiffy. Light the lamp, Polly, dear, and let's have things cheerful—just as glad to see you, Washington, as if you'd been lost a century and we'd found you again!"

By this time the Colonel was conveying a lighted match into a poor little stove. Then he propped the stove door to its place by leaning the poker against it, for the hinges had retired from business. This door framed a small square of isinglass, which now warmed up with a faint glow. Mrs. Sellers lit a cheap, showy lamp, which dissipated a good deal of the gloom, and then everybody gathered into the light and took the stove into close companionship.

The children climbed all over Sellers, fondled him, petted him, and were lavishly petted in return. Out from this tugging, laughing, chattering disguise of legs and arms and little faces, the Colonel's voice worked its way and his tireless tongue ran blithely on without interruption; and the purring little wife, diligent with her knitting, sat near at hand and looked happy and proud and grateful; and she listened as one who listens to oracles and gospels and whose grateful soul is being refreshed with the bread of life. By and by the children quieted down to listen; clustered about their father, and resting their elbows on his legs, they hung upon his words as if he were uttering the music of the spheres.

A dreary old hair-cloth sofa against the wall; a few damaged chairs; the small table the lamp stood on; the crippled stove—these things constituted the furniture of the room. There was no carpet on the floor; on the wall were occasional square-shaped interruptions of the general tint of the plaster which betrayed that there used to be pictures in the house—but there were none now. There were no mantel ornaments, unless one might bring himself to regard as an ornament a clock which never came within fifteen strokes of striking the right time, and whose hands always hitched together at twenty-two minutes past anything and traveled in company the rest of the way home.

"Remarkable clock!" said Sellers, and got up and wound it. "I've been offered—well, I wouldn't expect you to believe what I've been offered for that clock. Old Gov. Hager never sees me but he says, 'Come, now, Colonel, name your price—I *must* have that clock!' But my goodness I'd as soon think of selling my wife. As I was saying to———silence in the court, now, she's begun to strike! You can't talk against her—you have to just be patient and hold up till she's said her say. Ah—well, as I was saying, when—she's beginning again! Nineteen, twenty, twenty-one, twenty-two, twen———ah, that's all.—Yes, as I was saying to old Judge———go it, old girl, don't mind me.—

Now how is that?—isn't that a good, spirited tone? She can wake the dead! Sleep? Why you might as well try to sleep in a thunder-factory. Now just listen at that. She'll strike a hundred and fifty, now, without stopping,—you'll see. There ain't another clock like that in Christendom."

Washington hoped that this might be true, for the din was distracting—though the family, one and all, seemed filled with joy; and the more the clock "buckled down to her work" as the Colonel expressed it, and the more insupportable the clatter became, the more enchanted they all appeared to be. When there was silence, Mrs. Sellers lifted upon Washington a face that beamed with a childlike pride, and said:

"It belonged to his grandmother."

The look and the tone were a plain call for admiring surprise, and therefore Washington said—(it was the only thing that offered itself at the moment:)

"Indeed!"

"Yes, it did, didn't it father!" exclaimed one of the twins. "She was my great-grandmother—and George's too; wasn't she, father! *You* never saw her, but Sis has seen her, when Sis was a baby—didn't you, Sis! Sis has seen her most a hundred times. She was awful deef—she's dead, now. Ain't she, father!"

All the children chimed in, now, with one general Babel of information about deceased—nobody offering to read the riot act or seeming to discountenance the insurrection or disapprove of it in any way—but the head twin drowned all the turmoil and held his own against the field:

"It's our clock, now—and it's got wheels inside of it, and a thing that flutters every time she strikes—don't it, father? Great-grandmother died before hardly any of us was born—she was an Old-School Baptist and had warts all over her—you ask father if she didn't. She had an uncle that was bald-headed and used to have fits; he wasn't *our* uncle, I don't know what he was to us—some kin or another I reckon—father's seen him a thousand times—hain't you, father! We used to have a calf that et apples and just chawed up dishrags like nothing, and if you stay here you'll see lots of funerals—won't he, Sis! Did you ever see a house afire? *I* have! Once me and Jim Terry———"

But Sellers began to speak now, and the storm ceased. He began to tell about an enormous speculation he was thinking of embarking some capital in—a speculation which some London bankers had been over to consult with him about—and soon he was building glittering pyramids of coin, and Washington was presently growing opulent under the magic of his eloquence. But at the same time Washington was not able to ignore the cold entirely. He was nearly as close to the stove as he could get, and yet he could not persuade himself that he felt the slightest heat, notwithstanding the isinglass door was still gently and serenely glowing. He tried to get a trifle closer to the stove, and the consequence was, he tripped the supporting poker and the stove-door tumbled to the floor. And then there was a revelation—there was nothing in the stove but a lighted tallow-candle!

The poor youth blushed and felt as if he must die with shame. But the Colonel was only disconcerted for a moment—he straightaway found his voice again:

"A little idea of my own, Washington—one of the greatest things in the world! You must write and tell your father about it—don't forget that, now. I have been reading up some European Scientific reports—friend of mine, Count Fugier, sent them to me—sends me all sorts of things from Paris—he thinks the world of me, Fugier does. Well, I saw that the Academy of France had been testing the properties of heat, and they came to the conclusion that it was a non-conductor or something like that, and of course its influence must necessarily be deadly in nervous organizations with excitable temperaments, especially where there is any tendency toward rheumatic affections. Bless you I saw in a moment what was the matter with us, and says I, out goes your fires!—no more slow torture and certain death for me, sir. What you want is the *appearance* of heat, not the heat itself—that's the idea. Well how to do it was the next thing. I just put my head to work, pegged away a couple of days, and here you are! Rheumatism? Why a man can't any more start a case of rheumatism in this house than he can shake an opinion out of a mummy! Stove with a candle in it and a transparent door—that's it—it has been the salvation of this family. Don't you fail to write your father about it, Washington. And tell him the idea is mine—I'm no more conceited than most people, I reckon, but you know it is human nature for a man to want credit for a thing like that."

Washington said with his blue lips that he would, but he said in his secret heart that he would promote no such iniquity. He tried to believe in the healthfulness of the invention, and succeeded tolerably well; but after all he could not feel that good health in a frozen body was any real improvement on the rheumatism.

The supper at Col. Sellers's was not sumptuous, in the beginning, but it improved on acquaintance. That is to say, that what Washington regarded at first sight as mere lowly potatoes, presently became awe-inspiring agricultural productions that had been reared in some ducal garden beyond the sea, under the sacred eye of the duke himself, who had sent them to Sellers; the bread was from corn which could be grown in only one favored locality in the earth and only a favored few could get it; the Rio coffee, which at first seemed execrable to the taste, took to itself an improved flavor when Washington was told to drink it slowly and not hurry what should be a lingering luxury in order to be fully appreciated—it was from the private stores of a Brazilian nobleman with an unrememberable name. The Colonel's tongue was a magician's wand that turned dried apples into figs and water into wine as easily as it could change a hovel into a palace and present poverty into imminent future riches.

Washington slept in a cold bed in a carpetless room and woke up in a palace in the morning; at least the palace lingered during the moment that he was rubbing his eyes and getting his bearings—and then it disappeared and he recognized that the Colonel's inspiring talk had been influencing his dreams. Fatigue had made him sleep late; when he entered the sitting room he noticed that the old hair-cloth sofa was absent; when he sat down to breakfast the Colonel tossed six or seven dollars in bills on the table, counted them over, said he was a little short and must call upon his banker; then returned the bills to his wallet with the indifferent air of a man who is used to money. The breakfast was not an improvement upon the supper, but the Colonel talked it up and transformed it into an oriental feast. By and by, he said:

"I intend to look out for you, Washington, my boy. I hunted up a place for you yesterday, but I am not referring to that, now—that is a mere livelihood—mere bread and butter; but when I say I mean to look out for you I mean something very different. I mean to put things in your way that will make a mere livelihood a trifling thing. I'll put you in a way to make more money than you'll ever know what to do with. You'll be right here where I can put my hand on you when anything turns up. I've got some prodigious operations on foot; but I'm keeping quiet; mum's the word; your old hand don't go around pow-wowing and letting everybody see his k'yards and find out his little game. But all in good time, Washington, all in good time. You'll see. Now there's an operation in corn that looks well. Some New York men are trying to get me to go into it—buy up all the growing crops and just boss the market when they mature—ah I tell you it's a great thing. And it only costs a trifle; two millions or two and a half will do it. I haven't exactly promised yet—there's no hurry—the more indifferent I seem, you know, the more anxious those fellows will get. And then there is the hog speculation—that's bigger still. We've got quiet men at work," [he was very impressive here,] "mousing around, to get propositions out of all the farmers in the whole west and northwest for the hog-crop, and other agents quietly getting propositions and terms out of all the manufactories—and don't you see, if we can get all the hogs and all the slaughter houses into our hands on the dead quiet—whew! it would take three ships to carry the money.—I've looked into the thing—calculated all the chances for and all the chances against, and though I shake my head and hesitate and keep on thinking, apparently, I've got my mind made up that if the thing can be done on a capital of six millions, that's the horse to put up money on! Why Washington—but what's the use of talking about it—any man can see that there's whole Atlantic oceans of cash in it, gulfs and bays thrown in. But there's a bigger thing than that, yet—a bigger———"

"Why Colonel, you can't want anything bigger!" said Washington, his eyes blazing. "Oh, I wish I could go into either of those speculations—I only wish I had money—I wish I wasn't cramped and kept down and fettered with poverty, and such prodigious chances lying right here in sight! Oh, it is a fearful thing to be poor. But don't throw away those things—they are so splendid and I can see how sure they are. Don't throw them away for something still better and maybe fail in it! I wouldn't, Colonel. I would stick to these. I wish father were here and were his old self again—Oh, he never in his life had such chances as these are. Colonel, you *can't* improve on these—no man can improve on them!"

A sweet, compassionate smile played about the Colonel's features, and he leaned over the table with the air of a man who is "going to show you" and do it without the least trouble:

"Why Washington, my boy, these things are nothing. They *look* large—of course they look large to a novice, but to a man who has been all his life accustomed to large operations—shaw! They're well enough to while away an idle hour with, or furnish a bit of employment that will give a trifle of idle capital a chance to earn its bread while it is waiting for something to *do,* but—now just listen a moment—just let me give you an idea of what we old veterans of commerce call 'business.' Here's the Rothschilds' proposition—this is between you and me, you understand———"

Washington nodded three of four times impatiently, and his glowing eyes said, "Yes, yes—hurry—I understand———"

———"for I wouldn't have it get out for a fortune. They want me to go in with them on the sly—agent was here two weeks ago about it—go in on the sly" [voice down to an impressive whisper, now,] "and buy up a hundred and thirteen wild cat banks in Ohio, Indiana, Kentucky, Illinois and Missouri—notes of these banks are at all sorts of discount now—average discount of the hundred and thirteen is forty-four per cent.—buy them all up, you see, and then all of a sudden let the cat out of the bag! Whiz! the stock of every one of those wild cats would spin up to a tremendous premium before you could turn a handspring—profit on the speculation not a dollar less than forty millions!" [An eloquent pause, while the marvelous vision settled into W.'s focus.] "Where's your hogs now! Why my dear innocent boy, we would just sit down on the front doorsteps and peddle banks like lucifer matches!"

Washington finally got his breath and said:

"Oh, it is perfectly wonderful! Why couldn't these things have happened in father's day? And I—it's of no use—they simply lie before my face and mock me. There is nothing for me but to stand helpless and see other people reap the astonishing harvest."

"Never mind, Washington, don't you worry. I'll fix you. There's plenty of chances. How much money have you got?"

In the presence of so many millions, Washington could not keep from blushing when he had to confess that he had but eighteen dollars in the world.

"Well, all right—don't despair. Other people have been obliged to begin with less. I have a small idea that may develop into something for us both, all in good time. Keep your money close and add to it. I'll make it breed. I've been experimenting (to pass away the time,) on a little preparation for curing sore eyes—a kind of decoction nine-tenths water and the other tenth drugs that don't cost more than a dollar a barrel; I'm still experimenting; there's one ingredient wanted yet to perfect the thing, and somehow I can't just manage to hit upon the thing that's necessary, and I don't dare talk with a chemist, of course. But I'm progressing, and before many weeks I wager the country will ring with the fame of Beriah Sellers' Infallible Imperial Oriental Optic Liniment and Salvation for Sore Eyes—the Medical Wonder of the Age! Small bottles fifty cents, large ones a dollar. Average cost, five and seven cents for the two sizes. The first year sell, say, ten thousand bottles in Missouri, seven thousand in Iowa, three thousand in Arkansas, four thousand in Kentucky, six thousand in Illinois, and say twenty-five thousand in the rest of the country. Total, fifty-five thousand bottles;

profit clear of all expenses, twenty thousand dollars at the very lowest calculation. All the capital needed to manufacture the first two thousand bottles—say a hundred and fifty dollars—then the money would begin to flow in. The second year, sales would reach 200,000 bottles—clear profit, say, $75,000—and in the meantime the great factory would be building in St. Louis, to cost, say, $100,000. The third year we could easily sell 1,000,000 bottles in the United States and———"

"O, splendid!" said Washington. "Let's commence right away—let's———"

"———1,000,000 bottles in the United States—profit at least $350,000—and *then* it would begin to be time to turn our attention toward the *real* idea of the business."

"The *real* idea of it! Ain't $350,000 a year a pretty real——"

"Stuff! Why what an infant you are, Washington—what a guileless, short-sighted, easily-contented innocent you are, my poor little country-bred know-nothing! Would I go to all that trouble and bother for the poor crumbs a body might pick up in *this* country? Now do I look like a man who—does my history suggest that I am a man who deals in trifles, contents himself with the narrow horizon that hems in the common herd, sees no further than the end of his nose? Now *you* know that that is not me—couldn't *be* me. *You* ought to know that if I throw my time and abilities into a patent medicine, it's a patent medicine whose field of operations is the solid earth! its clients the swarming nations that inhabit it! Why what is the republic of America for an eye-water country? Lord bless you, it is nothing but a barren highway that you've got to cross to get *to* the true eye-water market! Why, Washington, in the Oriental countries people swarm like the sands of the desert; every square mile of ground upholds its thousands upon thousands of struggling human creatures—and every separate and individual devil of them's got the ophthalmia! It's as natural to them as noses are—and sin. It's born with them, it stays with them, it's all that some of them have left when they die. Three years of introductory trade in the orient and what will be the result? Why, our headquarters would be in Constantinople and our hindquarters in Further India! Factories and warehouses in Cairo, Ispahan, Bagdad, Damascus, Jerusalem, Yedo, Peking, Bangkok, Delhi, Bombay and Calcutta! Annual income—well, God only knows how many millions and millions apiece!"

Washington was so dazed, so bewildered—his heart and his eyes had wandered so far away among the strange lands beyond the seas, and such avalanches of coin and currency had fluttered and jingled confusedly down before him, that he was now as one who has been whirling round and round for a time, and, stopping all at once, finds his surroundings still whirling and all objects a dancing chaos. However, little by little the Sellers family cooled down and crystalized into shape, and the poor room lost its glitter and resumed its poverty. Then the youth found his voice and begged Sellers to drop everything and hurry up the eye-water; and he got his eighteen dollars and tried to force it upon the Colonel—pleaded with him to take it—implored him to do it. But the Colonel would not; said he would not need the capital (in his native magnificent way he called that eighteen dollars Capital) till the eye-water was an accomplished fact. He made Washington easy in his mind, though, by promising that he would call for it just as soon as the invention was finished, and he added the glad tidings that nobody but just they two should be admitted to a share in the speculation.

When Washington left the breakfast table he could have worshiped that man. Washington was one of that kind of people whose hopes are in the very clouds one day and in the gutter the next. He walked on air, now. The Colonel was ready to take him around and introduce him to the employment he had found for him, but Washington begged for a few moments in which to write home; with his kind of people, to ride today's new interest to death and put off yesterday's till another time, is nature itself. He ran up stairs and wrote glowingly, enthusiastically, to his mother about the hogs and the corn, the banks and the eye-water—and added a few inconsequential millions to each project. And he said that people little dreamed what a man Col. Sellers was, and that the world would open its eyes when it found out. And he closed his letter thus:

"So make yourself perfectly easy, mother—in a little while you shall have everything you want, and more. I am not likely to stint *you* in anything, I fancy. This money will not be for me, alone, but for all of us. I want all to share alike; and there is going to be far more for each than one person can spend. Break it to father cautiously—you understand the need of that—break it to him cautiously, for he has had such cruel hard fortune, and is so stricken by it that great good news might prostrate him more surely than even bad, for he is used to the bad but is grown sadly unaccustomed to the other. Tell Laura—tell all the children. And write to Clay about it if he is not with you yet. You may tell Clay that whatever I get he can freely share in—freely. He knows that that is true—there will be no need that I should swear to that to make him believe it. Good-bye—and mind what I say: Rest perfectly easy, one and all of you, for our troubles are nearly at an end."

Poor lad, he could not know that his mother would cry some loving, compassionate tears over his letter and put off the family with a synopsis of its contents which conveyed a deal of love to them but not much idea of his prospects or projects. And he never dreamed that such a joyful letter could sadden her and fill her night with sighs, and troubled thoughts, and bodings of the future, instead of filling it with peace and blessing it with restful sleep.

When the letter was done, Washington and the Colonel sallied forth, and as they walked along Washington learned what he was to be. He was to be a clerk in a real estate office. Instantly the fickle youth's dreams forsook the magic eye-water and flew back to the Tennessee Land. And the gorgeous possibilities of that great domain straightway began to occupy his imagination to such a degree that he could scarcely manage to keep even enough of his attention upon the Colonel's talk to retain the general run of what he was saying. He was glad it was a real estate office—he was a made man now, sure.

The Colonel said that General Boswell was a rich man and had a good and growing business; and that Washington's work would be light and he would get forty dollars a month and be boarded and lodged in the General's family—which was as good as ten dollars more; and even better, for he could not live as well even at the "City Hotel" as he would there, and yet the hotel charged fifteen dollars a month where a man had a good room.

General Boswell was in his office; a comfortable looking place, with plenty of outline maps hanging about the walls and in the windows, and a spectacled man was marking out another one on a long table. The office was in the principal street. The General received Washington with a kindly but reserved politeness. Washington rather liked his looks. He was about fifty years old, dignified, well preserved and well dressed. After the Colonel took his leave, the General talked a while with Washington—his talk consisting chiefly of instructions about the clerical duties of the place. He seemed satisfied as to Washington's ability to take care of the books, he was evidently a pretty fair theoretical book-keeper, and experience would soon harden theory into practice. By and by dinner-time came, and the two walked to the General's house; and now Washington noticed an instinct in himself that moved him to keep not in the General's rear, exactly, but yet not at his side—somehow the old gentleman's dignity and reserve did not inspire familiarity.

FROM

A TRAMP ABROAD

(1880)

In 1878, the Clemens family moved to Europe for fifteen months. Twain's minister and friend, Joseph Twichell, joined him for a "walking tour" through the Black Forest, the Swiss Alps and to Geneva. This experience provided the basis for his travel narrative. In point of fact, instead of walking, they typically took whatever mode of transportation was handy, and that became the thematic joke of *A Tramp Abroad*. The humor did not come easily at first, however. Twain complained to William Dean Howells, "a man can't write successful satire except he be in a calm judicial good-humor—whereas I *hate* travel, & I *hate* hotels, & *I hate* the Old Masters." He obviously recovered his good humor sufficiently to write an exquisite satire of the Old Masters in his paean to the Hair Trunk. And, somewhat gratuitously it appears, he interpolated into the travel narrative one of his finest tall tales—the blue-jay yarn.

"Jim Baker's Blue-Jay Yarn"

One never tires of poking about in the dense woods that clothe all these lofty Neckar hills to their tops. The great deeps of a boundless forest have a beguiling and impressive charm in any country; but German legends and fairy tales have given these an added charm. They have peopled all that region with gnomes, and dwarfs, and all sorts of mysterious and uncanny creatures. At the time I am writing of, I had been reading so much of this literature that sometimes I was not sure but I was beginning to believe in the gnomes and fairies as realities.

One afternoon I got lost in the woods about a mile from the hotel, and presently fell into a train of dreamy thought about animals which talk, and kobolds, and enchanted folk, and the rest of the pleasant legendary stuff; and so, by stimulating my fancy, I finally got to imagining I glimpsed small flitting shapes here and there down the columned aisles of the forest. It was a place which was peculiarly meet for the occasion. It was a pine wood, with so thick and soft a carpet of brown needles that one's footfall made no more sound than if he was treading on wool; the tree-trunks were as round and straight and smooth as pillars, and stood close together; they were bare of branches to a point about twenty-five feet above ground, and from there upward so thick with boughs that not a ray of sunlight could pierce through. The world was bright with sunshine outside, but a deep and mellow twilight reigned in there, and also a silence so profound that I seemed to hear my own breathings.

When I had stood ten minutes, thinking and imagining, and getting my spirit in tune with the place, and in the right mood to enjoy the supernatural, a raven suddenly uttered a hoarse croak over my head. It made me start; and then I was angry because I started. I looked up, and the creature was sitting on a limb right over me, looking down at me. I felt something of the same sense of humiliation and injury which one feels when he finds that a human stranger has been clandestinely inspecting him in his privacy and mentally commenting upon him. I eyed the raven, and the raven eyed me. Noting was said during some seconds. Then the bird stepped a little way along his limb to get a better point of observation, lifted his wings, stuck his head far down below his shoulders toward me, and croaked again—a croak with a distinctly insulting expression about it. If he had spoken in English he could not have said any more plainly than he did say in raven, "Well, what do *you* want here?" I felt as foolish as if I had been caught in some mean act by a responsible being, and reproved for it. However, I made no reply; I would not bandy words with a raven. The adversary waited a while, with his shoulders still lifted, his head thrust down between them, and his keen bright eye fixed on me; then he threw out two or three more insults, which I could not understand, further than that I knew a portion of them consisted of language not used in church.

I still made no reply. Now the adversary raised his head and called. There was an answering croak from a little distance in the wood,—evidently a croak of inquiry. The adversary explained with enthusiasm, and the other raven dropped everything and came. The two sat side by side on the limb and discussed me as freely and offensively as two great naturalists might discuss a new kind of bug. The thing became more and more embarrassing. They called in another friend. This was too much. I saw that they had the advantage of me, and so I concluded to get out of the scrape by walking out of it. They enjoyed my defeat as much as any low white people could have done. They craned their necks and laughed at me, (for a raven *can* laugh, just like a man,) they squalled insulting remarks after me as long as they could see me. They were nothing but ravens—I knew that,—what they thought about me could be a matter of no consequence,—and yet when even a raven shouts after you, "What a hat!" "O, pull down your vest!" and that sort of thing, it hurts you and humiliates you, and there is no getting around it with fine reasoning and pretty arguments.

Animals talk to each other, of course. There can be no question about that; but I suppose there are very few people who can understand them. I never knew but one man who could. I knew he could, however, because he told me so himself. He was a middle-aged, simple-hearted miner who had lived in a lonely corner of California, among the woods and mountains, a good many years, and had studied the ways of his only neighbors, the beasts and the birds, until he believed he could accurately translate any remark which they made. This was Jim Baker. According to Jim Baker, some animals have only a limited education, and use only very simple words, and scarcely ever a comparison or a flowery figure; whereas, certain other animals have a large vocabulary, a fine command of language and a ready and fluent delivery; consequently these latter talk a great deal; they like it; they are conscious of their talent, and they enjoy "showing off." Baker said, that after long and careful observation, he had come to the conclusion that the blue-jays were the best talkers he had found among birds and beasts. Said he:—

"There's more *to* a blue-jay than any other creature. He has got more moods, and more different kinds of feelings than other creature; and mind you, whatever a blue-jay feels, he can put into language. And no more commonplace language, either, but rattling, out-and-out book-talk—and bristling with metaphor, too—just bristling! And as for command of language—why *you* never see a blue-jay get stuck for a word. No man ever did. They just boil out of him! And another thing: I've noticed a good deal, and there's no bird, or cow, or anything that uses as good grammar as a blue-jay. You may say a cat uses good grammar. Well, a cat does—but you let a cat get excited, once; you let a cat get to pulling fur with another cat on a shed, nights, and you'll hear grammar that will give you the lockjaw. Ignorant people think it's the *noise* which fighting cats make that is so aggravating, but it ain't so; it's the sickening grammar they use. Now I've never heard a jay use bad grammar but very seldom; and when they do, they are as ashamed as a human; they shut right down and leave.

"You may call a jay a bird. Well, so he is, in a measure—because he's got feathers on him, and don't belong to no church, perhaps; but otherwise he is just as much a human as you be. And I'll tell you for why. A jay's gifts, and instincts, and feelings, and interests, cover the whole ground. A jay hasn't got any more principle than a Congressman. A jay will lie, a jay will steal, a jay will deceive, a jay will betray; and four times out of five, a jay will go back on his solemnest promise. The sacredness of an obligation is a thing which you can't cram into no blue-jay's head. Now on top of all this, there's another thing: a jay can out-swear any gentleman in the mines. You think a cat can swear. Well, a cat can; but you give a blue-jay a subject that calls for his reserve-powers, and where is your cat? Don't talk to *me*—I know too much about this thing. And there's yet another thing: in the one little particular of scolding—just good, clean, out-and-out scolding—a blue-jay can lay over anything, human or divine. Yes, sir, a jay is everything that a man is. A jay can cry, a jay can laugh, a jay can feel shame, a jay can reason and plan and discuss, a jay likes gossip and scandal, a jay has got a sense of humor, a jay knows when he is an ass just as well as you do—maybe better. If a jay ain't human, he better take in his sign, that's all. Now I'm going to tell you a perfectly true fact about some blue-jays."

"When I first begun to understand jay language correctly, there was a little incident happened here. Seven years ago, the last man in this region but me, moved away. There stands his house,—been empty ever since; a log house, with a plank roof—just one big room, and no more; no ceiling—nothing between the rafters and the floor. Well, one Sunday morning I was sitting out here in front of my cabin, with my cat, taking the sun, and looking at the blue hills, and listening to the leaves rustling so lonely in the trees, and thinking of the home away yonder in the States, that I hadn't heard from in thirteen years, when a blue jay lit on that house, with an acorn in his mouth, and says, 'Hello, I reckon I've struck something.' When he spoke, the acorn dropped out of his mouth and rolled down the roof, of course, but he didn't care; his mind was all on the thing he had struck. It was a knot-hole in the roof. He cocked his head to one side, shut one eye and put the other one to the hole, like a 'possum looking down a jug; then he glanced up with his bright eyes, gave a wink or two with his wings—which signifies gratification, you understand,—and says, 'It looks like a hole, it's located like a hole,—blamed if I don't believe it *is* a hole!'

"Then he cocked his head down and took another look; he glances up perfectly joyful, this time; winks his wings and his tail both, and says, 'O, no, this ain't no fat thing, I reckon! If I ain't in luck!—why it's a perfectly elegant hole!' So he flew down and got that acorn, and fetched it up and dropped it in, and was just tilting his head back, with the heavenliest smile on his face, when all of a sudden he was paralyzed into a listening attitude and that smile faded gradually out of his countenance like breath off'n a razor, and the queerest look of surprise took its place. Then he says, 'Why I didn't hear it fall!' He cocked his eye at the hole again, and took a long look; raised up and shook his head; stepped around to the other side of the hole and took another look from that side; shook his head again. He studied a while, then he just went into the *de*tails—walked round and round the hole and spied into it from every point of the compass. No use. Now he took a thinking attitude on the comb of the roof and scratched the back of his head with his right foot a minute, and finally says, 'Well, it's too many for *me,* that's certain; must be a mighty long hole; however, I ain't got time to fool around here, I got to 'tend to business; I reckon it's all right—chance it, anyway.'

"So he flew off and fetched another acorn and dropped it in, and tried to flirt, his eye to the hole quick enough to see what become of it, but he was too late. He held his eye there as much as a minute; then he raised up and sighed, and says, 'Consound it, I don't seem to understand this thing, no way; however, I'll tackle her again.' He fetched another acorn, and done his level best to see what become of it, but he couldn't. He says, 'Well, *I* never struck no such a hole as this, before; I'm of the opinion it's a totally new kind of a hole.' Then he began to get mad. He held in for a spell, walking up and down the comb of the roof and shaking his head and muttering to himself; but his feelings got the upper hand of him, presently, and he broke loose and cussed himself black in the face. I never see a bird take on so about a little thing. When he got through he walks to the hole and looks in again for half a minute; then he says, 'Well, you're a long hole, and a deep hole, and a mighty singular hole altogether—but I've started in to fill you, and I'm d—d if I *don't* fill you, if it takes a hundred years!'

"And with that, away he went. You never see a bird work so since you was born. He laid into his work like a nigger, and the way he hove acorns into that hole for about two hours and a half was one of the most exciting and astonishing spectacles I ever struck. He never stopped to take a look any more—he just hove 'em in and went for more. Well at last he could hardly flop his wings, he was so tuckered out. He comes a-dropping down, once more, sweating like an ice-pitcher, drops his acorn in and says, '*Now* I guess I've got the bulge on you by this time!' So he bent down for a look. If you'll believe me, when his head come up again he was just pale with rage. He says, 'I've shoveled acorns enough in there to keep the family thirty years, and if I can see a sign of one of 'em I wish I may land in a museum with a belly full of sawdust in two minutes!'

"He just had strength enough to crawl up on to the comb and lean his back agin the chimbly, and then he collected his impressions and began to free his mind. I see in a second that what I had mistook for profanity in the mines was only just the rudiments, as you may say.

"Another jay was going by, and heard him doing his devotions, and stops to inquire what was up. The sufferer told him the whole circumstance, and says, 'Now yonder's the hole, and if you don't believe me, go and look for yourself.' So this fellow went and looked, and comes back and says, 'How many did you say you put in there?' 'Not any less than two tons,' says the sufferer. The other jay went and looked again. He couldn't seem to make it out, so he raised a yell, and three more jays come. They all examined the hole, they all made the sufferer tell it over again, then they all discussed it, and got off as many leather-headed opinions about it as an average crowd of humans could have done.

"They called in more jays; then more and more, till pretty soon this whole region 'peared to have a blue flush about it. There must have been five thousand of them; and such another jawing and disputing and ripping and cussing, you never heard. Every jay in the whole lot put his eye to the hole and delivered a more chuckle-headed opinion about the mystery than the jay that went there before him. They examined the house all over, too. The door was standing half open, and at last one old jay happened to go and light on it and look in. Of course that knocked the mystery galley-west in a second. There lay the acorns, scattered all over the floor. He flopped his wings and raised a whoop. 'Come here!' he says, 'Come here, everybody; hang'd if this fool hasn't been trying to fill up a house with acorns!' They all came a-swooping down like a blue cloud, and as each fellow lit on the door and took a glance, the whole absurdity of the contract that that first jay had tackled hit him home and he fell over backwards suffocating with laughter, and the next jay took his place and done the same.

"Well, sir, they roosted around here on the house-top and the trees for an hour, and guffawed over that thing like human beings. It ain't any use to tell me a blue-jay hasn't got a sense of humor, because I know better. And memory, too. They brought jays here from all over the United States to look down that hole, every summer for three years. Other birds too. And they could all see the point, except an owl that come from Nova Scotia to visit the Yo Semite, and he took this thing in on his way back. He said he couldn't see anything funny in it. But then he was a good deal disappointed about Yo Semite, too."

"The Hair Trunk"

I found more pleasure in contemplating the Old Masters this time than I did when I was in Europe in former years, but still it was a calm pleasure; there was nothing over-heated about it. When I was in Venice before, I think I found no picture which stirred me much, but this time there were two which enticed me to the Doge's palace day after day, and kept me there hours at a time. One of these was Tintoretto's three-acre picture in the Grand Council Chamber. When I saw it twelve years ago I was not strongly attracted to it—the guide told me it was an insurrection in heaven—but this was an error.

The movement of this great work is very fine. There are ten thousand figures, and they are all doing something. There is a wonderful "go" to the whole composition. Some of the figures are diving headlong downward, with clasped hands, others are swimming through the cloud-shoals,—some on their faces, some on their backs—great processions of bishops, martyrs and angels are pouring swiftly centerwards from various outlying directions—everywhere is enthusiastic joy, there is rushing movement everywhere. There are fifteen or twenty figures scattered here and there, with books, but they cannot keep their attention on their reading—they offer the books to others, but no one wishes to read, now. The Lion of St. Mark is there with his book; St. Mark is there with his pen uplifted; he and the Lion are looking each other earnestly in the face, disputing about the way to spell a word—the Lion looks up in wrapt admiration while St. Mark spells. This is wonderfully interpreted by the artist. It is the master-stroke of this incomparable painting.

I visited the place daily, and never grew tired of looking at that grand picture. As I have intimated, the movement is almost unimaginably vigorous; the figures are singing, hosannahing, and many are blowing trumpets. So vividly is noise suggested, that spectators who become absorbed in the picture almost always fall to shouting comments in each other's ears, making ear-trumpets of their curved hands, fearing they may not otherwise be heard. One often sees a tourist, with the eloquent tears pouring down his cheeks, funnel his hands at his wife's ear, and hears him roar through them, "O, TO BE THERE AND AT REST!"

None but the supremely great in art can produce effects like these with the silent brush.

Twelve years ago I could not have appreciated this picture. One year ago I could not have appreciated it. My study of Art in Heidelberg has been a noble education to me. All that I am to-day in Art, I owe to that.

The other great work which fascinated me was Bassano's immortal Hair Trunk. This is in the Chamber of the Council of Ten. It is in one of the three forty-foot pictures which decorate the walls of the room. The composition of this picture is beyond praise. The Hair Trunk is not hurled at the stranger's head,—so to speak—as the chief feature of an immortal work so often is; no, it is carefully guarded from prominence, it is subordinated, it is restrained, it is most deftly and cleverly held in reserve, it is most cautiously and ingeniously led up to, by the master, and consequently when the spectator reaches it at last, he is taken unawares, he is unprepared, and it bursts upon him with a stupefying surprise.

One is lost in wonder at all the thought and care which this elaborate planning must have cost. A general glance at the picture could never suggest that there was a hair trunk in it; the Hair Trunk is not mentioned in the title even,—which is, "Pope Alexander III and the Doge Ziani, the Conqueror of the Emperor Frederick Barbarossa;" you see, the title is actually utilized to help divert attention from the Trunk; thus, as I say, nothing suggests the presence of the Trunk, by any hint, yet everything studiedly leads up to it, step by step. Let us examine into this, and observe the exquisitely artful artlessness of the plan.

At the extreme left end of the picture are a couple of women, one of them with a child looking over her shoulder at a wounded man sitting with bandaged head on the ground. These people seem needless, but no, they are there for a purpose; one cannot look at them without seeing the gorgeous procession of grandees, bishops, halberdiers, and banner-bearers which is passing along behind them; one cannot see the procession without feeling a curiosity to follow it and learn whither it is going; it leads him to the Pope, in the center of the picture, who is talking with the bonnetless Doge—talking tranquilly, too, although within 12 feet of them a man is beating a drum, and not far from the drummer two persons are blowing horns, and many horsemen are plunging and rioting about—indeed, 22 feet of this great work is all a deep and happy holiday serenity and Sunday School procession, and then we come suddenly upon 11½ feet of turmoil and racket and insubordination. This latter state of things is not an accident, it has its purpose. But for it, one would linger upon the Pope and the Doge, thinking them to be the motive and supreme feature of the picture; whereas one is drawn along, almost unconsciously, to see what the trouble is about. Now at the very *end* of this riot, within 4 feet of the end of the picture, and full 36 feet from the beginning of it, the Hair Trunk bursts with an electrifying suddenness upon the spectator, in all its matchless perfection, and the great master's triumph is sweeping and complete. From that moment no other thing in those forty feet of canvas has any charm; one sees the Hair Trunk, and the Hair Trunk only—and to see it is to worship it. Bassano even placed objects in the immediate vicinity of the Supreme Feature whose pretended purpose was to divert attention from it yet a little longer and thus delay and augment the surprise; for instance, to the right of it he has placed a stooping man with a cap so red that it is sure to hold the eye for a moment—to the left of it, some 6 feet away, he has placed a red-coated man on an inflated horse, and that coat plucks your eye to that locality the next moment—then, between the Trunk and the red horseman he has intruded a man, naked to his waist, who is carrying a fancy flour sack on the middle of his back instead of on his shoulder—this admirable feat interests you, of course—keeps you at bay a little longer, like a sock or a jacket thrown to the pursuing wolf—but at last, in spite of all distractions and detentions, the eye of even the most dull and heedless spectator is sure to fall upon the World's Masterpiece, and in that moment he totters to his chair or leans upon his guide for support.

Descriptions of such a work as this must necessarily be imperfect, yet they are of value. The top of the Trunk is arched; the arch is a perfect half circle, in the Roman style of architecture, for in the then rapid decadence of Greek art, the rising influence of Rome was already beginning to be felt in the art of the Republic. The Trunk is bound or bordered with leather all around where the lid joins the main body. Many critics consider this leather too cold in tone; but I consider this its highest merit, since it was evidently made so to emphasize by contrast the impassioned fervor of the hasp. The high lights in this part of the work are cleverly managed, the *motif* is admirably subordinated to the ground tints, and the *technique* is very fine. The brass nail-heads are in the purest style of the early renaissance. The strokes, here, are very firm and bold—every nail-head is a portrait. The handle on the end of the Trunk has evidently been retouched—I think, with a piece of chalk—but one can still see the inspiration of the Old Master in the tranquil, almost too tranquil, hang of it. The hair of this Trunk is *real* hair—so to speak—white in patches, brown in patches. The details are finely worked out; the repose proper to hair in a recumbent and inactive attitude is charmingly expressed. There is a feeling about this part of the work which lifts it to the highest altitudes of art; the sense of sordid realism vanishes away—one recognizes that there is *soul* here. View this Trunk as you will, it is a gem, it is a marvel, it is a miracle. Some of the effects are very daring, approaching even to the boldest flights of the rococo, the sirocco, and the Byzantine schools—yet the master's hand never falters—it moves on, calm, majestic, confident,—and with that art which conceals art, it finally casts over the *total ensemble*, by mysterious methods of its own, a subtle something which refines, subdues, etherealizes the arid components and endues them with the deep charm and gracious witchery of poesy.

Among the art treasures of Europe there are pictures which approach the Hair Trunk—there are two which may be said to equal it, possibly—but there is none that surpasses it. So perfect is the Hair Trunk that it moves even persons who ordinarily have no feeling for art. When an Erie baggage master saw it two years ago, he could hardly keep from checking it; and once when a customs inspector was brought into its presence, he gazed upon it in silent rapture for some moments, then slowly and unconsciously placed one hand behind him with the palm uppermost, and got out his chalk with the other. These facts speak for themselves.

FROM

LIFE ON THE MISSISSIPPI

(1883)

Largely through the invitation of William Dean Howells to contribute something to the *Atlantic* and the prodding of his friend Joseph Twichell, who, after hearing him speak of the glory days of Mississippi steamboating, exclaimed that this was "a virgin subject to hurl into a magazine," Twain published the several installments of "Old Times on the Mississippi" in 1875. He returned to the subject (and the Mississippi itself) seven years later with an eye to writing a full-length book treatment of life along the river. The "Old Times" chapters are generally considered superior to the other portions of *Life on the Mississippi,* however. "The Boy's Ambition," "Perplexing Lessons," and "Continued Perplexities" come from the earlier stint of writing; the remaining selections are from the later period. Twain's description of the "House Beautiful" and sunrise on the river may be profitably compared to Huck's idiomatic treatment of the same subjects in Chapters 17 and 19 of *Huckleberry Finn.*

"The River and Its History"

The Mississippi is well worth reading about. It is not a commonplace river, but on the contrary is in all ways remarkable. Considering the Missouri its main branch, it is the longest river in the world—four thousand three hundred miles. It seems safe to say that it is also the crookedest river in the world, since in one part of its journey it uses up one thousand three hundred miles to cover the same ground that the crow would fly over in six hundred and seventy-five. It discharges three times as much water as the St. Lawrence, twenty-five times as much as the Rhine, and three hundred and thirty-eight times as much as the Thames. No other river has so vast a drainage-basin: it draws its water supply from twenty-eight States and Territories; from Delaware, on the Atlantic seaboard, and from all the country between that and Idaho on the Pacific slope—a spread of forty-five degrees of longitude. The Mississippi receives and carries to the Gulf water from fifty-four subordinate rivers that are navigable by steamboats, and from some hundreds that are navigable by flats and keels. The area of its drainage-basin is as great as the combined areas of England, Wales, Scotland, Ireland, France, Spain, Portugal, Germany, Austria, Italy, and Turkey; and almost all this wide region is fertile; the Mississippi valley, proper, is exceptionally so.

It is a remarkable river in this: that instead of widening toward its mouth, it grows narrower; grows narrower and deeper. From the junction of the Ohio to a point half way down to the sea, the width averages a mile in high water: thence to the sea the width steadily diminishes, until, at the "Passes," above the mouth, it is but little over half a mile. At the junction of the Ohio the Mississippi's depth is eighty-seven feet; the depth increases gradually, reaching one hundred and twenty-nine just above the mouth.

The difference in rise and fall is also remarkable—not in the upper, but in the lower river. The rise is tolerably uniform down to Natchez (three hundred and sixty miles above the mouth)—about fifty feet. But at Bayou LaFourche the river rises only twenty-four feet; at New Orleans only fifteen, and just above the mouth only two and one half.

An article in the New Orleans "Times-Democrat," based upon reports of able engineers, states that the river annually empties four hundred and six million tons of mud into the Gulf of Mexico—which brings to mind Captain Marryat's rude name for the Mississippi—"the Great Sewer." This mud, solidified, would make a mass a mile square and two hundred and forty-one feet high.

The mud deposit gradually extends the land—but only gradually; it has extended it not quite a third of a mile in the two hundred years which have elapsed since the river took its place in history. The belief of the scientific people is, that the mouth used to be at Baton Rouge, where the hills cease, and that the two hundred miles of land between there and the Gulf was built by the river. This gives us the age of that piece of country, without any trouble at all—one hundred and twenty thousand years. Yet it is much the youthfulest batch of country that lies around there anywhere.

The Mississippi is remarkable in still another way—its disposition to make prodigious jumps by cutting through narrow necks of land, and thus straightening and shortening itself. More than once it has shortened itself thirty miles at a single jump! These cut-offs have had curious effects: they have thrown several river towns out into the rural districts, and built up sand bars and forests in front of them. The town of Delta used to be three miles below Vicksburg: a recent cut-off has radically changed the position, and Delta is now *two miles above* Vicksburg.

Both of these river towns have been retired to the country by that cut-off. A cut-off plays havoc with boundary lines and jurisdictions: for instance, a man is living in the State of Mississippi to-day, a cut-off occurs to-night, and to-morrow the man finds himself and his land over on the other side of the river, within the boundaries and subject to the laws of the State of Louisiana! Such a thing, happening in the upper river in the old times, could have transferred a slave from Missouri to Illinois and made a free man of him.

The Mississippi does not alter its locality by cut-offs alone: it is always changing its habitat *bodily*—it always moving bodily *sidewise.* At Hard Times, La., the river is two miles west of the region it used to occupy. As a result, the original *site* of that settlement is not now in Louisiana at all, but on the other side of the river, in the State of Mississippi. *Nearly the whole of that one thousand three hundred miles of old Mississippi River which La Salle floated down in his canoes, two hundred years ago, is good solid dry ground now.* The river lies to the right of it, in places, and to the left of it in other places.

Although the Mississippi's mud builds land but slowly, down at the mouth, where the Gulf's billows interfere with its work, it builds fast enough in better protected regions higher up: for instance, Prophet's Island contained one thousand five hundred acres of land thirty years ago; since then the river has added seven hundred acres to it.

But enough of these examples of the mighty stream's eccentricities for the present—I will give a few more of them further along in the book.

Let us drop the Mississippi's physical history, and say a word about its historical history—so to speak. We can glance briefly at the slumbrous first epoch in a couple of short chapters; at its second and wider-awake epoch in a couple more; at its flushest and widest-awake epoch in a good many succeeding chapters; and then talk about its comparatively tranquil present epoch in what shall be left of the book.

The world and the books are so accustomed to use, and overuse, the word "new" in connection with our country, that we early get and permanently retain the impression that there is nothing old about it. We do of course know that there are several comparatively old dates in American history, but the mere figures convey to our minds no just idea, no distinct realization, of the stretch of time which they represent. To say that De Soto, the first white man who ever saw the Mississippi River, saw it in 1542, is a remark which states a fact without interpreting it: it is something like giving the dimensions of a sunset by astronomical measurements, and cataloguing the colors by their scientific names;—as a result, you get the bald fact of the sunset, but you don't see the sunset. It would have been better to paint a picture of it.

The date 1542, standing by itself, means little or nothing to us; but when one groups a few neighboring historical dates and facts around it, he adds perspective and color, and then realizes that this is one of the American dates which is quite respectable for age.

For instance, when the Mississippi was first seen by a white man, less than a quarter of a century had elapsed since Francis I.'s defeat at Pavia; the death of Raphael; the death of Bayard, *sans peur et sans reproche;* the driving out of the Knights-Hospitallers from Rhodes by the Turks; and the placarding of the Ninety-Five Propositions,—the act which began the Reformation. When De Soto took his glimpse of the river, Ignatius Loyola was an obscure name; the order of the Jesuits was not yet a year old; Michael Angelo's paint was not yet dry on the Last Judgment in the Sistine Chapel; Mary Queen of Scots was not yet born, but would be before the year closed. Catherine de Medici was a child; Elizabeth of England was not yet in her teens; Calvin, Benvenuto Cellini, and the Emperor Charles V. were at the top of their fame, and each was manufacturing history after his own peculiar fashion; Margaret of Navarre was writing the "Heptameron" and some religious books,—the first survives, the others are forgotten, wit and indelicacy being sometimes better literature-preservers than holiness; lax court morals and the absurd chivalry business were in full feather, and the joust and the tournament were the frequent pastime of titled fine gentlemen who could fight better than they could spell, while religion was the passion of their ladies, and the classifying their offspring into children of full rank and children by brevet their pastime. In fact, all around, religion was in a peculiarly blooming condition: the Council of Trent was being called; the Spanish Inquisition was roasting, and racking, and burning, with a free hand; elsewhere on the continent the nations were being persuaded to holy living by the sword and fire; in England, Henry VIII. had suppressed the monasteries, burnt Fisher and another bishop or two, and was getting his English reformation and his harem effectively started. When De Soto stood on the banks of the Mississippi, it was still two years before Luther's death; eleven years before the burning of Servetus; thirty years before the St. Bartholomew slaughter; Rabelais was not yet published; "Don Quixote" was not yet written; Shakespeare was not yet born; a hundred long years still must elapse before Englishmen would hear the name of Oliver Cromwell.

Unquestionably the discovery of the Mississippi is a datable fact which considerably mellows and modifies the shiny newness of our country, and gives her a most respectable outside-aspect of rustiness and antiquity.

De Soto merely glimpsed the river, then died and was buried in it by his priests and soldiers. One would expect the priests and the soldiers to multiply the river's dimensions by ten—the Spanish custom of the day—and thus move other adventurers to go at once and explore it. On the contrary, their narratives when they reached home, did not excite that amount of curiosity. The Mississippi was left unvisited by whites during a term of years which seems incredible in our energetic days. One may "sense" the interval to his mind, after a fashion, by dividing it up in this way: After De Soto glimpsed the river, a fraction short of a quarter of a century elapsed, and then Shakespeare was born; lived a trifle more than half a century, then died; and when he had been in his grave considerably more than half a century, the *second* white man saw the Mississippi. In our day we don't allow a hundred and thirty years to elapse between glimpses of a marvel. If somebody should discover a creek in the county next to the one that the North Pole is in, Europe and America would start fifteen costly expeditions thither: one to explore the creek, and the other fourteen to hunt for each other.

For more than a hundred and fifty years there had been white settlements on our Atlantic coasts. These people were in intimate communication with the Indians: in the south the Spaniards were robbing, slaughtering, enslaving and converting them; higher up, the English were trading beads and blankets to them for a consideration, and throwing in civilization and whiskey, "for lagniappe;" and in Canada the French were schooling them in a rudimentary way, missionarying among them, and drawing whole populations of them at a time to Quebec, and later to Montreal, to buy furs of them. Necessarily, then, these various clusters of whites must have heard of the great river of the far west; and indeed, they did hear of it vaguely,—so vaguely and indefinitely, that its course, proportions, and locality were hardly even guessable. The mere mysteriousness of the matter ought to have fired curiosity and compelled exploration; but this did not occur. Apparently nobody happened to want such a river, nobody needed it, nobody was curious about it; so, for a century and a half the Mississippi remained out of the market and undisturbed. When De Soto found it, he was not hunting for a river, and had no present occasion for one; consequently he did not value it or even take any particular notice of it.

But at last La Salle the Frenchman conceived the idea of seeking out that river and exploring it. It always happens that when a man seizes upon a neglected and important idea, people inflamed with the same notion crop up all around. It happened so in this instance.

Naturally the question suggests itself, Why did these people want the river now when nobody had wanted it in the five preceding generations? Apparently it was because at this late day they thought they had discovered a way to make it useful; for it had come to be believed that the Mississippi emptied into the Gulf of California, and therefore afforded a short cut from Canada to China. Previously the supposition had been that it emptied into the Atlantic, or Sea of Virginia.

"The Boys' Ambition"

When I was a boy, there was but one permanent ambition among my comrades in our village* on the west bank of the Mississippi River. That was, to be a steamboatman. We had transient ambitions of other sorts, but they were only transient. When a circus came and went, it left us all burning to become clowns; the first negro minstrel show that came to our section left us all suffering to try that kind of life; now and then we had a hope that if we lived and were good, God would permit us to be pirates. These ambitions faded out, each in its turn; but the ambition to be a steamboatman always remained.

Once a day a cheap, gaudy packet arrived upward from St. Louis, and another downward from Keokuk. Before these events, the day was glorious with expectancy; after them, the day was a dead and empty thing. Not only the boys, but the whole village, felt this. After all these years I can picture that old time to myself now, just as it was then: the white town drowsing in the sunshine of a summer's morning; the streets empty, or pretty nearly so; one or two clerks sitting in front of the Water Street stores, with their splint-bottomed chairs tilted back against the wall, chins on breasts, hats slouched over their faces, asleep—with shingle-shavings enough around to show what broke them down; a sow and a litter of pigs loafing along the sidewalk, doing a good business in watermelon rinds and seeds; two or three lonely little freight piles scattered about the "levee;" a pile of "skids" on the slope of the stone-paved wharf, and the fragrant town drunkard asleep in the shadow of

*Hannibal, Missouri.

them; two or three wood flats at the head of the wharf, but nobody to listen to the peaceful lapping of the wavelets against them; the great Mississippi, the majestic, the magnificent Mississippi, rolling its mile-wide tide along, shining in the sun; the dense forest away on the other side; the "point" above the town, and the "point" below, bounding the river-glimpse and turning it into a sort of sea, and withal a very still and brilliant and lonely one. Presently a film of dark smoke appears above one of those remote "points;" instantly a negro drayman, famous for his quick eye and prodigious voice, lifts up the cry, "S-t-e-a-m-boat a-comin'!" and the scene changes! The town drunkard stirs, the clerks wake up, a furious clatter of drays follows, every house and store pours out a human contribution, and all in a twinkling the dead town is alive and moving. Drays, carts, men, boys, all go hurrying from many quarters to a common centre, the wharf. Assembled there, the people fasten their eyes upon the coming boat as upon a wonder they are seeing for the first time. And the boat *is* rather a handsome sight, too. She is long and sharp and trim and pretty; she has two tall, fancy-topped chimneys, with a gilded device of some kind swung between them; a fanciful pilot-house, all glass and "gingerbread," perched on top of the "texas" deck behind them; the paddle-boxes are gorgeous with a picture or with gilded rays above the boat's name; the boiler deck, the hurricane deck, and the texas deck are fenced and ornamented with clean white railings; there is a flag gallantly flying from the jack-staff; the furnace doors are open and the fires glaring bravely; the upper decks are black with passengers; the captain stands by the big bell, calm, imposing, the envy of all; great volumes of the blackest smoke are rolling and tumbling out of the chimneys—a husbanded grandeur created with a bit of pitch pine just before arriving at a town; the crew are grouped on the forecastle; the broad stage is run far out over the port bow, and an envied deck-hand stands picturesquely on the end of it with a coil of rope in his hand; the pent steam is screaming through the gauge-cocks; the captain lifts his hand, a bell rings, the wheels stop; then they turn back, churning the water to foam, and the steamer is at rest. Then such a scramble as there is to get aboard, and to get ashore, and to take in freight and to discharge freight, all at one and the same time; and such a yelling and cursing as the mates facilitate it all with! Ten minutes later the steamer is under way again, with no flag on the jack-staff and no black smoke issuing from the chimneys. After ten more minutes the town is dead again, and the town drunkard asleep by the skids once more.

My father was a justice of the peace, and I suppose he possessed the power of life and death over all men and could hang anybody that offended him. This was distinction enough for me as a general thing; but the desire to be a steamboatman kept intruding, nevertheless. I first wanted to be a cabin-boy, so that I could come out with a white apron on and shake a table-cloth over the side, where all my old comrades could see me; later I thought I would rather be the deck-hand who stood on the end of the stage-plank with the coil of rope in his hand, because he was particularly conspicuous. But these were only day-dreams,—they were too heavenly to be contemplated as real possibilities. By and by one of our boys went away. He was not heard of for a long time. At last he turned up as apprentice engineer or "striker" on a steamboat. This thing shook the bottom out of all my Sunday-school teachings. That boy had been notoriously worldly, and I just the reverse; yet he was exalted to this eminence, and I left in obscurity and misery. There was nothing generous about this fellow in his greatness. He would always manage to have a rusty bolt to scrub while his boat tarried at our town, and he would sit on the inside guard and scrub it where we could all see him and envy him and loathe him. And whenever his boat was laid up he would come home and swell around the town in his blackest and greasiest clothes, so that nobody could help remembering that he was a steamboatman; and he used all sorts of steamboat technicalities in his talk, as if he were so used to them that he forgot common people could not understand them. He would speak of the "labboard" side of a horse in an easy, natural way that would make one wish he was dead. And he was always talking about "St. Looy" like an old citizen; he would refer casually to occasions when he "was coming down Fourth Street," or when he was "passing by the Planter's House," or when there was a fire and he took a turn on the brakes of "the old big Missouri;" and then he would go on and lie about how many towns the size of ours were burned down there that day. Two or three of the boys had long been persons of consideration among us because they had been to St. Louis once and had a vague general knowledge of its wonders, but the day of their glory was over now. They lapsed into a humble silence, and learned to disappear when the ruthless "cub"-engineer approached. This fellow had money, too, and hair oil. Also an ignorant silver watch and a showy brass watch chain. He wore a leather belt and used no suspenders. If ever a youth was cordially admired and hated by his comrades, this one was. No girl could withstand his charms. He "cut out" every boy in the village. When his boat blew up at last, it diffused a tranquil contentment among us such as we had not known for months. But when he came home the next week, alive, renowned, and appeared in church all battered up and bandaged, a shining hero, stared at and wondered over by everybody, it seemed to us that the partiality of Providence for an undeserving reptile had reached a point where it was open to criticism.

This creature's career could produce but one result, and it speedily followed. Boy after boy managed to get on the river. The minister's son became an engineer. The doctor's and the post-master's sons became "mud clerks;" the wholesale liquor dealer's son became a bar-keeper on a boat; four sons of the chief merchant, and two sons of the county judge, became pilots. Pilot was the grandest position of all. The pilot, even in those days of trivial wages, had a princely salary—from a hundred and fifty to two hundred and fifty dollars a month, and no board to pay. Two months of his wages would pay a preacher's salary for a year. Now some of us were left disconsolate. We could not get on the river—at least our parents would not let us.

So by and by I ran away. I said I never would come home again till I was a pilot and could come in glory. But somehow I could not manage it. I went meekly aboard a few of the boats that lay packed together like sardines at the long St. Louis wharf, and very humbly inquired for the pilots, but got only a cold shoulder and short words from mates and clerks. I had to make the best of this sort of treatment for the time being, but I had comforting day-dreams of a future when I should be a great and honored pilot, with plenty of money, and could kill some of these mates and clerks and pay for them.

"Perplexing Lessons"

At the end of what seemed a tedious while, I had managed to pack my head full of islands, towns, bars, "points," and bends; and a curiously inanimate mass of lumber it was, too. However, inasmuch as I could shut my eyes and reel off a good long string of these names without leaving out more than ten miles of river in every fifty, I began to feel that I could take a boat down to New Orleans if I could make her skip those little gaps. But of course my complacency could hardly get start enough to lift my nose a trifle into the air, before Mr. Bixby would think of something to fetch it down again. One day he turned on me suddenly with this settler:—

"What is the shape of Walnut Bend?"

He might as well have asked me grandmother's opinion of protoplasm. I reflected respectfully, and then said I didn't know it had any particular shape. My gunpowdery chief went off with a bang, of course, and then went on loading and firing until he was out of adjectives.

I had learned long ago that he only carried just so many rounds of ammunition, and was sure to subside into a very placable and even remorseful old smooth-bore as soon as they were all gone. That word "old" is merely affectionate; he was not more than thirty-four. I waited. By and by he said,—

"My boy, you've got to know the *shape* of the river perfectly. It is all there is left to steer by on a very dark night. Everything else is blotted out and gone. But mind you, it hasn't the same shape in the night that it has in the day-time."

"How on earth am I ever going to learn it, then?"

"How do you follow a hall at home in the dark? Because you know the shape of it. You can't see it."

"Do you mean to say that I've got to know all the million trifling variations of shape in the banks of this interminable river as well as I know the shape of the front hall at home?"

"On my honor, you've got to know them *better* than any man ever did know the shapes of the halls in his own house."

"I wish I was dead!"

"Now I don't want to discourage you, but"—

"Well, pile it on me; I might as well have it now as another time."

"You see, this has got to be learned; there isn't any getting around it. A clear starlight night throws such heavy shadows that if you didn't know the shape of a shore perfectly you would claw away from every bunch of timber, because you would take the black shadow of it for a solid cape; and you see you would be getting scared to death every fifteen minutes by the watch. You would be fifty yards from shore all the time when you ought to be within fifty feet of it. You can't see a snag in one of those shadows, but you know exactly where it is, and the shape of the river tells you when you are coming to it. Then there's your pitch-dark night; the river is a very different shape on a pitch-dark night from what it is on a starlight night. All shores seem to be straight lines, then, and mighty dim ones, too; and you'd *run* them for straight lines only you know better. You boldly drive your boat right into what seems to be a solid, straight wall (you knowing very well that in reality there is a curve there), and that wall falls back and makes way for you. Then there's your gray mist. You take a night when there's one of these grisly, drizzly, gray mists, and then there isn't *any* particular shape to a shore. A gray mist would tangle the head of the oldest man that ever lived. Well, then, different kinds of *moonlight* change the shape of the river in different ways. You see"—

"Oh, don't say any more, please! Have I got to learn the shape of the river according to all these five hundred thousand different ways? If I tried to carry all that cargo in my head it would make me stoop-shouldered."

"*No!* you only learn *the* shape of the river; and you learn it with such absolute certainty that you can always steer by the shape that's *in your head,* and never mind the one that's before your eyes."

"Very well, I'll try it; but after I have learned it can I depend on it? Will it keep the same form and not go fooling around?"

Before Mr. Bixby could answer, Mr. W—came in to take the watch, and he said,—

"Bixby, you'll have to look out for President's Island and all that country clear away up above the Old Hen and Chickens. The banks are caving and the shape of the shores changing like everything. Why, you wouldn't know the point above 40. You can go up inside the old sycamore snag, now."*

So that question was answered. Here were leagues of shore changing shape. My spirits were down in the mud again. Two things seemed pretty apparent to me. One was, that in order to be a pilot a man had got to learn more than any one man ought to be allowed to know; and the other was, that he must learn it all over again in a different way every twenty-four hours.

That night we had the watch until twelve. Now it was an ancient river custom for the two pilots to chat a bit when the watch changed. While the relieving pilot put on his gloves and lit his cigar, his partner, the retiring pilot, would say something like this:—

"I judge the upper bar is making down a little at Hale's Point; had quarter twain with the lower lead and mark twain† with the other."

"Yes, I thought it was making down a little, last trip. Meet any boats?"

"Met one abreast the head of 21, but she was away over hugging the bar, and I couldn't make her out entirely. I took her for the 'Sunny South'—hadn't any skylights forward of the chimneys."

And so on. And as the relieving pilot took the wheel his

*It may not be necessary, but still it can do no harm to explain that "inside" means between the snag and the shore.—M.T.

†Two fathoms. Quarter twain is 2¼ fathoms, 13½ feet. Mark three is three fathoms.

partner* would mention that we were in such-and-such a bend, and say we were abreast of such-and-such a man's wood-yard or plantation. This was courtesy; I suppose it was *necessity.* But Mr. W—came on watch full twelve minutes late on this particular night,—a tremendous breach of etiquette; in fact, it is the unpardonable sin among pilots. So Mr. Bixby gave him no greeting whatever, but simply surrendered the wheel and marched out of the pilot-house without a word. I was appalled; it was a villainous night for blackness, we were in a particularly wide and blind part of the river, where there was no shape of substance to anything, and it seemed incredible that Mr. Bixby should have left that poor fellow to kill the boat trying to find out where he was. But I resolved that I would stand by him any way. He should find that he was not wholly friendless. So I stood around, and waited to be asked where we were. But Mr. W—plunged on serenely through the solid firmament of black cats that stood for an atmosphere, and never opened his mouth. Here is a proud devil, thought I; here is a limb of Satan that would rather send us all to destruction than put himself under obligations to me, because I am not yet one of the salt of the earth and privileged to snub captains and lord it over everything dead and alive in a steamboat. I presently climbed up on the bench; I did not think it was safe to go to sleep while this lunatic was on watch.

However, I must have gone to sleep in the course of time, because the next thing I was aware of was the fact that day was breaking, Mr. W—gone, and Mr. Bixby at the wheel again. So it was four o'clock and all well—but me; I felt like a skinful of dry bones and all of them trying to ache at once.

Mr. Bixby asked me what I had stayed up there for. I confessed that if was to do Mr. W—a benevolence,—tell him where he was. It took five minutes for the entire preposterousness of the thing to filter into Mr. Bixby's system, and then I judge it filled him nearly up to the chin; because he paid me a compliment—and not much of a one either. He said,—

"Well, taking you by-and-large, you do seem to be more dif-

*"Partner" is technical for "the other pilot."

ferent kinds of an ass than any creature I ever saw before. What did you suppose he wanted to know for?"

I said I thought it might be a convenience to him.

"Convenience! D-nation! Didn't I tell you that a man's got to know the river in the night the same as he'd know his own front hall?"

"Well, I can follow the front hall in the dark if I know it *is* the front hall; but suppose you set me down in the middle of it in the dark and not tell me which hall it is; how am *I* to know?"

"Well, you've *got* to, on the river!"

"All right. Then I'm glad I never said anything to Mr. W—"

"I should say so. Why, he'd have slammed you through the window and utterly ruined a hundred dollars' worth of window-sash and stuff."

I was glad this damage had been saved, for it would have made me unpopular with the owners. They always hated anybody who had the name of being careless, and injuring things.

I went to work now to learn the shape of the river; and of all the eluding and ungraspable objects that ever I tried to get mind or hands on, that was the chief. I would fasten my eyes upon a sharp, wooded point that projected far into the river some miles ahead of me, and go to laboriously photographing its shape upon my brain; and just as I was beginning to succeed to my satisfaction, we would draw up toward it and the exasperating thing would begin to melt away and fold back into the bank! If there had been a conspicuous dead tree standing upon the very point of the cape, I would find that tree inconspicuously merged into the general forest, and occupying the middle of a straight shore, when I got abreast of it! No prominent hill would stick to its shape long enough for me to make up my mind what its form really was, but it was as dissolving and changeful as if it had been a mountain of butter in the hottest corner of the tropics. Nothing ever had the same shape when I was coming down-stream that it had borne when I went up. I mentioned these little difficulties to Mr. Bixby. He said,—

"That's the very main virtue of the thing. If the shapes didn't change every three seconds they wouldn't be of any use. Take this place where we are now, for instance. As long as that hill over yonder is only one hill, I can boom right along the way I'm going; but the moment it splits at the top and forms a V, I know I've got to scratch to starboard in a hurry, or I'll bang this boat's brains out against a rock; and then the moment one of the prongs of the V swings behind the other, I've got to waltz to larboard again, or I'll have a misunderstanding with a snag that would snatch the keelson out of this steamboat as neatly as if it were a sliver in your hand. If that hill didn't change its shape on bad nights there would be an awful steamboat graveyard around here inside of a year."

It was plain that I had got to learn the shape of the river in all the different ways that could be thought of,—upside down, wrong end first, inside out, fore-and-aft, and "thort-ships,"—and then know what to do on gray nights when it hadn't any shape at all. So I set about it. In the course of time I began to get the best of this knotty lesson, and my self-complacency moved to the front once more. Mr. Bixby was all fixed, and ready to start it to the rear again. He opened on me after this fashion:—

"How much water did we have in the middle crossing at Hole-in-the-Wall, trip before last?"

I considered this an outrage. I said:—

"Every trip, down and up, the leadsmen are singing through that tangled place for three quarters of an hour on a stretch. How do you reckon I can remember such a mess as that?"

"My boy, you've got to remember it. You've got to remember the exact spot and the exact marks the boat lay in when we had the shoalest water, in every one of the five hundred shoal places between St. Louis and New Orleans; and you mustn't get the shoal soundings and marks of one trip mixed up with the shoal soundings and marks of another, either, for they're not often twice alike. You must keep them separate."

When I came to myself again, I said,—

"When I get so that I can do that, I'll be able to raise the dead, and then I won't have to pilot a steamboat to make a living. I want to retire from this business. I want a slush-bucket and a brush; I'm only fit for a roustabout. I haven't got brains enough to be a pilot; and if I had I wouldn't have strength enough to carry them around, unless I went on crutches."

"Now drop that! When I say I'll learn* a man the river, I mean it. And you can depend on it, I'll learn him or kill him."

* "Teach" is not in the river vocabulary.

"*Continued Perplexities*"

There was no use in arguing with a person like this. I promptly put such a strain on my memory that by and by even the shoal water and the countless crossing-marks began to stay with me. But the result was just the same. I never could more than get one knotty thing learned before another presented itself. Now I had often seen pilots gazing at the water and pretending to read it as if it were a book; but it was a book that told me nothing. A time came at last, however, when Mr. Bixby seemed to think me far enough advanced to bear a lesson on water-reading. So he began:—

"Do you see that long slanting line on the face of the water? Now, that's a reef. Moreover, it's a bluff reef. There is a solid sand-bar under it that is nearly as straight up and down as the side of a house. There is plenty of water close up to it, but mighty little on top of it. If you were to hit it you would knock the boat's brains out. Do you see where the line fringes out at the upper end and begins to fade away?"

"Yes, sir."

"Well, that is a low place; that is the head of the reef. You can climb over there, and not hurt anything. Cross over, now, and follow along close under the reef—easy water there—not much current."

I followed the reef along till I approached the fringed end. Then Mr. Bixby said,—

"Now get ready. Wait till I give the word. She won't want to mount the reef; a boat hates shoal water. Stand by—wait—*wait*—keep her well in hand. *Now* cramp her down! Snatch her! snatch her!"

He seized the other side of the wheel and helped to spin it around until it was hard down, and then we held it so. The boat resisted, and refused to answer for a while, and next she came surging to starboard, mounted the reef, and sent a long, angry ridge of water foaming away from her bows.

"Now watch her; watch her like a cat, or she'll get away from you. When she fights strong and the tiller slips a little, in a jerky, greasy sort of way, let up on her a trifle; it is the way she tells you at night that the water is too shoal; but keep edging her up, little by little, toward the point. You are well up on the bar, now; there is a bar under every point, because the water that comes down around it forms an eddy and allows the sediment to sink. Do you see those fine lines on the face of the water that branch out like the ribs of a fan? Well, those are little reefs; you want to just miss the ends of them, but run them pretty close. Now look out—look out! Don't you crowd that slick, greasy-looking place; there ain't nine feet there; she won't stand it. She begins to smell it; looks sharp, I tell you! Oh blazes, there you go! Stop the starboard wheel! Quick! Ship up the back! Set her back!"

The engine bells jingled and the engines answered promptly, shooting white columns of steam far aloft out of the 'scape pipes, but it was too late. The boat had "smelt" the bar in good earnest; the foamy ridges that radiated from her bows suddenly disappeared, a great dead swell came rolling forward and swept ahead of her, she careened far over to larboard, and went tearing away toward the other shore as if she were about scared to death. We were a good mile from where we ought to have been, when we finally got the upper hand of her again.

During the afternoon watch the next day, Mr. Bixby asked me if I knew how to run the next few miles. I said:—

"Go inside the first snag above the point, outside the next one, start out from the lower end of Higgin's wood-yard, make a square crossing and"—

"That's all right. I'll be back before you close up on the next point."

But he wasn't. He was still below when I rounded it and entered upon a piece of river which I had some misgivings about.

I did not know that he was hiding behind a chimney to see how I would perform. I went gayly along, getting prouder and prouder, for he had never left the boat in my sole charge such a length of time before. I even got to "setting" her and letting the wheel go, entirely, while I vaingloriously turned my back and inspected the stern marks and hummed a tune, a sort of easy indifference which I had prodigiously admired in Bixby and other great pilots. Once I inspected rather long, and when I faced to the front again my heart flew into my mouth so suddenly that if I hadn't clapped my teeth together I should have lost it. One of those frightful bluff reefs was stretching its deadly length right across our bows! My head was gone in a moment; I did not know which end I stood on; I gasped and could not get my breath; I spun the wheel down with such rapidity that it wove itself together like a spider's web; the boat answered and turned square away from the reef, but the reef followed her! I fled, and still it followed still it kept—right across my bows! I never looked to see where I was going, I only fled. The awful crash was imminent—why didn't that villain come! If I committed the crime of ringing a bell, I might get thrown overboard. But better that than kill the boat. So in blind desperation I started such a rattling "shivaree" down below as never had astounded an engineer in this world before, I fancy. Amidst the frenzy of the bells the engines began to back and fill in a furious way, and my reason forsook its throne—we were about to crash into the woods on the other side of the river. Just then Mr. Bixby stepped calmly into view on the hurricane deck. My soul went out to him in gratitude. My distress vanished; I would have felt safe on the brink of Niagara, with Mr. Bixby on the hurricane deck. He blandly and sweetly took his tooth-pick out of his mouth between his fingers, as if it were a cigar,—we were just in the act of climbing an overhanging big tree, and the passengers were scudding astern like rats,—and lifted up these commands to me ever so gently:—

"Stop the starboard. Stop the larboard. Set her back on both."

The boat hesitated, halted, pressed her nose among the boughs a critical instant, then reluctantly began to back away.

"Stop the larboard. Come ahead on it. Stop the starboard. Come ahead on it. Point her for the bar."

I sailed away as serenely as a summer's morning. Mr. Bixby came in and said, with mock simplicity,—

"When you have a hail, my boy, you ought to tap the big bell three times before you land, so that the engineers can get ready."

I blushed under the sarcasm, and said I hadn't had any hail.

"Ah! Then it was for wood, I suppose. The officer of the watch will tell you when he wants to wood up."

I went on consuming, and said I wasn't after wood.

"Indeed?" Why, what could you want over here in the bend, then? Did you ever know of a boat following a bend up-stream at this stage of the river?"

"No, sir,—and *I* wasn't trying to follow it. I was getting away from the bluff reef."

"No, it wasn't a bluff reef; there isn't one within three miles of where you were."

"But I saw it. It was as bluff as that one yonder."

"Just about. Run over it."

"Do you give it as an order?"

"Yes. Run over it."

"If I don't, I wish I may die."

"All right; I am taking the responsibility."

I was just as anxious to kill the boat, now, as I had been to save her before. I impressed my orders upon my memory, to be used at the inquest, and made a straight break for the reef. As it disappeared under our bows I held my breath; but we slid over it like oil.

"Now don't you see the difference? It wasn't anything but a *wind* reef. The wind does that."

"So I see. But it is exactly like a bluff reef. How am I ever going to tell them apart?"

"I can't tell you. It is an instinct. By and by you will just naturally *know* one from the other, but you never will be able to explain why or how you know them apart."

It turned out to be true. The face of the water, in time, became a wonderful book—a book that was a dead language to the uneducated passenger, but which told its mind to me without reserve, delivering its most cherished secrets as clearly as if it uttered them with a voice. And it was not a book to be read once and thrown aside, for it had new story to tell every day. Throughout the long twelve hundred miles there was never a page that was void of interest, never one that you could leave unread without loss, never one that you would want to skip, thinking you could find higher enjoyment in some other thing. There never was so wonderful a book written by man; never one whose interest was so absorbing, so unflagging, so sparklingly renewed with every re-perusal. The passenger who could not read it was charmed with a peculiar sort of faint dimple on its surface (on the rare occasions when he did not overlook it altogether); but to the pilot that was an *italicized* passage; indeed, it was more than that, it was a legend of the largest capitals, with a string of shouting exclamation points at the end of it; for it meant that a wreck or a rock was buried there that could tear the life out of the strongest vessel that ever floated. It is the faintest and simplest expression the water ever makes, and the most hideous to a pilot's eye. In truth, the passenger who could not read this book saw nothing but all manner of pretty pictures in it, painted by the sun and shaded by the clouds, whereas to the trained eye these were not pictures at all, but the grimmest and most dead-earnest of reading-matter.

Now when I had mastered the language of this water and had come to know every trifling feature that bordered the great river as familiarly as I knew the letters of the alphabet, I had made a valuable acquisition. But I had lost something, too. I had lost something which could never be restored to me while I lived. All the grace, the beauty, the poetry had gone out of the majestic river! I still keep in mind a certain wonderful sunset which I witnessed when steamboating was new to me. A broad expanse of the river was turned to blood; in the middle distance the red hue brightened into gold, through which a solitary log came floating, black and conspicuous; in one place a long, slanting mark lay sparkling upon the water; in another the surface was broken by boiling, tumbling rings, that were as many-tinted as an opal; where the ruddy flush was faintest, was a smooth spot that was covered with graceful circles and radiating lines, ever so delicately traced; the shore on our left was densely wooded, and the sombre shadow that fell from this forest was broken in one place by a long, ruffled trail that shone like silver; and high above the forest wall a clean-stemmed dead tree waved a single leafy bough that glowed like a flame in the unobstructed splendor that was flowing from the sun. There were graceful curves, reflected images, woody heights, soft distances; and over the whole scene, far and near, the dissolving lights drifted steadily, enriching it, every passing moment, with new marvels of coloring.

I stood like one bewitched. I drank it in, in a speechless rapture. The world was new to me, and I had never seen anything like this at home. But as I have said, a day came when I began to cease from noting the glories and the charms which the moon and the sun and the twilight wrought upon the river's face; another day came when I ceased altogether to note them. Then, if that sunset scene had been repeated, I should have looked upon it without rapture, and should have commented upon it, inwardly, after this fashion: This sun means that we are going to have wind to-morrow; that floating log means that the river is rising, small thanks to it; that slanting mark on the water refers to a bluff reef which is going to kill somebody's steamboat one of these nights, if it keeps on stretching out like that; those tumbling "boils" show a dissolving bar and a changing channel there; the lines and circles in the slick water over yonder are a warning that that troublesome place is shoaling up dangerously; that silver streak in the shadow of the forest is the "break" from a new snag, and he has located himself in the very best place he could have found to fish for steamboats; that tall dead tree, with a single living branch, is not going to last long, and then how is a body ever going to get through this blind place at night without the friendly old landmark?

No, the romance and the beauty were all gone from the river. All the value any feature of it had for me now was the amount of usefulness it could furnish toward compassing the safe piloting of a steamboat. Since those days, I have pitied doctors from my heart. What does the lovely flush in a beauty's cheek mean to a doctor but a "break" that ripples above some deadly disease? Are not all her visible charms sown thick with what are to him the signs and symbols of hidden decay? Does he ever see her beauty at all, or doesn't he simply view her professionally, and comment upon her unwholesomeness condition all to himself? And doesn't he sometimes wonder whether he has gained most or lost most by learning his trade?

"Sunrise on the River"

I had myself called with the four o'clock watch, mornings, for one cannot see too many summer sunrises on the Mississippi. They are enchanting. First, there is the eloquence of silence; for a deep hush broods everywhere. Next, there is the haunting sense of loneliness, isolation, remoteness from the worry and bustle of the world. The dawn creeps in stealthily; the solid walls of black forest soften to gray, and vast stretches of the river open up and reveal themselves; the water is glass-smooth, gives off spectral little wreaths of white mist, there is not the faintest breath of wind, nor stir of leaf; the tranquility is profound and infinitely satisfying. Then a bird pipes up, another follows, and soon the pipings develop into a jubilant riot of music. You see none of the birds; you simply move through an atmosphere of song which seems to sing itself. When the light has become a little stronger, you have one of the fairest and softest pictures imaginable. You have the intense green of the massed and crowded foliage near by; you see it paling shade by shade in front of you; upon the next projecting cape, a mile off or more, the tint has lightened to the tender young green of spring; the cape beyond that one has almost lost color, and the furthest one, miles away under the horizon, sleeps upon the water a mere dim vapor, and hardly separable from the sky above it and about it. And all this stretch of river is a mirror, and you have the shadowy reflections of the leafage and the curving shores and the receding capes pictured in it. Well, that is all beautiful; soft and rich and beautiful; and when the sun gets well up, and distributes a pink flush here and a powder of gold yonder and a purple haze where it will yield the best effect, you grant that you have seen something that is worth remembering.

"The House Beautiful"

We took passage in a Cincinnati boat for New Orleans; or on a Cinncincinnati boat—either is correct; the former is the eastern form of putting it, the latter the western.

Mr. Dickens declined to agree that the Mississippi steamboats were "magnificent," or that they were "floating palaces,"—terms which had always been applied to them; terms which did not over-express the admiration with which the people viewed them.

Mr. Dickens's position was unassailable, possibly; the people's position was certainly unassailable. If Mr. Dickens was comparing these boats with the crown jewels; or with the Taj, or with the Matterhorn; or with some other priceless or wonderful thing which he had seen, they were not magnificent—he was right. The people compared them with what *they* had seen; and, thus measured, thus judged, the boats were magnificent—the term was the correct one, it was not at all too strong. The people were as right as was Mr. Dickens. The steamboats were finer then anything on shore. Compared with superior dwelling-houses and first class hotels in the Valley, they were indubitably magnificent, they were "palaces." To a few people living in New Orleans and St. Louis, they were not magnificent, perhaps; not palaces; but to the great majority of those populations, and to the entire populations spread over both banks between Baton Rouge and St. Louis, they were palaces; they tallied with the citizen's dream of what magnificence was, and satisfied it.

Every town and village along that vast stretch of double river-frontage had a best dwelling, finest dwelling, mansion,—the home of its wealthiest and most conspicuous citizen. It is easy to describe it: large grassy yard, with paling fence painted white—in fair repair; brick walk from gate to door; big, square, two-story "frame" house, painted white and porticoed like a Grecian temple—with this difference, that the imposing fluted columns and Corinthian capitals were a pathetic sham, being made of white pine, and painted; iron knocker; brass door knob—discolored, for lack of polishing. Within, an uncarpeted hall, of planed boards; opening out of it, a parlor, fifteen feet by fifteen—in some instances five or ten feet larger; ingrain carpet; mahogany centre-table; lamp on it, with green-paper shade —standing on a gridiron, so to speak, made of high-colored yarns, by the young ladies of the house, and called a lampmat; several books, piled and disposed, with cast-iron exactness, according to an inherited and unchangeable plan; among them, Tupper, much pencilled; also, "Friendship's Offering," and "Affection's Wreath," with their sappy inanities illustrated in die-away mezzotints; also, Ossian; "Alonzo and Melissa;" maybe "Ivanhoe;" also "Album," full of original "poetry" of the Thou-hast-wounded-the-spirit-that-loved-thee breed; two or three goody-goody works—"Shepherd of Salisbury Plain," etc.; current number of the chaste and innocuous Godey's "Lady's Book," with painted fashion-plate of wax-figure women with mouths all alike—lips and eyelids the same size—each five-foot woman with a two-inch wedge sticking from under her dress and letting-on to be half her foot. Polished air-tight stove (new and deadly invention), with pipe passing through a board which closes up the discarded good old fireplace. On each end of the wooden mantel, over the fireplace, a large basket of peaches and other fruits, natural size, all done in plaster, rudely, or in wax, and painted to resemble the originals—which they don't. Over middle of mantel, engraving—Washington Crossing the Delaware; on the wall by the door, copy of it done in thunder-and-lightning crewels by one of the young ladies—work of art which would have made Washington hesitate about crossing, if he could have foreseen what advantage was going to be taken of it. Piano—kettle in disguise—with music, bound and unbound, piled on it, and on a stand near by: Battle of Prague; Bird Waltz; Arkansas Traveller; Rosin the Bow; Marseilles Hymn; On a Lone Barren Isle (St. Helena); The Last Link is Broken; She wore a Wreath of Roses the Night when we last met; Go, forget me, Why should Sorrow o're that Brow a Shadow fling; Hours there were to Memory Dearer; Long, Long Ago; Days of Absence; A Life on the Ocean Wave, a Home on the Rolling Deep; Bird at Sea; and spread open on the rack, where the plaintive singer has left it, *Ro*-holl on, silver *moo*-hoon, guide the *trav*-el-lerr his *way*, etc. Tilted pensively against the piano, a guitar—guitar capable of playing the Spanish Fandango by itself, if you give it a start. Frantic work of art on the wall—pious motto, done on the premises, sometimes in colored yarns, sometimes in faded grasses: progenitor of the "God Bless Our Home" of modern commerce. Framed in black mouldings on the wall, other works of art, conceived and committed on the premises, by the young ladies; being grim black-and-white crayons; landscapes, mostly: lake, solitary sail-boat, petrified clouds, pre-geological trees on shore, anthracite precipice; name of criminal conspicuous in the corner. Lithograph, Napoleon Crossing the Alps. Lithograph, The Grave at St. Helena. Steel-plates, Trumbull's Battle of Bunker Hill, and the Sally from Gibraltar. Copper-plates, Moses Smiting the Rock, and Return of the Prodigal Son. In big gilt frame, slander of the family in oil: papa holding a book ("Constitution of the United States"); guitar leaning against mamma, blue ribbons fluttering from its neck; the young ladies, as children, in slippers and scalloped pantelettes, one embracing toy horse, the other beguiling kitten with ball of yarn, and both simpering up at mamma, who simpers back. These persons all fresh, raw, and red—apparently skinned. Opposite, in gilt frame, grandpa and grandma, at thirty and twenty-two, stiff, old-fashioned, high-collared, puff-sleeved, glaring pallidly out from a background of solid Egyptian night. Under a glass French clock dome, large bouquet of stiff flowers done in corpsy white wax. Pyramidal what-not in the corner, the shelves occupied chiefly with bric-a-brac of the period, disposed with an eye to best effect; shell, with the Lord's Prayer carved on it; another shell—of the long-oval sort, narrow, straight orifice, three inches long, running from end to end—

portrait of Washington carved on it; not well done; the shell had Washington's mouth, originally—artist should have built to that. These two are memorials of the long-ago bridal trip to New Orleans and the French Market. Other bric-a-brac: California "specimens"—quartz, with gold wart adhering; old Guinea-gold locket, with circlet of ancestral hair in it; Indian arrow-heads, of flint; pair of bead moccasins, from uncle who crossed the Plains; three "alum" baskets of various colors—being skeleton-frame of wire, clothed-on with cubes of crystallized alum in the rock-candy style—works of art which were achieved by the young ladies; their doubles and duplicates to be found upon all what-nots in the land; convention of desiccated bugs and butterflies pinned to a card; painted toy-dog, seated upon bellows-attachment—drops its under jaw and squeaks when pressed upon; sugar-candy rabbit—limbs and features merged together, not strongly defined; pewter presidential-campaign medal; miniature card-board wood-sawyer, to be attached to the stove-pipe and operated by the heat; small Napoleon, done in wax; spread-open daguerreotypes of dim children, parents, cousins, aunts, and friends, in all attitudes but customary ones; no templed portico at back, and manufactured landscape stretching away in the distance—that came in later, with the photograph; all these vague figures lavishly chained and ringed—metal indicated and secured from doubt by stripes and splashes of vivid gold bronze; all of them too much combed, too much fixed up; and all of them uncomfortable in inflexible Sunday-clothes of a pattern which the spectator cannot realize could ever have been in fashion; husband and wife generally grouped together—husband sitting, wife standing, with hand on his shoulder—and both preserving, all these fading years, some traceable effect of the daguerreotypist's brisk "Now smile, if you please!" Bracketed over what-not—place of special sacredness—an outrage in water-color, done by the young niece that came on a visit long ago, and died. Pity, too; for she might have repented of this in time. Horse-hair chairs, horse-hair sofa which keeps sliding from under you. Window shades, of oil stuff, with milk-maids and ruined castles stencilled on them in fierce colors. Lambrequins dependent from gaudy boxings of beaten tin, gilded. Bedrooms with rag carpets; bedsteads of the "corded" sort, with a sag in the middle, the cords needing tightening; snuffy feather-bed—not aired often enough; cane-seat chairs, splint-bottomed rocker; looking-glass on wall, school-slate size, veneered frame; inherited bureau; wash-bowl and pitcher, possibly—but not certainly; brass candlestick, tallow candle, snuffers. Nothing else in the room. Not a bathroom in the house; and no visitor likely to come along who has ever seen one.

That was the residence of the principal citizen, all the way from the suburbs of New Orleans to the edge of St. Louis.

ADVENTURES OF HUCKLEBERRY FINN

(1885)

Mark Twain began writing *Huckleberry Finn* sometime in July, 1876; he would not finish the book until seven years later. Though he may have worked on the manuscript intermittently throughout this period, the novel was written in three principal stints of composition. That first burst of composition in 1876 took Huck to the point in Chapter 18 where Huck asks Buck Grangerford, "What's a feud?" For whatever reasons, Twain pigeonholed the manuscript and did no significant writing on it until sometime in late 1879 or early 1880. At that time, he resumed the story where he had left off, with the Grangerford–Sheperdson feud, and developed his story to the end of Chapter 21 when the mob is resolved to lynch Colonel Sherburn for the murder of Boggs. The final stint of composition occurred June–September 1883. He resumed the confrontation between Sherburn and the town, though contrary to expectation Sherburn faces down his adversaries, and in an energetic burst of composition Twain brought the book to its narrative conclusion. During this final phase of the composition, he also interpolated into the novel the *Walter Scott* episode and the argument between Huck and Jim about "King Sollermun" (Chapters 12½–14 from that point in Chapter 12 where Huck and Jim spot the grounded riverboat, the *Walter Scott,* through to the end of Chapter 14).

Quite apart from the segmented course of composition, apparently there were also significant shifts in interest and authorial intention during these seven years. When he began the book, Twain's initial interest was one of idle amusement, though the episodes increase in seriousness and satirical significance soon enough. When he is first introduced, the slave Jim does not seem destined to play an important role in the story, but by Chapter 11, the fortunes of Huck and Jim are sufficiently linked for Huck to return to Jackson's Island, after learning that there is a $300 reward for Jim's capture, and to shout, "There ain't a minute to lose. They're after us." Of course, "they" are not after Huck at all, for it is generally supposed that he has been murdered, perhaps by Jim himself. The picture of Huck and Jim floating down the Mississippi River on a raft has become a familiar image of idle and peaceful drift, but that raft was launched into the river on a note of fearful urgency.

From then on, if not before, Twain began to see proliferating comic and satiric opportunities. He could survey the manner of life along the river and describe it as would be perceived by a slightly quizzical, slightly perplexed, and wholly literal-minded boy and told in his distinctive voice. Twain's hatred of aristocratic privilege, his distrust of the mob, his suspiciousness of con men and hucksters and his mocking amusement of those gullible enough to be their prey, all of these mature convictions might be expressed effectively by having Huck describe a world in which these things disturb but do not outrage him. Because Huck does not quite understand the sloth, sentimentality, double-dealing, boastfulness, or cruelty he sees, he is, almost by definition, a satirical device. In order to dramatically satirize the object of his contempt, all Twain had to do was to have Huck try to admire it, as in his failed attempts to admire Emmeline Grangerford's poetry and drawings. But Huck's perceptions can also be refreshingly new and alive. In order to recapture the flavor of river talk, the beauty of sunrise on the river, or the majestically innocent speculations on the origins of stars, Twain has Huck report it, without judgment or explanation and without any attempt at rhetorical effect. In order to make his readers feel the force of the shamefulness of slavery, Twain has Huck, who is after all a mere boy, agonize over his moral predicament of helping Jim to freedom. In a word, by resolving to tell an extended narrative from Huckleberry Finn's point of view, Twain automatically created a multitude of imaginative possibilities, though he would necessarily have to develop the stylistic and technical means to develop them. He did this through painstaking revision and by setting aside his temptation to speak through Huck, so that an unlettered, unsophisticated boy might speak plainly and for himself. This required more artistic restraint than the opinionated Twain was accustomed to, but he rose to the challenge.

In the last phase of composition, however, Twain approached his material with mixed motives. He had acquired his own publishing house, and issuing *Adventures of Huckleberry Finn* would be a commercial as well as an artistic venture. He seems to have written those concluding chapters with an eye toward a popular readership who had certain established expectations of a literary comedian. In any event, many regret the reappearance of Tom Sawyer at the Phelps farm and have found the last chapters to contain altogether too much burlesque and too little serious moral reflection. And the character of Jim, who had become in the middle chapters a fully developed human being, dignified, sympathetic, and intelligent, appears in the end to be cast in the role of a comic figure, and not much more. Perhaps Hemingway was right in saying that the concluding chapters were just plain "cheating." That is a question individual readers will decide. It is more certain, however, that, even if there is a falling off at the end, Twain had created in *Huckleberry Finn* something quite distinctive and memorable.

NOTE: Twain published the "raftsmen" portion of the novel in Chapter 3 of *Life on the Mississippi* and had originally intended to include it in the finished manuscript of the novel. However, when it was thought that *Huckleberry Finn* might be published as a companion volume to *Tom Sawyer,* Charles Webster, Clemens's business manager and titular publisher for the book, convinced the author to remove the episode. He argued that the relative lengths of the two books were disproportionate and, besides, readers were already familiar with that episode. As it happened, the two books were not published as companion volumes but the raftsmen passage was not included in the first edition or in any subsequent edition published during Clemens's lifetime. In this edition, as in the authoritative version edited by The Mark Twain Project, this episode is restored to the narrative (pages 211-223) and set off by brackets.

Adventures of Huckleberry Finn

NOTICE.

Persons attempting to find a motive in this narrative will be prosecuted; persons attempting to find a moral in it will be banished; persons attempting to find a plot in it will be shot.

BY ORDER OF THE AUTHOR
PER G. G., CHIEF OF ORDNANCE.

EXPLANATORY.

In this book a number of dialects are used, to wit: the Missouri negro dialect; the extremest form of the backwoods South-Western dialect; the ordinary "Pike-County" dialect; and four modified varieties of this last. The shadings have not been done in a hap-hazard fashion, or by guess-work; but pains-takingly, and with the trustworthy guidance and support of personal familiarity with these several forms of speech.

I make this explanation for the reason that without it many readers would suppose that all these characters were trying to talk alike and not succeeding.

THE AUTHOR.

CHAPTER I

You don't know about me, without you have read a book by the name of "The Adventures of Tom Sawyer," but that ain't no matter. That book was made by Mr. Mark Twain, and he told the truth, mainly. There was things which he stretched, but mainly he told the truth. That is nothing. I never seen anybody but lied, one time or another, without it was Aunt Polly, or the widow, or maybe Mary. Aunt Polly—Tom's Aunt Polly, she is—and Mary, and the Widow Douglas, is all told about in that book—which is mostly a true book; with some stretchers, as I said before.

Now the way that the book winds up, is this: Tom and me found the money that the robbers hid in the cave, and it made us rich. We got six thousand dollars apiece—all gold. It was an awful sight of money when it was piled up. Well, Judge Thatcher, he took it and put it out at interest, and it fetched us a dollar a day apiece, all the year round—more than a body could tell what to do with. The Widow Douglas, she took me for her son, and allowed she would sivilize me; but it was rough living in the house all the time, considering how dismal regular and decent the widow was in all her ways; and so when I couldn't stand it no longer, I lit out. I got into my old rags, and my sugar-hogshead again, and was free and satisfied. But Tom Sawyer, he hunted me up and said he was going to start a band of robbers, and I might join if I would go back to the widow and be respectable. So I went back.

The widow she cried over me, and called me a poor lost lamb, and she called me a lot of other names, too, but she never meant no harm by it. She put me in them new clothes again, and I couldn't do nothing but sweat and sweat, and feel all cramped up. Well, then, the old thing commenced again. The widow rung a bell for supper, and you had to come to time. When you got to the table you couldn't go right to eating, but you had to wait for the widow to tuck down her head and grumble a little over the victuals, though there warn't really anything the matter with them. That is, nothing only everything was cooked by itself. In a barrel of odds and ends it is different; things get mixed up, and the juice kind of swaps around, and the things go better.

After supper she got out her book and learned me about Moses and the Bulrushers; and I was in a sweat to find out all about him; but by-and-by she let it out that Moses had been dead a considerable long time; so then I didn't care no more about him; because I don't take no stock in dead people.

Pretty soon I wanted to smoke, and asked the widow to let me. But she wouldn't. She said it was a mean practice and wasn't clean, and I must try to not to do it any more. That is just the way with some people. They get down on a thing when they don't know nothing about it. Here she was a bothering about Moses, which was no kin to her, and no use to anybody, being gone, you see, yet finding a power of fault with me for doing a thing that had some good in it. And she took snuff too; of course that was all right, because she done it herself.

Her sister, Miss Watson, a tolerable slim old maid, with goggles on, had just come to live with her, and took a set at me now, with a spelling-book. She worked me middling hard for about an hour, and then the widow made her ease up. I couldn't stood it much longer. Then for an hour it was deadly dull, and I was fidgety. Miss Watson would say, "Dont put your feet up there, Huckleberry;" and "dont scrunch up like that, Huckleberry—set up straight;" and pretty soon she would say, "Don't gap and stretch like that, Huckleberry—why don't you try to behave?" Then she told me all about that bad place, and I said I wished I was there. She got mad, then, but I didn't mean no harm. All I wanted was to go somewheres; all I wanted was a change, I warn't particular. She said it was wicked to say what I said; said she wouldn't say it for the whole world; *she* was going to live so as to go to the good place. Well, I couldn't see no advantage in going where she was going, so I made up my mind I wouldn't try for it. But I never said so, because it would only make trouble, and wouldn't do no good.

Now she had got a start, and she went on and told me all about the good place. She said all a body would have to do there was to go around all day long with a harp and sing, forever and ever. So I didn't think much of it. But I never said so. I asked her if she reckoned Tom Sawyer would go there, and, she said, not by a considerable sight. I was glad about that, because I wanted him and me to be together.

Miss Watson she kept pecking at me, and it got tiresome and lonesome. By-and-by they fetched the niggers in and had prayers, and then everybody was off to bed. I went up to my room with a piece of candle and put it on the table. Then I sat down in a chair by the window and tried to think of something cheerful, but it warn't no use. I felt so lonesome I most wished I was dead. The stars was shining, and the leaves rustled in the woods ever so mournful; and I heard an owl, away off, who-whooing about somebody that was dead, and a whippowill and a dog crying about somebody that was going to die; and the wind was trying to whisper something to me and I couldn't make out what it was, and so it made the cold shivers run over me. Then away out in the woods I heard that kind of a sound that a ghost makes when it wants to tell about something that's on its mind and can't make itself understood, and so can't rest easy in its grave and has to go about that way every night grieving. I got so down-hearted and scared, I did wish I had some company. Pretty soon a spider went crawling up my shoulder, and I flipped it off and it lit in the candle; and before I could budge it was all shriveled up. I didn't need anybody to tell me that that was an awful bad sign and would fetch me some bad luck, so I was scared and most shook the clothes off of me. I got up and turned around in my tracks three times and crossed my breast every time; and then I tied up a little lock of my hair with a thread to keep witches away. But I hadn't no confidence. You do that when you've lost a horse-shoe that you've found, instead of nailing it up over the door, but I hadn't ever heard anybody say it was any way to keep off bad luck when you'd killed a spider.

I set down again, a shaking all over, and got out my pipe for a smoke; for the house was all as still as death, now, and so the widow wouldn't know. Well, after a long time I heard the clock away off in the town go boom—boom—boom—twelve licks—and all still again—stiller than ever. Pretty soon I heard a twig snap, down in the dark amongst the trees—something was a stirring. I set still and listened. Directly I could just barely hear a *"me-yow! me-yow!"* down there. That was good! Says I, *"me-yow! me-yow!"* as soft as I could, and then I put out the light and scrambled out of the window onto the shed. Then I slipped down to the ground and crawled in amongst the trees, and sure enough there was Tom Sawyer waiting for me.

CHAPTER II

We went tip-toeing along a path amongst the trees back towards the end of the widow's garden, stooping down so as the branches wouldn't scrape our heads. When we was passing by the kitchen I fell over a root and made a noise. We scrouched down and laid still. Miss Watson's big nigger, named Jim, was setting in the kitchen door; we could see him pretty clear, because there was a light behind him. He got up and stretched his neck out about a minute, listening. Then he says,

"Who dah?"

He listened some more; then he come tip-toeing down and stood right between us; we could a touched him, nearly. Well, likely it was minutes and minutes that there warn't a sound, and we all there so close together. There was a place on my ankle that got to itching; but I dasn't scratch it; and then my ear begun to itch; and next my back, right between my shoulders. Seemed like I'd die if I couldn't scratch. Well, I've noticed that thing plenty of times since. If you are with the quality, or at a funeral, or trying to go to sleep when you ain't sleepy—if you are anywheres where it won't do for you to scratch, why you will itch all over in upwards of a thousand places. Pretty soon Jim says:

"Say—who is you? Whar is you? Dog my cats ef I didn' hear sumf'n. Well, I knows what I's gwyne to do. I's gwyne to set down here and listen tell I hears it agin."

So he set down on the ground betwixt me and Tom. He leaned his back up against a tree, and stretched his legs out till one of them most touched one of mine. My nose begun to itch.

It itched till the tears come into my eyes. But I dasn't scratch. Then it begun to itch on the inside. Next I got to itching underneath. I didn't know how I was going to set still. This miserableness went on as much as six or seven minutes; but it seemed a sight longer than that. I was itching in eleven different places now. I reckoned I couldn't stand it more'n a minute longer, but I set my teeth hard and got ready to try. Just then Jim begun to breathe heavy; next he begun to snore—and then I was pretty soon comfortable again.

Tom he made a sign to me—kind of a little noise with his mouth—and we went creeping away on our hands and knees. When we was ten foot off, Tom whispered to me and wanted to tie Jim to the tree for fun; but I said no; he might wake and make a disturbance, and then they'd find out I warn't in. Then Tom said he hadn't got candles enough, and he would slip in the kitchen and get some more. I didn't want him to try. I said Jim might wake up and come. But Tom wanted to resk it; so we slid in there and got three candles, and Tom laid five cents on the table for pay. Then we got out, and I was in a sweat to get away; but nothing would do Tom but he must crawl to where Jim was, on his hands and knees, and play something on him. I waited, and it seemed a good while, everything was so still and lonesome.

As soon as Tom was back, we cut along the path, around the garden fence, and by-and-by fetched up on the steep top of the hill the other side of the house. Tom said he slipped Jim's hat off of his head and hung it on a limb right over him, and Jim stirred a little, but he didn't wake. Afterwards Jim said the witches bewitched him and put him in a trance, and rode him all over the State, and then set him under the trees again and hung his hat on a limb to show who done it. And next time Jim told it said they rode him down to New Orleans; and after that, every time he told it he spread it more and more, till by-and-by he said they rode him all over the world, and tired him most to death, and his back was all over saddle-boils. Jim was monstrous proud about it, and he got so he wouldn't hardly notice the other niggers. Niggers would come miles to hear Jim tell about it, and he was more looked up to than any nigger in that country. Strange niggers would stand with their mouths open and look him all over, same as if he was a wonder. Niggers is always talking about witches in the dark by the kitchen fire; but whenever one was talking and letting on to know all about such things, Jim would happen in and say, "Hm! What you know 'bout witches?" and that nigger was corked up and had to take a back seat. Jim always kept that five-center piece around his neck with a string and said it was a charm the devil give to him with his own hands and told him he could cure anybody with it and fetch witches whenever he wanted to, just by saying something to it; but he never told what it was he said to it. Niggers would come from all around there and give Jim anything they had, just for a sight of that five-center piece; but they wouldn't touch it, because the devil had had his hands on it. Jim was most ruined, for a servant, because he got so stuck up on account of having seen the devil and been rode by witches.

Well, when Tom and me got to the edge of the hill-top, we looked away down into the village and could see three or four lights twinkling, where there was sick folks, may be; and the stars over us was sparkling ever so fine; and down by the village was the river, a whole mile broad, and awful still and grand. We went down the hill and found Jo Harper, and Ben Rogers, and two or three more of the boys, hid in the old tanyard. So we unhitched a skiff and pulled down the river two mile and a half, to the big scar on the hillside, and went ashore.

We went to a clump of bushes, and Tom made everybody swear to keep the secret, and then showed them a hole in the hill, right in the thickest part of the bushes. Then we lit the candles and crawled in on our hands and knees. We went about two hundred yards, and then the cave opened up. Tom poked about amongst the passages and pretty soon ducked under a wall where you wouldn't a noticed that there was a hole. We went along a narrow place and got into a kind of room, all damp and sweaty and cold, and there we stopped. Tom says:

"Now we'll start this band of robbers and call it Tom Sawyer's Gang. Everybody that wants to join has got to take an oath, and write his name in blood."

Everybody was willing. So Tom got out a sheet of paper that he had wrote the oath on, and read it. It swore every boy to stick to the band, and never tell any of the secrets; and if anybody done anything to any boy in the band, whichever boy was ordered to kill that person and his family must do it, and he mustn't eat and he mustn't sleep till he had killed them and hacked a cross in their breasts, which was the sign of the band. And nobody that didn't belong to the band could use that mark, and if he did he must be sued; and if he done it again he must be killed. And if anybody that belonged to the band told the secrets, he must have his throat cut, and then have his carcass burnt up and the ashes scattered all around, and his name blotted off the list with blood and never mentioned again by the gang, but have a curse put on it and be forgot, forever.

Everybody said it was a real beautiful oath, and asked Tom if he got it out of his own head. He said, some of it, but the rest was out of pirate books, and robber books, and every gang that was high-toned had it.

Some thought it would be good to kill the *families* of boys that told the secrets. Tom said it was a good idea, so he took a pencil and wrote it in. Then Ben Rogers said:

"Here's Huck Finn, he hain't got no family—what you going to do 'bout him?"

"Well, hain't he got a father?" says Tom Sawyer.

"Yes, he's got a father, but you can't never find him, these days. He used to lay drunk with the hogs in the tanyard, but he hain't been seen in these parts for a year or more."

They talked it over, and they was going to rule me out, because they said every boy must have a family or somebody to kill, or else it wouldn't be fair and square for the others. Well, nobody could think of anything to do—everybody was stumped, and set still. I was most ready to cry; but all at once I thought of a way, and so I offered them Miss Watson—they could kill her. Everybody said:

"Oh, she'll do, she'll do. That's all right. Huck can come in."

Then they all stuck a pin in their fingers to get blood to sign with, and I made my mark on the paper.

"Now," says Ben Rogers, "what's the line of business of this Gang?"

"Nothing only robbery and murder," Tom said.

"But who are we going to rob? houses—or cattle—or—"

"Stuff! stealing cattle and such things ain't robbery, it's burglary," says Tom Sawyer. "We ain't burglars. That ain't no sort of style. We are highwaymen. We stop stages and carriages on the road, with masks on, and kill the people and take their watches and money."

"Must we always kill the people?"

"Oh, certainly. It's best. Some authorities think different, but mostly it's considered best to kill them. Except some that you bring to the cave here and keep them till they're ransomed."

"Ransomed? What's that?"

"I don't know. But that's what they do. I've seen it in books; and so of course that's what we've got to do."

"But how can we do it if we don't know what it is?"

"Why blame it all, we've *got* to do it. Don't I tell you it's in the books? Do you want to go to doing different from what's in the books, and get things all muddled up?"

"Oh, that's all very fine to *say,* Tom Sawyer, but how in the nation are these fellows going to be ransomed if we don't know how to do it to them? that's the thing *I* want to get at. Now what do you *reckon* it is?"

"Well I don't know. But per'aps if we keep them till they're ransomed, it means that we keep them till they're dead."

"Now, that's something *like.* That'll answer. Why couldn't you said that before? We'll keep them till they're ransomed to death—and a bothersome lot they'll be, too, eating up everything and always trying to get loose."

"How you talk, Ben Rogers. How can they get loose when there's a guard over them, ready to shoot them down if they move a peg?"

"A guard. Well, that *is* good. So somebody's got to set up all night and never get any sleep, just so as to watch them. I think that's foolishness. Why can't a body take a club and ransom them as soon as they get here?"

"Because it ain't in the books so—that's why. Now Ben Rogers, do you want to do things regular, or don't you?—that's the idea. Don't you reckon that the people that made the books knows what's the correct thing to do? Do you reckon *you* can learn 'em anything? Not by a good deal. No, sir, we'll just go on and ransom them in the regular way."

"All right. I don't mind; but I say it's a fools way, anyhow. Say—do we kill the women, too?"

"Well, Ben Rogers, if I was as ignorant as you I wouldn't let on. Kill the women? No—nobody ever saw anything in the books like that. You fetch them to the cave, and you're always as polite as pie to them; and by-and-by they fall in love with you and never want to go home any more."

"Well, if that's the way, I'm agreed, but I don't take no stock in it. Mighty soon we'll have the cave so cluttered up with women, and fellows waiting to be ransomed, that there won't be no place for the robbers. But go ahead, I ain't got nothing to say."

Little Tommy Barnes was asleep, now, and when they waked him up he was scared, and cried, and said he wanted to go home to his ma, and didn't want to be a robber any more.

So they all made fun of him, and called him cry-baby, and that made him mad, and he said he would go straight and tell all the secrets. But Tom give him five cents to keep quiet, and said we would all go home and meet next week and rob somebody and kill some people.

Ben Rogers said he couldn't get out much, only Sundays, and so he wanted to begin next Sunday; but all the boys said it would be wicked to do it on Sunday, and that settled the thing. They agreed to get together and fix a day as soon as they could, and then we elected Tom Sawyer first captain and Jo Harper second captain of the gang, and so started home.

I clumb up the shed and crept into my window just before day was breaking. My new clothes was all greased up and clayey, and I was dog-tired.

CHAPTER III

Well, I got a good going-over in the morning, from old Miss Watson, on account of my clothes; but the widow she didn't scold, but only cleaned off the grease and clay and looked so sorry that I thought I would behave a while if I could. Then Miss Watson she took me in the closet and prayed, but nothing come of it. She told me to pray every day, and whatever I asked for I would get it. But it warn't so. I tried it. Once I got a fish-line, but no hooks. It warn't any good to me without hooks. I tried for the hooks three or four times, but somehow I couldn't make it work. By-and-by, one day, I asked Miss Watson to try for me, but she said I was a fool. She never told me why, and I couldn't make it out no way.

I set down, one time, back in the woods, and had a long think about it. I says to myself, if a body can get anything they pray for, why don't Deacon Winn get back the money he lost on pork? Why can't the widow get back her silver snuff-box that was stole? Why can't Miss Watson fat up? No, says I to myself, there ain't nothing in it. I went and told the widow about it, and she said the thing a body could get by praying for it was "spiritual gifts." This was too many for me, but she told me what she meant—I must help other people, and do everything I could for other people, and look out for them all the time, and never think about myself. This was including Miss Watson, as I took it. I went out in the woods and turned it over in my mind a long time, but I couldn't see no advantage about it—except for the other people—so at last I reckoned I wouldn't worry about it any more, but just let it go. Sometimes the widow would take me one side and talk about Providence in a way to make a body's mouth water; but maybe next day Miss Watson would take hold and knock it all down again. I judged I could see that there was two Providences, and a poor chap would stand considerable show with the widow's Providence, but if Miss Watson's got him there warn't no help for him any more. I thought it all out, and reckoned I would belong to the widow's, if he wanted me, though I couldn't make out how he was agoing to be any better off then than what he was before, seeing I was so ignorant and so kind of low-down and ornery.

Pap he hadn't been seen for more than a year, and that was comfortable for me; I didn't want to see him no more. He used to always whale me when he was sober and could get his hands on me; though I used to take to the woods most of the time when he was around. Well, about this time he was found in the river drowned, about twelve mile above town, so people said. They judged it was him, anyway; said this drowned man was just his size, and was ragged, and had uncommon long hair—which was all like pap—but they couldn't make nothing out of the face, because it had been in the water so long it warn't much like a face at all. They said he was floating on his back in the water. They took him and buried him on the bank. But I warn't comfortable long, because I happened to think of something. I knowed mighty well that a drownded man don't float on his back, but on his face. So I knowed, then, that this warn't pap, but a woman dressed up in a man's clothes. So I was uncomfortable again. I judged the old man would turn up again by-and-by, though I wished he wouldn't.

We played robber now and then about a month, and then I resigned. All the boys did. We hadn't robbed nobody, we hadn't killed any people, but only just pretended. We used to hop out of the woods and go charging down on hog-drovers and women in carts taking garden stuff to market, but we never hived any of them. Tom Sawyer called the hogs "ingots," and he called the turnips and stuff "julery" and we would go to the cave and pow-wow over what we had done and how many people we had killed and marked. But I couldn't see no profit in it. One time Tom sent a boy to run about town with a blazing stick, which he called a slogan (which was the sign for the Gang to get together), and then he said he had got secret news by his spies that next day a whole parcel of Spanish merchants and rich A-rabs was going to camp in Cave Hollow with two hundred elephants, and six hundred camels, and over a thousand "sumter" mules, all loaded down with di'monds, and they didn't have only a guard of four hundred soldiers, and so we would lay in ambuscade, as he called it, and kill the lot and scoop the things. He said we must slick up our swords and guns, and get ready. He never could go after even a turnip-cart but he must have the swords and guns all scoured up for it; though they was only lath and broom-sticks, and you might scour at them till you rotted and then they warn't worth a mouthful of ashes more than what they was before. I didn't believe we could lick such a crowd of Spaniards and A-rabs, but I wanted to see the camels and elephants, so I was on hand next day, Saturday, in the ambuscade; and when we got the word, we rushed out of the woods and down the hill. But there warn't no Spaniards and A-rabs, and there warn't no camels nor no elephants. It warn't anything but a Sunday-school picnic, and only a primer-class at that. We busted it up, and chased the children up the hollow; but we never got anything but some doughnuts and jam, though Ben Rogers got a rag doll, and Jo Harper got a hymn-book and a tract; and then the teacher charged in and made us drop everything and cut. I didn't see no di'monds, and I told Tom Sawyer so. He said there was loads of them there, anyway; and he said there was A-rabs there, too, and elephants and things. I said, why couldn't we see them, then? He said if I warn't so ignorant, but had read a book called "Don Quixote," I would know without asking. He said it was all done by enchantment. He said there was hundreds of soldiers there, and elephants and treasure, and so on, but we had enemies which he called magicians, and they had turned the whole thing into an infant Sunday school, just out of spite. I said, all right, then the thing for us to do was to go for the magicians. Tom Sawyer said I was a numskull.

"Why," says he, "a magician could call up a lot of genies, and they would hash you up like nothing before you could say Jack Robinson. They are as tall as a tree and as big around as a church."

"Well," I says, "s'pose we got some genies to help *us*—can't we lick the other crowd then?"

"How you going to get them?"

"I don't know. How do *they* get them?"

"Why they rub an old tin lamp or an iron ring, and then the genies come tearing in, with the thunder and lightning a-ripping around and the smoke a-rolling, and everything they're told to do they up and do it. They don't think nothing of pulling a shot tower up by the roots, and belting a Sunday-school superintendent over the head with it—or any other man."

"Who makes them tear around so?"

"Why, whoever rubs the lamp or the ring. They belong to whoever rubs the lamp or the ring, and they've got to do whatever he says. If he tells them to build a palace forty miles long, out of di'monds, and fill it full of chewing gum, or whatever you want, and fetch an emperor's daughter from China for you to marry, they've got to do it—and they've got to do it before sun-up next morning, too. And more—they've got to waltz that palace around over the country wherever you want it, you understand."

"Well," says I, "I think they are a pack of flatheads for not keeping the palace themselves 'stead of fooling them away like that. And what's more—if I was one of them I would see a man in Jericho before I would drop my business and come to him for the rubbing of an old tin lamp."

"How you talk, Huck Finn. Why, you'd *have* to come when he rubbed it, whether you wanted to or not."

"What, and I as high as a tree and as big as a church? All right, then; I *would* come; but I lay I'd make that man climb the highest tree there was in the country."

"Shucks, it ain't no use to talk to you, Huck Finn. You don't seem to know anything, somehow—perfect sap-head."

I thought all this over for two or three days, and then I reckoned I would see if there was anything in it. I got an old tin lamp and an iron ring and went out in the woods and rubbed and rubbed till I sweat like an Injun, calculating to build a palace and sell it; but it warn't no use, none of the genies come. So then I judged that all that stuff was only just one of Tom Sawyer's lies. I reckoned he believed in the A-rabs and the elephants, but as for me I think different. It had all the marks of a Sunday school.

CHAPTER IV

Well, three or four months run along, and it was well into the winter, now. I had been to school most all the time, and could spell, and read, and write just a little, and could say the multiplication table up to six times seven is thirty-five, and I don't reckon I could ever get any further than that if I was to live forever. I don't take no stock in mathematics, anyway.

At first I hated the school, but by-and-by I got so I could stand it. Whenever I got uncommon tired I played hookey, and the hiding I got next day done me good and cheered me up. So the longer I went to school the easier it got to be. I was getting sort of used to the widow's ways, too, and they warn't so raspy on me. Living in a house, and sleeping in a bed, pulled on me pretty tight, mostly, but before the cold weather I used to slide out and sleep in the woods, sometimes, and so that was a rest to me. I liked the old ways best, but I was getting so I liked the new ones, too, a little bit. The widow said I was coming along slow but sure, and doing very satisfactory. She said she warn't ashamed of me.

One morning I happened to turn over the salt-cellar at breakfast. I reached for some of it as quick as I could, to throw over my left shoulder and keep off the bad luck, but Miss Watson was in ahead of me, and crossed me off. She says, "Take your hands away, Huckleberry—what a mess you are always making." The widow put in a good word for me, but that warn't going to keep off the bad luck, I knowed that well enough. I started out, after breakfast, feeling worried and shaky, and wondering where it was going to fall on me, and what it was going to be. There is ways to keep off some kinds of bad luck, but this wasn't one of them kind; so I never tried to do anything, but just poked along low-spirited and on the watch-out.

I went down the front garden and clumb over the stile, where you go through the high board fence. There was an inch of new snow on the ground, and I seen somebody's tracks. They had come up from the quarry and stood around the stile awhile, and then went on around the garden fence. It was funny they hadn't come in, after standing around so. I couldn't make it out. It was very curious, somehow. I was going to follow around, but I stooped down to look at the tracks first. I didn't notice anything at first, but next I did. There was a cross in the left boot-heel made with big nails, to keep off the devil.

I was up in a second and shinning down the hill. I looked over my shoulder every now and then, but I didn't see nobody. I was at Judge Thatcher's as quick as I could get there. He said:

"Why, my boy, you are all out of breath. Did you come for your interest?"

"No sir," I says; "is there some for me?"

"Oh, yes, a half-yearly is in, last night. Over a hundred and fifty dollars. Quite a fortune for you. You better let me invest it along with your six thousand, because if you take it you'll spend it."

"No sir," I says, "I don't want to spend it. I don't want it at all—nor the six thousand, nurther. I want you to take it; I want to give it to you—the six thousand and all."

He looked surprised. He couldn't seem to make it out. He says:

"Why, what can you mean, my boy?"

I says, "Don't you ask me no questions about it, please. You'll take it—won't you?"

He says:

"Well I'm puzzled. Is something the matter?"

"Please take it," says I, "and don't ask me nothing—then I won't have to tell no lies."

He studied a while, and then he says:

"Oho-o. I think I see. You want to *sell* all your property to me—not give it. That's the correct idea."

Then he wrote something on a paper and read it over, and says:

"There—you see it says 'for a consideration.' That means I have bought it of you and paid you for it. Here's a dollar for you. Now, you sign it."

So I signed it, and left.

Miss Watson's nigger, Jim, had a hair-ball as big as your fist, which had been took out of the fourth stomach of an ox, and he used to do magic with it. He said there was a spirit inside of it, and it knowed everything. So I went to him that night and told him pap was here again, for I found his tracks in the snow. What I wanted to know, was, what he was going to do, and was he going to stay? Jim got out his hair-ball, and said something over it, and then he held it up and dropped it on the floor. It fell pretty solid, and only rolled about an inch. Jim tried it again, and then another time, and it acted just the same. Jim got down on his knees and put his ear against it and listened. But it warn't no use; he said it wouldn't talk. He said sometimes it wouldn't talk without money. I told him I had an old slick counterfeit quarter that warn't no good because the brass showed through the silver a little, and it wouldn't pass nohow, even if the brass didn't show, because it was so slick it felt greasy, and so that would tell on it every time. (I reckoned I wouldn't say nothing about the dollar I got from the judge.) I said it was pretty bad money, but maybe the hair-ball would take it, because maybe it wouldn't know the difference. Jim smelt it, and bit it, and rubbed it, and said he would manage so the hair-ball would think it was good. He said he would split open a raw Irish potato and stick the quarter in between and keep it there all night, and next morning you couldn't see no brass, and it wouldn't feel greasy no more, and so anybody in town would take it in a minute, let alone a hair-ball. Well, I knowed a potato would do that, before, but I had forgot it.

Jim put the quarter under the hair-ball and got down and listened again. This time he said the hair-ball was all right. He said it would tell my whole fortune if I wanted it to. I says, go on. So the hair-ball talked to Jim, and Jim told it to me. He says:

"Yo' ole father doan' know, yit, what he's a-gwyne to do. Sometimes he spec he'll go 'way, en den agin he spec he'll stay. De bes' way is to res' easy en let de ole man take his own way. Dey's two angels hoverin' roun' 'bout him. One uv 'em is white en shiny, en 'tother one is black. De white one gits him to go right, a little while, den de black one sail in en bust it all up. A body can't tell, yit, which one gwyne to fetch him at de las'. But you is all right. You gwyne to have considerable trouble in yo' life, en considerable joy. Sometimes you gwyne to git hurt, en sometimes you gwyne to get sick; but every time you's gwyne to git well agin. Dey's two gals flyin' 'bout you in yo' life. One uv 'em's light en 'tother one is dark. One is rich en 'tother is po'. You's gwyne to marry de po' one fust en de rich one by-en-by. You wants to keep 'way fum de water as much as you kin, en don't run no resk, 'kase it's down in de bills dat you's gwyne to git hung."

When I lit my candle and went up to my room that night, there set pap, his own self!

CHAPTER V

I had shut the door to. Then I turned around, and there he was. I used to be scared of him all the time, he tanned me so much. I reckoned I was scared now, too; but in a minute I see I was mistaken. That is, after the first jolt, as you may say, when my breath sort of hitched—he was being so unexpected; but right away after, I see I warn't scared of him worth bothering about.

He was most fifty, and he looked it. His hair was long and tangled and greasy, and hung down, and you could see his eyes shining through like he was behind vines. It was all black, no gray; so was his long, mixed-up whiskers. There warn't no color in his face, where his face showed; it was white; not like another man's white, but a white to make a body sick, a white to make a body's flesh crawl—a tree-toad white, a fish-belly white. As for his clothes—just rags, that was all. He had one ankle resting on 'tother knee; the boot on that foot was busted, and two of his toes stuck through, and he worked them now and then. His hat was laying on the floor; an old black slouch with the top caved in, like a lid.

I stood a-looking at him; he set there a-looking at me, with his chair tilted back a little. I set the candle down. I noticed the window was up; so he had clumb in by the shed. He kept a-looking at me all over. By-and-by he says:

"Starchy clothes—very. You think you're a good deal of a big-bug, *don't* you?"

"Maybe I am, maybe I ain't" I says.

"Don't you give me none o' your lip," says he. "You've put on considerable many frills since I been away. I'll take you down a peg before I get done with you. You're educated, too, they say; can read and write. You think you're better'n your father, now, don't you, because he can't? *I*'ll take it out of you. Who told you you might meddle with such hifalut'n foolishness, hey?—who told you you could?"

"The widow. She told me."

"The widow, hey?—and who told the widow she could put in her shovel about a thing that ain't none of her business?"

"Nobody never told her."

"Well, I'll learn her how to meddle. And looky here—you drop that school, you hear? I'll learn people to bring up a boy to put on airs over his own father and let on to be better'n what *he* is. You lemme catch you fooling around that school again, you hear? Your mother couldn't read, and she couldn't write, nuther, before she died. None of the family couldn't, before *they* died. *I* can't; and here you're a-swelling yourself up like this. I ain't the man to stand it—you hear? Say—lemme hear you read."

I took up a book and begun something about General Washington and the wars. When I'd read about a half a minute, he fetched the book a whack with his hand and knocked it across the house. He says:

"It's so. You can do it. I had my doubts when you told me. Now looky here; you stop that putting on frills. I won't have it. I'll lay for you, my smarty; and if I catch you about that school I'll tan you good. First you know you'll get religion, too. I never see such a son."

He took up a little blue and yaller picture of some cows and a boy, and says:

"What's this?"

"It's something they give me for learning my lessons good."

He tore it up, and says—

"I'll give you something better—I'll give you a cowhide."

He set there a-mumbling and a-growling a minute, and then he says—

"*Ain't* you a sweet-scented dandy, though? A bed; and bedclothes; and a look'n-glass; and a piece of carpet on the floor—and your own father got to sleep with the hogs in the tanyard. I never see such a son. I bet I'll take some o' these frills out o' you before I'm done with you. Why there ain't no end to your airs—they say you're rich. Hey?—how's that?"

"They lie—that's how."

"Looky here—mind how you talk to me; I'm a-standing

about all I can stand, now—so don't gimme no sass. I've been in town two days, and I hain't heard nothing but about you bein' rich. I heard about it away down the river, too. That's why I come. You get me that money to-morrow—I want it."

"I hain't got no money."

"It's a lie. Judge Thatcher's got it. You git it. I want it."

"I hain't got no money, I tell you. You ask Judge Thatcher; he'll tell you the same.

"All right. I'll ask him; and I'll make him pungle, too, or I'll know the reason why. Say—how much you got in your pocket? I want it."

"I hain't got only a dollar, and I want that to—"

"It don't make no difference what you want it for—you just shell it out."

He took it and bit it to see if it was good, and then he said he was going down town to get some whiskey; said he hadn't had a drink all day. When he had got out on the shed, he put his head in again, and cussed me for putting on frills and trying to be better than him; and when I reckoned he was gone, he come back and put his head in again, and told me to mind about that school, because he was going to lay for me and lick me if I didn't drop that.

Next day he was drunk, and he went to Judge Thatcher's and bullyragged him and tried to make him give up the money, but he couldn't, and then he swore he'd make the law force him.

The judge and the widow went to law to get the court to take me away from him and let one of them be my guardian; but it was a new judge that had just come, and he didn't know the old man; so he said courts mustn't interfere and separate families if they could help it; said he'd druther not take a child away from its father. So Judge Thatcher and the widow had to quit on the business.

That pleased the old man till he couldn't rest. He said he'd cowhide me till I was black and blue if I didn't raise some money for him. I burrowed three dollars from Judge Thatcher, and pap took it and got drunk and went a-blowing around and cussing and whooping and carrying on; and he kept it up all over town, with a tin pan, till most midnight; then they jailed him, and next day they had him before court, and jailed him again for a week. But he said *he* was satisfied; said he was boss of his son, and he'd make it warm for *him*.

When he got out the new judge said he was agoing to make a man of him. So he took him to his own house, and dressed him up clean and nice, and had him to breakfast and dinner and supper with the family, and was just old pie to him, so to speak. And after supper he talked to him about temperance and such things till the old man cried, and said he'd been a fool, and fooled away his life; but now he was agoing to turn over a new leaf and be a man nobody wouldn't be ashamed of, and he hoped the judge would help him and not look down on him. The judge said he could hug him for the words; so *he* cried, and his wife she cried again; pap said he'd been a man that had always been misunderstood before, and the judge said he believed it. The old man said that what a man wanted that was down, was sympathy; and the judge said it was so; so they cried again. And when it was bedtime, the old man rose up and held out his hand, and says:

"Look at it gentlemen, and ladies all; take ahold of it; shake it. There's a hand that was the hand of a hog; but it ain't so no more; it's the hand of a man that's started in on a new life, and 'll die before he'll go back. You mark them words—don't forget I said them. It's a clean hand now; shake it—don't be afeard."

So they shook it, one after the other, all around, and cried. The judge's wife she kissed it. Then the old man he signed a pledge—made his mark. The judge said it was the holiest time on record, or something like that. Then they tucked the old man into a beautiful room, which was the spare room, and in the night sometime he got powerful thirsty and clumb out onto the porch-roof and slid down a stanchion and traded his new coat for a jug of forty-rod, and clumb back again and had a good old time; and towards daylight he crawled out again, drunk as a fiddler, and rolled off the porch and broke his left arm in two places and was most froze to death when somebody found him after sun-up. And when they come to look at that spare room, they had to take soundings before they could navigate it.

The judge he felt kind of sore. He said he reckoned a body could reform the ole man with a shot-gun, maybe, but he didn't know no other way.

CHAPTER VI

Well, pretty soon the old man was up and around again, and then he went for Judge Thatcher in the courts to make him give up that money, and he went for me, too, for not stopping school. He catched me a couple of times and thrashed me, but I went to school just the same, and dodged him or out-run him most of the time. I didn't want to go to school much, before, but I reckoned I'd go now to spite pap. The law trial was a slow business; appeared like they warn't ever going to get started on it; so every now and then I'd borrow two or three dollars off of the judge for him, to keep from getting a cowhiding. Every time he got money he got drunk; and every time he got drunk he raised Cain around town; and every time he raised Cain he got jailed. He was just suited—this kind of thing was right in his line.

He got to hanging around the widow's too much, and so she told him at last, that if he didn't quit using around there she would make trouble for him. Well, *wasn't* he mad? He said he would show who was Huck Finn's boss. So he watched out for me one day in the spring, and catched me, and took me up the river about three mile, in a skiff, and crossed over to the Illinois shore where it was woody and there warn't no houses but an old log hut in a place where the timber was so thick you couldn't find it if you didn't know where it was.

He kept me with him all the time, and I never got a chance to run off. We lived in that old cabin, and he always locked the door and put the key under his head, nights. He had a gun which he had stole, I reckon, and we fished and hunted, and that was what we lived on. Every little while he locked me in and went down to the store, three miles, to the ferry, and traded fish and game for whiskey and fetched it home and got drunk and had a good time, and licked me. The widow she found out where I was, by-and-by, and she sent a man over to try to get hold of me, but pap drove him off with the gun, and it warn't long after that till I was used to being where I was, and liked it, all but the cowhide part.

It was kind of lazy and jolly, laying off comfortable all day, smoking and fishing, and no books nor study. Two months or more run along, and my clothes got to be all rags and dirt, and I didn't see how I'd ever got to like it so well at the widow's, where you had to wash, and eat on a plate, and comb up, and go to bed and get up regular, and be forever bothering over a book and have old Miss Watson pecking at you all the time. I didn't want to go back no more. I had stopped cussing, because the widow didn't like it; but now I took to it again because pap hadn't no objections. It was pretty good times up in the woods there, take it all around.

But by-and-by pap got too handy with his hick'ry, and I couldn't stand it. I was all over welts. He got to going away so much, too, and locking me in. Once he locked me in and was gone three days. It was dreadful lonesome. I judged he had got drowned and I wasn't ever going to get out any more. I was scared. I made up my mind I would fix up some way to leave there. I had tried to get out of that cabin many a time, but I couldn't find no way. There warn't a window to it big enought for a dog to get through. I couldn't get up the chimbly, it was too narrow. The door was thick solid oak slabs. Pap was pretty careful not to leave a knife or anything in the cabin when he was away; I reckon I had hunted the place over as much as a hundred times; well, I was 'most all the time at it, because it was about the only way to put in the time. But this time I found something at last; I found an old rust wood-saw without any handle; it was laid in between a rafter and the clapboards of the roof. I greased it up and went to work. There was an old horse-blanket nailed against the logs at the far end of the cabin behind the table, to keep the wind from blowing through the chinks and putting the candle out. I got under the table and raised the blanket and went to work to saw a section of the big bottom log out, big enough to let me through. Well, it was a good long job, but I was getting towards the end of it when I heard pap's gun in the woods. I got rid of the signs of my work, and dropped the blanket and hid my saw, and pretty soon pap come in.

Pap warn't in a good humor—so he was his natural self. He said he was down to town, and everything was going wrong. His lawyer said he reckoned he would win his lawsuit and get the money, if they ever got started on the trial; but then there was ways to put it off a long time, and Judge Thatcher knowed how to do it. And he said people allowed there'd be another trial to get me away from him and give me to the widow for my guardian, and they guessed it would win, this time. This shook me up considerable, because I didn't want to go back to the widow's any more and be so cramped up and sivilized, as they called it. Then the old man got to cussing, and cussed everything and everybody he could think of, and then cussed them all over again to make sure he hadn't skipped any, and after that he polished off with a kind of general cuss all round, including a considerable parcel of people which he didn't know the names of, and so called them what's-his-name, when he got to them, and went right along with his cussing.

He said he would like to see the widow get me. He said he would watch out, and if they tried to come any such game on him he knowed of a place six or seven mile off, to stow me in, where they might hunt till they dropped and they couldn't find me. That made me pretty uneasy again, but only for a minute; I reckoned I wouldn't stay on hand till he got that chance.

The old man made me go to the skiff and fetch the things he had got. There was a fifty-pound sack of corn meal, and a side of bacon, ammunition, and a four-gallon jug of whiskey, and an old book and two newspapers for wadding, besides some tow. I toted up a load, and went back and set down on the bow of the skiff to rest. I thought it all over, and I reckoned I would walk off with the gun and some lines, and take to the woods when I run away. I guessed I wouldn't stay in one place, but just tramp right across the country, mostly night times, and hunt and fish to keep alive, and so get so far away that the old man nor the widow couldn't ever find me any more. I judged I would saw out and leave that night if pap got drunk enough, and I reckoned he would. I got so full of it I didn't notice how long I was staying, till the old man hollered and asked me whether I was asleep or drownded.

I got the things all up to the cabin, and then it was about dark. While I was cooking supper the old man took a swig or two and got sort of warmed up, and went to ripping again. He had been drunk over in town, and laid in the gutter all night, and he was a sight to look at. A body would a thought he was Adam, he was just all mud. Whenever his liquor begun to work, he most always went for the govment. This time he says:

"Call this a govment! why, just look at it and see what it's like. Here's the law a-standing ready to take a man's son away from him—a man's own son, which he has had all the trouble and all the anxiety and all the expense of raising. Yes, just as that man has got that son raised at last, and ready to go to work and begin to du suthin' for *him* and give him a rest, the law up and goes for him. And they call *that* govment! That ain't all, nuther. The law backs that old Judge Thatcher up and helps him to keep me out o' my property. Here's what the law does. The law takes a man worth six thousand dollars and upwards, and jams him into an old trap of a cabin like this, and lets him go round in clothes that ain't fitten for a hog. They call that govment! A man can't get his rights in a govment like this. Sometimes I've a mighty notion to just leave the country for good and all. Yes, and I *told* 'em so; I told old Thatcher to his face. Lots of 'em heard me, and can tell what I said. Says I, for two cents I'd leave the blamed country and never come anear it agin. Them's the very words. I says, look at my hat—if you call it a hat—but the lid raised up and the rest of it goes down till it's below my chin, and then it ain't rightly a hat at all, but more like my head was shoved up through a jint o' stove-pipe. Look at it, says I—such a hat for me to wear—one of the wealthiest men in this town, if I could git my rights.

"Oh, yes, this is a wonderful govment, wonderful. Why, looky here. There was a free nigger there, from Ohio; a mulatter, most as white as a white man. He had the whitest shirt on you ever see, too, and the shinest hat; and there ain't a man in that town that's got as fine clothes as what he had; an he had a gold watch and chain, and a silver-headed cane—the awfulest old gray-headed nabob in the State. And what do you think? they said he was a p'fessor in a college, and could talk all kinds of languages, and knowed everything. And that ain't the wust. They said he could *vote,* when he was at home. Well, that let me out. Thinks I, what is the country a-coming to? It was 'lection day, and I was just about to go and vote, myself, if I warn't too drunk to get there; but when they told me there was a State in this country where they'd let that nigger vote, I drawed out. I says I'll never vote agin. Them's the very words I said; they all heard me; and the country may rot for all me—I'll never vote agin as long as I live. And to see the cool way of that nigger—why, he wouldn't give me the road if I hadn't shoved him out o' the way. I says to the people, why ain't this nigger put up at auction and sold?—that's what I want to know. And what do you reckon they said? Why, they said he couldn't be sold till he'd been in the State six months, and he hadn't been there that long yet. There, now—that's a specimen. They call that a govment that can't sell a free nigger till he's been in the State six months. Here's a govment that calls itself a govment, and lets on to be a govment, and thinks it is a govment, and yet's got to set stock-still for six whole months before it can take ahold of a prowling thieving, infernal, white-shirted free nigger, and—"

Pap was agoing on so, he never noticed where his old limber legs was taking him to, so he went head over heels over the tub of salt pork, and barked both shins, and the rest of his speech was all the hottest kind of language—mostly hove at the nigger and the govment, though he give the tub some, too, all along, here and there. He hopped around the cabin considerable, first on one leg and then on the other, holding first one shin and then the other one, and at last he let out with his left foot all of a sudden and fetched the tub a rattling kick. But it warn't good judgment, because that was the boot that had a couple of his toes leaking out of the front end of it; so now he raised a howl that fairly made a body's hair raise, and down he went in the dirt, and rolled there, and held his toes; and the cussing he done then laid over anything he had ever done previous. He said so his own self, afterwards. He had heard old Sowberry Hagan in his best days, and he said it laid over him, too; but I reckon that was sort of piling it on, maybe.

After supper pap took the jug, and said he had enough whiskey there for two drunks and one delirium tremens. That was always his word. I judged he would be blind drunk in about an hour, and then I would steal the key, or saw myself out, one or 'tother. He drank, and drank, and tumbled down on his blankets, by-and-by; but luck didn't run my way. He didn't go sound asleep, but was uneasy. He groaned, and moaned, and thrashed around this way and that, for a long time. At last I got so sleepy I couldn't keep my eyes open, all I could do, and so before I knowed what I was about I was sound asleep, and the candle burning.

I don't know how long I was asleep, but all of a sudden there was an awful scream and I was up. There was pap, looking wild and skipping around every which way and yelling about snakes. He said they was crawling up his legs; and then he would give a jump and scream, and say one had bit him on the cheek—but I couldn't see no snakes. He started and run round and round the cabin, hollering "take him off! take him off! he's biting me on the neck!" I never see a man look so wild in the eyes. Pretty soon he was all fagged out, and fell down panting; then he rolled over and over, wonderful fast, kicking things every which way, and striking and grabbing at the air with his hands, and screaming, and saying there was devils ahold of him. He wore out, by-and-by, and laid still a while, moaning. Then he laid stiller, and didn't make a sound. I could hear the owls and the wolves, away off in the woods, and it seemed terrible still. He was laying over by the corner. By-and-by he raised up, part way, and listened, with his head to one side. He says very low:

"Tramp—tramp—tramp; that's the dead; tramp—tramp—tramp; they're coming after me; but I won't go— Oh, they're here! don't touch me—don't! hands off—they're cold; let go— Oh, let a poor devil alone!"

Then he went down on all fours and crawled off begging them to let him alone, and he rolled himself up in his blanket and wallowed in under the old pine table, still a-begging; and then he went to crying. I could hear him through the blanket.

By-and-by he rolled out and jumped up on his feet looking wild, and he see me and went for me. He chased me round and round the place, with a clasp-knife, calling me the Angel of Death and saying he would kill me and then I couldn't come for him no more. I begged, and told him I was only Huck, but he laughed *such* a screechy laugh, and roared and cussed, and kept on chasing me up. Once when I turned short and dodged under his arm he made a grab and got me by the jacket between my shoulders, and I thought I was gone; but I slid out of the jacket quick as lightning, and saved myself. Pretty soon he was all tired out, and dropped down with his back against the door, and said he would rest a minute and then kill me. He put his knife under him, and said he would sleep and get strong, and then he would see who was who.

So he dozed off, pretty soon. By-and-by I got the old split-bottom chair and clumb up, as easy as I could, not to make any noise, and got down the gun. I slipped the ramrod down to make sure it was loaded, and then I laid it across the turnip barrel, pointing towards pap, and set down behind it to wait for him to stir. And how slow and still the time did drag along.

CHAPTER VII

Git up! what you 'bout!"

I opened my eyes and looked around, trying to make out where I was. It was after sun-up, and I had been sound asleep. Pap was standing over me, looking sour—and sick, too. He says—

"What you doin' with this gun?"

I judged he didn't know nothing about what he had been doing, so I says:

"Somebody tried to get in, so I was laying for him."

"Why didn't you roust me out?"

"Well I tried to, but I couldn't; I couldn't budge you."

"Well, all right. Don't stand there palavering all day, but out with you and see if there's a fish on the lines for breakfast. I'll be along in a minute."

He unlocked the door and I cleared out, up the river bank. I noticed some pieces of limbs and such things floating down, and a sprinkling of bark; so I knowed the river had begun to rise. I reckoned I would have great times, now, if I was over at the town. The June rise used to be always luck for me; because as soon as that rise begins, here comes cord-wood floating down, and pieces of log rafts—sometimes a dozen logs together; so all you have to do is to catch them and sell them to the wood yards and the sawmill.

I went along up the bank with one eye out for pap and 'tother one out for what the rise might fetch along. Well, all at once, here comes a canoe; just a beauty, too, about thirteen or fourteen foot long, riding high like a duck. I shot head first off of the bank, like a frog, clothes and all on, and struck out for the canoe. I just expected there'd be somebody laying down in it, because people often done that to fool folks, and when a chap had pulled a skiff out most to it they'd raise up and laugh at him. But it warn't so this time. It was a drift-canoe, sure enough, and I clumb in and paddled her ashore. Thinks I, the old man will be glad when he sees this—she's worth ten dollars. But when I got to shore pap wasn't in sight yet, and as I was running her into a little creek like a gully, all hung over with vines and willows, I struck another idea; I judged I'd hide her good, and then, stead of taking to the woods when I run off, I'd go down the river about fifty mile and camp in one place for good, and not have such a rough time tramping on foot.

It was pretty close to the shanty, and I thought I heard the old man coming, all the time; but I got her hid; and then I out and looked around a bunch of willows, and there was the old man down the path apiece just drawing a bead on a bird with his gun. So he hadn't seen anything.

When he got along, I was hard at it taking up a "trot" line. He abused me a little for being so slow, but I told him I fell in the river and that was what made me so long. I knowed he would see I was wet, and then he would be asking questions. We got five cat-fish off of the lines and went home.

While we laid off, after breakfast, to sleep up, both of us being about wore out, I got to thinking that if I could fix up some way to keep pap and the widow from trying to follow me, it would be a certainer thing than trusting to luck to get far enough off before they missed me; you see, all kinds of things might happen. Well, I didn't see no way for a while, but by-and-by pap raised up a minute, to drink another barrel of water, and he says:

"Another time a man comes a-prowling round here, you roust me out, you hear?" That man warn't here for no good. I'd a shot him. Next time, you roust me out, you hear?"

Then he dropped down and went to sleep again—but what he had been saying give me the very idea I wanted. I says to myself, I can fix it now so nobody won't think of following me.

About twelve o'clock we turned out and went along up the bank. The river was coming up pretty fast, and lots of drift-wood going by on the rise. By-and-by, along comes part of a log raft—nine logs fast together. We went out with the skiff and towed it ashore. Then we had dinner. Anybody but pap would a waited and seen the day through, so as to catch more stuff; but that warn't pap's style. Nine logs was enough for one time; he must shove right over to town and sell. So he locked me in and took the skiff and started off towing the raft about half-past three. I judged he wouldn't come back that night. I waited till I reckoned he had a good start, then I out with my saw and went to work on that log again. Before he was 'tother side of the river I was out of the hole; him and his raft was just a speck on the water away off yonder.

I took the sack of corn meal and took it to where the canoe was hid, and shoved the vines and branches apart and put it in; then I done the same with the side of bacon; then the whiskey jug; I took all the coffee and sugar there was, and all the ammunition; I took the wadding; I took the bucket and gourd, I took a dipper and a tin cup, and my old saw and two blankets, and the skillet and the coffee pot. I took fish-lines and matches and other things—everything that was worth a cent. I cleaned out the place. I wanted an axe, but there wasn't any, only the one out at the wood pile, and I knowed why I was going to leave that. I fetched out the gun, and now I was done.

I had wore the ground a good deal, crawling out of the hole

and dragging out so many things. So I fixed that as good as I could from the outside by scattering dust on the place, which covered up the smoothness and the sawdust. Then I fixed the piece of log back into its place, and put two rocks under it and one against it to hold it there,—for it was bent up at that place, and didn't quite touch ground. If you stood four or five foot away and didn't know it was sawed, you wouldn't ever notice it; and besides, this was the back of the cabin and it warn't likely anybody would go fooling around there.

It was all grass clear to the canoe; so I hadn't left a track. I followed around to see. I stood on the bank and looked out over the river. All safe. So I took the gun and went up a piece into the woods and was hunting around for some birds, when I see a wild pig; hogs soon went wild in them bottoms after they had got away from the prairie farms. I shot this fellow and took him into camp.

I took the axe and smashed in the door—I beat it and hacked it considerable, a-doing it. I fetched the pig in and took him back nearly to the table and hacked into his throat with the ax, and laid him down on the ground to bleed—I say ground, because it *was* ground—hard packed, and no boards. Well, next I took an old sack and put a lot of rocks in it,—all I could drag—and I started it from the pig and dragged it to the door and through the woods down to the river and dumped it in, and down it sunk, out of sight. You could easy see that something had been dragged over the ground. I did wish Tom Sawyer was there, I knowed he would take an interest in this kind of business, and throw in the fancy touches. Nobody could spread himself like Tom Sawyer in such a thing as that.

Well, last I pulled out some of my hair, and bloodied the ax good, and stuck it on the back side, and slung the ax in the corner. Then I took up the pig and held him to my breast with my jacket (so he couldn't drip) till I got a good piece below the house and then dumped him into the river. Now I thought of something else. So I went and got the bag of meal and my old saw out of the canoe and fetched them to the house. I took the bag to where it used to stand, and ripped a hole in the bottom of it with the saw, for there warn't no knives and forks on the place—pap done everything with his clasp-knife, about the cooking. Then I carried the sack about a hundred yards across the grass and through the willows east of the house, to a shallow lake that was five mile wide and full of rushes—and ducks too, you might say, in the season. There was a slough or a creek leading out of it on the other side, that went miles away, I don't know where, but it didn't go to the river. The meal sifted out and made a little track all the way to the lake. I dropped pap's whetstone there too, so as to look like it had been done by accident. Then I tied up the rip in the meal sack with a string, so it wouldn't leak no more, and took it and my saw to the canoe again.

It was about dark, now; so I dropped the canoe down the river under some willows that hung over the bank, and waited for the moon to rise. I made fast to a willow; then I took a bit to eat, and by-and-by laid down in the canoe to smoke a pipe and lay out a plan. I says to myself, they'll follow the track of that sackful of rocks to the shore and then drag the river for me. And they'll follow that meal track to the lake and go browsing down the creek that leads out of it to find the robbers that killed me and took the things. They won't ever hunt the river for anything but my dead carcass. They'll soon get tired of that, and won't bother no more about me. All right; I can stop anywhere I want to. Jackson's Island is good enough for me; I know that island pretty well, and nobody ever comes there. And then I can paddle over to town, nights, and slink around and pick up things I want. Jackson's Island's the place.

I was pretty tired, and the first thing I knowed, I was asleep. When I woke up I didn't know where I was, for a minute. I set up and looked around, a little scared. Then I remembered. The river looked miles and miles across. The moon was so bright I could a counted the drift logs that went a slipping along, black and still, hundred of yards out from shore. Everything was dead quiet, and it looked late, and *smelt* late. You know what I mean—I don't know the words to put it in.

I took a good gap and a stretch, and was just going to unhitch and start, when I heard a sound away over the water. I listened. Pretty soon I made it out. It was that dull kind of regular sound that comes from oars working in rowlocks when it's a still night. I peeped out through the willow branches, and there it was—a skiff, away across the water. I couldn't tell how many was in it. It kept a-coming, and when it was abreast of me I see there warn't but one man in it. Thinks I, maybe it's pap, though I warn't expecting him. He dropped below me, with the current, and by-and-by he come a-swinging up shore in the easy water, and he went so close I could a reached out the gun and touched him. Well, it *was* pap, sure enough—and sober, too, by the way he laid to his oars.

I didn't lose no time. The next minute I was a-spinning down stream soft but quick in the shade of the bank. I made two mile and a half, and then struck out a quarter of a mile or more towards the middle of the river, because pretty soon I would be passing the ferry landing and people might see me and hail me. I got out amongst the drift-wood and then laid down in the bottom of the canoe and let her float. I laid there and had a good rest and a smoke out of my pipe, looking away into the sky, not a cloud in it. The sky looks ever so deep when you lay down on your back in the moonshine; I never knowed it before. And how far a body can hear on the water such nights! I heard people talking at the ferry landing. I heard what they said, too, every word of it. One man said it was getting towards the long days and the short nights, now. 'Tother one said *this* warn't one of the short ones, he reckoned—and then they laughed, and he said it over again and they laughed again; then they walked up another fellow and told him, and laughed, but he didn't laugh; he ripped out something brisk and said let him alone. The first fellow said he 'lowed to tell it to his old woman—she would think it was pretty good; but he said that warn't nothing to some things he had said in his time. I heard one man say it was nearly three o'clock, and he hoped daylight wouldn't wait more than about a week longer. After that, the talk got further and further away, and I couldn't make out the words any more, but I could hear the mumble; and now and then a laugh, too, but it seemed a long ways off.

I was away below the ferry now. I rose up and there was Jackson's Island, about two mile and a half down stream, heavy-timbered and standing up out of the middle of the river, big and dark and solid, like a steamboat without any lights. There warn't any signs of the bar at the head—it was all under water, now.

It didn't take me long to get there. I shot past the head at a ripping rate, the current was so swift, and then I got into the dead water and landed on the side towards the Illinois shore. I run the canoe into a deep dent in the bank that I knowed about; I had to part the willow branches to get in; and when I made fast nobody could a seen the canoe from the outside.

I went up and set down on a log at the head of the island and looked out on the big river and the black driftwood, and away over to the town, three mile away, where there was three or four lights twinkling. A monstrous big lumber raft was about a mile up stream, coming along down, with a lantern in the middle of it. I watched it come creeping down, and when it was most abreast of where I stood I heard a man say, "Stern oars, there! heave her head to stabboard!" I heard that just as plain as if the man was by my side.

There was a little gray in the sky, now; so I stepped into the woods and laid down for a nap before breakfast.

CHAPTER VIII

The sun was up so high when I waked, that I judged it was after eight o'clock. I laid there in the grass and the cool shade, thinking about things and feeling rested and ruther comfortable and satisfied. I could see the sun out at one or two holes, but mostly it was big trees all about, and gloomy in there amongst them. There was freckled places on the ground where the light sifted down through the leaves, and the freckled places swapped about a little, showing there was a little breeze up there. A couple of squirrels set on a limb an jabbered at me very friendly.

I was powerful lazy and comfortable—didn't want to get up and cook breakfast. Well, I was dozing off again, when I thinks I hears a sound of "boom!" away up the river. I rouses up and rests on my elbow and listens; pretty soon I hears it again. I hopped up and went and looked out at a hole in the leaves, and I see a bunch of smoke laying on the water a long ways up—about abreast the ferry. And there was the ferry-boat full of people, floating along down. I knowed what was the matter, now. "Boom!" I see the white smoke squirt out of the ferry-boat's side. You see, they was firing cannon over the water, trying to make my carcass come to the top.

I was pretty hungry, but it warn't going to do for me to start a fire, because they might see the smoke. So I set there and watched the cannon-smoke and listened to the boom. The river was a mile wide, there, and it always looked pretty on a summer morning—so I was having a good enough time seeing them hunt for my remainders, if I only had a bite to eat. Well, then I happened to think how they always put quicksilver in loaves of bread and float them off because they always go right to the drownded carcass and stop there. So says I, I'll keep a lookout, and if any of them's floating around after me, I'll give them a show. I changed to the Illinois edge of the island to see what luck I could have, and I warn't disappointed. A big double loaf come along, and I most got it, with a long stick, but my foot slipped and she floated out further. Of course I was where the current set in the closest to the shore—I knowed enough for that. But by-and-by along comes another one, and this time I won. I took out the plug and shook out the little dab of quicksilver, and set my teeth in. It was "baker's bread"—what the quality eat—none of your low-down corn-pone.

I got a good place amongst the leaves, and set there on a log, munching the bread and watching the ferry-boat, and very well satisfied. And then something struck me. I says, now I reckon the widow of the parson or somebody prayed that this bread would find me, and there it has gone and done it. So there ain't no doubt but there is something in that thing. That is, there's something in it when a body like the widow or the parson prays, but it don't work for me, and I reckon it don't work for only just the right kind.

I lit a pipe and had a good long smoke and went on watching. The ferry-boat was floating with the current, and I allowed

I'd have a chance to see who was aboard when she come along, because she would come in close, where the bread did. When she'd got pretty well along down towards me, I put out my pipe and went to where I fished out the bread, and laid down behind a log on the bank in a little open place. Where the log forked I could peep through.

By-and-by she come along, and she drifted in so close that they could a run out a plank and walked ashore. Most everybody was on the boat. Pap, and Judge Thatcher, and Bessie Thatcher, and Jo Harper, and Tom Sawyer, and his old Aunt Polly, and Sid and Mary, and plenty more. Everybody was talking about the murder, but the captain broke in and says:

"Look sharp, now; the current sets in the closest here, and maybe he's washed ashore and got tangled amongst the brush at the water's edge. I hope so, anyway."

I didn't hope so. They all crowded up and leaned over the rails, nearly in my face, and kept still, watching with all their might. I could see them first-rate, but they couldn't see me. Then the captain sung out:

"Stand away!" and the cannon let off such a blast right before me that it made me deef with the noise and pretty near blind with the smoke, and I judged I was gone. If they'd a had some bullets in, I reckon they'd a got the corpse they was after. Well, I see I warn't hurt, thanks to goodness. The boat floated on and went out of sight around the shoulder of the island. I could hear the booming, now and then, further and further off, and by-and-by after an hour, I didn't hear it no more. The island was three mile long. I judged they had got to the foot, and was giving it up. But they didn't yet a while. They turned around the foot of the island and started up the channel on the Missouri side, under steam, and booming once in a while as they went. I crossed over to that side and watched them. When they got abreast the head of the island they quit shooting and dropped over to the Missouri shore and went home to the town.

I knowed I was all right now. Nobody else would come a-hunting after me. I got my traps out of the canoe and made me a nice camp in the thick woods. I made a kind of a tent out of my blankets to put my things under so the rain couldn't get at them. I catched a cat-fish and haggled him open with my saw, and towards sundown I started my camp fire and had supper. Then I set out a line to catch some fish for breakfast.

When it was dark I set by my camp fire smoking, and feeling pretty satisfied; but by-and-by it got sort of lonesome, and so I went and set on the bank and listened to the currents washing along, and counted the stars and drift-logs and rafts that come down, and then went to bed; there ain't no better way to put in time when you are lonesome; you can't stay so, you soon get over it.

And so for three days and nights. No difference—just the same thing. But the next day I went exploring around down through the island. I was boss of it; it all belonged to me, so to say, and I wanted to know all about it; but mainly I wanted to put in the time. I found plenty strawberries, ripe and prime; and green summer-grapes, and green razberries; and the green blackberries was just beginning to show. They would all come handy by-and-by, I judged.

Well, I went fooling along in the deep woods till I judged I warn't far from the foot of the island. I had my gun along, but I hadn't shot nothing; it was for protection; thought I would kill some game nigh home. About this time I mighty near stepped on a good sized snake, and it went sliding off through the grass and flowers, and I after it, trying to get a shot at it. I clipped along, and all of a sudden I bounded right on to the ashes of a camp fire that was still smoking.

My heart jumped up amongst my lungs. I never waited for to look further, but uncocked my gun and went sneaking back on my tip-toes as fast as ever I could. Every now and then I stopped a second, amongst the thick leaves, and listened; but my breath come so hard I couldn't hear nothing else. I slunk along another piece further, then listened again; and so on, and so on; if I see a stump, I took it for a man; if I trod on a stick and broke it, it made me feel like a person had cut one of my breaths in two and I only got half, and the short half, too.

When I got to camp I warn't feeling very brash, there warn't much sand in my craw; but I says, this ain't no time to be fooling around. So I got all my traps into my canoe again so as to have them out of sight, and I put out the fire and scattered the ashes around to look like an old last year's camp, and then clumb a tree.

I reckon I was up in the tree two hours; but I didn't see nothing, I didn't hear nothing—I only *thought* I heard and seen as much as a thousand things. Well, I couldn't stay up there forever; so at last I got down, but I kept in the thick woods and on the lookout all the time. All I could get to eat was berries and what was left over from breakfast.

By the time it was night I was pretty hungry. So when it was good and dark, I slid out from shore before moonrise and paddled over to the Illinois bank—about a quarter of a mile. I went out in the woods and cooked a supper, and I had about made up my mind I would stay there all night, when I hear a *plunkety-plunk, plunkety-plunk,* and says to myself, horses coming; and next I hear people's voices. I got everything into the canoe as quick as I could, and then went creeping through the woods to see what I could find out. I hadn't got far when I hear a man say:

"We better camp here, if we can find a good place; the horses is about beat out. Let's look around."

I didn't wait, but shoved out and paddled away easy. I tied up in the old place, and reckoned I would sleep in the canoe.

I didn't sleep much. I couldn't, somehow, for thinking. And every time I waked up I thought somebody had me by the neck. So the sleep didn't do me no good. By-and-by I says to myself, I can't live this way; I'm agoing to find out who it is that's here on the island with me; I'll find it out or bust. Well, I felt better, right off.

So I took my paddle and slid out from shore just a step or two, and then let the canoe drop along down amongst the shadows. The moon was shining, and outside of the shadows it made it most as light as day. I poked along well onto an hour, everything still as rocks and sound asleep. Well by this time I was most down to the foot of the island. A little ripply, cool breeze begun to blow, and that was as good as saying the night was about done. I give her a turn with the paddle and brung her nose to shore; then I got my gun and slipped out and into the edge of the woods. I set down there on a log and looked out through the leaves. I see the moon go off watch and the darkness begin to blanket the river. But in a little while I see a pale streak over the tree-tops, and knowed the day was coming. So I took my gun and slipped off towards where I had run across that camp fire, stopping every minute or two to listen. But I hadn't no luck, somehow; I couldn't seem to find the place. But by-and-by, sure enough I catched a glimpse of fire, away through the trees. I went for it, cautious and slow. By-and-by I was close enough to have a look, and there laid a man on the ground. It most give me the fan-tods. He had a blanket around his head, and his head was nearly in the fire. I set there behind a clump of bushes, in about six foot of him, and kept my eyes on him steady. It was getting gray daylight, now. Pretty soon he gapped, and stretched himself, and hove off the blanket, and it was Miss Watson's Jim! I bet I was glad to see him. I says:

"Hello, Jim!" and skipped out.

He bounced up and stared at me wild. Then he drops down on his knees, and puts his hands together and says:

"Doan' hurt me—don't! I hain't ever done no harm to a ghos'. I awluz liked dead people, en done all I could for 'em. You go en git in de river agin, whah you b'longs, en doan' do nuffn to Ole Jim, 'at 'uz awluz yo' fren'."

Well, I warn't long making him understand I warn't dead. I was ever so glad to see Jim. I warn't lonesome, now. I told him I warn't afraid of *him* telling the people where I was. I talked along, but he only set there and looked at me; never said nothing. Then I says:

"It's good daylight. Let's get breakfast. Make up your camp fire good."

"What's de use er makin' up de camp fire to cook strawbries en sich truck? But you got a gun, hain't you? Den we ken git sumfn better den strawbries."

"Strawberries and such truck," I says. "Is that what you live on?"

"I couldn't git nuffn else," he says.

"Why, how long you been on the island, Jim?"

"I come heah de night after you's killed."

"What, all that time?"

"Yes-indeedy."

"And ain't you had nothing but that kind of rubbage to eat?"

"No, sah—nuffn else."

"Well, you must be most starved, ain't you?"

"I reck'n I could eat a hoss. I think I could. How long you ben on de islan'?"

"Since the night I got killed."

"No! W'y, what has you lived on? But you got a gun. Oh, yes, you got a gun. Dat's good. Now you kill sumfn en I'll make up de fire."

So we went over to where the canoe was, and while he built a fire in a grassy open place amongst the trees, I fetched meal and bacon and coffee, and coffee-pot and frying-pan, and sugar and tin cups, and the nigger was set back considerable, because he reckoned it was all done with witchcraft. I catched a good big cat-fish, too, and Jim cleaned him with his knife, and fried him.

When breakfast was ready, we lolled on the grass and eat it smoking hot. Jim laid it in with all his might, for he was most about starved. Then when we had got pretty well stuffed, we laid off and lazied.

By-and-by Jim says:

"But looky here, Huck, who wuz it dat 'uz killed in dat shanty, ef it warn't you?"

Then I told him the whole thing, and he said it was smart. He said Tom Sawyer couldn't get up no better plan than what I had. Then I says:

"How do you come to be here, Jim, and how did you get here?"

He looked pretty uneasy, and didn't say nothing for a minute. Then he says:

"Maybe I better not tell."

"Why, Jim?"

"Well, dey's reasons. But you wouldn' tell on me ef I 'uz to tell you, would you, Huck?"

"Blamed if I would, Jim."

"Well, I b'lieve you, Huck. I—I *run off*."

"Jim!"

"But mind, you said you wouldn't tell—you know you said you wouldn't tell, Huck."

"Well, I did. I said I wouldn't, and I'll stick to it. Honest *injun* I will. People would call me a low down Abolitionist and despise me for keeping mum—but that don't make no difference. I ain't agoing to tell, and I ain't agoing back there anyways. So now, le's know all about it."

"Well, you see, it 'uz dis way. Ole Missus—dat's Miss Watson—she pecks on me all de time, en treats me pooty rough, but she awluz said she wouldn' sell me down to Orleans. But I noticed dey wuz a nigger trader roun' de place considable, lately, en I begin to git oneasy. Well, one night I creeps to de do', pooty late, en de do' warn't quite shet, en I hear ole missus tell de widder she gwyne to sell me down to Orleans, but she didn' want to, but she could git eight hund'd dollars for me, en it 'uz sich a big stack o' money she couldn' resis'. De widder she try to git her to say she wouldn' do it, but I never waited to hear de res'. I lit out might quick, I tell you.

"I tuck out en shin down de hill en 'spec to steal a skift 'long de sho' som'ers 'bove de town, but dey wuz people a-stirrin' yit, so I hid in de ole tumble-down cooper shop on de bank to wait for everybody to go 'way. Well, I wuz dah all night. Dey wuz somebody roun' all de time. 'Long 'bout six in de mawnin', skifts begin to go by, en 'bout eight er nine every skift dat went 'long wuz talkin' 'bout how yo' pap come over to de town en say you's killed. Dese las' skifts wuz full o' ladies en genlmen agoin' over for to see de place. Sometimes dey'd pull up at de sho' en take a res' b'fo' dey started acrost, so by de talk I got to know all 'bout de killin'. I 'uz powerful sorry you's killed, Huck, but I ain't no mo' now.

"I laid dah under de shavins all day. I 'uz hungry, but I warn't afraid; bekase I knowed ole missus en de widder wuz goin' to start to de camp-meetn' right arter breakfas' en be gone all day, en dey knows I goes off wid de cattle 'bout daylight, so dey wouldn' 'spec to see me roun' de place, en so dey wouldn' miss me, kase dey'd shin out en take holiday, soon as de ole folks 'uz out'n de way.

"Well, when it come dark I tuck out up de river road, en went 'bout two mile er more to whah dey warn't no houses. I'd made up my mine 'bout what I's agwyne to do. You see ef I kep' on tryin' to git away afoot, de dogs 'ud track me; ef I stole a skift to cross over, dey'd miss dat skift, you see, en dey'd know 'bout whah I'd lan' on de yuther side en whah to pick up my track. So I says, a raff is what I's arter; it doan' *make* no track.

"I see light a-comin' roun' de p'int, bymeby, so I wade' in en shove' a log ahead o' me, en swum more'n half-way acrost de river, en got in 'mongst de drift-wood, en kep' my head down low, en kinder swum agin de current tell de raff come along. Den I swum to de stern uv it, en tuck aholt. It clouded up en 'uz pooty dark for a little while. So I clumb up en laid down on de planks. De men 'uz all 'way yonder in de middle, whah de lantern wuz. De river wuz arisin' en dey wuz a good current; so I reck'n'd 'at by fo' in de mawnin' I'd be twenty-five mile down de river, en den I'd slip in, jis' b'fo' daylight, en swim asho' en take to de woods on de Illinois side.

"But I didn' have no luck. When we 'uz mos' down to de head er de islan', a man begin to come aft wid de lantern. I see it warn't no use fer to wait, so I slid overboard, en struck out fer de islan'. Well, I had a notion I could lan' mos' anywhers, but I couldn't—bank too bluff. I 'uz mos' to de foot er de islan' b'fo' I foun' a good place. I went into de woods en jedged I wouldn' fool wid raffs no mo', long as dey move de lantern roun' so. I had my pipe en a plug er dog-leg, en some matches in my cap, en dey warn't wet, so I 'uz all right."

"And so you ain't had no meat nor bread to eat all this time? Why didn't you get mud-turkles?"

"How you gwyne to git'm? You can't slip up on um en grab um; en how's a body gwyne to hit um wid a rock? How could a body do it in de night? en I warn't gwyne to show mysef on de bank in de daytime."

"Well, that's so. You've had to keep in the woods all the time, of course. Did you hear 'em shooting the cannon?"

"Oh, yes. I knowed dey was arter you. I see um go by heah; watched um thoo de bushes."

Some young birds come along, flying a yard or two at a time and lighting. Jim said it was a sign it was going to rain. He said it was a sign when young chickens flew that way, and so he reckoned it was the same way when young birds done it. I was going to catch some of them, but Jim wouldn't let me. He said it was death. He said his father laid mighty sick once, and some of them catched a bird, and his old granny said his father would die, and he did.

And Jim said you musn't count the things you are going to cook for dinner, because that would bring bad luck. The same if you shook the table-cloth after sundown. And he said if a man owned a bee-hive, and that man died, the bees must be told about it before sun-up next morning, or else the bees would all weaken down and quit work and die. Jim said bees wouldn't sting idiots; but I didn't believe that, because I had tried them lots of times myself, and they wouldn't sting me.

I had heard about some of these things before, but not all of them. Jim knowed all kinds of signs. He said he knowed most everything. I said it looked to me like all the signs was about bad luck, and so I asked him if there warn't any good-luck signs. He says:

"Mighty few—an' *dey* ain' no use to a body. What you want to know when good luck's a-comin' for? want to keep it off?" And he said: "Ef you's got hairy arms en a hairy breas', it's a sign dat you's agwyne to be rich. Well, dey's some use in a sign like dat, 'kase it's so fur ahead. You see, maybe you's got to be po' a long time fust, en so you might git discourage' en kill yo'sef 'f you did n' know by de sign dat you gwyne to be rich bymeby."

"Have you got hairy arms and a hairy breast, Jim?"

"What's de use to ax dat question? don' you see I has?"

"Well, are you rich?"

"No, but I ben rich wunst, and gwyne to be rich agin. Wunst I had foteen dollars, but I tuck to specalat'n', en got busted out."

"What did you speculate in, Jim?"

"Well, fust I tackled stock."

"What kind of stock?"

"Why, live stock. Cattle, you know. I put ten dollars in a cow. But I ain' gwyne to resk no mo' money in stock. De cow up 'n' died on my han's."

"So you lost the ten dollars."

"No, I didn' lose it all. I on'y los' 'bout nine of it. I sole de hide en taller for a dollar en ten cents."

"You had five dollars and ten cents left. Did you speculate any more?"

"Yes. You know dat one-laigged nigger dat b'longs to old Misto Bradish? well, he sot up a bank, en say anybody dat put in a dollar would git fo' dollars mo' at de en' er de year. Well, all de niggers went in, but dey didn' have much. I wuz de on'y one dat had much. So I stuck out for mo' dan fo' dollars, en I said 'f I didn' git it I'd start a bank mysef. Well o' course dat nigger want' to keep me out er de business, bekase he say dey warn't business 'nough for two banks, so he say I could put in my five dollars en he pay me thirty-five at de en' er de year.

"So I done it. Den I reck'n'd I'd inves' de thirty-five dollars right off en keep things a-movin'. Dey wuz a nigger name' Bob, dat had ketched a wood-flat, en his marster didn' know it; en I bought it off'n him en told him to take de thirty-five dollars when de en' er de year come; but somebody stole de wood-flat dat night, en nex' day de one-laigged nigger say de bank's busted. So dey didn' none uv us git no money."

"What did you do with the ten cents, Jim?"

"Well, I 'uz gwyne to spen' it, but I had a dream, en de dream tole me to give it to a nigger name' Balum—Balum's Ass dey call him for short, he's one er dem chuckle-heads, you know. But he's lucky, dey say, en I see I warn't lucky. De dream say let Balum inves' de ten cents en he'd make a raise for me. Well, Balum he tuck de money, en when he wuz in church he hear de preacher say dat whoever give to de po' len' to de Lord, en boun' to git his money back a hund'd times. So Balum he tuck en give de ten cents to do po,' en laid low to see what wuz gwyne to come of it."

"Well, what did come of it, Jim?"

"Nuffn' never come of it. I couldn' manage to k'leck dat money no way; en Balum he couldn'. I ain' gwyne to len' no mo' money 'dout I see de security. Boun' to git yo' money back a hund'd times, de preacher says! Ef I could git de ten *cents* back, I'd call it squah, en be glad er de chanst."

"Well, it's all right, anyway, Jim, long as you're going to be rich again some time or other."

"Yes—en I's rich now, come to look at it. I owns mysef, en I's wuth eight hund'd dollars. I wisht I had de money, I wouldn' want no mo'."

CHAPTER IX

I wanted to go and look at a place right about the middle of the island, that I'd found when I was exploring; so we started, and soon got to it, because the island was only three miles long and a quarter of a mile wide.

This place was a tolerable long steep hill or ridge, about forty foot high. We had a rough time getting to the top, the sides was so steep and the bushes so thick. We tramped and clumb around all over it, and by-and-by found a good big cavern in the rock, most up to the top on the side towards Illinois. The cavern was as big as two or three rooms bunched together, and Jim could stand up straight in it. It was cool in there. Jim was for putting our traps in there, right away, but I said we didn't want to be climbing up and down there all the time.

Jim said if we had the canoe hid in a good place, and had all the traps in the cavern, we could rush there if anybody was to come to the island, and they would never find us without dogs. And besides, he said them little birds had said it was going to rain, and did I want the things to get wet?

So we went back and got the canoe and paddled up abreast of the cavern, and lugged all the traps up there. Then we hunted up a place close by to hide the canoe in, amongst the thick willows. We took some fish off of the lines and set them again, and begun to get ready for dinner.

The door of the cavern was big enough to roll a hogshead in, and on one side of the door the floor stuck out a little bit and was flat and a good place to build a fire on. So we built it there and cooked dinner.

We spread the blankets inside for a carpet, and eat our dinner in there. We put all the other things handy at the back of the cavern. Pretty soon it darkened up and begun to thunder and lighten; so the birds was right about it. Directly it begun to rain, and it rained like all fury, too, and I never see the wind blow so. It was one of these regular summer storms. It would get so dark that it looked all blue-black outside, and lovely; and the rain would thrash along by so thick that the trees off a little ways looked dim and spider-webby; and here would come a blast of wind that would bend the trees down and turn up the pale underside of the leaves; and then a perfect ripper of a gust would follow along and set the branches to tossing their arms as if they was just wild; and next, when it was just about the bluest and blackest—*fst!* it was as bright as glory and you'd have a little glimpse of tree-tops a-plunging about, away off yonder in the storm, hundreds of yards further than you could see before; dark as sin again in a second, and now you'd hear the thunder let go with an awful crash and then go rumbling, grumbling, tumbling down the sky towards the under side of the world, like rolling empty barrels down stairs, where it's long stairs and they bounce a good deal, you know.

"Jim, this is nice," I says. "I wouldn't want to be nowhere else but here. Pass me along another hunk of fish and some hot corn-bread."

"Well, you wouldn't a ben here, 'f it hadn't ben for Jim. You'd a ben down dah in de woods widout any dinner, en gittin' mos' drownded, too, dat you would, honey. Chickens knows when its gwyne to rain, en so do de birds, chile."

The river went on raising and raising for ten or twelve days, till at last it was over the banks. The water was three or four foot deep on the island in the low places and on the Illinois bottom. On that side it was a good many miles wide; but on the Missouri side it was the same old distance across—a half a mile—because the Missouri shore was just a wall of high bluffs.

Daytimes we paddled all over the island in the canoe. It was mighty cool and shady in the deep woods even if the sun was blazing outside. We went winding in and out amongst the trees; and sometimes the vines hung so thick we had to back away and go some other way. Well, on every old broken-down tree, you could see rabbits, and snakes, and such things; and when the island had been overflowed a day or two, they got so tame, on account of being hungry, that you could paddle right up and put your hand on them if you wanted to; but not the snakes and turtles—they would slide off in the water. The ridge our cavern was in, was full of them. We could a had pets enough if we'd wanted them.

One night we catched a little section of a lumber raft—nine pine planks. It was twelve foot wide and about fifteen or sixteen foot long, and the top stood above water six or seven inches, a solid level floor. We could see saw-logs go by in the daylight, sometimes, but we let them go; we didn't show ourselves in daylight.

Another night, when we was up at the head of the island, just before daylight, here comes a frame house down, on the west side. She was a two-story, and tilted over, considerable. We paddled out and got aboard—clumb in at an up-stairs window. But it was too dark to see yet, so we made the canoe fast and set in her to wait for daylight.

The light begun to come before we got to the foot of the island. Then we looked in at the window. We could make out a bed, and a table, and two old chairs, and lots of things around about on the floor; and there was clothes hanging against the wall. There was something laying on the floor in the far corner that looked like a man. So Jim says:

"Hello, you!"

But it didn't budge. So I hollered again, and then Jim says:

"De man ain't asleep—he's dead. You hold still—I'll go en see."

He went and bent down and looked, and says:

"It's a dead man. Yes, indeedy; naked, too. He's ben shot in de back. I reck'n he's been dead two er three days. Come in, Huck, but doan' look at his face—it's too gashly."

I didn't look at him at all. Jim throwed some old rags over him, but he needn't done it; I didn't want to see him. There was heaps of old greasy cards scattered around over the floor, and old whiskey bottles, and a couple of masks made out of black cloth; and all over the walls was the ignorantest kind of words and pictures, made with charcoal. There was two old dirty calico dresses, and a sun-bonnet, and some women's under-clothes, hanging against the wall, and some men's clothing, too. We put the lot into the canoe; it might come good. There was a boy's old speckled straw hat on the floor; I took that too. And there was a bottle that had had milk in it; and it had a rag stopper for a baby to suck. We would a took the bottle, but it was broke. There was a seedy old chest, and an old hair trunk with the hinges broke. They stood open, but there warn't nothing left in them that was any account. The way things was scattered about, we reckoned the people left in a hurry and warn't fixed so as to carry off most of their stuff.

We got an old tin lantern, and a butcher knife without any handle, and a bran-new Barlow knife worth two bits in any store, and a lot of tallow candles, and a tin candlestick, and a gourd, and a tin cup, and a ratty old bed-quilt off the bed, and a reticule with needles and pins and beeswax and buttons and thread an all such truck in it, and a hatchet and some nails, and a fish-line as thick as my little finger, with some monstrous hooks on it, and a roll of buckskin, and a leather dog-collar, and a horse-shoe, and some vials of medicine that didn't have no label on them; and just as we was leaving I found a tolerable good curry-comb, and Jim he found a ratty old fiddle-bow, and a wooden leg. The straps was broke off of it, but barring that, it was a good enough leg, though it was too long for me and not long enough for Jim, and we couldn't find the other one, though we hunted all around.

And so, take it all around, we made a good haul. When we was ready to shove off, we was a quarter of a mile below the island, and it was pretty broad day; so I made Jim lay down in the canoe and cover up with the quilt, because if he set up, people could tell he was a nigger a good ways off. I paddled over to the Illinois shore, and drifted down most a half a mile doing it. I crept up the dead water under the bank, and hadn't no accidents and didn't see nobody. We got home all safe.

CHAPTER X

After breakfast I wanted to talk about the dead man and guess out how he come to be killed, but Jim didn't want to. He said it would fetch bad luck; and besides, he said, he might come and ha'nt us; he said a man that warn't buried was more likely to go a-ha'nting around than one that was planted and comfortable. That sounded pretty reasonable, so I didn't say no more; but I couldn't keep from studying over it and wishing I knowed who shot the man, and what they done it for.

We rummaged the clothes we'd got, and found eight dollars in silver sewed up in the lining of an old blanket overcoat. Jim said he reckoned the people in that house stole the coat, because if they'd a knowed the money was there they wouldn't a left it. I said I reckoned they killed him, too; but Jim didn't want to talk about that. I says:

"Now you think it's bad luck; but what did you say when I fetched in the snake-skin that I found on the top of the ridge day before yesterday? You said it was the worst bad luck in the world to touch a snake-skin with my hands. Well, here's your bad luck! We've raked in all this truck and eight dollars besides. I wish we could have some bad luck like this every day, Jim."

"Never you mind, honey, never you mind. Don't you git too peart. It's a-comin'. Mind I tell you, it's a-comin'."

It did come, too. It was a Tuesday that we had that talk. Well, after dinner Friday, we was laying around in the grass at the upper end of the ridge, and got out of tobacco. I went to the cavern to get some, and found a rattlesnake in there. I killed him, and curled him up on the foot of Jim's blanket, ever so natural, thinking there'd be some fun when Jim found him there. Well, by night I forgot all about the snake, and when Jim flung himself down on the blanket while I struck a light, the snake's mate was there, and bit him.

He jumped up yelling, and the first thing the light showed was the varmint curled up and ready for another spring. I laid him out in a second with a stick, and Jim grabbed pap's whiskey jug and begun to pour it down.

He was barefooted, and the snake bit him right on the heel. That all comes of my being such a fool as to not remember that whenever you leave a dead snake its mate always comes there and curls around it. Jim told me to chop off the snake's head and throw it away, and then skin the body and roast a piece of it. I done it, and he eat it and said it would help cure him. He made me take off the rattles and tie them around his wrist, too. He said that that would help. Then I slid out quiet and throwed the snakes clear away amongst the bushes; for I warn't going to let Jim find out it was all my fault, not if I could help it.

Jim sucked and sucked at the jug, and now and then he got out of his head and pitched around and yelled; but every time he come to himself he went to sucking at the jug again. His foot swelled up pretty big, and so did his leg; but by-and-by the drunk begun to come, and so I judged he was all right; but I'd druther been bit with a snake than pap's whiskey.

Jim was laid up for four days and nights. Then the swelling was all gone and he was around again. I made up my mind I wouldn't ever take aholt of a snake-skin again with my hands, now that I see what had come of it. Jim said he reckoned I would believe him next time. And he said that handling a snake-skin was such awful bad luck that maybe we hadn't got to the end of it yet. He said he druther see the new moon over his left shoulder as much as a thousand times than take up a snake-skin in his hand. Well, I was getting to feel that way myself, though I've always reckoned that looking at the new moon over your left shoulder is one of the carelessest and foolishest things a body can do. Old Hank Bunker done it once, and bragged about it; and in less than two years he got drunk and fell off of the shot tower and spread himself out so that he was just kind of a layer, as you may say; and they slid him edgeways between two barn doors for a coffin, and buried him so, so they say, but I didn't see it. Pap told me. But anyway, it all come of looking at the moon that way, like a fool.

Well, the days went along, and the river went down between its banks again; and about the first thing we done was to bait one of the big hooks with a skinned rabbit and set it and catch a cat-fish that was as big as a man, being six foot two inches long, and weighed over two hundred pounds. We couldn't handle him, of course; he would a flung us into Illinois. We just set there and watched him rip and tear around till he drowned. We found a brass button in his stomach, and a round ball, and lots of rubbage. We split the ball open with the hatchet, and there was a spool in it. Jim said he'd had it there a long time, to coat it over so and make a ball of it. It was as big a fish as was ever catched in the Mississippi, I reckon. Jim said he hadn't ever seen a bigger one. He would a been worth a good deal over at the village. They peddle out such a fish as that by the pound in the market house there; everybody buys some of him; his meat's as white as snow and makes a good fry.

Next morning I said it was getting slow and dull, and I wanted to get a stirring up, some way. I said I reckoned I would slip over the river and find out what was going on. Jim liked that notion; but he said I must go in the dark and look sharp. Then he studied it over and said, couldn't I put on some of them old things and dress up like a girl? That was a good notion, too. So we shortened up one of the calico gowns and I turned up my trowser-legs to my knees and got into it. Jim hitched it behind with the hooks, and it was a fair fit. I put on the sun-bonnet and tied it under my chin, and then for a body to look in and see my face was like looking down a joint of stove-pipe. Jim said nobody would know me, even in the daytime, hardly. I practiced around all day to get the hang of the things, and by-and-by I could do pretty well in them, only Jim said I didn't walk like a girl; and he said I must quit pulling up my gown to get at my britches pocket. I took notice, and done better.

I started up the Illinois shore in the canoe just after dark.

I started across to the town from a little below the ferry landing, and the drift of the current fetched me in at the bottom of the town. I tied up and started along the bank. There was a light burning in a little shanty that hadn't been lived in for a long time, and I wondered who had took up quarters there. I slipped up and peeped in at the window. There was a woman about forty year old in there, knitting by a candle that was on a pine table. I didn't know her face; she was a stranger, for you couldn't start a face in that town that I didn't know. Now this was lucky, because I was weakening; I was getting afraid I had come; people might know my voice and find me out. But if this woman had been in such a little town two days she could tell me all I wanted to know; so I knocked at the door, and made up my mind I wouldn't forget I was a girl.

CHAPTER XI

"Come in," says the woman, and I did. She says:

"Take a cheer."

I done it. She looked me all over with her shiny eyes, and says:

"What might your name be?"

"Sarah Williams."

"Where 'bouts do you live? In this neighborhood?"

"No'm. In Hookerville, seven mile below. I've walked all the way and I'm all tired out."

"Hungry, too, I reckon. I'll find you something."

"No'm, I ain't hungry. I was so hungry I had to stop two mile below here at a farm; so I ain't hungry no more. It's what makes me so late. My mother's down sick, and out of money and everything, and I come to tell my uncle Abner Moore. He lives at the upper end of the town, she says. I hain't ever been here before. Do you know him?"

"No; but I don't know everybody yet. I haven't lived here quite two weeks. It's a considerable ways to the upper end of the town. You better stay here all night. Take off your bonnet."

"No," I says, "I'll rest a while, I reckon, and go on. I ain't afeard of the dark."

She said she wouldn't let me go by myself, but her husband would be in by-and-by, maybe in an hour and a half, and she'd send him along with me. Then she got to talking about her husband, and about her relations up the river, and her relations down the river, and about how much better off they used to was, and how they didn't know but they'd made a mistake coming to our town, instead of letting well alone—and so on and so on, till I was afeard *I* had made a mistake coming to her to find out what was going on in town; but by-and-by she dropped onto pap and the murder, and then I was pretty willing to let her clatter right along. She told about me and Tom Sawyer finding the six thousand dollars (only she got it ten) and all about pap and what a hard lot he was, and what a hard lot I was, and at last she got down to where I was murdered. I says:

"Who done it? We've heard considerable about these goings on, down in Hookerville, but we don't know who 'twas that killed Huck Finn."

"Well, I reckon there's a right smart chance of people *here* that 'd like to know who killed him. Some thinks old Finn done it himself."

"No—is that so?"

"Most everybody thought it at first. He'll never know how nigh he come to getting lynched. But before night they changed around and judged it was done by a runaway nigger named Jim."

"Why *he*—"

I stopped. I reckoned I better keep still. She run on, and never noticed I had put in at all.

"The nigger run off the very night Huck Finn was killed. So there's a reward out for him—three hundred dollars. And there's a reward out for old Finn too—two hundred dollars. You see, he come to town the morning after the murder, and told about it, and was out with 'em on the ferry-boat hunt, and right away after he up and left. Before night they wanted to lynch him, but he was gone, you see. Well, next day they found out the nigger was gone; they found out he hadn't ben seen sence ten o'clock the night the murder was done. So then they put it on him, you see, and while they was full of it, next day back comes old Finn and went boo-hooing to Judge Thatcher to get money to hunt for the nigger all over Illinois with. The judge give him some, and that evening he got drunk and was around till after midnight with a couple of mighty hard looking strangers, and then went off with them. Well, he hain't come back sence, and they ain't looking for him back till this thing blows over a little, for people thinks now that he killed his boy and fixed things so folks would think robbers done it, and then he'd get Huck's money without having to bother a long time with a lawsuit. People do say he warn't any too good to do it. Oh, he's sly, I reckon. If he don't come back for a year, he'll be all right. You can't prove anything on him, you know; everything will be quieted down then, and he'll walk into Huck's money as easy as nothing."

"Yes, I reckon so, 'm. I don't see nothing in the way of it. Has everybody quit thinking the nigger done it?"

"Oh, no, not everybody. A good many thinks he done it. But they'll get the nigger pretty soon, now, and maybe they can scare it out of him."

"Why, are they after him yet?"

"Well, you're innocent, ain't you! Does three hundred dollars lay round every day for people to pick up? Some folks thinks the nigger ain't far from here. I'm one of them—but I hain't talked it around. A few days ago I was talking with an old couple that lives next door in the log shanty, and they happened to say hardly anybody ever goes to that island over yonder that they call Jackson's Island. Don't anybody live there? says I. No, nobody, says they. I didn't say any more, but I done some thinking. I was pretty near certain I'd seen smoke over there, about the head of the island, a day or two before that, so I says to myself, like as not that nigger's hiding over there; anyway, says I, it's worth the trouble to give the place a hunt. I hain't seen any smoke sence, so I reckon maybe he's gone, if it was him; but husband's going over to see—him and another man. He was gone up the river; but he got back to-day and I told him as soon as he got here two hours ago."

I had got so uneasy I couldn't set still. I had to do something with my hands; so I took up a needle off the table and went to threading it. My hands shook, and I was making a bad job of it. When the woman stopped talking, I looked up, and she was looking at me pretty curious, and smiling a little. I put down the needle and let on to be interested—and I was, too—and says:

"Three hundred dollars is a power of money. I wish my mother could get it. Is your husband going over there tonight?"

"Oh, yes. He went up town with the man I was telling you of, to get a boat and see if they could borrow another gun. They'll go over after midnight."

"Couldn't they see better if they was to wait till daytime?"

"Yes. And couldn't the nigger see better, too? After midnight he'll likely be asleep, and they can slip around through the woods and hunt up his camp fire all the better for the dark, if he's got one."

"I didn't think of that."

The woman kept looking at me pretty curious, and I didn't feel a bit comfortable. Pretty soon she says:

"What did you say your name was, honey?"

"M—Mary Williams."

Somehow it didn't seem to me that I said it was Mary before, so I didn't look up; seemed to me I said it was Sarah; so I felt sort of cornered, and was afeared maybe I was looking it, too. I wished the woman would say something more; the longer she set still, the uneasier I was. But now she says:

"Honey, I thought you said it was Sarah when you first come in?"

"Oh, yes'm, I did. Sarah Mary Williams. Sarah's my first name. Some calls me Sarah, some calls me Mary."

"Oh, that's the way of it?"

"Yes'm."

I was feeling better, then, but I wished I was out of there, anyway. I couldn't look up yet.

Well, the woman fell to talking about how hard times was, and how poor they had to live, and how the rats was as free as if they owned the place, and so forth, and so on, and then I got easy again. She was right about the rats. You'd see one stick his nose out of a hole in the corner every little while. She said she had to have things handy to throw at them when she was alone, or they wouldn't give her no peace. She showed me a bar of lead, twisted up into a knot, and said she was a good shot with it generly, but she'd wrenched her arm a day or two ago, and didn't know whether she could throw true, now. But she watched for a chance, and directly she banged away at a rat, but she missed him wide, and said "Ouch!" it hurt her arm so. Then she told me to try for the next one. I wanted to be getting away before the old man got back, but of course I didn't let on. I got the thing, and the first rat that showed his nose I let drive, and if he'd a stayed where he was he'd a been a tolerable sick rat. She said that that was first-rate, and she reckoned I would hive the next one. She went and got the lump of lead and fetched it back and brought along a hank of yarn, which she wanted me to help her with. I held up my two hands and put the hank over them and went on talking about her and her husband's matters. But she broke off to say:

"Keep your eye on the rats. You better have the lead in your lap, handy."

So she dropped the lump into my lap, just at that moment, and I clapped my legs together on it and she went on talking. But only about a minute. Then she took off the hank and looked me straight in the face, but very pleasant, and says:

"Come, now—what's your real name?"

"Wh-what, mum?"

"What's your real name? Is it Bill, or Tom, or Bob?—or what is it?"

I reckon I shook like a leaf, and I didn't know hardly what to do. But I says:

"Please to don't poke fun at a poor girl like me, mum. If I'm in the way, here, I'll—"

"No, you won't. Set down and stay where you are. I ain't going to hurt you, and I ain't going to tell on you, nuther. You just tell me your secret, and trust me. I'll keep it; and what's more, I'll help you. So'll my old man, if you want him to. You see, you're a runaway 'prentice—that's all. It ain't anything. There ain't any harm in it. You've been treated bad, and you made up your mind to cut. Bless you, child, I wouldn't tell on you. Tell me all about it, now—that's a good boy."

So I said it wouldn't be no use to try to play it any longer, and I would just make a clean breast and tell her everything, but she mustn't go back on her promise. Then I told her my father and mother was dead, and the law had bound me out to a mean old farmer in the country thirty mile back from the river, and he treated me so bad I couldn't stand it no longer; he went away to be gone a couple of days, and so I took my chance and stole some of his daughter's old clothes, and cleared out, and I had been three nights coming the thirty miles; I traveled nights, and hid day-times and slept, and the bag of bread and meat I carried from home lasted me all the way and I had plenty. I said I believed my uncle Abner Moore would take care of me, and so that was why I struck out for this town of Goshen.

"Goshen, child? This ain't Goshen. This is St. Petersburg. Goshen's ten mile further up the river. Who told you this was Goshen?"

"Why, a man I met at day-break this morning, just as I was going to turn into the woods for my regular sleep. He told me when the roads forked I must take the right hand, and five mile would fetch me to Goshen."

"He was drunk I reckon. He told you just exactly wrong."

"Well, he did act like he was drunk, but it ain't no matter now. I got to be moving along. I'll fetch Goshen before day-light."

"Hold on a minute. I'll put you up a snack to eat. You might want it."

So she put me up a snack, and says:

"Say—when a cow's laying down, which end of her gets up first? Answer us prompt, now—don't stop to study over it. Which end gets up first?"

"The hind end, mum."

"Well, then, a horse?"

"The for'rard end, mum."

"Which side of a tree does the most moss grow on?"

"North side."

"If fifteen cows is browsing on a hillside, how many of them eats with their heads pointed in the same direction?"

"The whole fifteen, mum."

"Well, I reckon you *have* lived in the country. I thought maybe you was trying to hocus me again. What's your real name, now?"

"George Peters, mum."

"Well, try to remember it, George. Don't forget and tell me it's Elexander before you go, and then get out by saying it's George-Elexander when I catch you. And don't go about women in that old calico. You do a girl tolerable poor, but you might fool men, maybe. Bless you, child, when you set out to thread a needle, don't hold the thread still and fetch the needle up to it; hold the needle still and poke the thread at it—that's the way a woman most always does; but a man always does 'tother way. And when you throw at a rat or anything, hitch yourself up a tip-toe, and fetch your hand up over your head as awkward as you can, and miss your rat about six or seven foot. Throw stiff-armed from the shoulder, like there was a pivot there for it to turn on—like a girl; not from the wrist and elbow, with your arm out to one side, like a boy. And mind you, when a girl tries to catch anything in her lap, she throws her knees apart; she don't clap them together, the way you did when you catched the lump of lead. Why, I spotted you for a boy when you was threading the needle; and I contrived the other things just to make certain. Now trot along to your uncle, Sarah Mary Williams George Elexander Peters, and if you get into trouble you send word to Mrs. Judith Loftus, which is me, and I'll do what I can to get you out of it. Keep the river road, all the way, and next time you tramp, take shoes and socks with you. The river road's a rocky one, and your feet 'll be in a condition when you get to Goshen, I reckon."

I went up the bank about fifty yards, and then I doubled on my tracks and slipped back to where my canoe was, a good piece below the house. I jumped in and was off in a hurry. I went up stream far enough to make the head of the island, and then started across. I took off the sun-bonnet, for I didn't want no blinders on, then. When I was about the middle, I hear the clock begin to strike; so I stops and listens; the sound come faint over the water, but clear—eleven. When I struck the head of the island I never waited to blow, though I was most winded, but I shoved right into the timber where my old camp used to be, and started a good fire there on a high-and-dry spot.

Then I jumped in the canoe and dug out for our place a mile

and a half below, as hard as I could go. I landed, and slopped through the timber and up the ridge and into the cavern. There Jim laid, sound asleep on the ground. I roused him out and says:

"Git up and hump yourself, Jim! There ain't a minute to lose. They're after us!"

Jim never asked no questions, he never said a word; but the way he worked for the next half an hour showed about how he was scared. By that time everything we had in the world was on our raft and she was ready to be shoved out from the willow cove where she was hid. We put out the camp fire at the cavern the first thing, and didn't show a candle outside after that.

I took the canoe out from shore a little piece and took a look, but if there was a boat around I couldn't see it, for stars and shadows ain't good to see by. Then we got out the raft and slipped along down in the shade, past the foot of the island dead still, never saying a word.

CHAPTER XII

It must a been close onto one o'clock when we got below the island at last, and the raft did seem to go mighty slow. If a boat was to come along, we was going to take to the canoe and break for the Illinois shore; and it was well a boat didn't come, for we hadn't ever thought to put the gun into the canoe, or a fishing-line or anything to eat. We was in ruther too much of a sweat to think of so many things. It warn't good judgment to put *everything* on the raft.

If the men went to the island, I just expect they found the camp fire I built, and watched it all night for Jim to come. Anyways, they stayed away from us, and if my building the fire never fooled them it warn't no fault of mine. I played it as low-down on them as I could.

When the first streak of day begun to show, we tied up to a tow-head in a big bend on the Illinois side, and hacked off cotton-wood branches with the hatchet and covered up the raft with them so she looked like there had been a cave-in in the bank there. A tow-head is a sand-bar that has cotton-woods on it as thick as harrow-teeth.

We had mountains on the Missouri shore and heavy timber on the Illinois side, and the channel was down the Missouri shore at that place, so we warn't afraid of anybody running across us. We laid there all day and watched the rafts and steamboats spin down the Missouri shore, and up-bound steamboats fight the big river in the middle. I told Jim all about the time I had jabbering with that woman; and Jim said she was a smart one, and if she was to start after us herself *she* wouldn't set down and watch a camp fire—no, sir, she'd fetch a dog. Well, then, I said, why couldn't she tell her husband to fetch a dog? Jim said he bet she did think of it by the time the men was ready to start, and he believed they must a gone up town to get a dog and so they lost all that time, or else we wouldn't be here on a tow-head sixteen or seventeen mile below the village—no, indeedy, we would be in that same old town again. So I said I didn't care what was the reason they didn't get us, as long as they didn't.

When it was beginning to come on dark, we poked our heads out of the cottonwood thicket and looked up, and down, and across; nothing in sight; so Jim took up some of the top planks of the raft and built a snug wigwam to get under in blazing weather and rainy, and to keep the things dry. Jim made a floor for the wigwam, and raised it a foot or more above the level of the raft, so now the blankets and all the traps was out of the reach of steamboat waves. Right in the middle of the wigwam we made a layer of dirt about five or six inches deep with a frame around it for to hold it to its place; this was to build a fire on in sloppy weather or chilly; the wigwam would keep it from being seen. We made an extra steering oar, too, because one of the others might get broke, on a snag or something. We fixed up a short forked stick to hang the old lantern on; because we must always light the lantern whenever we see a steamboat coming down stream, to keep from getting run over; but we wouldn't have to light it for upstream boats unless we see we was in what they call a "crossing;" for the river was pretty high yet, very low banks being still a little under water; so up-bound boats didn't always run the channel, but hunted easy water.

This second night we run between seven and eight hours, with a current that was making over four mile an hour. We catched fish, and talked, and we took a swim now and then to keep off sleepiness. It was kind of solemn, drifting down the big still river, laying on our backs looking up at the stars, and we didn't ever feel like talking loud, and it warn't often that we laughed, only a little kind of low chuckle. We had mighty good weather, as a general thing, and nothing ever happened to us at all, that night, nor the next, nor the next.

Every night we passed towns, some of them away up on black hillsides, nothing but just a shiny bed of lights, not a house could you see. The fifth night we passed St. Louis, and it was like the whole world lit up. In St. Petersburg they used to say there was twenty or thirty thousand people in St. Louis, but I never believed it till I see that wonderful spread of lights at two o'clock that still night. There warn't a sound there; everybody was asleep.

Every night, now, I used to slip ashore, towards ten o'clock, at some little village, and buy ten or fifteen cents' worth of meal or bacon or other stuff to eat; and sometimes I lifted a chicken that warn't roosting comfortable, and took him along. Pap always said, take a chicken when you get a chance, because if you don't want him yourself you can easy find somebody that does, and a good deed ain't ever forgot. I never see pap when he didn't want the chicken himself, but that is what he used to say, anyway.

Mornings, before daylight, I slipped into corn fields and borrowed a watermelon, or a mushmelon, or a punkin, or some new corn, or things of that kind. Pap always said it warn't no harm to borrow things, if you was meaning to pay them back, sometime; but the widow said it warn't anything but a soft name for stealing, and no decent body would do it. Jim said he reckoned the widow was partly right and pap was partly right; so the best way would be for us to pick out two or three things from the list and say we wouldn't borrow them any more—then he reckoned it wouldn't do no harm to borrow the others.

So we talked it over all one night, drifting along down the river, trying to make up our minds whether to drop the watermelons, or the cantelopes, or the mushmelons, or what. But towards daylight we got it all settled satisfactory, and concluded to drop crabapples and p'simmons. We warn't feeling just right, before that, but it was all comfortable now. I was glad the way it come out, too, because crabapples ain't ever good, and the p'simmons wouldn't be ripe for two or three months yet.

We shot a water-fowl, now and then, that got up too early in the morning or didn't go to bed early enough in the evening. Take it all around, we lived pretty high.

The fifth night below St. Louis we had a big storm after midnight, with a power of thunder and lightning, and the rain poured down in a solid sheet. We stayed in the wigwam and let the raft take care of itself. When the lightning glared out we could see a big straight river ahead, and high rocky bluffs on both sides. By-and-by says I, "Hel-*lo,* Jim, looky yonder!" It was a steamboat that had killed herself on a rock. We was drifting straight down for her. The lightning showed her very distinct. She was leaning over, with part of her upper deck above water, and you could see every little chimbly-guy clean and clear, and a chair by the big bell, with an old slouch hat hanging on the back of it when the flashes come.

Well, it being away in the night, and stormy, and all so mysterious-like, I felt just the way any other boy would a felt when I see that wreck laying there so mournful and lonesome in the middle of the river. I wanted to get aboard of her and slink around a little, and see what there was there. So I says:

"Le's land on her, Jim."

But Jim was dead set against it, at first. He says:

"I doan' want to go fool'n 'long er no wrack. We's doin blame' well, en we better let blame' well alone, as de good book says. Like as not dey's a watchman on dat wrack."

"Watchman your grandmother," I says; "there ain't nothing to watch but the texas and the pilot-house; and do you reckon anybody's going to resk his life for a texas and a pilot-house such a night as this, when it's likely to break up and wash off down the river any minute?" Jim couldn't say nothing to that, so he didn't try. "And besides," I says, "we might borrow something worth having, out of the captain's stateroom. Seegars, *I* bet you—and cost five cents apiece, solid cash. Steamboat captains is always rich, and get sixty dollars a month, and *they* don't care a cent what a thing costs, you know, long as they want it. Stick a candle in your pocket; I can't rest, Jim, till we give her a rummaging. Do you reckon Tom Sawyer would ever go by this thing? Not for pie, he wouldn't. He'd call it an adventure—that's what he'd call it; and he'd land on that wreck if it was his last act. And wouldn't he throw style into it?—wouldn't he spread himself, nor nothing? Why, you'd think it was Christopher C'lumbus discovering Kingdom-Come. I wish Tom Sawyer *was* here."

Jim he grumbled a little, but give in. He said we mustn't talk any more than we could help, and then talk mighty low. The lightning showed us the wreck again, just in time, and we fetched the starboard derrick, and made fast there.

The deck was high out, here. We went sneaking down the slope of it to labboard, in the dark, towards the texas, feeling our way slow with our feet, and spreading our hands out to fend off the guys, for it was so dark we couldn't see no sign of them. Pretty soon we struck the forward end of the skylight, and clumb onto it; and the next step fetched us in front of the captain's door, which was open, and by Jimminy, away down through the texas-hall we see a light! and all in the same second we seem to hear low voices in yonder!

Jim whispered and said he was feeling powerful sick, and told me to come along. I says, all right; and was going to start for the raft; but just then I heard a voice wail out and say:

"Oh, please don't, boys; I swear I won't ever tell!"

Another voice said, pretty loud:

"It's a lie, Jim Turner. You've acted this way before. You always want more'n your share of the truck, and you've always got it, too, because you've swore 't if you didn't you'd tell. But this time you've said it jest one time too many. You're the meanest, treacherousest hound in this country."

By this time Jim was gone for the raft. I was just a-biling with curiosity; and I says to myself, Tom Sawyer wouldn't back out now, and so I won't either; I'm agoing to see what's going on here. So I dropped on my hands and knees, in the little passage, and crept aft in the dark, till there warn't but about one stateroom betwixt me and the cross-hall of the texas. Then, in there I see a man stretched on the floor and tied hand and foot, and two men standing over him, and one of them had a dim lantern in his hand, and the other one had a pistol. This one kept pointing the pistol at the man's head on the floor and saying—

"I'd *like* to! And I orter, too, a mean skunk!"

The man on the floor would shrivel up, and say: "Oh, please don't, Bill—I hain't ever goin to tell."

And every time he said that, the man with the lantern would laugh, and say:

"'Deed you *ain't!* You never said no truer thing 'n that, you bet you." And once he said: "Hear him beg! and yit if we hadn't got the best of him and tied him, he'd a killed us both. And what *for?* Jist for noth'n. Jist because we stood on our *rights*—that's what for. But I lay you ain't agoin' to threaten nobody any more, Jim Turner. Put *up* that pistol, Bill."

Bill says:

"I don't want to, Jake Packard. I'm for killin' him—and didn't he kill old Hatfield jist the same way—and don't he deserve it?"

"But I don't *want* him killed, and I've got my reasons for it."

"Bless yo' heart for them words, Jake Packard! I'll never forgit you, long's I live!" says the man on the floor, sort of blubbering.

Packard didn't take no notice of that, but hung up his lantern on a nail, and started towards where I was, there in the dark, and motioned to Bill to come. I crawfished as fast as I could, about two yards, but the boat slanted so that I couldn't make very good time; so to keep from getting run over and catched I crawled into a stateroom on the upper side. The man come a-pawing along in the dark, and when Packard got to my stateroom, he says:

"Here—come in here."

And in he come, and Bill after him. But before they got in, I was up in the upper berth, cornered, and sorry I come. Then they stood there, with their hands on the ledge of the berth, and talked. I couldn't see them, but I could tell where they was, by the whisky they'd been having. I was glad I didn't drink whisky; but it wouldn't made much difference, anyway, because most of the time they couldn't a treed me because I didn't breathe. I was too scared. And besides, a body *couldn't* breathe, and hear such talk. They talked low and earnest. Bill wanted to kill Turner. He says:

"He's said he'll tell, and he will. If we was to give both our shares to him *now,* it wouldn't make no difference after the row, and the way we've served him. Shore's you're born, he'll turn State's evidence; now you hear *me.* I'm for putting him out of his troubles."

"So'm I," says Packard, very quiet.

"Blame it, I'd sorter begun to think you wasn't. Well, then, that's all right. Les' go and do it."

"Hold on a minute; I hain't had my say yit. You listen to me. Shooting's good, but there's quieter ways if the thing's *got* to be done. But what *I* say, is this; it ain't good sense to go court'n around after a halter, if you can git at what you're up to in some way that's jist as good and at the same time don't bring you into no resks. Ain't that so?"

"You bet it is. But how you goin' to manage it this time?"

"Well, my idea is this: we'll rustle around and gether up whatever pickins we've overlooked in the staterooms, and shove for shore and hide the truck. Then we'll wait. Now I say it ain't agoin' to be more 'n two hours befo' this wrack breaks up and washes off down the river. See? He'll be drownded, and won't have nobody to blame for it but his own self. I reckon that's a considerable sight better'n killin' of him. I'm unfavorable to killin' a man as long as you can git around it; it ain't good sense, it ain't good morals. Ain't I right?"

"Yes—I reck'n you are. But s'pose she *don't* break up and wash off?"

"Well, we can wait the two hours, anyway, and see, can't we?"

"All right, then; come along."

So they started, and I lit out, all in a cold sweat, and scrambled forward. It was dark as pitch there; but I said in a kind of a coarse whisper, "Jim!" and he answered up, right at my elbow, with a sort of a moan, and I says:

"Quick, Jim, it ain't no time for fooling around and moaning; there's a gang of murderers in yonder, and if we don't hunt up their boat and set her drifting down the river so these fellows can't get away from the wreck, there's one of 'em going to be in a bad fix. But if we find their boat we can put *all* of 'em in a bad fix—for the Sheriff 'll get 'em. Quick—hurry! I'll hunt the labboard side, you hunt the stabboard. You start at the raft, and—"

"Oh, my lordy, lordy! *Raf'?* Dey ain' no raf' no mo', she done broke loose en gone!—'en here we is!"

CHAPTER XIII

Well, I catched my breath and most fainted. Shut up on a wreck with such a gang as that! But it warn't no time to be sentimentering. We'd *got* to find that boat, now—had to have it for ourselves. So we went a-quaking and shaking down the stabboard side, and slow work it was, too—seemed a week before we got to the stern. No sign of a boat. Jim said he didn't believe he could go any further—so scared he hadn't hardly any strength left, he said. But I said come on, if we get left on this wreck, we are in a fix, sure. So on we prowled, again. We struck for the stern of the texas, and found it, and then scrabbled along forwards on the skylight, hanging on from shutter to shutter, for the edge of the skylight was in the water. When we got pretty close to the cross-hall door, there was the skiff, sure enough! I could just barely see her. I felt ever so thankful. In another second I would a been aboard of her; but just then the door opened. One of the men stuck his head out, only about a couple of foot from me, and I thought I was gone; but he jerked it in again, and says:

"Heave that blame lantern out o' sight, Bill!"

He flung a bag of something into the boat, and then got in himself, and set down. It was Packard. Then Bill *he* come out and got in. Packard says, in a low voice:

"All ready—shove off!"

I couldn't hardly hang onto the shutters, I was so weak. But Bill says:

"Hold on—'d you go through him?"

"No. Didn't you?"

"No. So he's got his share o' the cash, yet."

"Well, then, come along—no use to take truck and leave money."

"Say—won't he suspicion what we're up to?"

"Maybe he won't. But we got to have it anyway. Come along."

So they got out and went in.

The door slammed to, because it was on the careened side; and in a half second I was in the boat, and Jim come a tumbling after me. I out with my knife and cut the rope and away we went!

We didn't touch an oar, and we didn't speak nor whisper, nor hardly even breathe. We went gliding swift along, dead silent, past the tip of the paddlebox, and past the stern; then in a second or two more we was a hundred yards below the wreck, and the darkness soaked her up, every last sign of her, and we was safe, and knowed it.

When we was three or four hundred yards down stream, we see the lantern show like a little spark at the texas door, for a second, and we knowed by that that the rascals had missed their boat, and was beginning to understand that they was in just as much trouble, now, as Jim Turner was.

Then Jim manned the oars, and we took out after our raft. Now was the first time that I begun to worry about the men—I reckon I hadn't had time to before. I begun to think how dreadful it was, even for murderers, to be in such a fix. I says to myself, there ain't no telling but I might come to be a murderer myself, yet, and then how would *I* like it? So says I to Jim:

"The first light we see, we'll land a hundred yards below it or above it, in a place where it's a good hiding-place for you and the skiff, and then I'll go and fix up some kind of a yarn, and get somebody to go for that gang and get them out of their scrape, so they can be hung when their time comes."

But that idea was a failure; for pretty soon it begun to storm again, and this time worse than ever. The rain poured down, and never a light showed; everybody in bed, I reckon. We boomed along down the river, watching for lights and watching for our raft. After a long time the rain let up, but the clouds staid, and the lightning kept whimpering, and by-and-by a flash showed us a black thing ahead, floating, and we made for it.

It was the raft, and mighty glad was we to get aboard of it again. We seen a light, now, away down to the right, on shore. So I said I would go for it. The skiff was half full of plunder which that gang had stole, there on the wreck. We hustled it onto the raft in a pile, and I told Jim to float along down, and show a light when he judged he had gone about two mile, and keep it burning till I come; then I manned my oars an shoved for the light. As I got down towards it, three or four more showed—up on a hillside. It was a village. I closed in above the shore-light, and laid on my oars and floated. As I went by, I see it was a lantern hanging on the jackstaff of a double-hull ferry-boat. I skimmed around for the watchman, a-wondering whereabouts he slept; and by-and-by I found him roosting on the bitts, forward, with his head down between his knees. I give his shoulder two or three little shoves, and begun to cry.

He stirred up, in a kind of a startlish way; but when he see it was only me, he took a good gap, and stretch, and then he says:

"Hello, what's up? Don't cry, bub. What's the trouble?"

I says:

"Pap, and mam, and sis, and—"

Then I broke down. He says:

"Oh, dang it, now, *don't* take on so, we all has to have our troubles and this'n 'll come out all right. What's the matter with 'em?"

"They're—they're—are you the watchman of the boat?"

"Yes," he says, kind of pretty-well satisfied like. "I'm the captain and the owner, and the mate, and the pilot, and watchman, and head deck-hand; and sometimes I'm the freight and passengers. I ain't as rich as old Jim Hornback, and I can't be so blame' generous and good to Tom, Dick and Harry as what he is, and slam around money the way he does; but I've told him a many a time 't I wouldn't trade places with him; for, says I, a sailor's life's the life for me, and I'm derned if *I'd* live two mile out o' town, where there ain't nothing ever goin' on, not for all his spondulicks and as much more on top of it. Says I—"

I broke in and says:

"They're in an awful peck of trouble, and—"

"*Who* is?"

"Why, pap, and mam, and sis, and Miss Hooker; and if you'd take your ferry-boat and go up there—"

"Up where? Where are they?"

"On the wreck."

"What wreck?"

"Why, there ain't but one."

"What, you don't mean the *Walter Scott?*"

"Yes."

"Good land! what are they doin' *there,* for gracious sakes?"

"Well, they didn't go there a-purpose."

"I bet they didn't! Why, great goodness, there ain't no chance for 'em if they don't get off mighty quick! Why, how in the nation did they ever git into such a scrape?"

"Easy enough. Miss Hooker was a-visiting, up there to the town—"

"Yes, Booth's Landing—go on."

"She was a-visiting, there at Booth's Landing, and just in the edge of the evening she started over with her nigger woman in the horse-ferry, to stay all night at her friend's house, Miss What-you-may-call-her, I disremember her name, and they lost their steering-oar, and swung around and went a-floating down, stern-first, about two mile, and saddle-baggsed on the wreck, and the ferry man and the nigger woman and the horses was all lost, but Miss Hooker she made a grab and got aboard the wreck. Well, about an hour after dark, we come along down in our trading-scow, and it was so dark we didn't notice the wreck till we was right on it; and so *we* saddle-baggsed; but all of us was saved but Bill Whipple—and oh, he *was* the best cretur!—I most wish't it had been me, I do."

"My George! It's the beatenest thing I ever struck. And *then* what did you all do?"

"Well, we hollered and took on, but it's so wide there, we couldn't make nobody hear. So pap said somebody got to get ashore and get help somehow. I was the only one that could swim, so I made a dash for it, and Miss Hooker she said if I didn't strike help sooner, come here and hunt up her uncle, and he'd fix the thing. I made the land about a mile below, and been fooling along ever since, trying to get people to do something, but they said, 'What, in such a night and such a current? there ain't no sense in it; go for the steam-ferry.' Now if you'll go, and—"

"By Jackson, I'd *like* to, and blame it I don't know but I will; but who in the dingnation's agoin' to *pay* for it? Do you reckon your pap—"

"Why *that's* all right. Miss Hooker she told me, *particular,* that her uncle Hornback—"

"Great guns! is *he* her uncle? Looky here, you break for that light over yonder-way, and turn out west when you git there, and about a quarter of a mile out you'll come to the tavern; tell 'em to dart you out to Jim Hornback's and he'll foot the bill. And don't you fool around any, because he'll want to know the news. Tell him I'll have his niece all safe before he can get to town. Hump yourself, now; I'm agoing up around the corner here, to roust out my engineer."

I struck for the light, but as soon as he turned the corner I went back and got into my skiff and bailed her out and then pulled up shore in the easy water about six hundred yards, and tucked myself in among some woodboats; for I couldn't rest easy till I could see the ferry-boat start. But take it all around, I was feeling ruther comfortable on accounts of taking all this trouble for that gang, for not many would a done it. I wished the widow knowed about it. I judged she would be proud of me for helping these rapscallions, because rapscallions and dead beats is the kind the widow and good people takes the most interest in.

Well, before long, here comes the wreck, dim and dusky, sliding along down! A kind of cold shiver went through me, and then I struck out for her. She was very deep, and I see in a minute there warn't much chance for anybody being alive in her. I pulled all around her and hollered a little, but there wasn't any answer; all dead still. I felt a little bit heavy-hearted about the gang, but not much, for I reckoned if they could stand it, I could.

Then here comes the ferry-boat; so I shoved for the middle of the river on a long down-stream slant; and when I judged I was out of eye-reach, I laid on my oars, and looked back and see her go and smell around the wreck for Miss Hooker's remainders, because the captain would know her uncle Hornback would want them; and then pretty soon the ferry-boat give it up and went for shore, and I laid into my work and went a-booming down the river.

It did seem a powerful long time before Jim's light showed up; and when it did show, it looked like it was a thousand mile off. By the time I got there the sky was beginning to get a little gray in the east; so we struck for an island, and hid the raft, and sunk the skiff, and turned in and slept like dead people.

CHAPTER XIV

By-an-by, when we got up, we turned over the truck the gang had stole off of the wreck, and found boots, and blankets, and clothes, and all sorts of other things, and a lot of books, and a spyglass, and three boxes of seegars. We hadn't ever been this rich before, in neither of our lives. The seegars was prime. We laid off all the afternoon in the woods talking, and me reading the books, and having a general good time. I told Jim all about what happened inside the wreck, and at the ferry-boat; and I said these kinds of things was adventures; but he said he didn't want no more adventures. He said that when I went in the texas and he crawled back to get on the raft and found her gone, he nearly died; because he judged it was all up with *him*, anyway it could be fixed; for if he didn't get saved he would get drownded; and if he did get saved, whoever saved him would send him back home so as to get the reward, and then Miss Watson would sell him South, sure. Well, he was right; he was most always right; he had an uncommon level head, for a nigger.

I read considerable to Jim about kings, and dukes, and earls, and such, and how gaudy they dressed, and how much style they put on, and called each other your majesty, and your grace, and your lordship, and so on, 'stead of mister; and Jim's eyes bugged out, and he was interested. He says:

"I didn' know dey was so many un um. I hain't hearn 'bout none un um, skasely, but ole King Sollermun, onless you counts dem kings dat's in a pack er k'yards. How much do a king git?"

"Get?" I says; "why, they get a thousand dollars a month if they want it; they can have just as much as they want; everything belongs to them."

"*Ain'* dat gay? En what dey got to do, Huck?"

"*They* don't do nothing! Why how you talk. They just set around."

"No—is dat so?"

"Of course it is. They just set around. Except maybe when there 's a war; then they go to the war. But other times they just lazy around; or go hawking—just hawking and sp— Sh!—d' you hear a noise?"

We skipped out and looked; but it warn't nothing but the flutter of a steamboat's wheel, away down coming around the point; so we come back.

"Yes," says I, "and other times, when things is dull, they fuss with the parlyment; and if everybody don't go just so he whacks their heads off. But mostly they hang round the harem."

"Roun' de which?"

"Harem."

"What's de harem?"

"The place where he keeps his wives. Don't you know about the harem? Solomon had one; he had about a million wives."

"Why, yes, dat's so; I—I'd done forgot it. A harem's a bo'd'n-house, I reck'n. Mos' likely dey has rackety times in de nussery. En I reck'n de wives quarrels considable; en dat 'crease de racket. Yit dey say Sollermun de wises' man dat ever live'. I doan' take no stock in dat. Bekase why: would a wise man want to live in de mids' er sich a blimblammin' all de time? No—'deed he wouldn't. A wise man 'ud take en buil' a biler-factry; en den he sould shet *down* de biler-factry when he want to res'."

"Well, but he *was* the wisest man, anyway; because the widow she told me so, her own self."

"I doan k'yer what de widder say, he *warn't* no wise man, nuther. He had some er de dad-fetchedes' ways I ever see. Does you know 'bout dat chile dat he 'uz gwyne to chop in two?"

"Yes, the widow told me all about it."

"*Well,* den! Warn' dat de beatenes' notion in de worl'? You jes' take en look at it a minute. Dah's de stump, dah—dat's one er de women; heah's you—dat's de yuther one; I's Sollermun; en dish-yer dollar bill's de chile. Bofe un you claims it. What does I do? Does I shin aroun' mongs' de neighbors en fine out which un you de bill *do* b'long to, en han' it over to de right one, all safe en soun', de way dat anybody dat had any gumption would? No—I take en whack de bill in *two,* en give half un it to you, en de yuther half to de yuther woman. Dat's de way Sollermun was gwyne to do wid de chile. Now I want to ast you: what's de use er dat half a bill?—can't buy noth'n wid it. En what use is a half a chile? I would'n give a dern for a million un um."

"But hang it, Jim, you've clean missed the point—blame it, you've missed it a thousand mile."

"Who? Me? Go 'long. Doan' talk to *me* 'bout yo' pints. I reck'n I knows sense when I sees it; en dey ain' no sense in sich doin's as dat. De 'spute warn't 'bout half a chile, de 'spute was 'bout a whole chile; en de man dat think he kin settle a 'spute 'bout a whole chile wid a half a chile, doan' know enough to come in out'n de rain. Doan' talk to me 'bout Sollermun, Huck, I knows him by de back."

"But I tell you you don't get the point."

"Blame de pint! I reck'n I knows what I knows. En mine you, de *real* pint is down furder—it's down deeper. It lays in de way Sollermun was raised. You take a man dat's got on'y one er two chillen; is dat man gwyne to be waseful o' chillen? No, he ain't; he can't 'ford it. *He* know how to value 'em. But you take a man dat's got 'bout five million chillen runnin' roun' de house, en it's diffunt. *He* as soon chop a chile in two as a cat. Dey's plenty mo'. A chile er two, mo' er less, warn't no consekens to Sollermun, dad fetch him!"

I never see such a nigger. If he got a notion in his head once, there warn't no getting it out again. He was the most down on Solomon of any nigger I ever see. So I went to talking about other kings, and let Solomon slide. I told about Louis Sixteenth that got his head cut off in France long time ago; and about his little boy the dolphin, that would a been a king, but they took and shut him up in jail, and some say he died there.

"Po' little chap."

"But some says he got out and got away, and come to America."

"Dat's good! But he'll be pooty lonesome—dey ain' no kings here, is dey, Huck?"

"No."

"Den he cain't git no situation. What he gwyne to do?"

"Well, I don't know. Some of them gets on the police, and some of them learns people how to talk French."

"Why, Huck, doan' de French people talk de same way we does?"

"*No,* Jim; you couldn't understand a word they said—not a single word."

"Well, now, I be ding-busted! How do dat come?"

"*I* don't know; but it's so. I got some of their jabber out of a book. Spose a man was to come to you and say *Polly-voo-franzy*—what would you think?"

"I wouldn' think nuff'n; I'd take en bust him over de head. Dat is, if he warn't white. I wouldn't 'low no nigger to call me dat."

"Shucks, it ain't calling you anything. It's only saying do you know how to talk French."

"Well, den, why couldn't he *say* it?"

"Why, he *is* a-saying it. That's a Frenchman's *way* of saying it."

"Well, it's a blame' ridicklous way, en I doan' want to hear no mo' 'bout it. Dey ain' no sense in it."

"Looky here, Jim; does a cat talk like we do?"

"No, a cat don't."

"Well, does a cow?"

"No, a cow don't, nuther."

"Does a cat talk like a cow, or a cow talk like a cat?"

"No, dey don't."

"It's natural and right for 'em to talk different from each other, ain't it?"

"'Course."

"And ain't it natural and right for a cat and a cow to talk different from *us?*"

"Why, mos' sholy it is."

"Well, then, why ain't it natural and right for a *Frenchman* to talk different from us? You answer me that."

"Is a cat a man, Huck?"

"No."

"Well, den, dey ain't no sense in a cat talkin' like a man. Is a cow a man?—er is a cow a cat?"

"No, she ain't either of them."

"Well, den, she ain't got no business to talk like either one er the yuther of 'em. Is a Frenchman a man?"

"Yes."

"*Well,* den! Dad blame it, why doan' he *talk* like a man? You answer me *dat!*"

I see it warn't no use wasting words—you can't learn a nigger to argue. So I quit.

CHAPTER XV

We judged that three nights more would fetch us to Cairo, at the bottom of Illinois, where the Ohio River comes in, and that was what we was after. We would sell the raft and get on a steamboat and go way up the Ohio amongst the free States, and then be out of trouble.

Well, the second night a fog begun to come on, and we made for a tow-head to tie to, for it wouldn't do to try to run in fog; but when I paddled ahead in the canoe, with the line, to make fast, there warn't anything but little saplings to tie to. I passed the line around one of them right on the edge of the cut bank, but there was a stiff current, and the raft come booming down so lively she tore it out by the roots and away she went. I see the fog closing down, and it made me so sick and scared I couldn't budge for most a half a minute it seemed to me—and then there warn't no raft in sight; you couldn't see twenty yards. I jumped into the canoe and run back to the stern and grabbed the paddle and set her back a stroke. But she didn't come. I was in such a hurry I hadn't untied her. I got up and tried to untie her, but I was so excited my hands shook so I couldn't hardly do anything with them.

As soon as I got started I took out after the raft, hot and heavy, right down the tow-head. That was all right as far as it went, but the tow-head warn't sixty yards long, and the minute I flew by the foot of it I shot out into the solid white fog, and hadn't no more idea which way I was going than a dead man.

Thinks I, it won't do to paddle; first I know I'll run into the bank or a tow-head or something; I got to set still and float, and yet it's mighty fidgety business to have to hold your hands still at such a time. I whooped and listened. Away down there, somewheres, I hears a small whoop, and up comes my spirits. I went tearing after it, listening sharp to hear it again. The next time it come, I see I warn't heading for it but heading away to the right of it. And the next time, I was heading away to the left of it—and not gaining on it much, either, for I was flying around, this way and that and 'tother, but it was going straight ahead all the time.

I did wish the fool would think to beat a tin pan, and beat it all the time, but he never did, and it was the still places between the whoops that was making the trouble for me. Well, I fought along, and directly I hears the whoop *behind* me. I was tangled good, now. That was somebody else's whoop, or else I was turned around.

I throwed the paddle down. I heard the whoop again; it was behind me yet, but in a different place; it kept coming, and kept changing its place, and I kept answering, till by-and-by it was in front of me again and I knowed the current had swung the canoe's head down stream and I was all right, if that was Jim and not some other raftsman hollering. I couldn't tell nothing about voices in a fog, for nothing don't look natural nor sound natural in a fog.

The whooping went on, and in about a minute I come a booming down on a cut bank with smoky ghosts of big trees on it, and the current throwed me off to the left and shot by, amongst a lot of snags that fairly roared, the current was tearing by them so swift.

In another second or two it was solid white and still again. I set perfectly still, then, listening to my heart thump, and I reckon I didn't draw a breath while it thumped a hundred.

I just give up, then. I knowed what the matter was. That cut bank was an island, and Jim had gone down 'tother side of it. It warn't no tow-head, that you could float by in ten minutes. It had the big timber of a regular island; it might be five or six mile long and more than a half a mile wide.

I kept quiet, with my ears cocked, about fifteen minutes, I reckon. I was floating along, of course, four or five mile an hour; but you don't ever think of that. No, you *feel* like you are laying dead still on the water; and if a little glimpse of a snag slips by, you don't think to yourself how fast *you're* going, but you catch your breath and think, my! how that snag's tearing along. If you think it ain't dismal and lonesome out in a fog that way, by yourself, in the night, you try it once—you'll see.

Next, for about a half an hour, I whoops now and then; at last I hears the answer a long ways off, and tries to follow it, but I couldn't do it, and directly I judged I'd got into a nest of tow-heads, for I had little dim glimpses of them on both sides of me, sometimes just a narrow channel between; and some that I couldn't see, I knowed was there, because I'd hear the wash of the current against the old dead brush and trash that hung over the banks. Well, I warn't long losing the whoops, down amongst the tow-heads; and I only tried to chase them a little while, anyway, because it was worse than chasing a Jack-o-lantern. You never knowed a sound dodge around so, and swap places so quick and so much.

I had to claw away from the bank pretty lively, four or five times, to keep from knocking the islands out of the river; and so I judged the raft must be butting into the bank every now and then, or else it would get further ahead and clear out of hearing—it was floating a little faster than what I was.

Well, I seemed to be in the open river again, by-and-by, but I couldn't hear no sign of a whoop nowheres. I reckoned Jim had fetched up on a snag, maybe, and it was all up with him. I was good and tired, so I laid down in the canoe and said I wouldn't bother no more. I didn't want to go to sleep, of course; but I was so sleepy I couldn't help it; so I thought I would take just one little cat-nap.

But I reckon it was more than a cat-nap, for when I waked up the stars was shining bright, the fog was all gone, and I was spinning down a big bend stern first. First I didn't know where I was; I thought I was dreaming; and when things begun to come back to me, they seemed to come up dim out of last week.

It was a monstrous big river here, with the tallest and the thickest kind of timber on both banks; just a solid wall, as well as I could see, by the stars. I looked away down stream, and seen a black speck on the water. I took out after it; but when I got to it it warn't nothing but a couple of saw-logs made fast together. Then I see another speck, and chased that; then another, and this time I was right. It was the raft.

When I got to it Jim was setting there with his head down between his knees, asleep, with his right arm hanging over the steering oar. The other oar was smashed off, and the raft was littered up with leaves and branches and dirt. So she'd had a rough time.

I made fast and laid down under Jim's nose on the raft, and begun to gap, and stretch my fists out against Jim, and says:

"Hello, Jim, have I been asleep? Why didn't you stir me up?"

"Goodness gracious, is dat you, Huck? En you ain' dead—you ain' drownded—you's back agin? It's too good for true, honey, it's too good for true. Lemme look at you, chile, lemme feel o' you. No, you ain' dead! you's back agin,' live en soun', jis de same ole Huck—de same ole Huck, thanks to goodness!"

"What's the matter with you, Jim? You been a drinking?"

"Drinkin'? Has I ben a drinkin'? Has I had a chance to be a drinkin'?"

"Well, then, what makes you talk so wild?"

"How does I talk wild?"

"*How?* why, hain't you been talking about my coming back, and all that stuff, as if I'd been gone away?"

"Huck—Huck Finn, you look me in de eye; look me in de eye. *Hain't* you ben gone away?"

"Gone away? Why, what in the nation do you mean? *I* hain't been gone anywheres. Where would I go?"

"Well, looky here, boss, dey's sumf'n wrong, dey is. Is I *me*, or who *is* I? Is I heah, or whah *is* I? Now dat's what I wants to know?"

"Well, I think you're here, plain enough, but I think you're a tangle-headed old fool, Jim."

"I is, is I? Well you answer me dis. Didn't you tote out de line in de canoe, fer to make fas' to de tow-head?"

"No, I didn't. What tow-head? I hain't seen no tow-head."

"You hain't seen no tow-head? Looky here—didn't de line pull loose en de raf' go a hummin' down the river, en leave you en de canoe behine in de fog?"

"What fog?"

"Why *de* fog. De fog dat's ben aroun' all night. En didn't you whoop, en didn't I whoop, tell we got mix' up in de islands en one un us got los' en 'tother one was jis' as good as los', 'kase he didn't know whah he wuz? En didn't I bust up agin a lot er dem islands en have a turrible time en mos' git drownded? Now ain't dat so, boss—ain't it so? You answer me dat."

"Well, this is too many for me, Jim. I hain't seen no fog, nor no islands, nor no troubles, nor nothing. I been setting here talking with you all night till you went to sleep about ten minutes ago, and I reckon I done the same. You couldn't a got drunk in that time, so of course you've been dreaming."

"Dad fetch it, how is I gwyne to dream all dat in ten minutes?"

"Well, hang it all, you did dream it, because there didn't any of it happen."

"But Huck, it's all jis' as plain to me as—"

"It don't make no difference how plain it is, there ain't nothing in it. I know, because I've been here all the time."

Jim didn't say nothing for about five minutes, but set there studying over it. Then he says:

"Well, den, I reck'n I did dream it, Huck; but dog my cats ef it ain't de powerfullest dream I ever see. En I hain't ever had no dream b'fo' dat's tired me like dis one."

"Oh, well, that's all right, because a dream does tire a body like everything, sometimes. But this one was a staving dream—tell me all about it, Jim."

So Jim went to work and told me the whole thing right through, just as it happened, only he painted it up considerable. Then he said he must start in and "'terpret" it, because it was sent for a warning. He said the first tow-head stood for a man that would try to do us some good, but the current was another man that would get us away from him. The whoops was warnings that would come to us every now and then, and if we didn't try hard to make out to understand them they'd just take us into bad luck, 'stead of keeping us out of it. The lot of tow-heads was troubles we was going to get into with quarrelsome people and all kinds of mean folks, but if we minded our business and didn't talk back and aggravate them, we would pull through and get out of the fog and into the big clear river, which was the free States, and wouldn't have no more trouble.

It had clouded up pretty dark just after I got onto the raft, but it was clearing up again, now.

"Oh, well, that's all interpreted well enough, as far as it goes, Jim," I says; "but what does *these* things stand for?"

It was the leaves and rubbish on the raft, and the smashed oar. You could see them first rate, now.

Jim looked at the trash, and then looked at me, and back at the trash again. He had got the dream fixed so strong in his head that he couldn't seem to shake it loose and get the facts back into its place again, right away. But when he did get the thing straightened around, he looked at me steady, without ever smiling, and says:

"What do dey stan' for? I's gwyne to tell you. When I got all wore out wid work, en wid de callin' for you, en went to sleep, my heart wuz mos' broke bekase you wuz los', en I didn' k'yer no mo' what become er me en de raf'. En when I wake up and fine you back agin', all safe en soun', de tears come en I could a got down on my knees en kiss' yo' foot I's so thankful. En all you wuz thinkin 'bout wuz how you could make a fool uv ole Jim wid a lie. Dat truck dah is *trash;* en trash is what people is dat puts dirt on de head er dey fren's an makes 'em ashamed."

Then he got up slow, and walked to the wigwam, and went in there, without saying anything but that. But that was enough. It made me feel so mean I could almost kissed *his* foot to get him to take it back.

It was fifteen minutes before I could work myself up to go and humble myself to a nigger—but I done it, and I warn't ever sorry for it afterwards, neither. I didn't do him no more mean tricks, and I wouldn't done that one if I'd a knowed it would make him feel that way.

CHAPTER XVI

We slept most all day, and started out at night, a little ways behind a monstrous long raft that was as long going by as a procession. She had four long sweeps at each end, so we judged she carried as many as thirty men, likely. She had five big wigwams aboard, wide apart, and an open camp fire in the middle, and a tall flag-pole at each end. There was a power of style about her. It *amounted* to something being a raftsman on such a craft as that.

We went drifting down into a big bend, and the night clouded up and got hot. The river was very wide, and was walled with solid timber on both sides; you couldn't see a break in it hardly ever, or a light. We talked about Cairo, and wondered whether we would know it when we got to it. I said likely we wouldn't, because I had heard say there warn't but about a dozen houses there, and if they didn't happen to have them lit up, how was we going to know we was passing a town? Jim said if the two rivers joined together there, that would show. But I said maybe we might think we was passing the foot of an island and coming into the same old river again. That disturbed Jim—and me too. So the question was, what to do? I said, paddle ashore the first time a light showed, and tell them pap was behind, coming along with a trading-scow, and was a green hand at the business, and wanted to know how far it was to Cairo. Jim thought it was a good idea, so we took a smoke on it and waited.

[But you know a young person can't wait very well when he is impatient to find a thing out. We talked it over, and by and by Jim said it was such a black night, now, that it would n't be no risk to swim down to the big raft and crawl aboard and listen,—they would talk about Cairo, because they would be calculating to go ashore there for a spree, maybe, or anyway they would send boats ashore to buy whiskey or fresh meat or something. Jim had a wonderful level head, for a nigger: he could most always start a good plan when you wanted one.

I stood up and shook my rags off and jumped into the river, and struck out for the raft's light. By and by, when I got down nearly to her, I eased up and went slow and cautious. But everything was all right—nobody at the sweeps. So I swum down along the raft till I was most abreast the camp fire in the middle, then I crawled aboard and inched along and got in amongst some bundles of shingles on the weather side of the fire. There was thirteen men there—they was the watch on deck of course. And a mighty rough-looking lot, too. They had a jug, and tin cups, and they kept the jug moving. One man was singing—roaring, you may say; and it was n't a nice song—for a parlor anyway. He roared through his nose, and strung out the last word of every line very long. When he was done they all fetched a kind of Injun war-whoop and then another was sung: It begun:—

"There was a woman in our towdn,
In our towdn did dwed'l (dwell,)
She loved her husband dear-i-lee,
But another man twyste as wed'l.

Singing too, riloo, riloo, riloo,
Ri-too, riloo, rilay - - - e,

She loved her husband dear-i-lee,
But another man twyste as wed'l."

And so on—fourteen verses. It was kind of poor, and when he was going to start on the next verse one of them said it was the tune the old cow died on; and another one said, "Oh, give us a rest." And another one told him to take a walk. They made fun of him till he got mad and jumped up and begun to cuss the crowd, and said he could lam any thief in the lot.

They was all about to make a break for him, but the biggest man there jumped up and says:—

"Set whar you are, gentlemen. Leave him to me; he's my meat."

Then he jumped up in the air three times and cracked his heels together every time. He flung off a buckskin coat that was all hung with fringes, and says, "You lay thar tell the chawin-up's done;" and flung his hat down, which was all over ribbons, and says, "You lay thar tell his sufferins is over."

Then he jumped up in the air and cracked his heels together again and shouted out:—

"Whoo-oop! I'm the old original iron-jawed, brass-mounted, copper-bellied corpse-maker from the wilds of Arkansaw!—Look at me! I'm the man they call Sudden Death and General Desolation! Sired by a hurricane, dam'd by an earthquake, half-brother to the cholera, nearly related to the small-pox on the mother's side! Look at me! I take nineteen alligators and a bar'l of whiskey for breakfast when I'm in robust health, and a bushel of rattlesnakes and a dead body when I'm ailing! I split the everlasting rocks with my glance, and I squench the thunder when I speak! Whoo-oop! Stand back and give me room according to my strength! Blood's my natural drink, and the wails of the dying is music to my ears! Cast your eye on me, gentlemen!—and lay low and hold your breath, for I'm bout to turn myself loose!"

All the time he was getting this off, he was shaking his head and looking fierce, and kind of swelling around in a little circle, tucking up his wrist-bands, and now and then straightening up and beating his breast with his fist, saying, "Look at me gentlemen!" When he got through, he jumped up and cracked his heels together three times, and let off a roaring "Whoo-oop! I'm the bloodiest son of a wildcat that lives!"

Then the man that had started the row tilted his old slouch hat down over his right eye; then he bent stooping forward, with his back sagged and his south end sticking out far, and his fists a-shoving out and drawing in in front of him, and so went around in a little circle about three times, swelling himself up and breathing hard. Then he straightened, and jumped up and cracked his heels together three times before he lit again (that made them cheer), and he begun to shout like this:—

"Whoo-oop! bow your neck and spread, for the kingdom of sorrow's a-coming! Hold me down to the earth, for I feel my powers a-working! whoo-oop! I'm a child of sin, *don't* let me get a start! Smoked glass, here, for all! Don't attempt to look at me with the naked eye, gentlemen! When I'm playful I use the meridians of longitude and parallels of latitude for a seine, and drag the Atlantic Ocean for whales! I scratch my head with the lightning and purr myself to sleep with the thunder! When I'm cold, I bile the Gulf of Mexico and bathe in it; when I'm hot I fan myself with an equinoctial storm; when I'm thirsty I reach up and suck a cloud dry like a sponge; when I range the earth hungry, famine follows in my tracks! Whoo-oop! Bow your neck and spread! I put my hand on the sun's face and make it night in the earth; I bite a piece out of the moon and hurry the seasons; I shake myself and crumble the mountains! Contemplate me through leather—*don't* use the naked eye! I'm the man with a petrified heart and biler-iron bowels! The massacre of isolated communities is the pastime of my idle moments, the destruction of nationalities the serious business of my life! The boundless vastness of the great American desert is my enclosed property, and I bury my dead on my own premises!" He jumped up and cracked his heels together three times before he lit (they cheered him again), and as he come down he shouted out: "Whoo-oop! bow your neck and spread, for the Pet Child of Calamity's a-coming!"

Then the other one went to swelling around and blowing again—the first one—the one they called Bob; next, the Child of Calamity chipped in again, bigger than ever; then they both got at it at the same time, swelling round and round each other and punching their fists most into each other's faces, and whooping and jawing like Injuns; then Bob called the Child names, and the Child called him names back again: next, Bob called him a heap rougher names and the Child come back at him with the very worst kind of language; next, Bob knocked the Child's hat off, and the Child picked it up and kicked Bob's ribbony hat about six foot; Bob went and got it and said never mind, this war n't going to be the last of this thing, because he was a man that never forgot and never forgive, and so the Child better look out, for there was a time a-coming, just as sure as he was a living man, that he would have to answer to him with the best blood in his body. The Child said no man was willinger than he was for that time to come, and he would give Bob fair warning, *now,* never to cross his path again, for he could never rest till he had waded in his blood, for such was his nature, though he was sparing him now on account of his family, if he had one.

Both of them was edging away in different directions, growling and shaking their heads and going on about what they was going to do; but a little black-whiskered chap skipped up and says:—

"Come back here, you couple of chicken-livered cowards, and I'll thrash the two of ye!"

And he done it, too. He snatched them, he jerked them this way and that, he booted them around, he knocked them sprawling faster than they could get up. Why, it war n't two minutes till they begged like dogs—and how the other lot did yell and laugh and clap their hands all the way through, and shout "Sail in, Corpse-Maker!" "Hi! at him again, Child of Calamity!" "Bully for you, little Davy!" Well, it was a perfect pow-wow for a while. Bob and the Child had red noses and black eyes when they got through. Little Davy made them own up that they was sneaks and cowards and not fit to eat with a dog or drink with a nigger; then Bob and the Child shook hands with each other, very solemn, and said they had always respected each other and was willing to let bygones be bygones.

So then they washed their faces in the river; and just then there was a loud order to stand by for a crossing, and some of them went forward to man the sweeps there, and the rest went aft to handle the after-sweeps.

I laid still and waited for fifteen minutes, and had a smoke out of a pipe that one of them left in reach; then the crossing was finished, and they stumped back and had a drink around and went to talking and singing again. Next they got out an old fiddle, and one played, and another patted juba, and the rest turned themselves loose on a regular old-fashioned keel-boat break-down. They couldn't keep that up very long without getting winded, so by and by they settled around the jug again.

They sung "jolly, jolly raftsman's the life for me," with a rousing chorus, and then they got to talking about differences betwixt hogs, and their different kinds of habits; and next about women and their different ways; and next about the best ways to put out houses that was afire; and next about what ought to be done with the Injuns; and next about what a king had to do, and how much he got; and next about how to make cats fight; and next about what to do when a man has fits; and next about differences betwixt clear-water rivers and muddy-water ones. The man they called Ed said the muddy Mississippi water was wholesomer to drink than the clear water of the Ohio; he said if you let a pint of this yalier Mississippi water settle, you would have about a half to three quarters of an inch of mud in the bottom, according to the stage of the river, and then it war n't no better then Ohio water—what you wanted to do was to keep it sitrred up—and when the river was low, keep mud on hand to put in and thicken the water up the way it ought to be.

The Child of Calamity said that was so; he said there was nutritousness in the mud, and a man that drunk Mississippi water could grow corn in his stomach if he wanted to. He says:—

"You look at the graveyards; that tells the tale. Trees won't grow worth shucks in a Cincinnati graveyard, but in a Sent Louis graveyard they grow upwards of eight hundred foot high. It's all on account of the water the people drunk before they laid up. A Cincinnati corpse don't richen a soil any."

And they talked about how Ohio water did n't like to mix with Mississippi water. Ed said if you take the Mississippi on a rise when the Ohio is low, you'll find a wide band of clear water all the way down the east side of the Mississippi for a hundred mile or more, and the minute you get out a quarter of a mile from shore and pass the line, it is all thick and yaller the rest of the way across. Then they talked about how to keep tobacco from getting mouldy, and from that they went into ghosts and told about a lot that other folks had seen; but Ed says:—

"Why don't you tell something that you've seen yourselves? Now let me have a say. Five years ago I was on a raft as big as this, and right along here it was a bright moonshiny night, and I was on watch and boss of the stabboard oar forrard, and one of my pards was a man named Dick Allbright, and he come along to where I was sitting, forrard—gaping and stretching, he was—and stooped down on the edge of the raft and washed his face in the river, and come and set down by me and got out his pipe, and had just got it filled, when he looks up and says,—

"'Why looky-here,' he says, 'ain't that Buck Miller's place, over yander in the bend?'

"'Yes,' says I, 'it is—why?' He laid his pipe down and leant his head on his hand, and says,—

"'I thought we'd be furder down.' I says,—

"'I thought it too, when I went off watch'—we was standing six hours on and six off—'but the boys told me,' I says, 'that the raft didn't seem to hardly move, for the last hour,'—says I, 'though she's a slipping along all right, now,' says I. He give a kind of a groan, and says,—

"'I've seed a raft act so before, 'along here,' he says, ''pears to me the current has most quit above the head of this bend durin' the last two years,' he says.

"Well, he raised up two or three times, and looked away off and around on the water. That started me at it, too. A body is always doing what he sees somebody else doing, though there may n't be no sense in it. Pretty soon I see a black something floating on the water away off to stabboard and quartering behind us. I see he was looking at it, too. I says,—

"'What's that?' He says, sort of pettish,—

"'Tain't nothing but an old empty bar'l.'

"'An empty bar'l!' says I, 'why,' says I, 'a spy-glass is a fool to *your* eyes. How can you tell it's an empty bar'l?' He says,—

"'I don't know; I reckon it ain't a bar'l, but I thought it might be,' says he.

"'Yes,' I says, 'so it might be, and it might be anything else, too; a body can't tell nothing about it, such a distance as that,' I says.

"We had n't nothing else to do, so we kept on watching it. By and by I says,—

"'Why looky-here, Dick Allbright, that thing's a-gaining on us, I believe.'

"He never said nothing. The thing gained and gained, and I judged it must be a dog that was about tired out. Well, we swung down into the crossing, and the thing floated across the bright streak of the moonshine, and, by George, it *was* a bar'l. Says I,—

"'Dick Allbright, what made you think that thing was a bar'l, when it was a half a mile off,' says I. Says he,—

"'I don't know.' Says I,—

"'You tell me, Dick Allbright.' He says,—

"'Well, I knowed it was a bar'l; I've seen it before; lots has seen it; they says it's a hanted bar'l.'

"I called the rest of the watch, and they come and stood there, and I told them what Dick said. It floated right along abreast, now, and did n't gain any more. It was about twenty foot off. Some was for having it aboard, but the rest did n't want to. Dick Allbright said rafts that had fooled with it had got bad luck by it. The captain of the watch said he did n't believe in it. He said he reckoned the bar'l gained on us because it was in a little better current than what we was. He said it would leave by and by.

"So then we went to talking about other things, and we had a song, and then a breakdown; and after that the captain of the watch called for another song; but it was clouding up, now, and the bar'l stuck right thar in the same place, and the song did n't seem to have much warm-up to it, somehow, and so they did n't finish it, and there war n't any cheers, but it sort of dropped flat, and nobody said anything for a minute. Then everybody tried to talk at once, and one chap got off a joke, but it war n't no use, they did n't laugh, and even the chap that made the joke did n't laugh at it, which ain't usual. We all just settled down glum, and watched the bar'l, and was oneasy and oncomfortable. Well, sir, it shut down black and still, and then the wind begin to moan around, and next the lightning begin to play and the thunder to grumble. And pretty soon there was a regular storm, and in the middle of it a man that was running aft stumbled and fell and sprained his ankle so that he had to lay up. This made the boys shake their heads. And every time the lightning come, there was that bar'l with the blue lights winking around it. We was always on the look-out for it. But by and by, towards dawn, she was gone. When the day come we could n't see her anywhere, and we war n't sorry, neither.

"But next night about half-past nine, when there was songs and high jinks going on, here she comes again, and took her old roost on the stabboard side. There war n't no more high jinks. Everybody got solemn; nobody talked; you could n't get anybody to do anything but set around moody and look at the bar'l. It begun to cloud up again. When the watch changed, the off watch stayed up, 'stead of turning in. The storm ripped and roared around all night, and in the middle of it another man tripped and sprained his ankle, and had to knock off. The bar'l left towards day, and nobody see it go.

"Everybody was sober and down in the mouth all day. I don't mean the kind of sober that comes of leaving liquor alone,—not that. They was quiet, but they all drunk more than usual,—not together,—but each man sidled off and took it private, by himself.

"After dark the off watch did n't turn in; nobody sung, nobody talked; the boys did n't scatter around, neither; they sort of huddled together, forrard; and for two hours they set there, perfectly still, looking steady in the one direction, and heaving a sigh once in a while. And then, here comes the bar'l again. She took up her old place. She staid there all night; nobody turned in. The storm come on again, after midnight. It got awful dark; the rain poured down; hail, too; the thunder boomed and roared and bellowed; the wind blowed a hurricane; and the lightning spread over everything in big sheets of glare, and showed the whole raft as plain as day; and the river lashed up white as milk as far as you could see for miles, and there was that bar'l jiggering along, same as ever. The captain ordered the watch to man the after sweeps for a crossing, and nobody would go,—and no more sprained ankles for them, they said. They would n't even *walk* aft. Well then, just then the sky split wide open, with a crash, and the lightning killed two men of the after watch, and crippled two more. Crippled them how, says you? Why *sprained their ankles!*"

"The bar'l left in the dark betwixt lightnings, towards dawn. Well, not a body eat a bite at breakfast that morning. After that the men loafed around, in twos and threes, and talked low together. But none of them herded with Dick Allbright. They all give him the cold shake. If he come around where any of the men was, they split up and sidled away. They would n't man the sweeps with him. The captain had all the skiffs hauled up on the raft, alongside of his wigwam, and would n't let the dead men be took ashore to be planted; he did n't believe a man that got ashore would come back; and he was right.

"After night come, you could see pretty plain that there was going to be trouble if that bar'l come again; there was such a muttering going on. A good many wanted to kill Dick Allbright, because he'd seen the bar'l on other trips, and that had an ugly look. Some wanted to put him ashore. Some said, let's all go ashore in a pile, if the bar'l comes again.

"This kind of whispers was till going on, the men being bunched together forrard watching for the bar'l, when, lo and behold you, here she comes again. Down she comes, slow and steady, and settles into her old tracks. You could a heard a pin drop. Then up comes the captain, and says:—

"'Boys, don't be a pack of children and fools; I don't want this bar'l to be dogging us all the way to Orleans, and *you* don't; well, then, how's the best way to stop it? Burn it up,—that's the way. I'm going to fetch it aboard,' he says. And before anybody could say a word, in he went.

"He swum to it, and as he come pushing it to the raft, the men spread to one side. But the old man got it aboard and busted in the head, and there was a baby in it! Yes sir, a stark naked baby. It was Dick Allbright's baby; he owned up and said so.

"'Yes,' he says, a-leaning over it, 'yes, it is my own lamented darling, my poor lost Charles William Allbright deceased,' says he,—for he could curl his tongue around the bulliest words in the language when he was a mind to, and lay them before you without a jint started, anywheres. Yes, he said he used to live up at the head of this bend, and one night he choked his child, which was crying, not intending to kill it,—which was prob'ly a lie,—and then he was scared, and buried it in a bar'l, before his wife got home, and off he went, and struck the northern trail and went to rafting; and this was the third year that the bar'l had chased him. He said the bad luck always begun light, and lasted till four men was killed, and then the bar'l did n't come any more after that. He said if the men would stand it one more night,—and was a-going on like that,—but the men had got enough. They started to get out a boat to take him ashore and lynch him, but he grabbed the little child all of a sudden and jumped overboard with it hugged up to his breast and shedding tears, and we never see him again in this life, poor old suffering soul, nor Charles William neither."

"*Who* was shedding tears?" says Bob; "was it Allbright or the baby?"

"Why, Allbright, of course; didn't I tell you the baby was dead? Been dead three years—how could it cry?"

"Well, never mind how it could cry—how could it *keep* all that time?" says Davy. "You answer me that."

"I don't know how it done it," says Ed. "It done it though—that's all I know about it."

"Say—what did they do with the bar'l?" says the Child of Calamity.

"Why, they hove it overboard, and it sunk like a chunk of lead."

"Edward, did the child look like it was choked?" says one.

"Did it have its hair parted?" says another.

"What was the brand on that bar'l, Eddy?" says a fellow they called Bill.

"Have you got the papers for them statistics, Edmund?" says Jimmy.

"Say, Edwin, was you one of the men that was killed by the lightning?" says Davy

"Him? O, no, he was both of 'em," says Bob. Then they all haw-hawed.

"Say, Edward, don't you reckon you'd better take a pill? You look bad—don't you feel pale?" says the Child of Calamity.

"O, come, now, Eddy," says Jimmy, "show up; you must a kept part of the bar'l to prove the thing by. Show us the bung-hole—*do*—and we'll all believe you."

"Say, boys," says Bill, "less divide it up. Thar's thirteen of us. I can swaller a thirteenth of the yarn, if you can worry down the rest."

Ed got up mad and said they could all go to some place which he ripped out pretty savage, and then walked off aft cussing to himself, and they yelling and jeering at him, and roaring and laughing so you could hear them a mile.

"Boys, we'll split a watermelon on that," says the Child of Calamity; and he come rummaging around in the dark amongst the shingle bundles where I was, and put his hand on me. I was warm and soft and naked; so he says "Ouch!" and jumped back.

"Fetch a lantern or a chunk of fire here, boys—there's a snake here as big as a cow!"

So they run there with a lantern and crowded up and looked in on me.

"Come out of that, you beggar!" says one.

"Who are you?" says another.

"What are you after here? Speak up prompt, or overboard you go."

"Snake him out, boys. Snatch him out by the heels."

I began to beg, and crept out amongst them trembling. They looked me over, wondering, and the Child of Calamity says:—

"A cussed thief! Lend a hand and less heave him overboard!"

"No," says Big Bob, "less get out of the paint-pot and paint him a sky blue all over from head to heel, and *then* heave him over!"

"Good! that's it. Go for the paint, Jimmy."

When the paint come, and Bob took the brush and was just going to begin, the others laughing and rubbing their hands, I begun to cry, and that sort of worked on Davy, and he says:—

"'Vast there! He's nothing but a cub. I'll paint the man that tetches him!"

So I looked around on them, and some of them grumbled and growled, and Bob put down the paint, and the others did n't take it up.

"Come here to the fire, and less see what you're up to here," says Davy. "Now set down there and give an account of yourself. How long have you been aboard here?"

"Not over a quarter of a minute, sir," says I.

"How did you get dry so quick?"

"I don't know, sir. I'm always that way, mostly."

"Oh, you are, are you? What's your name?"

I war n't going to tell my name. I did n't know what to say, so I just says:

"Charles William Allbright, sir."

Then they roared—the whole crowd; and I was mighty glad I said that, because maybe laughing would get them in a better humor.

When they got done laughing, Davy says:—

"It won't hardly do, Charles William. You could n't have growed this much in five year, and you was a baby when you come out of the bar'l, you know, and dead at that. Come, now, tell a straight story, and nobody 'll hurt you, if you ain't up to anything wrong. What *is* your name?"

"Aleck Hopkins, sir. Aleck James Hopkins."

"Well, Aleck, where did you come from, here?"

"From a trading scow. She lays up the bend yonder. I was born on her. Pap has traded up and down here all his life; and he told me to swim off here, because when you went by he said he would like to get some of you to speak to a Mr. Jonas Turner, in Cairo, and tell him—"

"Oh, come!"

"Yes, sir, it's as true as the world; Pap he says—"

"Oh, your grandmother!"

They all laughed, and I tried again to talk, but they broke in on me and stopped me.

"Now, looky-here," says Davy; "you're scared, and so you talk wild. Honest, now, do you live in a scow, or is it a lie?"

"Yes, sir, in a trading scow. She lays up at the head of the bend. But I war n't born in her. It 's our first trip."

"Now you're talking! What did you come aboard here, for? To steal?"

"No, sir, I did n't.—It was only to get a ride on the raft. All boys does that."

"Well, I know that. But what did you hide for?"

"Sometimes they drive the boys off."

"So they do. They might steal. Looky-here; if we let you off this time, will you keep out of these kind of scrapes hereafter?"

"Deed I will, boss. You try me."

"All right, then. You ain't but little ways from shore. Overboard with you, and don't you make a fool of yourself another time this way.—Blast it, boy, some raftsmen would rawhide you till you were black and blue!"

I did n't wait to kiss good-bye, but went overboard and broke for shore. When Jim come along by and by, the big raft was away out of sight around the point. I swum out and got aboard, and was mighty glad to see home again.]

There warn't nothing to do, now, but to look out sharp for the town, and not pass it without seeing it. He said he'd be mighty sure to see it, because he'd be a free man the minute he seen it, but if he missed it he'd be in the slave country again and no more show for freedom. Every little while he jumps up and says:

"Dah she is!"

But it warn't. It was Jack-o-lanterns, or lightning-bugs; so he set down again, and went to watching, same as before. Jim said it made him all over trembly and feverish to be so close to freedom. Well, I can tell you it made me all over trembly and feverish, too, to hear him, because I begun to get it through my head that he *was* most free—and who was to blame for it? Why, *me*. I couldn't get that out of my conscience, no how nor no way. It got to troubling me so I couldn't rest; I couldn't stay still in one place. It hadn't ever come home to me before, what this thing was that I was doing. But now it did; and it staid with me, and scorched me more and more. I tried to make out to myself that *I* warn't to blame, because *I* didn't run Jim off from his rightful owner; but it warn't no use, conscience up and says, every time, "But you knowed he was running for his freedom, and you could a paddled ashore and told somebody." That was so—I couldn't get around that, noway. That was where it pinched. Conscience says to me, "What had poor Miss Watson done to you, that you could see her nigger go off right under your eyes and never say one single word? What did the poor old woman do to you, that you could treat her so mean? Why, she tried to learn you your book, she tried to learn you your manners, she tried to be good to you every way she knowed how. *That's* what she done."

I got to feeling so mean and so miserable I most wished I was dead. I fidgeted up and down the raft, abusing myself to myself, and Jim was fidgeting up and down past me. We neither of us could keep still. Every time he danced around and says, "Dah's Cairo!" it went through me like a shot, and I thought if it *was* Cairo I reckoned I would die of miserableness.

Jim talked out loud all the time while I was talking to myself. He was saying how the first thing he would do when he got to a free State he would go to saving up money and never spend a single cent, and when he got enough he would buy his wife, which was owned on a farm close to where Miss Watson lived; and then they would both work to buy the two children, and if their master wouldn't sell them, they'd get an Ab'litionist to go and steal them.

It most froze me to hear such talk. He wouldn't ever dared to talk such talk in his life before. Just see what a difference it made in him the minute he judged he was about free. It was according to the old saying, "give a nigger an inch and he'll take an ell." Thinks I, this is what comes of my not thinking. Here was this nigger which I had as good as helped to run away, coming right out flat-footed and saying he would steal his children—children that belonged to a man I didn't even know; a man that hadn't ever done me no harm.

I was sorry to hear Jim say that, it was such a lowering of him. My conscience got to stirring me up hotter than ever, until at last I says to it, "Let up on me—it ain't too late, yet—I'll paddle ashore at the first light, and tell." I felt easy, and happy, and light as a feather, right off. All my troubles was gone. I went to looking out sharp for a light, and sort of singing to myself. By-and-by one showed. Jim sings out:

"We's safe, Huck, we's safe! Jump up and crack yo' heels, dat's de good ole Cairo at las', I jis knows it!"

I says:

"I'll take the canoe and go see, Jim. It mightn't be, you know."

He jumped and got the canoe ready, and put his old coat in the bottom for me to set on, and give me the paddle; and as I shoved off, he says:

"Pooty soon I'll be a-shout'n for joy, en I'll say, it's all on accounts o' Huck; I's a free man, en I couldn't ever ben free ef it hadn't ben for Huck; Huck done it. Jim won't ever forgit you, Huck; you's de bes' fren' Jim's ever had; en you's de *only* fren' ole Jim's got now."

I was paddling off, all in a sweat to tell on him; but when he says this, it seemed to kind of take the tuck all out of me. I went along slow then, and I warn't right down certain whether I was glad I started or whether I warn't. When I was fifty yards off, Jim says:

"Dah you goes, de ole true Huck; de on'y white genlman dat ever kep' his promise to ole Jim."

Well, I just felt sick. But I says, I *got* to do it—I can't get *out* of it. Right then, along comes a skiff with two men in it, with guns, and they stopped and I stopped. One of them says:

"What's that, yonder?"

"A piece of a raft," I says.

"Do you belong on it?"

"Yes, sir."

"Any men on it?"

"Only one, sir."

"Well, there's five niggers run off to-night, up yonder above the head of the bend. Is your man white or black?"

I didn't answer prompt. I tried to, but the words wouldn't come. I tried, for a second or two, to brace up and out with it, but I warn't man enough—hadn't the spunk of a rabbit. I see I was weakening; so I just give up trying, and up and says—

"He's white."

"I reckon we'll go and see for ourselves."

"I wish you would," says I, "because it's pap that's there, and maybe you'd help me tow the raft ashore where the light is. He's sick—and so is mam and Mary Ann."

"Oh, the devil! we're in a hurry, boy. But I s'pose we've got to. Come—buckle to your paddle, and let's get along."

I buckled to my paddle and they laid to their oars. When we had made a stroke or two, I says:

"Pap'll be mighty much obleeged to you, I can tell you. Everybody goes away when I want them to help me tow the raft ashore, and I can't do it by myself."

"Well, that's infernal mean. Odd, too. Say, boy, what's the matter with your father?"

"It's the—a—the—well, it ain't anything, much."

They stopped pulling. It warn't but a mighty little ways to the raft, now. One says:

"Boy, that's a lie. What *is* the matter with your pap? Answer up square, now, and it'll be the better for you."

"I will, sir, I will, honest—but don't leave us, please. It's the—the—gentlemen, if you'll only pull ahead, and let me heave you the head-line, you won't have to come a-near the raft—please do."

"Set her back, John, set her back!" says one. They backed water. "Keep away, boy—keep to looard. Confound it, I just expect the wind has blowed it to us. Your pap's got the small-pox, and you know it precious well. Why didn't you come out and say so? Do you want to spread it all over?"

"Well," says I, a-blubbering, "I've told everybody before, and then they just went away and left us."

"Poor devil, there's something in that. We are right down sorry for you, but we—well, hang it, we don't want the small-pox, you see. Look here, I'll tell you what to do. Don't you try to land by yourself, or you'll smash everything to pieces. You float along down about twenty miles and you'll come to a town on the left-hand side of the river. It will be long after sun-up, then, and when you ask for help, you tell them your folks are all down with chills and fever. Don't be a fool again, and let people guess at what is the matter. Now we're trying to do you a kindness; so you just put twenty miles between us, that's a good boy. It wouldn't do any good to land yonder where the light is—it's only a wood-yard. Say—I reckon your father's poor, and I'm bound to say he's in pretty hard luck. Here—I'll put a twenty dollar gold piece on this board, and you get it when it floats by. I feel mighty mean to leave you, but my kingdom! it won't do to fool with small-pox, don't you see?"

"Hold on, Parker," says the other man, "here's a twenty to put on the board for me. Good-bye, you do as Mr. Parker told you, and you'll be all right."

"That's so, my boy—good-bye, good-bye. If you see any runaway niggers, you get help and nab them, and you can make some money by it."

"Good-bye, sir," says I, "I won't let no runaway niggers get by me if I can help it."

They went off, and I got aboard the raft, feeling bad and low, because I knowed very well I had done wrong, and I see it warn't no use for me to try to learn to do right; a body that don't get *started* right when he's little, ain't got no show—when the pinch comes there ain't nothing to back him up and keep him to his work, and so he gets beat. Then I thought a minute, and says to myself, hold on,—s'pose you'd a done right and give Jim up; would you felt better than what you do now? No, says I, I'd feel bad—I'd feel just the same way I do now. Well, then, says I, what's the use you learning to do right, when it's troublesome to do right and ain't no trouble to do wrong, and the wages is just the same? I was stuck. I couldn't answer that. So I reckoned I wouldn't bother no more about it, but after this always do whichever come handiest at the time.

I went into the wigwam; Jim warn't there. I looked all around; he warn't anywhere. I says:

"Jim!"

"Here I is, Huck. Is dey out o' sight yit? Don't talk loud."

He was in the river, under the stern oar, with just his nose out. I told him they was out of sight, so he come aboard. He says:

"I was a-listenin' to all de talk, en I slips into de river en was gwyne to shove for sho' if dey come aboard. Den I was gwyne to swim to de raf' agin when dey was gone. But lawsy, how did you fool 'em, Huck! Dat *wuz* de smartes' dodge! I tell you, chile, I 'speck it save' ole Jim—ole Jim ain't gwyne to forgit you for dat, honey."

Then we talked about the money. It was a pretty good raise, twenty dollars apiece. Jim said we could take deck passage on a steamboat now, and the money would last us far as we wanted to go in the free States. He said twenty mile more warn't far for the raft to go, but he wished we was already there.

Towards daybreak we tied up, and Jim was mighty particular about hiding the raft good. Then he worked all day fixing things in bundles, and getting all ready to quit rafting.

That night about ten we hove in sight of the lights of a town away down in a left-hand bend.

I went off in the canoe, to ask about it. Pretty soon I found a man out in the river with a skiff, setting a trot-line. I ranged up and says:

"Mister, is that town Cairo?"

"Cairo? no. You must be a blame' fool."

"What town is it, mister?"

"If you want to know, go and find out. If you stay here bothering' around me for about a half a minute longer, you'll get something you won't want."

I paddled to the raft. Jim was awful disappointed, but I said never mind, Cairo would be the next place, I reckoned.

We passed another town before daylight, and I was going out again; but it was high ground, so I didn't go. No high ground about Cairo, Jim said. I had forgot it. We laid up for the day, on a tow-head tolerable close to the left-hand bank. I begun to suspicion something. So did Jim. I says:

"Maybe we went by Cairo in the fog that night."

He says:

"Doan' less' talk about it, Huck. Po' niggers can't have no luck. I awluz 'spected dat rattle-snake skin warn't done wid it's work."

"I wish I'd never seen that snake-skin, Jim—I do wish I'd never laid eyes on it."

"It ain't yo' fault, Huck; you didn' know. Don't you blame yo'self 'bout it."

When it was daylight, here was the clear Ohio water in shore, sure enough, and outside was the old regular Muddy! So it was all up with Cairo.

We talked it all over. It wouldn't do to take to the shore; we couldn't take the raft up the stream, of course. There warn't no way but to wait for dark, and start back in the canoe and take the chances. So we slept all day amongst the cotton-wood thicket, so as to be fresh for the work, and when we went back to the raft about dark the canoe was gone!

We didn't say a word for a good while. There warn't anything to say. We both knowed well enough it was some more work of the rattle-snake skin; so what was the use to talk about it? It would only look like we was finding fault, and that would be bound to fetch more bad luck—and keep on fetching it, too, till we knowed enough to keep still.

By-and-by we talked about what we better do, and found there warn't no way but just to go along down with the raft till we got a chance to buy a canoe to go back in. We warn't going to borrow it when there warn't anybody around, the way pap would do, for that might set people after us.

So we shoved out, after dark, on the raft.

Anybody that don't believe yet, that it's foolishness to handle a snake-skin, after all that that snake-skin done for us, will believe it now, if they read on and see what more it done for us.

The place to buy canoes is off of rafts laying up at shore. But we didn't see no rafts laying up; so we went along during three hours and more. Well, the night got gray, and ruther thick, which is the next meanest thing to fog. You can't tell the shape of the river, and you can't see no distance. It got to be very late and still, and then along comes a steamboat up the river. We lit the lantern, and judged she would see it. Up-stream boats didn't generly come close to us; they go out and follow the bars and hunt for easy water under the reefs; but nights like this they bull right up the channel against the whole river.

We could hear her pounding along, but we didn't see her good till she was close. She aimed right for us. Often they do that and try to see how close they can come without touching; sometimes the wheel bites off a sweep, and then the pilot sticks his head out and laughs, and thinks he's mighty smart. Well, here she comes, and we said she was going to try to shave us; but she didn't seem to be sheering off a bit. She was a big one, and she was coming in a hurry, too, looking like a black cloud with rows of glow-worms around it; but all of a sudden she bulged out, big and scary, with a long row of wide-open furnace doors shining like red-hot teeth, and her monstrous bows and guards hanging right over us. There was a yell at us, and a jingling of bells to stop the engines, a pow-wow of cussing, and whistling of steam—and as Jim went overboard on one side and I on the other, she come smashing straight through the raft.

I dived—and I aimed to find the bottom, too, for a thirty-foot wheel had got to go over me, and I wanted it to have plenty of room. I could always stay under water a minute; this time I reckon I staid under water a minute and a half. Then I bounced for the top in a hurry, for I was nearly busting. I popped out to my arm-pits and blowed the water out of my nose, and puffed a bit. Of course there was a booming current; and of course that boat started her engines again ten seconds after she stopped them, for they never cared much for raftsmen; so now she was churning along up the river, out of sight in the thick weather, though I could hear her.

I sung out for Jim about a dozen times, but I didn't get any answer; so I grabbed a plank that touched me while I was "treading water," and struck out for shore, shoving it ahead of me. But I made out to see that the drift of the current was towards the left-hand shore, which meant that I was in a crossing; so I changed off and went that way.

It was one of these long, slanting, two-mile crossings; so I was a good long time in getting over. I made a safe landing, and clum up the bank. I couldn't see but a little ways, but I went poking along over rough ground for a quarter of a mile or more, and then I run across a big old-fashioned double log house before I noticed it. I was going to rush by and get away, but a lot of dogs jumped out and went to howling and barking at me, and I knowed better than to move another peg.

CHAPTER XVII

In about half a minute somebody spoke out of a window, without putting his head out, and says:

"Be done, boys! Who's there?"

I says:

"It's me."

"Who's me?"

"George Jackson, sir."

"What do you want?"

"I don't want nothing, sir. I only want to go along by, but the dogs won't let me."

"What are you prowling around here this time of night, for—hey?"

"I warn't prowling around, sir; I fell overboard off of the steamboat."

"Oh, you did, did you? Strike a light there, somebody. What did you say your name was?"

"George Jackson, sir. I'm only a boy."

"Look here; if you're telling the truth, you needn't be afraid—nobody'll hurt you. But don't try to budge; stand right where you are. Rouse out Bob and Tom, some of you, and fetch the guns. George Jackson, is there anybody with you?"

"No, sir, nobody."

I heard the people stirring around in the house, now, and see a light. The man sung out:

"Snatch that light away, Betsy, you old fool—ain't you got any sense? Put it on the floor behind the front door. Bob, if you and Tom are ready, take your places."

"All ready."

"Now, George Jackson, do you know the Shepherdsons?"

"No, sir—I never heard of them."

"Well, that may be so, and it mayn't. Now, all ready. Step forward, George Jackson. And mind, don't you hurry—come mighty slow. If there's anybody with you, let him keep back—if he shows himself he'll be shot. Come along, now. Come slow; push the door open, yourself—just enough to squeeze in, d' you hear?"

I didn't hurry, I couldn't if I'd a wanted to. I took one slow step at a time, and there warn't a sound, only I thought I could hear my heart. The dogs were as still as the humans, but they followed a little behind me. When I got to the three log door-steps, I heard them unlocking and unbarring and unbolting. I put my hand on the door and pushed it a little and a little more, till somebody said, "There, that's enough—put your head in." I done it, but I judged they would take it off.

The candle was on the floor, and there they all was, looking at me, and me at them, for about a quarter of a minute. Three big men with guns pointed at me, which made me wince, I tell you; the oldest, gray and about sixty, the other two thirty or more—all of them fine and handsome—and the sweetest old gray-headed lady, and back of her two young women which I couldn't see right well. The old gentleman says:

"There—I reckon it's all right. Come in."

As soon as I was in, the old gentleman he locked the door and barred it and bolted it, and told the young men to come in with their guns, and they all went in a big parlor that had a new rag carpet on the floor, and got together in a corner that was out of range of the front windows— there warn't none on the side. They held the candle, and took a good look at me, and all said, "Why *he* ain't a Shepherdson—no, there ain't any Shepherdson about him." Then the old man said he hoped I wouldn't mind being searched for arms, because he didn't mean no harm by it—it was only to make sure. So he didn't pry into my pockets, but only felt outside with his hands, and said it was all right. He told me to make myself easy and at home, and tell all about myself; but the old lady says:

"Why bless you, Saul, the poor thing's as wet as he can be; and don't you reckon it may be he's hungry?"

"True for you, Rachel—I forgot."

So the old lady says:

"Betsy" (this was a nigger woman), "you fly around and get him something to eat, as quick as you can, poor thing; and one of you girls go and wake up Buck and tell him—Oh, here he is himself. Buck, take this little stranger and get the wet clothes off from him and dress him up in some of yours that's dry."

Buck looked about as old as me—thirteen or fourteen or along there, though he was a little bigger than me. He hadn't on anything but a shirt, and he was very frowsy-headed. He come in gaping and digging one fist into his eyes, and he was dragging a gun along with the other one. He says:

"Ain't they no Shepherdsons around?"

They said, no, 'twas a false alarm.

"Well," he says, "if they'd a ben some, I reckon I'd a got one."

They all laughed, and Bob says: "Why, Buck, they might have scalped us all, you've been so slow in coming."

"Well, nobody come after me, and it ain't right. I'm always kep' down; I don't get no show."

"Never mind, Buck, my boy," says the old man, "you'll have show enough, all in good time, don't you fret about that. Go 'long with you now, and do as your mother told you."

When we got up stairs to his room, he got me a coarse shirt and a round-about and pants of his, and I put them on. While I was at it he asked me what my name was, but before I could tell him, he started to telling me about a blue jay and a young rabbit he had catched in the woods day before yesterday, and he asked me where Moses was when the candle went out. I said I didn't know; I hadn't heard about it before, no way.

"Well, guess," he says.

"How'm I going to guess," says I, "when I never heard tell about it before?"

"But you can guess, can't you? It's just as easy."

"*Which* candle?" I says.

"Why, any candle," he says.

"I don't know where he was," says I; "where was he?"

"Why he was in the *dark!* That's where he was!"

"Well, if you knowed where he was, what did you ask me for?"

"Why, blame it, it's a riddle, don't you see? Say, how long are you going to stay here? You got to stay always. We can just have booming times—they don't have no school now. Do you own a dog? I've got a dog—and he'll go in the river and bring out chips that you throw in. Do you like to comb up, Sundays, and all that kind of foolishness? You bet I don't, but ma she makes me. Confound these ole britches, I reckon I'd better put 'em on, but I'd ruther not, it's so warm. Are you all ready? All right—come along, old hoss."

Cold corn-pone, cold corn-beef, butter and butter-milk—that is what they had for me down there, and there ain't nothing better that ever I've come across yet. Buck and his ma and all of them smoked cob pipes, except the nigger woman, which was gone, and the two young women. They all smoked and talked, and I eat and talked. The young women had quilts around them, and their hair down their backs. They all asked me questions, and I told them how pap and me and all the family was living on a little farm down at the bottom of Arkansaw, and my sister Mary Ann run off and got married and never was heard of no more, and Bill went to hunt them and he warn't heard of no more, and Tom and Mort died, and then there warn't nobody but just me and pap left, and he was just trimmed down to nothing, on account of his troubles; so when he died I took what there was left, because the farm didn't belong to us, and started up the river, deck passage, and fell overboard; and that was how I come to be here. So they said I could have a home there as long as I wanted it. Then it was most daylight, and everybody went to bed, and I went to bed with Buck, and when I waked up in the morning, drat it all, I had forgot what my name was. So I laid there about an hour trying to think, and when Buck waked up, I say:

"Can you spell, Buck?"

"Yes," he says.

"I bet you can't spell my name," says I.

"I bet you what you dare I can," says he.

"All right," says I, "go ahead."

"G-o-r-g-e- J-a-x-o-n—there now," he says.

"Well," says I, "you done it, but I didn't think you could. It ain't no slouch of a name to spell—right off without studying."

I set it down, private, because somebody might want *me* to spell it, next, and so I wanted to be handy with it and rattle it off like I was used to it.

It was a mighty nice family, and a mighty nice house, too. I hadn't seen no house out in the country before that was so nice and has so much style. It didn't have an iron latch on the front door, nor a wooden one with a buckskin string, but a brass knob to turn, the same as houses in a town. There warn't no bed in the parlor, not a sign of a bed; but heaps of parlors in towns has beds in them. There was a big fireplace that was bricked on the bottom, and the bricks was kept clean and red by pouring water on them and scrubbing them with another brick; sometimes they washed them over with red water-paint that they call Spanish-brown, same as they do in town. They had big brass dog-irons that could hold up a saw-log. There was a clock on the middle of the mantel-piece, with a picture of a town painted on the bottom half of the glass front, and a round place in the middle of it for the sun, and you could see the pendulum swing behind it. It was beautiful to hear that clock tick; and sometimes when one of these peddlers had been along and scoured her up and got her in good shape, she would start in and strike a hundred and fifty before she got tuckered out. They wouldn't took any money for her.

Well, there was a big outlandish parrot on each side of the clock, made out of something like chalk, and painted up gaudy. By one of the parrots was a cat made of crockery, and a crockery dog by the other; and when you pressed down on them they squeaked, but didn't open their mouths nor look different nor interested. They squeaked through underneath. There was a couple of big wild-turkey-wing fans spread out behind those things. On a table in the middle of the room was a kind of a lovely crockery basket that had apples and oranges and peaches and grapes piled up in it which was much redder and yellower and prettier than real ones is, but they warn't real because you could see where pieces had got chipped off and showed the white chalk or whatever it was, underneath.

This table had a cover made out of beautiful oil-cloth, with a red and blue spread-eagle painted on it, and a painted border all around. It come all the way from Philadelphia, they said. There was some books too, piled up perfectly exact, on each corner of the table. One was a big family Bible, full of pictures. One was "Pilgrim's Progress," about a man that left his family it didn't say why. I read considerable in it now and then. The statements was interesting, but tough. Another was "Friendship's Offering," full of beautiful stuff and poetry; but I didn't read the poetry. Another was Henry Clay's Speeches, and another was Dr. Gunn's Family Medicine, which told you all about what to do if a body was sick or dead. There was a Hymn Book, and a lot of other books. And there was nice split-bottom chairs, and perfectly sound, too—not bagged down in the middle and busted, like an old basket.

They had pictures hung on the walls—mainly Washingtons and Lafayettes, and battles, and Highland Marys, and one called "Signing the Declaration." There was some that they called crayons, which one of the daughters which was dead made her own self when she was only fifteen years old. They was different from any pictures I ever see before; blacker, mostly, than is common. One was a woman in a slim black dress, belted small under the arm-pits, with bulges like a cabbage in the middle of the sleeves, and a large black scoop-shovel bonnet with a black veil, and white slim ankles crossed about with black tape, and very wee black slippers, like a chisel, and she was leaning pensive on a tombstone on her right elbow, under a weeping willow, and her other hand hanging down her side holding a white handkerchief and a reticule, and underneath the picture it said "Shall I Never See Thee More Alas." Another one was a young lady with her hair all combed up straight to the top of her head, and knotted there in front of a comb like a chair-back, and she was crying into a handkerchief and had a dead bird laying on its back in her other hand with its heels up, and underneath the picture it said "I Shall Never Hear Thy Sweet Chirrup More Alas." There was one where a young lady was at a window looking up at the moon, and tears running down her cheeks; and she had an open letter in one hand with black sealing-wax showing on one edge of it, and she was mashing a locket with a chain to it against her mouth, and underneath the picture it said "And Art Thou Gone Yes Thou Art Gone Alas." These was all nice pictures, I reckon, but I didn't somehow seem to take to them, because if ever I was down a little, they always give me the fan-tods. Everybody was sorry she died, because she had laid out a lot more of these pictures to do, and a body could see by what she had done what they had lost. But I reckoned, that with her disposition, she was having a better time in the graveyard. She was at work on what they said was her greatest picture when she took sick, and every day and every night it was her prayer to be allowed to live till she got it done, but she never got the chance. It was a picture of a young woman in a long white gown, standing on the rail of a bridge all ready to jump off, with her hair all down her back, and looking up to the moon, with the tears running down her face, and she had two arms folded across her breast, and two arms stretched out in front, and two more reaching up towards the moon—and the idea was, to see which pair would look best and then scratch out all the other arms; but, as I was saying, she died before she got her mind made up, and now they kept this picture over the head of the bed in her room, and every time her birthday come they hung flowers on it. Other times it was hid with a little curtain. The young woman in the picture had a kind of a nice sweet face, but there was so many arms it made her look too spidery, seemed to me.

This young girl kept a scrap-book when she was alive, and used to paste obituaries and accidents and cases of patient suffering in it out of the *Presbyterian Observer,* and write poetry after them out of her own head. It was very good poetry. This is what she wrote about a boy by the name of Stephen Dowling Bots that fell down a well and was drownded:

Ode to Stephen Dowling Bots, Dec'd

And did young Stephen sicken,
    And did young Stephen die?
And did the sad hearts thicken,
    And did the mourners cry?

No; such was not the fate of
    Young Stephen Dowling Bots;
Though sad hearts round him thickened,
    'Twas not from sickness' shots.

No whooping-cough did rack his frame,
    Nor measles drear, with spots;
Not these impaired the sacred name
    Of Stephen Dowling Bots.

Despised love struck not with woe
    That head of curly knots,
Nor stomach troubles laid him low,
    Young Stephen Dowling Bots.

O no. Then list with tearful eye,
    Whilst I his fate do tell.
His soul did from his cold world fly,
    By falling down a well.

They got him out and emptied him;
    Alas it was too late;
His spirit was gone for to sport aloft
    In the realms of the good and great.

If Emmeline Grangerford could make poetry like that before she was fourteen, there ain't no telling what she could a done by-and-by. Buck said she could rattle off poetry like nothing. She didn't ever have to stop to think. He said she would slap down a line, and if she couldn't find anything to rhyme with it she would just scratch it out and slap down another one, and go ahead. She warn't particular, she could write about anything you choose to give her to write about, just so it was sadful. Every time a man died, or a woman died, or a child died, she would be on hand with her "tribute" before he was cold. She called them tributes. The neighbors said it was the doctor first, then Emmeline, then the undertaker—the undertaker never got in ahead of Emmeline but once, and then she hung fire on a rhyme for the dead person's name, which was Whistler. She warn't ever the same, after that; she never complained, but she kind of pined away and did not live long. Poor thing, many's the time I made myself go up to the little room that used to be hers and get out her poor old scrapbook and read in it when her pictures had been aggravating me and I had soured on her a little. I liked all that family, dead ones and all, and warn't going to let anything come between us. Poor Emmeline made poetry about all the dead people when she was alive, and it didn't seem right that there warn't nobody to make some about her, now she was gone; so I tried to sweat out a verse or two myself, but I couldn't seem to make it go, somehow. They kept Emmeline's room trim and nice and all the things fixed in it just the way she liked to have them when she was alive, and nobody ever slept there. The old lady took care of the room herself, though there was plenty of niggers, and she sewed there a good deal and read her Bible there, mostly.

Well, as I was saying about the parlor, there was beautiful curtains on the windows: white, with pictures painted on them, of castles with vines all down the walls, and cattle coming down to drink. There was a little old piano, too, that had tin pans in it, I reckon, and nothing was ever so lovely as to hear the young ladies sing, "The Last Link is Broken" and play "The Battle of Prague" on it. The walls of all the rooms was plastered, and most had carpets on the floors, and the whole house was whitewashed on the outside.

It was a double house, and the big open place betwixt them was roofed and floored, and sometimes the table was set there in the middle of the day, and it was a cool, comfortable place. Nothing couldn't be better. And warn't the cooking good, and just bushels of it too!

CHAPTER XVIII

Grangerford was a gentleman, you see. He was a gentleman all over; and so was his family. He was well born, as the saying is, and that's worth as much in a man as it is in a horse, so the Widow Douglas said, and nobody ever denied that she was of the first aristocracy in our town; and pap he always said it, too, though he warn't no more quality than a mud-cat, himself. Col. Grangerford was very tall and very slim, and had a darkish-paly complexion, not a sign of red in it anywheres; he was clean-shaved every morning, all over his thin face, and he had the thinnest kind of lips, and the thinnest kind of nostrils, and a high nose, and heavy eyebrows, and the blackest kind of eyes, sunk so deep back that they seemed like they was looking out of caverns at you, as you may say. His forehead was high, and his hair was black and straight, and hung to his shoulders. His hands was long and thin, and every day of his life he put on a clean shirt and a full suit from head to foot made out of linen so white it hurt your eyes to look at it; and on Sundays he wore a blue tail-coat with brass buttons on it. He carried a mahogany cane with a silver head to it. There warn't no frivolishness about him, not a bit, and he warn't ever loud. He was as kind as he could be—you could feel that, you know, and so you had confidence. Sometimes he smiled, and it was good to see; but when he straightened himself up like a liberty-pole, and the lightning begun to flicker out from under his eyebrows you wanted to climb a tree first, and find out what the matter was afterwards. He didn't ever have to tell anybody to mind their manners—everybody was always good mannered where he was. Everybody loved to have him around, too; he was sunshine most always—I mean he made it seem like good weather. When he turned into a cloud-bank it was awful dark for a half a minute and that was enough; there wouldn't nothing go wrong again for a week.

When him and the old lady come down in the morning, all the family got up out of their chairs and give them good-day, and didn't set down again till they had set down. Then Tom and Bob went to the sideboard where the decanters was, and mixed a glass of bitters and handed it to him, and he held it in his hand and waited till Tom's and Bob's was mixed, and then they bowed and said "Our duty to you, sir, and madam;" and *they* bowed the least bit in the world and said thank you, and so they drank, all three, and Bob and Tom poured a spoonful of water on the sugar and the mite of whisky or apple brandy in the bottom of their tumblers, and give it to me and Buck, and we drank to the old people too.

Bob was the oldest, and Tom next. Tall, beautiful men with very broad shoulders and brown faces, and long black hair and black eyes. They dressed in white linen from head to foot, like the old gentleman, and wore broad Panama hats.

Then there was Miss Charlotte, she was twenty-five, and tall and proud and grand, but as good as she could be, when she warn't stirred up; but when she was, she had a look that would make you wilt in your tracks, like her father. She was beautiful.

So was her sister, Miss Sophia, but it was a different kind. She was gentle and sweet, like a dove, and she was only twenty.

Each person had their own nigger to wait on them—Buck, too. My nigger had a monstrous easy time, because I warn't used to having anybody do anything for me, but Buck's was on the jump most of the time.

This was all there was of the family, now; but there used to be more—three sons; they got killed; and Emmeline that died.

The old gentleman owned a lot of farms, and over a hundred niggers. Sometimes a stack of people would come there, horseback, from ten or fifteen mile around, and stay five or six days, and have such junketings round about and on the river, and dances and picnics in the woods, day-times, and balls at the house, nights. These people was mostly kin-folks of the family. The men brought their guns with them. It was a handsome lot of quality, I tell you.

There was another clan of aristocracy around there—five or six families—mostly of the name Shepherdson. They was as high-toned, and well born, and rich and grand, as the tribe of Grangerfords. The Shepherdsons and the Grangerfords used the same steamboat landing, which was about two mile above our house; so sometimes when I went up there with a lot of our folks I used to see a lot of the Shepherdsons there, on their fine horses.

One day Buck and me was away out in the woods, hunting, and heard a horse coming. We was crossing the road. Buck says:

"Quick! Jump for the woods!"

We done it, and then peeped down the woods through the leaves. Pretty soon a splendid young man come galloping down the road, settling his horse easy and looking like a soldier. He had his gun across his pommel. I had seen him before. It was young Harney Shepherdson. I heard Buck's gun go off at my ear, and Harney's hat tumbled off from his head. He grabbed his gun and rode straight to the place where we was hid. But we didn't wait. We started through the woods on a run. The woods warn't thick, so I looked over my shoulder, to dodge the bullet, and twice I seen Harney cover Buck with his gun; and then he rode away the way he come—to get his hat, I reckon, but I couldn't see. We never stopped running till we got home. The old gentleman's eyes blazed a minute—'twas pleasure, mainly, I judged—then his face sort of smoothed down, and he says, kind of gentle:

"I don't like that shooting from behind a bush. Why didn't you step into the road, my boy?"

"The Sheperdsons don't father. They always take advantage."

Miss Charlotte she held her head up like a queen while Buck was telling his tale, and her nostrils spread and her eyes snapped. The two young men looked dark, but never said nothing. Miss Sophia she turned pale, but the color come back when she found the man warn't hurt.

Soon as I could get Buck down by the corn-cribs under the trees by ourselves, I says:

"Did you want to kill him, Buck?"

"Well, I bet I did."

"What did he do to you?"

"Him? He never done nothing to me."

"Well, then, what did you want to kill him for?"

"Why nothing—only it's on account of the feud."

"What's a feud?"

"Why, where was you raised? Don't you know what a feud is?"

"Never heard of it before—tell me about it."

"Well," says Buck, "a feud is this way. A man has a quarrel with another man, and kills him; then that other man's brother kills *him;* then the other brothers, on both sides, goes for one another; then the *cousins* chip in—and by-and-by everybody's killed off, and there ain't no more feud. But it's kind of slow, and takes a long time."

"Has this one been going on long, Buck?"

"Well I should *reckon!* it started thirty year ago, or som'ers along there. There was trouble 'bout something and then a lawsuit to settle it; and the suit went agin one of the men, and so he up and shot the man that won the suit—which he would naturally do, of course. Anybody would."

"What was the trouble about, Buck?—land?"

"I reckon maybe—I don't know."

"Well, who done the shooting?—was it a Grangerford or a Shepherdson?"

"Laws, how do *I* know? it was so long ago."

"Don't anybody know?"

"Oh, yes, pa knows, I reckon, and some of the other old folks; but they don't know, now, what the row was about in the first place."

"Has there been many killed, Buck?"

"Yes—right smart chance of funerals. But they don't always kill. Pa's got a few buck-shot in him; but he don't mind it 'cuz he don't weigh much anyway. Bob's been carved up some with a bowie, and Tom's been hurt once or twice."

"Has anybody been killed this year, Buck?"

"Yes, we got one and they got one. 'Bout three months ago, my cousin Bud, fourteen year old, was riding through the woods, on t'other side of the river, and didn't have no weapon with him, which was blame' foolishness, and in a lonesome place he hears a horse a-coming behind him, and sees old Baldy Shepherdson a-linkin' after him with his gun in his hand and his white hair a-flying in the wind; and 'stead of jumping off and taking to the brush, Bud 'lowed he could outrun him; so they had it, nip and tuck, for five mile or more, the old man a-gaining all the time; so at last Bud seen it warn't any use, so he stopped and faced around so as to have the bullet holes in front, you know, and the old man he rode up and shot him down. But he didn't get much chance to enjoy his luck, for inside of a week our folks laid *him* out."

"I reckon that old man was a coward, Buck."

"I reckon he *warn't* a coward. Not by a blame' sight. There ain't a coward amongst them Shepherdsons—not a one. And there ain't no cowards amongst the Grangerfords, either. Why, that old man kep' up his end in a fight one day, for a half an hour, against three Grangerfords, and come out winner. They was all a-horseback; he lit off of his horse and got behind a little wood-pile, and kep' his horse before him to stop the bullets; but the Grangerfords staid on their horses and capered around the old man, and peppered away at him, and he peppered away at them. Him and his horse both went home pretty leaky and crippled, but the Grangerfords had to be *fetched* home—and one of 'em was dead, and another died the next day. No, sir, if a body's out hunting for cowards, he don't want to fool away any time amongst them Shepherdsons, becuz they don't breed any of that *kind*."

Next Sunday we all went to church, about three mile, everybody a-horseback. The men took their guns along, so did Buck, and kept them between their knees or stood them handy against the wall. The Shepherdsons done the same. It was pretty ornery preaching—all about brotherly love, and such-like tiresomeness; but everybody said it was a good sermon, and they all talked it over going home, and had such a powerful lot to say about faith, and good works, and free grace, and preforeordestination, and I don't know what all, that it did seem to me to be one of the roughest Sundays I had run across yet.

About an hour after dinner everybody was dozing around, some in their chairs and some in their rooms, and it got to be pretty dull. Buck and a dog was stretched out on the grass in the sun, sound asleep. I went up to our room, and judged I would take a nap myself. I found that sweet Miss Sophia standing in her door, which was next to ours, and she took me in her room and shut the door very soft, and asked me if I liked her, and I said I did; and she asked me if I would do something for her and not tell anybody, and I said I would. Then she said she'd forgot her Testament, and left it in the seat at church, between two other books and would I slip out quiet and go there and fetch it to her, and not say nothing to nobody. I said I would. So I slid out and slipped off up the road, and there warn't anybody at the church, except maybe a hog or two, for there warn't any lock on the door, and hogs like a puncheon floor in summer-time because it's cool. If you notice, most folks don't go to church only when they've got to; but a hog is different.

Says I to myself something's up—it ain't natural for a girl to be in such a sweat about a Testament; so I give it a shake, and out drops a little piece of paper with *"Half-past two"* wrote on it with a pencil. I ransacked it, but couldn't find anything else. I couldn't make anything out of that, so I put the paper in the book again, and when I got home and up stairs, there was Miss Sophia in her door waiting for me. She pulled me in and shut the door; then she looked in the Testament till she found the paper, and as soon as she read it she looked glad; and before a body could think, she grabbed me and give me a squeeze, and said I was the best boy in the world, and not to tell anybody. She was mighty red in the face, for a minute, and her eyes lighted up and it made her powerful pretty. I was a good deal astonished, but when I got my breath I asked her what the paper was about, and she asked me if I had read it, and I said no, and she asked me if I could read writing, and I told her "no, only coarse-hand," and then she said the paper warn't anything but a book-mark to keep her place, and I might go and play now.

I went off down to the river, studying over this thing, and pretty soon I noticed that my nigger was following along behind. When we was out of sight of the house, he looked back and around a second, and then comes a-running, and says:

"Mars Jawge, if you'll come down into de swamp, I'll show you a whole stack o' water-moccasins."

Thinks I, that's mighty curious; he said that yesterday. He

oughter know a body don't love water-moccasins enough to go around hunting for them. What is he up to anyway? So I says—

"All right, trot ahead."

I followed a half a mile, then he struck out over the swamp and waded ankle deep as much as another half mile. We come to a little flat piece of land which was dry and very thick with trees and bushes and vines, and he says—

"You shove right in dah, jist a few steps, Mars Jawge, dah's whah dey is. I's seed 'm befo', I don't k'yer to see 'em no mo'."

Then he slopped right along and went away, and pretty soon the trees hid him. I poked into the place a-ways, and come to a little open patch as big as a bedroom, all hung around with vines, and found a man laying there asleep—and by jings it was my old Jim!

I waked him up, and I reckoned it was going to be a grand surprise to him to see me again, but it warn't. He nearly cried, he was so glad, but he warn't surprised. Said he swum along behind me, that night, and heard me yell every time, but dasn't answer, because he didn't want nobody to pick *him* up, and take him into slavery again. Says he—

"I got hurt a little, en couldn't swim fas', so I wuz a considerable ways behine you, towards de las'; when you landed I reck'ned I could ketch up wid you on de lan' 'dout havin' to shout at you, but when I see dat house I begin to go slow. I 'uz off too fur to hear what dey say to you—I wuz 'fraid o' de dogs—but when it 'uz all quiet agin, I knowed you's in de house, so I struck out for de woods to wait for day. Early in de mawnin' some er de niggers come along, gwyne to de fields, en dey tuck me en showed me dis place, whah de dogs can't track me on accounts o' de water, en dey brings me truck to eat every night, en tells me how you's a gitt'n along."

"Why didn't you tell my Jack to fetch me here sooner, Jim?"

"Well, 'twarn't no use to 'sturb you, Huck, tell we could do sumfn—but we's all right, now. I ben a-buyin' pots en pans en vittles, as I got a chanst, en a patchin' up de raf', nights, when—"

"*What* raft, Jim?"

"Our ole raf'."

"You mean to say our old raft warn't smashed all to flinders?"

"No, she warn't. She was tore up a good deal—one en' of her was—but dey warn't no great harm done, on'y our traps was mos' all los'. Ef we hadn' dive' so deep en swum so fur under water, en de night hadn' ben so dark, en we warn't so sk'yerd, en ben sich punkin-heads, as de sayin' is, we'd a seed de raf'. But it's jis' as well we didn't, 'kase now she's all fixed up agin mos' as good as new, en we's got a new lot o' stuff, too, in de place o' what 'uz los'."

"Why, how did you get hold of the raft again, Jim—did you catch her?"

"How I gwyne to ketch her, en I out in de woods? No, some er de niggers foun' her ketched on a snag, along heah in de ben', en dey hid her in a crick, 'mongst de willows, en dey wuz so much jawin' 'bout which un 'um she b'long to de mos', dat I come to heah 'bout it pooty soon, so I ups en settles de trouble by tellin' 'um she don't b'long to none uv um, but to you en me; en I ast 'm if dey gwyne to grab a young white genlman's propaty, en git a hid'n for it? Den I gin 'm ten cents apiece, en dey 'uz mighty well satisfied, en wisht some mo' raf's 'ud come along en make 'm rich agin. Dey's mighty good to me, dese niggers is, en whatever I wants 'm to do fur me, I doan' have to ast 'm twice, honey. Dat Jack's a good nigger, en pooty smart."

"Yes, he is. He ain't ever told me you was here; told me to come, and he'd show me a lot of water-moccasins. If anything happens, *he* ain't mixed up in it. He can say he never seen us together, and it'll be the truth."

I don't want to talk much about the next day. I reckon I'll cut it pretty short. I waked up about dawn, and was agoing to turn over and go to sleep again, when I noticed how still it was—didn't seem to be anybody stirring. That warn't usual. Next I noticed that Buck was up and gone. Well, I gets up, a-wondering, and goes down stairs—nobody around; everything as still as a mouse. Just the same outside; thinks I, what does it mean? Down by the wood-pile I comes across my Jack, and says:

"What's it all about?"

Says he:

"Don't you know, Mars Jawge?"

"No," says I, "I don't."

"Well, den, Miss Sophia's run off! 'deed she has. She run off in de night, sometime—nobody don't know jis' when—run off to git married to dat young Harney Shepherdson, you know—leastways, so dey 'spec. De fambly foun' it out, 'bout half an hour ago—maybe a little mo'—en' I *tell* you dey warn't no time los'. Sich another hurryin' up guns en hosses *you* never see! De women folks has gone for to stir up de relations, en ole Mars Saul en de boys tuck dey guns en rode up de river road for to try to ketch dat young man en kill him 'fo' he kin get acrost de river wid Miss Sophia. I reck'n dey's gwyne to be mighty rough times."

"Buck went off 'thout waking me up."

"Well I reck'n he *did!* Dey warn't gwyne to mix you up in it. Mars Buck he loaded up his gun en 'lowed he's gwyne to fetch home a Shepherdson or bust. Well, dey'll be plenty un 'm dah, I reck'n, en you bet you he'll fetch one ef he gits a chanst."

I took up the river road as hard as I could put. By-and-by I begin to hear guns a good ways off. When I come in sight of the log store and the wood-pile where the steamboats lands, I worked along under the trees and brush till I got to a good place, and then I clumb up into the forks of a cotton-wood that was out of reach, and watched. There was a wood-rank four foot high, a little ways in front of the tree, and first I was going to hide behind that; but maybe it was luckier I didn't.

There was four or five men cavorting around on their horses in the open place before the log store, cussing and yelling, and trying to get at a couple of young chaps that was behind the wood-rank alongside of the steamboat landing—but they couldn't come it. Every time one of them showed himself on the river side of the wood-pile he got shot at. The two boys was squatting back to back behind the pile, so they could watch both ways.

By-and-by the men stopped cavorting around and yelling. They started riding towards the store; then up gets one of the boys, draws a steady bead over the wood-rank, and drops one of them out of his saddle. All the men jumped off of their horses and grabbed the hurt one and started to carry him to the store; and that minute the two boys started on the run. They got half-way to the tree I was in before the men noticed. Then the men see them, and jumped on their horses and took out after them. They gained on the boys, but it didn't do no good, the boys had too good a start; they got to the wood-pile that was in front of my tree, and slipped in behind it, and so they had the bulge on the men again. One of the boys was Buck, and the other was a slim young chap about nineteen years old.

The men ripped around awhile, and then rode away. As soon as they was out of sight, I sung out to Buck and told him. He didn't know what to make of my voice coming out of the tree, at first. He was awful surprised. He told me to watch out sharp and let him know when the men come in sight again; said they was up to some devilment or other—wouldn't be gone long. I wished I was out of that tree, but I dasn't come down. Buck begun to cry and rip, and 'lowed that him and his cousin Joe (that was the other young chap) would make up for this day, yet. He said his father and his two brothers was killed, and two or three of the enemy. Said the Shepherdsons laid for them, in ambush. Buck said his father and brothers ought to waited for their relations—the Shepherdsons was too strong for them. I asked him what was become of young Harney and Miss Sophia. He said they'd got across the river and was safe. I was glad of that; but the way Buck did take on because he didn't manage to kill Harney that day he shot at him—I hain't ever heard anything like it.

All of a sudden, bang! bang! bang! goes three or four guns—the men had slipped around through the woods and come in from behind without their horses! The boys jumped for the river—both of them hurt—and as they swum down the current the men run along the bank shooting at them and singing out, "Kill them, kill them!" It made me so sick I most fell out of the tree. I ain't agoing to tell *all* that happened—it would make be sick again if I was to do that. I wished I hadn't eve come ashore that night, to see such things. I ain't ever going to get shut of them—lots of times I dream about them.

I staid in the tree till it begun to get dark, afraid to come down. Sometimes I heard guns away off in the woods; and twice I seen little gangs of men gallop past the log store with guns; so I reckoned the trouble was still agoing on. I was mighty down-hearted; so I made up my mind I wouldn't ever go anear that house again, because I reckoned I was to blame, somehow. I judged that that piece of paper meant that Miss Sophia was to meet Harney somewheres at half-past two and run off; and I judged I ought to told her father about that paper and the curious way she acted, and then maybe he would a locked her up and this awful mess wouldn't ever happened.

When I got down out of the tree, I crept along down the river bank a piece, and found the two bodies laying in the edge of the water, and tugged at them till I got them ashore; then I covered up their faces, and got away as quick as I could. I cried a little when I was covering up Buck's face, for he was mighty good to me.

It was just dark, now. I never went near the house, but struck through the woods and made for the swamp. Jim warn't on his island, so I tramped off in a hurry for the crick, and crowded through the willows, red-hot to jump aboard and get out of that awful country—the raft was gone! My souls, but I was scared! I couldn't get my breath for most a minute. Then I raised a yell. A voice not twenty-five foot from me, says—

"Good lan'! is dat you, honey? Doan' make no noise."

It was Jim's voice—nothing ever sounded so good before. I run along the bank a piece and got aboard, and Jim he grabbed me and hugged me, he was so glad to see me. He says—

"Laws bless you, chile, I 'uz right down sho' you's dead agin. Jack's been heah, he say he reck'n you's ben shot, kase you didn't come home no mo'; so I's jes' dis minute a startin' de raf' down towards de mouf er de crick, so's to be all ready for to shove out en leave soon as Jack comes agin en tells me for certain you *is* dead. Lawsy, I's mighty glad to git you back agin, honey."

I says—

"All right—that's mighty good; they won't find me, and they'll think I've been killed, and floated down the river—there's something up there that'll help them to think so—so don't you lose no time, Jim, but just shove off for the big water as fast as ever you can."

I never felt easy till the raft was two mile below there and out in the middle of the Mississippi. Then we hung up our signal latern, and judged that we was free and safe once more. I hadn't had a bite to eat since yesterday; so Jim he got out some corn-dodgers and buttermilk, and pork and cabbage, and greens—there ain't nothing in the world so good, when it's cooked right—and whilst I eat my supper we talked, and had a good time. I was powerful glad to get away from the feuds, and so was Jim to get away from the swamp. We said there warn't no home like a raft, after all. Other places do seem so cramped up and smothery, but a raft don't. You feel mighty free and easy and comfortable on a raft.

CHAPTER XIX

Two or three days and nights went by; I reckon I might say they swum by, they slid along so quiet and smooth and lovely. Here is the way we put in the time. It was a monstrous big river down there—sometimes a mile and a half wide; we run nights, and laid up and hid day-times; soon as night was most gone, we stopped navigating and tied up—nearly always in the dead water under a tow-head; and then cut young cotton-woods and willows and hid the raft with them. Then we set out the lines. Next we slid into the river and had a swim, so as to freshen up and cool off; when we set down on the sandy bottom where the water was about knee deep, and watched the daylight come. Not a sound, anywheres—perfectly still—just like the whole world was asleep, only sometimes the bull-frogs a-cluttering, maybe. The first thing to see, looking away over the water, was a kind of dull line—that was the woods on the t'other side—you couldn't make nothing else out; then a pale place in the sky; then more paleness, spreading around; then the river softened up, away off, and warn't black any more, but gray; you could see little dark spots drifting along, ever so far away—trading scows, and such things; and long black streaks—rafts; sometimes you could hear a sweep screaking; or jumbled up voices, it was so still, and sounds come so far; and by-and-by you could see a streak on the water which you know by the look of the streak that there's a snag there in a swift current which breaks on it and makes that streak look that way; and you see the mist curl up off of the water, and the east reddens up, and the river, and you make out a log cabin in the edge of the woods, away on the bank on t'other side of the river, being a wood-yard, likely, and piled by them cheats so you can throw a dog through it anywheres; then the nice breeze springs up, and comes fanning you from over there, so cool and fresh, and sweet to smell, on account of the woods and the flowers; but sometimes not that way, because they've left dead fish laying around, gars, and such, and they do get pretty rank; and next you've got the full day, and everything smiling in the sun, and the song-birds just going it!

A little smoke couldn't be noticed, now, so we would take some fish off of the lines, and cook up a hot breakfast. And afterwards we would watch the lonesomeness of the river, and kind of lazy along, and by-and-by lazy off to sleep. Wake up, by-and-by, and look to see what done it, and maybe see a steamboat, coughing along up stream, so far off towards the other side you couldn't tell nothing about her only whether she was stern-wheel or side-wheel; then for about an hour there wouldn't be nothing to hear nor nothing to see—just solid lonesomeness. Next you'd see a raft sliding by, away off yonder, and maybe a galoot on it chopping, because they're most always doing it on a raft; you'd see the ax flash, and come down—you don't hear nothing; you see that ax go up again, and by the time it's above the man's head, then you hear the *k'chunk!*—it had took all that time to come over the water. So we would put in the day, lazying around, listening to the stillness. Once there was a thick fog, and the rafts and things that went by was beating tin pans so the steamboats wouldn't run over them. A scow or a raft went by so close we could hear them talking and cussing and laughing—heard them plain; but we couldn't see no sign of them; it made you feel crawly, it was like spirits carrying on that way in the air. Jim said he believed it was spirits; but I says:

"No, spirits wouldn't say, 'dern the dern fog.'"

Soon as it was night, out we shoved; when we got her out to about the middle, we let her alone, and let her float wherever the current wanted her to; then we lit the pipes, and dangled our legs in the water and talked about all kinds of things—we was always naked, day and night, whenever the mosquitoes would let us—the new clothes Buck's folks made for me was too good to be comfortable, and besides I didn't go much on clothes, nohow.

Sometimes we'd have that whole river all to ourselves for the longest time. Yonder was the banks and the islands, across the water; and maybe a spark—which was a candle in a cabin window—and sometimes on the water you could see a spark or two—on a raft or a scow, you know; and maybe you could hear a fiddle or a song coming over from one of them crafts. It's lovely to live on a raft. We had the sky, up there, all speckled with stars, and we used to lay on our backs and look up at them, and discuss about whether they was made, or only just happened—Jim he allowed they was made, but I allowed they happened; I judged it would have took too long to *make* so many. Jim said the moon could a *laid* them; well, that looked kind of reasonable, so I didn't say nothing against it, because I've seen a frog lay most as many, so of course it could be done. We used to watch the stars that fell, too, and see them streak down. Jim allowed they'd got spoiled and was hove out of the nest.

Once or twice of a night we would see a steamboat slipping along in the dark, and now and then she would belch a whole world of sparks up out of her chimbleys, and they would rain down in the river and look awful pretty; then she would turn a corner and her lights would wink out and her pow-wow shut off and leave the river still again; and by-and-by her waves would get to us, a long time after she was gone, and joggle the raft a bit, and after that you wouldn't hear nothing for you couldn't tell how long, except maybe frogs or something.

After midnight the people on shore went to bed, and then for two or three hours the shores was black—no more sparks in the cabin windows. These sparks was our clock—the first one that showed again meant morning was coming, so we hunted a place to hide and tie up, right away.

One morning about day-break, I found a canoe and crossed over a chute to the main shore—it was only two hundred yards—and paddled about a mile up a crick amongst the cypress woods, to see if I couldn't get some berries. Just as I was passing a place where a kind of a cow-path crossed the crick, here comes a couple of men tearing up the path as tight as they could foot it. I thought I was a goner, for whenever anybody was after anybody I judged it was *me*—or maybe Jim. I was about to dig out from there in a hurry, but they was pretty close to me then, and sung out and begged me to save their lives—said they hadn't been doing nothing, and was being chased for it—said there was men and dogs a-coming. They wanted to jump right in, but I says—

"Don't you do it. I don't hear the dogs and horses yet; you've got time to crowd through the brush and get up the crick a little ways; then you take to the water and wade down to me and get in—that'll throw the dogs off the scent."

They done it, and soon as they was aboard I lit out for our tow-head, and in about five or ten minutes we heard the dogs and the men away off, shouting. We heard them come along towards the crick, but couldn't see them; they seemed to stop and fool around a while; then, as we got further and further away all the time, we couldn't hardly hear them at all; by the time we had left a mile of woods behind us and struck the river, everything was quiet, and we paddled over to the tow-head and hid in the cotton-woods and was safe.

One of these fellows was about seventy, or upwards, and had a bald head and very gray whiskers. He had an old battered-up slouch hat on, and a greasy blue woolen shirt, and ragged old blue jeans britches stuffed into his boot tops, and home-knit galluses—no, he only had one. He had an old long-tailed blue jeans coat with slick brass buttons, flung over his arm, and both of them had big fat ratty-looking carpet-bags.

The other fellow was about thirty and dressed about as ornery. After breakfast we all laid off and talked, and the first thing that come out was that these chaps didn't know one another.

"What got you into trouble?" says the baldhead to t'other chap.

"Well, I'd been selling an article to take the tartar off the teeth—and it does take it off, too, and generally the enamel along with it—but I staid about one night longer than I ought to, and was just in the act of sliding out when I ran across you on the trail this side of town, and you told me they were coming, and begged me to help you to get off. So I told you I was expecting trouble myself and would scatter out *with* you. That's the whole yarn—what's yourn?"

"Well, I'd ben a-runnin' a little temperance revival thar, bout a week, and was the pet of the women-folks, big and little, for I was makin' it mighty warm for the rummies, I *tell* you, and takin' as much as five or six dollars a night—ten cents a head, children and niggers free—and business a growin' all the time; when somehow or another a little report got around, last night, that I had a way of puttin' in my time with a private jug, on the sly. A nigger rousted me out this mornin', and told me the people was getherin' on the quiet, with their dogs and horses, and they'd be along pretty soon and give me 'bout half an hour's start, and then run me down, if they could; and if they got me they'd tar and feather me and ride me on a rail, sure. I didn't wait for no breakfast—I warn't hungry."

"Old man," says the young one, "I reckon we might double-team it together; what do you think?"

"I ain't undisposed. What's your line—mainly?"

"Jour printer, by trade; do a little in patent medicines; theatre-actor—tragedy, you know; take a turn at mesmerism and phrenology when there's a chance; teach singing-geography school for a change; sling a lecture, sometimes—oh, I do lots of things—most anything that comes handy, so it ain't work. What's your lay?"

"I've done considerable in the doctoring way in my time. Layin' on o' hands is my best holt—for cancer, and paralysis, and sich things; and I k'n tell a fortune pretty good, when I've got somebody along to find out the facts for me. Preachin's my line, too; and workin' camp-meetin's; and missionaryin' around."

Nobody never said anything for a while; then the young man hove a sigh and says—

"Alas!"

"What're you alassin' about?" says the baldhead.

"To think I should have lived to be leading such a life, and be degraded down into such company." And he begun to wipe the corner of his eye with a rag.

"Dern your skin, ain't the company good enough for you?" says the baldhead, pretty pert and uppish.

"Yes, it *is* good enough for me; it's as good as I deserve; for who fetched me so low, when I was so high? *I* did myself. I don't blame *you*, gentlemen— far from it; I don't blame anybody. I deserve it all. Let the cold world do its worst; one thing I know—there's a grave somewhere for me. The world may go on just as its always done, and take everything from me—loved ones, property, everything—but it can't take that. Some day I'll lie down in it and forget it all, and my poor broken heart will be at rest." He went on a-wiping.

"Drot your pore broken heart," says the baldhead; "what are you heaving your pore broken heart at *us* f'r? *We* hain't done nothing."

"No, I know you haven't. I ain't blaming you, gentlemen. I brought my self down—yes, I did it myself. It's right I should suffer—perfectly right—I don't make any moan."

"Brought you down from whar? Whar was you brought down from?"

"Ah, you would not believe me; the world never believes—let it pass—'tis no matter. The secret of my birth——"

"The secret of your birth? Do you mean to say——"

"Gentlemen," says the young man, very solemn, "I will reveal it to you, for I feel I may have confidence in you. By rights I am a duke!"

Jim's eyes bugged out when he heard that; and I reckon mine did, too. Then the baldhead says: "No! you can't mean it?"

"Yes. My great-grandfather, eldest son of the Duke of Bridgewater, fled to this country about the end of the last century, to breathe the pure air of freedom; married here, and died, leaving a son, his own father dying about the same time. The second son of the late duke seized the title and estates—the infant real duke was ignored. I am the lineal descendant of that infant—I am the rightful Duke of Bridgewater; and here am I, forlorn, torn from my high estate, hunted of men, despised by the cold world, ragged, worn, heart-broken, and degraded to the companionship of felons on a raft!"

Jim pitied him ever so much, and so did I. We tried to comfort him, but he said it warn't much use, he couldn't be much comforted; said if we was a mind to acknowledge him, that would do him more good than most anything else; so we said we would, if he would tell us how. He said we ought to bow, when we spoke to him, and say "Your Grace," or "My Lord," or "Your Lordship"—and he wouldn't mind it if we called him plain "Bridgewater," which he said was a title, anyway, and not a name; and one of us ought to wait on him at dinner, and do any little thing for him he wanted done.

Well, that was all easy, so we done it. All through dinner Jim stood around and waited on him, and says, "Will yo' Grace have some o' dis, or some o' dat?" and so on, and a body could see it was mighty pleasing to him.

But the old man got pretty silent, by-and-by—didn't have much to say, and didn't look pretty comfortable over all that petting that was going on around that duke. He seemed to have something on his mind. So, along in the afternoon, he says:

"Looky here, Bilgewater," he says, "I'm nation sorry for you, but you ain't the only person that's had troubles like that."

"No?"

"No, you ain't. You ain't the only person that's ben snaked down wrongfully out'n a high place."

"Alas!"

"No, you ain't the only person that's had a secret of his birth." And by jings, *he* begins to cry.

"Hold! What do you mean?"

"Bilgewater, kin I trust you?" says the old man, still sort of sobbing.

"To the bitter death!" He took the old man by the hand and squeezed it, and says, "The secret of your being: speak!"

"Bilgewater, I am the late Dauphin!"

You bet you Jim and me stared, this time. Then the duke says:

"You are what?"

"Yes, my friend, it is too true—your eyes is lookin' at this very moment on the pore disappeared Dauphin, Looy the Seventeen, son of Looy the Sixteen and Marry Antonette."

"You! At your age! No! You mean you're the late Charlemagne; you must be six or seven hundred years old, at the very least."

"Trouble has done it, Bilgewater, trouble has done it; trouble has brung these gray hairs and this premature balditude. Yes, gentlemen, you see before you, in blue jeans and misery, the wanderin', exiled, trampled-on and sufferin' rightful King of France."

Well, he cried and took on so, that me and Jim didn't know hardly what to do, we was so sorry—and so glad and proud we'd got him with us, too. So we set in, like we done before with the duke, and tried to comfort *him*. But he said it warn't no use, nothing but to be dead and done with it all could do him any good; though he said it often made him feel easier and better for a while if people treated him according to his rights, and got down on one knee to speak to him, and always called him "Your Majesty," and waited on him first at meals, and didn't set down in his presence till he asked them. So Jim and me set to majestying him, and doing this and that and t'other for him, and standing up till he told us we might set down. This done him heaps of good, and so he got cheerful and comfortable. But the duke kind of soured on him, and didn't look a bit satisfied with the way things was going; still, the king acted real friendly towards him, and said the duke's great-grandfather and all the other Dukes of Bilgewater was a good deal thought of by *his* father and was allowed to come to the palace considerable; but the duke staid huffy a good while, till by-and-by the king says:

"Like as not we got to be together a blamed long time, on this h-yer raft, Bilgewater, and so what's the use o' your bein' sour? It'll only make things oncomfortable. It ain't my fault I warn't born a duke, it ain't your fault you warn't born a king—so what's the use to worry? Make the best o' things the way you find 'em, says I—that's my motto. This ain't no bad thing that we've struck here—plenty grub and an easy life—come, give us your hand, Duke, and less all be friends."

The duke done it, and Jim and me was pretty glad to see it. It took away all the uncomfortableness, and we felt mighty good over it, because it would a been a miserable business to have any unfriendliness on the raft; for what you want, above all things, on a raft, is for everybody to be satisfied, and feel right and kind towards the others.

It didn't take me long to make up my mind that these liars warn't no kings nor dukes, at all, but just low-down humbugs and frauds. But I never said nothing, never let on; kept it to myself; it's the best way; then you don't have no quarrels, and don't get into no trouble. If they wanted us to call them kings and dukes, I hadn't no objections, 'long as it would keep peace in the family; and it warn't no use to tell Jim, so I didn't tell him. If I never learnt nothing else out of pap, I learnt that the best way to get along with this kind of people is to let them have their own way.

CHAPTER XX

They asked us considerable many questions; wanted to know what we covered up the raft that way for, and laid by in the day-time instead of running—was Jim a runaway nigger? Says I—

"Goodness sakes, would a runaway nigger run *south?*"

No, they allowed he wouldn't. I had to account for things some way, so I says:

"My folks are living in Pike County, in Missouri, where I was born, and they all died off but me and pa and my brother Ike. Pa, he 'lowed he'd break up and go down and live with Uncle Ben, who's got a little one-horse place on the river, forty-four mile below Orleans. Pa was pretty poor, and had some debts; so when he'd squared up there warn't nothing left but sixteen dollars and our nigger, Jim. That warn't enough to take us forteen hundred mile, deck passage nor no other way. Well, when the river rose, pa had a streak of luck one day; he ketched this piece of raft; so we reckoned we'd go down to Orleans on it. Pa's luck didn't hold out; a steamboat run over the forrard corner of the raft, one night, and we all went overboard and dove under the wheel; Jim and me come up, all right, but pa was drunk, and Ike was only four years old, so they never come up no more. Well, for the next day or two we had considerable trouble, because people was always coming out in skiffs and trying to take Jim away from me, saying they believed he was a runaway nigger. We don't run day-times no more, now; nights they don't bother us."

The duke says—

"Leave me alone to cipher out a way so we can run in the day-time if we want to. I'll think the thing over—I'll invent a plan that'll fix it. We'll let it alone for to-day, because of course we don't want to go by that town yonder in day-light—it mightn't be healthy."

Towards night it begun to darken up and look like rain; the heat lightning was squirting around, low down in the sky, and the leaves was beginning to shiver—it was going to be pretty ugly, it was easy to see that. So the duke and the king went to overhauling our wigwam, to see what the beds was like. My bed was a straw tick—better than Jim's, which was a corn-shuck tick; there's always cobs around about in a shuck tick, and they poke into you and hurt; and when you roll over, the dry shucks sound like you was rolling over in a pile of dead leaves; it makes such a rustling that you wake up. Well, the duke allowed he would take my bed; but the king allowed he wouldn't. He says—

"I should a reckoned the difference in rank would a sejested to you that a corn-shuck bed warn't just fitten for me to sleep on. Your Grace'll take the shuck bed yourself."

Jim and me was in a sweat again, for a minute, being afraid there was going to be some more trouble amongst them; so we was pretty glad when the duke says—

"'Tis my fate to be always ground into the mire under the iron heel of oppression. Misfortune has broken my once haughty spirit; I yield, I submit; 'tis my fate. I am alone in the world—let me suffer; I can bear it."

We got away as soon as it was good and dark. The king told us to stand well out towards the middle of the river, and not show a light till we got a long ways below the town. We come in sight of the little bunch of lights by-and-by—that was the town, you know—and slid by, about a half a mile out, all right. When we was three-quarters of a mile below, we hoisted up our signal lantern; and about ten o'clock it come on to rain and blow and thunder and lighten like everything; so the king told us to both stay on watch till the weather got better; then him and the duke crawled into the wigwam and turned in for the night. It was my watch below, till twelve, but I wouldn't a turned in, anyway, if I'd had a bed; because a body don't see such a storm as that every day in the week, not by a long sight. My souls, how the wind did scream along! And every second or two there'd come a glare that lit up the white-caps for a half a mile around, and you'd see the islands looking dusty through the rain, and the trees thrashing aound in the wind; then comes a *h-wack!*—bum! bum! bumble-umble-umbum-bum-bum-bum—and the thunder would go rumbling and grumbling away, and quit—and then *rip* comes another flash and another sock-dolager. The waves most washed me off the raft, sometimes, but I hadn't any clothes on, and didn't mind. We didn't have no trouble about snags; the lightning was glaring and flittering around so constant that we could see them plenty soon enough to throw her head this way or that and miss them.

I had the middle watch, you know, but I was pretty sleepy by that time, so Jim he said he would stand the first half of it for me; he was always mighty good, that way, Jim was. I crawled into the wigwam, but the king and the duke had their legs sprawled around so there warn't no show for me; so I laid outside—I didn't mind the rain, because it was warm, and the waves warn't running so high, now. About two they come up again, though, and Jim was going to call me, but he changed his mind because he reckoned they warn't high enough yet to do any harm; but he was mistaken about that, for pretty soon all of a sudden along comes a regular ripper, and washed me overboard. It most killed Jim a-laughing. He was the easiest nigger to laugh that ever was, anyway.

I took the watch, and Jim he laid down and snored away; and by-and-by the storm let up for good and all; and the first cabin-light that showed, I rousted him out and we slid the raft into hiding-quarters for the day.

The king got out an old ratty deck of cards, after breakfast, and him and the duke played seven-up a while, five cents a game. Then they got tired of it, and allowed they would "lay out a campaign," as they called it. The duke went down into his carpet-bag and fetched up a lot of little printed bills, and read them out loud. One bill said "The celebrated Dr. Armand de Montalban of Paris," would "lecture on the Science of Phrenology" at such and such a place, on the blank day of blank, at ten cents admission, and "furnish charts of character at twenty-five cents apiece." The duke said that was *him*. In another bill he was the "world renowned Shaksperean tragedian, Garrick the Younger, of Drury Lane, London." In other bills he had a lot of other names and done other wonderful things, like finding water and gold with a "divining rod," "dissipating witch-spells," and so on. By-and-by he says—

"But the histrionic muse is the darling. Have you ever trod the boards, Royalty?"

"No," says the king.

"You shall, then, before you're three days older, Fallen Grandeur," says the duke. "The first good town we come to, we'll hire a hall and do the sword-fight in Richard III. and the balcony scene in Romeo and Juliet. How does that strike you?"

"I'm in, up to the hub, for anything that will pay, Bilgewater, but you see I don't know nothing about play-actn', and hain't ever seen much of it. I was too small when pap used to have 'em at the palace. Do you reckon you can learn me?"

"Easy!"

"All right. I'm jist a-freezn' for something fresh, anyway. Less commence, right away."

So the duke he told him all about who Romeo was, and who Juliet was, and said he was used to being Romeo, so the king could be Juliet.

"But if Juliet's such a young gal, Duke, my peeled head and my white whiskers is goin' to look oncommon odd on her, maybe."

"No, don't you worry—these country jakes won't ever think of that. Besides, you know, you'll be in costume, and that makes all the difference in the world; Juliet's in a balcony, enjoying the moonlight before she goes to bed, and she's got on her night-gown and her ruffled night-cap. Here are the costumes for the parts."

He got out two or three curtain-calico suits, which he said was meedyevil armor for Richard III. and t'other chap, and a long white cotton night-shirt and a ruffled night-cap to match. The king was satisfied; so the duke got out his book and read the parts over in the most splendid spread-eagle way, prancing around and acting at the same time, to show how it had got to be done; then he give the book to the king and told him to get his part by heart.

There was a little one-horse town about three mile down the bend, and after dinner the duke said he had ciphered out his idea about how to run in daylight without it being dangersome for Jim; so he allowed he would go down to the town and fix that thing. The king allowed he would go too, and see if he couldn't strike something. We was out of coffee, so Jim said I better go along with them in the canoe and get some.

When we got there, there warn't nobody stirring; streets empty, and perfectly dead and still, like Sunday. We found a sick nigger sunning himself in a back yard, and he said everybody that warn't too young or too sick or too old, was gone to camp-meeting, about two mile back in the woods. The king got the directions, and allowed he'd go and work that camp-meeting for all it was worth, and I might go, too.

The duke said what he was after was a printing office. We found it; a little bit of a concern, up over a carpenter shop—carpenters and printers all gone to the meeting, and no doors locked. It was a dirty, littered-up place, and had ink marks, and handbills with pictures of horses and runaway niggers on them, all over the walls. The duke shed his coat and said he was all right, now. So me and the king lit out for the camp-meeting.

We got there in about a half an hour, fairly dripping, for it was a most awful hot day. There was much as a thousand people there, from twenty mile around. The woods was full of teams and wagons, hitched everywheres, feeding out of the wagon troughs and stomping to keep off the flies. There was sheds made out of poles and roofed over with branches, where they had lemonade and gingerbread to sell, and piles of watermelons and green corn and such-like truck.

The preaching was going on under the same kinds of sheds, only they was bigger and held crowds of people. The benches was made out of outside slabs of logs, with holes bored in the round side to drive sticks into for legs. They didn't have no backs. The preachers had high platforms to stand on, at one end of the sheds. The women had on sunbonnets; and some had linsey-woolsey frocks, some gingham ones, and a few of the young ones had on calico. Some of the young men was barefooted, and some of the children didn't have on any clothes but just a tow-linen shirt. Some of the old women was knitting, and some of the young folks was courting on the sly.

The first shed we come to, the preacher was lining out a hymn. He lined out two lines, everybody sung it, and it was kind of grand to hear it, there was so many of them and they done it in such a rousing way; then he lined out two more for them to sing—and so on. The people woke up more and more, and sung louder and louder; and towards the end, some begun to groan, and some begun to shout. Then the preacher begun to preach; and begun in earnest, too; and went weaving first to one side of the platform and then the other, and then a leaning down over the front of it, with his arms and his body going all the time, and shouting his words out with all his might; and every now and then he would hold up his Bible and spread it open, and kind of pass it around this way and that, shouting, "It's the brazen serpent in the wilderness! Look upon it and live!" And people would shout out, "Glory!—A-a-*men!*" And so he went on, and the people groaning and crying and saying amen:

"Oh, come to the mourner's bench! come, black with sin! (*amen!*) come, sick and sore! (*amen!*) come, lame and halt, and blind! (*amen!*) come, pore and needy, sunk in shame! (*a-a-men!*) come all tha's worn, and soiled, and suffering!—come with a broken spirit! come with a contrite heart! come in your rags and sin and dirt! the waters that cleanse is free, the door of heaven stands open—oh, enter in and be at rest!" (*a-a-men! glory, glory hallelujah!*)

And so on. You couldn't make out what the preacher said,

any more, on account of the shouting and crying. Folks got up, everywheres in the crowd, and worked their way, just by main strength, to the mourners' bench, with the tears running down their faces; and when all the mourners had got up there to the front benches in a crowd, they sung, and shouted, and flung themselves down on the straw, just crazy and wild.

Well, the first I knowed, the king got a-going; and you could hear him over everybody; and next he went a-charging up on to the platform and the preacher he begged him to speak to the people, and he done it. He told them he was a pirate—been a pirate for thirty years, out in the Indian Ocean, and his crew was thinned out considerable, last spring, in a fight, and he was home now, to take out some fresh men, and thanks to goodness he'd been robbed last night, and put ashore off of a steamboat without a cent, and he was glad of it, it was the blessedest thing that ever happened to him, because he was a changed man now, and happy for the first time in his life; and poor as he was, he was going to start right off and work his way back to the Indian Ocean and put in the rest of his life trying to turn the pirates into the true path; for he could do it better than anybody else, being acquainted with all the pirate crews in that ocean; and though it would take him a long time to get there, without money, he would get there anyway, and every time he convinced a pirate he would say to him, "Don't you thank me, don't you give me no credit, it all belongs to them dear people in Pokeville camp-meeting, natural brothers and benefactors of the race—and that dear preacher there, the truest friend a pirate ever had!"

And then he busted into tears, and so did everybody. Then somebody sings out, "Take up a collection for him, take up a collection!" Well, a half a dozen made a jump to do it, but somebody sings out, "Let *him* pass the hat around!" Then everybody said it, the preacher too.

So the king went all through the crowd with his hat, swabbing his eyes, and blessing the people and praising them and thanking them for being so good to the poor pirates away off there; and every little while the prettiest kind of girls, with the tears running down their cheeks, would up and ask him would he let them kiss him, for to remember him by; and he always done it; and some of them he hugged and kissed as many as five or six times—and he was invited to stay a week; and everybody wanted him to live in their houses, and said they'd think it was an honor; but he said as this was the last day of the camp-meeting he couldn't do no good, and besides he was in a sweat to get to the Indian Ocean right off and go to work on the pirates.

When we got back to the raft and he come to count up, he found he had collected eighty-seven dollars and seventy-five cents. And then he had fetched away a three-gallon jug of whisky, too, that he found under a wagon when we was starting home through the woods. The king said, take it all around, it laid over any day he'd ever put in in the missionarying line. He said it warn't no use talking, heathens don't amount to shucks, alongside of pirates, to work a camp-meeting with.

The duke was thinking *he'd* been doing pretty well, till the king come to show up, but after that he didn't think so so much. He had set up and printed off two little jobs for farmers, in that printing office—horse bills—and took the money, four dollars. And he had got in ten dollars worth of advertisements for the paper, which he said he would put in for four dollars if they would pay in advance—so they done it. The price of the paper was two dollars a year, but he took in three subscriptions for half a dollar apiece on condition of them paying him in advance; they were going to pay in cord-wood and onions, as usual, but he said he had just bought the concern and knocked down the price as low as he could afford it, and was going to run it for cash. He set up a little piece of poetry, which he made, himself, out of his own head—three verses—kind of sweet and saddish—the name of it was, "Yes, crush, cold world, this breaking heart"—and he left that all set up and ready to print in the paper and didn't charge nothing for it. Well, he took in nine dollars and a half, and said he'd done a pretty square day's work for it.

Then he showed us another little job he's printed and hadn't charged for, because it was for us. It had a picture of a runaway nigger, with a bundle on a stick, over his shoulder, and "$200 reward" under it. The reading was all about Jim, and just described him to a dot. It said he run away from St. Jacques' plantation, forty mile below New Orleans, last winter, and likely went north, and whoever would catch him and send him back, he could have the reward and expenses.

"Now," says the duke, "after to-night we can run in the daytime if we want to. Whenever we see anybody coming, we can tie Jim hand and foot with a rope, and lay him in the wigwam and show this handbill and say we captured him up the river, and were too poor to travel on a steam boat, so we got this little raft on credit from our friends and are going down to get the reward. Handcuffs and chains would look still better on Jim, but it wouldn't go well with the story of us being so poor. Too much like jewelry. Ropes are the correct thing—we must preserve the unities, as we say on the boards."

We all said the duke was pretty smart, and there couldn't be no trouble about running daytimes. We judged we could make miles enough that night to get out of the reach of the pow-wow we reckoned the duke's work in the printing office was going to make in that little town—then we could boom right along, if we wanted to.

We laid low and kept still, and never shoved out till nearly ten o'clock; then we slid by, pretty wide away from the town, and didn't hoist our lantern till we was clear out of sight of it.

When Jim called me to take the watch at four in the morning, he says—

"Huck, does you reck'n we gwyne to run acrost any mo' kings on dis trip?"

"No," I says, "I reckon not."

"Well," says he, "dat's all right, den. I doan' mine one er two kings, but dat's enough. Dis one's powerful drunk, en de duke ain' much better."

I found Jim had been trying to get him to talk French, so he could hear what it was like; but he said he had been in this country so long, and had so much trouble, he'd forgot it.

CHAPTER XXI

It was after sun-up, now, but we went right on, and didn't tie up. The king and the duke turned out, by-and-by, looking pretty rusty; but after they'd jumped overboard and took a swim, it chippered them up a good deal. After breakfast the king he took a seat on a corner of the raft, and pulled off his boots and rolled up his britches, and let his legs dangle in the water, so as to be comfortable, and lit his pipe, and went to getting his Romeo and Juliet by heart. When he had got it pretty good, him and the duke begun to practice it together. The duke had to learn him over and over again, how to say every speech; and he made him sigh, and put his hand on his heart, and after a while he said he done it pretty well; "only," he says, "you mustn't bellow out *Romeo!* that way, like a bull—you must say it soft, and sick, and languishy, so—R-o-o-meo! that is the idea; for Juliet's a dear sweet mere child of a girl, you know, and she don't bray like a jackass."

Well, next they got out a couple of long swords that the duke made out of oak laths, and begun to practice the sword-fight—the duke called himself Richard III.; and the way they laid on, and pranced around the raft was grand to see. But by-and-by the king tripped and fell overboard, and after that they took a rest, and had a talk about all kinds of adventures they'd had in other times along the river.

After dinner, the duke says:

"Well, Capet, we'll want to make this a first-class show, you know, so I guess we'll add a little more to it. Want a little something to answer encores with, anyway."

"What's onkores, Bilgewater?"

The duke told him, and then says:

"I'll answer by doing the Highland fling or the sailor's hornpipe; and you—well, let me see—oh, I've got it—you can do Hamlet's soliloquy."

"Hamlet's which?"

"Hamlet's soliloquy, you know; the most celebrated thing in Shakespeare. Ah, it's sublime, sublime! Always fetches the house. I haven't got it in the book—I've only got one volume—but I reckon I can piece it out from memory. I'll just walk up and down a minute, and see if I can call it back from recollection's vaults."

So he went to marching up and down, thinking, and frowning horrible every now and then; then he would hoist up his eyebrows; next he would squeeze his hand on his forehead and stagger back and kind of moan; next he would sigh, and next he'd let on to drop a tear. It was beautiful to see him. By-and-by he got it. He told us to give attention. Then he strikes a most noble attitude, with one leg shoved forwards, and his arms stretched away up, and his head tilted back, looking up at the sky; and then he begins to rip and rave and grit his teeth; and after that, all through his speech he howled, and spread around, and swelled up his chest, and just knocked the spots out of any acting ever *I* see before. This is the speech— I learned it, easy enough, while he was learning it to the king:

To be, or not to be; that is the bare bodkin
That makes calamity of so long life;
For who would fardels bear, till Birnam Wood do come to Dunsinane,
But that the fear of something after death
Murders the innocent sleep,
Great nature's second course,
And makes us rather sling the arrows of outrageous fortune
Than fly to others that we know not of.
There's the respect must give us pause:
Wake Duncan with thy knocking! I would thou couldst;
For who would bear the whips and scorns of time,
The oppressor's wrong, the proud man's contumely,
The law's delay, and the quietus which his pangs might take,
In the dead waste and middle of the night, when churchyards yawn
In customary suits of solemn black,
But that the undiscovered country from whose bourne no traveler
returns,
Breathes forth contagion on the world,
And thus the native hue of resolution, like the poor cat i' the adage,
Is sicklied o'er with care,
And all the clouds that lowered o'er our housetops,
With this regard their currents turn awry,
And lose the name of action.
'Tis a consummation devoutly to be wished. But soft you, the fair
Ophelia:

Ope not thy ponderous and marble jaws,
But get thee to a nunnery—go!

Well, the old man he liked that speech, and he mighty soon got it so he could do it first rate. It seemed like he was just born for it; and when he had his hand in and was excited, it was perfectly lovely the way he would rip and tear and rair up behind when he was getting it off.

The first chance we got, the duke he had some show bills printed; and after that, for two or three days as we floated along, the raft was a most uncommon lively place, for there warn't nothing but sword-fighting and rehearsing—as the duke called it—going on all the time. One morning, when we was pretty well down the State of Arkansaw, we come in sight of a little one-horse town in a big bend; so we tied up about three-quarters of a mile above it, in the mouth of a crick which was shut in like a tunnel by the cypress trees, and all of us but Jim took the canoe and went down there to see if there was any chance in that place for our show.

We struck it mighty lucky; there was going to be a circus there that afternoon, and the country people was already beginning to come in, in all kinds of old shackly wagons, and on horses. The circus would leave before night, so our show would have a pretty good chance. The duke he hired the court house, and went around and stuck up our bills. They read like this:

Shaksperean Revival ! ! !
Wonderful Attraction !
For One Night Only !
The world renowned tragedians,
David Garrick the younger, of Drury Lane Theatre, London
and
Edmund Kean the elder, of the Royal Haymarket Theatre, Whitechapel, Pudding Lane, Piccadilly, London, and the
Royal Continental Theatres, in their sublime
Shaksperean Spectacle entitled
The Balcony Scene
in

Romeo and Juliet ! ! !

Romeo .... Mr. Garrick.

Juliet .... Mr. Kean.

Assisted by the whole strength of the company !

New costumes, new scenery, new appointments !

Also:

The thrilling, masterly, and blood-curdling

Broad-sword conflict

In Richard III. ! ! !

Richard III .... Mr. Garrick.

Richmond .... Mr. Kean.

also:

(by special request,)

Hamlet's Immortal Soliloquy ! !

By the Illustrious Kean !

Done by him 300 consecutive nights in Paris !

For One Night Only,

On account of imperative European engagements !

Admission 25 cents; children and servants, 10 cents.

Then we went loafing around the town. The stores and houses was most all old shackly dried-up frame concerns that hadn't ever been painted; they was set up three or four foot above ground on stilts, so as to be out of reach of the water when the river was overflowed. The houses had little gardens around them, but they didn't seem to raise hardly anything in them but jimpson weeds, and sunflowers, and ash-piles, and old curled-up boots and shoes, and pieces of bottles, and rags, and played-out tin-ware. The fences was made of different kinds of boards, nailed on at different times; and they leaned every which-way, and had gates that didn't generly have but one hinge—a leather one. Some of the fences had been whitewashed, some time or another, but the duke said it was in Columbus's time, like enough. There was generaly hogs in the garden, and people driving them out.

All the stores was along one street. They had white-domestic awnings in front, and the country people hitched their horses to the awning-posts. There was empty dry-goods boxes under the awnings, and loafers roosting on them all day long, whittling them with their Barlow knives; and chawing tobacco, and gaping and yawning and stretching—a mighty ornery lot. They generly had on yellow straw hats most as wide as an umbrella, but didn't wear no coats nor waistcoats; they called one another Bill, and Buck, and Hank, and Joe, and Andy, and talked lazy and drawly, and used considerable many cuss-words. There was as many as one loafer leaning up against every awning-post, and he most always had his hands in his britches pockets, except when he fetched them out to lend a chaw of tobacco or scratch. What a body was hearing amongst them, all the time was—

"Gimme a chaw 'v tobacker, Hank."

"Cain't—I hain't got but one chaw left. Ask Bill."

Maybe Bill he gives him a chaw; maybe he lies and says he ain't got none. Some of them kinds of loafers never has a cent in the world, nor a chaw of tobacco of their own. They get all their chawing by borrowing—they say to a fellow, "I wisht you'd len' me a chaw, Jack, I jist this minute give Ben Thompson the last chaw I had"—which is a lie, pretty much every time; it don't fool nobody but a stranger; but Jack ain't no stranger, so he says—

"*You* give him a chaw, did you? so did your sister's cat's grandmother. You pay me back the chaws you've awready borry'd off'n me, Lafe Buckner, then I'll loan you one or two ton of it, and won't charge you no back intrust, nuther."

"Well, I *did* pay you back some of it wunst."

"Yes, you did—'bout six chaws. You borry'd store tobacker and paid back nigger-head."

Store tobacco is flat black plug, but these fellows mostly chaws the natural leaf twisted. When they borrow a chaw, they don't generly cut it off with a knife, but they set the plug in between their teeth, and gnaw with their teeth and tug at the plug with their hands till they get it in two—then sometimes the one that owns the tobacco looks mournful at it when it's handed back, and says, sarcastic—

"Here, gimme the *chaw*, and you take the *plug*."

All the streets and lanes was just mud, they warn't nothing else *but* mud—mud as black as tar, and nigh about a foot deep in some places; and two or three inches deep in *all* the places. The hogs loafed and grunted around, everywheres. You'd see a muddy sow and a litter of pigs come lazying along the street and whollop herself right down in the way, where folks had to walk around her, and she'd stretch out, and shut her eyes, and wave her ears, whilst the pigs was milking her, and look as happy as if she was on salary. And pretty soon you'd hear a loafer sing out, "Hi! *so* boy! sick him, Tige!" and away the sow would go, squealing most horrible, with a dog or two swinging to each ear, and three or four dozen more a-coming; and then you would see all the loafers get up and watch the thing out of sight, and laugh at the fun and look grateful for the noise. Then they'd settle back again till there was a dog-fight. There couldn't anything wake them up all over, and make them happy all over, like a dog-fight—unless it might be putting turpentine on a stray dog and setting fire to him, or tying a tin pan to his tail and see him run himself to death.

On the river-front some of the houses was sticking out over the bank, and they was bowed and bent, and about ready to tumble in. The people had moved out of them. The bank was caved away under one corner of some others, and that corner was hanging over. People lived in them yet, but it was dangersome, because sometimes a strip of land as wide as a house caves in at a time. Sometimes a belt of land a quarter of a mile deep will start in and cave along and cave along till it all caves into the river in one summer. Such a town as that has to be always moving back, and back, and back, because the river's always gnawing at it.

The nearer it got to noon that day, the thicker and thicker was the wagons and horses in the streets, and more coming all the time. Families fetched their dinners with them, from the country, and eat them in the wagons. There was considerable whiskey drinking going on, and I seen three fights. By-and-by somebody sings out—

"Here comes old Boggs!—in from the country for his little old monthly drunk—here he comes, boys!"

All the loafers looked glad—I reckoned they was used to having fun out of Boggs. One of them says—

"Wonder who he's a gwyne to chaw up this time. If he'd a chawed up all the men he's ben a gwyne to chaw up in the last twenty year, he'd have considerable ruputation, now."

Another one says, "I wisht old Boggs'd threaten me, 'cuz then I'd know I warn't gwyne to die for a thousan' year."

Boggs comes a-tearing along on his horse, whooping and yelling like an Injun, and singing out—

"Cler the track, thar. I'm on the waw-path, and the price uv coffins is a gwyne to raise."

He was drunk, and weaving about in his saddle; he was over fifty year old, and had a very red face. Everybody yelled at him, and laughed at him, and sassed him, and he sassed back, and said he'd attend to them and lay them out in their regular turns, but he couldn't wait now, because he'd come to town to kill old Colonel Sherburn, and his motto was, "meat first, and spoon vittles to top off on."

He see me, and rode up and says—

"Whar'd you come f'm, boy? You prepared to die?"

Then he rode on. I was scared; but a man says—

"He don't mean nothing; he's always a carryin' on like that, when he's drunk. He's the best-naturedest old fool in Arkansaw—never hurt nobody, drunk nor sober."

Boggs rode up before the biggest store in town and bent his head down so he could see under the curtain of the awning, and yells—

"Come out here, Sherburn! Come out and meet the man you've swindled. You're the houn' I'm after, and I'm a gwyne to have you, too!"

And so he went on, calling Sherburn everything he could lay his tongue to, and the whole street packed with people listening and laughing and going on. By-and-by a proud-looking man about fifty-five—and he was a heap the best dressed man in that town, too—steps out of the store, and the crowd drops back on each side to let him come. He says to Boggs, mighty ca'm and slow—he says:

"I'm tired of this; but I'll endure it till one o'clock. Till one o'clock, mind—no longer. If you open your mouth against me only once, after that time, you can't travel so far but I will find you."

Then he turns and goes in. The crowd looked mighty sober; nobody stirred, and there warn't no more laughing. Boggs rode off blackguarding Sherburn as loud as he could yell, all down the street; and pretty soon back he comes and stops before the store, still keeping it up. Some men crowded around him and tried to get him to shut up, but he wouldn't; they told him it would be one o'clock in about fifteen minutes and so he *must* go home—he must go right away. But it didn't do no good. He cussed away, with all his might, and throwed his hat down in the mud and rode over it, and pretty soon away he went a-raging down the street again, with his gray hair a-flying. Everybody that could get a chance at him tried their best to coax him off of his horse so they could lock him up and get him sober; but it warn't no use—up the street he would tear again, and give Sherburn another cussing. By-and-by somebody says—

"Go for his daughter!—quick, go for his daughter; sometimes he'll listen to her. If anybody can persuade him, she can."

So somebody started on a run. I walked down street a ways, and stopped. In about five or ten minutes, here comes Boggs again—but not on his horse. He was a-reeling across the street towards me, bareheaded, with a friend on both sides of him aholt of his arms and hurrying him along. He was quiet, and looked uneasy; and he warn't hanging back any, but was doing some of the hurrying himself. Somebody sings out—

"Boggs!"

I looked over there to see who said it, and it was that Colonel Sherburn. He was standing perfectly still, in the street, and had a pistol raised in his right hand—not aiming it, but holding it out with the barrel tilted up towards the sky. The same second I see a young girl coming on the run, and two men with her. Boggs and the men turned round, to see who called him, and when they see the pistol the men jumped to one side, and the pistol barrel come down slow and steady to a level—both barrels cocked. Boggs throws up both of his hands, and says, "O

Lord, don't shoot!" Bang! goes the first shot, and he staggers back clawing at the air—bang! goes the second one, and he tumbles backwards onto the ground, heavy and solid, with his arms spread out. That young girl screamed out, and comes rushing, and down she throws herself on her father, crying, and saying, "Oh, he's killed him, he's killed him!" The crowd closed up around them, and shouldered and jammed one another, with their necks stretched, trying to see, and people on the inside trying to shove them back, and shouting, "Back, back! give him air, give him air!"

Colonel Sherburn he tossed his pistol onto the ground, and turned around on his heels and walked off.

They took Boggs to a little drug store, the crowd pressing around, just the same, and the whole town following, and I rushed and got a good place at the window, where I was close to him and could see in. They laid him on the floor, and put one large Bible under his head, and opened another one and spread it on his breast—but they tore open his shirt first, and I seen where one of the bullets went in. He made about a dozen long gasps, his breast lifting the Bible up when he drawed in his breath, and letting it down again when he breathed it out—and after that he laid still; he was dead. Then they pulled his daughter away from him, screaming and crying, and took her off. She was about sixteen, and very sweet and gentle-looking, but awful pale and scared.

Well, pretty soon the whole town was there, squirming and scrouging and pushing and shoving to get at the window and have a look, but people that had the places wouldn't give them up, and folks behind them was saying all the time, "Say, now, you've looked enough, you fellows; 'taint right and 'taint fair, for you to stay thar all the time, and never give nobody a chance; other folks has their rights as well as you."

There was considerable jawing back, so I slid out, thinking maybe there was going to be trouble. The streets was full, and everybody was excited. Everybody that seen the shooting was telling how it happened, and there was a big crowd packed around each one of these fellows, stretching their necks and listening. One long lanky man, with long hair and a big white fur stove-pipe hat on the back of his head, and a crooked-handled cane, marked out the places on the ground where Boggs stood, and where Sherburn stood, and the people, following him around from one place to t'other and watching everything he done, and bobbing their heads to show they understood, and stooping a little and resting their hands on their thighs to watch him mark the places on the ground with his cane; and then he stood up straight and stiff where Sherburn had stood, frowning and having his hat-brim down over his eyes, and sung out, "Boggs!" and then fetched his cane down slow to a level, and says "Bang!" staggered backwards, says "Bang!" again, and fell down flat on his back. The people that had seen the thing said he done it perfect; said it was just exactly the way it all happened. Then as much as a dozen people got out their bottles and treated him.

Well, by-and-by somebody said Sherburn ought to be lynched. In about a minute everybody was saying it; so away they went, mad and yelling, and snatching down every clothes-line they come to, to do the hanging with.

CHAPTER XXII

They swarmed up the street towards Sherburn's house, a-whopping and yelling and raging like Injuns, and everything had to clear the way or get run over and tromped to mush, and it was awful to see. Children was heeling it ahead of the mob, screaming and trying to get out of the way; and every window along the road was full of women's heads, and there was nigger boys in every tree, and bucks and wenches looking over every fence; and as soon as the mob would get nearly to them they would break and skaddle back out of reach. Lots of the women and girls was crying and taking on, scared most to death.

They swarmed up in front of Sherburn's palings as thick as they could jam together, and you couldn't hear yourself think for the noise. It was a little twenty-foot yard. Some sung out

"Tear down the fence! tear down the fence!" Then there was a racket of ripping and tearing and smashing, and down she goes, and the front wall of the crowd begins to roll in like a wave.

Just then Sherburn steps out on to the roof of his little front porch, with a double-barrel gun in his hand, and takes his stand, perfectly ca'm and deliberate, not saying a word. The racket stopped, and the wave sucked back.

Sherburn never said a word—just stood there, looking down. The stillness was awful creepy and uncomfortable. Sherburn run his eye slow along the crowd; and wherever it struck, the people tried a little to outgaze him, but they couldn't; they dropped their eyes and looked sneaky. Then pretty soon Sherburn sort of laughed; not the pleasant kind, but the kind that makes you feel like when you are eating bread that's got sand in it.

Then he says, slow and scornful:

"The idea of *you* lynching anybody! It's amusing. The idea of you thinking you had pluck enough to lynch a *man!* Because you're brave enough to tar and feather poor friendless cast-out women that come along here, did that make you think you had grit enough to lay your hands on a *man?* Why, a *man's* safe in the hands of ten thousand of your kind—as long as it's day-time and you're not behind him.

"Do I know you? I know you clear through. I was born and raised in the South, and I've lived in the North; so I know the average all around. The average man's a coward. In the North he lets anybody walk over him that wants to, and goes home and prays for a humble spirit to bear it. In the South one man, all by himself, has stopped a stage full of men, in the day-time, and robbed the lot. Your newspapers call you a brave people so much that you think you *are* braver than any other people—whereas you're just *as* brave, and no braver. Why don't your juries hang murderers? Because they're afraid the man's friends will shoot them in the back, in the dark—and it's just what they *would* do.

"So they always acquit; and then a *man* goes in the night, with a hundred masked cowards at his back, and lynches the rascal. Your mistake is, that you didn't bring a man with you;

that's one mistake, and the other is that you didn't come in the dark, and fetch your masks. You brought *part* of a man—Buck Harkness, there—and if you hadn't had him to start you, you'd a taken it out in blowing.

"You didn't want to come. The average man don't like trouble and danger. *You* don't like trouble and danger. But if only *half* a man—like Buck Harkness, there—shouts 'Lynch him, lynch him!' you're afraid to back down—afraid you'll be found out to be what you are—*cowards*—and so you raise a yell, and hang yourselves onto that half-a-man's coat tail, and come raging up here, swearing what big things you're going to do. The pitifulest thing out is a mob; that's what an army is—a mob; they don't fight with courage that's born in them, but with courage that's borrowed from their mass, and from their officers. But a mob without any *man* at the head of it, is *beneath* pitifulness. Now the thing for *you* to do, is to droop your tails and go home and crawl in a hole. If any real lynching's going to be done, it will be done in the dark, Southern fashion; and when they come they'll bring their masks, and fetch a *man* along. Now *leave*—and take your half-a-man with you"—tossing his gun up across his left arm and cocking it, when he says this.

The crowd washed back sudden, and then broke all apart and went tearing off every which way, and Buck Harkness he heeled it after them, looking tolerable cheap. I could a staid, if I'd a wanted to, but I didn't want to.

I went to the circus, and loafed around the back side till the watchman went by, and then dived in under the tent. I had my twenty-dollar gold piece and some other money, but I reckoned I better save it, because there ain't no telling how soon you are going to need it, away from home and amongst strangers, that way. You can't be too careful. I ain't opposed to spending money on circuses, when there ain't no use in *wasting* it on them.

It was a real bully circus. It was the splendidest sight that ever was, when they all come riding in, two and two, a gentleman and a lady, side by side, the men just in their drawers and under-shirts, and no shoes nor stirrups, and resting their hands on their thighs, easy and comfortable—there must a' been twenty of them—and every lady with a lovely complexion, and perfectly beautiful, and looking just like a gang of real sure-enough queens, and dressed in clothes that cost millions of dollars, and just littered with diamonds. It was a powerful fine sight; I never see anything so lovely. And then one by one they got up and stood, and went a-weaving around the ring so gentle and wavy and graceful, the men looking ever so tall and airy and straight, with their heads bobbing and skimming along, away up there under the tent-roof, and every lady's rose-leafy dress flapping soft and silky around her hips, and she looking like the most loveliest parasol.

And then faster and faster they went, all of them dancing, first one foot stuck out in the air and then the other, the horses leaning more and more, and the ring-master going round and round the centre-pole, cracking his whip and shouting "hi!—hi!" and the clown cracking jokes behind him; and by-and-by all hands dropped the reins, and every lady put her knuckles on her hips and every gentleman folded his arms, and then how the horses did lean over and hump themselves! And so, one after the other they all skipped off into the ring, and made the sweetest bow I ever see, and then scampered out, and everybody clapped their hands and went just about wild.

Well, all through the circus they done the most astonishing things; and all the time that clown carried on so it most killed the people. The ring-master couldn't ever say a word to him but he was back at him quick as a wink with the funniest things a body ever said; and how he ever *could* think of so many of them, and so sudden and so pat, was what I couldn't noway understand. Why, I couldn't a thought of them in a year. And by-and-by a drunk man tried to get into the ring—said he wanted to ride; said he could ride as well as anybody that ever was. They argued and tried to keep him out, but he wouldn't listen, and the whole show came to a standstill. Then the people begun to holler at him and make fun of him, and that made him mad, and he begun to rip and tear; so that stirred up the people, and a lot of men begun to pile down off of the benches and swarm towards the ring, saying, "Knock him down! throw him out!" and one or two women begun to scream. So, then, the ring-master he made a little speech, and said he hoped there wouldn't be no disturbance, and if the man would promise he wouldn't make no more trouble, he would let him ride, if he thought he could stay on the horse. So everybody laughed and said all right, and the man got on. The minute he was on, the horse begun to rip and tear and jump and cavort around, with two circus men hanging onto his bridle trying to hold him, and the drunk man hanging onto his neck, and his heels flying in the air every jump, and the whole crowd of people standing up shouting and laughing till the tears rolled down. And at last, sure enough, all the circus men could do, the horse broke loose, and away he went like the very nation, round and round the ring, with that sot laying down on him and hanging to his neck, with first one leg hanging most to the ground on one side, and then t'other one on t'other side, and the people just crazy. It warn't funny to me, though; I was all of a tremble to see his danger. But pretty soon he struggled up astraddle and grabbed the bridle, a-reeling this way and that; and the next minute he sprung up and dropped the bridle and stood! and the horse agoing like a house afire too. He just stood up there, a-sailing around as easy and comfortable as if he warn't ever drunk in his life—and then he begun to pull off his clothes and sling them. He shed them so thick they kind of clogged up the air, and altogether he shed seventeen suits. And then, there he was, slim and handsome, and dressed the gaudiest and prettiest you ever saw, and he lit into that horse with his whip and made him fairly hum—and finally skipped off, and made his bow and danced off to the dressing-room, and everybody just a-howling with pleasure and astonishment.

Then the ring-master he see how he had been fooled, and he *was* the sickest ring-master you ever see, I reckon. Why, it was one of his own men! He had got up that joke all out of his own head, and never let on to nobody. Well, I felt sheepish enough, to be took in so, but I wouldn't a been in that ring-master's place, not for a thousand dollars. I don't know; there may be bullier circuses than what that one was, but I never struck them yet. Anyways it was plenty good enough for *me;* and wherever I run across it, it can have all of *my* custom, every time.

Well, that night we had *our* show; but there warn't only

about twelve people there; just enough to pay expenses. And they laughed all the time, and that made the duke mad; and everybody left, anyway, before the show was over, but one boy which was asleep. So the duke said these Arkansas lunkheads couldn't come up to Shakspeare; what they wanted was low comedy—and may be something ruther worse than low comedy, he reckoned. He said he could size their style. So next morning he got some big sheets of wrapping-paper and some black paint, and drawed off some handbills and stuck them up all over the village. The bills said:

AT THE COURT HOUSE!
FOR 3 NIGHTS ONLY!
The World-Renowned Tragedians
DAVID GARRICK THE YOUNGER!
AND
EDMUND KEAN THE ELDER!
Of the London and Continental
Theatres,
In their Thrilling Tragedy of
THE KING'S CAMELOPARD
OR
THE ROYAL NONESUCH!!!
Admission 50 cents.

Then at the bottom was the biggest line of all—which said:

LADIES AND CHILDREN NOT ADMITTED.

"There," says he, "if that line don't fetch them, I dont know Arkansaw!"

CHAPTER XXIII

Well, all day him and the king was hard at it, rigging up a stage, and a curtain, and a row of candles for footlights; and that night the house was jam full of men in no time. When the place couldn't hold no more, the duke he quit tending door and went around the back way and come onto the stage and stood up before the curtain, and made a little speech, and praised up this tragedy, and said it was the most thrillingest one that ever was; and so he went on a-bragging about the tragedy and about Edmund Kean the Elder, which was to play the main principal part in it; and at last when he'd got everybody's expectations up high enough, he rolled up the curtain, and the next minute the king come a-prancing out on all fours, naked; and he was painted all over, ring-streaked-and-striped, all sorts of colors, as splendid as a rainbow. And—but never mind the rest of his outfit, it was just wild, but it was awful funny. The people most killed themselves laughing; and when the king got done capering, and capered off behind the scenes, they roared and clapped and stormed and haw-hawed till he come back and done it over again; and after that, they made him do it another time. Well, it would a made a cow laugh to see the shines that old idiot cut.

Then the duke he lets the curtain down, and bows to the people, and says the great tragedy will be performed only two nights more, on accounts of pressing London engagements, where the seats is all sold aready for it in Drury Lane; and then he makes them another bow, and says if he has succeeded in pleasing them and instructing them, he will be deeply obleeged if they will mention it to their friends and get them to come and see it.

Twenty people sings out:

"What, is it over? Is that *all?*"

The duke says yes. Then there was a fine time. Everybody sings out "sold," and rose up mad, and was agoing for that stage and them tragedians. But a big fine-looking man jumps up on a bench, and shouts:

"Hold on! Just a word, gentlemen." They stopped to listen. "We are sold—mighty badly sold. But we don't want to be the laughing-stock of this whole town, I reckon, and never hear the last of this thing as long as we live. *No*. What we want, is to go out of here quiet, and talk this show up, and sell the *rest* of the town! Then we'll all be in the same boat. Ain't that sensible?" ("You bet it is!—the jedge is right!" everybody sings out.) "All right, then—not a word about any sell. Go along home, and advise everybody to come and see the tragedy."

Next day you couldn't hear nothing around that town but how splendid that show was. House was jammed again, that night, and we sold this crowd the same way. When me and the king and the duke got home to the raft, we all had a supper; and by-and-by, about midnight, they made Jim and me back her out and float her down the middle of the river and fetch her in and hide her about two mile below town.

The third night the house was crammed again—and they warn't new-comers, this time, but people that was at the show the other two nights. I stood by the duke at the door, and I see that every man that went in had his pockets bulging, or something muffled up under his coat—and I see it warn't no perfumery neither, not by a long sight. I smelt sickly eggs by the barrel, and rotten cabbages, and such things; and if I know the signs of a dead cat being around, and I bet I do, there was sixty-four of them went in. I shoved in there for a minute, but it was too various for me, I couldn't stand it. Well, when the place couldn't hold no more people, the duke he give a fellow a quarter and told him to tend door for him a minute, and then he started around for the stage door, I after him; but the minute we turned the corner and was in the dark, he says:

"Walk fast, now, till you get away from the houses, and then shin for the raft like the dickens was after you!"

I done it, and he done the same. We struck the raft at the same time, and in less than two seconds we was gliding down stream, all dark and still, and edging towards the middle of the river, nobody saying a word. I reckoned the poor king was in for a gaudy time of it with the audience; but nothing of the sort; pretty soon he crawls out from under the wigwam, and says:

"Well, how'd the old thing pan out this time, Duke?"

He hadn't been up town at all.

We never showed a light till we was about ten mile below that village. Then we lit up and had a supper, and the king and the duke fairly laughed their bones loose over the way they'd served them people. The duke says:

"Greenhorns, flatheads! *I* knew the first house would keep

mum and let the rest of the town get roped in; and I knew they'd lay for us the third night, and consider it was *their* turn now. Well, it *is* their turn, and I'd give something to know how much they'd take for it. I *would* just like to know how they're putting in their opportunity. They can turn it into a picnic, if they want to—they brought plenty provisions."

Them rapscallions took in four hundred and sixty-five dollars in that three nights. I never see money hauled in by the wagon-load like that, before.

By-and by, when they was asleep and snoring, Jim says:

"Don't it 'sprise you, de way dem kings carries on, Huck?"

"No," I says, "it don't."

"Why don't it, Huck?"

"Well, it don't, because it's in the breed. I reckon they're all alike."

"But, Huck, dese kings o' ourn is regular rapscallions; dat's jist what dey is; dey's reglar rapscallions."

"Well, that's what I'm a-saying; all kings is mostly rapscallions, as fur as I can make out."

"Is dat so?"

"You read about them once—you'll see. Look at Henry the Eight; this'n 'sa Sunday-School Superintendent to *him*. And look at Charles Second, and Louis Fourteen, and Louis Fifteen, and James Second, and Edward Second, and Richard Third, and forty more; besides all them Saxon heptarchies that used to rip around so in old times and raise Cain. My, you ought to seen old Henry the Eight when he was in bloom. He *was* a blossom. He used to marry a new wife every day, and chop off her head next morning. And he would do it just as indifferent as if he was ordering up eggs. 'Fetch up Nell Gwynn,' he says. They fetch her up. Next morning, 'Chop off her head!' And they chop it off. 'Fetch up Jane Shore,' he says; and up she comes. Next morning 'Chop off her head'—and they chop it off. 'Ring up Fair Rosamun.' Fair Rosamun answers the bell. Next morning, 'Chop off her head.' And he made every one of them tell him a tale every night; and he kept that up till he had hogged a thousand and one tales that way, and then he put them all in a book, and called it Domesday Book—which was a good name and stated the case. You don't know kings, Jim, but I know them; and this old rip of ourn is one of the cleanest I've struck in history. Well, Henry he takes a notion he wants to get up some trouble with this country. How does he go at it—give notice?—give the country a show? No. All of a sudden he heaves all the tea in Boston Harbor overboard, and whacks out a declaration of independence, and dares them to come on. That was *his* style—he never give anybody a chance. He had suspicions of his father, the Duke of Wellington. Well, what did he do?—ask him to show up? No—drownded him in a butt of mamsey, like a cat. Spose people left money laying around where he was—what did he do? He collared it. Spose he contracted to do a thing; and you paid him, and didn't set down there and see that he done it—what did he do? He always done the other thing. Spose he opened his mouth—what then? If he didn't shut it up powerful quick, he'd lose a lie, every time. That's the kind of a bug Henry was; and if we'd a had him along 'stead of our kings, he'd a fooled that town a heap worse than ourn done. I don't say that ourn is lambs, because they ain't, when you come right down to the cold facts; but they ain't nothing to *that* old ram, anyway. All I say is, kings is kings, and you got to make allowances. Take them all around, they're a mighty ornery lot. It's the way they're raised."

"But dis one do *smell* so like de nation, Huck."

"Well, they all do, Jim. *We* can't help the way a king smells; history don't tell no way."

"Now de duke, he's a tolerable likely man, in some ways."

"Yes, a duke's different. But not very different. This one's a middling hard lot, for a duke. When he's drunk, there ain't no near-sighted man could tell him from a king."

"Well, anyways, I doan' hanker for no mo' un um, Huck. Dese is all I kin stan'."

"It's the way I feel, too, Jim. But we've got them on our hands, and we got to remember what they are, and make allowances. Sometimes I wish we could hear of a country that's out of kings."

What was the use to tell Jim these warn't real kings and

dukes? It wouldn't a done no good; and besides, it was just as I said; you couldn't tell them from the real kind.

I went to sleep, and Jim didn't call me when it was my turn. He often done that. When I waked up, just at day-break, he was setting there with his head down betwixt his knees, moaning and mourning to himself. I didn't take notice, nor let on. I knowed what it was about. He was thinking about his wife and his children, away up yonder, and he was low and homesick; because he hadn't ever been away from home before in his life; and I do believe he cared just as much for his people as white folks does for their'n. It don't seem natural, but I reckon it's so. He was often moaning and mourning that way, nights, when he judged I was asleep, and saying, "Po' little 'Lizabeth! po' little Johnny! it's mighty hard; I spec' I ain't ever gwyne to see you no mo', no mo'!" He was a mighty good nigger, Jim was.

But this time I somehow got to talking to him about his wife and young ones; and by-and-by he says:

"What makes me feel so bad dis time, 'uz bekase I hear sumpn over yonder on de bank like a whack, er a slam, while ago, en it mine me er de time I treat my little 'Lizabeth so ornery. She warn't on'y 'bout fo' year ole, en she tuck de sk'yarlet-fever, en had a powful rough spell; but she got well, en one day she was a-stannin' aroun', en I says to her, I says:

"Shet de do'.'

"She never done it; jis' stood dah, kiner smilin' up at me. It make me mad; en I says agin, mighty loud, I says:

"'Doan' you hear me?—shet de do'!'

"She jis' stood de same way, kiner smilin' up. I was a-bilin'! I says:

"'I lay I *make* you mine!'

"En wid dat I fetch' her a slap side de head dat sont her a-sprawlin'. Den I went into de yuther room, en 'uz gone 'bout ten minutes; en when I come back, dah was dat do' a-stannin' open *yit,* en dat chile stannin' mos' right in it, a-lookin' down and mournin', en de tears runnin' down. My, but I *wuz* mad, I was agwyne for de chile, but jis' den—it was a do' dat open innerds—jis' den, 'long came de wind en slam it to, behine de chile, ker-*blam!*—en my lan', de chile never move'! My breff mos' hop outer me; en I feel so—so—I doan' know *how* I feel. I crope out, all a-tremblin', en crope aroun' en open de do' easy en slow, en poke my head in behine de chile, sof' en still, en all uv a sudden, I says *pow!* jis' as loud as I could yell. *She never budge!* Oh, Huck, I bust out a-cryin' en grab her up in my arms, en say, 'Oh, de po' little thing! de Lord God Amighty forgiv po' ole Jim, kaze he never gwyne to forgive hisself as long's he live!' Oh, she was plumb deef en dumb, Huck, plumb deef en dumb—en I'd been a-treat'n her so!"

CHAPTER XXIV

Next day, towards night, we laid up under a little willow towhead out in the middle, where there was a village on each side of the river, and the duke and the king begun to lay out a plan for working them towns. Jim he spoke to the duke, and said he hoped it wouldn't take but a few hours, because it got mighty heavy and tiresome to him when we had to lay all day in the wigwam tied with the rope. You see, when we left him all alone we had to tie him, because if anybody happened on him all by himself and not tied, it wouldn't look much like he was a runaway nigger, you know. So the duke said it *was* kind of hard to have to lay roped all day, and he'd cipher out some way to get around it.

He was uncommon bright, the duke was, and he soon struck it. He dressed Jim up in King Lear's outfit—it was a long curtain-calico gown, and a white horse-hair wig and whiskers; and then he took his theater-paint and painted Jim's face and hands and ears and neck all over a dead dull solid blue, like a man that's been drownded nine days. Blamed if he warn't the horriblest looking outrage I ever see. Then the duke took and wrote out a sign on a shingle so—

Sick Arab—but harmless when not out of his head.

And he nailed that shingle to a lath, and stood the lath up four or five foot in front of the wigwam. Jim was satisfied. He said it was a sight better than laying tied a couple of years every day and trembling all over every time there was a sound. The duke told him to make himself free and easy, and if anybody ever come meddling around, he must hop out of the wigwam, and carry on a little, and fetch a howl or two like a wild beast, and he reckoned they would light out and leave him alone. Which was sound enough judgment; but you take the average man, and he wouldn't wait for him to howl. Why, he didn't only look like he was dead, he looked considerable more than that.

These rapscallions wanted to try the Nonesuch again, because there was so much money in it, but they judged it wouldn't be safe, because maybe the news might a worked along down by this time. They couldn't hit no project that suited, exactly; so at last the duke said he reckoned he'd lay off and work his brains an hour or two and see if he couldn't put up something on the Arkansaw village; and the king he allowed he would drop over to t'other village, without any plan, but just trust in Providence to lead him the profitable way—meaning the devil, I reckon. We had all bought store clothes where we stopped last; and now the king put his'n on, and he told me to put mine on. I done it, of course. The king's duds was all black, and he did look real swell and starchy. I never knowed how clothes could change a body before. Why, before, he looked like the orneriest old rip that ever was; but now, when he'd take off his new white beaver and make a bow and do a smile, he looked that grand and good and pious that you'd say he had walked right out of the ark, and maybe was old Leviticus himself. Jim cleaned up the canoe, and I got my paddle ready. There was a big steamboat laying at the shore away up under the point, about three mile above town—been there a couple of hours, taking on freight. Says the king:

"Seein' how I'm dressed, I reckon maybe I better arrive down from St. Louis or Cincinnati, or some other big place. Go for the steamboat, Huckleberry; we'll come down to the village on her."

I didn't have to be ordered twice, to go and take a steamboat ride. I fetched the shore a half a mile above the village, and then went scooting along the bluff bank in the easy water. Pretty soon we come to a nice innocent-looking young country jake setting on a log swabbing the sweat off of his face, for it was powerful warm weather; and he had a couple of big carpet-bags by him.

"Run her nose in shore," says the king. I done it. "Wher' you bound for, young man?"

"For the steamboat; going to Orleans."

"Git aboard," says the king. "Hold on a minute, my servant'll he'p you with them bags. Jump out and he'p the gentleman, Adolphus"—meaning me, I see.

I done so, and then we all three started on again. The young chap was mighty thankful; said it was tough work toting his baggage such weather. He asked the king where he was going, and the king told him he'd come down the river and landed at the other village this morning, and now he was going up a few mile to see an old friend on a farm up there. The young fellow says:

"When I first see you, I says to myself, 'It's Mr. Wilks, sure, and he come mighty near getting here in time.' But then I says again, 'No, I reckon it ain't him, or else he wouldn't be paddling up the river.' You *ain't* him, are you?"

"No, my name's Blodgett—Elexander Blodgett—*Reverend* Elexander Blodgett, I spose I must say, as I'm one o' the Lord's poor servants. But still I'm jist as able to be sorry for Mr. Wilks for not arriving in time, all the same, if he's missed anything by it—which I hope he hasn't."

"Well, he don't miss any property by it, because he'll get that all right; but he's missed seeing his brother Peter die—which he mayn't mind, nobody can tell as to that—but his brother would a give anything in this world to see *him* before he died; never talked about nothing else all these three weeks; hadn't seen him since they was boys together—and hadn't ever seen his brother William at all—that's the deef and dumb one—William ain't more than thirty or thirty-five. Peter and George was the only ones that come out here; George was the married brother; him and his wife both died last year. Harvey and William's the only ones that's left now; and, as I was saying, they haven't got here in time."

"Did anybody send 'em word?"

"Oh, yes; a month or two ago, when Peter was first took; because Peter said then that he sorter felt like he warn't going to get well this time. You see, he was pretty old, and George's g'yirls was too young to be much company for him, except Mary Jane the red-headed one; and so he was kinder lonesome after George and his wife died, and didn't seem to care much to live. He most desperately wanted to see Harvey—and William too, for that matter—because he was one of them kind that can't bear to make a will. He left a letter behind for Harvey, and said he'd told in it where his money was hid, and how he wanted the rest of the property divided up so George's g'yirls would be all right—for George didn't leave nothing. And that letter was all they could get him to put a pen to."

"Why do you reckon Harvey don't come? Wher' does he live?"

"Oh, he lives in England—Sheffield—preaches there—hasn't ever been in this country. He hasn't had any too much time—and besides he mightn't a got the letter at all, you know."

"Too bad, too bad he couldn't a lived to see his brothers, poor soul. You going to Orleans, you say?"

"Yes, but that ain't only a part of it. I'm going in a ship, next Wednesday, for Ryo Janeero, where my uncle lives."

"It's a pretty long journey. But it'll be lovely; I wisht I was agoing. Is Mary Jane the oldest? How old is the others?"

"Mary Jane's nineteen, Susan's fifteen, and Joanna's about fourteen—that's the one that gives herself to good works and has a hare-lip."

"Poor things! to be left alone in the cold world so."

"Well, they could be worse off. Old Peter had friends, and they ain't going to let them come to no harm. There's Hobson, the Babtis' preacher; and Deacon Lot Hovey, and Ben Rucker, and Abner Shackleford, and Levi Bell, the lawyer; and Dr. Robinson, and their wives, and the widow Bartley, and—well, there's a lot of them; but these are the ones that Peter was thickest with, and used to write about sometimes, when he wrote home; so Harvey'll know where to look for friends when he get's here."

Well, the old man he went on asking questions till he just fairly emptied that young fellow. Blamed if he didn't inquire about everybody and everything in that blessed town, and all about all the Wilkses; and about Peter's business—which was a tanner; and about George's—which was a carpenter; and about Harvey's—which was a dissentering minister; and so on, and so on. Then he says:

"What did you want to walk all the way up to the steamboat for?"

"Because she's a big Orleans boat, and I was afeard she mightn't stop there. When they're deep they won't stop for a hail. A Cincinnati boat will, but this is a St. Louis one."

"Was Peter Wilks well off?"

"Oh, yes, pretty well off. He had houses and land, and it's reckoned he left three or four thousand in cash hid up som'ers."

"When did you say he died?"

"I didn't say, but it was last night."

"Funeral to-morrow, likely?"

"Yes, 'bout the middle of the day."

"Well, it's all terrible sad; but we've all got to go, one time or another. So what we want to do is to be prepared; then we're all right."

"Yes, sir, it's the best way. Ma used to always say that."

When we struck the boat, she was about done loading, and pretty soon she got off. The king never said nothing about going aboard, so I lost my ride after all. When the boat was gone, the king made me paddle up another mile to a lonesome place, and then he got ashore, and says:

"Now hustle back, right off, and fetch the duke up here, and the new carpet-bags. And if he's gone over to t'other side, go over there and git him. And tell him to git himself up regardless. Shove along, now."

I see what *he* was up to; but I never said nothing, of course. When I got back with the duke, we hid the canoe and then they set down on a log, and the king told him everything, just like the young fellow had said it—every last word of it. And all the time he was a doing it, he tried to talk like an Englishman; and he done it pretty well too, for a slouch. I can't imitate him, and so I ain't agoing to try to; but he really done it pretty good. Then he says:

"How are you on the deef and dumb, Bilgewater?"

The duke said, leave him alone for that; said he had played a deef and dumb person on the histrionic boards. So then they waited for a steamboat.

About the middle of the afternoon a couple of little boats come along, but they didn't come from high enough up the river; but at last there was a big one, and they hailed her. She sent out her yawl, and we went aboard, and she was from Cincinnati; and when they found we only wanted to go four or five mile, they was booming mad, and give us a cussing, and said they wouldn't land us. But the king was ca'm. He says:

"If gentlemen kin afford to pay a dollar a mile apiece, to be took on and put off in a yawl, a steamboat kin afford to carry 'em, can't it?"

So they softened down and said it was all right; and when we got to the village, they yawled us ashore. About two dozen men flocked down, when they see the yawl a coming; and when the king says—

"Kin any of you gentlemen tell me wher' Mr. Peter Wilks lives?" they give a glance at one another, and nodded their heads, as much as to say, "What d' I tell you?" Then one of them says, kind of soft and gentle:

"I'm sorry, sir, but the best we can do is to tell you where he *did* live yesterday evening."

Sudden as winking, the ornery old cretur went all to smash, and fell up against the man, and put his chin on his shoulder, and cried down his back, and says:

"Alas, alas, our poor brother—gone, and we never got to see him; oh, it's too, *too* hard!"

Then he turns around, blubbering, and makes a lot of idiotic signs to the duke on his hands, and blamed if *he* didn't drop a carpet-bag and bust out a-crying. If they warn't the beatenest lot, them two frauds, that ever I struck.

Well, the men gathered around, and sympathized with them, and said all sorts of kind things to them, and carried their carpet-bags up the hill for them, and let them lean on them and cry, and told the king all about his brother's last moments, and the king he told it all over again on his hands to the duke, and both of them took on about that dead tanner like they'd lost the twelve disciples. Well, if ever I struck anything like it, I'm a nigger. It was enough to make a body ashamed of the human race.

CHAPTER XXV

The news was all over town in two minutes, and you could see the people tearing down on the run, from every which way, some of them putting on their coats as they come. Pretty soon we was in the middle of a crowd, and the noise of the tramping was like a soldier-march. The windows and dooryards was full; and every minute somebody would say, over a fence:

"Is it *them?*"

And somebody trotting along with the gang would answer back and say,

"You bet it is."

When we got to the house, the street in front of it was packed, and the three girls was standing in the door. Mary Jane *was* red-headed, but that don't make no difference, she was most awful beautiful, and her face and her eyes was all lit up like glory, she was so glad her uncles was come. The king he spread his arms, and Mary Jane she jumped for them, and the hare-lip jumped for the duke and there they *had* it! Everybody most, leastways women, cried for joy to see them meet again at last and have such good times.

Then the king he hunched the duke, private—I see him do it—and then he looked around and see the coffin, over in the corner on two chairs; so then, him and the duke, with a hand across each other's shoulder, and t'other hand to their eyes, walked slow and solemn over there, everybody dropping back to give them room, and all the talk and noise stopping, people saying "Sh!" and all the men taking their hats off and drooping their heads, so you could a heard a pin fall. And when they got there, they bent over and looked in the coffin, and took one sight, and then they bust out a crying so you could a heard them to Orleans, most; and then they put their arms around each other's necks, and hung their chins over each other's shoulders; and then for three minutes, or maybe four, I never see two men leak the way they done. And mind you, everybody was doing the same; and the place was that damp I never see anything like it. Then one of them got on one side of the coffin, and t'other on t'other side, and they kneeled down and rested their foreheads on the coffin, and let on to pray all to their-selves. Well, when it come to that, it worked the crowd like you never see anything like it, and so everybody broke down and went to sobbing right out loud—the poor girls, too; and every woman, nearly, went up to the girls, without saying a word, and kissed them, solemn, on the forehead, and then put their hand on their head, and looked up towards the sky, with the tears running down, and then busted out and went off sobbing and swabbing, and give the next woman a show. I never see anything so disgusting.

Well, by-and-by the king he gets up and comes forward a little, and works himself up and slobbers out a speech, all full of tears and flapdoodle about its being a sore trial for him and his poor brother to lose the diseased, and to miss seeing diseased alive, after the long journey of four thousand mile, but its a trial that's sweetened and sanctified to us by this dear sympathy and these holy tears, and so he thanks them out of his heart and out of his brother's heart, because out of their mouths they can't, words being too weak and cold, and all that kind of rot and slush, till it was just sickening; and then he blubbers out a pious goody-goody Amen, and turns himself loose and goes to crying fit to bust.

And the minute the words was out of his mouth somebody over in the crowd struck up the doxolojer, and everybody joined in with all their might, and it just warmed you up and made you feel as good as church letting out. Music *is* a good thing; and after all that soul-butter and hogwash, I never see it freshen up things so, and sound so honest and bully.

Then the king begins to work his jaw again, and says how him and his nieces would be glad if a few of the main principal friends of the family would take supper here with them this evening, and help set up with the ashes of the diseased; and says if his poor brother laying yonder could speak, he knows who he would name, for they was names that was very dear to him, and mentioned often in his letters; and so he will name the same, to-wit, as follows, vizz:—Rev. Mr. Hobson, and Deacon Lot Hovey, and Mr. Ben Rucker, and Abner Shackleford, and Levi Bell, and Dr. Robinson, and their wives, and the widow Bartley.

Rev. Hobson and Dr. Robinson was down to the end of the town, a-hunting together; that is, I mean the doctor was shipping a sick man to t'other world, and the preacher was pinting him right. Lawyer Bell was away up to Louisville on some business. But the rest was on hand, and so they all come and shook hands with the king and thanked him and talked to him; and then they shook hands with the duke, and didn't say nothing but just kept a-smiling and bobbing their heads like a passel of sapheads whilst he made all sorts of signs with his hands and said "Goo-goo—goo-goo-goo," all the time, like a baby that can't talk.

So the king he blatted along, and managed to inquire about pretty much everybody and dog in town, by his name, and mentioned all sorts of little things that happened one time or another in the town, or to George's family, or to Peter; and he always let on that Peter wrote him the things, but that was a lie, he got every blessed one of them out of that young flathead that we canoed up to the steamboat.

Then Mary Jane she fetched the letter her father left behind, and the king he read it out loud and cried over it. It give the dwelling-house and three thousand dollars, gold, to the girls; and it give the tanyard (which was doing a good business), along with some other houses and land (worth about seven thousand), and three thousand dollars in gold to Harvey and William, and told where the six thousand cash was hid, down cellar. So these two frauds said they'd go and fetch it up, and have everything square and above-board; and told me to come with a candle. We shut the cellar door behind us, and when they found the bag they spilt it out on the floor, and it was a lovely sight, all them yaller-boys. My, the way the king's eyes did shine! He slaps the duke on the shoulder, and says:

"Oh, *this* ain't bully, nor noth'n! Oh, no, I reckon not! Why, Biljy, it beats the Nonesuch, *don't* it!"

The duke allowed it did. They pawed the yaller-boys, and sifted them through their fingers and let them jingle down on the floor; and the king says:

"It ain't no use talkin'; bein' brothers to a rich dead man, and representatives of furrin heirs that's got left, is the line for you and me, Bilge. Thish-yer comes of trust'n to Providence. It's the best way, in the long run. I've tried 'em all, and ther' ain't no better way."

Most everybody would a been satisfied with the pile, and took it on trust; but no, they must count it. So they counts it, and it comes out four hundred and fifteen dollars short. Says the king:

"Dern him, I wonder what he done with that four hundred and fifteen dollars?"

They worried over that a while, and ransacked all around for it. Then the duke says:

"Well, he was a pretty sick man, and likely he made a mistake—I reckon that's the way of it. The best way's to let it go, and keep still about it. We can spare it."

"Oh, shucks, yes, we can *spare* it. I don't k'yer noth'n 'bout that—it's the *count* I'm thinkin' about. We want to be awful square and open and aboveboard, here, you know. We want to lug this h-yer money up stairs and count it before everybody—then there' ain't noth'n suspicious. But when the dead man says ther's six thous'n dollars, you know, we don't want to—"

"Hold on," says the duke. "Less make up the deffisit"—and he begun to haul out yaller-boys out of his pocket.

"It's a most amaz'n' good idea, duke—you *have* got a rattlin' clever head on you," says the king. "Blest if the old None-such ain't a heppin' us out agin"—and *he* begun to haul out yaller-jackets and stack them up.

It most busted them, but they made up the six thousand clean and clear.

"Say," says the duke, "I got another idea. Le's go up stairs and count this money, and then take and *give it to the girls.*"

"Good land, duke, lemme hug you! It's the most dazzling idea 'at ever a man struck. You have cert'nly got the most astonishin' head I ever see. Oh, this is the boss dodge, ther' ain't no mistake 'bout it. Let 'em fetch along their suspicions now, if they want to—this'll lay 'em out."

When we got up stairs, everybody gethered around the table, and the king he counted it and stacked it up, three hundred dollars in a pile—twenty elegant little piles. Everybody looked hungry at it, and licked their chops. Then they raked it into the bag again, and I see the king begin to swell himself up for another speech. He says:

"Friends all, my poor brother that lays yonder, has done generous by them that's left behind in the vale of sorrers. He has done generous by these-yer poor little lambs that he loved and sheltered, and that's left fatherless and motherless. Yes, and we that knowed him, knows that he would a done *more* generous by 'em if he hadn't ben afeard o' woundin' his dear William and me. Now, *wouldn't* he? Ther' ain't no question 'bout it, in *my* mind. Well, then—what kind o' brothers would it be, that'd stand in his way at sech a time? And what kind o' uncles would it be that'd rob—yes, *rob*—sech poor sweet lambs as these 'at he loved so, at sech a time? If I know William—and I *think* I do—he—well, I'll jest ask him." He turns around and begins to make a lot of signs to the duke with his hands; and the duke he looks at him stupid and leather-headed a while, then all of a sudden he seems to catch his meaning, and jumps for the king, goo-gooing with all his might for joy, and hugs him about fifteen times before he lets up. Then the king says, "I knowed it; I reckon *that* 'll convince anybody the way *he* feels about it. Here, Mary Jane, Susan, Joanner, take the money—take it *all.* It's the gift of him that lays yonder, cold but joyful."

Mary Jane she went for him, Susan and the hare-lip went for the duke, and then such another hugging and kissing I never see yet. And everybody crowded up with the tears in their eyes, and most shook the hands off of them frauds, saying all the time:

"You *dear* good souls!—how *lovely!*—how *could* you!"

Well, then, pretty soon all hands got to talking about the diseased again, and how good he was, and what a loss he was, and all that; and before long a big iron-jawed man worked himself in there from outside, and stood a listening and looking, and not saying anything; and nobody saying anything to him either, because the king was talking and they was all busy listening. The king was saying—in the middle of something he'd started in on—

"—they bein' partickler friends o' the diseased. That's why they're invited here this evenin'; but to-morrow we want *all* to come—everybody; for he respected everybody, he liked everybody, and so it's fittin that his funeral orgies h'd be public."

And so he went a-mooning on and on, liking to hear himself talk, and every little while he fetched in his funeral orgies again, till the duke he couldn't stand it no more; so he writes on a little scrap of paper, "*obsequies,* you old fool," and folds it up and goes too goo-gooing and reaching it over people's heads to him. The king he reads it, and puts it in his pocket, and says:

"Poor William, afflicted as he is, his *heart's* aluz right. Asks me to invite everybody to come to the funeral—wants me to make 'em all welcome. But he needn't a worried—it was jest what I was at."

Then he weaves along again, perfectly ca'm, and goes to dropping in his funeral orgies again every now and then, just like he done before. And when he done it the third time, he says:

"I say orgies, not because it's the common term, because it ain't—obsequies bein' the common term—but because orgies is the right term. Obsequies ain't used in England no more, now—it's gone out. We say orgies now, in England. Orgies is better, because it means the thing you're after, more exact. It's a word that's made up out'n the Greek *orgo,* outside, open, abroad; and the Hebrew *jeesum,* to plant, cover up; hence in*ter.* So, you see, funeral orgies is an open er public funeral."

He was the *worst* I ever struck. Well, the iron-jawed man he laughed right in his face. Everybody was shocked. Everybody says, "Why *doctor!*" and Abner Shackleford says:

"Why, Robinson, hain't you heard the news? This is Harvey Wilks."

The king he smiled eager, and shoved out his flapper, and says:

"*Is* it my poor brother's dear good friend and physician? I—"

"Keep your hands off of me!" says the doctor. "*You* talk like an Englishman—*don't* you? It's the worse imitation I ever heard. *You* Peter Wilks's brother. You're a fraud, that's what you are!"

Well, how they all took on! They crowded around the doctor, and tried to quiet him down, and tried to explain to him, and tell him how Harvey'd showed in forty ways that he *was* Harvey, and knowed everybody by name, and the names of the very dogs, and begged and *begged* him not to hurt Harvey's feelings and the poor girls' feelings, and all that; but it warn't no use, he stormed right along, and said any man that pretended to be an Englishman and couldn't imitate the lingo no better than what he did, was a fraud and a liar. The poor girls was hanging to the king and crying; and all of a sudden the doctor ups and turns on *them*. He says:

"I was your father's friend, and I'm your friend; and I warn you *as* a friend, and an honest one, that wants to protect you and keep you out of harm and trouble, to turn your backs on that scoundrel, and have nothing to do with him, the ignorant tramp, with his idiotic Greek and Hebrew as he calls it. He is the thinnest kind of an impostor—has come here with a lot of empty names and facts which he has picked up somewheres, and you take them for *proofs*, and are helped to fool yourselves by these foolish friends here, who ought to know better. Mary Jane Wilks, you know me for your friend, and for your unselfish friend, too. Now listen to me; turn this pitiful rascal out—I *beg* you to do it. Will you?"

Mary Jane straightened herself up, and my, but she was handsome! She says:

"*Here* is my answer." She hove up the bag of money and put it in the king's hands, and says, "Take this six thousand dollars, and invest for me and my sisters any way you want to, and don't give us no receipt for it."

Then she put her arm around the king on one side, and Susan and the hare-lip done the same on the other. Everybody clapped their hands and stomped on the floor like a perfect storm, whilst the king held up his head and smiled proud. The doctor says:

"All right, I wash *my* hands of the matter. But I warn you all that a time's coming when you're going to feel sick whenever you think of this day"—and away he went.

"All right, doctor," says the king, kinder mocking him, "we'll try and get 'em to send for you"—which made them all laugh, and they said it was a prime good hit.

CHAPTER XXVI

Well when they was all gone, the king he asks Mary Jane how they was off for spare rooms, and she said she had one spare room, which would do for Uncle William, and she'd give her own room to Uncle Harvey, which was a little bigger, and she would turn into the room with her sisters and sleep on a cot; and up garret was a little cubby, with a pallet in it. The king said the cubby would do for his valley—meaning me.

So Mary Jane took us up, and she showed them their rooms, which was plain but nice. She said she'd have her frocks and a lot of other traps took out of her room if they was in Uncle Harvey's way, but he said they warn't. The frocks was hung along the wall, and before them was a curtain made out of calico that hung down to the floor. There was an old hair trunk in one corner, and a guitar box in another, and all sorts of little knick-knacks and jimcracks around, like girls brisken up a room with. The king said it was all the more homely and more pleasanter for these fixings, and so don't disturb them. The duke's room was pretty small, but plenty good enough, and so was my cubby.

That night they had a big supper, and all them men and women was there, and I stood behind the king and the duke's chairs and waited on them, and the niggers waited on the rest. Mary Jane she set at the head of the table, with Susan along side of her, and said how bad the biscuits was, and how mean the preserves was, and how ornery and tough the fried chickens was—and all that kind of rot, the way women always do for to force out compliments; and the people all knowed everything was tip-top, and said so—said "How *do* you get biscuits to brown so nice?" and "Where, for the land's sake *did* you get these amaz'n pickles?" and all that kind of humbug talky-talk, just the way people always does at a supper, you know.

And when it was all done, me and the hare-lip had supper in the kitchen off of the leavings, whilst the others was helping the niggers clean up the things. The hare-lip she got to pumping me about England, and blest if I didn't think the ice was getting mighty thin, sometimes. She says:

"Did you ever see the king?"

"Who? William Fourth? Well, I bet I have—he goes to our church." I knowed he was dead years ago, but I never let on. So when I says he goes to our church, she says:

"What—regular?"

"Yes—regular. His pew's right over opposite ourn—on 'tother side the pulpit."

"I thought he lived in London?"

"Well, he does. Where *would* he live?"

"But I thought *you* lived in Sheffield?"

I see I was up a stump. I had to let on to get choked with a chicken bone, so as to get time to think how to get down again. Then I says:

"I mean he goes to our church regular when he's in Sheffield. That's only in the summer-time, when he comes there to take the sea baths."

"Why, how you talk—Sheffield ain't on the sea."

"Well, who said it was?"

"Why, you did."

"I *didn't,* nuther."

"You did!"

"I didn't."

"You did."

"I never said nothing of the kind."

"Well, what *did* you say, then?"

"Said he come to take the sea *baths*— that's what I said."

"Well, then! how's he going to take the sea baths if it ain't on the sea?"

"Looky here," I says; "did you ever see any Congress water?"

"Yes."

"Well, did you have to go to Congress to get it?"

"Why, no."

"Well, neither does William Fourth have to go to the sea to get a sea bath."

"How does he get it, then?"

"Gets it the way people down here gets Congress-water—in barrels. There in the palace at Sheffield they've got furnaces, and he wants his water hot. They can't bile that amount of water away off there at the sea. They haven't got no conveniences for it."

"Oh, I see, now. You might a said that in the first place and saved time."

When she said that, I see I was out of the woods again, and so I was comfortable and glad. Next, she says:

"Do you go to church, too?"

"Yes—regular."

"Where do you set?"

"Why, in our pew."

"*Whose* pew?"

"Why, *ourn*—your Uncle Harvey's."

"His'n? What does *he* want with a pew?"

"Wants it to set in. What did you *reckon* he wanted with it?"

"Why, I thought he'd be in the pulpit."

Rot him, I forgot he was a preacher. I see I was up a stump again, so I played another chicken bone and got another think. Then I says:

"Blame it, do you suppose there ain't but one preacher to a church?"

"Why, what do they want with more?"

"What!—to preach before a king? I never see such a girl as you. They don't have no less than seventeen."

"Seventeen! My land! Why, I wouldn't set out such a string as that, not if I *never* got to glory. It must take 'em a week."

"Shucks, they don't *all* of 'em preach the same day—only *one* of 'em."

"Well, then, what does the rest of 'em do?"

"Oh, nothing much. Loll around, pass the plate—and one thing or another. But mainly they don't do nothing."

"Well, then, what are they *for?*"

"Why, they're for *style.* Don't you know nothing?"

"Well, I don't *want* to know no such foolishness as that. How is servants treated in England? Do they treat 'em better 'n we treat our niggers?"

"*No!*" A servant ain't nobody there. They treat them worse than dogs."

"Don't they give 'em holidays, the way we do, Christmas and New Year's week, and Fourth of July?"

"Oh, just listen! A body could tell *you* hain't ever been to England, by that. Why, Hare-l—why, Joanna, they never see a holiday from year's end to year's end; never go to the circus, nor theatre, nor nigger shows, nor nowheres."

"Nor church?"

"Nor church."

"But *you* always went to church."

Well, I was gone up again. I forgot I was the old man's servant. But next minute I whirled in on a kind of an explanation how a valley was different from a common servant, and *had* to go to church whether he wanted to or not, and set with the family, on account of it's being the law. But I didn't do it pretty good, and when I got done I see she warn't satisfied. She says:

"Honest injun, now, hain't you been telling me a lot of lies?"

"Honest injun," says I.

"None of it at all?"

"None of it at all. Not a lie in it," says I.

"Lay your hand on this book and say it."

I see it warn't nothing but a dictionary, so I laid my hand on it and said it. So then she looked a little better satisfied, and says:

"Well, then, I'll believe some of it; but I hope to gracious if I'll believe the rest."

"What is it you won't believe, Joe?" says Mary Jane, stepping in with Susan behind her. "It ain't right nor kind for you to talk so to him, and him a stranger and so far from his people. How would you like to be treated so?"

"That's always your way, Maim—always sailing in to help

somebody before they're hurt. I hain't done nothing to him. He's told some stretchers, I reckon; and I said I wouldn't swallow it all; and that's every bit and grain I *did* say. I reckon he can stand a little thing like that, can't he?"

"I don't care whether 'twas little or whether 'twas big, he's here in our house and a stranger, and it wasn't good of you to say it. If you was in his place, it would make you feel ashamed; and so you oughtn't to say a thing to another person that will make *them* feel ashamed."

"Why, Maim, he said—"

"It don't make no difference what he *said*—that ain't the thing. The thing is for you to treat him *kind,* and not be saying things to make him remember he ain't in his own country and amongst his own folks."

I says to myself, *this* is the girl that I'm letting that old reptle rob her of her money!

Then Susan *she* waltzed in; and if you'll believe me, she did give Hare-lip hark from the tomb!

Says I to myself, And this is *another* one that I'm letting him rob her of her money!

Then Mary Jane she took another inning, and went in sweet and lovely again—which was her way—but when she got done there warn't hardly anything left o' poor Hare-lip. So she hollered.

"All right, then," says the other girls, "you just ask his pardon."

She done it, too. And she done it beautiful. She done it so beautiful it was good to hear; and I wished I could tell her a thousand lies, so she could do it again.

I says to myself, this is *another* one that I'm letting him rob her of her money. And when she got through, they all jest laid theirselves out to make me feel at home and know I was amongst friends. I felt so ornery and low down and mean, that I says to myself, My mind's made up; I'll hive that money for them or bust.

So then I lit out—for bed, I said, meaning some time or another. When I got by myself, I went to thinking the thing over. I says to myself, shall I go to that doctor, private, and blow on these frauds? No—that won't do. He might tell who told him; then the king and the duke would make it warm for me. Shall I go, private, and tell Mary Jane? No—I dasn't do it. Her face would give them a hint, sure; they've got the money, and they'd slide right out and get away with it. If she was to fetch in help, I'd get mixed up in the business, before it was done with, I judge. No, there ain't no good way but one. I got to steal that money, somehow; and I got to steal it some way that they won't suspicion that I done it. They've got a good thing, here; and they ain't agoing to leave till they've played this family and town for all they're worth, so I'll find a chance time enough. I'll steal it, and hide it; and by-and-by, when I'm away down the river, I'll write a letter and tell Mary Jane where it's hid. But I better hive it to-night, if I can, because the doctor maybe hasn't let up as much as he lets on he has; he might scare them out of here, yet.

So, thinks I, I'll go and search them rooms. Up stairs the hall was dark, but I found the duke's room, and started to paw around it with my hands; but I recollected it wouldn't be much like the king to let anybody else take care of that money but his own self; so then I went to his room and begun to paw around there. But I see I couldn't do nothing without a candle, and I dasn't light one, of course. So I judged I'd got to do the other thing—lay for them, and eavesdrop. About that time, I hears their footsteps coming, and was going to skip under the bed; I reached for it, but it wasn't where I thought it would be; but I touched the curtain that hid Mary Jane's frocks, so I jumped in behind that and snuggled in amongst the gowns, and stood there perfectly still.

They come in and shut the door; and the first thing the duke done was to get down and look under the bed. Then I was glad I hadn't found the bed when I wanted it. And yet, you know, it's kind of natural to hide under the bed when you are up to anything private. They sets down, then, and the king says:

"Well, what is it? and cut it middlin' short, because it's better for us to be down there a whoopin'-up the mournin', than up here givin' 'em a chance to talk us over."

"Well, this is it, Capet. I ain't easy; I ain't comfortable. That doctor lays on my mind. I wanted to know your plans. I've got a notion, and I think it's a sound one."

"What is it, duke?"

"That we better glide out of this, before three in the morning, and clip it down the river with what we've got. Specially, seeing we got it so easy—*given* back to us, flung at our heads, as you may say, when of course we allowed to have to steal it back. I'm for knocking off and lighting out."

That made me feel pretty bad. About an hour or two ago, it would a been a little different, but now it made me feel bad and disappointed. The king rips out and says:

"What! And not sell out the rest o' the property? March off like a passel o' fools and leave eight or nine thous'n' dollars' worth o' property layin' around jest sufferin' to be scooped in?—and all good salable stuff, too."

The duke he grumbled; said the bag of gold was enough, and he didn't want to go no deeper—didn't want to rob a lot of orphans of *everything* they had.

"Why, how you talk!" says the king. "We shan't rob 'em of nothing at all but jest this money. The people that *buys* the property is the suff'rers; because as soon's it's found out 'at we didn't own it—which won't be long after we've slid—the sale won't be valid, and it'll all go back to the estate. These-yer orphans'll git their house back agin, and that's enough for *them;* they're young and spry, and k'n easy earn a livin'. *They* ain't agoing to suffer. Why, jest think—there's thous'n's and thous'n's that ain't nigh so well off. Bless you, *they* ain't got noth'n to complain of."

Well, the king he talked him blind; so at last he give in, and said all right, but said he believed it was blame foolishness to stay, and that doctor hanging over them. But the king says:

"Cuss the doctor! What do we k'yer for *him?* Hain't we got all the fools in town on our side? and ain't that a big enough majority in any town?"

So they got ready to go down stairs again. The duke says:

"I don't think we put that money in a good place."

That cheered me up. I'd begun to think I warn't going to get a hint of no kind to help me. The king says:

"Why?"

"Because Mary Jane'll be in mourning from this out; and first you know the nigger that does up the rooms will get an order to box these duds up and put 'em away; and do you reckon a nigger can run across money and not borrow some of it?"

"Your head's level, agin, duke," says the king; and he come a fumbling under the curtain two or three foot from where I was. I stuck tight to the wall, and kept mighty still, though quivery; and I wondered what them fellows would say to me if they catched me; and I tried to think what I'd better do if they did catch me. But the king he got the bag before I could think more than about a half a thought, and he never suspicioned I was around. They took and shoved the bag through a rip in the straw tick that was under the feather bed, and crammed it in a foot or two amongst the straw and said it was all right, now, because a nigger only makes up the feather bed, and don't turn over the straw tick only about twice a year, and so it warn't in no danger of getting stole, now.

But I knowed better. I had it out of there before they was half-way down stairs. I groped along up to my cubby, and hid it there till I could get a chance to do better. I judged I better hide it outside of the house somewheres, because if they missed it they would give the house a good ransacking. I knowed that very well. Then I turned in, with my clothes all on; but I couldn't a gone to sleep, if I'd a wanted to, I was in such a sweat to get through with the business. By-and-by I heard the king and the duke come up; so I rolled off my pallet and laid with my chin at the top of my ladder and waited to see if anything was going to happen. But nothing did.

So I held on till all the late sounds had quit and the early ones hadn't begun yet; and then I slipped down the ladder.

CHAPTER XXVII

I crept to their doors and listened; they was snoring, so I tiptoed along, and got down stairs all right. There warn't a sound anywheres. I peeped through a crack of the dining-room door, and see the men that was watching the corpse all sound asleep on their chairs. The door was open into the parlor, where the corpse was laying, and there was a candle in both rooms. I passed along, and the parlor door was open; but I see there warn't nobody in there but the remainders of Peter; so I shoved on by; but the front door was locked, and the key wasn't there. Just then I heard somebody coming down the stairs, back behind me. I run in the parlor, and took a swift look around, and the only place I see to hide the bag was in the coffin. The lid was shoved along about a foot, showing the dead man's face down in there, with a wet cloth over it, and his shroud on. I tucked the money-bag in under the lid, just down beyond where his hands was crossed, which made me creep, they was so cold, and then I run back across the room and in behind the door.

The person coming was Mary Jane. She went to the coffin, very soft, and kneeled down and looked in; then she put up her handkerchief and I see she begun to cry, though I couldn't hear her, and her back was to me. I slid out, and as I passed the dining-room I thought I'd make sure them watchers hadn't seen me; so I looked through the crack and everything was all right. They hadn't stirred.

I slipped up to bed, feeling ruther blue, on accounts of the thing playing out that way after I had took so much trouble and run so much resk about it. Says I, if it could stay where it is, all right; because when we get down the river a hundred mile or two, I could write back to Mary Jane, and she could dig him up again and get it; but that ain't the thing that's going to happen; the thing that's going to happen is, the money'll be found when they come to screw on the lid. Then the king'll get it again, and it'll be a long day before he gives anybody another chance to smouch it from him. Of course I *wanted* to slide down and get it out of there, but I dasn't try it. Every minute it was getting earlier, now, and pretty soon some of them watchers would begin to stir, and I might get catched—catched with six thousand dollars in my hands that nobody hadn't hired me to take care of. I don't wish to be mixed up in no such business as that, I says to myself.

When I got down stairs in the morning, the parlor was shut

up, and the watchers was gone. There warn't nobody around but the family and the widow Bartley and our tribe. I watched their faces to see if anything had been happening, but I couldn't tell.

Towards the middle of the day the undertaker come, with his man, and they set the coffin in the middle of the room on a couple of chairs, and then set all our chairs in rows, and borrowed more from the neighbors till the hall and the parlor and the dining-room was full. I see the coffin lid was the way it was before, but I dasn't go to look in under it, with folks around.

Then the people begun to flock in, and the beats and the girls took seats in the front row at the head of the coffin, and for a half an hour the people filed around slow, in single rank, and looked down at the dead man's face a minute, and some dropped in a tear, and it was all very still and solemn, only the girls and the beats holding handkerchiefs to their eyes and keeping their heads bent, and sobbing a little. There warn't no other sound but the scraping of the feet on the floor, and blowing noses—because people always blows them more at a funeral than they do at other places except church.

When the place was packed full, the undertaker he slid around in his black gloves with his softy soothering ways, putting on the last touches, and getting people and things all shipshape and comfortable, and making no more sound than a cat. He never spoke; he moved people around, he squeezed in late ones, he opened up passage-ways, and done it all with nods, and signs with his hands. Then he took his place over against the wall. He was the softest, glidingest, stealthiest man I ever see; and there warn't no more smile to him than there is to a ham.

They had borrowed a melodeum—a sick one; and when everything was ready, a young woman set down and worked it, and it was pretty skreeky and colicky, and everybody joined in and sung, and Peter was the only one that had a good thing, according to my notion. Then the Reverend Hobson opened up, slow and solemn, and begun to talk; and straight off the most outrageous row busted out in the cellar a body every heard; it was only one dog, but he made a most powerful racket, and he kept it up, right along; the parson he had to stand there, over the coffin, and wait—you couldn't hear yourself think. It was right down awkward, and nobody didn't seem to know what to do. But pretty soon they see that long-legged undertaker make a sign to the preacher as much as to say, "Don't you worry—just depend on me." Then he stooped down and begun to glide along the wall, just his shoulders showing over the people's heads. So he glided along, and the pow-wow and racket getting more and more outrageous all the time; and at last, when he had gone around two sides of the room, he disappears down cellar. Then, in about two seconds we heard a whack, and the dog he finished up with a most amazing howl or two, and then everything was dead still, and the parson begun his solemn talk where he left off. In a minute or two here comes this undertaker's back and shoulders gliding along the wall again; and so he glided, and glided, around three sides of the room, and then rose up, and shaded his mouth with his hands, and stretched his neck out towards the preacher, over the people's heads, and says, in a kind of a coarse whisper, *"He had a rat!"* Then he drooped down and glided along the wall again to his place. You could see it was a great satisfaction to the people, because naturally they wanted to know. A little thing like that don't cost nothing, and it's just the little things that makes a man to be looked up to and liked. There warn't no more popular man in town than what that undertaker was.

Well, the funeral sermon was very good, but pison long and tiresome; and then the king he shoved in and got off some of his usual rubbage, and at last the job was through, and the undertaker begun to sneak up on the coffin with his screw-driver. I was in a sweat then, and watched him pretty keen. But he never meddled at all; just slid the lid along, as soft as mush, and screwed it down tight and fast. So there I was! I didn't know whether the money was in there, or not. So, says I, spose somebody had hogged that bag on the sly?—now how do *I* know whether to write to Mary Jane or not? 'Spose she dug him up and didn't find nothing—what would she think of me? Blame it, I says, I might get hunted up and jailed; I'd better lay low and keep dark, and not write at all; the thing's awful mixed, now; trying to better it, I've worsened it a hundred times, and I wish to goodness I'd just let it alone, dad fetch the whole business!

They buried him, and we come back home, and I went to watching faces again—I couldn't help it, and I couldn't rest easy. But nothing come of it; the faces didn't tell me nothing.

The king he visited around, in the evening, and sweetened every body up, and made himself ever so friendly; and he give out the idea that his congregration over in England would be in a sweat about him, so he must hurry and settle up the estate right away, and leave for home. He was very sorry he was so pushed, and so was everybody; they wished he could stay longer, but they said they could see it couldn't be done. And he said of course him and William would take the girls home with them; and that pleased everybody too, because then the girls would be well fixed, and amongst their own relations; and it pleased the girls; too—tickled them so they clean forgot they ever had a trouble in the world; and told him to sell out as quick as he wanted to, they would be ready. Them poor things was that glad and happy it made my heartache to see them getting fooled and lied to so, but I didn't see no safe way for me to chip in and change the general tune.

Well, blamed if the king didn't bill the house and the niggers and all the property for auction straight off—sale two days after the funeral; but anybody could buy private beforehand if they wanted to.

So the next day after the funeral, along about noontime, the girls' joy got the first jolt; a couple of nigger traders come along, and the king sold them the niggers reasonable, for three-day drafts as they called it, and away they went, the two sons up the river to Memphis, and their mother down the river to Orleans. I thought them poor girls and them niggers would break their hearts for grief; they cried around each other, and took on so it most made me down sick to see it. The girls said they hadn't ever dreamed of seeing the family separated or sold away from the town. I can't ever get it out of my memory, the sight of them poor miserable girls and niggers hanging around each other's necks and crying; and I reckon I couldn't a stood it all but would a had to bust out and tell on our gang if I hadn't knowed the sale warn't no account and the niggers would be back home in a week or two.

The thing made a big stir in the town, too, and a good many

come out flat-footed and said it was scandalous to separate the mother and the children that way. It injured the frauds some; but the old fool he bulled right along, spite of all the duke could say or do, and I tell you the duke was powerful uneasy.

Next day was auction day. About broad-day in the morning, the king and the duke come up in the garret and woke me up, and I see by their look that there was trouble. The king says:

"Was you in my room night before last?"

"No, your majesty"—which was the way I always called him when nobody but our gang warn't around.

"Was you in there yisterday er last night?"

"No, your majesty."

"Honor bright, now—no lies."

"Honor bright, your majesty, I'm telling you the truth. I hain't been anear your room since Miss Mary Jane took you and the duke and showed it to you."

The duke says:

"Have you seen anybody else go in there?"

"No, your grace, not as I remember, I believe."

"Stop and think."

I studied a while, and see my chance, then I says:

"Well, I see the niggers go in there several times."

Both of them give a little jump; and looked like they hadn't ever expected it, and then like they *had*. Then the duke says:

"What, *all* of them?"

"No—leastways not all at once. That is, I don't think I ever see them all come *out* at once but just one time."

"Hello—when was that?"

"It was the day we had the funeral. In the morning. It warn't early, because I overslept. I was just starting down the ladder, and I see them."

"Well, go on, *go* on—what did they do? How'd they act?"

"They didn't do nothing. And they didn't act anyway, much, as fur as I see. They tip-toed away; so I seen, easy enough, that they'd shoved in there to do up your majesty's room, or something, sposing you was up; and found you *warn't* up, and so they was hoping to slide out of the way of trouble without waking you up, if they hadn't already waked you up."

"Great guns, *this* is a go!" says the king; and both of them looked pretty sick and tolerable silly. They stood there a thinking and scratching their heads, a minute, and then the duke he bust into a kind of a little raspy chuckle, and says:

"It does beat all, how neat the niggers played their hand. They let on to be *sorry* they was going out of this region! and I believed they *was* sorry. And so did you, and so did everybody. Don't ever tell *me* any more that a nigger ain't got any histrionic talent. Why, the way they played that thing, it would fool *anybody*. In my opinion there's a fortune in 'em. If I had capital and a theatre, I wouldn't want a better lay out than that—and here we've gone and sold 'em for a song. Yes, and ain't privileged to sing the song, yet. Say, where *is* that song?—that draft."

"In the bank for to be collected. Where *would* it be?"

"Well, *that's* all right then, thank goodness."

Says I, kind of timid-like:

"Is something gone wrong?"

The king whirls on me and rips out:

"None o' your business! You keep your head shet, and mind y'r own affairs—if you got any. Long as you're in this town, don't you forgit *that*, you hear?" Then he says to the duke, "We got to jest swaller it, and say noth'n: mum's the word for *us*."

As they was starting down the ladder, the duke he chuckles again, and says:

"Quick sales *and* small profits! It's a good business—yes."

The king snarls around on him and says,

"I was trying to do for the best, in sellin' 'm out so quick. If the profits has turned out to be none, lackin' considable, and none to carry, is it my fault any more'n it's yourn?"

"Well, *they'd* be in this house yet, and we *wouldn't* if I could a got my advice listened to."

The king sassed back, as much as was safe for him, and then swapped around and lit into *me* again. He give me down the banks for not coming and *telling* him I see the niggers come out of his room acting that way—said any fool would a *knowed* something was up. And then waltzed in and cussed *himself* a while; and said it all come of him not laying late and taking his natural rest that morning, and he'd be blamed if he'd ever do it again. So they went off a jawing; and I felt dreadful glad I'd worked it all off onto the niggers and yet hadn't done the niggers no harm by it.

CHAPTER XXVIII

By and-by it was getting-up time; so I come down the ladder and started for down stairs, but as I come to the girls' room, the door was open, and I see Mary Jane setting by her old hair trunk, which was open and she'd been packing things in it—getting ready to go to England. But she had stopped now, with a folded gown in her lap, and had her face in her hands, crying. I felt awful bad to see it; of course anybody would. I went in there, and says:

"Miss Mary Jane, you can't abear to see people in trouble, and *I* can't—most always. Tell me about it."

So she done it. And it was the niggers—I just expected it. She said the beautiful trip to England was most about spoiled for her; she didn't know *how* she was every going to be happy there, knowing the mother and the children warn't ever going to see each other no more—and then busted out bitterer than ever, and flung up her hands, and says

"Oh, dear, dear, to think they ain't *ever* going to see each other any more!"

"But they *will*—and inside of two weeks—and I *know* it!" says I.

Laws it was out before I could think!—and before I could budge, she throws her arms around my neck, and told me to say it *again,* say it *again,* say it *again!*

I see I had spoke too sudden, and said too much, and was in a close place. I asked her to let me think a minute; and she set there, very impatient and excited, and handsome, but looking kind of happy and eased-up, like a person that's had a tooth pulled out. So I went to studying it out. I says to myself, I reckon a body that ups and tells the truth when he is in a tight place, is taking considerable many resks, though I ain't had no experience, and can't say for certain; but it looks so to me, anyway; and yet here's a case where I'm blest if it don't look to me like the truth is better, and actuly *safer,* than a lie. I must lay it by in my mind, and think it over some time or other, it's so kind of strange and unregular. I never see nothing like it. Well, I says to myself at last, I'm agoing to chance it; I'll up and tell the truth this time, though it does seem most like setting down on a kag of powder and touching it off just to see where you'll go to. Then I says:

"Miss Mary Jane, is there any place out of town a little ways, where you could go and stay three or four days?"

"Yes—Mr. Lothrop's. Why?"

"Never mind why, yet. If I'll tell you how I know the niggers will see each other again—inside of two weeks—here in this house—and *prove* how I know it—will you go to Mr. Lothrop's and stay four days?"

"Four days!" she says; "I'll stay a year!"

"All right," I says, "I don't want nothing more out of *you* than just your word—I druther have it than another man's kiss-the-Bible." She smiled, and reddened up very sweet, and I says, "If you don't mind it, I'll shut the door—and bolt it."

Then I come back and set down again, and says:

"Don't you holler. Just set still, and take it like a man. I got to tell the truth, and you want to brace up, Miss Mary, because it's a bad kind, and going to be hard to take, but there ain't no help for it. These uncles of yourn ain't no uncles at all—they're a couples of frauds—regular dead-beats. There, now we're over the worst of it—you can stand the rest middling easy."

It jolted her up like everything, of course; but I was over the shoal water now, so I went right along, her eyes a blazing higher and higher all the time, and told her every blame thing, from where we first struck that young fool going up to the steamboat, clear through to where she flung herself onto the king's breast at the front door and he kissed her sixteen or seventeen times—and then up she jumps, with her face afire like sunset, and says:

"The brute! Come—don't waste a minute—not a *second*—we'll have them tarred and feathered, and flung in the river!"

Says I:

"Cert'nly. But do you mean, *before* you go to Mr. Lothrop's, or—"

"Oh," she says, "What am I *thinking* about!" she says, and set right down again. "Don't mind what I said—please don't—you *won't,* now, *will* you?" Laying her silky hand on mine in that kind of a way that I said I would die first. "I never thought, I was so stirred up," she says; "now go on, and I won't do so any more. You tell me what to do, and whatever you say, I'll do it."

"Well," I says, "it's a rough gang, them two frauds, and I'm fixed so I got to travel with them a while longer, whether I want to or not—I druther not tell you why—and if you was to blow on them this town would get me out of their claws, and *I'*d be all right, but there'd be another person that you don't know about who'd be in big trouble. Well, we got to save *him,* hain't we? Of course. Well, then, we won't blow on them."

Saying them words put a good idea in my head. I see how maybe I could get me and Jim rid of the frauds; get them jailed here, and then leave. But I didn't want to run the raft in daytime, without anybody aboard to answer questions but me; so I didn't want the plan to begin working till pretty late to-night. I says:

"Miss Mary Jane, I'll tell you what we'll do—and you won't have to stay at Mr. Lothrop's so long, nuther. How fur is it?"

"A little short of four miles—right out in the country, back here."

"Well, that'll answer. Now you go along out there, and lay low till nine or half-past, to-night, and then get them to fetch you home again—tell them you've thought of something. If you get here before eleven, put a candle in this window, and if I don't turn up, wait *till* eleven, and *then* if I don't turn up it means I'm gone, and out of the way, and safe. Then you come out and spread the news around, and get these beats jailed."

"Good," she says, "I'll do it."

"And if it just happens so that I don't get away, but get took up along with them, you must up and say I told you the whole thing beforehand, and you must stand by me all you can."

"Stand by you, indeed I will. They sha'n't touch a hair of

your head!" she says, and I see her nostrils spread and her eyes snap when she said it, too.

"If I get away, I sha'n't be here," I says, "to prove these rapscallions ain't your uncles, and I couldn't do it if I *was* here. I could swear they was beats and bummers, that's all; though that's worth something. Well, there's others can do that better than what I can—and they're people that ain't going to be doubted as quick as I'd be. I'll tell you how to find them. Gimme a pencil and a piece of paper. There—'*Royal Nonesuch, Bricksville.*' Put it away, and don't lose it. When the court wants to find out something about these two, let them send up to Bricksville and say they've got the men that played the Royal Nonesuch, and ask for some witnesses—why, you'll have that entire town down here before you can hardly wink, Miss Mary. And they'll come a-biling, too."

I judged we had got everything fixed about right, now. So I says:

"Just let the auction go right along, and don't worry. Nobody don't have to pay for the things they buy till a whole day after the auction, on accounts of the short notice, and they ain't going out of this till they get that money—and the way we've fixed it the sale ain't going to count, and they ain't going to *get* no money. It's just like the way it was with the niggers—it warn't no sale, and the niggers will be back before long. Why, they can't collect the money for the *niggers,* yet—they're in the worst kind of fix, Miss Mary."

"Well," she says, "I'll run down to breakfast now, and then I'll start straight for Mr. Lothrop's."

" 'Deed, *that* ain't the ticket, Miss Mary Jane," I says, "by no manner of means; go *before* breakfast."

"Why?"

"What did you reckon I wanted you to go at all for, Miss Mary?"

"Well, I never thought—and come to think, I don't know. What was it?"

"Why, it's because you ain't one of these leather-face people. I don't want no better book that what your face is. A body can set down and read it off like coarse print. Do you reckon you can go and face your uncles, when they come to kiss you good-morning, and never—"

"There, there, don't! Yes, I'll go before breakfast—I'll be glad to. And leave my sisters with them?"

"Yes—never mind about them. They've got to stand it yet a while. They might suspicion something if all of you was to go. I don't want you to see them, nor your sisters, nor nobody in this town—if a neighbor was to ask how is your uncles this morning, your face would tell something. No, you go right along, Miss Mary Jane, and I'll fix it with all of them. I'll tell Miss Susan to give your love to your uncles and say you've went away for a few hours for to get a little rest and change, or to see a friend, and you'll be back to-night or early in the morning."

"Gone to see a friend is all right, but I won't have my love given to them."

"Well, then, it sha'n't be." It was well enough to tell *her* so—no harm in it. It was only a little thing to do, and no trouble; and it's the little things that smoothes people's roads the most, down here below; it would make Mary Jane comfortable, and it wouldn't cost nothing. Then I says: "There's one more thing—that bag of money."

"Well, they've got that; and it makes me feel pretty silly to think *how* they got it."

"No, you're out, there. They hain't got it."

"Why, who's got it?"

"I wish I knowed, but I don't. I *had* it, because I stole it from them: and I stole it to give to you; and I know where I hid it, but I'm afraid it ain't there no more. I'm awful sorry, Miss Mary Jane, I'm just as sorry as I can be; but I done the best I could; I did, honest. I come nigh getting caught, and I had to shove it into the first place I come to, and run—and it warn't a good place."

"Oh, stop blaming yourself—it's too bad to do it, and I won't allow it—you couldn't help it; it wasn't your fault. Where did you hide it?"

I didn't want to set her to thinking about her troubles again; and I couldn't seem to get my mouth to tell her what would make her see that corpse laying in the coffin with that bag of money on his stomach. So for a minute I didn't say nothing—then I says:

"I'd ruther not *tell* you where I put it, Miss Mary Jane, if you don't mind letting me off; but I'll write it for you on a piece of paper, and you can read it along the road to Mr. Lothrop's, if you want to. Do you reckon that'll do?"

"Oh, yes."

So I wrote: "I put it in the coffin. It was in there when you was crying there, away in the night. I was behind the door, and I was mighty sorry for you, Miss Mary Jane."

It made my eyes water a little, to remember her crying there all by herself in the night, and them devils laying there right under her own roof, shaming her and robbing her; and when I folded it up and give it to her, I see the water come into her eyes, too; and she shook me by the hand, hard, and says:

"*Good*-bye—I'm going to do everything just as you've told me; and if I don't ever see you again, I sha'n't ever forget you, and I'll think of you a many and a many a time, and I'll *pray* for you, too!"—and she was gone.

Pray for me! I reckoned if she knowed me she'd take a job that was more nearer her size. But I bet she done it, just the same—she was just that kind. She had the grit to pray for Judus if she took the notion—there warn't no back-down to her, I judge. You may say what you want to, but in my opinion she had more sand in her than any girl I ever see; in my opinion she was just full of sand. It sounds like flattery, but it ain't no flattery. And when it comes to beauty—and goodness too—she lays over them all. I hain't ever seen her since that time that I see her go out of that door; no, I hain't ever seen her since, but I reckon I've thought of her a many and a many a million times, and of her saying she would pray for me; and if ever I'd a thought it would do any good for me to pray for *her*, blamed if I wouldn't a done it or bust.

Well, Mary Jane she lit out the back way, I reckon; because nobody see her go. When I struck Susan and the hare-lip, I says:

"What's the name of them people over on t'other side of the river that you, all goes to see sometimes?"

They says:

"There's several; but it's the Proctors, mainly."

"That's the name," I says; "I most forgot it. Well, Miss Mary Jane she told me to tell you she's gone over there in a dreadful hurry—one of them's sick."

"Which one?"

"I don't know; leastways I kinder forget; but I think it's—"

"Sakes alive, I hope it ain't *Hanner?*"

"I'm sorry to say it," I says, "but Hanner's the very one."

"My goodness—and she so well only last week! Is she took bad?"

"It ain't no name for it. They set up with her all night, Miss Mary Jane said, and they don't think she'll last many hours."

"Only think of that, now! What's the matter with her!"

I couldn't think of anything reasonable, right off that way, so I says:

"Mumps."

"Mumps your granny! They don't set up with people that's got the mumps."

"They don't, don't they? You better bet they do with *these* mumps. These mumps is different. It's a new kind, Miss Mary Jane said."

"How's it a new kind?"

"Because it's mixed up with other things."

"What other things?"

"Well, measles, and whooping-cough, and erysiplas, and consumption, and yaller janders, and brain fever, and I don't know what all."

"My land! And they call it the *mumps?*"

"That's what Miss Mary Jane said."

"Well, what in the nation do they call it the *mumps* for?"

"Why, because it *is* the mumps. That's what it starts with."

"Well, ther' ain't no sense in it. A body might stump his toe, and take pison, and fall down the well, and break his neck, and bust his brains out, and somebody come along and ask what killed him, and some numskull up and say, 'Why, he stumped his *toe.*' Would ther' be any sense in that? *No.* And ther' ain't no sense in *this,* nuther. Is it ketching?"

"Is it *ketching*? Why, how you talk. Is a *harrow* catching?—in the dark? If you don't hitch onto one tooth, you're bound to on another, ain't you? And you can't get away with that tooth without fetching the whole harrow along, can you? Well, these kind of mumps is a kind of a harrow, as you may say—and it ain't no slouch of a harrow, nuther, you come to get it hitched on good."

"Well, it's awful, *I* think," says the hare-lip. "I'll go to Uncle Harvey and—"

"Oh, yes," I says, "I *would*. Of *course* I would. I wouldn't lose no time."

"Well, why wouldn't you?"

"Just look at it a minute, and maybe you can see. Hain't your uncles obleeged to get along home to England as fast as they can? And do you reckon they'd be mean enough to go off and leave you to go all that journey by yourselves? *You* know they'll wait for you. So fur, so good. Your uncle Harvey's a preacher, ain't he? Very well, then; is a *preacher* going to deceive a steamboat clerk? is he going to deceive a *ship clerk?*—so as to get them to let Miss Mary Jane go aboard? Now *you* know he ain't. What *will* he do, then? Why, he'll say, 'It's a great pity, but my church matters had got to get along the best way they can; for my niece has been exposed to the dreadful pluribus-unum mumps, and so it's my bounden duty to set down here and wait the three months it takes to show on her if she's got it.' But never mind, if you think it's best to tell your uncle Harvey—"

"Shucks, and stay fooling around here when we could all be having good times in England whilst we was waiting to find out whether Mary Jane's got it or not? Why, you talk like a muggins."

"Well, anyway, maybe you better tell some of the neighbors."

"Listen at that, now. You do beat all, for natural stupidness. Can't you *see* that *they'd* go and tell? Ther' ain't no way but just to not tell anybody at *all*."

"Well, maybe you're right—yes, I judge you *are* right."

"But I reckon we ought to tell Uncle Harvey she's gone out a while, anyway, so he wont be uneasy about her?"

"Yes, Miss Mary Jane she wanted you to do that. She says, "Tell them to give Uncle Harvey and William my love and a kiss, and say I've run over the river to see Mr.—Mr.—what *is* the name of that rich family our uncle Peter used to think so much of?—I mean the one that—"

"Why, you must mean the Apthorps, ain't it?"

"Of course; bother them kind of names, a body can't ever seem to remember them, half the time, somehow. Yes, she said, say she has run over for to ask the Apthorps to be sure and come to the auction and buy this house, because she allowed her uncle Peter would ruther they had it than anybody else; and she's going to stick to them till they say they'll come, and then, if she ain't too tired, she's coming home; and if she is, she'll be home in the morning anyway. She said, don't say nothing about the Proctors, but only about the Apthorps—which'll be perfectly true, because she *is* going there to speak about their buying the house; I know it, because she told me so, herself."

"All right," they said, and cleared out to lay for their uncles, and give them the love and kisses, and tell them the message.

Everything was all right now. The girls wouldn't say nothing because they wanted to go to England; and the king and the duke would ruther Mary Jane was off working for the auction than around in reach of Doctor Robinson. I felt very good; I judged I had done it pretty neat—I reckoned Tom Sawyer couldn't a done it no neater himself. Of course he would a throwed more style into it, but I can't do that very handy, not being brung up to it.

Well, they held the auction in the public square, along towards the end of the afternoon, and it strung along, and strung along, and the old man he was on hand and looking his level pisonest, up there longside of the auctioneer, and chipping in a little Scripture, now and then, or a little goody-goody saying, of some kind, and the duke he was around goo-gooing for sympathy all he knowed how, and just spreading himself generly.

But by-and-by the thing dragged through, and everything was sold. Everything but a little old trifling lot in the graveyard. So they'd got to work *that* off—I never see such a girafft as the king was for wanting to swallow *everything*. Well, whilst they was at it, a steamboat landed, and in about two minutes up comes a crowd a whooping and yelling and laughing and carrying on, and singing out:

"*Here's* your opposition line! here's your two sets o' heirs to old Peter Wilks—and you pays your money and you takes your choice!"

CHAPTER XXIX

They was fetching a very nice looking old gentleman along, and a nice looking younger one, with his right arm in a sling. And my souls, how the people yelled, and laughed, and kept it up. But I didn't see no joke about it, and I judged it would strain the duke and the king some to see any. I reckoned they'd turn pale. But no, nary a pale did *they* turn. The duke he never let on he suspicioned what was up, but just went a goo-gooing around, happy and satisfied, like a jug that's googling out buttermilk; and as for the king, he just gazed and gazed down sorrowful on them newcomers like it give him the stomach-ache in his very heart to think there could be such frauds and rascals in the world. Oh, he done it admirable. Lots of the principal people gethered around the king, to let him see they was on his side. That old gentleman that had just come looked all puzzled to death. Pretty soon he begun to speak, and I see, straight off, he pronounced *like* an Englishman, not the king's way, though the king's *was* pretty good, for an imitation. I can't give the old gent's words, nor I can't imitate him; but he turned around to the crowd, and says, about like this:

"This is a surprise to me which I wasn't looking for; and I'll acknowledge, candid and frank, I ain't very well fixed to meet it and answer it; for my brother and me has had misfortunes, he's broke his arm, and our baggage got put off at a town above here, last night in the night by a mistake. I am Peter Wilks's brother Harvey, and this is his brother William, which can't hear nor speak—and can't even make signs to amount to much, now't he's only got one hand to work them with. We are who we say we are; and in a day or two, when I get the baggage, I can prove it. But, up till then, I won't say nothing more, but go to the hotel and wait."

So him and the new dummy started off; and the king he laughs, and blethers out:

"Broke his arm—*very* likely *ain't* it?—and very convenient, too, for a fraud that's got to make signs, and hain't learnt how. Lost their baggage! That's *mighty* good!—and mighty ingenious—under the *circumstances!*"

So he laughed again; and so did everybody else, except three or four, or maybe half a dozen. One of these was that doctor; another one was a sharp looking gentleman, with a carpet-bag of the old-fashioned kind made out of carpet-stuff, that had just come off of the steamboat and was talking to him in a low voice, and glancing towards the king now and then and nodding their heads—it was Levi Bell, the lawyer that was gone up to Louisville; and another one was a big rough husky that come along and listened to all the old gentleman said, and was listening to the king now. And when the king got done, this husky up and says:

"Say, looky here; if you are Harvey Wilks, when'd you come to this town?"

"The day before the funeral, friend," says the king.

"But what time o' day?"

"In the evenin'—'bout an hour er two before sundown."

"*How'd* you come?"

"I come down on the *Susan Powell,* from Cincinnati."

"Well, then, how'd you come to be up at the Pint in the *mornin'*—in a canoe?"

"I warn't up at the Pint in the mornin'."

"It's a lie."

Several of them jumped for him and begged him not to talk that way to an old man and a preacher.

"Preacher be hanged, he's a fraud and a liar. He was up at the Pint that mornin'. I live up there, don't I? Well, I was up there, and he was up there. I *see* him there. He come in a canoe, along with Tim Collins and a boy."

The doctor he up and says:

"Would you know the boy again if you was to see him, Hines?"

"I reckon I would, but I don't know. Why, yonder he is, now. I know him perfectly easy."

It was me he pointed at. The doctor says:

"Neighbors, I don't know whether the new couple is frauds or not; but if *these* two ain't frauds, I am an idiot, that's all. I think it's our duty to see that they don't get away from here till we've looked into this thing. Come along, Hines; come along, the rest of you. We'll take these fellows to the tavern and affront them with t'other couple, and I reckon we'll find out *something* before we get through."

It was nuts for the crowd, though maybe not for the king's friends; so we all started. It was about sundown. The doctor he led me along by the hand, and was plenty kind enough, but he never let *go* my hand.

We all got in a big room in the hotel, and lit up some candles, and fetched in the new couple. First, the doctor says:

"I don't wish to be too hard on these two men, but *I* think they're frauds, and they may have complices that we don't know nothing about. If they have, won't the complices get away with that bag of gold Peter Wilks left? It ain't unlikely. If these men ain't frauds, they won't object to sending for that money and letting us keep it till they prove they're all right—ain't that so?"

Everybody agreed to that. So I judged they had our gang in a pretty tight place, right at the outstart. But the king he only looked sorrowful, and says:

"Gentlemen, I wish the money was there, for I ain't got no disposition to throw anything in the way of a fair, open, out-and-out investigation o' this misable business; but alas, the money ain't there; you k'n send and see, if you want to."

"Where is it, then?"

"Well, when my niece give it to me to keep for her, I took and hid it inside o' the straw tick o' my bed, not wishin' to bank it for the few days we'd be here, and considerin' the bed a safe place, we not bein' used to niggers, and suppos'n' 'em honest, like servants in England. The niggers stole it the very next mornin' after I had went down stairs; and when I sold 'em, I hadn't missed the money yit, so they got clean away with it. My servant here k'n tell you 'bout it gentlemen."

The doctor and several said "Shucks!" and I see nobody didn't altogether believe him. One man asked me if I see the niggers steal it. I said no, but I see them sneaking out of the room and hustling away, and I never thought nothing, only I reckoned they was afraid they had waked up my master and was trying to get away before he made trouble with them. That was all they asked me. Then the doctor whirls on me and says:

"Are *you* English too?"

I says yes; and him and some others laughed, and said, "Stuff!"

Well, then they sailed in on the general investigation, and there we had it, up and down, hour in, hour out, and nobody never said a word about supper, nor ever seemed to think about it—and so they kept it up, and kept it up; and it *was* the worst mixed-up thing you ever see. They made the king tell his yarn, and they made the old gentleman tell his'n; and anybody but a lot of prejudiced chuckleheads would a *seen* that the old gentleman was spinning truth and t'other one lies. And by-and-by they had me up to tell what I knowed. The king he give me a left-handed look out of the corner of his eye, and so I knowed enough to talk on the right side. I begun to tell about Sheffield, and how we lived there, and all about the English Wilkses, and so on; but I didn't get pretty fur till the doctor begun to laugh; and Levi Bell, the lawyer says:

"Set down, my boy, I wouldn't strain myself, if I was you. I reckon you ain't used to lying, it don't seem to come handy; what you want is practice. You do it pretty awkward."

I didn't care nothing for the compliment, but I was glad to be let off, anyway.

The doctor he started to say something, and turns and says:

"If you'd been in town at first, Levi Bell—"

The king broke in and reached out his hand, and says:

"Why, is this my poor dead brother's old friend that he's wrote so often about?"

The lawyer and him shook hands, and the lawyer smiled and looked pleased, and they talked right along a while, and then got to one side and talked low; and at last the lawyer speaks up and says:

"That'll fix it. I'll take the order and send it, along with your brother's and then they'll know it's all right."

So they got some paper and a pen, and the king he set down and twisted his head to one side, and chawed his tongue, and scrawled off something; and then they give the pen to the duke—and then for the first time, the duke looked sick. But he took the pen and wrote. So then the lawyer turns to the new old gentleman and says:

"You and your brother please write a line or two and sign your names."

The old gentleman wrote, but nobody couldn't read it. The lawyer looked powerful astonished, and says:

"Well, it beats *me*"—and snaked a lot of old letters out of his pocket, and examined them, and then examined the old man's writing, and then *them* again; and then says: "These old letters is from Harvey Wilks; and here's *these* two's handwritings, and anybody can see *they* didn't write them" (the king and the duke looked sold and foolish, I tell you, to see how the lawyer had took them in), "and here's *this* old gentleman's handwriting, and anybody can tell, easy enough, *he* didn't write them—fact is, the scratches he makes ain't properly *writing*, at all. Now here's some letters from—"

The new old gentleman says:

"If you please, let me explain. Nobody can read my hand but my brother there—so he copies for me. It's *his* hand you've got there, not mine."

"*Well!*" says the lawyer, "this *is* a state of things. I've got some of William's letters too; so if you'll get him to write a line or so we can com—"

"He *can't* write with his left hand," says the old gentleman. "If he could use his right hand, you would see that he wrote his own letters and mine too. Look at both, please—they're by the same hand."

The lawyer done it, and says:

"I believe it's so—and if it ain't so, there's a heap stronger resemblance than I'd noticed before, anyway. Well, well, well! I thought we was right on the track of a slution, but it's gone to grass, partly. But anyway, *one* thing is proved—*these* two ain't either of 'em Wilkses"—and he wagged his head toward the king and the duke.

Well, what do you think?—that muleheaded old fool wouldn't give in *then!* Indeed he wouldn't. Said it warn't no fair test. Said his brother William was the cussedest joker in the world, and hadn't *tried* to write—*he* see William was going to play one of his jokes the minute he put the pen to paper. And so he warmed up and went warbling and warbling right along, till he was actuly beginning to believe what he was saying, *himself*—but pretty soon the new old gentleman broke in, and says:

"I've thought of something. Is there anybody here that helped to lay out my br—helped to lay out the late Peter Wilks for burying?"

"Yes," says somebody, "me and Ab Turner done it. We're both here."

Then the old man turns towards the king, and says:

"Peraps this gentleman can tell me what was tatooed on his breast?"

Blamed if the king didn't have to brace up mighty quick, or he'd a squshed down like a bluff bank that the river has cut under, it took him so sudden—and mind you, it was a thing that was calculated to make most *anybody* sqush to get fetched such a solid one as that without any notice—because how was *he* going to know what was tatooed on the man? He whitened a little; he couldn't help it; and it was mighty still in there, and everybody bending a little forwards and gazing at him. Says I to myself, *Now* he'll throw up the sponge—there ain't no more use. Well, did he? A body can't hardly believe it, but he didn't. I reckon he thought he'd keep the thing up till he tired them people out, so they'd thin out, and him and the duke could break loose and get away. Anyway, he set there, and pretty soon he begun to smile, and says:

"Mf! It's a *very* tough question, *ain't* it! *Yes,* sir, I k'n tell you what's tatooed on his breast. It's jest a small, thin, blue arrow—

that's what it is; and if you don't look clost, you can't see it. *Now* what do you say—hey?"

Well, *I* never see anything like that old blister for clean out-and-out cheek.

The new old gentleman turns brisk towards Ab Turner and his pard, and his eye lights up like he judged he'd got the king *this* time, and says:

"There—you've heard what he said! Was there any such mark on Peter Wilks's breast?"

Both of them spoke up and says:

"We didn't see no such mark."

"Good!" says the old gentleman. "Now, what you *did* see on his breast was a small dim P, and a B (which is an initial he dropped when he was young), and a W, with dashes between them, so: P—B—W"—and he marked them that way on a piece of paper. "Come—ain't that what you saw?"

Both of them spoke up again, and says:

"No, we *didn't*. We never seen any marks at all."

Well, everybody *was* in a state of mind, now; and they sings out:

"The whole *bilin'* of 'm's frauds! Le's duck 'em! le's drown 'em! le's ride 'em on a rail!" and everybody was whooping at once, and there was a rattling pow-wow. But the lawyer he jumps on the table and yells, and says:

"Gentlemen—gentle*men!* Hear me just a word—just a *single* word—if you PLEASE! There's one way yet—let's go and dig up the corpse and look."

That took them.

"Hooray!" they all shouted, and was starting right off; but the lawyer and the doctor sung out:

"Hold on, hold on! Collar all these four men and the boy, and fetch *them* along, too!"

"We'll do it!" they all shouted: "and if we don't find them marks we'll lynch the whole gang!"

I *was* scared, now, I tell you. But there warn't no getting away, you know. They gripped us all, and marched us right along, straight for the graveyard, which was a mile and a half down the river, and the whole town at our heels, for we made noise enough, and it was only nine in the evening.

As we went by our house I wished I hadn't sent Mary Jane out of town; because now if I could tip her the wink, she'd light out and save me, and blow on our dead-beats.

Well, we swarmed along down the river road, just carrying on like wild-cats; and to make it more scary, the sky was darking up, and the lightning beginning to wink and flitter, and the wind to shiver amongst the leaves. This was the most awful trouble and most dangersome I ever was in; and I was kinder stunned; everything was going so different from what I had allowed for; stead of being fixed so I could take my own time, if I wanted to, and see all the fun, and have Mary Jane at my back to save me and set me free when the close-fit come, here was nothing in the world betwixt me and sudden death but just them tatoo-marks. If they didn't find them—

I couldn't bear to think about it; and yet, somehow, I couldn't think about nothing else. It got darker and darker, and it was a beautiful time to give the crowd the slip; but that big husky had me by the wrist—Hines—and a body might as well try to give Goliar the slip. He dragged me right along, he was so excited; and I had to run to keep up.

When they got there they swarmed into the graveyard and washed over it like an overflow. And when they got to the grave, they found they had about a hundred times as many shovels as they wanted, but nobody hadn't thought to fetch a lantern. But they sailed into digging, anyway, by the flicker of the lightning, and sent a man to the nearest house a half a mile off, to borrow one.

So they dug and dug, like everything; and it got awful dark, and the rain started, and the wind swished and swushed along, and the lightning come brisker and brisker, and the thunder boomed; but them people never took no notice of it, they was so full of this business; and one minute you could see everything and every face in that big crowd, and the shovelfuls of dirt sailing up out of the grave, and the next second the dark wiped it all out, and you couldn't see nothing at all.

At last they got out the coffin, and begun to unscrew the lid, and then such another crowding, and shouldering, and shoving as there was, to scrouge in and get a sight, you never see; and in the dark, that way, it was awful. Hines he hurt my wrist dreadful, pulling and tugging so, and I reckon he clean forgot I was in the world, he was so excited and panting.

All of a sudden the lightning let to a perfect sluice of white glare, and somebody sings out:

"By the living jingo, here's the bag of gold on his breast!"

Hines let out a whoop, like everybody else, and dropped my wrist and give a big surge to bust his way in and get a look, and the way I lit out and shinned for the road in the dark, there ain't nobody can tell.

I had the road all to myself, and I fairly flew—leastways I had it all to myself except the solid dark, and the now-and-then glares, and the buzzing of the rain, and the thrashing of the wind, and the splitting of the thunder; and sure as you are born I did clip it along!

When I struck the town, I see there warn't nobody out in the storm, so I never hunted for no back streets, but humped it straight through the main one; and when I begun to get towards our house I aimed my eye and set it. No light there; the house all dark—which made me feel sorry and disappointed, I didn't know why. But at last, just as I was sailing by, *flash* comes the light in Mary Jane's window! and my heart swelled up sudden, like to bust; and the same second the house and all was behind me in the dark, and wasn't ever going to be before me no more in this world. She *was* the best girl I ever see, and had the most sand.

The minute I was far enough above the town to see I could make the towhead, I begun to look sharp for a boat to borrow; and the first time the lightning showed me one that wasn't chained, I snatched it and shoved. It was a canoe, and warn't fastened with nothing but a rope. The towhead was a rattling big distance off, away out there in the middle of the river, but I didn't lose no time; and when I struck the raft at last, I was so fagged I would a just laid down to blow and gasp if I could afforded it. But I didn't. As I sprung aboard I sung out:

"Out with you Jim, and set her loose! Glory be to goodness, we're shut of them!"

Jim lit out, and was a coming for me with both arms spread, he was so full of joy; but when I glimpsed him in the lightning, my heart shot up in my mouth, and I went overboard backwards; for I forgot he was old King Lear and a drownded A-rab all in one, and it most scared the livers and lights out of me. But Jim fished me out, and was going to hug me and bless me, and so on, he was so glad I was back and we was shut of the king and the duke, but I says:

"Not now—have it for breakfast, have it for breakfast! Cut loose and let her slide!"

So, in two seconds, away we went, a sliding down the river, and it *did* seem so good to be free again and all by ourselves on the big river and nobody to bother us. I had to skip around a bit, and jump up and crack my heels a few times, I couldn't help it; but about the third crack, I noticed a sound that I knowed mighty well—and held my breath and listened and waited—and sure enough, when the next flash busted out over the water, here they come!—and just a laying to their oars and making their skiff hum! It was the king and the duke.

So I wilted right down onto the planks, then, and give up; and it was all I could do to keep from crying.

CHAPTER XXX

When they got aboard, the king went for me, and shook me by the collar, and says:

"Tryin' to give us the slip, was ye, you pup! Tired of our company—hey?"

I says:

"No, your majesty, we warn't—*please* don't, your majesty!"

"Quick, then, and tell us what *was* your idea, or I'll shake the insides out o' you!"

"Honest, I'll tell you everything, just as it happened, your majesty. The man that had aholt of me was very good to me, and kept saying he had a boy about as big as me that died last year, and he was sorry to see a boy in such a dangerous fix; and when they was all took by surprise by finding the gold, and made a rush for the coffin, he lets go of me and whispers, 'Heel it, now, or they'll hang ye, sure!' and I lit out. It didn't seem no good for *me* to stay—*I* couldn't do nothing, and I didn't want to be hung if I could get away. So I never stopped running till I found the canoe; and when I got here I told Jim to hurry, or they'd catch me and hang me yet, and said I was afeard you and the duke wasn't alive, now, and I was awful sorry, and so was Jim, and was awful glad when we see you coming, you may ask Jim if I didn't."

Jim said it was so; and the king told him to shut up, and said, "Oh, yes, it's *mighty* likely!" and shook me up again, and said he reckoned he'd drownd me. But the duke says:

"Leggo the boy, you old idiot! Would *you* a done any different? Did you inquire around for *him,* when you got loose? *I* don't remember it."

So the king let go of me, and begun to cuss that town and everybody in it. But the duke says:

"You better a blame sight give *yourself* a good cussing, for you're the one that's entitled to it most. You hain't done a thing, from the start, that had any sense in it, except coming out so cool and cheeky with that imaginary blue-arrow mark. That *was* bright—it was right down bully; and it was the thing that saved us. For if it hadn't been for that, they'd a jailed us till them Englishmen's baggage come—and then—the penitentiary, you bet! But that trick took 'em to the graveyard, and the gold done us a still bigger kindness; for if the excited fools hadn't let go all holts and made that rush to get a look, we'd a slept in our cravats to-night—cravats warranted to *wear*, too—longer than *we'd* need 'em."

They was still a minute—thinking—then the king says, kind of absentminded like:

"Mf! And we reckoned the *niggers* stole it!"

That made me squirm!

"Yes," says the duke, kinder slow, and deliberate, and sarcastic, "*We* did."

After about a half a minute, the king drawls out:

"Leastways—*I* did."

The duke says, the same way:

"On the contrary—*I* did."

The king kind of ruffles up, and says:

"Looky here, Bilgewater, what'r you referrin' to?"

The duke says, pretty brisk:

"When it comes to that, maybe you'll let me ask, what was *you* referring to?"

"Shucks!" says the king, very sarcastic; "but *I* don't know—maybe you was asleep, and didn't know what you was about."

The duke bristles right up, now, and says:

"Oh, let *up* on this cussed nonsense—do you take me for a blame' fool? Don't you reckon *I* know who hid that money in that coffin?"

"*Yes,* sir! I know you *do* know—because you done it yourself!"

"It's a lie!"—and the duke went for him. The king sings out:

"Take y'r hands off!—leggo my throat!—I take it all back!"

The duke says:

"Well, you just own up, first, that you *did* hide that money there, intending to give me the slip one of these days, and come back and dig it up, and have it all to yourself."

"Wait jest a minute, duke—answer me this one question, honest and fair; if you didn't put the money there, say it, and I'll b'lieve you, and take back everything I said."

"You old scoundrel, I didn't, and you know I didn't. There, now!"

"Well, then, I b'lieve you. But answer me only jest this one more—now *don't* git mad; didn't you have it in your *mind* to hook the money and hide it?"

The duke never said nothing for a little bit; then he says:

"Well—I don't care if I *did,* I didn't *do* it, anyway. But you not only had it in mind to do it, but you *done* it."

"I wisht I may never die if I done it, duke, and that's honest. I won't say I warn't *goin'* to do it, because I *was;* but you—I mean somebody—got in ahead o' me."

"It's a lie! You done it, and you got to *say* you done it, or—"

The king begun to gurgle, and then he gasps out:

"'Nough!—*I own up!*"

I was very glad to hear him say that, it made me feel much more easier than what I was feeling before. So the duke took his hands off, and says:

"If you ever deny it again, I'll drown you. It's *well* for you to set there and blubber like a baby—it's fitten for you, after the way you've acted. I never see such an old ostrich for wanting to gobble everything—and I a trusting you all the time, like you was my own father. You ought to been ashamed of yourself to stand by and hear it saddled onto a lot of poor niggers and you never say a word for 'em. It makes me feel ridiculous to think I was soft enough to *believe* that rubbage. Cuss you, I can see, now, why you was so anxious to make up the deffesit—you wanted to get what money I'd got out of the Nonesuch and one thing or another, and scoop it *all!*"

The king says, timid, and still a snuffling:

"Why, duke, it was you that said make up the deffersit, it warn't me."

"Dry up! I don't want to hear no more *out* of you!" says the duke. "And *now* you see what you *got* by it. They've got all their own money back, and all of *ourn* but a shekel or two, *besides*. G'long to bed—and don't you deffersit *me* no more deffersits, long's *you* live!"

So the king sneaked into the wigwam, and took to his bottle for comfort; and before long the duke tackled *his* bottle; and so in about a half an hour they was as thick as thieves again, and the tighter they got, the lovinger they got; and went off a snoring in each other's arms. They both got powerful mellow, but I noticed the king didn't get mellow enough to forget to remember to not deny about hiding the money-bag again. That made me feel easy and satisfied. Of course when they got to snoring, we had a long gabble, and I told Jim everything.

CHAPTER XXXI

We dasn't stop again at any town, for days and days; kept right along down the river. We was down south in the warm weather, now, and a mighty long ways from home. We begun to come to trees with Spanish moss on them, hanging down from the limbs like long gray beards. It was the first I ever see it growing, and it made the woods look solemn and dismal. So now the frauds reckoned they was out of danger, and they begun to work the villages again.

First they done a lecture on temperance; but they didn't make enough for them both to get drunk on. Then in another village they started a dancing school; but they didn't know no more how to dance than a kangaroo does; so the first prance they made, the general public jumped in and pranced them out of town. Another time they tried a go at yellocution; but they didn't yellocute long till the audience got up and give them a solid good cussing and made them skip out. They tackled missionarying, and mesmerizering, and doctoring, and telling fortunes, and a little of everything; but they couldn't seem to have no luck. So at last they got just about dead broke, and laid around the raft, as she floated along, thinking, and thinking, and never saying nothing, by the half a day at a time, and dreadful blue and desperate.

And at last they took a change, and begun to lay their heads together in the wigwam and talk low and confidential two or three hours at a time. Jim and me got uneasy. We didn't like the look of it. We judged they was studying up some kind of worse deviltry than ever. We turned it over and over, and at last we made up our minds they was going to break into somebody's house or store, or was going into the counterfeit-money business, or something. So then we was pretty scared, and made up an agreement that we wouldn't have nothing in the world to do with such actions, and if we ever got the least show we would give them the cold shake, and clear out and leave them behind. Well, early one morning we hid the raft in a good safe place about two mile below a little bit of a shabby village, named Pikesville, and the king he went ashore, and told us all to stay hid whilst he went up to town and smelt around to see if anybody had got any wind of the Royal Nonesuch there yet. ("House to rob, you *mean,*" says I to myself; "and when you get through robbing it you'll come back here and wonder what's become of me and Jim and the raft—and you'll have to take it out in wondering.") And he said if he warn't back by midday, the duke and me would know it was all right, and we was to come along.

So we staid where we was. The duke he fretted and sweated around, and was in a mighty sour way. He scolded us for everything, and we couldn't seem to do nothing right; he found fault with every little thing. Something was a-brewing, sure. I was good and glad when midday come and no king; we could have a change, anyway—and maybe a chance for *the* change, on top of it. So me and the duke went up to the village, and hunted around there for the king, and by-and-by we found him in the back room of a little low doggery, very tight, and a lot of loafers bullyragging him for sport, and he a cussing and threatening with all his might, and so tight he couldn't walk, and couldn't do nothing to them. The duke he begun to abuse him for an old fool, and the king begun to sass back; and the minute they was fairly at it, I lit out, and shook the reefs out of my hind legs, and spun down the river road like a deer—for I see our chance; and I made up my mind that it would be a long day before they ever see me and Jim again. I got down there all out of breath but loaded up with joy, and sung out—

"Set her loose, Jim, we're all right, now!"

But there warn't no answer, and nobody come out of the wigwam. Jim was gone! I set up a shout—and then another—and then another one; and run this way and that in the woods, whooping and screeching; but it warn't no use—old Jim was gone. Then I set down and cried; I couldn't help it. But I couldn't set still long. Pretty soon I went out on the road, trying to think what I better do, and I run across a boy walking, and asked him if he'd seen a strange nigger, dressed so and so, and he says:

"Yes."

"Whereabouts?" says I.

"Down to Silas Phelps's place, two mile below here. He's a runaway nigger, and they've got him. Was you looking for him?"

"You bet I ain't! I run across him in the woods about an hour or two ago, and he said if I hollered he'd cut my livers out—

and told me to lay down and stay where I was; and I done it. Been there ever since; afeard to come out."

"Well," he says, "you needn't be afeard no more, becuz they've got him. He run off f'm down South, som'ers."

"It's a good job they got him."

"Well, I *reckon!* There's two hunderd dollars reward on him. It's like picking up money out'n the road."

"Yes, it is—and *I* could a had it if I'd been big enough; I see him *first.* Who nailed him?"

"It was an old fellow—a stranger—and he sold out his chance in him for forty dollars, becuz he's got to go up the river and can't wait. Think o' that, now! You bet *I'd* wait, if it was seven year."

"That's me, every time," says I. "But maybe his chance ain't worth no more than that, if he'll sell it so cheap. Maybe there's something ain't straight about it."

"But it *is,* though—straight as a string. I see the handbill myself. It tells all about him, to a dot—paints him like a picture, and tells the plantation he's frum, below Newr*leans.* No-sirree-*bob,* they ain't no trouble 'bout *that* speculation, you bet you. Say, gimme a chaw tobacker, won't ye?"

I didn't have none, so he left. I went to the raft, and set down in the wigwam to think. But I couldn't come to nothing. I thought till I wore my head sore, but I couldn't see no way out of the trouble. After all this long journey, and after all we'd done for them scoundrels, here was it all come to nothing, everything all busted up and ruined, because they could have the heart to serve Jim such a trick as that, and make him a slave again all his life, and amongst strangers, too, for forty dirty dollars.

Once I said to myself it would be a thousand times better for Jim to be a slave at home where his family was, as long as he'd *got* to be a slave, and so I'd better write a letter to Tom Sawyer and tell him to tell Miss Watson where he was. But I soon give up that notion, for two things; she'd be mad and disgusted at his rascality and ungratefulness for leaving her, and so she'd sell him straight down the river again; and if she didn't, everybody naturally despises an ungrateful nigger, and they'd make

Jim feel it all the time, and so he'd feel ornery and disgraced. And then think of *me!* It would get all around, that Huck Finn helped a nigger to get his freedom; and if I was to ever see anybody from that town again, I'd be ready to get down and lick his boots for shame. That's just the way: a person does a low-down thing, and then he don't want to take no consequences of it. Thinks as long as he can hide it, it ain't no disgrace. That was my fix exactly. The more I studied about this, the more my conscience went to grinding me, and the more wicked and low-down and ornery I got to feeling. And at last, when it hit me all of a sudden that here was the plain hand of Providence slapping me in the face and letting me know my wickedness was being watched all the time from up there in heaven, whilst I was stealing a poor old woman's nigger that hadn't ever done me no harm, and now was showing me there's One that's always on the lookout, and ain't agoing to allow no such miserable doings to go only just so fur and no further, I most dropped in my tracks I was so scared. Well, I tried the best I could to kinder soften it up somehow for myself, by saying I was brung up wicked, and so I warn't so much to blame; but something inside of me kept saying, "There was the Sunday school, you could a gone to it; and if you'd a done it they'd a learnt you, there, that people that acts as I'd been acting about that nigger goes to everlasting fire."

It made me shiver. And I about made up my mind to pray; and see if I couldn't try to quit being the kind of a boy I was, and be better. So I kneeled down. But the words wouldn't come. Why wouldn't they? It warn't no use to try and hide it from Him. Nor from *me*, neither. I knowed very well why they wouldn't come. It was because my heart warn't right; it was because I warn't square; it was because I was playing double. I was letting *on* to give up sin, but away inside of me I was holding on to the biggest one of all. I was trying to make my mouth *say* I would do the right thing and the clean thing, and go and write to that nigger's owner and tell where he was; but deep down in me I knowed it was a lie—and He knowed it. You can't pray a lie—I found that out.

So I was full of trouble, full as I could be; and didn't know what to do. At last I had an idea; and I says, I'll go and write the letter—and *then* see if I can pray. Why, it was astonishing, the way I felt as light as a feather, right straight off, and my troubles all gone. So I got a piece of paper and a pencil, all glad and excited, and set down and wrote:

Miss Watson your runaway nigger Jim is down here two mile below Pikesville and Mr. Phelps has got him and he will give him up for the reward if you send. HUCK FINN.

I felt good and all washed clean of sin for the first time I had ever felt so in my life, and I knowed I could pray now. But I didn't do it straight off, but laid the paper down and set there thinking—thinking how good it was all this happened so, and how near I come to being lost and going to hell. And went on thinking. And got to thinking over our trip down the river; and I see Jim before me, all the time, in the day, and in the night-time, sometimes moonlight, sometimes storms, and we a floating along, talking, and singing, and laughing. But somehow I couldn't seem to strike no places to harden me against him, but only the other kind. I'd see him standing my watch on top of his'n, stead of calling me, so I could go on sleeping; and see him how glad he was when I come back out of the fog; and when I come to him again in the swamp, up there where the feud was; and such-like times; and would always call me honey, and pet me, and do everything he could think of for me, and how good he always was; and at last I struck the time I saved him by telling the men we had small-pox aboard, and he was so grateful, and said I was the best friend old Jim ever had in the world, and the *only* one he's got now; and then I happened to look around, and see that paper.

It was a close place. I took it up, and held it in my hand. I was a trembling, because I'd got to decide, forever, betwixt two things, and I knowed it. I studied a minute, sort of holding my breath, and then says to myself:

"All right, then, I'll *go* to hell"—and tore it up.

It was awful thoughts, and awful words, but they was said. And I let them stay said; and never thought no more about reforming. I shoved the whole thing out of my head; and said I would take up wickedness again, which was in my line, being brung up to it, and the other warn't. And for a starter, I would go to work and steal Jim out of slavery again; and if I could think up anything worse, I would do that, too; because as long as I was in, and in for good, I might as well go the whole hog.

Then I set to thinking over how to get at it, and turned over considerable many ways in my mind; and at last fixed up a plan that suited me. So then I took the bearings of a woody island that was down the river a piece, and as soon as it was fairly dark I crept out with my raft and went for it, and hid it there, and then turned in. I slept the night through, and got up before it was light, and had my breakfast, and put on my store clothes, and tied up some others and one thing or another in a bundle, and took the canoe and cleared for shore. I landed below where I judged was Phelps's place, and hid my bundle in the woods, and then filled up the canoe with water, and loaded rocks into her and sunk her where I could find her again when I wanted her, about a quarter of a mile below a little steam sawmill that was on the bank.

Then I struck up the road, and when I passed the mill I see a sign on it, "Phelps's Sawmill," and when I come to the farm-houses, two or three hundred yards further along, I kept my eyes peeled, but didn't see nobody around, though it was good daylight, now. But I didn't mind, because I didn't want to see nobody just yet—I only wanted to get a lay of the land. According to my plan, I was going to turn up there from the village, not from below. So I just took a look, and shoved along, straight for town. Well, the very first man I see, when I got there, was the duke. He was sticking up a bill for the Royal Nonesuch—three-night performance—like that other time. *They* had the cheek, them frauds! I was right on him, before I could shirk. He looked astonished, and says:

"Hel-*lo!* Where'd *you* come from?" Then he says, kind of glad and eager, "Where's the raft?—got her in a good place?"

I says:

"Why, that's just what I was agoing to ask your grace."

Then he didn't look so joyful—and says:

"What was your idea for asking *me?*" he says.

"Well," I says, "when I see the king in that doggery yesterday, I says to myself, we can't get him home for hours, till he's soberer; so I went a loafing around town to put in the time, and wait. A man up and offered me ten cents to help him pull a skiff over the river and back to fetch a sheep, and so I went along; but when we was dragging him to the boat, and the man left me aholt of the rope and went behind him to shove him along, he was too strong for me, and jerked loose and run, and we after him. We didn't have no dog, and so we had to chase him all over the country till we tired him out. We never got him till dark, then we fetched him over, and I started down for the raft. When I got there and see it was gone, I says to myself, 'they've got into trouble and had to leave; and they've took my nigger, which is the only nigger I've got in the world, and now I'm in a strange country, and ain't got no property no more, nor nothing, and no way to make my living;' so I set down and cried. I slept in the woods all night. But what *did* become of the raft then?—and Jim, poor Jim!"

"Blamed if *I* know—that is, what's become of the raft. That old fool had made a trade and got forty dollars, and when we found him in the doggery the loafers had matched half dollars with him and got every cent but what he'd spent for whisky; and when I got him home late last night and found the raft gone, we said, 'That little rascal has stole our raft and shook us, and run off down the river.'

"I wouldn't shake my *nigger,* would I?—the only nigger I had in the world, and the only property."

"We never thought of that. Fact is, I reckon we'd come to consider him *our* nigger; yes, we did consider him so—goodness knows we had trouble enough for him. So when we see the raft was gone, and we flat broke, there warn't anything for it but to try the Royal Nonesuch another shake. And I've pegged along ever since, dry as powder-horn. Where's that ten cents? Give it here."

I had considerable money, so I give him ten cents, but begged him to spend it for something to eat, and give me some, because it was all the money I had, and I hadn't had nothing to eat since yesterday. He never said nothing. The next minute he whirls on me and says:

"Do you reckon that nigger would blow on us? We'd skin him if he done that!"

"How can he blow? Hain't he run off?"

"No! That old fool sold him, and never divided with me, and the money's gone."

"*Sold* him?" I says, and begun to cry; "why, he was *my* nigger, and that was my money. Where is he?—I want my nigger."

"Well, you can't *get* your nigger, that's all—so dry up your blubbering. Looky here—do you think *you'd* venture to blow on us? Blamed if I think I'd trust you. Why, if you *was* to blow on us—"

He stopped, but I never see the duke look so ugly out of his eyes before. I went on a-whimpering, and says:

"I don't want to blow on nobody; and I ain't got no time to blow, nohow. I got to turn out and find my nigger."

He looked kinder bothered, and stood there with his bills fluttering on his arm, thinking, and wrinkling up his forehead. At last he says:

"I'll tell you something. We got to be here three days. If you'll promise you won't blow, and won't let the nigger blow, I'll tell you where to find him."

So I promised, and he says:

"A farmer by the name of Silas Ph—" and then he stopped. You see he started to tell me the truth; but when he stopped, that way, and begun to study and think again, I reckoned he was changing his mind. And so he was. He wouldn't trust me; he wanted to make sure of having me out of the way the whole three days. So pretty soon he says: "The man that bought him is named Abram Foster—Abram G. Foster—and he lives forty mile back here in the country, on the road to Lafayette."

"All right," I says, "I can walk it in three days. And I'll start this very afternoon."

"No you won't, you'll start *now;* and don't you lose any time about it, neither, nor do any gabbling by the way. Just keep a tight tongue in your head and move right along, and then you won't get into trouble with *us,* d'ye hear?"

That was the order I wanted, and that was the one I played for. I wanted to be left free to work my plans.

"So clear out," he says; "and you can tell Mr. Foster whatever you want to. Maybe you can get him to believe that Jim *is* your nigger—some idiots don't require documents—leastways I've heard there's such down South here. And when you tell him the handbill and the reward's bogus, maybe he'll believe you when you explain to him what the idea was for getting 'em out. Go 'long, now, and tell him anything you want to; but mind you won't work your jaw any *between* here and there."

So I left, and struck for the back country. I didn't look around, but I kinder felt like he was watching me. But I knowed I could tire him out at that. I went straight out in the country as much as a mile, before I stopped; then I doubled back through the woods toward Phelps's. I reckoned I better start in on my plan straight off, without fooling around, because I wanted to stop Jim's mouth till these fellows could get away. I didn't want no trouble with their kind. I'd seen all I wanted to of them, and wanted to get entirely shut of them.

CHAPTER XXXII

When I got there it was all still and Sunday-like, and hot and sunshiny—the hands was gone to the fields; and there was them kind of faint dronings of bugs and flies in the air that makes it seem so lonesome and like everybody's dead and gone; and if a breeze fans along and quivers the leaves, it makes you feel mournful, because you feel like it's spirits whispering—spirits that's been dead ever so many years—and you always think they're talking about *you*. As a general thing it makes a body wish *he* was dead, too, and done with it all.

Phelps's was one of these little one-horse cotton plantations; and they all look alike. A rail fence round a two-acre yard; a stile, made out of logs sawed off and up-ended, in steps, like barrels of a different length, to climb over the fence with, and for the women to stand on when they are going to jump onto a horse; some sickly grass-patches in the big yard, but mostly it was bare and smooth, like an old hat with the nap rubbed off; big double log house for the white folks—hewed logs, with the chinks stopped up with mud or mortar, and these mud-stripes been whitewashed some time or another; round-log kitchen, with a big broad, open but roofed passage joining it to the house; log smoke-house back of the kitchen; three little log nigger-cabins in a row t'other side the smokehouse; one little hut all by itself away down against the back fence, and some out-buildings down a piece the other side; ash-hopper, and big kettle to bile soap in, by the little hut; bench by the kitchen door, with bucket of water and a gourd; hound asleep there, in the sun; more hounds asleep, round about; about three shade-trees away off in a corner; some currant bushes and gooseberry bushes in one place by the fence; outside of the fence a garden and a water-melon patch; then the cotton fields begins; and after the fields, the woods.

I went around and clumb over the back stile by the ash-hopper, and started for the kitchen. When I got a little ways, I heard the dim hum of a spinning-wheel wailing along up and sinking along down again; and then I knowed for certain I wished I was dead—for that *is* the lonesomest sound in the whole world.

I went right along, not fixing up any particular plan, but just trusting to Providence to put the right words in my mouth when the time come; for I'd noticed that Providence always did put the right words in my mouth, if I left it alone.

When I got half-way, first one hound and then another got up and went for me, and of course I stopped and faced them, and kept still. And such another pow-wow as they made! In a quarter of a minute I was a kind of a hub of a wheel, as you may say—spokes made out of dogs—circle of fifteen of them packed together around me, with their necks and noses stretched up towards me, a barking and howling; and more a coming; you could see them sailing over fences and around corners from everywheres.

A nigger woman come tearing out of the kitchen with a rolling-pin in her hand, singing out, "Begone! *you* Tige! you Spot! begone, sah!" and she fetched first one and then another of them a clip and sent him howling, and then the rest followed; and the next second, half of them come back, wagging their tails around me and making friends with me. There ain't no harm in a hound, nohow.

And behind the woman comes a little nigger girl and two little nigger boys, without anything on but tow-linen shirts, and they hung onto their mother's gown, and peeped out from behind her at me, bashful, the way they always do. And here comes the white woman running from the house, about forty-five or fifty year old, bareheaded, and her spinning-stick in her hand; and behind her comes her little white children, acting the same way the little niggers was doing. She was smiling all over so she could hardly stand—and says:

"It's *you,* at last!—*ain't* it?"

I out with a "Yes'm," before I thought.

She grabbed me and hugged me tight; and then gripped me by both hands and shook and shook; and the tears come in her eyes, and run down over; and she couldn't seem to hug and shake enough, and kept saying, "You don't look as much like your mother as I reckoned you would, but law sakes, I don't care for that, I'm *so* glad to see you! Dear, dear, it does seem like I could eat you up! Childern, it's your cousin Tom!—tell him howdy."

But they ducked their heads, and put their fingers in their mouths, and hid behind her. So she run on:

"Lize, hurry up and get him a hot breakfast, right away—or did you get your breakfast on the boat?"

I said I had got it on the boat. So then she started for the house, leading me by the hand, and the children tagging after. When we got there, she set me down in a split-bottomed chair, and set herself down on a little low stool in front of me, holding both of my hands, and says:

"Now I can have a *good* look at you; and laws-a-me, I've been hungry for it a many and a many a time, all these long years, and it's come at last! We been expecting you a couple of days and more. What's kep' you?—boat get aground?"

"Yes'm—she—"

"Don't say yes'm—say Aunt Sally. Where'd she get aground?"

I didn't rightly know what to say, because I didn't know whether the boat would be coming up the river or down. But I go a good deal on instinct; and my instinct said she would be coming up—from down towards Orleans. That did'nt help me much, though; for I didn't know the names of bars down that way. I see I'd got to invent a bar, or forget the name of the one we got aground on—or—Now I struck an idea, and fetched it out:

"It warn't the grounding—that didn't keep us back but a little. We blowed out a cylinder-head."

"Good gracious! anybody hurt?"

"No'm. Killed a nigger."

"Well, it's lucky; because sometimes people do get hurt. Two years ago last Christmas, your uncle Silas was coming up from Newrleans on the old *Lally Rook,* and she blowed out a cylinder-head and crippled a man. And I think he died afterwards. He was a Babtist. Your uncle Silas knowed a family in Baton Rouge that knowed his people very well. Yes, I remember, now he *did* die. Mortification set in, and they had to amputate him. But it didn't save him. Yes, it was mortification—that was it. He turned blue all over, and died in the hope of a glorious resurrection. They say he was a sight to look at. Your uncle's been up to the town every day to fetch you. And he's gone again, not more'n an hour ago; he'll be back any minute, now. You must a met him on the road, didn't you?—oldish man, with a—"

"No, I didn't see nobody, Aunt Sally. The boat landed just at daylight, and I left my baggage on the wharf-boat and went looking around the town and out a piece in the country, to put in the time and not get here too soon; and so I come down the back way."

"Who'd you give the baggage to?"

"Nobody."

"Why, child, it'll be stole!"

"Not where *I* hid it I reckon it won't," I says.

"How'd you get your breakfast so early on the boat?"

It was kinder thin ice, but I says:

"The captain see me standing around, and told me I better have something to eat before I went ashore; so he took me in the texas to the officers' lunch, and give me all I wanted."

I was getting so uneasy I couldn't listen good. I had my mind on the children all the time; I wanted to get them out to one side, and pump them a little, and find out who I was. But I couldn't get no show, Mrs. Phelps kept it up and run on so. Pretty soon she made the cold chills streak all down my back, because she says:

"But here we're a running on this way, and you hain't told me a word about Sis, nor any of them. Now I'll rest my works a little, and you start up yourn; just tell me *everything*—tell me all about 'm all—every one of 'm; and how they are, and what they're doing, and what they told you to tell me; and every last thing you can think of."

Well, I see I was up a stump—and up it good. Providence had stood by me this fur, all right, but I was hard and tight aground, now. I see it warn't a bit of use to try to go ahead—I'd *got* to throw up my hand. So I says to myself, here's another place where I got to resk the truth. I opened my mouth to begin; but she grabbed me and hustled me in behind the bed, and says:

"Here he comes! stick your head down lower—there, that'll do; you can't be seen, now. Don't you let on you're here. I'll play a joke on him. Children, don't you say a word."

I see I was in a fix, now. But it warn't no use to worry; there warn't nothing to do but just hold still, and try and be ready to stand from under when the lightning struck.

I had just one little glimpse of the old gentleman when he come in, then the bed hid him. Mrs. Phelps she jumps for him and says:

"Has he come?"

"No," says her husband.

"Good-*ness* gracious!" she says, "what in the world *can* have become of him?"

"I can't imagine," says the old gentleman; "and I must say, it makes me dreadful uneasy."

"Uneasy!" she says, "I'm ready to go distracted! He *must* a come; and you've missed him along the road. I *know* it's so—something *tells* me so."

"Why Sally, I *couldn't* miss him along the road—*you* know that."

"But oh, dear, dear, what *will* Sis say! He must a come! You must a missed him. He—"

"Oh, don't distress me any more'n I'm already distressed. I don't know what in the world to make of it. I'm at my wit's end, and I don't mind acknowledging 't I'm right down scared. But there's no hope that he's come; for he *couldn't* come and me miss him. Sally, it's terrible—just terrible—something's happened to the boat, sure!"

"Why, Silas! Look yonder!—up the road!—ain't that somebody coming?"

He sprung to the window at the head of the bed, and that give Mrs Phelps the chance she wanted. She stooped down quick, at the foot of the bed, and give me a pull, and out I come; and when he turned back from the window, there she stood, a-beaming and a-smiling like a house afire, and I standing pretty meek and sweaty alongside. The old gentleman stared, and says:

"Why, who's that?"

"Who do you reckon 't is?"

"I haint no idea. Who *is* it?"

"It's *Tom Sawyer!*"

By jings, I most slumped though the floor. But there warn't no time to swap knives; the old man grabbed me by the hand and shook, and kept on shaking; and all the time, how the woman did dance around and laugh and cry; and then how they both did fire off questions about Sid, and Mary, and the rest of the tribe.

But if they was joyful, it warn't nothing to what I was; for it was like being born again, I was so glad to find out who I was. Well, they froze to me for two hours; and at last when my chin was so tired it couldn't hardly go, any more, I had told them more about my family—I mean the Sawyer family—than ever happened to any six Sawyer families. And I explained all about how we blowed out a cylinder-head at the mouth of White River and it took us three days to fix it. Which was all right, and worked first rate; because *they* didn't know but what it would take three days to fix it. If I'd a called it a bolt-head it would a done just as well.

Now I was felling pretty comfortable all down one side, and pretty uncomfortable all up the other. Being Tom Sawyer was easy and comfortable; and it stayed easy and comfortable till by-and-by I hear a steamboat coughing along down the river—then I says to myself, spose Tom Sawyer come down on that boat?—and spose he steps in here, any minute, and sings out my name before I can throw him a wink to keep quiet? Well, I couldn't *have* it that way—it wouldn't do at all. I must go up the road and waylay him. So I told the folks I reckoned I would go up to the town and fetch down my baggage. The old gentleman was for going along with me, but I said no, I could drive the horse myself, and I druther he wouldn't take no trouble about me.

CHAPTER XXXIII

So I started for town, in the wagon, and when I was half-way I see a wagon coming, and sure enough it was Tom Sawyer, and I stopped and waited till he come along. I says "Hold on!" and it stopped alongside, and his mouth opened up like a trunk, and staid so; and he swallowed two or three times like a person that's got a dry throat, and then says:

"I hain't ever done you no harm. You know that. So then, what you want to come back and ha'nt *me* for?"

I says:

"I hain't come back—I hain't been *gone.*"

When he heard my voice, it righted him up some, but he warn't quite satisfied yet. He says:

"Don't you play nothing on me, because I wouldn't on you. Honest injun, now, you ain't a ghost?"

"Honest injun, I ain't," I says.

"Well—I—I—well, that ought to settle it, of course; but I can't somehow seem to understand it, no way. Looky here, warn't you ever murdered *at all?*"

"No. I warn't ever murdered at all—I played it on them. You come in here and feel of me if you don't believe me."

So he done it; and it satisfied him; and he was that glad to see me again, he didn't know what to do. And he wanted to know all about it right off; because it was a grand adventure, and mysterious, and so it hit him where he lived. But I said, leave it along till by-and-by; and told his driver to wait, and we drove off a little piece, and I told him the kind of a fix I was in, and what did he reckon we better do? He said, let him alone a minute, and don't disturb him. So he thought and thought, and pretty soon he says:

"It's all right, I've got it. Take my trunk in your wagon, and let on it's your'n; and you turn back and fool along slow, so as to get to the house about the time you ought to; and I'll go towards town a piece, and take a fresh start, and get there a quarter or a half an hour after you; and you needn't let on to know me, at first."

I says:

"All right; but wait a minute. There's one more thing—a thing that *nobody* don't know but me. And that is, there's a nigger here that I'm trying to steal out of slavery—and his name is *Jim*—old Miss Watson's Jim."

He says:

"What! Why Jim is—"

He stopped and went to studying. I says:

"*I* know what you'll say. You'll say it's dirty low-down business; but what if it is?—*I*'m low down; and I'm agoing to steal him, and I want you to keep mum and not let on. Will you?"

His eye lit up, and he says:

"I'll *help* you steal him!"

Well, I let go all holts then, like I was shot. It was the most astonishing speech I ever heard—and I'm bound to say Tom Sawyer fell, considerable, in my estimation. Only I couldn't believe it. Tom Sawyer a *nigger stealer!*

"Oh, shucks," I says, "you're joking."

"I ain't joking, either."

"Well, then," I says, "joking or no joking, if you hear anything said about a runaway nigger, don't forget to remember that *you* don't know nothing about him, and *I* don't know nothing about him."

Then we took the trunk and put it in my wagon, and he drove off his way, and I drove mine. But of course I forgot all about driving slow, on accounts of being glad and full of thinking; so I got home a heap too quick for that length of a trip. The old gentleman was at the door, and he says:

"Why, this is wonderful. Who ever would a thought it was in that mare to do it. I wish we'd a timed her. And she hain't sweated a hair—not a hair. It's wonderful. Why, I wouldn't take a hunderd dollars for that horse now; I wouldn't honest; and yet I'd a sold her for fifteen before, and thought 'twas all she was worth."

That's all he said. He was the innocentest, best old soul I ever see. But it warn't surprising; because he warn't only just a farmer, he was a preacher, too, and had a little one-horse log church down back of the plantation, which he built it himself at his own expense, for a church and school-house, and never charged nothing for his preaching, and it was worth it, too. There was plenty of other farmer-preachers like that, and done the same way, down South.

In about half an hour Tom's wagon drove up to the front stile, and Aunt Sally she see it through the window because it was only about fifty yards, and says:

"Why, there's somebody come! I wonder who 'tis? Why, I do believe it's a stranger. Jimmy" (that's one of the children), "run and tell Lize to put on another plate for dinner."

Everybody made a rush for the front door, because, of course, a stranger don't come *every* year, and so he lays over the yaller fever, for interest, when he does come. Tom was over the stile and starting for the house; the wagon was spinning up the road for the village, and we was all bunched in the front door. Tom had his store clothes on, and an audience—and that was always nuts for Tom Sawyer. In them circumstances it warn't no trouble to him to throw in an amount of style that was suitable. He warn't a boy to meeky along up that yard like a sheep; no, he come ca'm and important, like the ram. When he got afront of us, he lifts his hat ever so gracious and dainty, like it was the lid of a box that had butterflies asleep in it and he didn't want to disturb them, and says:

"Mr. Archibald Nichols, I presume?"

"No, my boy," says the old gentleman, "I'm sorry to say 't

your driver has deceived you; Nichols's place is down a matter of three mile more. Come in, come in."

Tom he took a look back over his shoulder, and says, "Too late—he's out of sight."

"Yes, he's gone, my son, and you must come in and eat your dinner with us; and then we'll hitch up and take you down to Nichols's."

"Oh, I *can't* make you so much trouble; I couldn't think of it. I'll walk—I don't mind the distance."

"But we won't *let* you walk—it wouldn't be Southern hospitality to do it. Come right in."

"Oh, *do,*" says Aunt Sally; "it ain't a bit of trouble to us, not a bit in the world. You *must* stay. It's a long, dusty three mile, and we *can't* let you walk. And besides, I've already told 'em to put on another plate, when I see you coming; so you mustn't disappoint us. Come right in, and make yourself at home."

So Tom he thanked them very hearty and handsome, and let himself be persuaded, and come in; and when he was in, he said he was a stranger from Hicksville, Ohio, and his name was William Thompson—and he made another bow.

Well, he run on, and on, making up stuff about Hicksville and everybody in it he could invent, and I getting a little nervous, and wondering how this was going to help me out of my scrape; and at last, still talking along, he reached over and kissed Aunt Sally right on the mouth, and then settled back again in his chair, comfortable, and was going on talking; but she jumped up and wiped it off with the back of her hand, and says:

"You owdacious puppy!"

He looked kind of hurt, and says:

"I'm surprised at you, m'am."

"You're s'rp— Why, what do you reckon *I* am? I've a good notion to take and—say, what do you mean by kissing me?"

He looked kind of humble, and says:

"I didn't mean nothing, m'am. I didn't mean no harm. I—I—thought you'd like it."

"Why, you born fool!" She took up the spinning-stick, and it looked like it was all she could do to keep from giving him a crack with it. "What made you think I'd like it?"

'Well, I don't know. Only, they—they—told me you would."

"*They* told you I would. Whoever told you's *another* lunatic. I never heard the beat of it. Who's *they?*"

"Why—everybody. They all said so, m'am."

It was all she could do to hold in; and her eyes snapped, and her fingers worked like she wanted to scratch him; and she says:

"Who's 'everybody?' Out with their names—or ther'll be an idiot short."

He got up and looked distressed, and fumbled his hat, and says:

"I'm sorry, and I warn't expecting it. They told me to. They all told me to. They all said kiss her; and said she'll like it. They all said it—every one of them. But I'm sorry, m'am, and I won't do it no more—I won't, honest."

"You won't, won't you? Well, I sh'd *reckon* you won't!"

"No'm, I'm honest about it; I won't ever do it again. Till you ask me."

"Till I *ask* you! Well, I never see the beat of it in my born days! I lay you'll be the Methusalem-numskull of creation before ever *I* ask you—or the likes of you."

"Well," he says, "it does surprise me so. I can't make it out, somehow. They said you would, and I thought you would. But—" He stopped and looked around slow, like he wished he could run across a friendly eye, somewhere's; and fetched up on the old gentleman's, and says, "Didn't *you* think she'd like me to kiss her, sir?"

"Why, no, I—I—well, no, I b'lieve I didn't."

Then he looks on around, the same way, to me—and says:

"Tom, didn't *you* think Aunt Sally'd open out her arms and say, 'Sid Sawyer—'"

"My land!" she says, breaking in and jumping for him, "you impudent young rascal, to fool a body so—" and was going to hug him, but he fended her off, and says:

"No, not till you've asked me, first."

So she didn't lose no time, but asked him; and hugged him and kissed him, over and over again, and then turned him over to the old man, and he took what was left. And after they got a little quiet again, she says:

"Why, dear me, I never see such a surprise. We warn't looking for *you,* at all, but only Tom. Sis never wrote to me about anybody coming but him."

"It's because it warn't *intended* for any of us to come but Tom," he says; "but I begged and begged, and at the last minute she let me come, too; so, coming down the river, me and Tom thought it would be a first-rate surprise for him to come here to the house first, and for me to by-and-by tag along and drop in and let on to be a stranger. But it was a mistake, Aunt Sally. This ain't no healthy place for a stranger to come."

"No—not impudent whelps, Sid. You ought to had your jaws boxed; I hain't been so put out since I don't know when. But I don't care, I don't mind the terms—I'd be willing to stand a thousand such jokes to have you here. Well, to think of that performance! I don't deny it, I was most putrified with astonishment when you give me that smack."

We had dinner out in that broad open passage betwixt the house and the kitchen; and there was things enough on that table for seven families—and all hot, too; none of your flabby tough meat that's laid in a cupboard in a damp cellar all night and tastes like a hunk of old cold cannibal in the morning. Uncle Silas he asked a pretty long blessing over it, but it was worth it; and it didn't cool it a bit, neither, the way I've seen them kind of interruptions do, lots of times.

There was a considerable good deal of talk, all the afternoon, and me and Tom was on the lookout all the time, but it warn't no use, they didn't happen to say nothing about any runaway nigger, and we was afraid to try to work up to it. But at supper, at night, one of the little boys says:

"Pa, mayn't Tom and Sid and me go to the show?"

"No," says the old man, "I reckon there ain't going to be any; and you couldn't go if there was; because the runaway nigger told Burton and me all about that scandalous show, and Burton said he would tell the people; so I reckon they've drove the owdacious loafers out of town before this time."

So there it was!—but *I* couldn't help it. Tom and me was to sleep in the same room and bed; so, being tired, we bid good-night and went up to bed, right after supper, and clumb out of the window and down the lightning-rod, and shoved for the town; for I didn't believe anybody was going to give the king and the duke a hint, and so, if I didn't hurry up and give them one they'd get into trouble sure.

On the road Tom he told me all about how it was reckoned I was murdered, and how pap disappeared, pretty soon, and didn't come back no more, and what a stir there was when Jim run away; and I told Tom all about our Royal Nonesuch rapscallions, and as much of the raft-voyage as I had time to; and as we struck into the town and up through the middle of it—it was as much as half-after eight, then—here comes a raging rush of people, with torches, and an awful whooping and yelling, and banging tin pans and blowing horns; and we jumped to one side to let them go by; and as they went by, I see they had the king and the duke astraddle of a rail—that is, I knowed it *was* the king and the duke, though they was all over tar and feathers, and didn't look like nothing in the world that was human—just looked like a couple of monstrous big soldier-plumes. Well, it made me sick to see it; and I was sorry for them poor pitiful rascals, it seemed like I couldn't ever feel any hardness against them any more in the world. It was a dreadful thing to see. Human beings *can* be awful cruel to one another.

We see we was too late—couldn't do no good. We asked some stragglers about it, and they said everybody went to the show looking very innocent; and laid low and kept dark till the poor old king was in the middle of his cavortings on the stage; then somebody give a signal, and the house rose up and went for them.

So we poked along back home, and I warn't feeling so brash as I was before, but kind of ornery, and humble, and to blame, somehow—though *I* hadn't done nothing. But that's always the way; it don't make no difference whether you do right or wrong, a person's conscience ain't got no sense, and just goes for him *anyway.* If I had a yaller dog that didn't know no more than a person's conscience does, I would pison him. It takes up more room than all the rest of a person's insides, and yet ain't no good, nohow. Tom Sawyer he says the same.

CHAPTER XXXIV

We stopped talking, and got to thinking.

By-and-by Tom says:

"Looky here, Huck, what fools we are, to not think of it before! I bet I know where Jim is."

"No! Where?"

"In that hut down by the ash-hopper. Why, looky here. When we was at dinner, didn't you see a nigger man go in there with some vittles?"

"Yes."

"What did you think the vittles was for?"

"For a dog."

"So'd I. Well, it wasn't for a dog."

"Why?"

"Because part of it was watermelon."

"So it was—I noticed it. Well, it does beat all, that I never thought about a dog not eating watermelon. It shows how a body can see and don't see at the same time."

"Well, the nigger unlocked the padlock when he went in, and he locked it again when he come out. He fetched uncle a key, about the time we got up from table—same key, I bet. Watermelon shows man, lock shows prisoner; and it ain't likely there's two prisoners on such a little plantation, and where the people's all so kind and good. Jim's the prisoner. All right—I'm glad we found it out detective fashion; I wouldn't give shucks for any other way. Now you work your mind and study out a plan to steal Jim, and I will study out one, too; and we'll take the one we like the best."

What a head for just a boy to have! If I had Tom Sawyer's head, I wouldn't trade it off to be a duke, nor mate of a steamboat, nor clown in a circus, nor nothing I can think of. I went to thinking out a plan, but only just to be doing something; I knowed very well where the right plan was gong to come from. Pretty soon, Tom says:

"Ready?"

"Yes," I says.

"All right—bring it out."

"My plan is this," I says. "We can easy find out if it's Jim in there. Then get up my canoe to-morrow night, and fetch my raft over from the island. Then the first dark night that comes, steal the key out of the old man's britches, after he goes to bed, and shove off down the river on the raft, with Jim, hiding daytimes and running nights, the way me and Jim used to do before. Wouldn't that plan work?"

"*Work?* Why cert'nly, it would work, like rats a fighting. But it's too blame' simple; there ain't nothing *to* it. What's the good of a plan that ain't no more trouble than that? It's as mild as goose-milk. Why, Huck, it wouldn't make no more talk than breaking into a soap factory."

I never said nothing, because I warn't expecting nothing different; but I knowed mighty well that whenever he got *his* plan ready it wouldn't have none of them objections to it.

And it didn't. He told me what it was, and I see in a minute it was worth fifteen of mine, for style, and would make Jim just as free a man as mine would, and maybe get us all killed besides. So I was satisfied, and said we would waltz in on it. I needn't tell what it was, here, because I knowed it wouldn't stay the way it was. I knowed he would be changing it around, every which way, as we went along, and heaving in new bullinesses whenever he got a chance. And that is what he done.

Well, one thing was dead sure; and that was, that Tom Sawyer was in earnest and was actuly going to help steal that nigger out of slavery. That was the thing that was too many for me. Here was a boy that was respectable, and well brung up; and had a character to lose; and folks at home that had characters; and he was bright and not leather-headed; and knowing and not ignorant; and not mean, but kind; and yet here he was, without any more pride, or rightness, or feeling, than to stoop to this business, and make himself a shame, and his family a shame, before everybody. I *couldn't* understand it, no way at all. It was outrageous, and I knowed I ought to just up and tell him so; and so be his true friend, and let him quit the thing right where he was, and save himself. And I *did* start to tell him; but he shut me up, and says:

"Don't you reckon I know what I'm about? Don't I generly know what I'm about?"

"Yes."

"Didn't I *say* I was going to help steal the nigger?"

"Yes."

"*Well* then."

That's all he said, and that's all I said. It warn't no use to say any more; because when he said he'd do a thing, he always done it. But *I* couldn't make out how he was willing to go into this thing; so I just let it go, and never bothered no more about it. If he was bound to have it so, *I* couldn't help it.

When we got home, the house was all dark and still; so we went on down to the hut by the ash hopper, for to examine it. We went through the yard, so as to see what the hounds would do. They knowed us, and didn't make no more noise than country dogs is always doing when anything comes by in the night. When we got to the cabin, we took a look at the front and the two sides; and on the side I warn't acquainted with—which was the north side—we found a square window-hole, up tolerable high, with just one stout board nailed across it. I says:

"Here's the ticket. This hole's big enough for Jim to get through, if we wrench off the board."

Tom says:

"It's as simple as tit-tat-toe, three-in-a-row, and as easy as playing hooky. I should *hope* we can find a way that's a little more complicated than *that,* Huck Finn."

"Well, then," I says, "how'll it do to saw him out, the way I done before I was murdered, that time?"

"That's more *like,*" he says. "It's real mysterious, and troublesome, and good," he says; "but I bet we can find a way that's twice as long. There ain't no hurry; le's keep on looking around."

Betwixt the hut and the fence, on the back side, was a lean-to, that joined the hut at the eaves, and was made out of plank. It was as long as the hut, but narrow—only about six foot wide. The door to it was at the south end, and was padlocked. Tom he went to the soap kettle, and searched around and fetched back the iron thing they lift the lid with; so he took it and prized out one of the staples. The chain fell down, and we opened the door and went in, and shut it, and struck a match, and see the shed was only built against the cabin and hadn't no connection with it; and there warn't no floor to the shed, nor nothing in it but some old rusty played-out hoes, and spades, and picks, and a crippled plow. The match went out, and so did we, and shoved in the staple again, and the door was locked as good as ever. Tom was joyful. He says:

"Now we're all right. We'll *dig* him out. It'll take about a week!"

Then we started for the house, and I went in the back door—you only have to pull a buckskin latch-string, they don't fasten the doors—but that warn't romantical enough for Tom Sawyer: no way would do him but he must climb up the lightning-rod. But after he got up half-way about three times, and missed fire and fell every time, and the last time most busted his brains out, he thought he'd got to give it up; but after he was rested, he allowed he would give her one more turn for luck, and this time he made the trip.

In the morning we was up at break of day, and down to the nigger cabins to pet the dogs and make friends with the nigger that fed Jim—if it *was* Jim that was being fed. The niggers was just getting through breakfast and starting for the fields; and Jim's nigger was piling up a tin pan with bread and meat and things; and whilst the others was leaving, the key come from the house.

This nigger had a good-natured, chuckle-headed face, and his wool was all tied up in little bunches with thread. That was to keep witches off. He said the witches was pestering him awful, these nights, and making him see all kinds of strange things, and hear all kinds of strange words and noises, and he didn't believe he was ever witched so long, before, in his life. He got so worked up, and got to running on so about his troubles, he forgot all about what he'd been agoing to do. So Tom says:

"What's the vittles for? Going to feed the dogs?"

The nigger kind of smiled around graduly over his face, like when you heave a brickbat in a mud puddle, and he says:

"Yes, Mars Sid, *a* dog. Cur'us dog, too. Does you want to go en look at 'im?"

"Yes."

I hunched Tom, and whispers:

"You going, right here in the day-break? *That* warn't the plan."

"No, it warn't—but it's the plan *now.*"

So, drat him, we went along, but I didn't like it much. When we got in, we couldn't hardly see anything, it was so dark; but Jim was there, sure enough, and could see us; and he sings out:

"Why, *Huck!* En good *lan'!* ain't dat Misto Tom?"

I just knowed how it would be; I just expected it. *I* didn't know nothing to do; and if I had, I couldn't a done it; because that nigger busted in and says:

"Why, de gracious sakes! do he know you genlmen?"

We could see pretty well, now. Tom he looked at the nigger, steady and kind of wondering, and says:

"Does *who* know us?"

"Why, dish-yer runaway nigger."

"I don't reckon he does; but what put that into your head?"

"What *put* it dar? Didn' he jis' dis minute sing out like he knowed you?"

Tom says, in a puzzled-up kind of way:

"Well, that's mighty curious. *Who* sung out? *When* did he sing out? *What* did he sing out?" And turns to me, perfectly c'am, and says, "Did *you* hear anybody sing out?"

Of course there warn't nothing to be said but one thing; so I says:

"No; *I* ain't heard nobody say nothing."

Then he turns to Jim, and looks him over like he never see him before; and says:

"Did you sing out?"

"No, sah," says Jim; "*I* hain't said nothing, sah."

"Not a word?"

"No, sah, I hain't said a word."

"Did you ever see us before?"

"No, sah; not as *I* knows on."

So Tom turns to the nigger, which was looking wild and distressed, and says, kind of severe:

"What do you reckon's the matter with you, anyway? What made you think somebody sung out?"

"Oh, it's de dad-blame' witches, sah, en I wisht I was dead, I do. Dey's awluz at it, sah, en dey do mos' kill me, dey sk'yers me so. Please to don't tell nobody 'bout it sah, er old Mars Silas he'll scole me; 'kase he say dey *ain't* no witches. I jis' wish to goodness he was heah now—*den* what would he say! I jis' bet he couldn' fine no way to git aroun' it *dis* time. But it's awluz jis' so; people dat's *sot,* stays sot; dey won't look into nothn' en fine it out f'r deyselves, en when *you* fine it out en tell um 'bout it, dey doan' b'lieve you."

Tom give him a dime, and said we wouldn't tell nobody; and told him to buy some more thread to tie up his wool with; and then looks at Jim, and says:

"I wonder if Uncle Silas is going to hang this nigger. If I was to catch a nigger that was ungrateful enough to run away, *I* wouldn't give him up, I'd hang him." And whilst the nigger stepped to the door to look at the dime and bite it to see if it was good, he whispers to Jim, and says:

"Don't ever let on to know us. And if you hear any digging going on nights, it's us: we're going to set you free."

Jim only had time to grab us by the hand and squeeze it, then the nigger come back, and we said we'd come again some time if the nigger wanted us to; and he said he would, more particular if it was dark, because the witches went for him mostly in the dark, and it was good to have folks around then.

CHAPTER XXXV

It would be most an hour, yet, till breakfast, so we left, and struck down into the woods; because Tom said we got to have *some* light to see how to dig by, and a lantern makes too much, and might get us into trouble; what we must have was a lot of them rotten chunks that's called fox-fire and just makes a soft kind of a glow when you lay them in a dark place. We fetched an armful and hid it in the weeds, and set down to rest, and Tom says, kind of dissatisfied:

"Blame it, this whole thing is just as easy and awkard as it can be. And so it makes it so rotten difficult to get up a difficult plan. There ain't no watchman to be drugged—now there *ought* to be a watchman. There ain't even a dog to give a sleeping-mixture to. And there's Jim chained by one leg, with a ten-foot chain, to the leg of his bed: why, all you got to do is to lift up the bedstead and slip off the chain. And Uncle Silas he trusts everybody; sends the key to the punkin-headed nigger, and don't send nobody to watch the nigger. Jim could a got out of that window hole before this, only there wouldn't be no use trying to travel with a ten-foot chain on his leg. Why, drat it, Huck, it's the stupidest arrangement I ever see. You got to invent *all* the difficulties. Well, we can't help it, we got to do the best we can with the materials we've got. Anyhow, there's one thing—there's more honor in getting him out through a lot of difficulties and dangers, where there warn't one of them furnished to you by the people who it was their duty to furnish them, and you had to contrive them all out of your own head. Now look at just that one thing of the lantern. When you come down to the cold facts, we simply got to *let on* that a lantern's resky. Why, we could work with a torchlight procession if we wanted to, *I* believe. Now, whilst I think of it, we got to hunt up something to make a saw out of, the first chance we get."

"What do we want of a saw?"

"What do we *want* of it? Hain't we got to saw the leg of Jim's bed off, so as to get the chain loose?"

"Why, you just said a body could lift up the bedstead and slip the chain off."

"Well, if that ain't just like you, Huck Finn. You *can* get up the infant-schooliest ways of going at a thing. Why, hain't you ever read any books at all?—Baron Trenck, nor Casanova, nor Benvenuto Chelleeny, nor Henri IV., nor none of them heroes? Whoever heard of getting a prisoner loose in such an old-maidy way as that? No; the way all the best authorities does, is to saw the bed-leg in two, and leave it just so, and swallow the sawdust, so it can't be found, and put some dirt and grease around the sawed place so the very keenest seneskal can't see no sign of it's being sawed, and thinks the bed-leg is perfectly sound. Then, the night you're ready, fetch the leg a kick, down she goes; slip off your chain, and there you are. Nothing to do but hitch your rope-ladder to the battlements, shin down it, break your leg in the moat—because a rope-ladder is nineteen foot too short, you know—and there's your horses and your trusty vassles, and they scoop you up and fling you across a saddle and away you go, to your native Langudoc, or Navarre, or wherever it is. It's gaudy, Huck. I wish there was a moat to this cabin. If we get time, the night of the escape, we'll dig one."

I says:

"What do we want of a moat, when we're going to snake him out from under the cabin?"

But he never heard me. He had forgot me and everything else. He had his chin in his hand, thinking. Pretty soon, he sighs, and shakes his head; then sighs again, and says:

"No, it wouldn't do—there's ain't necessity enough for it."

"For what?" I says.

"Why, to saw Jim's leg off," he says.

"Good land!" I says, "why, there ain't *no* necessity for it. And what would you want to saw his leg off for, anyway?"

"Well, some of the best authorities has done it. They couldn't get the chain off, so they just cut their hand off, and shoved. And a leg would be better still. But we got to let that go. There ain't necessity enough in this case; and besides, Jim's a nigger and wouldn't understand the reasons for it, and how it's the custom in Europe; so we'll let it go. But there's one thing—he can have a rope-ladder; we can tear up our sheets and make him a rope-ladder easy enough. And we can send it to him in a pie; it's mostly done that way. And I've et worse pies."

"Why, Tom Sawyer, how you talk," I says; "Jim ain't got no use for a rope-ladder."

"He *has* got use for it. How *you* talk, you better say; you don't know nothing about it. He's *got* to have a rope ladder; they all do."

"What in the nation can he *do* with it?"

"*Do* with it? He can hide it in his bed, can't he? That's what they all do; and *he's* got to, too. Huck, you don't ever seem to want to do anything that's regular; you want to be starting something fresh all the time. Spose he *don't* do nothing with it? ain't it there in his bed, for a clew, after he's gone? and don't you reckon they'll want clews? Of course they will. And you wouldn't leave them any? That would be a *pretty* howdy-do, *wouldn't* it! I never heard of such a thing."

"Well," I says, "if it's in the regulations, and he's got to have it, all right, let him have it; because I don't wish to go back on no regulations; but there's one thing, Tom Sawyer—if we go to tearing up our sheets to make Jim a rope-ladder, we're going to get into trouble with Aunt Sally, just as sure as you're born. Now, the way I look at it, a hickry-bark ladder don't cost nothing, and don't waste nothing, and is just as good to load up a pie with, and hide in a straw tick, as any rag ladder you can start; and as for Jim, he ain't had no experience, and so *he* don't care what kind of a—"

"Oh, shucks, Huck Finn, if I was as ignorant as you, I'd keep still—that's what *I'd* do. Who ever heard of a state prisoner escaping by a hickry-bark ladder? Why, it's perfectly ridiculous."

"Well, all right, Tom, fix it your own way; but if you'll take my advice, you'll let me borrow a sheet off of the clothes-line."

He said that would do. And that give him another idea, and he says:

"Borrow a shirt, too."

"What do we want of a shirt, Tom?"

"Want it for Jim to keep a journal on."

"Journal your granny—*Jim* can't write."

"Spose he *can't* write—he can make marks on the shirt, can't he, if we make him a pen out of an old pewter spoon or a piece of an old iron barrel-hoop?"

"Why, Tom, we can pull a feather out of a goose and make him a better one; and quicker, too."

"*Prisoners* don't have geese running around the donjon-keep to pull pens out of, you muggins. They *always* make their pens out of the hardest, toughest, troublesomest piece of old brass candlestick or something like that they can get their hands on;

and it takes them weeks and weeks, and months and months to file it out, too, because they've got to do it by rubbing it on the wall. *They* wouldn't use a goose-quill if they had it. It ain't regular."

"Well, then, what'll we make him the ink out of?"

"Many makes it out of iron-rust and tears; but that's the common sort and women; the best authorities uses their own blood. Jim can do that; and when he wants to send any little common ordinary mysterious message to let the world know where he's captivated, he can write it on the bottom of a tin plate with a fork and throw it out of the window. The Iron Mask always done that, and it's a blame' good way, too."

"Jim ain't got no tin plates. They feed him in a pan."

"That ain't anything; we can get him some."

"Can't nobody *read* his plates."

"That ain't got nothing to *do* with it, Huck Finn. All *he's* got to do is to write on the plate and throw it out. You don't *have* to be able to read it. Why, half the time you can't read anything a prisoner writes on a tin plate, or anywhere else."

"Well, then, what's the sense in wasting the plates?"

"Why, blame it all, it ain't the *prisoner's* plates."

"But it's *somebody's* plates, ain't it?"

"Well, spos'n it is? What does the *prisoner* care whose—"

He broke off there, because we heard the breakfast-horn blowing. So we cleared out for the house.

Along during that morning I borrowed a sheet and a white shirt off of the clothes-line; and I found an old sack and put them in it, and we went down and got the fox-fire, and put that in too. I called it borrowing, because that was what pap always called it; but Tom said it warn't borrowing, it was stealing. He said we was representing prisoners; and prisoners don't care how they get a thing so they get it, and nobody don't blame them for it, either. It ain't no crime in a prisoner to steal the thing he needs to get away with, Tom said; it's his right; and so, as long as we was representing a prisoner, we had a perfect right to steal anything on this place we had the least use for, to get ourselves out of prison with. He said if we warn't prisoners it would be a very different thing, and nobody but a mean ornery person would steal when he warn't a prisoner. So we allowed we would steal everything there was that come handy. And yet he made a mighty fuss, one day, after that, when I stole a water-melon out of the nigger patch and eat it; and he made me go and give the niggers a dime, without telling them what it was for. Tom said that what he meant was, we could steal anything we *needed,* Well, I says, I needed the watermelon. But he said I didn't need it to get out of prison with, there's where the difference was. He said if I'd a wanted it to hide a knife in, and smuggle it to Jim to kill the sensekal with, it would a been all right. So I let it go at that, though I couldn't see no advantage in my representing a prisoner, if I got to set down and chaw over a lot of gold-leaf distinctions like that, every time I see a chance to hog a watermelon.

Well, as I was saying, we waited that morning till everybody was settled down to business, and nobody in sight around the yard; then Tom he carried the sack into the lean-to whilst I stood off a piece to keep watch. By-and-by he come out, and we went to set down on the wood-pile, to talk. He says:

"Everything's all right, now, except tools; and that's easy fixed."

"Tools?" I says.

"Yes."

"Tools for what?"

"Why, to dig with. We ain't agoing to *gnaw* him out, are we?"

"Ain't them old crippled picks and things in there good enough to dig a nigger out with?" I says.

He turns on me looking pitying enough to make a body cry, and says:

"Huck Finn, did you *ever* hear of a prisoner having picks and shovels, and all the modern conveniences in his wardrobe to dig himself out with? Now I want to ask you—if you got any reasonableness in you at all—what kind of a show would *that* give him to be a hero? Why, they might as well lend him the key, and done with it. Picks and shovels—why they wouldn't furnish 'em to a king."

"Well, then," I says, "if we don't want the picks and shovels, what do we want?"

"A couple of case-knives."

"To dig the foundations out from under that cabin with?"

"Yes."

"Confound it, it's foolish, Tom."

"It don't make no difference how foolish it is, it's the *right* way—and it's the regular way. And there ain't no *other* way, that ever *I* heard of, and I've read all the books that gives any information about these things. They always dig out with a case-knife—and not through dirt, mind you; generly it's through solid rock. And it takes them weeks and weeks and weeks, and for ever and ever. Why, look at one of them prisoners in the bottom dungeon of the Castle Deef, in the harbor of Marseilles, that dug himself out that way; how long was *he* at it, you reckon?"

"I don't know."

"Well, guess."

"I don't know. A month and a half?"

"*Thirty-seven year*—and he come out in China. *That's* the kind. I wish the bottom of *this* fortress was solid rock."

"*Jim* don't know nobody in China."

"What's *that* got to do with it? Neither did that other fellow. But you're always a-wandering off on a side issue. Why can't you stick to the main point?"

"All right—*I* don't care where he comes out, so he *comes* out; and Jim don't, either, I reckon. But there's one thing, anyway—Jim's too old to be dug out with a case-knife. He won't last."

"Yes he will *last,* too. You don't reckon it's going to take thirty-seven years to dig out through a *dirt* foundation, do you?"

"How long will it take, Tom?"

"Well, we can't resk being as long as we ought to, because it mayn't take very long for Uncle Silas to hear from down there by New Orleans. He'll hear Jim ain't from there. Then his next move will be to advertise Jim, or something like that. So we can't resk being as long digging him out as we ought to. By rights I reckon we ought to be a couple of years; but we can't. Things being so uncertain, what I recommend is this: that we really dig right in, as quick as we can; and after that, we can *let on,* to ourselves, that we was at it thirty-seven years. Then we can snatch him out and rush him away the first time there's an alarm. Yes, I reckon that'll be the best way."

"Now, there's *sense* in that," I says. "Letting on don't cost nothing; letting on ain't no trouble; and if it's any object, I don't mind letting on we was at it a hundred and fifty year. It wouldn't strain me none, after I got my hand in. So I'll mosey along now, and smouch a couple of case-knives."

"Smouch three," he says; "we want one to make a saw out of."

"Tom, if it ain't unregular and irreligious to sejest it," I says, "there's an old rusty saw-blade around yonder sticking under the weatherboarding behind the smoke-house."

He looked kind of weary and discouraged-like, and says:

"It ain't no use to try to learn you nothing, Huck. Run along and smouch the knives—three of them." So I done it.

CHAPTER XXXVI

As soon as we reckoned everybody was asleep, that night, we went down the lightning-rod, and shut ourselves up in the lean-to, and got out our pile of fox-fire, and went to work. We cleared everything out of the way, about four or five foot along the middle of the bottom log. Tom said he was right behind Jim's bed now, and we'd dig in under it, and when we got through there couldn't nobody in the cabin ever know there was any hole there, because Jim's counterpin hung down most to the ground, and you'd have to raise it up and look under to see the hole. So we dug and dug, with the case-knives, till most midnight; and then we was dog-tired, and our hands was blistered, and yet you couldn't see we'd done anything, hardly. At last I says:

"This ain't no thirty-seven year job, this is a thirty-eight year job, Tom Sawyer."

He never said nothing. But he sighed, and pretty soon he stopped digging, and then for a good little while I knowed he was thinking. Then he says:

"It ain't no use, Huck, it ain't agoing to work. If we was prisoners it would, because then we'd have as many years as we wanted, and no hurry; and we wouldn't get but a few minutes to dig, every day, while they was changing watches, and so our hands wouldn't get blistered, and we could keep it up right along, year in and year out, and do it right, and the way it ought to be done. But *we* can't fool along, we got to rush; we ain't got no time to spare. If we was to put in another night this way, we'd have to knock off for a week to let our hands get well—couldn't touch a case-knife with them sooner."

"Well, then, what we going to do, Tom?"

"I'll tell you. It ain't right, and it ain't moral, and I wouldn't like it to get out—but there ain't only just the one way; we got to dig him out with the picks, and *let on* it's case-knives."

"*Now* you're *talking!*" I says; "your head gets leveler and leveler all the time, Tom Sawyer," I says. "Picks is the thing, moral or no moral; and as for me, I don't care shucks for the morality of it, nohow. When I start in to steal a nigger, or a watermelon, or a Sunday-school book, I ain't no ways particular how it's done so it's done. What I want is my nigger; or what I want is my watermelon; or what I want is my Sunday-school book; and if a pick's the handiest thing, that's the thing I'm agoing to dig that nigger or that watermelon or that Sunday-school book out with; and I don't give a dead rat what the authorities thinks about it nuther."

"Well," he says, "there's excuse for picks and letting-on in a case like this; if it warn't so, I wouldn't approve of it, nor I wouldn't stand by and see the rules broke—because right is right, and wrong is wrong, and a body ain't got no business doing wrong when he ain't ignorant and knows better. It might answer for *you* to dig Jim out with a pick, *without* any letting-on, because you don't know no better; but it wouldn't for me, because I do know better. Gimme a case-knife."

He had his own by him, but I handed him mine. He flung it down, and says:

"Gimme a *case-knife.*"

I didn't know just what to do—but then I thought. I scratched around amongst the old tools, and got a pick-ax and give it to him, and he took it and went to work, and never said a word.

He was always just that particular. Full of principle.

So then I got a shovel, and then we picked and shoveled, turn about, and made the fur fly. We stuck to it about a half an hour, which was as long as we could stand up; but we had a good deal of a hole to show for it. When I got up stairs, I looked out at the window and see Tom doing his level best with the lightning-rod, but he couldn't come it, his hands was so sore. At last he says:

"It ain't no use, it can't be done. What you reckon I better do? Can't you think up no way?"

"Yes," I says, "but I reckon it ain't regular. Come up the stairs, and let on it's a lightning-rod."

So he done it.

Next day Tom stole a pewter spoon and a brass candlestick in the house, for to make some pens for Jim out of, and six tallow candles; and I hung around the nigger cabins, and laid for a chance, and stole three tin plates. Tom said it wasn't enough; but I said nobody wouldn't ever see the plates that Jim throwed out, because they'd fall in the dog-fennel and jimpson weeds under the window-hole—then we could tote them back and he could use them over again. So Tom was satisfied. Then he says:

"Now, the thing to study out is, how to get the things to Jim."

"Take them in through the hole," I says, "when we get it done."

He only just looked scornful, and said something about nobody ever heard of such an idiotic idea, and then he went to studying. By-and-by he said he had ciphered out two or three ways, but there warn't no need to decide on any of them yet. Said we'd got to post Jim first.

That night we went down the lightning-rod a little after ten, and took one of the candles along, and listened under the window-hole, and heard Jim snoring; so we pitched it in, and it didn't wake him. Then we whirled in with the pick and shovel, and in about two hours and a half the job was done. We crept in under Jim's bed and into the cabin, and pawed around and found the candle and lit it, and stood over Jim a while, and found him looking hearty and healthy, and then we woke him up gentle and gradual. He was so glad to see us he most cried; and called us honey, and all the pet names he could think of; and was for having us hunt up a cold chisel to cut the chain off his leg with, right away, and clearing out without losing any time. But Tom he showed him how unregular it would be, and set down and told him all about our plans, and how we could alter them in a minute any time there was an alarm; and not to be the least afraid, because we would see he got away, *sure*. So Jim said he was all right, and we set there and talked over old times a while, and then Tom asked a lot of questions, and when Jim told him Uncle Silas come in every day or two to pray with him, and Aunt Sally come in to see if he was comfortable and had plenty to eat, and both of them was kind as they could be, Tom says:

"*Now* I know how to fix it. We'll send you some things by them."

I said, "Don't do nothing of the kind; it's one of the most jackass ideas I ever struck;" but he never paid no attention to me; went right on. It was his way when he'd got his plans set.

So he told Jim how we'd have to smuggle in the rope-ladder pie, and other large things, by Nat, the nigger that fed him, and he must be on the lookout, and not be surprised, and not let Nat see him open them; and we would put small things in uncle's coat pockets and he must steal them out; and we would tie things to aunt's apron strings or put them in her apron pocket, if we got a chance; and told him what they would be and what they was for. And told him how to keep a journal on the shirt with his blood, and all that. He told him everything. Jim he couldn't see no sense in most of it, but he allowed we was white folks and knowed better than him; so he was satisfied, and said he would do it all just as Tom said.

Jim had plenty corn-cob pipes and tobacco; so we had a right down good sociable time; then we crawled out through the hole, and so home to bed, with hands that looked like they'd been chawed. Tom was in high spirits. He said it was the best fun he ever had in his life, and the most intellectural; and said if he only could see his way to it we would keep it up all the rest of our lives and leave Jim to our children to get out; for he believed Jim would come to like it better and better the more he got used to it. He said that in that way it could be strung out to as much as eighty year, and would be the best time on record. And he said it would make us all celebrated that had a hand in it.

In the morning we went out to the wood-pile and chopped up the brass candlestick into handy sizes, and Tom put them and the pewter spoon in his pocket. Then we went to the nigger cabins, and while I got Nat's notice off, Tom shoved a piece of candlestick into the middle of a corn-pone that was in Jim's pan, and we went along with Nat to see how it would work, and it just worked noble; when Jim bit into it it most mashed all his teeth out; and there warn't ever anything could a worked better. Tom said so himself. Jim he never let on but what it was only just a piece of rock or something like that that's always getting into bread, you know; but after that he never bit into nothing but what he jabbed his fork into it three or four places, first.

And whilst we was a standing there in the dimmish light, here comes a couple of the hounds bulging in, from under Jim's bed; and they kept on piling in till there was eleven of them, and there warn't hardly room in there to get your breath. By jings, we forgot to fasten that lean-to door. The nigger Nat he only just hollered "witches!" once, and keeled over onto the floor amongst the dogs, and begun to groan like he was dying. Tom jerked the door open and flung out a slab of Jim's meat, and the dogs went for it, and in two seconds he was out himself and back again and shut the door, and I knowed he'd fixed the other door too. Then he went to work on the nigger, coaxing him and petting him, and asking him if he'd been imagining he saw something again. He raised up, and blinked his eyes around, and says:

"Mars Sid, you'll say I's a fool, but if I didn't b'lieve I see most a million dogs, er devils, er some'n, I wisht I may die right heah in dese tracks. I did, mos' sholy. Mars Sid, I *felt* um—I *felt* um, sah; dey was all over me. Dad fetch it, I jis' wisht I could git my han's on one er dem witches jis' wunst—on'y jis' wunst—it's all *I*'d ast. But mos'ly I wisht dey'd lemme 'lone, I does."

Tom says:

"Well, I tell you what *I* think. What makes them come here just at this runaway nigger's breakfast-time? It's because they're hungry; that's the reason. You make them a witch pie; that's the thing for *you* to do."

"But my lan', Mars Sid, how's *I* gwyne to make 'm a witch pie? I doan' know how to make it. I hain't ever hearn er sich a thing b'fo.'"

"Well, then, I'll have to make it myself."

"Will you do it, honey?—will you? I'll wusshup de groun' und' yo' foot, I will!"

"All right, I'll do it, seeing it's you, and you've been good to us and showed us the runaway nigger. But you got to be mighty careful. When we come around, you turn your back; and whatever we've put in the pan, don't you let on you see it at all. And don't you look, when Jim unloads the pan—something might happen, I don't know what. And above all, don't you *handle* the witch-things."

"*Hannel* 'm Mars Sid? What *is* you a talkin' 'bout? I wouldn' lay de weight er my finger on um, not f'r ten hund'd thous'n' billion dollars, I wouldn't."

CHAPTER XXXVII

That was all fixed. So then we went away and went to the rubbage-pile in the back yard where they keep the old boots, and rags, and pieces of bottles, and wore-out tin things, and all such truck, and scratched around and found an old tin wash-pan and stopped up the holes as well as we could, to bake the pie in, and took it down cellar and stole it full of flour, and started for breakfast and found a couple of shingle-nails that Tom said would be handy for a prisoner to scrabble his name and sorrows on the dungeon walls with, and dropped one of them in Aunt Sally's apron pocket which was hanging on a chair, and t'other we stuck in the band of Uncle Silas's hat, which was on the bureau, because we heard the children say their pa and ma was going to the runaway nigger's house this morning, and then went to breakfast, and Tom dropped the pewter spoon in Uncle Silas's coat pocket, and Aunt Sally wasn't come yet, so we had to wait a little while.

And when she come she was hot, and red, and cross, and couldn't hardly wait for the blessing; and then she went to sluicing out coffee with one hand and cracking the handiest child's head with her thimble with the other, and says:

"I've hunted high, and I've hunted low, and it does beat all, what *has* become of your other shirt."

My heart fell down amongst my lungs and livers and things, and a hard piece of corn-crust started down my throat after it and got met on the road with a cough and was shot across the table and took one of the children in the eye and curled him up like a fishing-worm, and let a cry out of him the size of a war-whoop, and Tom he turned kinder blue around the gills, and it all amounted to a considerable state of things for about a quarter of a minute or as much as that, and I would a sold out for half price if there was a bidder. But after that we was all right again—it was the sudden surprise of it that knocked us so kind of cold. Uncle Silas he says:

"It's most uncommon curious, I can't understand it. I know perfectly well I took it *off,* because—"

"Because you hain't got but one *on.* Just *listen* at the man! *I* know you took it off, and know it by a better way than your wool-gethering memory, too, because it was on the clo'es-line yesterday—I see it there myself. But it's gone—that's the long and the short of it, and you'll just have to change to a red flan-n'l one till I can get time to make a new one. And it'll be the third I've made in two years; it just keeps a body on the jump to keep you in shirts; and whatever you do manage to *do* with 'm all, is more'n *I* can make out. A body'd think you *would* learn to take some sort of care of 'em, at your time of life."

"I know it, Sally, and I do try all I can. But it oughtn't to be altogether my fault, because you know I don't see them nor have nothing to do with them except when they're on me; and I don't believe I've ever lost one of them *off* of me."

"Well, it ain't *your* fault if you haven't, Silas—you'd a done it if you could, I reckon. And the shirt ain't all that's gone, nuther. Ther's a spoon gone; and *that* ain't all. There was ten, and now ther's only nine. The calf got the shirt I reckon, but the calf never took the spoon, *that's* certain."

"Why, what else is gone, Sally?"

"Ther's six *candles* gone—that's what. The rats could a got the candles, and I reckon they did; I wonder they don't walk off with the whole place, the way you're always going to stop their holes and don't do it; and if they warn't fools they'd sleep in your hair, Silas—*you'd* never find it out; but you can't lay the *spoon* on the rats, and that I *know*."

"Well, Sally, I'm in fault, and I acknowledge it; I've been remiss; but I won't let to-morrow go by without stopping up them holes."

"Oh, I wouldn't hurry, next year'll do. Matilda Angelina Araminta *Phelps!*"

Whack comes the thimble, and the child snatches her claws out of the sugar-bowl without fooling around any. Just then, the nigger woman steps onto the passage, and says:

"Missus, dey's a sheet gone."

"A *sheet* gone! Well, for the land's sake!"

"I'll stop up them holes *to-day*," says Uncles Silas, looking sorrowful.

"Oh, *do* shet up!—spose the rats took the *sheet*? *Where's* it gone, Lize?"

"Clah to goodness I hain't no notion, Miss Sally. She wuz on de clo's-line yistiddy, but she done gone; she ain' dah no mo,' now."

"I reckon the world *is* coming to an end. I *never* see the beat of it, in all my born days. A shirt, and a sheet, and a spoon, and six can—"

"Missus," comes a young yaller wench, "dey's a brass cannelstick miss'n."

"Cler out from here, you hussy, er I'll take a skillet to ye!"

Well, she was just a biling. I begun to lay for a chance; I reckoned I would sneak out and go for the woods till the weather moderated. She kept a raging right along, running her insurrection all by herself, and everybody else mighty meek and quiet; and at last Uncle Silas, looking kind of foolish, fishes up that spoon out of his pocket. She stopped, with her mouth open and her hands up; and as for me, I wished I was in Jeruslem or somewheres. But not long; because she says:

"It's *just* as I expected. So you had it in your pocket all the time; and like as not you've got the other things there, too. How'd it get there?"

"I reely don't know, Sally," he says, kind of apologizing, "or you know I would tell. I was a-studying over my text in Acts Seventeen, before breakfast, and I reckon I put it in there, not noticing, meaning to put my Testament in, and it must be so, because my Testament ain't in, but I'll go and see, and if the Testament is where I had it, I'll know I didn't put it in, and that will show that I laid the Testament down and took up the spoon, and—"

"Oh, for the land's sake! Give a body a rest! Go 'long now, the whole kit and biling of ye; and don't come nigh me again till I've got back my peace of mind."

I'd a heard her, if she'd a said it to herself, let alone speaking it out; and I'd a got up and obeyed her, if I'd a been dead. As we was passing through the setting-room, the old man he took up his hat, and the shingle-nail fell out on the floor, and he just merely picked it up and laid it on the mantel-shelf, and never said nothing, and went out. Tom see him do it, and remembered about the spoon, and says:

"Well, it ain't no use to send things by *him* no more, he ain't reliable." Then he says: "But he done us a good turn with the spoon, anyway, without knowing it, and so we'll go and do him one without *him* knowing it—stop up his rat-holes."

There was a noble good lot of them, down cellar, and it took us a whole hour, but we done the job tight and good, and shipshape. Then we heard steps on the stairs, and blowed out our light, and hid; and here comes the old man, with a candle in one hand and a bundle of stuff in t'other, looking as absent-minded as year before last. He went a mooning around, first to one rat-hole and then another, till he'd been to them all. Then he stood about five minutes, picking tallow-drip off of his candle and thinking. Then he turns off slow and dreamy towards the stairs, saying:

"Well, for the life of me I can't remember when I done it. I could show her now that I warn't to blame on account of the rats. But never mind—let it go. I reckon it wouldn't do no good."

And so he went on a mumbling up stairs, and then we left. He was a mighty nice old man. And always is.

Tom was a good deal bothered about what to do for a spoon, but he said we'd got to have it; so he took a think. When he had ciphered it out, he told me how we was to do; then we went and waited around the spoon-basket till we see Aunt Sally coming, and then Tom went to counting the spoons and laying them out to one side, and I slid one of them up my sleeve, and Tom says:

"Why, Aunt Sally, there ain't but nine spoons, *yet.*"

She says:

"Go 'long to your play, and don't bother me. I know better, I counted 'm myself."

"Well, I've counted them twice, Aunty, and *I* can't make but nine."

She looked out of all patience, but of course she come to count—anybody would.

"I declare to gracious ther' *ain't* but nine!" she says. "Why, what in the world—plague *take* the things, I'll count 'm again."

So I slipped back the one I had, and when she got done counting, she says:

"Hang the troublesome rubbage, ther's *ten,* now!" and she looked huffy and bothered both. But Tom says:

"Why, Aunty, *I* don't think there's ten."

"You numskull, didn't you see me *count* 'm?"

"I know, but—"

"Well, I'll count 'm *again.*"

So I smouched one, and they come out nine same as the other time. Well, she *was* in a tearing way—just a trembling all over, she was so mad. But she counted and counted, till she got that addled she'd start to count-in the *basket* for a spoon, sometimes; and so, three times they come out right, and three times they come out wrong. Then she grabbed up the basket and slammed it across the house and knocked the cat galley-west; and she said cle'r out and let her have some peace, and if we come bothering around her again betwixt that and dinner, she'd skin us. So we had the odd spoon; and dropped it in her apron pocket whilst she was giving us our sailing-orders, and Jim got it all right, along with her shingle-nail, before noon. We was very well satisfied with this business, and Tom allowed it was worth twice the trouble it took, because he said *now* she couldn't ever count them spoons twice alike again to save her life; and wouldn't believe she'd counted them right, if she *did;* and said that after she'd about counted her head off, for the next three days, he judged she'd give it up and offer to kill anybody that wanted her to ever count them any more.

So we put the sheet back on the line, that night, and stole one out of her closet; and kept on putting it back and stealing it again, for a couple of days, till she didn't know how many sheets she had, any more, and said she didn't *care,* and warn't agoing to bullyrag the rest of her soul out about it, and wouldn't count them again not to save her life, she druther die first.

So we was all right now, as to the shirt and the sheet and the spoon and the candles, by the help of the calf and the rats and the mixed-up counting; and as to the candlestick, it warn't no consequence, it would blow over by-and-by.

But that pie was a job; we had no end of trouble with that pie. We fixed it up away down in the woods, and cooked it there; and we got it done at last, and very satisfactory, too; but not all in one day; and we had to use up three washpans full of flour, before we got through, and we got burnt pretty much all over, in places, and eyes put out with the smoke; because, you see, we didn't want nothing but a crust, and we couldn't prop it up right, and she would always cave in. But of course we thought of the right way at last; which was to cook the ladder, too, in the pie. So then we laid in with Jim, the second night, and tore up the sheet all in little strings, and twisted them together, and long before daylight we had a lovely rope, that you could a hung a person with. We let on it took nine months to make it.

And in the forenoon we took it down to the woods, but it

wouldn't go in the pie. Being made of a whole sheet, that way, there was rope enough for forty pies, if we'd a wanted them, and plenty left over for soup, or sausage, or anything you choose. We could a had a whole dinner.

But we didn't need it. All we needed was just enough for the pie, and so we throwed the rest away. We didn't cook none of the pies in the washpan, afraid the solder would melt; but Uncle Silas he had a noble brass warming-pan which he thought considerable of, because it belonged to one of his ancesters with a long wooden handle that come over from England with William the Conqueror in the *Mayflower* or one of them early ships and was hid away up garret with a lot of other old pots and things that was valuable, not on account of being any account because they warn't, but on account of them being relicts, you know, and we snaked her out, private, and took her down there, but she failed on the first pies, because we didn't know how, but she come up smiling on the last one. We took and lined her with dough, and set her on the coals, and loaded her up with rag-rope, and put on a dough roof, and shut down the lid, and put hot embers on top, and stood off five foot, with the long handle, cool and comfortable, and in fifteen minutes she turned out a pie that was a satisfaction to look at. But the person that et it would want to fetch a couple of kags of toothpicks along, for if that rope-ladder wouldn't cramp him down to business, I don't know nothing what I'm talking about, and lay him in enough stomach-ache to last him till next time, too.

Nat didn't look, when we put the witch-pie in Jim's pan; and we put the three tin plates in the bottom of the pan under the vittles; and so Jim got everything all right, and as soon as he was by himself he busted into the pie and hid the rope-ladder inside his straw tick, and scratched some marks on a tin plate and throwed it out of the window-hole.

CHAPTER XXXVIII

Making them pens was a distressid-tough job, and so was the saw; and Jim allowed the inscription was going to be the toughest of all. That's the one which the prisoner has to scrabble on the wall. But we had to have it; Tom said we'd *got* to; there warn't no case of a state prisoner not scrabbling his inscription to leave behind, and his coat of arms.

"Look at Lady Jane Grey," he says; "look at Gilford Dudley; look at old Northumberland! Why, Huck, spose it *is* considerable trouble?—what you going to do?—how you going to get around it? Jim's *got* to do his inscription and coat of arms. They all do."

Jim says:

"Why, Mars Tom, I hain't got no coat o' arms; I hain't got nuffn but dish-yer ole shirt, en you knows I got to keep de journal on dat."

"Oh, you don't understand, Jim; a coat of arms is very different."

"Well," I says, "Jim's right, anyway, when he says he hain't got no coat of arms, because he hain't."

"I reckon *I* knowed that," Tom says, "but you bet he'll have one before he goes out of this—because he's going out *right*, and there ain't going to be no flaws in his record."

So whilst me and Jim filed away at the pens on a brickbat apiece, Jim a making his'n out of the brass and I making mine out of the spoon, Tom set to work to think out the coat of arms. By-and-by he said he'd struck so many good ones he didn't hardly know which to take, but there was one which he reckoned he'd decide on. He says:

"On the scutcheon we'll have a bend *or* in the dexter base, a saltire *murrey* in the fess, with a dog, couchant, for common charge, and under his foot a chain embattled, for slavery, with a chevron *vert* in a chief engrailed, and three invected lines on a field *azure*, with the nombril points rampant on a dancette indented; crest, a runaway nigger, *sable*, with his bundle over his shoulder on a bar sinister: and a couple of gules for supporters, which is you and me; motto, *Maggiore fretta, minore atto*. Got it out of a book—means, the more haste, the less speed."

"Geewhillikins," I says, "but what does the rest of it mean?"

"We ain't got no time to bother over that," he says, "we got to dig in like all git-out."

"Well, anyway," I says, "what's *some* of it? What's a fess?"

"A fess—a fess is—*you* don't need to know what a fess is. I'll show him how to make it when he gets to it."

"Shucks, Tom," I says, "I think you might tell a person. What's a bar sinister?"

"Oh, *I* don't know. But he's got to have it. All the nobility does."

That was just his way. If it didn't suit him to explain a thing to you, he wouldn't do it. You might pump at him a week, it wouldn't make no difference.

He'd got all that coat of arms business fixed, so now he started in to finish up the rest of that part of the work, which was to plan out a mournful inscription—said Jim got to have one, like they all done. He made up a lot, and wrote them out on a paper, and read them off, so:

1. *Here a captive heart busted.*

2. *Here a poor prisoner, forsook by the world and friends, fretted out his sorrowful life.*

3. *Here a lonely heart broke, and a worn spirit went to its rest, after thirty-seven years of solitary captivity.*

4. *Here, homeless and friendless, after thirty-seven years of bitter captivity, perished a noble stranger, natural son of Louis XIV.*

Tom's voice trembled, whilst he was reading them, and he most broke down. When he got done, he couldn't no way make up his mind which one for Jim to scrabble onto the wall, they was all so good; but at last he allowed he would let him scrabble them all on. Jim said it would take him a year to scrabble such a lot of truck onto the logs with a nail, and he didn't know how to make letters, besides; but Tom said he would block them out for him, and then he wouldn't have nothing to do but just follow the lines. Then pretty soon he says:

"Come to think, the logs ain't agoing to do; they don't have log walls in a dungeon: we got to dig the inscriptions into a rock. We'll fetch a rock."

Jim said the rock was worse than the logs; he said it would

take him such a pison long time to dig them into a rock, he wouldn't ever get out. But Tom said he would let me help him do it. Then he took a look to see how me and Jim was getting along with the pens. It was most pesky tedious hard work and slow, and didn't give my hands no show to get well of the sores, and we didn't seem to make no headway, hardly. So Tom says:

"I know how to fix it. We got to have a rock for the coat of arms and mournful inscriptions, and we can kill two birds with that same rock. There's a gaudy big grindstone down at the mill, and we'll smouch it, and carve the things on it, and file out the pens and the saw on it, too."

It warn't no slouch of an idea; and it warn't no slouch of a grindstone nuther; but we allowed we'd tackle it. It warn't quite midnight, yet, so we cleared out for the mill, leaving Jim at work. We smouched the grindstone, and set out to roll her home, but it was a most nation tough job. Sometimes, do what we could, we couldn't keep her from falling over, and she come mighty near mashing us, every time. Tom said she was going to get one of us, sure, before we got through. We got her half way; and then we was plumb played out, and most drownded with sweat. We see it warn't no use, we got to go and fetch Jim. So he raised up his bed and slid the chain off the bed-leg, and wrapt it round and round his neck, and we crawled out through our hole and down there, and Jim and me laid into that grindstone and walked her along like nothing; and Tom superintended. He could out-superintend any boy I ever see. He knowed how to do everything.

Our hole was pretty big, but it warn't big enough to get the grindstone through; but Jim he took the pick and soon made it big enough. Then Tom marked out them things on it with the nail, and set Jim to work on them, with the nail for a chisel and an iron bolt from the rubbage in the lean-to for a hammer, and told him to work till the rest of his candle quit on him, and then he could go to bed, and hide the grindstone under his straw tick and sleep on it. Then we helped him fix his chain back on the bed-leg, and was ready for bed ourselves. But Tom thought of something, and says:

"You got any spiders in here, Jim?"

"No, sah, thanks to goodness I hain't, Mars Tom."

"All right, we'll get you some."

"But bless you, honey, I doan' *want* none. I's afeard un um. I jis' 's soon have rattlesnakes aroun'."

Tom thought a minute or two, and says:

"It's a good idea. And I reckon it's been done. It *must* a been done; it stands to reason. Yes, it's a prime good idea. Where could you keep it?"

"Keep what, Mars Tom?"

"Why, a rattlesnake."

"De goodness gracious alive, Mars Tom! Why, if dey was a rattlesnake to come in heah, I'd take en bust right out thoo dat log wall, I would, wid my head."

"Why, Jim, you wouldn't be afraid of it, after a little. You could tame it."

"*Tame* it!"

"Yes—easy enough. Every animal is grateful for kindness and petting, and they wouldn't *think* of hurting a person that pets them. Any book will tell you that. You try—that's all I ask; just try for two or three days. Why, you can get him so, in a little while, that he'll love you; and sleep with you; and won't stay away from you a minute; and will let you wrap him round your neck and put his head in your mouth."

"*Please,* Mars Tom—*doan'* talk so! I can't *stan'* it! He'd *let* me shove his head in my mouf—fer a favor, hain't it? I lay he'd wait a pow'ful long time 'fo' I *ast* him. En mo' en dat, I doan' *want* him to sleep wid me."

"Jim, don't act so foolish. A prisoner's *got* to have some kind of a dumb pet, and if a rattlesnake hain't ever been tried, why, there's more glory to be gained in your being the first to ever try it than any other way you could ever think of to save your life."

"Why, Mars Tom, I doan' *want* no sich glory. Snake take 'n bite Jim's chin off, den *whah* is de glory? No, sah, I doan' want no sich doin's."

"Blame it, can't you *try?* I only *want* you to try—you needn't keep it up if it don't work."

"But de trouble all *done,* ef de snake bite me while I's a tryin' him. Mars Tom, I's willin' to tackle mos' anything 'at ain't on-reasonable, but ef you en Huck fetches a rattlesnake in heah for me to tame, I's gwyne to *leave,* dat's *shore.*"

"Well, then, let it go, let it go, if you're so bullheaded about it. We can get you some garter-snakes and you can tie some buttons on their tails, and let on they're rattlesnakes, and I reckon that'll have to do."

"I k'n stan' *dem,* Mars Tom, but blame' 'f I couldn' get along widout um, I tell you dat. I never knowed b'fo', 't was so much bother and trouble to be a prisoner."

"Well, it *always* is, when it's done right. You got any rats around here?"

"No, sah, I hain't seed none."

"Well, we'll get you some rats."

"Why, Mars Tom, I doan' *want* no rats. Dey's de dad-blamedest creturs to sturb a body, en rustle roun' over 'im, en bite his feet, when he's tryin' to sleep, I ever see. No, sah, gimme g'yarter-snakes, 'f I's got to have 'm, but doan' gimme no rats, I ain' got no use f'r um, skasely."

"But Jim, you *got* to have 'em—they all do. So don't make no more fuss about it. Prisoners ain't ever without rats. There ain't no instance of it. And they train them, and pet them, and learn them tricks, and they get to be as sociable as flies. But you got to play music to them. You got anything to play music on?"

"I ain' got nuffn but a coase comb en a piece o' paper, en a juice-harp; but I reck'n dey wouldn' take no stock in a juice-harp."

"Yes they would. *They* don't care what kind of music 'tis. A jews-harp's plenty good enough for a rat. All animals likes music—in a prison they dote on it. Specially, painful music; and you can't get no other kind out of a jews-harp. It always interests them; they come out to see what's the matter with you. Yes, you're all right; you're fixed very well. You want to set on your bed, nights, before you go to sleep, and early in the mornings, and play your jews-harp; play The Last Link Is Broken—that's the thing that'll scoop a rat, quicker'n anything else: and when you've played about two minutes, you'll see all the rats, and the snakes, and spiders, and things begin to feel worried about you, and come. And they'll just fairly swarm over you, and have a noble good time."

"Yes, *dey* will, I reck'n, Mars Tom, but what kine er time is *Jim* havin'? Blest if I kin see de pint. But I'll do it ef I got to. I reck'n I better keep de animals satisfied, en not have no trouble in de house."

Tom waited to think over, and see if there wasn't nothing else; and pretty soon he says:

"Oh—there's one thing I forgot. Could you raise a flower here, do you reckon?"

"I doan' know but maybe I could, Mars Tom; but it's tolable dark in heah, en I ain' got no use f'r no flower, nohow, en she'd be a pow'ful sight o' trouble."

"Well, you try it, anyway. Some other prisoners has done it."

"One er dem big cat-tail-lookin' mullen-stalks would grow in heah, Mars Tom, I reck'n, but she wouldn' be wuth half de trouble she'd coss."

"Don't you believe it. We'll fetch you a little one, and you plant it in the corner, over there, and raise it. And don't call it mullen, call it Pitchiola—that's its right name, when it's in a prison. And you want to water it with your tears."

"Why, I got plenty spring water, Mars Tom."

"You don't *want* spring water; you want to water it with your tears. It's the way they always do."

"Why, Mars Tom, I lay I kin raise one er dem mullen-stalks twyste wid spring water whiles another man's a *start'n* one wid tears."

"That ain't the idea. You *got* to do it with tears."

"She'll die on my han's, Mars Tom, she sholy will; kase I doan' skasely ever cry."

So Tom was stumped. But he studied it over, and then said Jim would have to worry along the best he could with an onion. He promised he would go to the nigger cabins and drop one, private, in Jim's coffee-pot, in the morning. Jim said he would "jis' 's soon have tobacker in his coffee;" and found so much fault with it, and with the work and bother of raising the mullen, and jews-harping the rats, and petting and flattering up the snakes and spiders and things, on top of all the other work he had to do on pens, and inscriptions, and journals, and things, which made it more trouble and worry and responsibility to be a prisoner than anything he ever undertook, that Tom most lost all patience with him; and said he was just loadened down with more gaudier chances than a prisoner ever had in the world to make a name for himself, and yet he didn't know enough to appreciate them, and they was just about wasted on him. So Jim he was sorry, and said he wouldn't behave so no more, and then me and Tom shoved for bed.

CHAPTER XXXIX

In the morning we went up to the village and bought a wire rat trap and fetched it down, and unstopped the best rat hole, and in about an hour we had fifteen of the bulliest kind of ones; and then we took it and put it in a safe place under Aunt Sally's bed. But while we was gone for spiders, little Thomas Franklin Benjamin Jefferson Elexander Phelps found it there, and opened the door of it to see if the rats would come out, and they did; and Aunt Sally she come in, and when we got back she was standing on top of the bed raising Cain, and the rats was doing what they could to keep off the dull times for her. So she took and dusted us both with the hickry, and we was as much as two hours catching another fifteen or sixteen, drat that meddlesome cub, and they warn't the likeliest, nuther, because the first haul was the pick of the flock. I never see a likelier lot of rats than what that first haul was.

We got a splendid stock of sorted spiders, and bugs, and frogs, and caterpillars, and one thing or another; and we liketo got a hornet's nest, but we didn't. The family was at home. We didn't give it right up, but staid with them as long as we could; because we allowed we'd tire them out or they'd got to tire us out, and they done it. Then we got allycumpain and rubbed on the places, and was pretty near all right again, but couldn't set down convenient. And so we went for the snakes, and grabbed a couple of dozen garters and house-snakes, and put them in a bag, and put it in our room, and by that time it was supper time, and a rattling good honest day's work; and hungry?—oh, no, I reckon not! And there warn't a blessed snake up there, when we went back—we didn't half tie the sack, and they worked out, somehow, and left. But it didn't matter much, because they was still on the premises somewheres. So we judged we could get some of them again. No, there warn't no real scarcity of snakes about the house for a considerable spell. You'd see them dripping from the rafters and places, every now and then; and they generly landed in your plate, or down the back of your neck, and most of the time where you didn't want them. Well, they was handsome, and striped, and there warn't no harm in a million of them; but that never made no difference to Aunt Sally, she despised snakes, be the breed what they might, and she couldn't stand them no way you could fix it; and every time one of them flopped down on her, it didn't make no difference what she was doing, she would just lay that work down and light out. I never see such a woman. And you could hear her whoop to Jericho. You couldn't get her to take aholt of one of them with the tongs. And if she turned over and found one in bed, she would scramble out and lift a howl that you would think the house was afire. She disturbed the old man so, that he said he could most wish there hadn't ever been no snakes created. Why, after every last snake had been gone clear out of the house for as much as a week, Aunt Sally warn't over it yet; she warn't near over it; when she was setting thinking about something, you could touch her on the back of her neck with a feather and she would jump right out of her stockings. It was very curious. But Tom said all women was just so. He said they was made that way; for some reason or other.

We got a licking every time one of our snakes come in her way; and she allowed these lickings warn't nothing to what she would do if we ever loaded up the place again with them. I didn't mind the lickings, because they didn't amount to nothing; but I minded the trouble we had, to lay in another lot. But we got them laid in, and all the other things; and you never see a cabin as blithesome as Jim's was when they'd all swarm out for music and go for him. Jim didn't like the spiders, and the spiders didn't like Jim; and so they'd lay for him and make it mighty warm for him. And he said that between the rats, and the snakes, and the grindstone, where warn't no room in bed for him, skasely; and when there was, a body couldn't sleep, it was so lively, and it was always lively, he said, because *they* never all slept at one time, but took turn about, so when the snakes was asleep the rats was on deck, and when the rats turned in the snakes come on watch, so he always had one gang under him, in his way, and t'other gang having a circus over him, and if he got up to hunt a new place, the spiders would take a chance at him as he crossed over. He said if he ever got out, this time, he wouldn't ever be a prisoner again, not for a salary.

Well, by the end of three weeks, everything was in pretty good shape. The shirt was sent in early, in a pie, and every time a rat bit Jim he would get up and write a little in his journal whilst the ink was fresh; the pens was made, the inscriptions and so on was all carved on the grindstone; the bed-leg was sawed in two, and we had et up the sawdust, and it give us a most amazing stomach-ache. We reckoned we was all going to die, but didn't. It was the most indigestible sawdust I ever see; and Tom said the same. But as I was saying, we'd got all the work done, now, at last; and we was all pretty much fagged out, too, but mainly Jim. The old man had wrote a couple of times to the plantation below Orleans to come and get their runaway nigger, but hadn't got no answer, because there warn't no such plantation; so he allowed he would advertise Jim in the St. Louis and New Orleans papers; and when he mentioned the St. Louis ones, it give me the cold shivers, and I see we hadn't no time to lose. So Tom said, now for the nonnamous letters.

"What's them?" I says.

"Warnings to the people that something is up. Sometimes it's done one way, sometimes another. But there's always somebody spying around, that gives notice to the governor of the castle. When Louis XVI. was going to light out of the Tooleries, a servant girl done it. It's a very good way, and so is the nonnamous letters. We'll use them both. And it's usual for the prisoner's mother to change clothes with him, and she stays in, and he slides out in her clothes. We'll do that too."

"But looky here, Tom, what do we want to *warn* anybody for, that something's up? Let them find it out for themselves—it's their lookout."

"Yes, I know; but you can't depend on them. It's the way they've acted from the very start—left us to do *everything*. They're so confiding and mullet-headed they don't take notice of nothing at all. So if we don't *give* them notice, there won't be nobody nor nothing to interfere with us, and so after all our hard work and trouble this escape'll go off perfectly flat: won't amount to nothing—won't be nothing *to* it."

"Well, as for me, Tom, that's the way I'd like."

"Shucks," he says, and looked disgusted. So I says:

"But I ain't going to make no complaint. Anyway that suits you suits me. What you going to do about the servant-girl?"

"You'll be her. You slide in, in the middle of the night, and hook that yaller girl's frock."

"Why, Tom, that'll make trouble next morning; because of course she prob'-bly hain't got any but that one."

"I know; but you don't want it but fifteen minutes, to carry the nonnamous letter and shove it under the front door."

"All right, then, I'll do it; but I could carry it just as handy in my own togs."

"You wouldn't look like a servant-girl *then,* would you?"

"No, but there won't be nobody to see what I look like, *anyway.*"

"That ain't got nothing to do with it. The thing for us to do, is just to do our *duty,* and not worry about whether anybody *sees* us do it or not. Hain't you got no principle at all?"

"All right, I ain't saying nothing; I'm the servant-girl. Who's Jim's mother?"

"I'm his mother. I'll hook a gown from Aunt Sally."

"Well, then, you'll have to stay in the cabin when me and Jim leaves."

"Not much. I'll stuff Jim's clothes full of straw and lay it on his bed to represent his mother in disguise, and Jim'll take the nigger woman's gown off of me and wear it, and we'll all evade together. When a prisoner of style escapes, it's called an evasion. It's always called so when a king escapes, f'rinstance. And the same with a king's son; it don't make no difference whether he's a natural one or an unnatural one."

So Tom he wrote the nonnamous letter, and I smouched the yaller wench's frock, that night, and put it on, and shoved it under the front door, the way Tom told me to. It said:

Beware. Trouble is brewing. Keep a sharp lookout.

UNKNOWN FRIEND.

Next night we stuck a picture which Tom drawed in blood, of a skull and crossbones, on the front door; and next night another one of a coffin, on the back door. I never see a family in such a sweat. They couldn't a been worse scared if the place had a been full of ghosts laying for them behind everything and under the beds and shivering through the air. If a door banged, Aunt Sally she jumped, and said "ouch!" if anything fell, she jumped and said "ouch!" if you happened to touch her, when she warn't noticing, she done the same; she couldn't face noway and be satisfied, because she allowed there was something behind her every time—so she was always a whirling around, sudden, and saying "ouch," and before she'd get two-thirds around, she'd whirl back again, and say it again; and she was afraid to go to bed, but she dasn't set up. So the thing was working very well, Tom said; he said he never see a thing work more satisfactory. He said it showed it was done right.

So he said, now for the grand bulge! So the very next morning at the streak of dawn we got another letter ready, and was wondering what we better do with it, because we heard them say at supper they was going to have a nigger on watch at both doors all night. Tom he went down the lightning-rod to spy around; and the nigger at the back door was asleep, and he stuck it in the back of his neck and come back. This letter said:

> Don't betray me, I wish to be your friend. There is a desprate gang of cutthroats from over in the Ingean Territory going to steal your runaway nigger to-night, and they have been trying to scare you so as you will stay in the house and not bother them. I am one of the gang, but have got religgion and wish to quit it and lead a honest life again, and will betray the helish design. They will sneak down from northards, along the fence, at midnight exact, with a false key, and go in the nigger's cabin to get him. I am to be off a piece and blow a tin horn if I see any danger; but stead of that, I will BA like a sheep soon as they get in and not blow at all; then whilst they are getting his chains loose, you slip there and lock them in, and can kill them at your leasure. Don't do anything but just the way I am telling you, if you do they will suspicion something and raise whoopjamboreehoo. I do not wish any reward but to know I have done the right thing.
>
> UNKNOWN FRIEND

CHAPTER XL

We was feeling pretty good, after breakfast, and took my canoe and went over the river a fishing, with a lunch, and had a good time, and took a look at the raft and found her all right, and got home late to supper, and found them in such a sweat and worry they didn't know which end they was standing on, and made us go right off to bed the minute we was done supper, and wouldn't tell us what the trouble was, and never let on a word about the new letter, but didn't need to, because we knowed as much about it as anybody did, and as soon as we was half up stairs and her back was turned, we slid for the cellar cubboard and loaded up a good lunch and took it up to our room and went to bed, and got up about half-past eleven, and Tom put on Aunt Sally's dress that he stole and was going to start with the lunch, but says:

"Where's the butter?"

"I laid out a hunk of it," I says, "on a piece of corn-pone."

"Well, you *left* it laid out, then—it ain't here."

"We can get along without it," I says.

"We can get along *with* it, too," he says; "just you slide down cellar and fetch it. And then mosey right down the lightning-rod and come along. I'll go and stuff the straw into Jim's clothes to represent his mother in disguise, and be ready to *ba* like a sheep and shove soon as you get there."

So out he went, and down cellar went I. The hunk of butter, big as a person's fist, was where I had left it, so I took up the slab of corn-pone with it on, and blowed out my light, and started up stairs, very stealthy, and got up to the main floor all right, but here comes Aunt Sally with a candle, and I clapped the truck in my hat, and clapped my hat on my head, and the next second she see me; and she says:

"You been down cellar?"

"Yes'm."

"What you been doing down there?"

"Noth'n."

"*Noth'n!*"

"No'm."

"Well, then, what possessed you to go down there, this time of night?"

"I don't know'm."

"You don't *know*? Don't answer me that way, Tom, I want to know what you been *doing* down there?"

"I hain't been doing a single thing, Aunt Sally, I hope to gracious if I have."

I reckoned she'd let me go, now, and as a generl thing she would; but I spose there was so many strange things going on she was just in a sweat about every little thing that warn't yard-stick straight; so she says, very decided:

"You just march into that setting-room and stay there till I come. You been up to something you no business to, and I lay I'll find out what it is before *I'm* done with you."

So she went away as I opened the door and walked into the setting-room. My, but there was a crowd there! Fifteen farmers, and every one of them had a gun. I was most powerful sick, and slunk to a chair and set down. They was setting around, some of them talking a little, in a low voice, and all of them fidgety and uneasy, but trying to look like they warn't; but I knowed they was, because they was always taking off their hats, and putting them on, and scratching their heads, and changing their seats, and fumbling with their buttons. I warn't easy myself, but I didn't take my hat off, all the same.

I did wish Aunt Sally would come, and get done with me, and lick me, if she wanted to, and let me get away and tell Tom how we'd overdone this thing, and what a thundering hornet's nest we'd got ourselves into, so we could stop fooling around, straight off, and clear out with Jim before these rips got out of patience and come for us.

At last she come, and begun to ask me questions, but I *couldn't* answer them straight, I didn't know which end of me was up; because these men was in such a fidget now, that some was wanting to start right *now* and lay for them desperadoes, and saying it warn't but a few minutes to midnight; and others was trying to get them to hold on and wait for the sheep-signal; and here was aunty pegging away at the questions, and me a shaking all over and ready to sink down in my tracks I was that scared; and the place getting hotter and hotter, and the butter beginning to melt and run down my neck and behind my ears; and pretty soon, when one of them says, "*I'm* for going and getting in the cabin *first,* and right *now,* and catching them when they come," I most dropped; and a streak of butter come a trickling down my forehead, and Aunt Sally she see it, and turns white as a sheet, and says:

"For the land's sake what *is* the matter with the child!—he's got the brain fever as shore as you're born, and they're oozing out!"

And everybody runs to see, and she snatches off my hat, and out comes the bread, and what was left of the butter, and she grabbed me, and hugged me, and says:

"Oh, what a turn you did give me! and how glad and grateful I am it ain't no worse; for luck's against us, and it never rains but it pours, and when I see that truck I thought we'd lost you, for I knowed by the color and all, it was just like your brains would be if— Dear, dear, whyd'nt you *tell* me that was what you'd been down there for, *I* wouldn't a cared. Now cler out to bed, and don't lemme see no more of you till morning!"

I was up the stairs in a second, and down the lightning-rod in another one, and shinning through the dark to the lean-to. I couldn't hardly get my words out, I was so anxious; but I told Tom as quick as I could, we must jump for it, now, and not a minute to lose—the house full of men, yonder, with guns!

His eyes just blazed; and he says:

"No!—is that so? *Ain't* it bully! Why, Huck if it was to do over again, I bet I could fetch two hundred! If we could put it off till—"

"Hurry! *hurry!*" I says. "Where's Jim?"

"Right at your elbow; if you reach out your arm you can touch him. He's dressed, and everything's ready. Now we'll slide out and give the sheep-signal."

But then we heard the tramp of men, coming to the door, and heard them begin to fumble with the padlock; and heard a man say:

"I *told* you we'd be too soon; they haven't come—the door is locked. Here, I'll lock some of you into the cabin and you lay for 'em in the dark and kill 'em when they come; and the rest scatter around a piece, and listen if you can hear 'em coming."

So in they come, but couldn't see us in the dark, and most trod on us whilst we was hustling to get under the bed. But we got under all right, and out through the hole, swift but soft—Jim first, me next, and Tom last, which was according to Tom's orders. Now we was in the lean-to, and heard trampings close by outside. So we crept to the door, and Tom stopped us there and put his eye to the crack, but couldn't make out nothing, it was so dark; and whispered and said he would listen for the steps to get further, and when he nudged us Jim must glide out first, and him last. So he set his ear to the crack and listened, and listened, and listened, and the steps a scraping around, out there, all the time; and at last he nudged us, and we slid out, and stooped down, not breathing, and not making the least noise, and slipped stealthy towards the fence, in Injun file, and got to it, all right, and me and Jim over it; but Tom's britches catched fast on a splinter on the top rail, and then he hear the steps coming, so he had to pull loose, which snapped the splinter and made a noise; and as he dropped in our tracks and started, somebody sings out:

"Who's that? Answer, or I'll shoot!"

But we didn't answer; we just unfurled our heels and shoved. Then there was a rush, and a *bang, bang, bang!* and the bullets fairly whizzed around us! We heard them sing out:

"Here they are! They've broke for the river! after 'em boys! And turn loose the dogs!"

So here they come, full tilt. We could hear them, because they wore boots, and yelled, but we didn't wear no boots, and didn't yell. We was in the path to the mill; and when they got pretty close onto us, we dodged into the bush and let them go by, and then dropped in behind them. They'd had all the dogs shut up, so they wouldn't scare off the robbers; but by this time somebody had let them loose, and here they come, making pow-wow enough for a million; but they was our dogs; so we stopped in our tracks till they catched up; and when they see it warn't nobody but us, and no excitement to offer them, they only just said howdy, and tore right ahead towards the shouting and clattering; and then we up steam again and whizzed along after them till we was nearly to the mill, and then struck up through the bush to where my canoe was tied, and hopped in and pulled for dear life towards the middle of the river, but didn't make no more noise than we was obleeged to. Then we struck out, easy and comfortable, for the island where my raft was; and we could hear them yelling and barking at each other all up and down the bank, till we was so far away the sounds got dim and died out. And when we stepped onto the raft, I says:

"*Now,* old Jim, you're a free man *again,* and I bet you won't ever be a slave no more."

"En a mighty good job it wuz, too, Huck. It 'uz planned beautiful, en it 'uz *done* beautiful; en dey ain't *nobody* kin git up a plan dat's mo' mixed-up en splendid den what dat one wuz."

We was all as glad as we could be, but Tom was the gladdest of all, because he had a bullet in the calf of his leg.

When me and Jim heard that, we didn't feel so brash as what we did before. It was hurting him considerble, and bleeding; so we laid him in the wigwam and tore up one of the duke's shirts for to bandage him, but he says:

"Gimme the rags, I can do it myself. Don't stop, now; don't fool around here, and the evasion booming along so handsome; man the sweeps, and set her loose! Boys, we done it elegant!—'deed we did. I wish *we'd* a had the handling of Louis XVI., there wouldn't a been no 'Son of Saint Louis, ascend to heaven!' wrote down in *his* biography: no, sir, we'd a whooped him over the *border*—that's what we'd a done with *him*—and done it just as slick as nothing at all, too. Man the sweeps—man the sweeps!"

But me and Jim was consulting—and thinking. And after we'd thought a minute, I says:

"Say it, Jim."

So he says:

"Well, den, dis is de way it look to me, Huck. Ef it wuz *him* dat 'uz bein' sot free, en one er de boys wuz to git shot, would he say, 'Go on en save me, nemmine 'bout a doctor f'r to save dis one? Is dat like Mars Tom Sawyer? Would he say dat? You *bet* he wouldn't! *Well,* den, is *Jim* gwyne to say it? No, sah—I doan' budge a step out'n dis place, 'dout a *doctor;* not if it's forty year!"

I knowed he was white inside, and I reckoned he'd say what he did say—so it was all right, now, and I told Tom I was agoing for a doctor. He raised considerable row about it, but me and Jim stuck to it and wouldn't budge; so he was for crawling out and setting the raft loose himself; but we wouldn't let him. Then he give us a piece of his mind—but it didn't do no good.

So when he see me getting the canoe ready, he says:

"Well, then, if you're bound to go, I'll tell you the way to do, when you get to the village. Shut the door, and blindfold the doctor tight and fast, and make him swear to be silent as the grave, and put a purse full of gold in his hand, and then take and lead him all around the back alleys and everywheres, in the dark, and then fetch him here in the canoe, in a roundabout way amongst the islands, and search him and take his chalk away from him, and don't give it back to him till you get him back to the village, or else he will chalk this raft so he can find it again. It's the way they all do."

So I said I would, and left, and Jim was to hide in the woods when he see the doctor coming, till he was gone again.

CHAPTER XLI

The doctor was an old man; a very nice, kind-looking old man, when I got him up. I told him me and my brother was over on Spanish Island hunting, yesterday afternoon, and camped on a piece of a raft we found, and about midnight he must a kicked his gun in his dreams, for it went off and shot him in the leg, and we wanted him to go over there and fix it and not say nothing about it, nor let anybody know, because we wanted to come home this evening, and surprise the folks.

"Who is your folks?" he says.

"The Phelpses, down yonder."

"Oh," he says. And after a minute, he says: "How'd you say he got shot?"

"He had a dream," I says, "and it shot him."

"Singular dream," he says.

So he lit up his lantern, and got his saddle-bags, and we started. But when he see the canoe, he didn't like the look of her—said she was big enough for one, but didn't look pretty safe for two. I says:

"Oh, you needn't be afeard, sir, she carried the three of us, easy enough."

"What three?"

"Why, me and Sid, and—and—and the *guns;* that's what I mean."

"Oh," he says.

But he put his foot on the gunnel, and rocked her; and shook his head, and said he reckoned he'd look around for a bigger one. But they was all locked and chained; so he took my canoe, and said for me to wait till he come back, or I could hunt around further, or maybe I better go down home and get them ready for the surprise, if I wanted to. But I said I didn't; so I told him just how to find the raft, and then he started.

I struck an idea, pretty soon. I says to myself, spos'n he can't fix that leg just in three shakes of a sheep's tail, as the saying is? spos'n it takes him three or four days? What are we going to do?—lay around there till he lets the cat out of the bag? No, sir, I know what *I'll* do. I'll wait, and when he comes back, if he says he's got to go any more, I'll get down there, too, if I swim; and we'll take and tie him, and keep him, and shove out down the river; and when Tom's done with him, we'll give him what it's worth, or all we got, and then let him get shore.

So then I crept into a lumber pile to get some sleep; and next time I waked up the sun was away up over my head! I shot out and went for the doctor's house, but they told me he'd gone away in the night, some time or other, and warn't back yet. Well, thinks I, that looks powerful bad for Tom, and I'll dig out for the island right off. So away I shoved, and turned the corner, and nearly rammed my head into Uncle Silas's stomach! He says:

"Why, *Tom!* Where you been, all this time, you rascal?"

"*I* hain't been nowheres," I says, "only just hunting for the runaway nigger—me and Sid."

"Why, where ever did you go?" he says. "Your aunt's been mighty uneasy."

"She needn't," I says, "because we was all right. We followed the men and the dogs, but they out-run us, and we lost them; but we thought we heard them on the water, so we got a canoe and took out after them, and crossed over but couldn't find nothing of them; so we cruised along up-shore till we got kind of tired and beat out; and tied up the canoe and went to sleep, and never waked up till about an hour ago, then we paddled over here to hear the news, and Sid's at the post-office to see what he can hear, and I'm a branching out to get something to eat for us, and then we're going home."

So then we went to the post-office to get "Sid"; but just as I suspicioned, he warn't there; so the old man he got a letter out of the office, and we waited a while longer but Sid didn't come; so the old man said come along, let Sid foot it home, or canoe-it, when he got done fooling around—but we would ride. I couldn't get him to let me stay and wait for Sid; and he said there warn't no use in it, and I must come along, and let Aunt Sally see we was all right.

When we got home, Aunt Sally was that glad to see me she laughed and cried both, and hugged me, and give me one of them lickings of hern that don't amount to shucks, and said she'd serve Sid the same when he come.

And the place was plumb full of farmers and farmers' wives, to dinner; and such another clack a body never heard. Old Mrs. Hotchkiss was the worst; her tongue was agoing all the time. She says:

"Well, Sister Phelps, I've ransacked that-air cabin over an' I b'lieve the nigger was crazy. I says so to Sister Damrell—didn't I, Sister Damrell?—s'I, he's crazy, s'I—them's the very words I said. You all hearn me: he's crazy, s'I; everything shows it, s'I. Look at that-air grindstone, s'I; want to tell *me*'t any cretur 'ts in his right mind's agoin' to scrabble all them crazy things onto a grindstone, s'I? Here sich 'n' sich a person busted his heart; 'n' here so 'n' so pegged along for thirty-seven year, 'n' all that—natcherl son o' Louis somebody, 'n' sich everlast'n rubbage. He's plumb crazy, s'I; it's what I says in the fust place, it's what I says in the middle, 'n' it's what I says last 'n' all the time—the nigger's crazy—crazy's Nebokoodneezer, s'I."

"An' look at that-air ladder made out'n rags, Sister Hotchkiss," says old Mrs. Damrell, "what in the name o' goodness *could* he ever want of—"

"The very words I was a-sayin' no longer ago th'n this minute to Sister Utterback, 'n' she'll tell you so herself. Sh-she, look at that-air rag ladder, sh-she; 'n' s'I, yes, *look* at it, s'I—what *could* he a wanted of it, s'I. Sh-she, Sister Hotchkiss, sh-she—"

"But how in the nation'd they ever *git* that grindstone *in* there, *any*way, 'n' who dug that-air *hole?* 'n' who—"

"My very *words,* Brer Penrod! I was a-sayin'—pass that-air sasser o' m'lasses, won't ye?—I was a-sayin' to Sister Dunlap, jist this minute, how *did* they git that grindstone in there, s'I.

Without *help,* mind you—'thout *help! Thar's* wher' 'tis. Don't tell *me,* s'I; there *wuz* help, s'I; 'n' ther' wuz a *plenty* help, too, s'I; ther's ben a *dozen* a-helpin' that nigger, 'n' I lay I'd skin every last nigger on this place, but *I'd* find out who done it, s'I; 'n' moreover, s'I—"

"A *dozen* says you!—*forty* couldn't a done everything that's been done. Look at them case-knife saws and things, how tedious they've been made; look at that bed-leg sawed off with 'm, a week's work for six men; look at that nigger made out'n straw on the bed; and look at—"

"You may *well* say it, Brer Hightower! It's jist as I was a-sayin' to Brer Phelps, his own self. S'e, what do *you* think of it, Sister Hotchkiss, s'e? think o' what, Brer Phelps, s'I? think o' that bed-leg sawed off that a way, s'e? *think* of it, s'I? I lay it never sawed *itself* off, s'I—somebody *sawed* it, s'I; that's my opinion, take it or leave it, it mayn't be no 'count, s'I, but sich as 't is, it's my opinion, s'I, 'n' if anybody k'n start a better one, s'I, let him *do* it, s'I, that's all. I says to Sister Dunlap, s'I—"

"Why, dog my cats, they must a ben a house-full o'niggers in there every night for four weeks, to a done al that work, Sister Phelps. Look at that shirt—every last inch of it kivered over with secret African writ'n done with blood! Must a ben a raft uv'm at it right along, all the time, amost. Why? I'd give two dollars to have it read to me; 'n' as for the niggers that wrote it, I 'low I'd take 'n' lash 'm t'll—"

"People to *help* him, Brother Marples! Well, I reckon you'd *think* so, if you'd a been in this house for a while back. Why, they've stole everything they could lay their hands on—and we a watching, all the time, mind you. They stole that shirt right off o' the line! and as for that sheet they made the rag ladder out of ther' ain't no telling how many times they *didn't* steal that; and flour, and candles, and candlesticks, and spoons, and the old warming-pan, and most a thousand things that I disremember, now, and my new calico dress; and me, and Silas, and my Sid and Tom on the constant watch day *and* night, as I was a telling you, and not a one of us could catch hide nor hair, nor sight nor sound of them; and here at the last minute, lo an behold you, they slides right in under our noses, and fools us, and not only fools *us* but the Injun Territory robbers too, and actuly gets *away* with that nigger, safe and sound, and that with sixteen men and twenty-two dogs right on their very heels at that very time! I tell you, it just bangs anything I ever *heard* of. Why, *sperits* couldn't a done better, and been no smarter. And I reckon they must a *been* sperits—because, *you* know our dogs, and ther' ain't no better; well, them dogs never even got on the *track* of 'm, once! You explain *that* to me, if you can!—*any* of you!"

"Well, it does beat—"

"Laws alive, I never—"

"So help me, I wouldn't a be—"

"*House*-thieves as well as—"

"Goodnessgracioussakes, I'd a ben afeard to *live* in sich a—"

"'Fraid to *live!*—why, I was that scared I das'nt hardly go to bed, or get up, or lay down, or *set* down, Sister Ridgeway. Why, they'd steal the very—why, goodness sakes, you can guess what kind of a fluster *I* was in by the time midnight come, last night. I hope to gracious if I warn't afraid they'd steal some o' the family! I was just to that pass, I didn't have no reasoning faculties no more. It looks foolish enough, *now,* in the day-time; but I says to myself, there's my two poor boys asleep, 'way up stairs in that lonesome room, and I declare to goodness I was that uneasy 't I crep' up there and locked 'em in! I *did.* And anybody would. Because, you know, when you get scared, that way, and it keeps running on, and getting worse and worse, all the time, and your wits gets to addling, and you get to doing all sorts o' wild things, and by-and-by you think to yourself, spos'n *I* was a boy, and was away up there, and the door ain't locked, and you—" She stopped, looking kind of wondering, and then she turned her head around slow, and when her eye lit on me—I got up and took a walk.

Says I to myself, I can explain better how we come to not be in that room this morning, if I go out to one side and study over it a little. So I done it. But I dasn't go fur, or she'd a sent for me. And when it was late in the day, the people all went, and then I come in and told her the noise and shooting waked me up and "Sid," and the door was locked, and we wanted to see the fun, so we went down the lightning-rod, and both of us got hurt a little, and we didn't never want to try *that* no more. And then I went on and told her all what I told Uncle Silas before; and then she said she'd forgive us, and maybe it was all right enough anyway, and about what a body might expect of boys, for all boys was a pretty harum-scarum lot, as fur as she could see; and so, as long as no harm hadn't come of it, she judged she better put in her time being grateful we was alive and well and she had us still, stead of fretting over what was past and done. So then she kissed me, and patted me on the head, and dropped into a kind of a brown study; and pretty soon jumps up, and says:

"Why lawsamercy, it's most night, and Sid not come yet! What *has* become of that boy?"

I see my chance; so I skips up and says:

"I'll run right up to town and get him," I says.

"No you won't," she says. "You'll stay right wher' you are; *one's* enough to be lost at a time. If he ain't here to supper, your uncle'll go."

Well, he warn't there to supper; so right after supper uncle went.

He came back about ten, a little bit uneasy; hadn't run across Tom's track. Aunt Sally was a good *deal* uneasy; but Uncle Silas he said there warn't no occasion to be—boys will be boys, he said, and you'll see this one turn up in the morning, all sound and right. So she had to be satisfied. But she said she'd set up for him a while, anyway, and keep a light burning, so he could see it.

And then when I went up to bed she come up with me and fetched her candle, and tucked me in, and mothered me so good I felt mean, and like I couldn't look her in the face; and she set down on the bed and talked with me a long time, and said what a splendid boy Sid was, and didn't seem to want to ever stop talking about him; and kept asking me every now and then, if I reckoned he could a got lost, or hurt, or maybe drownded, and might be laying at this minute, somewheres, suffering or dead, and she not by him to help him, and so the tears would drip down, silent, and I would tell her that Sid was all right, and would be home in the morning, sure; and she would squeeze my hand, or maybe kiss me, and tell me to say it again, and keep on saying it, because it done her good, and she was in so much trouble. And when she was going away, she looked down in my eyes, so steady and gentle, and says:

"The door ain't going to be locked, Tom; and there's the window and the rod; but you'll be good, *won't* you? And you won't go? For *my* sake."

Laws knows I *wanted* to go, bad enough, to see about Tom, and was all intending to go; but after that, I wouldn't a went, nor for kingdoms.

But she was on my mind, and Tom was on my mind; so I slept very restless. And twice I went down the rod, away in the night, and slipped around front, and see her setting there by her candle in the window with her eyes towards the road and the tears in them; and I wished I could do something for her, but I couldn't, only to swear that I wouldn't never do nothing to grieve her any more. And the third time, I waked up at dawn, and slid down, and she was there yet, and her candle was most out, and her old gray head was resting on her hand, and she was asleep.

CHAPTER XLII

The old man was up town again, before breakfast, but couldn't get no track of Tom; and both of them set at the table, thinking, and not saying nothing, and looking mournful, and their coffee getting cold, and not eating anything. And by-and-by the old man says:

"Did I give you the letter?"

"What letter?"

"The one I got yesterday out of the post-office."

"No, you didn't give me no letter."

"Well, I must a forgot it."

So he rummaged in his pockets, and then went off somewheres where he had laid it down, and fetched it, and give it to her. She says:

"Why, it's from St. Petersburg—it's from Sis."

I allowed another walk would do me good; but I couldn't stir. But before she could break it open, she dropped it and run—for she see something. And so did I. It was Tom Sawyer on a mattress; and that old doctor; and Jim, in *her* calico dress, with his hands tied behind him; and a lot of people. I hid the letter behind the first thing that come handy, and rushed. She flung herself at Tom, crying, and says:

"Oh, he's dead, he's dead, I know he's dead!"

And Tom he turned his head a little, and muttered something or other, which showed he warn't in his right mind; then she flung up her hands, and says:

"He's alive, thank God! And that's enough!" and she snatched a kiss of him, and flew for the house to get the bed ready, and scattering orders right and left at the niggers and everybody else, as fast as her tongue could go, every jump of the way.

I followed the men to see what they was going to do with Jim; and the old doctor and Uncle Silas followed after Tom into the house. The men was very huffy, and some of them wanted to hang Jim, for an example to all the other niggers around there, so they wouldn't be trying to run away, like Jim done, and making such a raft of trouble, and keeping a whole family scared most to death for days and nights. But the others said, don't do it, it wouldn't answer at all, he ain't our nigger, and his owner would turn up and make us pay for him, sure. So that cooled them down a little, because the people that's always the most anxious for to hang a nigger that hain't done just right, is always the very ones that ain't the most anxious to pay for him when they've got their satisfaction out of him.

They cussed Jim considerable, though, and give him a cuff or two, side the head, once in a while, but Jim never said nothing, and he never let on to know me, and they took him to the same cabin, and put his own clothes on him, and chained him again, and not to no bed-leg this time, but to a big staple drove into the bottom log, and chained his hands, too, and both legs, and said he warn't to have nothing but bread and water to eat, after this, till his owner come or he was sold at auction, because he didn't come in a certain length of time, and filled up our hole, and said a couple of farmers with guns must stand watch around about the cabin every night, and a bull-dog tied to the door in the day-time; and about this time they was through with the job and was tapering off with a kind of generl good-bye cussing, and then the old doctor comes and takes a look, and says:

"Don't be no rougher on him that you're obleeged to, because he ain't a bad nigger. When I got to where I found the boy, I see I couldn't cut the bullet out without some help, and he warn't in no condition for me to leave, to go and get help; and he got a little worse and a little worse, and after a long time he went out of his head, and wouldn't let me come anigh him, any more, and said if I chalked his raft he'd kill me, and no end of wild foolishness like that, and I see I couldn't do anything at all with him; so I says, I got to have *help,* somehow; and the minute I says it, out crawls this nigger from somewheres, and says he'll help, and he done it, too, and done it very well. Of course I judged he must be a runaway nigger, and there I *was!* and there I had to stick, right straight along all the rest of the day, and all night. It was a fix, I tell you! I had a couple of patients with the chills, and of course I'd of liked to run up to town and see them, but I dasn't, because the nigger might get away, and then I'd be to blame; and yet never a skiff come close enough for me to hail. So there I had to stick, plumb till daylight this morning; and I never see a nigger that was a better nuss or faithfuller, and yet he was resking his freedom to do it, and was all tired out, too, and I see plain enough he'd been worked main hard, lately. I liked the nigger for that; I tell you, gentlemen, a nigger like that is worth a thousand dollars—and kind treatment, too. I had everything I needed, and the boy was doing as well there as he would a done at home—better, maybe, because it was so quiet; but there I *was,* with both of 'm on my hands; and there I had to stick, till about dawn this morning; then some men in a skiff come by, and as good luck would have it, the nigger was setting by the pallet with his head propped on his knees, sound asleep; so I motioned them in, quiet, and they slipped up on him and grabbed him and tied him before he knowed what he was about, and we never had no trouble. And the boy being in a kind of a flighty sleep, too, we muffled the oars and hitched the raft on, and towed her over very nice and quiet, and the nigger never made the least row nor said a word, from the start. He ain't no bad nigger, gentlemen; that's what I think about him."

Somebody says:

"Well, it sounds very good, doctor, I'm obleeged to say."

Then the others softened up a little, too, and I was mighty thankful to that old doctor for doing Jim that good turn; and I was glad it was according to my judgment of him, too; because I thought he had a good heart in him and was a good man, the first time I see him. Then they all agreed that Jim had acted very well, and was deserving to have some notice took of it, and reward. So every one of them promised, right out and hearty, that they wouldn't cuss him no more.

Then they come and locked him up. I hoped they was going to say he could have one or two of the chains took off, because they was rotten heavy, or could have meat and greens with his bread and water, but they didn't think of it, and I reckoned it warn't best for me to mix in, but I judged I'd get the doctor's yarn to Aunt Sally, somehow or other, as soon as I'd got through the breakers that was laying just ahead of me. Explanations, I mean, of how I forgot to mention about Sid being shot, when I was telling how him and me put in that dratted night paddling around hunting the runaway nigger.

But I had plenty time. Aunt Sally she stuck to the sick-room all day and all night; and every time I see Uncle Silas mooning around, I dodged him.

Next morning I heard Tom was a good deal better, and they said Aunt Sally was gone to get a nap. So I slips to the sick-room, and if I found him awake I reckoned we could put up a yarn for the family that would wash. But he was sleeping, and sleeping very peaceful, too; and pale, not fire-faced the way he was when he come. So I set down and laid for him to wake. In about a half an hour, Aunt Sally comes gliding in, and there I was, up a stump again! She motioned me to be still, and set down by me and begun to whisper, and said we could all be joyful now, because all the symptoms was first rate, and he'd been sleeping like that for ever so long, and looking better and peacefuller all the time, and ten to one he'd wake up in his right mind.

So we set there watching, and by-and-by he stirs a bit, and opened his eyes very natural, and takes a look, and says:

"Hello, why I'm at *home!* How's that? Where's the raft?"

"It's all right," I says.

"And *Jim?*"

"The same," I says, but couldn't say it pretty brash. But he never noticed, but says:

"Good! Splendid! *Now* we're all right and safe! Did you tell Aunty?"

I was going to say yes; but she chipped in and says:

"About what, Sid?"

"Why, about the way the whole thing was done."

"What whole thing?"

"Why, *the* whole thing. There ain't but one; how we set the runaway nigger free—me and Tom."

"Good land! Set the run— What *is* the child talking about! Dear, dear, out of his head again!"

"*No,* I ain't out of my HEAD; I know all what I'm talking about. We *did* set him free—me and Tom. We laid out to do it, and we *done* it. And we done it elegant, too." He'd got a start, and she never checked him up, just set and stared and stared, and let him clip along, and I see it warn't no use for *me* to put in. "Why, Aunty, it cost us a power of work—weeks of it—hours and hours, every night, whilst you was all asleep. And we had to steal candles, and the sheet, and the shirt, and your dress, and spoons, and tin plates, and case-knives, and the warming-pan, and the grindstone, and flour, and just no end of things, and you can't think what work it was to make the saws, and pens, and inscriptions, and one thing or another, and you can't think *half* the fun it was. And we had to make up the pictures of coffins and things, and nonnamous letters from the robbers, and get up and down the lightning-rod, and dig the hole into the cabin, and make the rope-ladder and send it in cooked up in a pie, and send in spoons and things to work with, in your apron pocket"—

"Mercy sakes!"

—"and load up the cabin with rats and snakes and so on, for company for Jim; and then you kept Tom here so long with the butter in his hat that you come near spiling the whole business, because the men come before we was out of the cabin, and we had to rush, and they heard us and let drive at us, and I got my share, and we dodged out of the path and let them go by, and when the dogs come they warn't interested in us, but went for the most noise, and we got our canoe, and made for the raft, and was all safe, and Jim was a free man, and we done it all by ourselves, and *wasn't* it bully, Aunty!"

"Well, I never heard the likes of it all in my born days! So it was *you*, you little rapscallions, that's been making all this trouble, and turned everybody's wits clean inside out and scared us all most to death. I've as good a notion as ever I had in my life, to take it out o' you this very minute. To think, here I've been, night after night, a—*you* just get well once, you young scamp, and I lay I'll tan the Old Harry out o' both o' ye!"

But Tom, he *was* so proud and joyful, he just *couldn't* hold in, and his tongue just *went* it—she a-chipping in, and spitting fire all along, and both of them going it at once, like a cat-convention; and she says:

"*Well*, you get all the enjoyment you can out of it *now*, for mind I tell you if I catch you meddling with him again—"

"Meddling with *who?*" Tom says, dropping his smile and looking surprised.

"With *who?* Why, the runaway nigger, of course. Who'd you reckon?"

Tom looks at me very grave, and says:

"Tom, didn't you just tell me he was all right? Hasn't he got away?"

"*Him?*" says Aunt Sally; "the runaway nigger? 'Deed he hasn't. They've got him back, safe and sound, and he's in that cabin again, on bread and water, and loaded down with chains, till he's claimed or sold!"

Tom rose square up in bed, with his eye hot, and his nostrils opening and shutting like gills, and sings out to me:

"They hain't no *right* to shut him up! *Shove!*—and don't you lose a minute. Turn him loose! he ain't no slave; he's as free as any cretur that walks this earth!"

"What *does* the child mean?"

"I mean every word I *say,* Aunt Sally, and if somebody don't go, *I'll* go. I've knowed him all his life, and so has Tom, there. Old Miss Watson died two months ago, and she was ashamed she ever was going to sell him down the river, and *said* so; and she set him free in her will."

"Then what on earth did *you* want to set him free for, seeing he was already free?"

"Well that *is* a question, I must say; and *just* like women! Why, I wanted the *adventure* of it; and I'd a waded neck-deep in blood too—goodness alive, AUNT POLLY!"

If she warn't standing right there, just inside the door, looking as sweet and contented as an angel half-full of pie, I wish I may never!

Aunt Sally jumped for her, and most hugged the head off of her, and cried over her, and I found a good enough place for me under the bed, for it was getting pretty sultry for *us,* seemed to me. And I peeped out, and in a little while Tom's Aunt Polly shook herself loose and stood there looking across at Tom over her spectacles—kind of grinding him into the earth, you know. And then she says:

"Yes, you *better* turn y'r head away—I would if I was you, Tom."

"Oh, deary me!" says Aunt Sally; "*is* he changed so? Why, that ain't *Tom* it's Sid; Tom's—Tom's—why, where is Tom? He was here a minute ago."

"You mean where's Huck *Finn*—that's what you mean! I reckon I hain't raised such a scamp as my Tom all these years, not to know him when I *see* him. That *would* be a pretty howdy-do. Come out from under that bed, Huck Finn."

So I done it. But not feeling brash.

Aunt Sally she was one of the mixed-upest looking persons I ever see; except one, and that was Uncle Silas, when he come in, and they told it all to him. It kind of made him drunk, as you may say, and he didn't know nothing at all the rest of the day, and preached a prayer-meeting sermon that night that give him a rattling reputation, because the oldest man in the world couldn't a understood it. So Tom's Aunt Polly, she told all about who I was, and what; and I had to up and tell how I was in such a tight place that when Mrs. Phelps took me for Tom Sawyer—she chipped in and says, "Oh, go on and call me Aunt Sally, I'm used to it, now, and 'tain't no need to change—that when Aunt Sally took me for Tom Sawyer, I had to stand it—there warn't no other way, and I knowed he wouldn't mind, because it would be nuts for him, being a mystery, and he'd make an adventure out of it and be perfectly satisfied. And so it turned out, and he let on to be Sid, and made things as soft as he could for me.

And his Aunt Polly she said Tom was right about old Miss Watson setting Jim free in her will; and so, sure enough, Tom Sawyer had gone and took all that trouble and bother to set a free nigger free! and I couldn't ever understand, before, until that minute and that talk, how he *could* help a body set a nigger free, with his bringing-up.

Well, Aunt Polly she said that when Aunt Sally wrote to her that Tom and *Sid* had come, all right and safe, she says to herself:

"Look at that now! I might have expected it, letting him go off that way without anybody to watch him. So now I got to go and trapse all the way down the river, eleven hundred mile, and find out what that creetur's up to, *this* time; as long as I couldn't seem to get any answer out of you about it."

"Why, I never heard nothing from you," says Aunt Sally.

"Well, I wonder! Why, I wrote to you twice, to ask you what you could mean by Sid being here."

"Well, I never got 'em, Sis."

Aunt Polly, she turns around slow and severe, and says:

"You, Tom!"

"Well—*what?*" he says, kind of pettish.

"Don't you what *me,* you impudent thing—hand out them letters."

"What letters?"

"*Them* letters. I be bound, if I have to take aholt of you I'll—"

"They're in the trunk. There, now. And they're just the same as they was when I got them out of the office. I hain't looked into them, I hain't touched them. But I knowed they'd make trouble, and I thought if you warn't in no hurry, I'd—"

"Well, you *do* need skinning, there ain't no mistake about it. And I wrote another one to tell you I was coming; and I spose he—"

"No, it come yesterday; I hain't read it yet, but *it's* all right, I've got that one."

I wanted to offer to bet two dollars she hadn't, but I reckoned maybe it was just as safe not to. So I never said nothing.

CHAPTER THE LAST

The first time I catched Tom, private, I asked him what was his idea, time of the evasion?—what it was he'd planned to do if the evasion worked all right and he managed to set a nigger free that was already free before? And he said, what he had planned in his head, from the start, if we got Jim out all safe, was for us to run him down the river, on the raft, and have adventures plumb to the mouth of the river, and then tell him about his being free, and take him back up home on a steamboat, in style, and pay him for his lost time, and write word ahead and get out all the niggers around, and have them waltz him into town with a torchlight procession and a brass band, and then he would be a hero, and so would we. But I reckened it was about as well the way it was.

We had Jim out of the chains in no time, and when Aunt Polly and Uncle Silas and Aunt Sally found out how good he helped the doctor nurse Tom, they made a heap of fuss over him, and fixed him up prime, and give him all he wanted to eat, and a good time, and nothing to do. And we had him up to the sick-room; and had a high talk; and Tom give Jim forty dollars for being prisoner for us so patient, and doing it up so good, and Jim was pleased most to death, and busted out, and says:

"*Dah*, now, Huck, what I tell you?—what I tell you up dah on Jackson islan'? I *tole* you I got a hairy breas', en what's de sign un it; en I *tole* you I ben rich wunst, en gwineter to be rich *agin;* en it's come true; en heah she *is! Dah,* now! doan' talk to *me*—signs is *signs,* mine I tell you; en I knowed jis' 's well 'at I 'uz gwineter be rich agin as I's a stannin' heah dis minute!"

And then Tom he talked along, and talked along, and says, le's all three slide out of here, one of these nights, and get an outfit, and go for howling adventures amongst the Injuns, over in the Territory, for a couple of weeks or two; and I says, all right, that suits me, but I ain't got no money for to buy the outfit, and I reckon I couldn't get none from home, because it's likely pap's been back before now, and got it all away from Judge Thatcher and drunk it up.

"No he hain't," Tom says; "it's all there, yet—six thousand dollars and more; and your pap hain't ever been back since. Hadn't when I come away, anyhow."

Jim says, kind of solemn:

"He ain't a comin' back no mo', Huck."

I says:

"Why, Jim?"

"Nemmine why, Huck—but he ain't comin' back no mo'."

But I kept at him; so at last he says:

"Doan' you 'member de house dat was float'n down de river, en dey wuz a man in dah, kivered up, en I went in en unkivered him and didn' let you come in? Well, den, you k'n git yo' money when you wants it; kase dat wuz him."

Tom's most well, now, and got his bullet around his neck on a watch-guard for a watch, and is always seeing what time it is, and so there ain't nothing more to write about, and I'm rotten glad of it, because if I'd a knowed what a trouble it was to make a book I wouldn't a tackled it and ain't agoing to no more. But I reckon I got to light out for the Territory ahead of the rest, because Aunt Sally she's going to adopt me and sivilize me and I can't stand it. I been there before.

THE END, YOURS TRULY HUCK FINN

THE PRIVATE HISTORY OF A CAMPAIGN THAT FAILED

(1885)

In May, 1885, an editor for the *Century* magazine asked Twain to contribute a piece to their "Battles and Leaders of the Civil War" series. Surprisingly, Twain accepted the assignment, and the reminiscence was published the following December. There were reasons he might not have wanted to write the essay. For one thing, Clemens's military history was checkered, and he had no battle experience to speak of—he participated in no skirmishes and he was certainly no military "leader." At the time of the request, he was also busy preparing *Huckleberry Finn* for publication. In addition, as it happened, his publishing firm had an agreement to publish Ulysses S. Grant's *Personal Memoirs,* and Clemens had received some criticism for this contract because Grant was a dying man and some thought he was taking advantage of the nation's war hero. Whatever his reasons for composing it, "The Private History of a Campaign That Failed" is a masterful piece of writing.

The beginnings of the war meant that Clemens's days as a riverboat pilot were over, unless he wished to remain to be impressed as a gunboat pilot for the Union, something that in no way appealed to him. He returned to Hannibal and soon joined the pro-Confederate Marion Rangers, composed mostly of his old schoolmates. Because Missouri never seceded from the Union, it is not really accurate to say Clemens served as a Confederate soldier. In any event, after only two weeks half the group disbanded, and Clemens himself traveled with his brother Orion for the Nevada Territory in July, 1865. Contrary to what he says in "The Private History," the Marion Rangers never came within "a few hours of encountering General Grant" on the battlefield. Nor, in all likelihood, was there a shooting of an innocent stranger, or any shooting at all. These were fictional touches that served the author well in burlesquing his own, brief military history, but they also served to extenuate his conduct and to present himself as one "not rightly equipped for this awful business" of war. Clemens left the war, we are to believe, in order to retain some portion of his self-respect, much as his created character Huck had decided to "light out for the territory" in order to avoid the contaminating effects of so-called "civilization."

"The Private History of a Campaign That Failed"

You have heard from a great many people who did something in the war; is it not fair and right that you listen a little moment to one who started out to do something in it, but didn't? Thousands entered the war, got just a taste of it, and then stepped out again, permanently. These, by their very numbers, are respectable, and are therefore entitled to a sort of voice,—not a loud one, but a modest one; not a boastful one, but an apologetic one. They ought not to be allowed much space among better people—people who did something—I grant that; but they ought at least to be allowed to state why they didn't do anything, and also to explain the process by which they didn't do anything. Surely this kind of light must have a sort of value.

Out West there was a good deal of confusion in men's minds during the first months of the great trouble—a good deal of unsettledness, of leaning first this way, then that, then the other way. It was hard for us to get our bearings. I call to mind an instance of this. I was piloting the Mississippi when the news came that South Carolina had gone out of the Union on the 20th of December, 1860. My pilot-mate was a New Yorker. He was strong for the Union; so was I. But he would not listen to me with any patience; my loyalty was smirched, to his eye, because my father had owned slaves. I said, in palliation of this dark fact, that I had heard my father say, some years before he died, that slavery was a great wrong, and that he would free the solitary negro he then owned if he could think it right to give away the property of the family when he was so straitened in means. My mate retorted that a mere impulse was nothing—anybody could pretend to a good impulse; and went on decrying my Unionism and libeling my ancestry. A month later the secession atmosphere had considerably thickened on the Lower Mississippi, and I became a rebel; so did he. We were together in New Orleans, the 26th of January, when Louisiana went out of the Union. He did his full share of the rebel shouting, but was bitterly opposed to letting me do mine. He said that I came of bad stock—of a father who had been willing to set slaves free. In the following summer he was piloting a Federal gunboat and shouting for the Union again, and I was in the Confederate army. I held his note for some borrowed money. He was one of the most upright men I ever knew; but he repudiated that note without hesitation, because I was a rebel, and the son of a man who owned slaves.

In that summer—of 1861—the first wash of the wave of war broke upon the shores of Missouri. Our State was invaded by the Union forces. They took possession of St. Louis, Jefferson Barracks, and some other points. The Governor, Claib Jackson, issued his proclamation calling out fifty thousand militia to repel the invader.

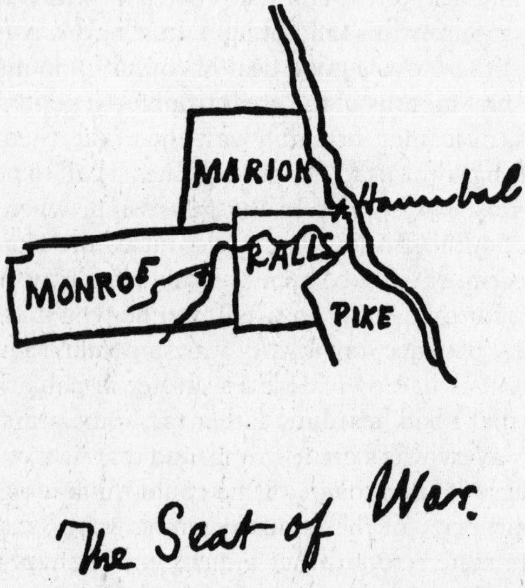

I was visiting in the small town where my boyhood had been spent—Hannibal, Marion County. Several of us got together in a secret place by night and formed ourselves into a military company. One Tom Lyman, a young fellow of a good deal of spirit but of no military experience, was made captain; I was made second lieutenant. We had no first lieutenant; I do not know why; it was long ago. There were fifteen of us. By the advice of an innocent connected with the organization, we called ourselves the Marion Rangers. I do not remember that any one found fault with the name. I did not; I thought it sounded quite well. The young fellow who proposed this title was perhaps a fair sample of the kind of stuff we were made of. He was young, ignorant, good-natured, well-meaning, trivial, full of romance, and given to reading chivalric novels and singing forlorn love-ditties. He had some pathetic little nickel-plated aristocratic instincts, and detested his name, which was Dunlap; detested it, partly because it was nearly as common in that region as Smith, but mainly because it had a plebeian sound to his ear. So he tried to ennoble it by writing it in this way: *d'Unlap*. That contented his eye, but left his ear unsatisfied, for people gave the new name the same old pronunciation—emphasis on the front end of it. He then did the bravest thing that can be imagined,—a thing to make one shiver when one remembers how the world is given to resenting shams and affectations; he began to write his name so: *d'Un Lap*. And he waited patiently through the long storm of mud that was flung at this work of art, and he had his reward at last; for he lived to see that name accepted, and the emphasis put where he wanted it, by people who had known him all his life, and to whom the tribe of Dunlaps had been as familiar as the rain and the sunshine for forty years. So sure of victory at last is the courage that can wait. He said he had found, by consulting some ancient French chronicles, that the name was rightly and originally written d'Un Lap; and said that if it were translated into English it would mean Peterson: *Lap,* Latin or Greek, he said, for stone or rock, same as the French *pierre,* that is to say, Peter; *d',* of or from; *un,* a or one; hence, d'Un Lap, of or from a stone or a Peter; that is to say, one who is the son of a stone, the son of a Peter—Peterson. Our militia company were not learned, and the explanation confused them; so they called him Peterson Dunlap. He proved useful to us in his way; he named our camps for us, and he generally struck a name that was "no slouch," as the boys said.

That is one sample of us. Another was Ed Stevens, son of the town jeweler,—trim-built, handsome, graceful, neat as a cat; bright, educated, but given over entirely to fun. There was nothing serious in life to him. As far as he was concerned, this military expedition of ours was simply a holiday. I should say that about half of us looked upon it in the same way; not consciously, perhaps, but unconsciously. We did not think; we were not capable of it. As for myself, I was full of unreasoning joy to be done with turning out of bed at midnight and four in the morning, for a while; grateful to have a change, new scenes, new occupations, a new interest. In my thoughts that was as far as I went; I did not go into the details; as a rule one doesn't at twenty-four.

Another sample was Smith, the blacksmith's apprentice. This vast donkey had some pluck, of a slow and sluggish nature, but a soft heart; at one time he would knock a horse down for some impropriety, and at another he would get homesick and cry. However, he had one ultimate credit to his account which some of us hadn't: he stuck to the war, and was killed in battle at last.

Jo Bowers, another sample, was a huge, good-natured, flax-headed lubber; lazy, sentimental, full of harmless brag, a grumbler by nature; an experienced, industrious, ambitious, and often quite picturesque liar, and yet not a successful one, for he had had no intelligent training, but was allowed to come up just any way. This life was serious enough to him, and seldom satisfactory. But he was a good fellow anyway, and the boys all liked him. He was made orderly sergeant; Stevens was made corporal.

These samples will answer—and they are quite fair ones. Well, this herd of cattle started for the war. What could you expect of them? They did as well as they knew how, but really what was justly to be expected of them? Nothing, I should say. That is what they did.

We waited for a dark night, for caution and secrecy were necessary; then, toward midnight, we stole in couples and from various directions to the Griffith place, beyond the town; from that point we set out together on foot. Hannibal lies at the extreme southeastern corner of Marion County, on the Mississippi River; our objective point was the hamlet of New London, ten miles away, in Ralls County.

The first hour was all fun, all idle nonsense and laughter. But that could not be kept up. The steady trudging came to be like work; the play had somehow oozed out of it; the stillness of the woods and the somberness of the night began to throw a depressing influence over the spirits of the boys, and presently the talking died out and each person shut himself up in his own thoughts. During the last half of the second hour nobody said a word.

Now we approached a log farm-house where, according to report, there was a guard of five Union soldiers. Lyman called a halt; and there, in the deep gloom of the overhanging branches, he began to whisper a plan of assault upon that house, which made the gloom more depressing than it was before. It was a crucial moment; we realized, with a cold suddenness, that here was no jest—we were standing face to face with actual war. We were equal to the occasion. In our response there was no hesitation, no indecision: we said that if Lyman wanted to meddle with those soldiers, he could go ahead, and do it; but if he waited for us to follow him, he would wait a long time.

Lyman urged, pleaded, tried to shame us, but it had no effect. Our course was plain, our minds were made up: we would flank the farm-house—go out around. And that is what we did.

We struck into the woods and entered upon a rough time, stumbling over roots, getting tangled in vines, and torn by briers. At last we reached an open place in a safe region, and sat down, blown and hot, to cool off and nurse our scratches and bruises. Lyman was annoyed, but the rest of us were cheerful; we had flanked the farm-house, we had made our first military movement, and it was a success; we had nothing to fret about, we were feeling just the other way. Horse-play and laughing began again; the expedition was become a holiday frolic once more.

Then we had two more hours of dull trudging and ultimate silence and depression; then, about dawn, we straggled into New London, soiled, heel-blistered, fagged with our little march, and all of us except Stevens in a sour and raspy humor and privately down on the war. We stacked our shabby old shot-guns in Colonel Ralls's barn, and then went in a body and breakfasted with that veteran of the Mexican war. Afterwards he took us to a distant meadow, and there in the shade of a tree we listened to an old-fashioned speech from him, full of gunpowder and glory, full of that adjective-piling, mixed metaphor, and windy declamation which was regarded as eloquence in that ancient time and that remote region; and then he swore us on the Bible to be faithful to the State of Missouri and drive all invaders from her soil, no matter whence they might come or under what flag they might march. This mixed us considerably, and we could not make out just what service we were embarked in; but Colonel Ralls, the practiced politician and phrase-juggler, was not similarly in doubt; he knew quite clearly that he had invested us in the cause of the Southern Confederacy. He closed the solemnities by belting around me the sword which his neighbor, Colonel Brown, had worn at Buena Vista and Molino del Rey; and he accompanied this act with another impressive blast.

Then we formed in line of battle and marched four miles to a shady and pleasant piece of woods on the border of the far-reaching expanses of a flowery prairie. It was an enchanting region for war—our kind of war.

We pierced the forest about half a mile, and took up a strong position, with some low, rocky, and wooded hills behind us, and a purling, limpid creek in front. Straightway half the command were in swimming, and the other half fishing. The ass with the French name gave this position a romantic title, but it was too long, so the boys shortened and simplified it to Camp Ralls.

We occupied an old maple-sugar camp, whose half-rotted troughs were still propped against the trees. A long corn-crib served for sleeping quarters for the battalion. On our left, half a mile away, was Mason's farm and house; and he was a friend to the cause. Shortly after noon the farmers began to arrive from several directions, with mules and horses for our use, and these they lent us for as long as the war might last, which they judged would be about three months. The animals were of all sizes, all colors, and all breeds. They were mainly young and frisky, and nobody in the command could stay on them long at a time; for we were town boys, and ignorant of horsemanship. The creature that fell to my share was a very small mule, and yet so quick and active that it could throw me without difficulty; and it did this whenever I got on it. Then it would bray—stretching its neck out, laying its ears back, and spreading its jaws till you could see down to its works. It was a disagreeable animal, in every way. If I took it by the bridle and tried to lead it off the grounds, it would sit down and brace back, and no one could budge it. However, I was not entirely destitute of military resources, and I did presently manage to spoil this game; for I had seen many a steamboat aground in my time, and knew a trick or two which even a grounded mule would be obliged to respect. There was a well by the corn-crib; so I substituted thirty fathom of rope for the bridle, and fetched him home with the windlass.

I will anticipate here sufficiently to say that we did learn to ride, after some days' practice, but never well. We could not learn to like our animals; they were not choice ones, and most of them had annoying peculiarities of one kind or another. Stevens's horse would carry him, when he was not noticing, under the huge excrescences which form on the trunks of oak-trees, and wipe him out of the saddle; in this way Stevens got several bad hurts. Sergeant Bowers's horse was very large and tall, with slim, long legs, and looked like a railroad bridge. His size enabled him to reach all about, and as far as he wanted to, with his head; so he was always biting Bowers's legs. On the march, in the sun, Bowers slept a good deal; and as soon as the horse recognized that he was asleep he would reach around and bite him on the leg. His legs were black and blue with bites. This was the only thing that could ever make him swear, but this always did; whenever the horse bit him he always swore, and of course Stevens, who laughed at everything, laughed at this, and would even get into such convulsions over it as to lose his balance and fall off his horse; and then Bowers, already irritated by the pain of the horse-bite, would resent the laughter with hard language, and there would be a quarrel; so that horse made no end of trouble and bad blood in the command.

However, I will get back to where I was—our first afternoon in the sugar-camp. The sugar-troughs came very handy as horse-troughs, and we had plenty of corn to fill them with. I ordered Sergeant Bowers to feed my mule; but he said that if I reckoned he went to war to be dry-nurse to a mule, it wouldn't take me very long to find out my mistake. I believed that this was insubordination, but I was full of uncertainties about everything military, and so I let the thing pass, and went and ordered Smith, the blacksmith's apprentice, to feed the mule; but he merely gave me a large, cold, sarcastic grin, such as an ostensibly seven-year-old horse gives you when you lift his lip and find he is fourteen, and turned his back on me. I then went to the captain, and asked if it was not right and proper and military for me to have an orderly. He said it was, but as there was only one orderly in the corps, it was but right that he himself should have Bowers on his staff. Bowers said he wouldn't serve on anybody's staff; and if anybody thought he could make him, let him try it. So, of course, the thing had to be dropped; there was no other way.

Next, nobody would cook; it was considered a degradation; so we had no dinner. We lazied the rest of the pleasant afternoon away, some dozing under the trees, some smoking cob-pipes and talking sweethearts and war, some playing games. By late suppertime all hands were famished; and to meet the difficulty all hands turned to, on an equal footing, and gathered wood, built fires, and cooked the meal. Afterward everything was smooth for a while; then trouble broke out between the corporal and the sergeant, each claiming to rank the other. Nobody knew which was the higher office; so Lyman had to settle the matter by making the rank of both officers equal. The commander of an ignorant crew like that has many troubles and vexations which probably do not occur in the regular army at all. However, with the song-singing and yarn-spinning around the camp-fire, everything presently became serene again; and by and by we raked the corn down level in one end of the crib, and all went to bed on it, tying a horse to the door, so that he would neigh if any one tried to get in.*

We had some horsemanship drill every forenoon; then, afternoons, we rode off here and there in squads a few miles, and visited the farmers' girls, and had a youthful time, and got an honest good dinner or supper, and then home again to camp, happy and content.

For a time, life was idly delicious, it was perfect; there was nothing to mar it. Then came some farmers with an alarm one day. They said it was rumored that the enemy were advancing in our direction, from over Hyde's prairie. The result was a sharp stir among us, and general consternation. It was a rude awakening from our pleasant trance. The rumor was but a rumor—nothing definite about it; so, in the confusion, we did not know which way to retreat. Lyman was for not retreating at all, in these uncertain circumstances; but he found that if he tried to maintain that attitude he would fare badly, for the command were in no humor to put up with insubordination. So he yielded the point and called a council of war—to consist of himself and the three other officers; but the privates made such a fuss about being left out, that we had to allow them to be present. I mean we had to allow them to remain, for they were already present, and doing the most of the talking too. The question was, which way to retreat; but all were so flurried that nobody seemed to have even a guess to offer. Except Lyman. He explained in a few calm words, that inasmuch as the

*It was always my impression that that was what the horse was there for, and I know that it was also the impression of at least one other of the command, for we talked about it at the time, and admired the military ingenuity of the device; but when I was out West three years ago I was told by Mr. A. G. Fuqua, a member of our company, that the horse was his, that the leaving him tied at the door was a matter of mere forgetfulness, and that to attribute it to intelligent invention was to give him quite too much credit. In support of his position, he called my attention to the suggestive fact that the artifice was not employed again. I had not thought of that before.

enemy were approaching from over Hyde's prairie, our course was simple: all we had to do was not to retreat *toward* him; any other direction would answer our needs perfectly. Everybody saw in a moment how true this was, and how wise; so Lyman got a great many compliments. It was now decided that we should fall back on Mason's farm.

It was after dark by this time, and as we could not know how soon the enemy might arrive, it did not seem best to try to take the horses and things with us; so we only took the guns and ammunition, and started at once. The route was very rough and hilly and rocky, and presently the night grew black and rain began to fall; so we had a troublesome time of it, struggling and stumbling along in the dark; and soon some person slipped and fell, and then the next person behind stumbled over him and fell, and so did the rest, one after the other; and then Bowers came with the keg of powder in his arms, whilst the command were all mixed together, arms and legs, on the muddy slope; and so he fell, of course, with the keg, and this started the whole detachment down the hill in a body, and they landed in the brook at the bottom in a pile, and each that was undermost pulling the hair and scratching and biting those that were on top of him; and those that were being scratched and bitten scratching and biting the rest in their turn, and all saying they would die before they would ever go to war again if they ever got out of this brook this time, and the invader might rot for all they cared, and the country along with him—and all such talk as that, which was dismal to hear and take part in, in such smothered, low voices, and such a grisly dark place and so wet, and the enemy may be coming any moment.

The keg of powder was lost, and the guns too; so the growling and complaining continued straight along whilst the brigade pawed around the pasty hillside and slopped around in the brook hunting for these things; consequently we lost considerable time at this; and then we heard a sound, and held our breath and listened, and it seemed to be the enemy coming, though it could have been a cow, for it had a cough like a cow; but we did not wait, but left a couple of guns behind and struck out for Mason's again as briskly as we could scramble along in the dark. But we got lost presently among the rugged little ravines, and wasted a deal of time finding the way again, so it was after nine when we reached Mason's stile at last; and then before we could open our mouths to give the countersign, several dogs came bounding over the fence, with great riot and noise, and each of them took a soldier by the slack of his trousers and began to back away with him. We could not shoot the dogs without endangering the persons they were attached to; so we had to look on, helpless, at what was perhaps the most mortifying spectacle of the civil war. There was light enough, and to spare, for the Masons had now run out on the porch with candles in their hands. They old man and his son came and undid the dogs without difficulty, all but Bowers's; but they couldn't undo his dog, they didn't know his combination; he was of the bull kind, and seemed to be set with a Yale time-lock; but they got him loose at last with some scalding water, of which Bowers got his share and returned thanks. Peterson Dunlap afterwards made up a fine name for this engagement, and also for the night march which preceded it, but both have long ago faded out of my memory.

We now went into the house, and they began to ask us a world of questions, whereby it presently came out that we did not know anything concerning who or what we were running from; so the old gentleman made himself very frank, and said we were a curious breed of soldiers, and guessed we could be depended on to end up the war in time, because no government could stand the expense of the shoe-leather we should cost it trying to follow us around. "Marion *Rangers!* good name, b'gosh!" said he. And wanted to know why we hadn't had a picket-guard at the place where the road entered the prairie, and why we hadn't sent out a scouting party to spy out the enemy and bring us an account of his strength, and so on, before jumping up and stampeding out of a strong position upon a mere vague rumor—and so on and so forth, till he made us all feel shabbier than the dogs had done, not half so enthusiastically welcome. So we went to bed shamed and low-spirited; except Stevens. Soon Stevens began to devise a garment for Bowers which could be made to automatically display his battle-scars to the grateful, or conceal them from the envious, according to his occasions; but Bowers was in no humor for this, so there was a fight, and when it was over Stevens had some battle-scars of his own to think about.

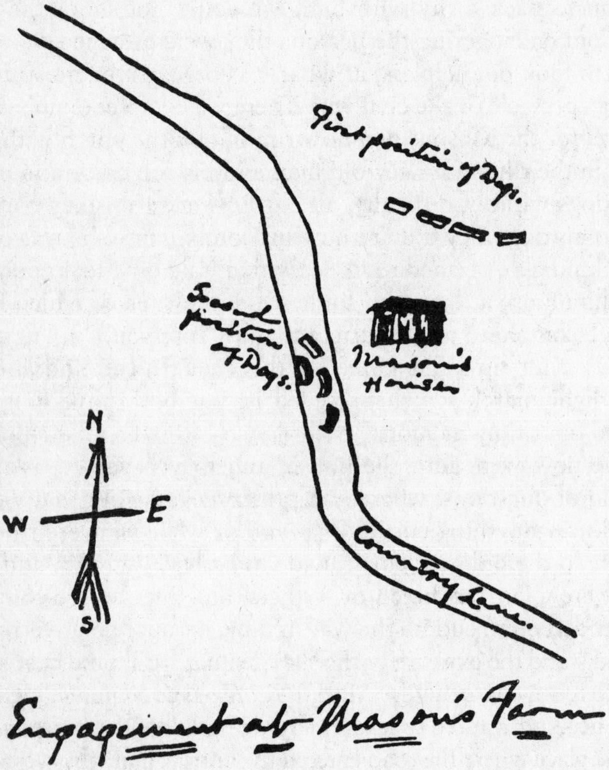

Then we got a little sleep. But after all we had gone through, our activities were not over for the night; for about two o'clock in the morning we heard a shout of warning from down the lane, accompanied by a chorus from all the dogs, and in a moment everybody was up and flying around to find out what the alarm was about. The alarmist was a horseman who gave notice that a detachment of Union soldiers was on its way from Hannibal with orders to capture and hang any bands like ours which it could find, and said we had no time to lose. Farmer Mason was in a flurry this time, himself. He hurried us out of the house with all haste, and sent one of his negroes with us to show us where to hide ourselves and our tell-tale guns among the ravines half a mile away. It was raining heavily.

We struck down the lane, then across some rocky pasture-land which offered good advantages for stumbling; consequently we were down in the mud most of the time, and every time a man went down he blackguarded the war, and the people that started it, and everybody connected with it, and gave himself the master dose of all for being so foolish as to go into it. At last we reached the wooded mouth of a ravine, and there we huddled ourselves under the streaming trees, and sent the negro back home. It was a dismal and heart-breaking time. We were like to be drowned with the rain, deafened with the howling wind and the booming thunder, and blinded by the lightning. It was indeed a wild night. The drenching we were getting was misery enough, but a deeper misery still was the reflection that the halter might end us before we were a day older. A death of this shameful sort had not occurred to us as being among the possibilities of war. It took the romance all out of the campaign, and turned our dreams of glory into a repulsive nightmare. As for doubting that so barbarous an order had been given, not one of us did that.

The long night wore itself out at last, and then the negro came to us with the news that the alarm had manifestly been a false one, and that breakfast would soon be ready. Straightaway we were light-hearted again, and the world was bright, and life as full of hope and promise as ever—for we were young then. How long ago that was! Twenty-four years.

The mongrel child of philology named the night's refuge Camp Devastation, and no soul objected. The Masons gave us a Missouri country breakfast, in Missourian abundance, and we needed it: hot biscuits; hot "wheat bread" prettily criss-crossed in a lattice pattern on top; hot corn pone; fried chicken; bacon, coffee, eggs, milk, buttermilk, etc.;—and the world may be confidently challenged to furnish the equal to such a breakfast, as it is cooked in the South.

We staid several days at Mason's; and after all these years the memory of the dullness, the stillness and lifelessness of that slumberous farm-house still oppresses my spirit as with a sense of the presence of death and mourning. There was nothing to do, nothing to think about; there was no interest in life. The male part of the household were away in the fields all day, the women were busy and out of our sight; there was no sound but the plaintive wailing of a spinning-wheel, forever moaning out from some distant room,—the most lonesome sound in nature, a sound steeped and sodden with homesickness and the emptiness of life. The family went to bed about dark every night, and as we were not invited to intrude any new customs, we naturally followed theirs. Those nights were a hundred years long to youths accustomed to being up till twelve. We lay awake and miserable till that hour every time, and grew old and decrepit waiting through the still eternities for the clock-strikes. This was no place for town boys. So at last it was with something very like joy that we received news that the enemy were on our track again. With a new birth of the old warrior spirit, we sprang to our places in line of battle and fell back on Camp Ralls.

Captain Lyman had taken a hint from Mason's talk, and he now gave orders that our camp should be guarded against surprise by the posting of pickets. I was ordered to place a picket at the forks of the road in Hyde's prairie. Night shut down black and threatening. I told Sergeant Bowers to go out to that place and stay till midnight; and, just as I was expecting, he said he wouldn't do it. I tried to get others to go, but all refused. Some excused themselves on account of the weather; but the rest were frank enough to say they wouldn't go in any kind of weather. This kind of thing sounds odd now, and impossible, but there was no surprise in it at the time. On the contrary, it seemed a perfectly natural thing to do. There were scores of little camps scattered over Missouri where the same thing was happening. These camps were composed of young men who had been born and reared to a sturdy independence, and who did not know what it meant to be ordered around by Tom, Dick, and Harry, whom they had known familiarly all their lives, in the village or on the farm. It is quite within the probabilities that this same thing was happening all over the South. James Redpath recognized the justice of this assumption, and furnished the following instance in support of it. During a short stay in East Tennessee he was in a citizen colonel's tent one day, talking, when a big private appeared at the door, and without salute or other circumlocution said to the colonel:

"Say, Jim, I'm a-goin' home for a few days."

"What for?"

"Well, I hain't b'en there for a right smart while, and I'd like to see how things is comin' on."

"How long are you going to be gone?"

"'Bout two weeks."

"Well, don't be gone longer than that; and get back sooner if you can."

That was all, and the citizen officer resumed his conversation where the private had broken it off. This was in the first months of the war, of course. The camps in our part of Missouri were under Brigadier-General Thomas H. Harris. He was a townsman of ours, a first-rate fellow, and well liked; but we had all familiarly known him as the sole and modest-salaried operator in our telegraph office, where he had to send about one dispatch a week in ordinary times, and two when there was a rush of business; consequently, when he appeared in our midst one day, on the wing, and delivered a military command of some sort, in a large military fashion, nobody was surprised at the response which he got from the assembled soldiery:

"Oh, now, what'll you take to *don't,* Tom Harris!"

It was quite the natural thing. One might justly imagine that we were hopeless material for war. And so we seemed, in our ignorant state; but there were those among us who afterward learned the grim trade; learned to obey like machines; became valuable soldiers; fought all through the war, and came out at the end with excellent records. One of the very boys who refused to go out on picket duty that night, and called me an ass for thinking he would expose himself to danger in such a foolhardy way, had become distinguished for intrepidity before he was a year older.

I did secure my picket that night—not by authority, but by diplomacy. I got Bowers to go, by agreeing to exchange ranks with him for the time being, and go along and stand the watch with him as his subordinate. We staid out there a couple of dreary hours in the pitchy darkness and the rain, with nothing to modify the dreariness but Bowers's monotonous growlings at the war and the weather; then we began to nod, and presently found it next to impossible to stay in the saddle; so we gave up the tedious job, and went back to the camp without waiting for the relief guard. We rode into camp without interruption or objection from anybody, and the enemy could have done the same, for there were no sentries. Everybody was asleep; at midnight there was nobody to send out another picket, so none was sent. We never tried to establish a watch at night again, as far as I can remember, but we generally kept a picket out in the daytime.

In that camp the whole command slept on the corn in the big corn-crib; and there was usually a general row before morning, for the place was full of rats, and they would scramble over the boys' bodies and faces, annoying and irritating everybody; and now and then they would bite some one's toe, and the person who owned the toe would start up and magnify his English and begin to throw corn in the dark. The ears were half as heavy as bricks, and when they struck they hurt. The persons struck would respond, and inside of five minutes every man would be locked in a death-grip with his neighbor. There was a grievous deal of blood shed in the corn-crib, but this was all that was spilt while I was in the war. No, that is not quite true. But for one circumstance it would have been all. I will come to that now.

Our scares were frequent. Every few days rumors would come that the enemy were approaching. In these cases we always fell back on some other camp of ours; we never staid where we were. But the rumors always turned out to be false; so at last even we began to grow indifferent with them. One night a negro was sent to our corn-crib with the same old warning: the enemy was hovering in our neighborhood. We all said let him hover. We resolved to stay still and be comfortable.

It was a fine warlike resolution, and no doubt we all felt the stir of it in our veins—for a moment. We had been having a very jolly time, that was full of horse-play and school-boy hilarity; but that cooled down now, and presently the fast-waning fire of forced jokes and forced laughs died out altogether, and the company became silent. Silent and nervous. And soon uneasy—worried—apprehensive. We had said we would stay, and we were committed. We could have been persuaded to go, but there was nobody brave enough to suggest it. An almost noiseless movement presently began in the dark, by a general but unvoiced impulse. When the movement was completed, each man knew that he was not the only person who had crept to the front wall and had his eye at a crack between the logs. No, we were all there; all there with our hearts in our throats, and staring out toward the sugar-troughs where the forest foot-path came through. It was late, and there was a deep woodsy stillness everywhere. There was a veiled moonlight, which was only just strong enough to enable us to mark the general shape of objects. Presently a muffled sound caught our ears, and we recognized it as the hoof-beats of a horse or horses. And right away a figure appeared in the forest path; it could have been made of smoke, its mass had so little sharpness of outline. It was a man on horseback; and it seemed to me that there were others behind him. I got hold of a gun in the dark, and pushed it through a crack between the logs, hardly knowing what I was doing, I was so dazed with fright. Somebody said, "Fire!" I pulled the trigger. I seemed to see a hundred flashes and hear a hundred reports, then I saw the man fall down out of the saddle. My first feeling was of surprised gratification; my first impulse was an apprentice-sportsman's impulse to run and pick up his game. Somebody said, hardly audibly, "Good—we've got him!—wait for the rest." But the rest did not come. We waited—listened—still no more came. There was not a sound, not the whisper of a leaf; just perfect stillness; an uncanny kind of stillness, which was all the more uncanny on account of the damp, earthy, late-night smells now rising and pervading it. Then, wondering, we crept stealthily out, and approached the man. When we got to him the moon revealed him distinctly. He was lying on his back, with his arms abroad; his mouth was open and his chest heaving with long gasps, and his white shirt-front was all splashed with blood. The thought shot through me that I was a murderer; that I had killed a man—a man who had never done me any harm. That was the coldest sensation that ever went through my marrow. I was down by him in a moment, helplessly stroking his forehead; and I would have given anything then—my own life freely—to make him again what he had been five minutes before. And all the boys seemed to be feeling in the same way; they hung over him, full of pitying interest, and tried all they could to help him, and said all sorts of regretful things. They had forgotten all about the enemy; they thought only of this one forlorn unit of the foe. Once my imagination persuaded me that the dying man gave me a reproachful look out of his shadowy eyes, and it seemed to me that I would rather he had stabbed me than done that. He muttered and mumbled like a dreamer in his sleep, about his wife and his child; and I thought with a new despair, "This thing that I have done does not end with him; it falls upon *them* too, and they never did me any harm, any more than he."

In a little while the man was dead. He was killed in war; killed in fair and legitimate war; killed in battle, as you may say; and yet he was as sincerely mourned by the opposing force as if he had been their brother. The boys stood there a half hour sorrowing over him, and recalling the details of the tragedy, and wondering who he might be, and if he were a spy, and saying that if it were to do over again they would not hurt him unless he attacked them first. It soon came out that mine was not the only shot fired; there were five others,—a division of the guilt which was a grateful relief to me, since it in some degree lightened and diminished the burden I was carrying. There were six shots fired at once; but I was not in my right mind at the time, and my heated imagination had magnified my one shot into a volley.

The man was not in uniform, and was not armed. He was a stranger in the country; that was all we ever found out about him. The thought of him got to preying upon me every night; I could not get rid of it. I could not drive it away, the taking of the unoffending life seemed such a wanton thing. And it seemed an epitome of war; that all war must be just that—the killing of strangers against whom you feel no personal animosity; strangers whom, in other circumstances, you would help if you found them in trouble, and who would help you if you needed it. My campaign was spoiled. It seemed to me that I was not rightly equipped for this awful business; that war was intended for men, and I for a child's nurse. I resolved to retire from this avocation of sham soldiership while I could save some remnant of my self-respect. These morbid thoughts clung to me against reason; for at bottom I did not believe I had touched that man. The law of probabilities decreed me guiltless of his blood; for in all my small experience with guns I had never hit anything I had tried to hit, and I knew I had done my best to hit him. Yet there was no solace in the thought. Against a diseased imagination, demonstration goes for nothing.

The rest of my war experience was of a piece with what I have already told of it. We kept monotonously falling back upon one camp or another, and eating up the country. I marvel now at the patience of the farmers and their families. They ought to have shot us; on the contrary, they were as hospitably kind and courteous to us as if we had deserved it. In one of these camps we found Ab Grimes, an Upper Mississippi pilot, who afterwards became famous as a dare-devil rebel spy, whose career bristled with desperate adventures. The look and style of his comrades suggested that they had not come into the war to play, and their deeds made good the conjecture later. They were fine horsemen and good revolver-shots; but their favorite arm was the lasso. Each had one at his pommel, and could snatch a man out of the saddle with it every time, on a full gallop, at any reasonable distance.

In another camp the chief was a fierce and profane old blacksmith of sixty, and he had furnished his twenty recruits with gigantic home-made bowie-knives, to be swung with two hands, like the *machetes* of the Isthmus. It was a grisly spectacle to see that earnest band practicing their murderous cuts and slashes under the eye of that remorseless old fanatic.

The last camp which we fell back upon was in a hollow near

the village of Florida, where I was born—in Monroe County. Here we were warned, one day, that a Union colonel was sweeping down on us with a whole regiment at his heels. This looked decidedly serious. Our boys went apart and consulted; then we went back and told the other companies present that the war was a disappointment to us and we were going to disband. They were getting ready, themselves, to fall back on some place or other, and were only waiting for General Tom Harris, who was expected to arrive at any moment; so they tried to persuade us to wait a little while, but the majority of us said no, we were accustomed to falling back, and didn't need any of Tom Harris's help; we could get along perfectly well without him—and save time too. So about half of our fifteen, including myself, mounted and left on the instant; the others yielded to persuasion and staid—staid through the war.

An hour later we met General Harris on the road, with two or three people in his company—his staff, probably, but we could not tell; none of them were in uniform; uniforms had not come into vogue among us yet. Harris ordered us back; but we told him there was a Union colonel coming with a whole regiment in his wake, and it looked as if there was going to be a disturbance; so we had concluded to go home. He raged a little, but it was of no use; our minds were made up. We had done our share; had killed one man, exterminated one army, such as it was; let him go and kill the rest, and that would end the war. I did not see that brisk young general again until last year; then he was wearing white hair and whiskers.

In time I came to know that Union colonel whose coming frightened me out of the war and crippled the Southern cause to that extent—General Grant. I came within a few hours of seeing him when he was as unknown as I was myself; at a time when anybody could have said, "Grant?—Ulysses S. Grant? I do not remember hearing the name before." It seems difficult to realize that there was once a time when such a remark could be rationally made; but there *was,* and I was within a few miles of the place and the occasion too, though proceeding in the other direction.

The thoughtful will not throw this war-paper of mine lightly aside as being valueless. It has this value: it is a not unfair picture of what went on in many and many a militia camp in the first months of the rebellion, when the green recruits were without discipline, without the steadying and heartening influence of trained leaders; when all their circumstances were new and strange, and charged with exaggerated terrors, and before the invaluable experience of actual collision in the field had turned them from rabbits into soldiers. If this side of the picture of that early day has not before been put into history, then history has been to that degree incomplete, for it had and has its rightful place there. There was more Bull Run material scattered through the early camps of this country than exhibited itself at Bull Run. And yet it learned its trade presently, and helped to fight the great battles later. I could have become a soldier myself, if I had waited. I had got part of it learned; I knew more about retreating than the man that invented retreating.

FROM

A CONNECTICUT YANKEE IN KING ARTHUR'S COURT

(1889)

Twain was an avid reader of history and knew much about feudalism and Arthurian legend before he read Thomas Malory's *Le Morte D'Arthur,* the book that inspired *A Connecticut Yankee in King Arthur's Court.* In 1884, Clemens and George Washington Cable were on a joint lecture tour, and, while browsing in a bookstore, Cable encouraged Clemens to buy the volume, for he was sure Clemens would find it fascinating. Cable was right. Twain praised Malory's description of the death of Arthur as "one of the most beautiful things ever written in English, and written when we had no vocabulary."

When Twain began in earnest to write his novel, he envisioned a comic fable about a nineteenth-century man, Hank Morgan, who awakes in sixth-century England. By pretending to have supernatural powers, including blotting out the sun (he knows that an eclipse is about to occur), Morgan escapes death and acquires authority second only to the King. He becomes known as "the Boss" and undertakes to quietly transform the kingdom into a modern republic. The novel soon becomes a satire of feudalism, aristocracy, and established religion, and then a double-edged satire, in which nineteenth-century survivals of the same tendencies toward oppression, demagoguery, greed, and sham are also ridiculed. In the end, Hank Morgan and his small band of allies do battle against all of England. In the "battle of the sand belt," Morgan's technological sophistication gives him a clear advantage, and he kills around 25,000 knights with alarming efficiency. Modern readers have tended to view this ending as apocalyptic, though there is little evidence that Twain's contemporaries read the book this way.

Just prior to the first excerpt below, Demoiselle Alisande la Carteloise has come to court and announced that an ogre has imprisoned her mistress and forty-four beautiful young women. King Arthur appoints Morgan to go on an expedition to free them. Outfitted in the metal garb of a knight errant, he travels with the woman he has come to call "Sandy" in search of the ogre's castle. (The imprisoned women, it turns out, are in fact hogs kept by a swineherd.) In the second excerpt, Hank learns that a sacred fountain has stopped flowing and that his arch enemy, Merlin, is attempting to restore the fountain through incantation. Hank discovers that the problem is a simple leak in the well, but before repairing the fountain himself, Morgan allows Merlin to wear himself out trying his magic. Meanwhile, Hank and Sandy take in the sights, including the local hermits.

"The Yankee in Search of Adventures"

My expedition was all the talk that day and that night, and the boys were very good to me, and made much of me, and seemed to have forgotten their vexation and disappointment, and come to be as anxious for me to hive those ogres and set those ripe old virgins loose as if it were themselves that had the contract. Well, they *were* good children—but just children, that is all. And they gave me no end of points about how to scout for giants, and how to scoop them in; and they told me all sorts of charms against enchantments, and gave me salves and other rubbish to put on my wounds. But it never occurred to one of them to reflect that if I was such a wonderful necromancer as I was pretending to be, I ought not to need salves or instructions, or charms against enchantments, and least of all, arms and armor, on a foray of any kind—even against fire-spouting dragons, and devils hot from perdition, let alone such poor adversaries as these I was after, these commonplace ogres of the back settlements.

I was to have an early breakfast, and start at dawn, for that was the usual way; but I had the demon's own time with my armor, and this delayed me a little. It is troublesome to get into, and there is so much detail. First you wrap a layer or two of blanket around your body, for a sort of cushion to keep off the cold iron; then you put on your sleeves and shirt of chain-mail—these are made of small steel links woven together, and they form a fabric so flexible that if you toss your shirt onto the floor, it slumps into a pile like a peck of wet fish-net; it is very heavy and is nearly the uncomfortablest material in the world for a night-shirt, yet plenty used it for that—tax collectors, and reformers, and one-horse kings with a defective title, and those sorts of people; then you put on your shoes—flat-boats roofed over with interleaving bands of steel—and screw your clumsy spurs into the heels. Next you buckle your greaves on your legs, and your cuisses on your thighs; then come your back-plate and your breastplate, and you begin to feel crowded; then you hitch onto the breastplate the half-petticoat of broad overlapping bands of steel which hangs down in front but is scolloped out behind so you can sit down, and isn't any real improvement on an inverted coal scuttle, either for looks or for wear, or to wipe your hands on; next you belt on your sword; then you put your stove-pipe joints onto your arms, your iron gauntlets onto your hands, your iron rat-trap onto your head, with a rag of steel web hitched onto it to hang over the back of your neck—and there you are, snug as a candle in a candle-mould. This is no time to dance. Well, a man that is packed away like that, is a nut that isn't worth the cracking, there is so little of the meat, when you get down to it, by comparison with the shell.

The boys helped me, or I never could have got in. Just as we finished, Sir Bedivere happened in, and I saw that as like as not I hadn't chosen the most convenient outfit for a long trip. How stately he looked; and tall and broad and grand. He had on his head a conical steel casque that only came down to his ears, and for visor had only a narrow steel bar that extended down to his upper lip and protected his nose; and all the rest of him, from neck to heel, was flexible chain-mail, trowsers and all. But pretty much all of him was hidden under his outside garment, which of course was of chain-mail, as I said, and hung straight from his shoulders to his ancles; and from his middle to the bottom, both before and behind, was divided, so that he could ride and let the skirts hang down on each side. He was going grailing, and it was just the outfit for it, too. I would have given a good deal for that ulster, but it was too late now to be fooling around. The sun was just up, the king and the court were all on hand to see me off and wish me luck; so it wouldn't be etiquette for me to tarry. You don't get on your horse yourself; no, if you tried it you would get disappointed. They carry you out, just as they carry a sun-struck man to the drug store, and put you on, and help get you to rights, and fix your feet in the stirrups; and all the while you do feel so strange and stuffy and like somebody else—like somebody that has been married on a sudden, or struck by lightning, or something like that, and hasn't quite fetched around, yet, and is sort of numb, and can't just get his bearings. Then they stood up the mast they called a spear, in its socket by my left foot, and I gripped it with my hand; lastly they hung my shield around my neck, and I was all complete and ready to up anchor and get to sea. Everybody was as good to me as they could be, and a maid of honor gave me the stirrup-cup her own self. There was nothing more to do, now, but for that damsel to get up behind me on a pillion, which she did, and put an arm or so around me to hold on.

And so we started; and everybody gave us a good-bye and waved their handkerchiefs or helmets. And everybody we met, going down the hill and through the village was respectful to us, except some shabby little boys on the outskirts. They said—

"Oh, what a guy!" And hove clods at us.

In my experience boys are the same in all ages. They don't respect anything, they don't care for anything or anybody. They say "Go up, baldhead" to the prophet going his unoffending way in the gray of antiquity; they sass me in the holy gloom of the Middle Ages; and I had seen them act the same way in Buchanan's administration; I remember, because I was there and helped. The prophet had his bears and settled with his boys; and I wanted to get down and settle with mine, but it wouldn't answer, because I couldn't have got up again. I hate a country without a derrick.

Straight off, we were in the country. It was mostly lovely and pleasant in those sylvan solitudes in the early cool morning in the first freshness of autumn. From hilltops we saw fair green valleys lying spread out below, with streams winding through them, and island-groves of trees here and there, and huge lonely oaks scattered about and casting black blots of shade; and beyond the valleys we saw the ranges of hills, blue with haze, stretching away in billowy perspective to the horizon, with at wide intervals a dim fleck of white or gray on a wave-summit, which we knew was a castle. We crossed broad natural lawns sparkling with dew, and we moved like spirits, the cushioned turf giving out no sound of foot-fall; we dreamed along through glades in a mist of green light that got its tint from the sun-drenched roof of leaves overhead, and by our feet the clearest and coldest of runlets went frisking and gossiping over its reefs and making a sort of whispering music comfortable to hear; and at times we left the world behind and entered into the solemn great deeps and rich gloom of the forest, where furtive wild things whisked and scurried by and were gone before you could even get your eye on the place where the noise was; and where only the earliest birds were turning out and getting to business with a song here and a quarrel yonder and a mysterious far-off hammering and drumming for worms on a tree-trunk away somewhere in the impenetrable remotenesses of the woods. And by and by out we would swing again into the glare.

About the third or fourth or fifth time we swung out into the glare—it was along there somewhere, a couple of hours or so after sun-up—it wasn't as pleasant as it had been. It was beginning to get hot. This was quite noticeable. We had a very long pull, after that, without any shade. Now it is curious how progressively little frets grow and multiply after they once get a start. Things which I didn't mind at all, at first, I began to mind now—and more and more, too, all the time. The first ten or fifteen times I wanted my handkerchief I didn't seem to care; I got along, and said never mind, it isn't any matter, and dropped it out of my mind. But now it was different; I wanted it all the time; it was nag, nag, nag, right alone, and no rest; I couldn't get it out of my mind; and so at last I lost my temper and said hang a man that would make a suit or armor without any pockets in it. You see I had my handkerchief in my helmet; and some other things; but it was that kind of a helmet that you can't take off by yourself. That hadn't occurred to me when I put it there; and in fact I didn't know it. I supposed it would be particularly convenient there. And so now, the thought of its being there, so handy and close by, and yet not get-at-able, made it all the worse and the harder to bear. Yes, the thing that you can't get is the thing that you want, mainly; everyone has noticed that. Well, it took my mind off from everything else; took it clear off, and centred it in my helmet; and mile after mile, there it staid, imagining the handkerchief, picturing the handkerchief; and it was bitter and aggravating to have the salt sweat keep trickling down into my eyes, and I couldn't get at it. It seems like a little thing, on paper, but it was not a little thing at all; it was the most real kind of misery. I would not say it if it was not so. I made up my mind that I would carry along a reticule next time, let it look how it might, and people say what they would. Of course these iron dudes of the Round Table would think it was scandalous, and maybe raise Sheol about it, but as for me, give me comfort first, and style afterwards. So we jogged along, and now and then we struck a stretch of dust, and it would tumble up in clouds and get into my nose and make me sneeze and cry; and of course I said things I oughtn't to have said, I don't deny that. I am not better than others. We couldn't seem to meet anybody in this lonesome Britain, not even an ogre; and in the mood I was in then, it was well for the ogre; that is, an ogre with a handkerchief. Most knights would have thought of nothing but getting his armor; but so I got his bandanna, he could keep his hardware, for all me.

Meantime it was getting hotter and hotter in there. You see, the sun was beating down and warming up the iron more and more all the time. Well, when you are hot, that way, every little thing irritates you. When I trotted, I rattled like a crate of dishes, and that annoyed me; and moreover I couldn't seem to stand that shield slatting and banging, now about my breast, now around my back; and if I dropped into a walk my joints creaked and screeched in that wearisome way that a wheelbarrow does, and as we didn't create any breeze at that gait, I was like to get fried in that stove; and besides, the quieter you went the heavier the iron settled down on you and the more and more tons you seemed to weigh every minute. And you had to be always changing hands, and passing your spear over to the other foot, it got so irksome for one hand to hold it long at a time.

Well, you know, when you perspire that way, in rivers, there comes a time when you—when you—well, when you itch. You are inside, your hands are outside; so there you are; nothing but iron between. It is not a light thing, let it sound as it may. First it is one place; then another; then some more; and it goes on spreading and spreading, and at last the territory is all occupied, and nobody can imagine what you feel like, nor how unpleasant it is. And when it had got to the worst, and it seemed to me that I could not stand anything more, a fly got in through the bars and settled on my nose, and the bars were stuck and wouldn't work, and I couldn't get the visor up; and I could only shake my head, which was baking hot by this time, and the fly—well, you know how a fly acts when he has got a certainty—he only minded the shaking enough to change from nose to lip, and lip to ear, and buzz and buzz all around in there, and keep on lighting and biting, in a way that a person already so distressed as I was, simply could not stand. So I gave in, and got Alisande to unship the helmet and relieve me of it. Then she emptied the conveniences out of it and fetched it full of water, and I drank and then stood up and she poured the rest down inside the armor. One cannot think how refreshing it was. She continued to fetch and pour until I was well soaked and thoroughly comfortable.

It was good to have a rest—and peace. But nothing is quite perfect in this life, at any time. I had made a pipe a while back, and also some pretty fair tobacco; not the real thing, but what some of the Indians use: the inside bark of the willow, dried. These comforts had been in the helmet, and now I had them again, but no matches.

Gradually, as the time wore along, one annoying fact was borne in upon my understanding—that we were weather-bound. An armed novice cannot mount his horse without help and plenty of it. Sandy was not enough; not enough for me, anyway. We had to wait until somebody should come along. Waiting, in silence, would have been agreeable enough, for I was full of matter for reflection, and wanted to give it a chance to work. I wanted to try and think out how it was that rational or even half-rational men could ever have learned to wear armor, considering its inconveniences; and how they had managed to keep up such a fashion for generations when it was plain that what I had suffered to-day they had had to suffer all the days of their lives. I wanted to think that out; and moreover I wanted to think out some way to reform this evil and persuade the people to let the foolish fashion die out; but thinking was out of the question in the circumstances. You couldn't think, where Sandy was. She was a quite biddable creature and good-hearted, but she had a flow of talk that was as steady as a mill, and made your head sore like the drays and wagons in a city. If she had had a cork she would have been a comfort. But you can't cork that kind; they would die. Her clack was going all day, and you would think something would surely happen to her works, by and by; but no, they never got out of order; and she never had to slack up for words. She could grind, and pump, and churn and buzz by the week, and never stop to oil up or blow out. And yet the result was just nothing but wind. She never had any ideas, any more than a fog has. She was a perfect blatherskite; I mean for jaw, jaw, jaw, talk, talk, talk, jabber, jabber, jabber; but just as good as she could be. I hadn't minded her mill that morning, on account of having that hornet's nest of other troubles; but more than once in the afternoon I had to say—

"Take a rest, child; the way you are using up all the domestic air, the kingdom will have to go to importing it by to-morrow, and it's a low enough treasury without that."

"The Holy Fountain"

I was at the well next day betimes. Merlin was there, enchanting away like a beaver, but not raising the moisture. He was not in a pleasant humor; and every time I hinted that perhaps this contract was a shade too hefty for a novice he unlimbered his tongue and cursed like a bishop—French bishop of the Regency days, I mean.

Matters were about as I expected to find them. The "fountain" was an ordinary well, it had been dug in the ordinary way, and stoned up in the ordinary way. There was no miracle about it. Even the lie that had created its reputation was not miraculous; I could have told it myself, with one hand tied behind me. The well was in a dark chamber which stood in the centre of a cut-stone chapel, whose walls were hung with pious pictures of a workmanship that would have made a chromo feel good; pictures historically commemorative of curative miracles which had been achieved by the waters when nobody was looking. That is, nobody but angels: they were always on deck when there is a miracle to the fore—so as to get put in the picture, perhaps. Angels are as fond of that as a fire company; look at the old masters.

The well-chamber was dimly lighted by lamps; the water was drawn with a windlass and chain, by monks, and poured into troughs which delivered it into stone reservoirs outside, in the chapel—when there was water to draw, I mean—and none but monks could enter the well-chamber. I entered it, for I had temporary authority to do so, by courtesy of my professional brother and subordinate. But he hadn't entered it himself. He did everything by incantations; he never worked his intellect. If he had stepped in there and used his eyes, instead of his disordered mind, he could have cured the well by natural means, and then turned it into a miracle in the customary way; but no, he was an old numskull, a magician who believed in his own magic; and no magician can thrive who is handicapped with a superstition like that.

I had an idea that the well had sprung a leak; that some of the wall stones near the bottom had fallen and exposed fissures that allowed the water to escape. I measured the chain—98 feet. Then I called in a couple of monks, locked the door, took a candle, and made them lower me in the bucket. When the chain was all paid out, the candle confirmed my suspicion; a considerable section of the wall was gone, exposing a good big fissure.

I almost regretted that my theory about the well's trouble was correct, because I had another one that had a showy point or two about it for a miracle. I remembered that in America, many centuries later, when an oil well ceased to flow, they used to blast it out with a dynamite torpedo. If I should find this well dry, and no explanation of it, I could astonish these people most nobly by having a person of no especial value drop a dynamite bomb into it. It was my idea to appoint Merlin. However, it was plain that there was no occasion for the bomb. One cannot have everything the way he would like it. A man has no business to be depressed by a disappointment, anyway; he ought to make up his mind to get even. That is what I did. I said to myself, I am in no hurry, I can wait; that bomb will come good, yet. And it did, too.

When I was above ground again, I turned out the monks, and let down a fish-line: the well was a hundred and fifty feet deep, and there was forty-one feet of water in it! I called in a monk and asked:

"How deep is the well?"

"That, sir, I wit not, having never been told."

"How does the water usually stand in it?"

"Near to the top, these two centuries, as the testimony goeth, brought down to us through our predecessors."

It was true—as to recent times at least—for there was witness to it, and better witness than a monk: only about twenty or thirty feet of the chain showed wear and use, the rest of it was unworn and rusty. What had happened when the well gave out that other time? Without doubt some practical person had come along and mended the leak, and then had come up and told the abbot he had discovered by divination that if the sinful bath were destroyed the well would flow again. The leak had befallen again, now, and these children would have prayed, and processioned, and tolled their bells for heavenly succor till they all dried up and blew away, and no innocent of them all would ever have thought to drop a fish-line into the well or go down in it and find out what was really the matter. Old habit of mind is one of the toughest things to get away from in the world. It transmits itself like physical form and feature; and for a man, in those days, to have had an idea that his ancestors hadn't had, would have brought him under suspicion of being illegitimate. I said to the monk:

"It is a difficult miracle to restore water in a dry well, but we will try, if my brother Merlin fails. Brother Merlin is a very passable artist, but only in the parlor-magic line, and he may not succeed; in fact is not likely to succeed. But that should be nothing to his discredit; the man that can do *this* kind of miracle knows enough to keep hotel."

"Hotel? I mind not to have heard—"

"Of hotel? It's what you call hostel. The man that can do this miracle can keep hostel. I can do this miracle; I shall do this miracle; yet I do not try to conceal from you that it is a miracle to tax the occult powers to the last strain."

"None knoweth that truth better than the brotherhood, indeed; for it is of record that aforetime it was parlous difficult and took a year. Natheless, God send you good success, and to that end will we pray."

As a matter of business it was a good idea to get the notion around that the thing was difficult. Many a small thing has been made large by the right kind of advertising. That monk was filled up with the difficulty of this enterprise; he would fill up the others. In two days the solicitude would be booming.

On my way home at noon, I met Sandy. She had been sampling the hermits. I said:

"I would like to do that, myself. This is Wednesday. Is there a matinèe?"

"A which, please you, sir?"

"Matinèe. Do they keep open, afternoons?"

"Who?"

"The hermits, of course."

"Keep open?"

"Yes, keep open. Isn't that plain enough? Do they knock off at noon?"

"Knock off?"

"Knock off?—yes, knock off. What is the matter with knock off? I never saw such a dunderhead; can't you understand anything at all? In plain terms, do they shut up shop, draw the game, bank the fires—"

"Shut up shop, draw—"

"There, never mind, let it go; You make me tired. You can't seem to understand the simplest thing."

"I would I might please thee, sir, and it is to me dole and sorrow that I fail, albeit sith I am but a simple damsel and taught of none, being from the cradle unbaptised in those deep waters of learning that do anoint with a sovereignty him that partaketh of that most noble sacrament, investing him with reverend state to the mental eye of the humble mortal who, by bar and lack of that great consecration seeth in his own unlearned estate but a symbol of that other sort of lack and loss which men do publish to the pitying eye with sackcloth trappings whereon the ashes of grief do lie bepowdered and bestrewn, and so, when such shall in the darkness of his mind encounter these golden phrases of high mystery, these shut-up-shops, and draw-the-game, and bank-the-fires, it is but by the grace of God that he burst not for envy of the mind that can beget, and tongue that can deliver so great and mellow-sounding miracles of speech, and if there do ensue confusion in that humbler mind, and failure to divine the meanings of these wonders, then if so be this miscomprehension is not vain but sooth and true, wit ye well it is the very substance of worshipful dear homage and may not lightly be misprized, nor had been, an ye had noted this complexion of my mood and mind and understood that that I would I could not, and that I could not I might not, nor yet nor might *nor* could, nor might-not nor could-not, might be by advantage turned to the desired *would,* and so I pray you mercy of my fault, and that ye will of your kindness and your charity forgive it, good my master and most dear lord."

I couldn't make it all out—that is, the details—but I got the general idea; and enough of it, too, to be ashamed. It was not fair to spring those nineteenth century technicalities upon the untutored infant of the sixth and then rail at her because she couldn't get their drift; and when she was making the honest best drive at it she could, too, and no fault of hers that she couldn't fetch the home-plate; and so I apologized. Then we meandered pleasantly away toward the hermit-holes in sociable converse together, and better friends than ever.

I was gradually coming to have a mysterious and shuddery reverence for this girl; for nowadays whenever she pulled out from the station and got her train fairly started on one of those horizonless transcontinental sentences of hers, it was borne in upon me that I was standing in the awful presence of the Mother of the German Language. I was so impressed with this, that sometimes when she began to empty one of these sentences on me I unconsciously took the very attitude of reverence, and stood uncovered; and if words had been water, I had been drowned, sure. She had exactly the German way: whatever was in her mind to be delivered, whether a mere remark, or a sermon, or a cyclopedia, or the history of a war, she would get it into a single sentence or die. Whenever the literary German dives into a sentence, that is the last you are going to see of him till he emerges on the other side of his Atlantic with his verb in his mouth.

We drifted from hermit to hermit all the afternoon. It was a most strange menagerie. The chief emulation among them seemed to be, to see which could manage to be the uncleanest and most prosperous with vermin. Their manner and attitudes were the last expression of complacent self-righteousness. It was one anchorite's pride to lie naked in the mud and let the insects bite him and blister him unmolested; it was another's to lean against a rock, all day long, conspicuous to the admiration of the throng of pilgrims, and pray; it was another's to go naked, and crawl around on all fours; it was another's to drag about with him, year in and year out, eighty pounds of iron; it was another's to never lie down when he slept, but to stand among the thorn-bushes and snore when there were pilgrims around to look; a woman, who had the white hair of age, and no other apparel, was black from crown to heel with forty-seven years of holy abstinence from water. Groups of gazing pilgrims stood around all and every of these strange objects, lost in reverent wonder, and envious of the fleckless sanctity which these pious austerities had won for them from an exacting heaven.

By and by we went to see one of the supremely great ones. He was a mighty celebrity; his fame had penetrated all Christendom; the noble and the renowned journeyed from the remotest lands on the globe to pay him reverence. His stand was in the centre of the widest part of the valley; and it took all that space to hold his crowds.

His stand was a pillar sixty feet high, with a broad platform on the top of it. He was now doing what he had been doing every day for twenty years up there—bowing his body ceaselessly and rapidly almost to his feet. It was his way of praying. I timed him with a stop-watch, and he made 1244 revolutions in 24 minutes and 46 seconds. It seemed a pity to have all this power going to waste. It was one of the most useful motions in mechanics, the pedal-movement; so I made a note in my memorandum book, purposing some day to apply a system of elastic cords to him and run a sewing-machine with it. I afterwards carried out that scheme, and got five years' good service out of him; in which time he turned out upwards of eighteen thousand first-rate tow-linen shirts, which was ten a day. I worked him Sundays and all; he was going, Sundays, the same as week-days, and it was no use to waste the power. These shirts cost me nothing but just the mere trifle for the materials—I furnished those myself, it would not have been right to make him do that—and they sold like smoke to pilgrims at a dollar and a half apiece, which was the price of fifty cows or a blooded racehorse in Arthurdom. They were regarded as a perfect protection against sin, and advertised as such by my knights everywhere, with the paint-pot and stencil-plate; insomuch that there was not a cliff or a boulder or a dead-wall in England but you could read on it at a mile distance:

> "Buy the only genuine St. Stylite; patronized by the Nobility. Patent applied for."

There was more money in the business than one knew what to do with. As it extended, I brought out a line of goods suitable for kings, and a nobby thing for duchesses and that sort, with ruffles down the fore-hatch and the running-gear clewed up with a feather-stitch to leeward and then hauled aft with a back-stay and triced up with a half-turn in the standing rigging forward of the weather-gaskets. Yes, it was a daisy.

But about that time I noticed that the motive power had taken to standing on one leg, and I found that there was something the matter with the other one; so I stocked the business and unloaded, taking Sir Bors de Ganis into camp financially along with certain of his friends: for the works stopped within a year, and the good saint got him to his rest. But he had earned it. I can say that for him.

EXTRACTS FROM ADAM'S DIARY

(1893)

Clemens knew the Bible well and wrote often about biblical subjects, though typically with comic irreverence. Many of his antediluvian stories—his "Noah's Ark book" (now lost), "Methuselah's Diary," "Adam's Expulsion," and others—were not published during his lifetime. The figure of Adam seems to have been a particular favorite, and the humorous account of Twain standing at the Tomb of Adam in *The Innocents Abroad* (1869) was not the first time he used the original parent for broad farce. "Extracts from Adam's Diary" was the first of his biblical narratives to see print, however. Even so, Clemens had to revise the piece before it would be published. He had finished the manuscript in 1892, but he had trouble finding a publisher for it at first. A friend proposed that it might be revised and included in a collection of articles to be titled *The Niagara Book* (1893). The volume was meant to advertise the Falls as a tourist attraction and as an attractive side-trip for those bound for the Columbian Exposition in Chicago. Clemens made the necessary changes, including transplanting the Garden of Eden to Niagara Falls. Some years later, Twain decided that Eve should have a chance to tell her version of the story, and he wrote "Eve's Diary" (1906).

The Earliest Authentic Mention of Niagara Falls

"Extracts from Adam's Diary Translated from the Original MS"

By Mark Twain

MONDAY.—This new creature with the long hair is a good deal in the way. It is always hanging around and following me about. I don't like this; I am not used to company. I wish it would stay with the other animals. . . . Cloudy today, wind in the east; think we shall have rain. . . . *We?* Where did I get that word? . . . I remember now,—the new creature uses it.

TUESDAY.—Been examining the great waterfall. It is the finest thing on the estate, I think. The new creature calls it Niagara Falls—why, I am sure I do not know. Says it *looks* like Niagara Falls. That is not a reason, it is mere waywardness and imbecility. I get no chance to name anything myself. The new creature names everything that comes along, before I can get in a protest. And always the same pretext is offered—it *looks* like the thing. There is the dodo, for instance. Says the moment one looks at it one sees at a glance that it "looks like a dodo." It will have to keep that name, no doubt. It wearies me to fret about it, but it does no good, anyway. Dodo! It looks no more like a dodo than I do.

WEDNESDAY.—Built me a shelter against the rain, but could not have it to myself in peace. The new creature intruded. When I tried to put it out it shed water out of the holes it looks with, and wiped it away with the back of its paws, and made a noise such as some of the other animals make when they are in distress. I wish it would not talk, it is always talking. That sounds like a cheap fling at the poor creature, a slur; but I do not mean it so. I have never heard the human voice before, and any new and strange sound intruding itself here upon the solemn hush of these dreaming solitudes offends my ear and seems a false note. And this new sound is so close to me; it is right at my shoulder, right at my ear, first on one side then on the other, and I am used only to sounds that are more or less distant from me.

FRIDAY.—The naming goes recklessly on, in spite of anything I can do. I had a very good name for the estate, and it was musical and pretty—GARDEN-OF-EDEN. Privately, I continue to call it that, but not any longer publicly. The new creature says it is all woods and rocks and scenery, and therefore has no resemblance to a garden. Says it *looks* like a park, and does not look like anything *but* a park. Consequently, without consulting me it has been new named—NIAGARA FALLS PARK. This is sufficiently high-handed, it seems to me. And already there is a sign up:

KEEP OFF
THE GRASS

My life is not as happy as it was.

SATURDAY.—The new creature eats too much fruit. We are going to run short, most likely. "We" again—that is *its* word; mine, too, now, from hearing it so much. Good deal of fog this morning. I do not go out in the fog, myself. The new creature does. It goes out in all weathers, and stumps right in with its muddy feet. And talks. It used to be so pleasant and quiet here.

SUNDAY.—Pulled through. This day is getting to be more and more trying. It was selected and set apart last November as a day of rest. I already had six of them per week before. This is another of those unaccountable things. There seems to be too much legislation; too much fussing, and fixing, and tidying up, and not enough of the better-let-well-enough-alone policy. [*Mem.*—Must keep that sort of opinions to myself.] This morning found the new creature trying to clod apples out of that forbidden tree.

MONDAY.—The new creature says its name is Eve. That is all right, I have no objections. Says it is to call it by when I want it to come. I said it was superfluous, then. The word evidently raised me in its respect; and indeed it is a large, good word and will bear repetition. It says it is not an It, it is a She. This is probably doubtful, yet it is all one to me; what she is were nothing to me if she would but go by herself and not talk.

TUESDAY.—She has littered the whole estate with execrable names and offensive signs:

☛ THIS WAY TO THE WHIRLPOOL.
☛ THIS WAY TO GOAT ISLAND.
☛ CAVE OF THE WINDS THIS WAY.

She says this park would make a tidy summer resort, if there were any custom for it. Summer resort—another invention of hers—just words, without any meaning. What is a summer resort? But it is best not to ask her, she has such a rage for explaining.

FRIDAY.—She has taken to begging and imploring me to stop going over the Falls. What harm does it do? Says it makes her shudder. I wonder why; I have always done it—always liked the plunge, and the excitement and the coolness. I supposed it was what the Falls were for. They have no other use that I can see, and they must have been made for something. She says they were only made for scenery—like the rhinoceros and the mastodon.

I went over the Falls in a barrel—not satisfactory to her. Went over in a tub—still not satisfactory. Swam the Whirlpool and the Rapids in a fig-leaf suit. It got much damaged. Hence, tedious complaints about my extravagance. I am too much hampered here. What I need is change of scene.

SATURDAY.—I escaped last Tuesday night, and traveled two days, and built me another shelter, in a secluded place, and obliterated my tracks as well as I could, but she hunted me out by means of a beast which she has tamed and calls a wolf, and came making that pitiful noise again, and shedding that water out of the places she looks with. I was obliged to return with her, but will presently emigrate again, when occasion offers. She engages herself in many foolish things: among others, trying to study out why the animals called lions and tigers live on grass and flowers, when, as she says, the sort of teeth they wear would indicate that they were intended to eat each other. This is foolish, because to do that would be to kill each other, and that would introduce what, as I understand it, is called "death"; and death, as I have been told, has not yet entered the Park. Which is a pity, on some accounts.

SUNDAY.—Pulled through.

MONDAY.—I believe I see what the week is for: it is to give time to rest up from the weariness of Sunday. It seems a good idea, in a region where good ideas are rather conspicuously scarce. Will try it. [*Mem.*—Must keep this sort of remarks private.]. . . . She has been climbing that tree again. Clodded her out of it. She said nobody was looking. Seems to consider that a sufficient justification for chancing any dangerous thing. Told her that. The word justification moved her admiration—and envy, too, I thought. It is a good word.

THURSDAY.—She told me she was made out of a rib taken from my body. This is at least doubtful, if not more than that. I have not missed any rib. . . . She is in much trouble about the buzzard; says grass does not agree with it; is afraid she can't raise it; thinks it was intended to live on decayed flesh. The buzzard must get along the best it can with what is provided. We cannot overturn the whole scheme to accommodate the buzzard.

SATURDAY.—She fell in the pond yesterday, when she was looking at herself in it, which she is always doing. She nearly strangled, and said it was most uncomfortable. This made her sorry for the creatures which live in there, which she calls fish, for she continues to fasten names on to things that don't need them and don't come when they are called by them, which is a matter of no consequence to her, she is such a fool anyway; so she got a lot of them out and brought them in and put them in my bed to keep warm, but I have noticed them now and then all day and I don't see that they are any happier there than they were before. When night comes I shall throw them outdoors; I will not sleep with them, for I find them clammy and unpleasant to lie among when a person hasn't anything on.

SUNDAY.—Pulled through.

TUESDAY.—She has taken up with a snake, now. The other animals are glad, for she was always experimenting with them and bothering them; and I am glad, because the snake talks, and this enables me to get a rest.

FRIDAY.—She says the snake advises her to try the fruit of that tree, and says the result will be a great and fine and noble education. I told her there would be another result, too—it would introduce death into the world. That was a mistake—it had been better to keep the remark to myself: it only gave her an idea—she could save the sick buzzard, and furnish fresh meat to the despondent lions and tigers. I advised her to keep away from the tree. She said she wouldn't. I foresee trouble. Will emigrate.

WEDNESDAY.—I have had a variegated time. I escaped that night, and rode a horse all night as fast as he could go, hoping to get clear out of the Garden and hide in some other country before the trouble should begin; but it was not to be. About an hour after sun-up, as I was riding through a flowery plain where thousands of animals were grazing, slumbering, or playing with each other, according to their common wont, all of a sudden they broke into a tempest of frightful noises and in one moment the plain was a frantic commotion and every beast was destroying its neighbor. I knew what it meant—Eve had eaten that fruit, and death was come into the world. . . . The tigers ate my horse, paying no attention when I ordered them to desist, and they would have eaten me if I had stayed—which I didn't, but went away in much haste. . . . I found this place, outside the Garden, and was fairly comfortable for a few days, but she has found me out. Found me out, and has named the place Tonawanda—says it *looks* like that. In fact I was not sorry she came, for there are but meagre pickings here, and she brought some of those apples. I was obliged to eat them, I was so hungry. It was against my principles, but I find that principles have no real force except when one is well fed. . . . She came curtained in boughs and bunches of leaves, and when I asked her what she meant by such nonsense, and snatched them away and threw them down, she tittered and blushed. I had never seen a person titter and blush before, and to me it seemed unbecoming and idiotic. She said I would soon know how it was myself. This was correct. Hungry as I was, I laid down the apple half eaten—certainly the best one I ever saw, considering the lateness of the season—and arrayed myself in the discarded boughs and branches, and then spoke to her with some severity and ordered her to go and get some more and not make such a spectacle of herself. She did it, and after this we crept down to where the wild-beast battle had been, and collected some skins, and I made her patch together a couple of suits proper for public occasions. They are uncomfortable, it is true, but stylish, and that is the main point about clothes. . . . I find she is a good deal of a companion. I see I should be lonesome and depressed without her, now that I have lost my property. Another thing, she says it is ordered that we work for our living hereafter. She will be useful. I will superintend.

TEN DAYS LATER.—She accuses *me* of being the cause of our disaster! She says, with apparent sincerity and truth, that the Serpent assured her that the forbidden fruit was not apples, it was chestnuts. I said I was innocent, then, for I had not eaten any chestnuts. She said the Serpent informed her that "chestnut" was a figurative term meaning an aged and mouldy joke. I turned pale at that, for I have made many jokes to pass the weary time, and some of them could have been of that sort, though I had honestly supposed they were new when I made them. She asked me if I had made one just at the time of the catastrophe. I was obliged to admit that I had made one to myself, though not aloud. It was this. I was thinking about the Falls, and I said to myself, "How wonderful it is to see that vast body of water tumble down there!" Then in an instant a bright thought flashed into my head, and I let it fly, saying, "It would be a deal more wonderful to see it tumble *up* there!"—and I was just about to kill myself with laughing at it when all nature broke loose in war and death and I had to flee for my life. "There," she said, with triumph, "that is just it; the Serpent mentioned that very jest, and called it the First Chestnut, and said it was coeval with the creation." Alas, I am indeed to blame. Would that I were not witty; oh, would that I never had that radiant thought!

NEXT YEAR.—We have named it Cain. She caught it while I was up country, trapping on the North Shore of the Erie; caught it in the timber a couple of miles from our dug-out—or it might have been four, she isn't certain which. It resembles us in some ways, and may be a relation. That is what she thinks, but this is an error, in my judgment. The difference in size warrants the conclusion that it is a different and new kind of animal—a fish, perhaps, though when I put it in the water to see, it sank, and she plunged in and snatched it out before there was opportunity for the experiment to determine the matter. I still think it is a fish, but she is indifferent about what it is, and will not let me have it to try. I do not understand this. The coming of the creature seems to have changed her whole nature, and made her unreasonable about experiments. She thinks more of it than she does of any of the other animals, but is not able to explain why. Her mind is disordered—everything shows it. Sometimes she carries the fish in her arms half the night when it complains and wants to get to the water. At such times the water comes out of the places in her face that she looks out of, and she pats the fish on the back and makes soft sounds with her mouth to soothe it, and betrays sorrow and solicitude in a hundred ways. I have never seen her do like this with any other fish, and it troubles me greatly. She used to carry the young tigers around so, and play with them, before we lost our property, but it was only play; she never took on about them like this when their dinner disagreed with them.

SUNDAY.—She don't work, Sundays, but lies around all tired out, and likes to have the fish wallow over her; and she makes fool noises to amuse it, and pretends to chew its paws, and that makes it laugh. I have not seen a fish before that could laugh. This makes me doubt. . . . I have come to like Sunday myself. Superintending all the week tires a body so. There ought to be more Sundays. In the old days they were tough, but now they come handy.

WEDNESDAY.—It isn't a fish. I cannot quite make out what it is. It makes curious devilish noises when not satisfied, and says "goo-goo" when it is. It is not one of us, for it doesn't walk;

it is not a bird, for it doesn't fly; it is not a frog, for it doesn't hop; it is not a snake, for it doesn't crawl; I feel sure it is not a fish, though I cannot get a chance to find out whether it can swim or not. It merely lies around, and mostly on its back, with its feet up. I have not seen any other animal do that before. I said I believed it was an enigma; but she only admired the word without understanding it. In my judgment it is either an enigma or some kind of bug. If it dies I will take it apart and see what its arrangements are. I never had a thing perplex me so.

THREE MONTHS LATER.–The perplexity merely augments instead of diminishing. I sleep but little. It has ceased from lying around, and goes about on its four legs, now. Yet it differs from the other four-legged animals, in that its front legs are unusually short, consequently this causes the main part of its person to stick up uncomfortably high in the air, and this is not attractive. It is built much as we are, but its method of traveling shows that it is not of our breed. The short front legs and long hind ones indicate that it is of the kangaroo family, but it is a marked variation on the species, since the true kangaroo hops, whereas this one never does. Still it is a curious and interesting variety, and has not been catalogued before. As I discovered it, I have felt justified in securing the credit of the discovery by attaching my name to it, and hence have called it *Kagaroorum Adamiensis*. . . . It must have been a young one when it came, for it has grown exceedingly since. It must be five times as big, now, as it was then, and when discontented is able to make from twenty-two to thirty-eight times the noise it made at first. Coercion does not modify this, but has the contrary effect. For this reason I discontinued the system. She reconciles it by persuasion, and by giving it things which she had told it she wouldn't give it, before. As observed previously, I was not at home when it first came, and she told me she found it in the woods. It seems odd that it should be the only one, yet it must be so, for I have worn myself out these many weeks trying to find another one to add to my collection, and for this one to play with; for surely then it would be quieter and we could tame it more easily. But I find none, nor any vestige of any; and strangest of all, no tracks. It has to live on the ground, it cannot help itself; therefore, how does it get about without leaving a track? I have set a dozen traps, but they do no good; I catch all small animals except that one; animals that merely go into the trap out of curiosity, I think, to see what the milk is there for. They never drink it.

THREE MONTHS LATER.—The Kangaroo still continues to grow, which is very strange and perplexing. I never knew one to be so long getting its growth. It has fur on its head, now; not like kangaroo fur, but exactly like our hair except that it is much finer and softer, and instead of being black, is red. I am like to lose my mind over the capricious and harassing developments of this unclassifiable zoological freak. If I could catch another one—but that is hopeless; it is a new variety, and the only sample; this is plain. But I caught a true kangaroo and brought it in, thinking that this one, being lonesome, would rather have that for company than have no kin at all, or any animal it could feel a nearness to or get sympathy from in its forlorn condition here among strangers who do not know its ways or habits, or what to do to make it feel that it is among friends; but it was a mistake—it went into such fits at the sight of the kangaroo that I was convinced it had never seen one before. I pity the poor noisy little animal, but there is nothing I can do to make it happy. If I could tame it—but that is out of the question; the more I try the worse I seem to make it. It grieves me to the heart to see it in its little storms of sorrow and passion. I wanted to let it go, but she wouldn't hear of it. That seemed cruel, and not like her; and yet she may be right. It might be lonelier than ever; for since I cannot find another one, how could *it?*

FIVE MONTHS LATER.—It is not a kangaroo. No, for it supports itself by holding to her finger, and thus goes a few steps on its hind legs, and then falls down. It is probably some kind of bear; and yet it has no tail—as yet—and no fur, except on its head. It still keeps on growing—that is a curious circumstance, for bears get their growth earlier than this. Bears are dangerous—since our catastrophe—and I shall not be satisfied to have this one prowling about the place much longer without a muzzle on. I have offered to get her a kangaroo if she would let this one go, but it did no good—she is determined to run us into all sorts of foolish risks, I think. She was not like this before she lost her mind.

A Fortnight Later.—I examined its mouth. There is no danger yet; it has only one tooth. It has no tail yet. It makes more noise, now, than it ever did before—and mainly at night. I have moved out. But I shall go over, mornings, to breakfast, and to see if it has more teeth. If it gets a mouthful of teeth it will be time for it to go, tail or no tail, for a bear does not need a tail in order to be dangerous.

Four Months Later.—I have been off hunting and fishing for a month up in the region that she calls Buffalo; I don't know why, unless it is because there are not any buffalos there. Meantime the bear has learned to paddle around all by itself on its hind legs, and says "poppa" and "momma." It is certainly a new species. This resemblance to words may be purely accidental, of course, and may have no purpose or meaning; but even in that case it is still extraordinary, and is a thing which no other bear can do. This imitation of speech, taken together with general absence of fur and entire absence of tail, sufficiently indicates that this is a new kind of bear. The further study of it will be exceedingly interesting. Meantime I will go off on a far expedition among the forests of the north and make an exhaustive search. There must certainly be another one somewhere, and this one will be less dangerous when it has company of its own species. I will go straightway; but I will muzzle this one first.

Three Months Later.—It has been a weary, weary hunt, yet I have had no success. In the meantime, without stirring from the home-estate, she has caught another one! I never saw such luck. I might have hunted these woods a hundred years, I never would have run across that thing.

Next Day.—I have been comparing the new one with the old one, and it is perfectly plain that they are the same breed. I was going to stuff one of them for my collection, but she is prejudiced against it for some reason or other; so I have relinquished the idea, though I think it is a mistake. It would be an irreparable loss to science if they should get away. The old one is tamer than it was, and can laugh and talk like the parrot, having learned this, no doubt, from being with the parrot so much, and having the imitative faculty in a highly developed degree. I shall be astonished if it turns out to be a new kind of parrot; and yet I ought not to be astonished, for it has already been everything else it could think of, since those first days when it was a fish. The new one is as ugly now as the old one was at first; has the same sulphur-and-raw-meat complexion and the same singular head without any fur on it. She calls it Abel.

TEN YEARS LATER.—They are boys; we found it out long ago. It was their coming in that small, immature shape that fooled us; we were not used to it. There are some girls now. Abel is a good boy, but if Cain had stayed a bear it would have improved him. After all these years, I see that I was mistaken about Eve in the beginning; it is better to live outside the Garden with her than inside without her. At first I thought she talked too much; but now, I should be sorry to have that voice fall silent and pass out of my life. Blessed be the chestnut that brought us near together and taught me to know the goodness of her heart and the sweetness of her spirit!

FROM

THE TRAGEDY OF PUDD'NHEAD WILSON

(1894)

FROM

FOLLOWING THE EQUATOR

(1897)

Mark Twain had a longstanding affection for the maxim. Early in his career, he was content with parodies and burlesques of Franklinseque words of advice, but by the time he came to write the sayings purportedly excerpted from Pudd'nhead Wilson's "Calendar," he had declared bankruptcy and his aphorisms frequently turned biting and cynical. David Wilson, the "pudd'nhead," is a character in the novel bearing his name, but this story of babies switched at birth, one black and the other white, has relatively little to do with him. He does solve the mystery of identity at the end of the novel, but whatever "tragedy" there is in the tale is not Wilson's. Nevertheless, each chapter is rather gratuitously introduced with one or more of his maxims, though their thematic relation to the narrative events is questionable at best. Pudd'nhead Wilson plays no part in *Following the Equator.* Nevertheless, Twain revived the device for this book, perhaps merely to introduce levity into a subject that was not nearly so playful as his earlier travel narratives had been. *Following the Equator* is a record of his round-the-world lecture tour, though the fact he is lecturing at all is barely mentioned. Instead, Twain somewhat plays the role of cultural anthropologist. Most of the book casts a jaundiced eye on the effects of colonialism throughout the world, and if Twain is still a believer in the blessings of "civilization" and progress and not yet the card-carrying anti-imperialist he would become in later years, he is nevertheless superbly damning of the savagery of some of the supposedly enlightened colonizers. This is clear in the chapter from *Following the Equator* that follows.

FROM

The Tragedy of Pudd'nhead Wilson (1894)

"PUDD'NHEAD WILSON'S CALENDAR"

There is no character, howsoever good and fine, but it can be destroyed by ridicule, howsoever poor and witless. Observe the ass, for instance: his character is about perfect, he is the choicest spirit among all the humbler animals, yet see what ridicule has brought him to. Instead of feeling complimented when we are called an ass, we are left in doubt.

Tell the truth or trump—but get the trick.

Adam was but human—this explains it all. He did not want the apple for the apple's sake, he wanted it only because it was forbidden. The mistake was in not forbidding the serpent; then he would have eaten the serpent.

Whoever has lived long enough to find out what life is, knows how deep a debt of gratitude we owe to Adam, the first great benefactor of our race. He brought death into the world.

Adam and Eve had many advantages, but the principal one was that they escaped teething.

There is this trouble about special providences—namely, there is so often a doubt as to which party was intended to be the beneficiary. In the case of the children, the bears, and the prophet, the bears got more real satisfaction out of the episode than the prophet did, because they got the children.

Training is everything. The peach was once a bitter almond; cauliflower is nothing but cabbage with a college education.

Remark of Dr. Baldwin's, concerning upstarts: We don't care to eat toadstools that think they are truffles.

Let us endeavor so to live that when we come to die even the undertaker will be sorry.

Habit is habit and not to be flung out of the window by any man but coaxed down-stairs a step at a time.

One of the most striking differences between a cat and a lie is that a cat has only nine lives.

The holy passion of Friendship is of so sweet and steady and loyal and enduring a nature that it will last through a whole lifetime, if not asked to lend money.

Consider well the proportions of things. It is better to be a young June-bug than an old bird of paradise.

Why is it that we rejoice at a birth and grieve at a funeral? It is because we are not the person involved.

It is easy to find fault, if one has that disposition. There was once a man who, not being able to find any other fault with his coal, complained that there were too many prehistoric toads in it.

All say, "How hard it is that we have to die"—a strange complaint to come from the mouths of people who have had to live.

When angry, count four; when very angry, swear.

There are three infallible ways of pleasing an author and the three form a rising scale of compliment: 1, to tell him you have read one of his books; 2, to tell him you have read all of his books; 3, to ask him to let you read the manuscript of his forthcoming book. No. 1 admits you to his respect; No. 2 admits you to his admiration; No. 3 carries you clear into his heart.

As to the Adjective: when in doubt, strike it out.

Courage is resistance to fear, mastery of fear—not absence of fear. Except a creature be part coward it is not a compliment to say it is brave; it is merely a loose misapplication of the word. Consider the flea!—incomparably the bravest of all the creatures of God, if ignorance of fear were courage. Whether you are asleep or awake he will attack you, caring nothing for the fact that in bulk and strength you are to him as are the massed armies of the earth to a sucking child; he lives both day and night and all days and nights in the very lap of peril and the immediate presence of death, and yet is no more afraid than is the man who walks the streets of a city that was threatened by an earthquake ten centuries before. When we speak of Clive, Nelson, and Putnam as men who "didn't know what fear was," we ought always to add the flea—and put him at the head of the procession.

When I reflect upon the number of disagreeable people who I know have gone to a better world, I am moved to lead a different life.

October. This is one of the peculiarly dangerous months to speculate in stocks. The others are July, January, September, April, November, May, March, June, December, August, and February.

The true Southern watermelon is a boon apart and not to be mentioned with commoner things. It is chief of this world's luxuries, king by grace of God over all the fruits of the earth. When one has tasted it, he knows what the angels eat. It was not a Southern watermelon that Eve took; we know it because she repented.

Nothing so need reforming as other people's habits.

Behold, the fool saith, "Put not all thine eggs in the one basket"—which is but a manner of saying, "Scatter your money and your attention"; but the wise man saith, "Put all your eggs in the one basket and—WATCH THAT BASKET."

If you pick up a starving dog and make him prosperous, he will not bite you. This is the principal difference between a dog and a man.

We know all about the habits of the ant, we know all about the habits of the bee, but we know nothing at all about the habits of the oyster. It seems almost certain that we have been choosing the wrong time for studying the oyster.

Even popularity can be overdone. In Rome, along at first, you are full of regrets that Michelangelo died, but by and by you only regret that you didn't see him do it.

July 4. Statistics show that we lose more fools on this day than in all the other days of the year put together. This proves, by the number left in stock, that one Fourth of July per year is now inadequate, the country has grown so.

Gratitude and treachery are merely the two extremities of the same procession. You have seen all of it that is worth staying for when the band and the gaudy officials have gone by.

Thanksgiving Day. Let all give humble, hearty, and sincere thanks, now, but the turkeys. In the island of Fiji they do not use turkeys; they use plumbers. It does not become you and me to sneer at Fiji.

Few things are harder to put up with than the annoyance of a good example.

It were not best that we should all think alike; it is difference of opinion that makes horse-races.

Even the clearest and most perfect circumstantial evidence is likely to be at fault, after all, and therefore ought to be received with great caution. Take the case of any pencil sharpened by any woman: if you have witnesses you will find she did it with a knife, but if you take simply the aspect of the pencil you will say she did it with her teeth.

He is useless on top of the ground; he ought to be under it, inspiring the cabbages.

April 1. This is the day upon which we are reminded of what we are on the other three hundred and sixty-four.

It is often the case that the man who can't tell a *lie* thinks he is the best judge of one.

October 12, the Discovery. It was wonderful to find America, but it would have been more wonderful to miss it.

FROM
Following the Equator (1897)

"PUDD'NHEAD WILSON'S NEW CALENDAR"

A man may have no bad habits and have worse.

When in doubt, tell the truth.

It is more trouble to make a maxim than it is to do right.

A dozen direct censures are easier to bear than one morganatic compliment.

Noise proves nothing. Often a hen who has merely laid an egg cackles as if she had laid an asteroid.

He was as shy as a newspaper is when referring to its own merits.

Truth is the most valuable thing we have. Let us economize it.

It could probably be shown by facts and figures that there is no distinctly native American criminal class except Congress.

It is your human environment that makes climate.

Everything human is pathetic. The secret source of Humor itself is not joy but sorrow. There is no humor in heaven.

We should be careful to get out of an experience only the wisdom that is in it—and stop there; lest we be like the cat that sits down on a hot stove-lid. She will never sit down on a hot stove-lid again, and that is well; but also she will never sit down on a cold one any more.

There are those who scoff at the school-boy, calling him frivolous and shallow. Yet it was the school-boy who said, "Faith is believing what you know ain't so."

The timid man yearns for full value and demands a tenth. The bold man strikes for double value and compromises on par.

We can secure other people's approval if we do right and try hard, but our own is worth a hundred of it and no way has been found out of securing that.

Truth is stranger than fiction—to some people, but I am measurably familiar with it.

Truth is stranger than Fiction, but it is because Fiction is obliged to stick to possibilities; Truth isn't.

There is a Moral Sense and there is an Immoral Sense. History shows us that the Moral Sense enables us to perceive morality and how to avoid it, and that the Immoral Sense enables us to perceive immorality and how to enjoy it.

The English are mentioned in the Bible: Blessed are the meek, for they shall inherit the earth.

It is easier to stay out than get out.

Pity is for the living, envy is for the dead.

It is by the goodness of God that in our country we have those three unspeakably precious things: freedom of speech, freedom of conscience, and the prudence never to practise either of them.

Man will do many things to get himself loved, he will do all things to get himself envied.

Nothing is so ignorant as a man's left hand, except a lady's watch.

Be careless in your dress if you must but keep a tidy soul.

There is no such thing as "the Queen's English." The property has gone into the hands of a joint stock company and we own the bulk of the shares.

"*Classic.*" A book which people praise and don't read.

There are people who can do all fine and heroic things but one: keep from telling their happiness to the unhappy.

Man is the Only Animal that blushes. Or needs to.

The universal brotherhood of man is our most precious possession, what there is of it.

Let us be thankful for the fools. But for them the rest of us could not succeed.

When people do not respect us we are sharply offended; yet deep down in his private heart no man much respects himself.

Nature makes the locust with an appetite for crops; man would have made him with an appetite for sand.

The spirit of wrath—not the words—is the sin; and the spirit of wrath is cursing. We begin to swear before we can talk.

The man with a new idea is a Crank until the idea succeeds.

Let us be grateful to Adam our benefactor. He cut us out of the "blessing" of idleness and won for us the "curse" of labor.

Let us not be too particular. It is better to have second-hand diamonds than none at all.

The Autocrat of Russia possesses more power than any other man in the earth, but he cannot stop a sneeze.

There are several good protections against temptations but the surest is cowardice.

Names are not always what they seem. The common Welsh name Bzjxxllwep is pronounced Jackson.

To succeed in the other trades, capacity must be shown; in the law, concealment of it will do.

Prosperity is the best protector of principle.

By trying we can easily learn to endure adversity. Another man's, I mean.

Few of us can stand prosperity. Another man's, I mean.

There is an old-time toast which is golden for its beauty, "When you ascend the hill of prosperity may you not meet a friend."

Each person is born to one possession which outvalues all his others—his last breath.

Hunger is the handmaid of genius.

The old saw says, "Let a sleeping dog lie." Right. Still, when there is much at stake it is better to get a newspaper to do it.

It takes your enemy and your friend, working together, to hurt you to the heart, the one to slander you and the other to get the news to you.

If the desire to kill and the opportunity to kill came always together, who would escape hanging?

Simple rules for saving money: To save half, when you are fired by an eager impulse to contribute to a charity, wait and count forty. To save three-quarters, count sixty. To save it all, count sixty-five.

Grief can take care of itself, but to get the full value of a joy you must have somebody to divide it with.

He had had much experience of physicians, and said "the only way to keep your health is to eat what you don't want, drink what you don't like, and do what you'd druther not."

The man who is ostentatious of his modesty is twin of the statue that wears a fig-leaf.

Let me make the superstitions of a nation and I care not who makes its laws or its songs either.

Wrinkles should merely indicate where smiles have been.

True irreverence is disrespect for another man's god.

Do not undervalue the headache. While it is at its sharpest it seems a bad investment, but when relief begins the unexpired remainder is worth four dollars a minute.

There are eight hundred and sixty-nine different forms of lying, but only one of them has been squarely forbidden. Thou shalt not bear false witness against thy neighbor.

There are two times in a man's life when he should not speculate: when he can't afford it and when he can.

She was not quite what you would call refined. She was not

quite what you would call unrefined. She was the kind of person that keeps a parrot.

Make it a point to do something every day that you don't want to do. This is the golden rule for acquiring the habit of doing your duty without pain.

Don't part with your illusions. When they are gone you may still exist but you have ceased to live.

Often, the surest way to convey misinformation is to tell the strict truth.

SATAN (impatiently) to NEW-COMER. The trouble with you Chicago people is that you think you are the best people down here, whereas you are merely the most numerous.

In the first place God made idiots. This was for practice. Then He made School Boards.

There are no people who are quite so vulgar as the over-refined ones.

When your watch gets out of order you have choice of two things to do: throw it in the fire or take it to the watch-tinker. The former is the quickest.

In statesmanship get the formalities right, never mind about the moralities.

Every one is a moon and has a dark side which he never shows to anybody.

First catch your Boer, then kick him.

None of us can have as many virtues as the fountain-pen, or half its cussedness; but we can try.

The very ink with which all history is written is merely fluid prejudice.

There isn't a Parallel of Latitude but thinks it would have been the Equator if it had had its rights.

I have traveled more than any one else and I have noticed that even the angels speak English with an accent.

"DECIMATING THE SAVAGES"

There must have been a large distribution of acuteness among those naked skinny aboriginals, or they couldn't have been such unapproachable trackers and boomerangers and weet-weeters. It must have been race-aversion that put upon them a good deal of the low-rate intellectual reputation which they bear and have borne this long time in the world's estimate of them.

They were lazy—always lazy. Perhaps that was their trouble. It is a killing defect. Surely they could have invented and built a competent house, but they didn't. And they could have invented and developed the agricultural arts, but they didn't. They went naked and houseless, and lived on fish and grubs and worms and wild fruits, and were just plain savages, for all their smartness.

With a country as big as the United States to live and multiply in, and with no epidemic diseases among them till the white man came with those and his other appliances of civilization, it is quite probable that there was never a day in his history when he could muster 100,000 of his race in all Australia. He diligently and deliberately kept population down by infanticide—largely; but mainly by certain other methods. He did not need to practise these artificialities any more after the white man came. The white man knew ways of keeping down population which were worth several of his. The white man knew ways of reducing a native population 80 percent in 20 years. The native had never seen anything as fine as that before.

For example, there is the case of the country now called Victoria—a country eighty times as large as Rhode Island, as I have already said. By the best official guess there were 4,500 aboriginals in it when the whites came along in the middle of the 'Thirties. Of these, 1,000 lived in Gippsland, a patch of territory the size of fifteen or sixteen Rhode Islands: they did not diminish as fast as some of the other communities; indeed, at the end of forty years there were still 200 of them left. The Geelong tribe diminished more satisfactorily: from 173 persons it faded to 34 in twenty years; at the end of another twenty the tribe numbered one person altogether. The two Melbourne tribes could muster about 300 when the white man came; they could muster but twenty, thirty-seven years later, in 1875. In that year there were still odds and ends of tribes scattered about the colony of Victoria, but I was told that natives of full blood are very scarce now. It is said that the aboriginals continue in some force in the huge territory called Queensland.

The early whites were not used to savages. They could not understand the primary law of savage life: that if a man do you a wrong, his whole tribe is responsible—each individual of it—and you may take your change out of any individual of it, without bothering to seek out the guilty one. When a white killed an aboriginal, the tribe applied the ancient law, and killed the first white they came across. To the whites this was a monstrous thing. Extermination seemed to be the proper medicine for such creatures as this. They did not kill all the blacks, but they promptly killed enough of them to make their own persons safe. From the dawn of civilization down to this day the white man has always used that very precaution. Mrs. Campbell Praed lived in Queensland, as a child, in the early days, and in her "Sketches of Australian life," we get informing pictures of the early struggles of the white and the black to reform each other.

Speaking of pioneer days in the mighty wilderness of Queensland, Mrs. Praed says:

> "At first the natives retreated before the whites; and, except that they every now and then speared a beast in one of the herds, gave little cause for uneasiness. But, as the number of squatters increased, each one taking up miles of country and bringing two or

three men in his train, so that shepherds' huts and stockmen's camps lay far apart, and defenseless in the midst of hostile tribes, the Blacks' depredations became more frequent and murder was no unusual event.

"The loneliness of the Australian bush can hardly be painted in words. Here extends mile after mile of primeval forest where perhaps foot of white man has never trod—interminable vistas where the eucalyptus trees rear their lofty trunks and spread forth their lanky limbs, from which the red gum oozes and hangs in fantastic pendants like crimson stalactites; ravines along the sides of which the long-bladed grass grows rankly; level untimbered plains alternating with undulating tracts of pasture, here and there broken by a stony ridge, steep gully, or dried-up creek. All wild, vast and desolate; all the same monotonous gray coloring, except where the wattle, when in blossom, shows patches of feathery gold, or a belt of scrub lies green, glossy, and impenetrable as Indian jungle.

"The solitude seems intensified by the strange sounds of reptiles, birds, and insects, and by the absence of larger creatures; of which in the daytime, the only audible signs are the stampede of a herd of kangaroo, or the rustle of a wallabi, or a dingo stirring the grass as it creeps to its lair. But there are the whirring of locusts, the demoniac chuckle of the laughing jackass, the screeching of cockatoos and parrots, the hissing of the frilled lizard, and the buzzing of innumerable insects hidden under the dense undergrowth. And then at night, the melancholy wailing of the curlews, the dismal howling of dingoes, the discordant croaking of tree-frogs, might well shake the nerves of the solitary watcher."

That is the theater for the drama. When you comprehend one or two other details, you will perceive how well suited for trouble it was, and how loudly it invited it. The cattlemen's stations were scattered over that profound wilderness miles and miles apart—at each station half a dozen persons. There was a plenty of cattle, the black natives were always ill-nourished and hungry. The land belonged to *them*. The whites had not bought it, and couldn't buy it; for the tribes had no chiefs; nobody in authority, nobody competent to sell and convey; and the tribes themselves had no comprehension of the idea of transferable ownership of land. The ousted owners were despised by the white interlopers, and this opinion was not hidden under a bushel. More promising materials for a tragedy could not have been collated. Let Mrs. Praed speak:

> "At Nie Nie station, one dark night, the unsuspecting hut-keeper, having, as he believed, secured himself against assault, was lying wrapped in his blankets sleeping profoundly. The Blacks crept stealthily down the chimney and battered in his skull while he slept."

One could guess the whole drama from that little text. The curtain was up. It would not fall until the mastership of one party or the other was determined—and permanently:

> "There was treachery on both sides. The Blacks killed the Whites when they found them defenseless, and the Whites slew the Blacks in a wholesale and promiscuous fashion which offended against my childish sense of justice.
>
> . . . They were regarded as little above the level of brutes, and in some cases *were destroyed like vermin.*
>
> "Here is an instance. A squatter, whose station was surrounded by Blacks, whom he suspected to be hostile and from whom he feared an attack, parleyed with them from his house-door. He told them it was Christmas-time—a time at which all men, black or white, feasted; that there were flour, sugar-plums, good things in plenty in the store, and that he would make for them such a pudding as they had never dreamed of—a great pudding of which all might eat and be filled. The Blacks listened and were lost. The pudding was made and distributed. Next morning there was howling in the camp, for it had been sweetened with sugar and arsenic!"

The white man's spirit was right, but his method was wrong. His spirit was the spirit which the civilized white has always exhibited toward the savage, but the use of poison was a departure from custom. True, it was merely a technical departure, not a real one; still, it was a departure, and therefore a mistake, in my opinion. It was better, kinder, swifter, and much more humane than a number of the methods which have been sanctified by custom, but that does not justify its employment. That is, it does not wholly justify it. Its unusual nature makes it stand out and attract an amount of attention which it is not entitled to. It takes hold upon morbid imaginations and they work it up into a sort of exhibition of cruelty, and this smirches the good name of our civilization, whereas one of the old harsher methods would have had no such effect because usage had made those methods familiar to us and innocent. In many countries we have chained the savage and starved him to death; and this we do not care for, because custom has inured us to it; yet a quick death by poison is lovingkindness to it. In many countries we have burned the savage at the stake; and this we do not care for, because custom has inured us to it; yet a quick death is lovingkindness to it. In more than one country we have hunted the savage and his little children and their mother with dogs and guns through the woods and swamps for an afternoon's sport, and filled the region with happy laughter over their sprawling and stumbling flight, and their wild supplications for mercy; but this method we do not mind, because custom has inured us to it; yet a quick death by poison is lovingkindness to it. In many countries we have taken the savage's land from him, and made him our slave, and lashed him every day, and broken his pride, and made death his only friend, and overworked him till he dropped in his tracks; and this we do not care for, because custom has inured us to it; yet a quick death by poison is lovingkindness to it. In the Matabeleland today—why, there we are confining ourselves to sanctified custom, we Rhodes-Beit millionaires in South Africa and Dukes in London; and nobody cares, because we are used to the old holy customs, and all we ask is that no notice-inviting new ones shall be intruded upon the attention of our comfortable consciences. Mrs. Praed says of the poisoner, "That squatter deserves to have his name handed down to the contempt of posterity."

I am sorry to hear her say that. I myself blame him for one thing, and severely, but I stop there. I blame him for the indiscretion of introducing a novelty which was calculated to attract attention to our civilization. There was no occasion to do that. It was his duty, and it is every loyal man's duty to protect that heritage in every way he can; and the best way to do that is to attract attention elsewhere. The squatter's judgment was bad—that is plain; but his heart was right. He is almost the only pioneering representative of civilization in history who has risen above the prejudices of his caste and his heredity and tried to introduce the element of mercy into the superior race's dealings with the savage. His name is lost, and it is a pity; for it deserves to be handed down to posterity with homage and reverence.

This paragraph is from a London journal:

> "To learn what France is doing to spread the blessings of civilization in her distant dependencies we may turn with advantage to New Caledonia. With a view to attracting free settlers to that penal colony, M. Feillet, the Governor, forcibly expropriated the Kanaka cultivators from the best of their plantations, with a derisory compensation, in spite of the protests of the Council General of the island. Such immigrants as could be induced to cross the seas thus found themselves in possession of thousands of coffee, cocoa, banana, and bread-fruit trees, the raising of which had cost the wretched natives years of toil, whilst the latter had a few five-franc pieces to spend in the liquor stores of Noumea."

You observe the combination? It is robbery, humiliation, and slow, slow murder, through poverty and the white man's whisky. The savage's gentle friend, the savage's noble friend, the only magnanimous and unselfish friend the savage has ever had, was not there with the merciful swift release of his poisoned pudding.

There are many humorous things in the world; among them the white man's notion that he is less savage than the other savages.

TO THE PERSON SITTING IN DARKNESS

(1901)

The following essay was published in the *North American Review* in January, 1901; some 125,000 copies were later distributed by the Anti-Imperialist League. There was considerable reaction, both favorable and unfavorable, to the essay in the press, and Twain was sometimes accused of having lost touch with American ideals. His rebuttal was that America had lost sight of its own democratic values and that the U.S. soldiers in the Philippines were in fact no better than "Christian butchers." "To the Person Sitting in Darkness" is, in any event, his most eloquent, if not his most venomous, attack on imperialism. At first, Clemens was in favor of the war because he believed the United States meant to restore the country to and confer political liberty upon its native citizens. When it became clear that this was not to be our national policy, his change of heart was swift and complete. Because its satiric target is broad, including diverse imperialist wars going on at the time and examining the venal motives behind such territorial expansion, this essay has retained a certain currency well beyond its appointed hour.

"To the Person Sitting in Darkness"

"Christmas will dawn in the United States over a people full of hope and aspiration and good cheer. Such a condition means contentment and happiness. The carping grumbler who may here and there go forth will find few to listen to him. The majority will wonder what is the matter with him and pass on."—*New York Tribune,* on Christmas Eve.

From *The Sun,* of New York:

"The purpose of this article is not to describe the terrible offences against humanity committed in the name of Politics in some of the most notorious East Side districts. *They could not be described, even verbally.* But it is the intention to let the great mass of more or less careless citizens of this beautiful metropolis of the New World get some conception of the havoc and ruin wrought to man, woman and child in the most densely populated and least known section of the city. Name, date and place can be supplied to those of little faith—or to any man who feels himself aggrieved. It is a plain statement of record and observation, written without license and without garnish.

"Imagine, if you can, a section of the city territory completely dominated by one man, without whose permission neither legitimate nor illegitimate business can be conducted; *where illegitimate business is encouraged and legitimate business discouraged;* where the respectable residents have to fasten their doors and windows summer nights and sit in their rooms with asphyxiating air and 100-degree temperature, rather than try to catch the faint whiff of breeze in their natural breathing places, the stoops of their homes; *where naked women dance by night in the streets, and unsexed men prowl like vultures through the darkness on 'business'* not only permitted but encouraged by the police; *where the education of infants begins with the knowledge of prostitution* and the training of little girls is training in the arts of Phryne; where *American* girls brought up with the refinements of *American* homes are imported from small towns up-State, Massachusetts, Connecticut and New Jersey, and kept as virtually prisoners as if they were locked up behind jail bars until they have lost all semblance of womanhood; *where small boys are taught to solicit for the women of disorderly houses;* where there is an organized society of young men *whose sole business in life is to corrupt young girls and turn them over to bawdy houses;* where men walking with their wives along the street are openly insulted; *where children that have adult diseases are the chief patrons of the hospitals and dispensaries;* where it is the rule, rather than the exception, that *murder, rape, robbery and theft go unpunished*—in short where the Premium of the most awful forms of Vice is the Profit of the politicians."

The following news from China appeared in *The Sun,* of New York, on Christmas Eve. The italics are mine:

"The Rev. Mr. Ament, of the American Board of Foreign Missions, has returned from a trip which he made for the purpose of collecting indemnities for damages done by Boxers. *Everywhere he went he compelled the Chinese to pay.* He says that all his native Christians are now provided for. He had 700 of them under his charge, and 300 were killed. He has *collected 300 taels for each* of these murders, and has *compelled full payment for all the property belonging to Christians* that was destroyed. He also assessed *fines* amounting to THIRTEEN TIMES the amount of the indemnity. *This money will be used for the propagation of the Gospel.*

"Mr. Ament declares that the compensation he has collected is *moderate,* when compared with the amount secured by the Catholics, who demand, in addition to money, *head for head.* They collect 500 taels for each murder of a Catholic. In the

Wenchiu country, 680 Catholics were killed, and for this the European Catholics here demand 750,000 strings of cash and 680 *heads*.

"In the course of a conversation, Mr. Ament referred to the attitude of the missionaries toward the Chinese. He said:

"'I deny emphatically that the missionaries are *vindictive*, that they *generally* looted, or that they have done anything *since* the siege that *the circumstances did not demand*. I criticise the Americans. *The soft hand of the Americans is not as good as the mailed fist of the Germans*. If you deal with the Chinese with a soft hand they will take advantage of it.'

"The statement that the French Government will return the loot taken by the French soldiers, is the source of the greatest amusement here. The French soldiers were more systematic looters than the Germans, and it is a fact that to-day *Catholic Christians*, carrying French flags and armed with modern guns, *are looting villages* in the Province of Chili."

By happy luck, we get all these glad tidings on Christmas Eve—just in time to enable us to celebrate the day with proper gaiety and enthusiasm. Our spirits soar, and we find we can even make jokes: Taels I win, Heads you lose.

Our Reverend Ament is the right man in the right place. What we want of our missionaries out there is, not that they shall merely represent in their acts and persons the grace and gentleness and charity and loving kindness of our religion, but that they shall also represent the American spirit. The oldest Americans are the Pawnees. Macallum's History says:

"When a white Boxer kills a Pawnee and destroys his property, the other Pawnees do not trouble to seek *him* out, they kill any white person that comes along; also, they make some white village pay deceased's heirs the full cash value of deceased, together with full cash value of the property destroyed; they also make the village pay, in addition, *thirteen times* the value of that property into a fund for the dissemination of the Pawnee religion, which they regard as the best of all religions for the softening and humanizing of the heart of man. It is their idea that it is only fair and right that the innocent should be made to suffer for the guilty, and that it is better that ninety and nine innocent should suffer than the one guilty person should escape."

Our Reverend Ament is justifiably jealous of those enterprising Catholics, who not only get big money for each lost convert, but get "head for head" besides. But he should soothe himself with the reflection that the entirety of their exactions are for their own pockets, whereas he, less selfishly, devotes only 300 taels per head to that service, and gives the whole vast thirteen repetitions of the property-indemnity to the service of propagating the Gospel. His magnanimity has won him the approval of his nation, and will get him a monument. Let him be content with these rewards. We all hold him dear for manfully defending his fellow missionaries from exaggerated charges which were beginning to distress us, but which his testimony has so considerably modified that we can now contemplate them without noticeable pain. For now we know that, even before the siege, the missionaries were not "generally" out looting, and that, "since the siege," they have acted quite handsomely, except when "circumstances" crowded them. I am arranging for the monument. Subscriptions for it can be sent to the American Board; designs for it can be sent to me. Designs must allegorically set forth the Thirteen Reduplications of the Indemnity, and the Object for which they were exacted; as Ornaments, the designs must exhibit 680 Heads, so disposed as to give a pleasing and pretty effect; for the Catholics have done nicely, and are entitled to notice in the monument. Mottoes may be suggested, if any shall be discovered that will satisfactorily cover the ground.

Mr. Ament's financial feat of squeezing a thirteen-fold indemnity out of the pauper peasants to square other people's offenses, thus condemning them and their women and innocent little children to inevitable starvation and lingering death, in order that the blood-money so acquired might be *"used for the propagation of the Gospel,"* does not flutter my serenity; although the act and the words, taken together, concrete a blasphemy so hideous and so colossal that, without doubt, its mate is not findable in the history of this or of any other age. Yet, if a layman had done that thing and justified it with those words, I should have shuddered, I know. Or, if I had done the thing and said the words myself—however, the thought is unthinkable, irreverent as some imperfectly informed people think me. Sometimes an ordained minister sets out to be blasphemous. When this happens, the layman is out of the running; he stands no chance.

We have Mr. Ament's impassioned assurance that the missionaries are not "vindictive." Let us hope and pray that they will never become so, but will remain in the almost morbidly fair and just and gentle temper which is affording so much satisfaction to their brother and champion to-day.

The following is from the *New York Tribune* of Christmas Eve. It comes from that journal's Tokio correspondent. It has a strange and impudent sound, but the Japanese are but partially civilized as yet. When they become wholly civilized they will not talk so:

> "The missionary question, of course, occupies a foremost place in the discussion. It is now felt as essential that the Western Powers take cognizance of the sentiment here, that religious invasions of Oriental countries by powerful Western organizations are tantamount to filibustering expeditions, and should not only be discountenanced, but that stern measures should be adopted for their suppression. The feeling here is that the missionary organizations constitute a constant menace to peaceful international relations."

Shall we? That is, shall we go on conferring our Civilization upon the peoples that sit in darkness, or shall we give those poor things a rest? Shall we bang right ahead in our old-time, loud, pious way, and commit the new century to the game; or shall we sober up and sit down and think it over first? Would it not be prudent to get our Civilization-tools together, and see how much stock is left on hand in the way of Glass Beads and Theology, and Maxim Guns and Hymn Books, and Trade-Gin and Torches of Progress and Enlightenment (patent adjustable ones, good to fire villages with, upon occasion), and balance the books, and arrive at the profit and loss, so that we may intelligently decide whether to continue the business or sell out the property and start a new Civilization Scheme on the proceeds?

Extending the Blessings of Civilization to our Brother who Sits in Darkness has been a good trade and has paid well, on the whole; and there is money in it yet, if carefully worked—but not enough, in my judgment, to make any considerable risk advisable. The People that Sit in Darkness are getting to be too scarce—too scarce and too shy. And such darkness as is now left is really of but an indifferent quality, and not dark enough for the game. The most of those People that Sit in Darkness have been furnished with more light than was good for them or profitable for us. We have been injudicious.

The Blessings-of-Civilization Trust, wisely and cautiously administered, is a Daisy. There is more money in it, more territory, more sovereignty, and other kinds of emolument, than there is in any other game that is played. But Christendom has been playing it badly of late years, and must certainly suffer by it, in my opinion. She has been so eager to get every stake that appeared on the green cloth, that the People who Sit in Darkness have noticed it—they have noticed it, and have begun to show alarm. They have become suspicious of the Blessings of Civilization. More—they have begun to examine them. This is not well. The Blessings of Civilization are all right, and a good commercial property; there could not be a better, in a dim light. In the right kind of light, and at a proper distance, with the goods a little out of focus, they furnish this desirable exhibit to the Gentlemen who Sit in Darkness:

LOVE,
JUSTICE,
GENTLENESS,
CHRISTIANITY,
PROTECTION TO THE WEAK,
TEMPERANCE,
LAW AND ORDER,
LIBERTY,
EQUALITY,
HONORABLE DEALING,
MERCY,
EDUCATION,

—and so on.

There. Is it good? Sir, it is pie. It will bring into camp any idiot that sits in darkness anywhere. But not if we adulterate it. It is proper to be emphatic upon that point. This brand is strictly for Export—apparently. *Apparently.* Privately and confidentially, it is nothing of the kind. Privately and confidentially, it is merely an outside cover, gay and pretty and attractive, displaying the special patterns of our Civilization which we reserve for Home Consumption, while *inside* the bale is the Actual Thing that the Customer Sitting in Darkness buys with his blood and tears and land and liberty. That Actual Thing is, indeed, Civilization, but it is only for Export. Is there a difference between the two brands? In some of the details, yes.

We all know that the Business is being ruined. The reason is not far to seek. It is because our Mr. McKinley, and Mr. Chamberlain, and the Kaiser, and the Czar and the French have been exporting the Actual Thing *with the outside cover left off.* This is bad for the Game. It shows that these new players of it are not sufficiently acquainted with it.

It is a distress to look on and note the mismoves, they are so strange and so awkward. Mr. Chamberlain manufactures a war out of materials so inadequate and so fanciful that they make the boxes grieve and the gallery laugh, and he tries hard to persuade himself that it isn't purely a private raid for cash, but has a sort of dim, vague respectability about it somewhere, if he could only find the spot; and that, by and by, he can scour the flag clean again after he has finished dragging it through the mud, and make it shine and flash in the vault of heaven once more as it had shone and flashed there a thousand years in the world's respect until he laid his unfaithful hand upon it. It is bad play—bad. For it exposes the Actual Thing to Them that Sit in Darkness, and they say: "What! Christian against Christian? And only for money? Is *this* a case of magnanimity, forbearance, love, gentleness, mercy, protection of the weak—this strange and over-showy onslaught of an elephant upon a nest of field-mice, on the pretext that the mice had squeaked an insolence at him—conduct which 'no self-respecting government could allow to pass unavenged?' as Mr. Chamberlain said. Was that a good pretext in a small case, when it had not been a good pretext in a large one?—for only recently Russia had affronted the elephant three times and survived alive and unsmitten. Is this Civilization and Progress? Is it something better than we already possess? These harryings and burnings and desert-makings in the Transvaal—is this an improvement on our darkness? Is it, perhaps, possible that there are two kinds of Civilization—one for home consumption and one for the heathen market?"

Then They that Sit in Darkness are troubled, and shake their heads; and they read this extract from a letter of a British private, recounting his exploits in one of Methuen's victories, some days before the affair of Magersfontein, and they are troubled again:

> "We tore up the hill and into the intrenchments, and the Boers saw we had them; so they dropped their guns and went down on their knees and put up their hands clasped, and begged for mercy. And we gave it them—*with the long spoon.*"

The long spoon is the bayonet. See *Lloyd's Weekly,* London, of those days. The same number—and the same column—contained some quite unconscious satire in the form of shocked and bitter upbraidings of the Boers for their brutalities and inhumanities!

Next, to our heavy damage, the Kaiser went to playing the game without first mastering it. He lost a couple of missionaries in a riot in Shantung, and in his account he made an overcharge for them. China had to pay a hundred thousand dollars apiece for them, in money; twelve miles of territory, containing several millions of inhabitants and worth twenty million dollars; and to build a monument, and also a Christian church; whereas the people of China could have been depended upon to remember the missionaries without the help of these expensive memorials. This was all bad play. Bad, because it would not, and could not, and will not now or ever, deceive the Person Sitting in Darkness. He knows that it was an overcharge. He knows that a missionary is like any other man: he is worth merely what you can supply his place for, and no more. He is useful, but so is a doctor, so is a sheriff, so is an editor; but a just Emperor does not charge war-prices for such. A diligent, intelligent, but obscure missionary, and a diligent, intelligent country editor are worth much, and we know it; but they are not worth the earth. We esteem such an editor, and we are sorry to see him go; but, when he goes, we should consider twelve miles of territory, and a church, and a fortune, over-compensation for his loss. I mean, if he was a Chinese editor, and we had to settle for him. It is no proper figure for an editor or a missionary; one can get shop-worn kings for less. It was bad play on the Kaiser's part. It got this property, true; but it *produced the Chinese revolt,* the indignant uprising of China's traduced patriots, the Boxers. The results have been expensive to Germany, and to the other Disseminators of Progress and the Blessings of Civilization.

The Kaiser's claim was paid, yet it was bad play, for it could not fail to have an evil effect upon Persons Sitting in Darkness in China. They would muse upon the event, and be likely to say: "Civilization is gracious and beautiful, for such is its reputation; but can we afford it? There are rich Chinamen, perhaps they could afford it; but this tax is not laid upon them, it is laid upon the peasants of Shantung; it is they that must pay this mighty sum, and their wages are but four cents a day. Is this a better civilization than ours, and holier and higher and nobler? Is not this rapacity? Is not this extortion? Would Germany charge America two hundred thousand dollars for two missionaries, and shake the mailed fist in her face, and send warships, and send soldiers, and say: 'Seize twelve miles of territory, worth twenty millions of dollars, as additional pay for the missionaries; and make those peasants build a monument to the missionaries, and a costly Christian church to remember them by?' And later would Germany say to her soldiers: 'March through America and slay, *giving no quarter;* make the German face there, as has been our Hunface here, a terror for a thousand years; march through the Great Republic and slay, slay, slay, carving a road for our offended religion through its heart and bowels?' Would Germany do like this to America, to England, to France, to Russia? Or only to China the helpless—imitating the elephant's assault upon the field-mice? Had we better invest in this Civilization—this Civilization which called Napoleon a buccaneer for carrying off Venice's bronze horses, but which steals our ancient astronomical instruments from our walls, and goes looting like common bandits—that is, all the alien soldiers except America's; and (Americans again excepted) storms frightened villages and cables the result to glad journals at home every day: 'Chinese losses, 450 killed; ours, *one officer and two men wounded.* Shall proceed against neighboring village to-morrow, where a *massacre* is reported.' Can we afford Civilization?"

And, next, Russia must go and play the game injudiciously. She affronts England once or twice—with the Person Sitting in Darkness observing and noting; by moral assistance of France and Germany, she robs Japan of her hard-earned spoil, all swimming in Chinese blood—Port Arthur—with the Person again observing and noting; then she seizes Manchuria, raids its villages, and chokes its great river with the swollen corpses of countless massacred peasants—that astonished Person still observing and noting. And perhaps he is saying to himself: "It is yet *another* Civilized Power, with its banner of the Prince of Peace in one hand and its loot-basket and its butcher-knife in the other. Is there no salvation for us but to adopt Civilization and lift ourselves down to its level?"

And by and by comes America, and our Master of the Game plays it badly—plays it as Mr. Chamberlain was playing it in South Africa. It was a mistake to do that; also, it was one which was quite unlooked for in a Master who was playing it so well in Cuba. In Cuba, he was playing the usual and regular *American* game, and it was winning, for there is no way to beat it. The Master, contemplating Cuba, said: "Here is an oppressed and friendless little nation which is willing to fight to be free; we go partners, and put up the strength of seventy million sympathizers and the resources of the United States: play!" Nothing but Europe combined could call that hand: and Europe cannot combine on anything. There, in Cuba, he was following our great tradition in a way which made us very proud of him, and proud of the deep dissatisfaction which his play was provoking in Continental Europe. Moved by a high inspiration, he threw out those stirring words which proclaimed that forcible annexation would be "criminal aggression;" and in that utterance fired another "shot heard round the world." The memory of that fine saying will be outlived by the remembrance of no act of his but one—that he forgot it within the twelvemonth, and its honorable gospel along with it.

For, presently, came the Philippine temptation. It was strong; it was too strong, and he made that bad mistake: he played the European game, the Chamberlain game. It was a pity; it was a great pity, that error; that one grievous error, that irrevocable error. For it was the very place and time to play the American game again. And at no cost. Rich winnings to be gathered in, too; rich and permanent; indestructible; a fortune transmissible forever to the children of the flag. Not land, not money, not dominion—no, something worth many times more than that dross: our share, the spectacle of a nation of long harassed and persecuted slaves set free through our influence; our posterity's share, the golden memory of that fair deed. The game was in our hands. If it had been played according to the American rules, Dewey would have sailed away from Manila as soon as he had destroyed the Spanish fleet—after putting up a sign on shore guaranteeing foreign property and life against damage by the Filipinos, and warning the Powers that interference with the emancipated patriots would be regarded as an act unfriendly to the United States. The Powers cannot combine, in even a bad cause, and the sign would not have been molested.

Dewey could have gone about his affairs elsewhere, and left the competent Filipino army to starve out the little Spanish garrison and send it home, and the Filipino citizens to set up the form of government they might prefer, and deal with the friars and their doubtful acquisitions according to Filipino ideas of fairness and justice—ideas which have since been tested and found to be of as high an order as any that prevail in Europe or America.

But we played the Chamberlain game, and lost the chance to add another Cuba and another honorable deed to our good record.

The more we examine the mistake, the more clearly we perceive that it is going to be bad for the Business. The Person Sitting in Darkness is almost sure to say: "There is something curious about this—curious and unaccountable. There must be two Americas: one that sets the captive free, and one that takes a once-captive's new freedom away from him, and picks a quarrel with him with nothing to found it on; then kills him to get his land."

The truth is, the Person Sitting in Darkness *is* saying things like that; and for the sake of the Business we must persuade him to look at the Philippine matter in another and healthier way. We must arrange his opinions for him. I believe it can be done; for Mr. Chamberlain has arranged England's opinion of the South African matter, and done it most cleverly and successfully. He presented the facts—some of the facts—and showed those confiding people what the facts meant. He did it statistically, which is a good way. He used the formula: "Twice 2 are 14, and 2 from 9 leaves 35." Figures are effective; figures will convince the elect.

Now, my plan is a still bolder one than Mr. Chamberlain's, though apparently a copy of it. Let us be franker than Mr. Chamberlain; let us audaciously present the whole of the facts, shirking none, then explain them according to Mr. Chamberlain's formula. This daring truthfulness will astonish and dazzle the Person Sitting in Darkness, and he will take the Explanation down before his mental vision had had time to get back into focus. Let us say to him:

"Our case is simple. On the 1st of May, Dewey destroyed the Spanish fleet. This left the Archipelago in the hands of its proper and rightful owners, the Filipino nation. Their army numbered 30,000 men, and they were competent to whip out or starve out the little Spanish garrison; then the people could set up a government of their own devising. Our traditions required that Dewey should now set up his warning sign, and go away. But the Master of the Game happened to think of another plan—the European plan. He acted upon it. This was, to send out an army—ostensibly to help the native patriots put the finishing touch upon their long and plucky struggle for independence, but really to take their land away from them and keep it. That is, in the interest of Progress and Civilization. The plan developed, stage by stage, and quite satisfactorily. We entered into a military alliance with the trusting Filipinos, and they hemmed in Manila on the land side, and by their valuable help the place, with its garrison of 8,000 or 10,000 Spaniards, was captured—a thing which we could not have accomplished unaided at that time. We got their help by—by ingenuity. We knew they were fighting for their independence, and that they had been at it for two years. We knew they supposed that we also were fighting in their worthy cause—just as we had helped the Cubans fight for Cuban independence—and we allowed them to go on thinking so. *Until Manila was ours and we could get along without them.* Then we showed our hand. Of course, they were surprised—that was natural; surprised and disappointed; disappointed and grieved. To them it looked un-American; uncharacteristic; foreign to our established traditions. And this was natural, too; for we were only playing the American Game in public—in private it was the European. It was neatly done, very neatly, and it bewildered them. They could not understand it; for we had been so friendly—so affectionate, even—with those simple-minded patriots! We, our own selves, had brought back out of exile their leader, their hero, their hope, their Washington—Aguinaldo; brought him in a warship, in high honor, under the sacred shelter and hospitality of the flag; brought him back and restored him to his people, and got their moving and eloquent gratitude for it. Yes, we had been so friendly to them, and had heartened them up in so many ways! We had lent them guns and ammunition; advised with them; exchanged pleasant courtesies with them; placed our sick and wounded in their kindly care; entrusted our Spanish prisoners to their humane and honest hands; fought shoulder to shoulder with them against 'the common enemy' (our own phrase); praised their courage, praised their gallantry, praised their mercifulness, praised their fine and honorable conduct; borrowed their trenches, borrowed strong positions which they had previously captured from the Spaniard; petted them, lied to them—officially proclaiming that our land and naval forces came to give them their freedom and displace the bad Spanish Government—fooled them, used them until we needed them no longer; then derided the sucked orange and threw it away. We kept the positions which we had beguiled them of; by and by, we moved a force forward and overlapped patriot ground—a clever thought, for we needed trouble, and this would produce it. A Filipino soldier, crossing the ground, where no one had a right to forbid him, was shot by our sentry. The badgered patriots resented this with arms, without waiting to know whether Aguinaldo, who was absent, would approve or not. Aguinaldo did not approve; but that availed nothing. What we wanted, in the interest of Progress and Civilization, was the Archipelago, unencumbered by patriots struggling for independence; and War was what we needed. We clinched our opportunity. It is Mr. Chamberlain's case over again—at least in its motive and intention; and we played the game as adroitly as he played it himself."

At this point in our frank statement of fact to the Person Sitting in Darkness, we should throw in a little trade-taffy about the Blessings of Civilization—for a change, and for the refreshment of his spirit—then go on with our tale:

"We and the patriots having captured Manila, Spain's ownership of the Archipelago and her sovereignty over it were at an end—obliterated—annihilated—not a rag or shred of either remaining behind. It was then that we conceived the divinely humorous idea of *buying* both of these spectres from Spain! [It is quite safe to confess this to the Person Sitting in Darkness, since neither he nor any other sane person will believe it.] In buying those ghosts for twenty millions, we also contracted to take care of the friars and their accumulations. I think we also agreed to propagate leprosy and smallpox, but as to this there is doubt. But it is not important; persons afflicted with the friars do not mind other diseases.

"With our Treaty ratified, Manila subdued, and our Ghosts secured, we had not further use for Aguinaldo and the owners of the Archipelago. We forced a war, and we have been hunting America's guest and ally through the woods and swamps ever since."

At this point in the tale, it will be well to boast a little of our war-work and our heroisms in the field, so as to make our performance look as fine as England's in South Africa; but I believe it will not be best to emphasize this too much. We must be cautious. Of course, we must read the war-telegrams to the Person, in order to keep up our frankness; but we can throw an air of humorousness over them, and that will modify their grim eloquence a little, and their rather indiscreet exhibitions of gory exultation. Before reading to him the following display heads of the dispatches of November 18, 1900, it will be well to practice on them in private first, so as to get the right tang of lightness and gaiety into them:

"ADMINISTRATION WEARY OF PROTRACTED HOSTILITIES!"
"REAL WAR AHEAD FOR FILIPINO REBELS!"*
"WILL SHOW NO MERCY!"
"KITCHENER'S PLAN ADOPTED!"

Kitchener knows how to handle disagreeable people who are fighting for their homes and their liberties, and we must let on that we are merely imitating Kitchener, and have no national interest in the matter, further than to get ourselves admired by the Great Family of Nations, in which august company our Master of the Game has bought a place for us in the back row. Of course, we must not venture to ignore our General MacArthur's reports—oh, why do they keep on printing those embarrassing things?—we must drop them trippingly from the tongue and take the chances:

> "During the last ten months our losses have been 268 killed and 750 wounded; Filipino loss; *three thousand two hundred and twenty-seven killed*, and 694 wounded."

We must stand ready to grab the Person Sitting in Darkness, for he will swoon away at this confession, saying: "Good God, those 'niggers' spare their wounded, and the Americans massacre theirs!"

*"Rebels!" Mumble that funny word—don't let the Person catch it distinctly.

We must bring him to, and coax him and coddle him, and assure him that the ways of Providence are best, and that it would not become us to find fault with them; and then, to show him that we are only imitators, not originators, we must read the following passage from the letter of an American soldier-lad in the Philippines to his mother, published in *Public Opinion*, of Decorah, Iowa, describing the finish of a victorious battle:

> "We never left one alive. If one was wounded, we would run our bayonets through him."

Having now laid all the historical facts before the Person Sitting in Darkness, we should bring him to again, and explain them to him. We should say to him:

"They look doubtful, but in reality they are not. There have been lies; yes, but they were told in a good cause. We have been treacherous; but that was only in order that real good might come out of apparent evil. True, we have crushed a deceived and confiding people; we have turned against the weak and the friendless who trusted us; we have stamped out a just and intelligent and well-ordered republic; we have stabbed an ally in the back and slapped the face of a guest; we have bought a Shadow from an enemy that hadn't it to sell; we have robbed a trusting friend of his land and his liberty; we have invited our clean young men to shoulder a discredited musket and do bandit's work under a flag which bandits have been accustomed to fear, not to follow; we have debauched America's honor and blackened her face before the world; but each detail was for the best. We know this. The Head of every State and Sovereignty in Christendom and ninety per cent of every legislative body in Christendom, including our Congress and our fifty State Legislatures, are members not only of the church, but also of the Blessings-of-Civilization Trust. This world-girdling accumulation of trained morals, high principles, and justice, cannot do an unright thing, an unfair thing, and ungenerous thing, an unclean thing. It knows what it is about. Give yourself no uneasiness; it is all right."

Now then, that will convince the Person. You will see. It will restore the Business. Also, it will elect the Master of the Game to the vacant place in the Trinity of our national gods; and there on their high thrones the Three will sit, age after age, in the people's sight, each bearing the Emblem of his service: Washington, the Sword of the Liberator; Lincoln, the Slave's Broken Chains; the Master, the Chains Repaired.

It will give the Business a splendid new start. You will see.

Everything is prosperous, now; everything is just as we should wish it. We have got the Archipelago, and we shall never give it up. Also, we have every reason to hope that we shall have an opportunity before very long to slip out of our Congressional contract with Cuba and give her something better in the place of it. It is a rich country, and many of us are already beginning to see that the contract was a sentimental mistake. But now—right now—is the best time to do some profitable rehabilitating work—work that will set us up and make us comfortable, and discourage gossip. We cannot conceal from ourselves that, privately, we are a little troubled about our uniform. It is one of our prides; it is acquainted with honor; it is familiar with great deeds and noble; we love it, we revere it; and so this errand it is on makes us uneasy. And our flag—another pride of ours, our chiefest! We have worshipped it so; and when we have seen it in far lands—glimpsing it unexpectedly in that strange sky, waving its welcome and benediction to us—we have caught our breath, and uncovered our heads, and couldn't speak, for a moment, for the thought of what it was to us and the great ideals it stood for. Indeed, we *must* do something about these things; we must not have the flag out there, and the uniform. They are not needed there; we can manage in some other way. England manages, as regards the uniform, and so can we. We have to send soldiers—we can't get out of that—but we can disguise them. It is the way England does in South Africa. Even Mr. Chamberlain himself takes pride in England's honorable uniform, and makes the army down there wear an ugly and odious and appropriate disguise, of yellow stuff such as quarantine flags are made of, and which are hoisted to warn the healthy away from unclean disease and repulsive death. This cloth is called khaki. We could adopt it. It is light, comfortable, grotesque, and deceives the enemy, for he cannot conceive of a soldier being concealed in it.

And as for a flag for the Philippine Province, it is easily managed. We can have a special one—our States do it: we can have just our usual flag, with the white stripes painted black and the stars replaced by the skull and cross-bones.

And we do not need the Civil Commission out there. Having no powers, it has to invent them, and that kind of work cannot be effectively done by just anybody; an expert is required. Mr. Croker can be spared. We do not want the United States represented there, but only the Game.

By help of these suggested amendments, Progress and Civilization in that country can have a boom, and it will take in the Persons who are Sitting in Darkness, and we can resume Business at the old stand.

CORN-PONE OPINIONS

(1901)

"Corn-Pone Opinions" was written in 1901 but was first published in *Europe and Elsewhere* (1923). It is one of the more clever statements of Twain's philosophy. The supposed germ for the piece, the recollected "sermons" of a slave named Jerry, may have been an invention; at least such a man has not yet been identified. Twain's refinement and elaboration of a bit of folk wisdom turns the reminiscence into an argument that human beings are incapable of independent rational thought and are ruled by influences from without.

"Corn-Pone Opinions"

Fifty years ago, when I was a boy of fifteen and helping to inhabit a Missourian village on the banks of the Mississippi, I had a friend whose society was very dear to me because I was forbidden by my mother to partake of it. He was a gay and impudent and satirical and delightful young black man—a slave—who daily preached sermons from the top of his master's woodpile, with me for sole audience. He imitated the pulpit style of the several clergymen of the village, and did it well and with fine passion and energy. To me he was a wonder. I believed he was the greatest orator in the United States and would some day be heard from. But it did not happen; in the distribution of rewards he was overlooked. It is the way, in this world.

He interrupted his preaching now and then to saw a stick of wood, but the sawing was a pretense—he did it with his mouth, exactly imitating the sound the bucksaw makes in shrieking its way through the wood. But it served its purpose, it kept his master from coming out to see how the work was getting along. I listened to the sermons from the open window of a lumber room at the back of the house. One of his texts was this:

"You tell me whar a man gits his corn pone, en I'll tell you what his 'pinions is."

I can never forget it. It was deeply impressed upon me. By my mother. Not upon my memory, but elsewhere. She had slipped in upon me while I was absorbed and not watching. The black philosopher's idea was that a man is not independent and cannot afford views which might interfere with his bread and butter. If he would prosper, he must train with the majority; in matters of large moment, like politics and religion, he must think and feel with the bulk of his neighbors or suffer damage in his social standing and in his business prosperities. He must restrict himself to corn-pone opinions—at least on the surface. He must get his opinions from other people, he must reason out none for himself, he must have no first-hand views.

I think Jerry was right, in the main, but I think he did not go far enough.

1. It was his idea that a man conforms to the majority view of his locality by calculation and intention.

This happens, but I think it is not the rule.

2. It was his idea that there is such a thing as a first-hand opinion, an original opinion, an opinion which is coldly reasoned out in a man's head by a searching analysis of the facts involved, with the heart unconsulted and the jury room closed against outside influences. It may be that such an opinion has been born somewhere at some time or other, but I suppose it got away before they could catch it and stuff it and put it in the museum.

I am persuaded that a coldly-thought-out and independent verdict upon a fashion in clothes, or manners, or literature, or politics, or religion, or any other matter that is projected into the field of our notice and interest is a most rare thing—if it has indeed ever existed.

A new thing in costume appears—the flaring hoopskirt, for example—and the passers-by are shocked, and the irreverent laugh. Six months later everybody is reconciled; the fashion has established itself; it is admired now and no one laughs. Public opinion resented it before, public opinion accepts it now and is happy in it. Why? Was the resentment reasoned out? Was the acceptance reasoned out? No. The instinct that moves to conformity did the work. It is our nature to conform; it is a force which not many can successfully resist. What is its seat? The inborn requirement of self-approval. We all have to bow to that; there are no exceptions. Even the woman who refuses from first to last to wear the hoopskirt comes under the law and is its slave; she could not wear the skirt and have her own approval, and that she *must* have, she cannot help herself. But as a rule our self-approval has its source in but one place and not elsewhere—the approval of other people. A person of vast consequences can introduce any kind of novelty in dress and the general world will presently adopt it—moved to do it in the first place by the natural instinct to passively yield to that vague something recognized as authority, and in the second place by the human instinct to train with the multitude and have its approval. An empress introduced the hoopskirt and we know the result. If Eve should come again in her ripe renown, and reintroduce her quaint styles—well, we know what would happen. And we should be cruelly embarrassed, along at first.

The hoopskirt runs its course and disappears. Nobody reasons about it. One woman abandons the fashion, her neighbor notices this and follows her lead, this influences the next woman and so on and so on, and presently the skirt has vanished out of the world, no one knows how nor why; nor cares, for that matter. It will come again by and by, and in due course will go again.

Twenty-five years ago in England, six or eight wine glasses stood grouped by each person's plate at a dinner party, and they were used, not left idle and empty; to-day there are but three or four in the group and the average guest sparingly uses about two of them. We have not adopted this new fashion yet, but we shall do it presently. We shall not think it out, we shall merely conform and let it go at that. We get our notions and habits and opinions from outside influences; we do not have to study them out.

Our table manners and company manners and street manners change from time to time, but the changes are not reasoned out; we merely notice and conform. We are creatures of outside influences; as a rule we do not think, we only imitate. We cannot invent standards that will stick; what we mistake for standards are only fashions, and perishable. We may continue to admire them but we drop the use of them. We notice this in literature. Shakespeare is a standard, and fifty years ago we used to write tragedies which we couldn't tell from—from somebody else's, but we don't do it any more now. Our prose standard three quarters of a century ago was ornate and diffuse; some authority or other changed it in the direction of compactness and simplicity, and conformity followed without argument. The historical novel starts up suddenly and sweeps the land. Everybody writes one and the nation is glad. We had historical novels before; but nobody read them and the rest of us conformed—without reasoning it out. We are conforming in the other way now, because it is another case of everybody.

The outside influences are always pouring in upon us and we are always obeying their orders and accepting their verdicts. The Smiths like the new play, the Joneses go to see it and they copy the Smith verdict. Morals, religions, politics, get their following from surrounding influences and atmospheres almost entirely; not from study, not from thinking. A man must and will have his own approval first of all, in each and every moment and circumstance of his life—even if he must repent of a self-approved act the moment after its commission in order to get his self-approval *again:* but speaking in general terms, a man's self-approval in the large concerns of life has its source in the approval of the peoples about him, and not in a searching personal examination of the matter. Mohammedans are Mohammedans because they are born and reared among that sect; not because they have thought it out and can furnish sound reasons for being Mohammedans; we know why Catholics are Catholics, why Presbyterians are Presbyterians, why Baptists are Baptists, why Mormons are Mormons, why thieves are thieves, why monarchists are monarchists, why Republicans are Republicans and Democrats, Democrats. We know it is a matter of association and sympathy, not reasoning and examination; that hardly a man in the world has an opinion upon morals, politics, or religion which he got otherwise than through his associations and sympathies. Broadly speaking, there are none but corn-pone opinions. And broadly speaking, corn-pone stands for self-approval. Self-approval is acquired mainly from the approval of other people. The result is conformity. Sometimes conformity has a sordid business interest—the bread-and-butter interest—but not in most cases, I think. I think that in the majority of cases it is unconscious and not calculated, that it is born of the human being's natural yearning to stand well with his fellows and have their inspiring approval and praise—a yearning which is commonly so strong and so insistent that it cannot be effectually resisted and must have its way.

A political emergency brings out the corn-pone opinion in fine force in its two chief varieties—the pocketbook variety, which has its origin in self-interest, and the bigger variety, the sentimental variety—the one which can't bear to be outside the pale; can't bear to be in disfavor, can't endure the averted face and the cold shoulder, wants to stand well with his friends, wants to be smiled upon, wants to be welcome, wants to hear the precious words, "*He's* on the right track!" Uttered perhaps by an ass, but still an ass of high degree, an ass whose approval is gold and diamonds to a smaller ass, and confers glory and honor and happiness and membership in the herd. For these guads many a man will dump his life-long principles into the street, and his conscience along with them. We have seen it happen. In some millions of instances.

Men think they think upon great political questions, and they do; but they think with their party, not independently; they read its literature but not that of the other side; they arrive at convictions but they are drawn from a partial view of the matter in hand and are of no particular value. They swarm with their party, they feel with their party, they are happy in their party's approval; and where the party leads they will follow, whether for right and honor or through blood and dirt and a mush of mutilated morals.

In our late canvass half of the nation passionately believed that in silver lay salvation, the other half as passionately believed that that way lay destruction. Do you believe that a tenth part of the people on either side had any rational excuse for having an opinion about the matter at all? I studied that mighty question to the bottom—came out empty. Half of our people passionately believe in high tariff, the other half believe otherwise. Does this mean study and examination or only feeling? The latter, I think. I have deeply studied that question, too—and didn't arrive. We all do no end of feeling and we mistake it for thinking. And out of it we get an aggregation which we consider a boon. Its is held in reverence. It settles everything. Some think it the Voice of God.

EARLY DAYS

(1907)

Mark Twain chose to publish selected chapters from his ongoing "Autobiography" in the *North American Review.* "Early Days" appeared in the March, 1907, issue. Apart from its interest as pure reminiscence, this piece sheds light on the literary resources his youth provided him in later years. It also demonstrates, palpably, Twain's mastery of evocative memory. Written at a rather cheerless time in his life, "Early Days" reveals the author's artistic capacity to displace a world that was, at times, too much with him by indulging in vivid and often delicious remembrance.

"Early Days"

As I have said, that vast plot of Tennessee land* was held by my father twenty years—intact. When he died in 1847, we began to manage it ourselves. Forty years afterward, we had managed it all away except 10,000 acres, and gotten nothing to remember the sales by. About 1887—possibly it was earlier—the 10,000 went. My brother found a chance to trade it for a house and lot in the town of Corry, in the oil regions of Pennsylvania. About 1894 he sold this property for $250. That ended the Tennessee Land.

If any penny of cash ever came out of my father's wise investment but that, I have no recollection of it. No, I am overlooking a detail. It furnished me a field for Sellers and a book. Out of my half of the book I got $15,000 or $20,000; out of the play I got $75,000 or $80,000—just about a dollar an acre. It is curious: I was not alive when my father made the investment, therefore he was not intending any partiality; yet I was the only member of the family that ever profited by it. I shall have the occasion to mention this land again, now and then, as I go along, for it influenced our life in one way or another during more than a generation. Whenever things grew dark it rose and put out its hopeful Sellers hand and cheered us up, and said "Do not be afraid—trust in me—wait." It kept us hoping and hoping, during forty years, and forsook us at last. It put our energies to sleep and made visionaries of us—dreamers and indolent. We were always going to be rich next year—no occasion to work. It is good to begin life poor; it is good to begin life

*100,000 acres.

rich—these are wholesome; but to begin it *prospectively* rich! The man who has not experienced it cannot imagine the curse of it.

My parents removed to Missouri in the early thirties; I do not remember just when, for I was not born then, and cared nothing for such things. It was a long journey in those days, and must have been a rough and tiresome one. The home was made in the wee village of Florida, in Monroe county, and I was born there in 1835. The village contained a hundred people and I increased the population by one per cent. It is more than the best man in history ever did for any other town. It may not be modest in me to refer to this, but it is true. There is no record of a person doing as much—not even Shakespeare. But I did it for Florida, and it shows that I could have done it for any place—even London, I suppose.

Recently some one in Missouri has sent me a picture of the house I was born in. Heretofore I have always stated that it was a palace, but I shall be more guarded, now.

I remember only one circumstance connected with my life in it. I remember it very well, though I was but two and a half years old at the time. The family packed up everything and started in wagons for Hannibal, on the Mississippi, thirty miles away. Toward night, when they camped and counted up the children, one was missing. I was the one. I had been left behind. Parents ought always to count the children before they start. I was having a good enough time playing by myself until I found that the doors were fastened and that there was a grisly deep silence brooding over the place. I knew, then, that the family were gone, and that they had forgotten me. I was well frightened, and I made all the noise I could, but no one was near and it did no good. I spent the afternoon in captivity and was not rescued until the gloaming had fallen and the place was alive with ghosts.

My brother Henry was six months old at that time. I used to remember his walking into a fire outdoors when he was a week old. It was remarkable in me to remember a thing like that, which occurred when I was so young. And it was still more remarkable that I should cling to the delusion, for thirty years, that I *did* remember it—for of course it never happened; he would not have been able to walk at that age. If I had stopped to reflect, I should not have burdened my memory with that impossible rubbish so long. It is believed by many people that an impression deposited in a child's memory within the first two years of its life cannot remain there five years, but that is an error. The incident of Benvenuto Cellini and the salamander must be accepted as authentic and trustworthy; and then that remarkable and indisputable instance in the experience of Helen Keller—however, I will speak of that at another time. For many years I believed that I remembered helping my grandfather drink his whiskey toddy when I was six weeks old, but I do not tell about that any more, now; I am grown old, and my memory is not as active as it used to be. When I was younger I could remember anything, whether it had happened or not; but my faculties are decaying, now, and soon I shall be so I cannot remember any but the things that happened. It is sad to go to pieces like this, but we all have to do it.

My uncle, John A. Quarles, was a farmer, and his place in the country four miles from Florida. He had eight chi and fifteen or twenty negroes, and was also fortunate ways. Particularly in his character. I have not come acro better man than he was. I was his guest for two or three months every year, from the fourth year after we removed to Hannibal till I was eleven or twelve years old. I have never consciously used him or his wife in a book, but his farm has come very handy to me in literature, once or twice. In "Huck Finn" and in "Tom Sawyer Detective" I moved it down to Arkansas. It was all of six hundred miles, but it was no trouble, it was not a very large farm; five hundred acres, perhaps, but I could have done it if it had been twice as large. And as for the morality of it, I cared nothing for that; I would move a State if the exigencies of literature required it.

It was a heavenly place for a boy, that farm of my uncle John's. The house was a double log one, with a spacious floor (roofed in) connecting it with the kitchen. In the summer the table was set in the middle of that shady and breezy floor, and the sumptuous meals—well, it makes me cry to think of them.

Fried chicken, roast pig, wild and tame turkeys, ducks and geese; venison just killed; squirrels, rabbits, pheasants, partridges, prairie-chickens; biscuits, hot batter cakes, hot buckwheat cakes, hot "wheat bread," hot rolls, hot corn pone; fresh corn boiled on the ear, succotash, butter-beans, string-beans, tomatoes, pease, Irish potatoes, sweet-potatoes; buttermilk, sweet milk, "clabber"; watermelons, muskmelons, cantaloups,—all fresh from the garden—apple pie, peach pie, pumpkin pie, apple dumplings, peach cobbler—I can't remember the rest. The way that the things were cooked was perhaps the main splendor—particularly a certain few of the dishes. For instance, the corn bread, the hot biscuits and wheat bread, and the fried chicken. These things have never been properly cooked in the North—in fact, no one there is able to learn the art, so far as my experience goes. The North thinks it knows how to make corn bread, but this is gross superstition. Perhaps no bread in the world is quite as good as Southern corn bread, and perhaps no bread in the world is quite so bad as the Northern imitation of it. The North seldom tries to fry chicken, and this is well, the art cannot be learned north of the line of Mason and Dixon, nor anywhere in Europe. This is not hearsay; it is experience that is speaking. In Europe it is imagined that the custom of serving various kinds of bread blazing hot is "American," but that is too broad a spread; it is custom in the South, but is much less than that in the North. In the North and in Europe hot bread is considered unhealthy. This is probably another fussy superstition, like the European superstition that ice-water is unhealthy. Europe does not need ice-water, and does not drink it; and yet, notwithstanding this, its word for it is better than ours, because it describes it, whereas ours doesn't. Europe calls it "iced" water. Our word describes water made from melted ice—a drink which we have but little acquaintance with.

It seems a pity that the world should throw away so many good things merely because they are unwholesome. I doubt if God has given us any refreshment which, taken in moderation, is unwholesome, except microbes. Yet there are people who strictly deprive themselves of each and every eatable, drinkable and smokable which has in any way acquired a shady reputation. They pay this price for health. And health is all they get for it. How strange it is; it is like paying out your whole fortune for a cow that has gone dry.

The farmhouse stood in the middle of a very large yard, and the yard was fenced on three sides with rails and on the rear side with high palings; against these stood the smokehouse; beyond the palings was the orchard; beyond the orchard were the negro quarter and the tobacco-fields. The front yard was entered over a stile, made of sawed-off logs of graduated heights; I do not remember any gate. In a corner of the front yard were a dozen lofty hickory-trees and a dozen black-walnuts, and in the nutting season riches were to be gathered there.

Down a piece, abreast the house, stood a little log cabin against the rail fence; and there the woody hill fell sharply away, past the barns, the corn-crib, the stables and the tobacco-curing house, to a limpid brook which sang along over its gravelly bed and curved and frisked in and out and here and there and yonder in the deep shade of overhanging foliage and vines—a divine place for wading, and it had swimming-pools, too, which were forbidden to us and therefore much frequented by us. For we were little Christian children, and had early been taught the value of forbidden fruit.

In the little log cabin lived a bedridden white-headed slave woman whom we visited daily, and looked upon with awe, for we believed she was upwards of a thousand years old and had talked with Moses. The younger negroes credited these statistics, and had furnished them to us in good faith. We accommodated all the details which came to us about her; and so we believed that she had lost her health in the long desert trip coming out of Egypt, and had never been able to get it back again. She had a round bald place on the crown of her head, and we used to creep around and gaze at it in reverent silence, and reflect that it was caused by fright through seeing Pharaoh drowned. We called her "Aunt" Hannah, Southern fashion. She was superstitious like the other negroes; also, like them, she was deeply religious. Like them, she had great faith in prayer, and employed it in all ordinary exigencies, but not in cases where a dead certainty of result was urgent. Whenever witches were around she tied up the remnant of her wool in little tufts, with white thread, and this promptly made the witches impotent.

All the negroes were friends of ours, and with those of our own age we were in effect comrades. I say in effect, using the phrase as a modification. We were comrades, and yet not comrades; color and condition interposed a subtle line which both parties were conscious of, and which rendered complete fusion impossible. We had a faithful and affectionate good friend, ally and adviser in "Uncle Dan'l," a middle-aged slave whose head was the best one in the negro quarter, whose sympathies were wide and warm, and whose heart was honest and simple and knew no guile. He has served me well, these many, many years. I have not seen him for more than half a century, and yet spiritually I have had his welcome company a good part of that time, and have staged him in books under his own name and as "Jim," and carted him all around—to Hannibal, down the Mississippi on a raft, and even across the Desert of Sahara in a balloon—and he has endured it all with the patience and friendliness and loyalty which were his birthright. It was on the farm that I got my strong liking for his race and my appreciation of certain of its fine qualities. This feeling and this estimate have stood the test of sixty years and more and have suffered no impairment. The black face is as welcome to me now as it was then.

In my schoolboy days I had no aversion to slavery. I was not aware that there was anything wrong about it. No one arraigned it in my hearing; the local papers said nothing against it; the local pulpit taught us that God approved it, that it was a holy thing, and that the doubter need only look in the Bible if he wished to settle his mind—and then the texts were read aloud to us to make the matter sure; if the slaves themselves had an aversion to slavery they were wise and said nothing. In Hannibal we seldom saw a slave misused; on the farm, never.

There was, however, one small incident of my boyhood days which touched this matter, and it must have meant a good deal to me or it would not have stayed in my memory, clear and sharp, vivid and shadowless, all these slow-drifting years. We had a little slave boy whom we had hired from some one, there in Hannibal. He was from the Eastern Shore of Maryland, and had been brought away from his family and his friends, half-way across the American continent, and sold. He was a cheery spirit, innocent and gentle, and the noisiest creature that ever was, perhaps. All day long he was singing, whistling, yelling, whooping, laughing—it was maddening, devastating, unendurable. At last, one day, I lost all my temper, and went raging to my mother, and said Sandy had been singing for an hour without a single break, and I couldn't stand it, and *wouldn't* she please shut him up. The tears came into her eyes, and her lip trembled, and she said something like this—

"Poor thing, when he sings, it shows that he is not remembering, and that comforts me; but when he is still, I am afraid he is thinking, and I cannot bear it. He will never see his mother again; if he can sing, I must not hinder it, but be thankful for it. If you were older, you would understand me; then that friendless child's noise would make you glad."

It was a simple speech, and made up of small words, but it went home, and Sandy's noise was not a trouble to me any more. She never used large words, but she had a natural gift for making small ones do effective work. She lived to reach the neighborhood of ninety years, and was capable with her tongue to the last—especially when a meanness or an injustice roused her spirit. She has come handy to me several times in my books, where she figures as Tom Sawyer's "Aunt Polly." I fitted her out with a dialect, and tried to think up other improvements for her, but did not find any. I used Sandy once, also; it was in "Tom Sawyer"; I tried to get him to whitewash the fence, but it did not work. I do not remember what name I called him by in the book.

I can see the farm yet, with perfect clearness. I can see all its belongings, all its details; the family room of the house, with a "trundle" bed in one corner and a spinning-wheel in another—a wheel whose rising and falling wail, heard from a distance, was the mournfulest of all sounds to me, and made me homesick and low-spirited, and filled my atmosphere with the wandering spirits of the dead; the vast fireplace, piled high, on winter nights, with flaming hickory logs from whose ends a sugary sap bubbled out but did not go to waste, for we scraped it off and ate it; the lazy cat spread out on the rough hearthstones, the drowsy dogs braced against the jambs and blinking; my aunt in one chimney-corner knitting, my uncle in the other smoking his corn-cob pipe; the slick and carpetless oak floor faintly mirroring the dancing flame-tongues and freckled with black indentations where fire-coals had popped out and died a leisurely death; half a dozen children romping in the background twilight; "split"-bottomed chairs here and there, some with rockers; a cradle—out of service, but waiting, with confidence; in the early cold mornings a snuggle of children, in shirts and chemises, occupying the hearthstone and procrastinating—they could not bear to leave that comfortable place and go out on the wind-swept floor-space between the house and the kitchen where the general tin basin stood, and wash.

Along outside of the front fence ran the country road; dusty in the summertime, and a good place for snakes—they liked to lie in it and sun themselves; when they were rattlesnakes, or puff adders, we killed them; when they were black snakes, or racers, or belonged to the fabled "hoop" breed, we fled, without shame; when they were "house snakes" or "garters" we carried them home and put them in Aunt Patsy's work-basket for a surprise; for she was prejudiced against snakes, and always when she took the basket in her lap and they began to climb out of it disordered her mind. She never could seem to get used to them; her opportunities went for nothing. And she was always cold toward bats, too, and could not bear them; and yet I think a bat is as friendly a bird as there is. My mother was Aunt Patsy's sister, and had the same wild superstitions. A bat is beautifully soft and silky; I do not know any creature that is pleasanter to the touch, or is more grateful for caressings, if offered in the right spirit. I know all about these coleoptera, because our great cave, three miles below Hannibal, was multitudinously stocked with them, and often I brought them home to amuse my mother with. It was easy to manage if it was a school day, because then I had ostensibly been to school and hadn't any bats. She was not a suspicious person, but full of trust and confidence; and when I said "There's something in my coat pocket for you," she would put her hand in. But she always took it out again, herself; I didn't have to tell her. It was remarkable, the way she couldn't learn to like private bats.

I think she was never in the cave in her life; but everybody else went there. Many excursion parties came from considerable distances up and down the river to visit the cave. It was miles in extent, and was a tangled wilderness of narrow and lofty clefts and passages. It was an easy place to get lost in; anybody could do it—including the bats. I got lost in it myself, along with a lady, and our last candle burned down to almost nothing before we glimpsed the search-party's lights winding about in the distance.

"Injun Joe" the half-breed got lost in there once, and would have starved to death if the bats had run short. But there was no chance of that; there were myriads of them. He told me all his story. In the book called "Tom Sawyer" I starved him entirely to death in the cave, but that was in the interest of art; it never happened. "General" Gaines, who was our first town drunkard before Jimmy Finn got the place, was lost in there for the space of a week, and finally pushed his handkerchief out of a hole in a hilltop near Saverton, several miles down the river from the cave's mouth, and somebody saw it and dug him out. There is nothing the matter with his statistics except the handkerchief. I knew him for years, and he hadn't any. But it could have been his nose. That would attract attention.

Beyond the road where the snakes sunned themselves was a dense young thicket, and through it a dim-lighted path led a quarter of a mile; then out of the dimness one emerged abruptly upon a level great prairie which was covered with wild strawberry-plants, vividly starred with prairie pinks, and walled in on all sides by forests. The strawberries were fragrant and fine, and in the season we were generally there in the crisp freshness of the early morning, while the dew-beads still sparkled upon the grass and the woods were ringing with the first songs of the birds.

Down the forest slopes to the left were the swings. They were made of bark stripped from hickory saplings. When they became dry they were dangerous. They usually broke when a child was forty feet in the air, and this was why so many bones had to be mended every year. I had no ill-luck myself, but none of my cousins escaped. There were eight of them, and at one time and another they broke fourteen arms among them. But it cost next to nothing, for the doctor worked by the year—$25 for the whole family. I remember two of the Florida doctors, Chowning and Meredith. They not only tended an entire family for $25 a year, but furnished the medicines themselves. Good measure, too. Only the largest persons could hold a whole dose. Castor-oil was the principal beverage. The dose was half a dipperful, with half a dipperful of New Orleans molasses added to help it down and make it taste good, which it never did. The next standby was calomel; the next, rhubarb; and the next, jalap. Then they bled the patient, and put mustard-plasters on him. It was a dreadful system, and yet the death-rate was not heavy. The calomel was nearly sure to salivate the patient and cost him some of his teeth. There were no dentists. When teeth became touched with decay or were otherwise ailing, the doctor knew of but one thing to do: he fetched his tongs and dragged them out. If the jaw remained, it was not his fault.

Doctors were not called, in cases of ordinary illness; the family's grandmother attended to those. Every old woman was a doctor, and gathered her own medicines in the woods, and knew how to compound doses that would stir the vitals of a cast-iron dog. And then there was the "Indian doctor"; a grave savage, remnant of his tribe, deeply read in the mysteries of nature and the secret properties of herbs; and most backwoodsmen had high faith in his powers and could tell of wonderful cures achieved by him. In Mauritius, away off yonder in the solitudes of the Indian Ocean, there is a person who answers to our Indian doctor of the old times. He is a negro, and he had no teaching as a doctor, yet there is one disease which he is master of and can cure, and the doctors can't. They send for him when they have a case. It is a child's disease of a strange and deadly sort, and the negro cures it with a herb medicine which he makes, himself, from a prescription which has come down to him from his father and grandfather. He will not let any one see it. He keeps the secret of its components to himself, and it is feared that he will die without divulging it; then there will be consternation in Mauritius. I was told these things by the people there, in 1896.

We had the "faith doctor," too, in those early days—a woman. Her specialty was toothache. She was a farmer's old wife, and lived five miles from Hannibal. She would lay her hand on the patient's jaw and say "Believe!" and the cure was prompt. Mrs. Utterback. I remember her very well. Twice I rode out there behind my mother, horseback, and saw the cure performed. My mother was the patient.

Dr. Meredith removed to Hannibal, by and by, and was our family physician there, and saved my life several times. Still, he was a good man and meant well. Let it go.

I was always told that I was a sickly and precarious and tiresome and uncertain child, and lived mainly on allopathic medicines during the first seven years of my life. I asked my mother about this, in her old age—she was in her 88th year—and said:

"I suppose that during all that time you were uneasy about me?"

"Yes, the whole time."

"Afraid I wouldn't live?"

After a reflective pause—ostensibly to think out the facts—

"No—afraid you would."

It sounds like a plagiarism, but it probably wasn't. The country schoolhouse was three miles from my uncle's farm. It stood in a clearing in the woods, and would hold about twenty-five boys and girls. We attended the school with more or less regularity once or twice a week, in summer, walking to it in the cool of the morning by the forest paths, and back in the gloaming at the end of the day. All the pupils brought their dinners in baskets—corn-dodger, buttermilk and other good things—and sat in the shade of the trees at noon and ate them. It is the part of my education which I look back upon with the most satisfaction. My first visit to the school was when I was seven. A strapping girl of fifteen, in the customary sunbonnet and calico dress, asked me if I "used tobacco"—meaning did I chew it. I said, no. It roused her scorn. She reported me to all the crowd, and said—

"Here is a boy seven years old who can't chaw tobacco."

By the looks and comments which this produced, I realized that I was a degraded object; I was cruelly ashamed of myself. I determined to reform. But I only made myself sick; I was not able to learn to chew tobacco. I learned to smoke fairly well, but that did not conciliate anybody, and I remained a poor thing, and characterless. I longed to be respected, but I never was able to rise. Children have but little charity for each other's defects.

As I have said, I spent some part of every year at the farm until I was twelve or thirteen years old. The life which I led there with my cousins was full of charm, and so is the memory of it yet. I can call back the solemn twilight and mystery of the deep woods, the earthy smells, the faint odors of the wild flowers, the sheen of rain-washed foliage, the rattling clatter of drops when the wind shook the trees, the far-off hammering of woodpeckers and the muffled drumming of wood-pheasants in the remoteness of the forest, the snap-shot glimpses of disturbed wild creatures skurrying through the grass,—I can call it all back and make it as real as it ever was, and as blessed. I can call back the prairie, and its loneliness and peace, and a vast hawk hanging motionless in the sky, with his wings spread wide and the blue of the vault showing through the fringe of their end-feathers. I can see the woods in their autumn dress, the oaks purple, the hickories washed with gold, the maples and sumacs luminous with crimson fires, and I can hear the rustle made by the fallen leaves as we ploughed through them. I can see the blue clusters of wild grapes hanging amongst the foliage of the saplings, and I remember the taste of them and the smell. I know how the wild blackberries looked, and how they tasted; and the same with the pawpaws, the hazelnuts and the persimmons; and I can feel the thumping rain, upon my head, of hickory-nuts and walnuts when we were out in the frosty dawn to scramble for them with the pigs, and the gusts of wind loosed them and sent them down. I know the stain of blackberries, and how pretty it is; and I know the stain of walnut hulls, and how little it minds soap and water; also what grudged experience it had of either of them. I know the taste of maple sap, and when to gather it, and how to arrange the troughs and the delivery tubes, and how to boil down the juice, and how to hook the sugar after it is made; also how much better hooked sugar tastes than any that is honestly come by, let bigots say what they will. I know how a prize watermelon looks when it is sunning its fat rotundity among pumpkin-vines and "simblins"; I know how to tell when it is ripe without "plugging" it; I know how inviting it looks when it is cooling itself in a tub of water under the bed, waiting; I know how it looks when it lies on the table in the sheltered great floor-space between house and kitchen, and the children gathered for the sacrifice and their mouths watering; I know the crackling sound it makes when the carving-knife enters its end, and I can see the split fly along in front of the blade as the knife cleaves its way to the other end; I can see its halves fall apart and display the rich red meat and the black seeds, and the heart standing up, a luxury fit for the elect; I know how a boy looks, behind a yard-long slice of that melon, and I know how he feels; for I have been there. I know the taste of the watermelon which has been honestly come by, and I know the taste of the watermelon which has been acquired by art. Both taste good, but the experienced know which tastes best. I know the look of green apples and peaches and pears on the trees, and I know how entertaining they are when they are inside of a person. I know how ripe ones look when they are piled in pyramids under the trees, and how pretty they are and how vivid their colors. I know how a frozen apple looks, in a barrel down cellar in the winter-time, and how hard it is to bite, and how the frost makes the teeth ache, and yet how good it is, notwithstanding. I know the disposition of elderly people to select the speckled apples for the children, and I once knew ways to beat the game. I know the look of an apple that is roasting and sizzling on a hearth on a winter's evening, and I know the comfort that comes of eating it hot, along with some sugar and a drench of cream. I know the delicate art and mystery of so cracking hickory-nuts and walnuts on a flatiron with a hammer that the kernels will be delivered whole, and I know how the nuts, taken in conjunction with winter apples, cider and doughnuts, make old people's tales and old jokes sound fresh and crisp and enchanting, and juggle an evening away before you know what went with the time. I know the look of Uncle Dan'l's kitchen as it was on privileged nights when I was a child, and I can see the white and black children grouped on the hearth, with the firelight playing on their faces and the shadows flickering upon the walls, clear back toward the cavernous gloom of the rear, and I can hear Uncle Dan'l telling the immortal tales which Uncle Remus Harris was to gather into his books and charm the world with, by and by; and I can feel again the creepy joy which quivered through me when the time for the ghost-story of the "Golden Arm" was reached—and the sense of regret, too, which came over me, for it was always the last story of the evening, and there was nothing between it and the unwelcome bed.

I can remember the bare wooden stairway in my uncle's house, and the turn to the left above the landing, and the rafters and the slanting roof over my bed, and the squares of moonlight on the floor, and the white cold world of snow outside, seen through the curtainless window. I can remember the howling of the wind and the quaking of the house on stormy nights, and how snug and cozy one felt, under the blankets, listening, and how the powdery snow used to sift in, around the sashes, and lie in little ridges on the floor, and make the place look chilly in the morning, and curb the wild desire to get up—in case there was any. I can remember how very dark that room was, in the dark of the moon, and how packed it was with ghostly stillness when one woke up by accident away in the night, and forgotten sins came flocking out of the secret chambers of the memory and wanted a hearing; and how ill chosen the time seemed for this kind of business; and how dismal was the hoo-hooing of the owl and the wailing of the wolf, sent mourning by on the night wind.

I remember the raging of the rain on the roof, summer nights, and how pleasant it was to lie and listen to it, and enjoy the white splendor of the lightning and the majestic booming and crashing of the thunder. It was a very satisfactory room;

and there was a lightning-rod which was reachable from the window, an adorable and skittish thing to climb up and down, summer nights, when there were duties on hand of a sort to make privacy desirable.

I remember the 'coon and 'possum hunts, nights, with the negroes, and the long marches through the black gloom of the woods, and the excitement which fired everybody when the distant bay of an experienced dog announced that the game was treed; then the wild scramblings and stumblings through briars and bushes and over roots to get to the spot; then the lighting of a fire and the felling of the tree; the joyful frenzy of the dogs and the negroes, and the weird picture it all made in the red glare—I remember it all well, and the delight that every one got out of it, except the 'coon.

I remember the pigeon seasons, when the birds would come in millions, and cover the trees, and by their weight break down the branches. They were clubbed to death with sticks; guns were not necessary, and were not used. I remember the squirrel hunts, and the prairie-chicken hunts, and the wild-turkey hunts, and all that; and how we turned out, mornings, while it was still dark, to go on these expeditions, and how chilly and dismal it was, and how often I regretted that I was well enough to go. A toot on a tin horn brought twice as many dogs as were needed, and in their happiness they raced and scampered about, and knocked small people down, and made no end of unnecessary noise. At the word, they vanished away toward the woods, and we drifted silently after them in the melancholy gloom. But presently the gray dawn stole over the world, the birds piped up, then the sun rose and poured light and comfort all around, everything was fresh and dewy and fragrant, and life was a boon again. After three hours of tramping we arrived back wholesomely tired, overladen with game, very hungry, and just in time for breakfast.

SPEECHES

After-dinner speaking was a form of entertainment in the nineteenth century. A given banquet might have from ten to fifteen speakers, each speaking from five to twenty minutes and each proposing a "toast" to someone or some idea. In an age that regarded oratory as a fine art, Mark Twain was reckoned one of the nation's best speakers, and he could always turn to the lecture circuit when he needed money. Around two hundred of Twain's speeches have been published, but he may have made many more. Twain typically memorized the text of his prepared speech and delivered it in an off-hand, impromptu manner, sometimes adjusting his remarks to the mood of the audience. Twain always worked best in small compass, and the speech was a genre congenial to his sociable manner and his playful wit. The speeches printed below suggest a range of his thought and feeling and his invention in this form.

Farewell Banquet for Bayard Taylor

Dinner Speech, Delmonico's, New York

April 4, 1878

Mr. Chairman: I had intended to make an address of some length here tonight, and in fact wrote out an impromptu speech, but have had no time to memorize it. I cannot make a speech on the moment, and therefore being unprepared I am silent and undone. However, I will say this much for the speech that I had written out—that it was a very good one, and I gave it away as I had no further use for it, and saw that I could not deliver it. Therefore I will ask the indulgence of the company here to let me retire without speaking. I will make my compliments to our honored friend, Mr. Taylor, but I will make them on board ship where I shall be a fellow passenger.

[The following is the speech Mark Twain had prepared.]

I have been warned—as, no doubt, have all among you that are inexperienced—that a dinner to our Ambassador is an occasion which demands, and even requires, a peculiar caution and delicacy in the handling of the dangerous weapon of speech. I have been warned to avoid all mention of international politics, and all criticisms, however mild, of countries with which we are at peace, lest such utterances embarrass our minister and our government in their dealings with foreign states. In a word, I have been cautioned to talk, but be careful not to say anything. I do not consider this a difficult task.

Now, it has often occurred to me that the conditions under which we live at the present day, with the revelations of geology all about us, viewing, upon the one hand, the majestic configurations of the silurian, oolitic, old red sandstone periods, and, upon the other, the affiliations, and stratifications, and ramifications of the prehistoric, post-pliocene, antepenultimate epochs, we are stricken dumb with amazed surprise, and can only lift up our hands and say with that wise but odious Frenchman: "It was a slip of the tongue, sir, and wholly unintentional—entirely unintentional." It would ill become me, upon an occasion like this, purposely to speak slightingly of a citizen of a country with whom we are at peace—and especially great and gracious France, whom God preserve! The subject, however, is a delicate one, and I will not pursue it.

But—as I was about to remark—cast your eye abroad, sir, for one pregnant moment over the vista which looms before you in the mighty domain of intellectual progression and contemplate the awe-compelling theory of the descent of man! Development, sir! Development! Natural selection! Correlation of the sexes! Spontaneous combustion!—what gulfs and whirlwinds of intellectual stimulus these magic words fling upon the burning canvas of the material universe of soul! Across the chasm of the ages we take the oyster by the hand and call him brother; and back, and still further back, we go, and breathe the germ we cannot see, and know, in him, our truer Adam! And as we stand, dazed, transfixed, exalted, and gaze down the long procession of life, marking how steadily, how symmetrically we have ascended, step by step, to our sublime estate and dignity of humanity—out of one lowly form into a higher and a little higher forms—adding grace after every change—developing from tadpoles into frogs, frogs into fishes, fishes into birds, birds into reptiles, reptiles into Russians—I beg a million pardons, sir and gentlemen—it was a wholly innocent slip of the tongue, and due only to the excitement of debate—for far be it from me, on such an occasion as this, to cast a seeming slur upon a great nation with which we are at peace—a great and noble and Christian nation—whom God expand!

But, as I was about to remark, I maintain—and nothing can ever drive me from that position—that the contributions of the nineteenth century to science and the industrial arts are—are—but, of course they are. There is no need to dwell upon that. You look at it yourself. Look at steam! Look at the steamboat, look at the railway, look at the steamship! Look at the telegraph, which enables you to flash your thoughts from world to world, ignoring intervening seas. Look at the telephone, which enables you to speak into affection's remote ear the word that cheers, and into that ear of the foe the opinion which you ought not to risk at shorter range. Look at the sewing machine, look at the foghorn, look at the bell punch, look at the book agent. And, more than all, a thousand times, look at the last and greatest, the aerophone, which will enable Moody and Sankey to stand on the tallest summit of the Rocky Mountains and deliver their message to listening America!—and necessarily it will annul and do away with the pernicious custom of taking up a collection. Look at all these things, sir, and say if it is not a far prouder and more precious boon to have been born in the nineteenth century than in any century that went before it. Ah, sir, clothed with the all-sufficient grandeur of citizenship in the nineteenth century, even the wild and arid New Jerseyman might—a mistake, sir, a mistake, and entirely unintentional. Of all the kingdoms, principalities and countries with which it is our privilege to hold peaceful relations, I regard New Jersey as dearest to our admiration, nearest to our heart, the wisest and the purest among the nations. I retire the undiplomatic language, and beg your sympathy and indulgence.

But, as I was about to remark, it has always seemed to me—that is, of course, since I reached a reasoning age—that this much agitated question of future rewards and punishments was one upon which honest and sincere differences of opinion might exist; one individual, with more or less justice, leaning to the radical side of it, whilst another individual, with apparently equal justice, but with infinitely more common sense, more intelligence, more justification, leans to a bitter and remorseless detestation of the pitiless Prince of Perdition—a slip of the tongue, I do sincerely assure you—I beg you to let me withdraw that unintentional slur upon the character of that great and excellent personage with whom and whose country we are upon the closest and warmest terms, and who—it is no use, sir, I will sit down; I don't seem to have any knack at a diplomatic speech. I have probably compromised the country enough for the present.

Nonsense aside, sir, I am most sincerely glad to assist at this public expression of appreciation of Mr. Taylor's character, scholarship, and distinguished literary service. I am sure he was not merely one of the fittest men we had for the place, but the fittest. In so honoring him, our country has conspicuously honored herself.

Plymouth Rock and the Pilgrims

Address at the First Annual Dinner, N. E. Society, Philadelphia, December 22, 1881

On calling Mr. Clemens to make response, President Rollins said:

"This sentiment has been assigned to one who was never *exactly* born in New England, nor, perhaps, were any of his ancestors. He is not *technically,* therefore of New England descent. Under the painful circumstances in which he has found himself, however, he has done the best he could—he has had all his children born there, and has made of *himself* a New England *ancestor.* He is a self-made man. More than this, and better even, in cheerful, hopeful, helpful literature he is of New England *ascent.* To *ascend* there in anything that's reasonable is difficult, for—confidentially, with the door shut—we all know that they are the brightest, ablest sons of the goodly land who never leave it, and it is among and above *them* that Mr. Twain has made his brilliant and permanent ascent—become a man of mark."

I rise to protest. I have kept still for years, but really I think there is no sufficient justification for this sort of thing. What do you want to celebrate those people for?—those ancestors of yours of 1620—the *Mayflower* tribe, I mean. What do you want to celebrate *them* for? Your pardon: the gentleman at my left assures me that you are not celebrating the Pilgrims themselves, but the landing of the Pilgrims at Plymouth Rock on the 22nd of December. So you are celebrating their landing. Why, the other pretext was thin enough, but this is thinner than ever; the other was tissue, tinfoil, fish-bladder, but this is gold-leaf. Celebrating their landing! What was there remarkable about it,

I would like to know? What can you be thinking of? Why, those Pilgrims had been at sea three or four months. It was the very middle of winter: it was cold as death off Cape Cod there. Why shouldn't they come ashore? If they *hadn't* landed there would be some reason for celebrating the fact. It would have been a case of monumental leatherheadedness which the world would not willingly let die. If it had been *you,* gentlemen, you probably wouldn't have landed, but you have no shadow of right to be celebrating, in your ancestors, gifts which they did not exercise, but only transmitted. Why, to be celebrating the mere landing of the Pilgrims—to be trying to make out that this most natural and simple and customary procedure was an extraordinary circumstance—a circumstance to be amazed at, and admired, aggrandized and glorified, at orgies like this for two hundred and sixty years—hang it, a horse would have known enough to land; a horse—Pardon again; the gentleman on my right assures me that it was not merely the landing of the Pilgrims that we are celebrating, but the Pilgrims themselves. So we have struck an inconsistency here—one says it was the landing, the other says it was the Pilgrims. It is an inconsistency characteristic of your intractable and disputatious tribe, for you never agree about anything but Boston. Well, then, what do you want to celebrate those Pilgrims for? They were a mighty hard lot—you know it. I grant you, without the slightest unwillingness, that they were a deal more gentle and merciful and just than were the people of Europe of that day; I grant you that they are better than their predecessors. But what of that?—that is nothing. People always progress. You are better than your fathers and grandfathers were (this it the first time I have ever aimed a measureless slander at the departed, for I consider such things improper). Yes, those among you who have not been in the penitentiary, if such there be, are better than your fathers and grandfathers were; but is that any sufficient reason for getting up annual dinners and celebrating you? No, by no means—by no means. Well, I repeat, those Pilgrims were a hard lot. They took good care of themselves, but they abolished everybody else's ancestors. I am a border-ruffian from the State of Missouri. I am a Connecticut Yankee by adoption. In me, you have

Missouri morals, Connecticut culture; this, gentlemen, is the combination which makes the perfect man. But where are my ancestors? Whom shall I celebrate? Where shall I find the raw materials?

My first American ancestor, gentlemen, was an Indian—an early Indian. Your ancestors skinned him alive, and I am an orphan. Not one drop of my blood flows in that Indian's veins today. I stand here, lone and forlorn, without an ancestor. They skinned him! I do not object to that, if they needed his fur; but alive, gentlemen—alive! They skinned him alive—and before men—alive! They skinned him alive—and before company! This is what rankles. Think how he must have felt; for he was a sensitive person and easily embarrassed. If he had been a bird, it would have been all right, and no violence done to his feelings, because he would have been considered "dressed." But he was not a bird, gentlemen, he was a man, and probably one of the most undressed men that ever was. I ask you to put yourselves in his place. I ask it as a favor; I ask it as a tardy act of justice; I ask it in the interest of fidelity to the traditions of your ancestors; I ask it that the world may contemplate, with vision unobstructed by disguising swallow-tails and white cravats, the spectacle which the true New England Society ought to present. Cease to come to these annual orgies in this hollow modern mockery—the surplusage of raiment. Come in character; come in the summer grace, come in the unadorned simplicity, come in the free and joyous costume which your sainted ancestors provided for mine.

Later ancestors of mine were the Quakers William Robinson, Marmaduke Stevenson, *et al.* Your tribe chased them out of the country for their religion's sake; promised them death if they came back; for your ancestors had forsaken the homes they loved, and braved the perils of the sea, the implacable climate, and the savage wilderness, to acquire that highest and most precious of boons, freedom for every man on this broad continent to worship according to the dictates of his own conscience—and they were not going to allow a lot of pestiferous Quakers to interfere with it. Your ancestors broke forever the chains of political slavery, and gave the vote to every man in this wide land, excluding none!—none except those who did not belong to the orthodox church. Your ancestors—yes, they were a hard lot; but, nevertheless, they gave us religious liberty to worship as they required us to worship, and political liberty to vote as the church required; and so I the bereft one, I the forlorn one, am here to do my best to help you celebrate them right.

The Quaker woman Elizabeth Hooton was an ancestress of mine. Your people were pretty severe with her—you will confess that. But, poor thing! I believe they changed her opinions before she died, and took her into their fold; and so we have every reason to presume that when she died she went to the same place which your ancestors went to. It is a great pity, for she was a good woman. Roger Williams was an ancestor of mine. I don't really remember what your people did with him. But they banished him to Rhode Island, anyway. And then, I believe, recognizing that this was really carrying harshness to an unjustifiable extreme, they took pity on him and burned him. They were a hard lot! All those Salem witches were ancestors of mine! Your people made it tropical for them. Yes, they did; by pressure and the gallows they made such a clean deal with them that there hasn't been a witch and hardly a halter in our family from that day to this, and that is one hundred and eighty-nine years. The first slave brought into New England out of Africa by your progenitors was an ancestor of mine—for I am of a mixed breed, an infinitely shaded and exquisite Mongrel. I'm not one of your sham meerschaums that you can color in a week. No, my complexion is the patient art of eight generations. Well, in my own time, I had acquired a lot of my kin—by purchase, and swapping around, and one way and another—and was getting along very well. Then, with the inborn perversity of your lineage, you got up a war, and took them all away from me. And so, again am I bereft, again am I forlorn; no drop of my blood flows in the veins of any living being who is marketable.

O my friends, hear me and reform! I seek your good, not mine. You have heard the speeches. Disband these New England societies—nurseries of a system of steadily augmenting laudation and hosannaing, which, if persisted in uncurbed, may some day in the remote future beguile you into prevaricating and bragging. Oh, stop, stop, while you are still temperate in your appreciation of your ancestors! Hear me, I beseech you, get up an auction and sell Plymouth Rock! The Pilgrims were a simple and ignorant race. They never had seen any good rocks before, or at least any that were not watched, and so they were excusable for hopping ashore in frantic delight and clapping an iron fence around this one. But you, gentlemen, are educated; you are enlightened; you know that in the rich land of your nativity, opulent New England, overflowing with rocks, this one isn't worth, at the outside, more than thirty-five cents. Therefore, sell it, before it is injured by exposure, or at least throw it open to the patent-medicine advertisements, and let it earn its taxes.

Yes, hear your true friend—your only true friend—list to his voice. Disband these societies, hotbeds of vice, or moral decay—perpetuators of ancestral superstition. Here on this board I see water, I see milk, I see the wild and deadly lemonade. These are but steps upon the downward path. Next we shall see tea, then chocolate, then coffee—hotel coffee. A few more years—all too few, I fear—mark my words, we shall have cider! Gentlemen, pause ere it be too late. You are on the broad road which leads to dissipation, physical ruin, moral decay, gory crime and the gallows! I beseech you, I implore you, in the name of your anxious friends, in the name of your suffering families, in the name of your impending widows and orphans, stop ere it be too late. Disband these New England societies, renounce these soul-blistering saturnalia, cease from varnishing the rusty reputations of your long-varnished ancestors—the super-high-moral old iron-clads of Cape Cod, the pious buccaneers of Plymouth Rock—go home, and try to learn to behave!

However, chaff and nonsense aside, I think I honor and appreciate your Pilgrim stock as much as you do yourselves, perhaps; and I endorse and adopt a sentiment uttered by a grandfather of mine once—a man of sturdy opinions, of sincere make of mind, and not given to flattery. He said: "People may talk as they like about that Pilgrim stock, but, after all's said and done, it would be pretty hard to improve on those people; and, as for me, I don't mind coming out flatfooted and saying there ain't any way to improve on them—except having them born in Missouri!"

Advice to Youth

Saturday Morning Club, Boston

April 15, 1882

Being told I would be expected to talk here, I inquired what sort of talk I ought to make. They said it should be something suitable to youth—something didactic, instructive, or something in the nature of good advice. Very well; I have a few things in my mind which I have often longed to say for the instruction of the young; for it is in one's tender early years that such things will best take root and be most enduring and most valuable. First, then, I will say to you, my young friends—and say it beseechingly, urgingly—.

Always obey your parents, when they are present. This is the best policy in the long run; because if you don't, they will make you. Most parents think they know better than you do; and you can generally make more by humoring that superstition then you can by acting on your own better judgment.

Be respectful to your superiors, if you have any; also to strangers, and sometimes to others. If a person offend you, and you are in doubt as to whether it was intentional or not, do not resort to extreme measures; simply watch your chance and hit him with a brick. That will be sufficient. If you shall find that he had not intended any offense, come out frankly and confess yourself in the wrong when you struck him; acknowledge it like a man, and say you didn't mean to. Yes, always avoid violence; in this age of charity and kindliness, the time has gone by for such things. Leave dynamite to the low and unrefined.

Go to bed early, get up early—this is wise. Some authorities say get up with one thing, some with another. But a lark is really the best thing to get up with. It gives you a splendid reputation with everybody to know that you get up with the lark;

and if you get the right kind of lark, and work at him right, you can easily train him to get up at half-past nine, every time—it is no trick at all.

Now as to the matter of lying. You want to be very careful about lying; otherwise you are nearly sure to get caught. Once caught, you can never again be, in the eyes of the good and the pure, what you were before. Many a young person has injured himself permanently through a single clumsy and ill-finished lie, the result of carelessness born of incomplete training. Some authorities hold that the young ought not to lie at all. That, of course, is putting it rather stronger than necessary; still, while I cannot go quite so far as that, I do maintain, and I believe I am right, that the young ought to be temperate in the use of this great art until practice and experience shall give them that confidence, elegance and precision which alone can make the accomplishment graceful and profitable. Patience, diligence, painstaking attention to detail—these are the requirements; these, in time, will make the student perfect; upon these, and upon these only, may he rely as the sure foundation for future eminence. Think what tedious years of study, thought, practice, experience, went to the equipment of that peerless old master who was able to impose upon the whole world the lofty and sounding maxim that "Truth is mighty and will prevail"—the most majestic compound fracture of fact which any of woman born has yet achieved. For the history of our race, and each individual's experience, are sown thick with evidences that a truth is not hard to kill, and that a lie well told is immortal. There in Boston is a monument to the man who discovered anesthesia; many people are aware, in these latter days, that that man didn't discover it at all, but stole the discovery from another man. Is this truth mighty, and will it prevail? Ah, no, my hearers, the monument is made of hardy material, but the lie it tells will outlast it a million years. An awkward, feeble, leaky lie is a thing which you ought to make it your unceasing study to avoid; such a lie as that has no more real permanence than an average truth. Why, you might as well tell the truth at once and be done with it. A feeble, stupid, preposterous lie will not live two years—except it be a slander upon somebody. It is indestructible, then, of course, but that is no merit of yours. A final word: begin your practice of this gracious and beautiful art early—begin now. If I had begun earlier, I could have learned how.

Never handle firearms carelessly. The sorrow and suffering that have been caused through the innocent but heedless handling of firearms by the young! Only four days ago, right in the next farmhouse to the one where I am spending the summer, a mother, old and gray and sweet, one of the loveliest spirits in the land, was sitting at her work, when her young son crept in and got down an old battered, rusty gun which had not been touched for many years, and was supposed not to be loaded, and pointed it at her, laughing and threatening to shoot. In her fright she ran screaming and pleading toward the door on the other side of the room; but as she passed him he placed the gun almost against her very breast and pulled the trigger! He had supposed it was not loaded. And he was right: it wasn't. So there wasn't any harm done. It is the only case of the kind I ever heard of. Therefore, just the same, don't you meddle with old unloaded firearms; they are the most deadly and unerring things that have ever been created by man. You don't have to take any pains at all, with them; you don't have to have a rest, you don't have to have any sights on the gun, you don't have to take aim, even. No, you just pick out a relative and bang away, and you are sure to get him. A youth who can't hit a cathedral at thirty yards with a Gatling gun in three-quarters of an hour, can take up an old empty musket and bag his mother every time, at a hundred. Think what Waterloo would have been if one of the armies had been boys armed with old rusty muskets supposed not to be loaded, and the other army had been composed of their female relations. The very thought of it makes me shudder.

There are many sorts of books; but good ones are the sort for the young to read. Remember that. They are a great, an inestimable, an unspeakable means of improvement. Therefore be careful in your selection, my young friends; be very careful; confine yourself exclusively to Robertson's *Sermons,* Baxter's *Saint's Rest, The Innocents Abroad,* and works of that kind.

But I have said enough. I hope you will treasure up the instructions which I have given you, and make them a guide to your feet and a light to your understanding. Build your character thoughtfully and painstakingly upon these precepts; and by and by, when you have got it built, you will be surprised and gratified to see how nicely and sharply it resembles everybody else's.

The Alphabet and Simplified Spelling

Address at the Dinner Given to Mr. Carnegie at the Dedication of the New York Engineers' Club, December 9, 1907

Mr. Clemens was introduced by the president of the club, who, quoting from the Mark Twain autobiography, recalled the day when the distinguished writer came to New York with $3 in small change in his pockets and a $10 bill sewed in his clothes.

It seems to me that I was around here in the neighborhood of the Public Library about fifty or sixty years ago. I don't deny the circumstance, although I don't see how you got it out of my autobiography, which was not to be printed until I am dead, unless I'm dead now. I had that $3 in change, and I remember well the $10 which was sewed in my coat. I have prospered since. Now I have plenty of money and a disposition to squander it, but I can't. One of those trust companies is taking care of it.

Now, as this is probably the last time I shall be out after nightfall this winter, I must say that I have come here with a mission, and I would make my errand of value.

Many compliments have been paid to Mr. Carnegie to-night. I was expecting them. They are very gratifying to me.

I have been a guest of honor myself, and I know what Mr. Carnegie is experiencing now. It is embarrassing to get compliments and compliments and only compliments, particularly when he knows as well as the rest of us that on the other side of him there are all sorts of things worthy of our condemnation.

Just look at Mr. Carnegie's face. It is fairly scintillating with fictitious innocence. You would think, looking at him, that he had never committed a crime in his life. But no—look at his pestiferious simplified spelling. You can't any of you imagine what a crime that has been. Torquemada was nothing to Mr. Carnegie. That old fellow shed some blood in the Inquisition, but Mr. Carnegie has brought destruction to the entire race. I know he didn't mean it to be a crime, but it was just the same. He's got us all so we can't spell anything.

The trouble with him is that he attacked orthography at the wrong end. He meant well, but he attacked the symptoms and not the cause of the disease. He ought to have gone to work on the alphabet. There's not a vowel in it with a definite value, and not a consonant that you can hitch anything to. Look at the "h's" distributed all around. There's "gherkin." What are you going to do with the "h" in that? What the devil's the use of "h" in gherkin, I'd like to know. It's one thing I admire the English for: they just don't mind anything about them at all.

But look at the "pneumatics" and the "pneumonias" and the rest of them. A real reform would settle them once and for all, and wind up by giving us an alphabet that we wouldn't have to spell with at all, instead of this present silly alphabet, which I fancy was invented by a drunken thief. Why, there isn't a man who doesn't have to throw out some fifteen hundred words a day when he writes his letters because he can't spell them! It's like trying to do a St. Vitus's dance with wooden legs.

Now I'll bet there isn't a man here who can spell "pterodactyl," not even the prisoner at the bar. I'd like to hear him try once—but not in public, for it's too near Sunday, when all extravagant histrionic entertainments are barred. I'd like to hear him try in private, and when he got through trying to spell "pterodactyl" you wouldn't know whether it was a fish or a beast or a bird, and whether it flew on its legs or walked with its wings. The chances are that he would give it tusks and make it lay eggs.

Let's get Mr. Carnegie to reform the alphabet, and we'll pray for him—if he'll take the risk.

If we had adequate, competent vowels, with a system of accents, giving to each vowel its own soul and value, so every shade of that vowel would be shown in its accent, there is not a word in any tongue that we could not spell accurately. That would be competent, adequate, simplified spelling, in contrast to the clipping, the hair punching, the carbuncles, and the cancers which go by the name of simplified spelling. If I ask you what b-o-w spells you can't tell me unless you know which b-o-w I mean, and it is the same with r-o-w, b-o-r-e, and the whole family of words which were born out of lawful wedlock and don't know their own origin.

Now, if we had an alphabet that was adequate and competent, instead of inadequate and incompetent, things would be different. Spelling reform has only made it bald-headed and unsightly. There is the whole tribe of them, "row" and "read" and "lead"—a whole family who don't know who they are. I ask you to pronounce s-o-w, and you ask me what kind of a one.

If we had the same, determinate alphabet, instead of a hospital of comminuted eunuchs, you would know whether one referred to the act of a man casting the seed over the ploughed land or whether one wished to recall the lady hog and the future ham.

It's a rotten alphabet. I appoint Mr. Carnegie to get after it, and leave simplified spelling alone. Simplified spelling brought about the sun-spots, the San Francisco earthquake, and the recent business depression, which we would never have had if spelling had been left alone.

Now, I hope I have soothed Mr. Carnegie and made him more comfortable than he would have been had he received only compliment after compliment, and I wish to say to him that simplified spelling is all right, but like chastity, you can carry it too far.

Education and Citizenship

On the evening of May 14, 1908, the alumni of the College of the City of New York celebrated the opening of the new college buildings at a banquet in the Waldorf Astoria. Mr. Clemens followed Mayor McClellan.

I agreed when the Mayor said that there was not a man within hearing who did not agree that citizenship should be placed above everything else, even learning.

Have you ever thought about this? Is there a college in the whole country where there is a chair of good citizenship? There is a kind of bad citizenship which is taught in the schools, but no real good citizenship taught. There are some which teach insane citizenship, bastard citizenship, but that is all. Patriotism! Yes; but patriotism is usually the refuge of the scoundrel. He is the man who talks the loudest.

You can begin that chair of citizenship in the College of the City of New York. You can place it above mathematics and literature, and that is where it belongs.

We used to trust in God. I think it was in 1863 that some genius suggested that it be put upon the gold and silver coins which circulated among the rich. They didn't put it on the nickels and coppers because they didn't think the poor folks had any trust in God.

Good citizenship would teach accuracy of thinking and accuracy of statement. Now, that motto on the coin is an overstatement. Those Congressmen had no right to commit this whole country to a theological doctrine. But since they did, Congress ought to state what our creed should be.

There was never a nation in the world that put its whole trust in God. It is a statement made on insufficient evidence. Leaving out the gamblers, the burglars, and the plumbers, perhaps we do put our trust in God after a fashion. But, after all, it is an overstatement.

If the cholera or black plague should come to these shores, perhaps the bulk of the nation would pray to be delivered from it, but the rest would put their trust in the Health Board of the City of New York.

I read in the papers within the last day or two of a poor young girl who they said was a leper. Did the people in that populous section of the country where she was—did they put their trust in God? The girl was afflicted with the leprosy, a disease which cannot be communicated from one person to another.

Yet, instead of putting their trust in God, they harried that poor creature, shelterless and friendless, from place to place, exactly as they did in the Middle Ages, when they made lepers wear bells, so that people could be warned of their approach and avoid them. Perhaps those people in the Middle Ages thought they were putting their trust in God.

The President ordered the removal of that motto from the coin, and I thought that it was well. I thought that the overstatement should not stay there. But I think it would better read, "Within certain judicious limitations we trust in God," and if there isn't enough room on the coin for this, why, enlarge the coin.

Now I want to tell a story about jumping at conclusions. It was told to me by Bram Stoker, and it concerns a christening. There was a little clergyman who was prone to jump at conclusions sometimes. One day he was invited to officiate at a christening. He went. There sat the relatives—intelligent-looking relatives they were. The little clergyman's instinct came to him to make a great speech. He was given to flights of oratory that way—a very dangerous thing, for often the wings which take one into clouds of oratorical enthusiasm are wax and melt up there, and down you come.

But the little clergyman couldn't resist. He took the child in his arms, and, holding it, looked at it a moment. It wasn't much of a child. It was little, like a sweet-potato. Then the little clergyman waited impressively, and then: "I see in your countenances," he said, "disappointment of him. I see you are disappointed with this baby. Why? Because he is so little. My friends, if you had but the power of looking into the future you might see that great things may come of little things. There is the great ocean, holding the navies of the world, which comes from little drops of water no larger than a woman's tears. There are the great constellations in the sky, made up of little bits of stars. Oh, if you could consider his future you might see that he might become the greatest poet of the universe, the greatest warrior the world has ever known, greater than Caesar, than Hannibal, than—er—er" (turning to the father)—"what's his name?"

The father hesitated, then whispered back: "His name? Well, his name is Mary Ann."

LETTERS

Samuel Clemens was an indefatigable letter-writer. By some conservative estimates, he wrote 50,000 letters during his lifetime and may have written twice as many. As it stands, the approximately 12,000 extant letters will occupy many volumes of the authoritative California edition of his works. In an age when letter writing was considered an art, Twain was widely reckoned a masterful correspondent, and typically adjusted his manner to fit the recipient. He was sometimes ardent (as in his many courtship letters to Olivia Langdon)—alternately playful, refined, pleading. At other times (as in a scolding letter to a childhood friend or his letter to the Gas Company) he was impatient, indulging freely in the spontaneous overflow of cantankerous feelings. Often, particularly in his correspondence to Howells, he was merely antic, delivering himself of what amounts to a comic sketch. Eventually, he came to believe that the freest and most truthful sort of expression might be contained in unsent letters to select friends, letters that, because they would never be mailed, permit "unallowable frankness & freedom."

Letters

To Mrs. Jane Clemens and Mrs. Moffett, in St. Louis:

SAN FRANCISCO, JAN. 20, 1866.

MY DEAR MOTHER AND SISTER,—I do not know what to write; my life is so uneventful. I wish I was back there piloting up and down the river again. Verily, all is vanity and little worth—save piloting.

To think that, after writing many an article a man might be excused for thinking tolerably good, those New York people should single out a villainous backwoods sketch to compliment me on!—"Jim Smiley and His Jumping Frog"—a squib which would never have been written but to please Artemus Ward, and then it reached New York too late to appear in his book.

But no matter. His book was a wretchedly poor one, generally speaking, and it could be no credit to either of us to appear between its covers. . . .

To W. D. Howells, in Boston:

H'T'F'D. DEC. 8, 1874.

MY DEAR HOWELLS,—It isn't the Atlantic audience that distresses me; for *it* is the only audience that I sit down before in perfect serenity (for the simple reason that it doesn't require a "humorist" to paint himself stripèd and stand on his head every fifteen minutes.) The trouble was, that I was only bent on "working up an atmosphere" and that is to me a most fidgety and irksome thing, sometimes. I avoid it, usually, but in this case it was absolutely necessary, else every reader would be applying the atmosphere of his own or sea experiences, and *that* shirt wouldn't fit, you know.

I could have sent this Article II a week ago, or more, but I couldn't bring myself to the drudgery of revising and correcting it. I have been at that tedious work 3 hours, now, and by *George* but I am glad it is over.

Say—I am as prompt as a clock, if I only know the *day* a thing is wanted—otherwise I am a natural procrastinaturalist. Tell me what day and date you want Nos. 3 and 4, and I will tackle and revise them and they'll be there to the minute.

I could wind up with No. 4, but there are some things more which I am powerfully moved to write. Which is natural enough, since I am a person who would quit authorizing in a minute to go to piloting, if the madam would stand it. I would rather sink a steamboat than eat, any time.

My wife was afraid to write you—so I said with simplicity, "I will give you the language—and ideas." Through the infinite grace of God there has not been such another insurrection in the family before as followed this. However, the letter was written, and promptly, too—whereas, heretofore she has *remained* afraid to do such things.

With kind regards to Mrs. Howells,

Yrs ever,

MARK

To W. D. Howells, in Boston:

ELMIRA, AUG. 9, 1876.

MY DEAR HOWELLS,—I was just about to write you when your letter came—and not one of those obscene postal cards, either, but reverently, upon paper.

I shall read that biography, though the letter of acceptance was amply sufficient to corral my vote without any further knowledge of the man. Which reminds me that a campaign club in Jersey City wrote a few days ago and invited me to be present at the raising of a Tilden and Hendricks flag there, and to take the stand and give them some "counsel." Well, I could not go, but gave them counsel and advice by letter, and in the kindliest terms as to the raising of the flag—advised them "not to raise it."

Get your book out quick, for this is a momentous time. If Tilden is elected I think the entire country will go pretty straight to—Mrs. Howells's bad place.

I am infringing on your patent—I started a record of our children's sayings, last night. Which reminds me that last week I sat down and got Susie a vast pair of shoes of a most villainous pattern, for I discovered that her feet were being twisted and cramped out of shape by a smaller and prettier article. She did not complain, but looked degraded and injured. At night her mamma gave her the usual admonition when she was about to say her prayers—to wit:

"Now, Susie—think about God."

"Mamma, I can't, with those shoes."

The farm is perfectly delightful this season. It is as quiet and peaceful as a South Sea Island. Some of the sunsets which we have witnessed from this commanding eminence were marvelous. One evening a rainbow spanned an entire range of hills with its mighty arch, and from a black hub resting upon the hilltop in the exact centre, black rays diverged upward in perfect regularity to the rainbow's arch and created a very strongly defined and altogether the most majestic, magnificent and startling half-sunk wagon wheel you can imagine. After that, a world of tumbling and prodigious clouds came drifting up out of the West and took to themselves a wonderfully rich and brilliant *green* color—the decided green of new spring foliage. Close by them we saw the intense blue of the skies, through rents in the cloudrack, and away off in another quarter were drifting clouds of a delicate pink color. In one place hung a pall of dense black clouds, like compacted pitch-smoke. And the stupendous wagon wheel was still in the supremacy of its unspeakable grandeur. So you see, the colors present in the sky at once and the same time were blue, green, pink, black, and the vari-colored splendors of the rainbow. All strong and decided colors, too. I don't know whether this weird and astounding spectacle most suggested heaven, or hell. The wonder, with its constant, stately, and always surprising changes, lasted upwards of two hours, and we all stood on the top of the hill by my study till the final miracle was complete and the greatest day ended that we ever saw.

Our farmer, who is a grave man, watched that spectacle, to the end, and then observed that it was "dam funny."

The double-barreled novel lies torpid. I found I could not go on with it. The chapters I had written were still too new and familiar to me. I may take it up next winter, but cannot tell yet; I waited and waited to see if my interest in it would not revive, but gave it up a month ago and began another boys' book—more to be at work than anything else. I have written 400 pages on it—therefore it is very nearly half done. It is Huck Finn's Autobiography. I like it only tolerably well, as far as I have got, and may possibly pigeonhole or burn the MS when it is done.

So the comedy is done, and with a "fair degree of satisfaction." That rejoices me, and makes me mad, too—for I can't plan a comedy, and what have you done that God should be so good to you? I have racked myself bald-headed trying to plan a comedy harness for some promising characters of mine to work in, and had to give it up. It is a noble lot of blooded stock and worth no end of money, but they must stand in the stable and be profitless. I want to be present when the comedy is produced and help enjoy the success.

Warner's book is mighty readable, I think.

Love to yez.

Yrs ever

MARK

To J. H. Burrough of Cape Girardeau, Missouri

HARTFORD, NOVEMBER 1, 1876.

MY DEAR BURROUGH:

As you describe me I can picture myself as I was 22 years ago. The portrait is correct. You think I have grown some; upon my word there was room for it. You have described a callow fool, a self-sufficient ass, a mere human tumble-bug, stern in air, heaving at his bit of dung and imagining he is re-molding the world and is entirely capable of doing it right. Ignorance, intolerance, egotism, self-assertion, opaque perception, dense and pitiful chuckle-headedness—and an almost pathetic unconsciousness of it all. That is what I was at 19-20, and that is what the average Southerner is at 60 today. Northerners too, of a certain grade. It is of children like this that voters are made. And such is the primal source of our government! A man hardly knows whether to swear or cry over it.

I think I comprehend their position there—perfect freedom to vote just as you choose, provided you choose to vote as other people think, social ostracism otherwise. The same thing exists here among the Irish. An Irish Republican is a pariah among his people. Yet that race find fault with the same spirit in Know-Nothingism.

Fortunately a good deal of experience of men enabled me to choose my residence wisely. I live in the freest corner of the country. There are no social disabilities between me and my democratic personal friends. We break the bread and eat the salt of hospitality freely together and never dream of such a thing as offering impertinent interference in each other's political opinions. . . .

Yes, Will Bowen and I have exchanged letters now and then for several years but I suspect that I made him mad with my last—shortly after you saw him in St. Louis, I judge. There is one thing which I can't stand, and won't stand from many people. That is sham sentimentality—the kind a school-girl puts into her graduation composition; the sort that makes up the Original Poetry column of a country newspaper; the rot that deals in "the happy days of yore," "the sweet yet melancholy past," with its "blighted hopes" and its "vanished dreams"—and all that sort of drivel. Will's were always of this stamp. I stood it years. When I get a letter like that from a grown man and he a widower with a family, it gives me the bowel complaint. And I just told Will Bowen so, last summer. I told him to stop being 16 at 40; told him to stop drooling about the sweet yet melancholy past and take a pill. I said there was but one solitary thing about the past worth remembering and that was the fact that it *is* the past—can't be restored. Well, I exaggerated some of these truths a little—but only a little—but my idea was to kill his nasty sham sentimentality once and forever and so make a good fellow of him again. I went to the unheard of trouble of re-writing the letter and saying the same harsh things softly, so as to sugar-coat the anguish and make it a little more endurable, and I asked him to write and thank me honestly for doing him the best and kindliest favor that any friend ever *had* done him—but he hasn't done it yet. Maybe he will some time. I am grateful to God that I got that letter off before he was married (I get that news from you), else he would just have slobbered all over me and drowned me when that event happened.

I enclose photograph for the young ladies. I will remark that I do not wear seal-skin for grandeur but because I found, when I used to lecture in the winter, that nothing else was able to keep a man warm sometimes, in these high latitudes. I wish you had sent pictures of yourself and family—I'll trade picture for picture with you, straight through, if you are commercially inclined.

Your old friend

SAML L. CLEMENS

To the Reverend J. H. Twichell

MUNICH, JANUARY 26, 1879.

DEAR OLD JOE:

Sunday. Your delicious letter arrived exactly at the right time. It was laid by my plate as I was finishing breakfast at 12 noon. Livy and Clara [Spaulding] arrived from church 5 minutes later; I took a pipe and spread myself out on the sofa and Livy sat by and read, and I warmed to that butcher the moment he began to swear. There is more than one way of praying and I like the butcher's way because the petitioner is so apt to be in earnest. I was peculiarly alive to his performance just at this time for another reason, to wit: Last night I awoke at 3 this morning and after raging to myself for 2 interminable hours, I gave it up. I rose, assumed a catlike stealthiness, to keep from waking Livy, and proceeded to dress in the pitch dark. Slowly but surely I got on garment after garment—all down to one sock; I had one slipper on and the other in my hand. Well, on my hands and knees I crept softly around, pawing and feeling and scooping along the carpet and among chair-legs for the missing sock; I kept that up;—and still kept it up and kept it up. At first I only said to myself "Blame that sock," but that soon ceased to answer; my expletives grew steadily stronger and stronger and at last, when I found I was lost, I had to sit flat down on the floor and take hold of something to keep from lifting the roof off with the profane explosion that was trying to get out of me. I could see the dim blur of the window, but of course it was in the wrong place and could give me no information as to where I was. But I had one comfort, I had not waked Livy; I believed I could find that sock in silence if the night lasted long enough. So I started again and softly pawed all over the place, and sure enough at the end of half an hour I laid my hand on the missing article. I rose joyfully up and butted the wash-bowl and pitcher off the stand and simply raised—so to speak. Livy screamed, then said, "Who is that? what is the matter?" I said "There ain't anything the matter—I'm hunting for my sock." She said, "Are you hunting for it with a club?" . . .

To Orion Clemens and family, in Keokuk, Ia.:

ELMIRA, JULY 21, '83.

Private

DEAR MA AND ORION AND MOLLIE,—I don't know that I have anything new to report, except that Livy is still gaining, and all the rest of us flourishing. I haven't had such booming working-days for many years. I am piling up manuscript in a really astonishing way. I believe I shall complete, in two months, a book which I have been fooling over for 7 years. This summer it is no more trouble to me to write than it is to lie.

Day before yesterday I felt slightly warned to knock off work for one day. So I did it, and took the open air. Then I struck an idea of the instruction of the children, and went to work and carried it out. It took me all day. I measured off 817 feet of the roadway in our farm grounds, with a foot-rule, and then divided it up among the English reigns, from the Conqueror down to 1883, allowing one foot to the year. I whittled out a basket of little pegs and drove one in the ground at the beginning of each reign, and gave it that King's name—thus:

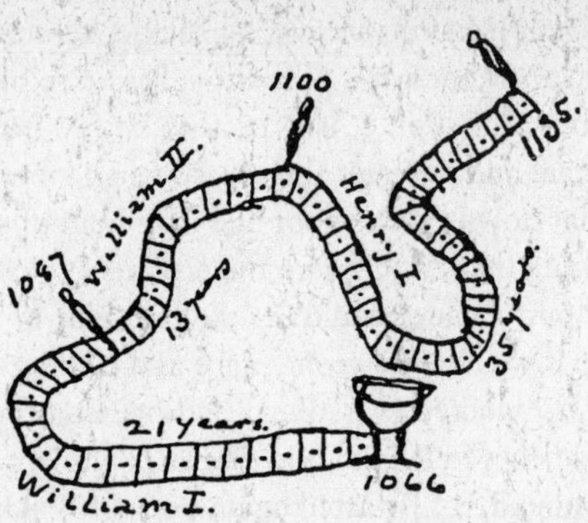

I measured all the reigns exactly—as many feet to the reign as there were years in it. You can look out over the grounds and see the little pegs from the front door—some of them close together, like Richard II, Richard Cromwell, James II, &c; and some prodigiously wide apart, like Henry III, Edward III, George III, &c. It gives the children a realizing sense of the length or brevity of a reign. Shall invent a violent game to go with it.

And in bed, last night, I invented a way to play it indoors—in a far more voluminous way, as to multiplicity of dates and events—on a *cribbage board.*

Hello, supper's ready. Love to all. Good bye.

SAML.

To Frank A. Nichols, Secretary, Concord Free Trade Club

[Previously published only in part]
HARTFORD, MARCH, 1885.

DEAR SIR:

I am in receipt of your favor of the 24th inst., conveying the gratifying intelligence that I have been made an honorary member of the Free Trade Club of Concord, Massachusetts, and I desire to express to the Club, through you, my grateful sense of the high compliment thus paid me.

It does look as if Massachusetts were in a fair way to embarrass me with kindnesses this year. In the first place a Massachusetts Judge has just decided in open court that a Boston publisher may sell not only his own property in a free and unfettered way, but may also as freely sell property which does not belong to him but to me—property which he has not bought and which I have not sold. Under this ruling I am now advertising that judge's homestead for sale; and if I make as good a sum out of it as I expect I shall go on and sell the rest of his property.

In the next place, a committee of the public library of your town has condemned and excommunicated my last book, and doubled its sale. This generous action of theirs must necessarily benefit me in one or two additional ways. For instance, it will deter other libraries from buying the book and you are doubtless aware that one book in a public library prevents the sale of a sure ten and possible hundred of its mates. And secondly it will cause the purchasers of the book to read it, out of curiosity, instead of merely intending to do so after the usual way of the world and library committees; and then they will discover, to my great advantage and their own indignant disappointment, that there is nothing objectional in the book, after all.

And finally, the Free Trade Club of Concord comes forward and adds to the splendid burden of obligations already conferred upon me by the Commonwealth of Massachusetts, an honorary membership which is more worth than all the rest since it endorses me as worthy to associate with certain gentlemen whom even the moral icebergs of the Concord library committee are bound to respect.

May the Commonwealth of Massachusetts endure forever, is the heartfelt prayer of one who, long a recipient of her mere general good will, is proud to realize that he is at last become her pet.

Thanking you again, dear sir and gentlemen, I remain

Your obliged servant

S. L. Clemens

(known to the Concord Winter School of Philosophy as "Mark Twain.")

To Jeannette Gilder (not mailed):

HARTFORD, MAY 14, '87.

MY DEAR MISS GILDER,—We shall spend the summer at the same old place—the remote farm called "Rest-and-be-Thankful," on top of the hills three miles from Elmira, N.Y. Your other question is harder to answer. It is my habit to keep four or five books in process of erection all the time, and every summer add a few courses of bricks to two or three of them; but I cannot forecast which of the two or three it is going to be. It takes seven years to complete a book by this method, but still it is a good method: gives the public a rest. I have been accused of "rushing into print" prematurely, moved thereto by greediness for money; but in truth I have never done that. Do you care for trifles of information? Well, then, "Tom Sawyer" and "The Prince and the Pauper" were each on the stocks two or three years, and "Old Times on the Mississippi" eight. One of my unfinished books has been on the stocks sixteen years; another seventeen. This latter book could have been finished in a day, at any time during the past five years. But as in the first of these two narratives all the action takes place in Noah's ark, and as in the other the action takes place in heaven, there seems to be no hurry, and so I have not hurried. Tales of stirring adventure in those localities do not need to be rushed to publication lest they get stale by waiting. In twenty-one years, with all my time at my free disposal I have written and completed only eleven books, whereas with half the labor that a journalist does I could have written sixty in that time. I do not greatly mind being accused of a proclivity for rushing into print, but at the same time I don't believe that the charge is really well founded. Suppose I did write eleven books, have you nothing to be grateful for? Go to—remember the forty-nine which I didn't write.

truly Yours

S. L. CLEMENS

To Andrew Lang

[EARLY 1890]

. . . The little child is permitted to label its drawings "This is a cow—this is a horse" and so on. This protects the child. It saves it from the sorrow and wrong of hearing its cows and horses criticised as kangaroos and work-benches. A man who is whitewashing a fence is doing a useful thing, so also is the man who is adorning a rich man's house with costly frescoes; and all of us are sane enough to judge these performances by standards proper to each. Now then, to be fair an author ought to be allowed to put upon his book an explanatory line: "This is written for the Belly and the Members." And the critic ought to hold himself in honor bound to put away from his ancient habit of judging all books by one standard and thenceforth follow a fairer course.

The critic assumes every time that if a book doesn't meet the cultivated-class standard, it isn't valuable. Let us apply his law all around: for if it is sound in the case of novels, narratives, pictures, and such things, it is certainly sound and applicable to all the steps which lead up to culture and make culture possible. It condemns the spelling book, for a spelling book is of no use to a person of culture; it condemns all school books and all schools which lie between the child's primer and Greek, and between the infant school and the university; it condemns all the rounds of art which lie between the cheap terra cotta groups and the Venus de Medici, and between the chromo and the Transfiguration; it requires Whitcomb Riley to sing no more till he can sing like Shakespeare, and it forbids all amateur music and will grant its sanction to nothing below the "classic."

Is this an extravagant statement? No, it is a mere statement of fact. It is the fact itself that is extravagant and grotesque. And what is the result? This, and it is sufficiently curious: the critic has actually imposed upon the world the superstition that a painting by Raphael is more valuable to the civilizations of the earth than is a chromo; and the august opera than the hurdy-gurdy and the villagers' singing society; and Homer than the little everybody's-poet whose rhymes are in all mouths to-day and will be in nobody's mouth next generation; and the Latin classics than Kipling's far-reaching bugle-note; and Jonathan Edwards than the Salvation Army; and the Venus di Medici than the plaster-cast peddler; the superstition, in a word, that the vast and awful comet that trails its cold lustre through the remote abysses of space once a century and interests and instructs a cultivated handful of astronomers is worth more to the world than the sun which warms and cheers all the nations every day and makes the crops to grow.

If a critic should start a religion it would not have any object but to convert angels, and they wouldn't need it. The thin top crust of humanity—the cultivated—are worth pacifying, worth pleasing, worth coddling, worth nourishing and preserving with dainties and delicacies, it is true; but to be caterer to that little faction is no very dignified or valuable occupation, it seems to me; it is merely feeding the over-fed and there must be small satisfaction in that. It is not that little minority who are already saved that are best worth lifting at, I should think, but the mighty mass of the uncultivated who are underneath. That mass will never see the Old Masters—that sight is for the few; but the chromo maker can lift them all one step upward toward appreciation of art; they cannot have the opera, but the hurdy-gurdy and the singing class lift them a little way toward that far light; they will never know Homer, but the passing rhymester of their day leaves them higher than he found them; they may never hear of the Latin classics but they will strike step with Kipling's drumbeat, and they will march; for all Jonathan Edwards's help they would die in their slums, but the Salvation Army will beguile some of them up to pure air and a cleaner life; they know no sculpture, the Venus is not even a name to them, but they are a grade higher in the scale of civilization by the ministrations of the plaster-cast than they were before it took its place upon their mantel and made it beautiful to their unexacting eyes.

Indeed I have been misjudged from the very first. I have never tried in even one single little instance to help cultivate the cultivated classes. I was not equipped for it, either by native gifts or training. And I never had any ambition in that direction, but always hunted for bigger game—the masses. I have seldom deliberately tried to instruct them but have done my best to entertain them. To simply amuse them would have satisfied my dearest ambition at any time; for they could get instruction elsewhere and I had two chances to help to the teacher's one: for amusement is a good preparation for study and a good healer of fatigue after it. My audience is dumb, it has no voice in print, and so I cannot know whether I have won its approbation or only got its censure.

Yes, you see, I have always catered for the Belly and the Members but have been served like the others—*criticized* from the culture-standard—to my sorrow and pain; because, honestly, I never cared what became of the cultured classes; they could go to the theatre and the opera, they had no use for me and the melodeon.

And now at last I arrive at my object and tender my petition, making supplication to this effect: that the critics adopt a rule recognizing the Belly and the Members and formulate a standard whereby work done for them shall be judged. Help me, Mr. Lang; no voice can reach further than yours in a case of this kind, or carry greater weight of authority.

Fragment of Letter to —, 1891:

. . . I confine myself to life with which I am familiar when pretending to portray life. But I confined myself to the boy-life out on the Mississippi because that had a peculiar charm for me, and not because I was not familiar with other phases of life. I was a *soldier* two weeks once in the beginning of the war, and was hunted like a rat the whole time. Familiar? My splendid Kipling himself hasn't a more burnt-in, hard-baked and unforgettable familiarity with that death-on-the-pale-horse-with-hell-following-after, which is a raw soldier's first fortnight in the field—and which, without any doubt, is the most tremendous fortnight and the vividest he is ever going to see.

Yes, and I have shoveled silver tailings in a quartz-mill a couple of weeks, and acquired the last possibilities of culture in *that* direction. And I've done "pocket-mining" during three months in the one little patch of ground in the whole globe where Nature conceals gold in pockets—or *did,* before we robbed all of those pockets and exhausted, obliterated, annihilated the most curious freak Nature ever indulged in. There are not thirty men left alive who, being told there was a pocket hidden on the broad slope of a mountain, would know how to go and find it, or have even the faintest idea of how to set about it; but I am one of the possible 20 or 30 who possess the secret, and I could go and put my hand on that hidden treasure with a most deadly precision.

And I've been a prospector, and know pay rock from poor when I find it—just with a touch of the tongue. And I've been a *silver* miner and know how to dig and shovel and drill and put in a blast. And so I know the mines and the miners interiorly as well as Bret Harte knows them exteriorly.

And I was a newspaper reporter four years in cities, and so saw the inside of many things; and was reporter in a legislature two sessions and the same in Congress one session, and thus learned to know personally three sample bodies of the smallest minds and the selfishest souls and the cowardliest hearts that God makes.

And I was some years a Mississippi pilot, and familiarly knew all the different kinds of steamboatmen—a race apart, and not like other folk.

And I was for some years a traveling "jour" printer, and wandered from city to city—and so I know *that* sect familiarly.

And I was a lecturer on the public platform a number of seasons and was a responder to toasts at all the different kinds of banquets—and so I know a great many secrets about audiences—secrets not to be got out of books, but only acquirable by experience.

And I watched over one dear project of mine for years, spent a fortune on it, and failed to make it go—and the history of that would make a large book in which a million men would see themselves as in a mirror; and they would testify and say, Verily, this is not imagination; this fellow has been there—and after would cast dust upon their heads, cursing and blaspheming.

And I am a publisher and did pay to one author's widow (General Grant's) the largest copyright checks this world has seen—aggregating more the £80,000 in the first year.

And I have been an author for 20 years and an ass for 55.

Now then; as the most valuable capital or culture or education usable in the building of novels is personal experience, I ought to be well equipped for that trade.

I surely have the equipment, a wide culture, and all of it real, none of it artificial, for I don't know anything about books.

[No signature.]

From a letter to Susan Crane, March 19, 1893, Florence, Italy

Susy dear, this is Susy [Clemens]'s birth day & she is 21—facts which will be drifting through your mind as you sit at your breakfast three hours from now—& there will be pictures drifting with the facts,—& ghosts. Well-a-day!

I dreamed I was born, & grew up, & was a pilot on the Mississippi, & a miner & journalist in Nevada, & a pilgrim in the Quaker City, & had a wife & children & went to live in a Villa out of Florence—& this dream goes on & *on* & sometimes seems *so* real that I almost believe it *is* real. I wonder if it is? But there is no way to tell, for if one applied tests, *they* would be part of the dream, too, & so would simply aid the deceit. I wish I knew whether it is a dream or real.

Betty the perfect-tempered left last night for Bad-Nauheim—her mother is dying. It is only a dream, probably, & doubtless there is no Betty & no mother; but it all has the effect of reality. Jean cried a good deal. . . .

Love to you & all.

Saml.*

To Major "Jack" Downing, in Middleport, Ohio:

Hotel Krantz, Wein, I, Neuer Markt 6,
Feb. 26, 1899.

Dear Major,—No; it was to Bixby that I was apprenticed. He was to teach me the river for a certain specified sum. I have forgotten what it was, but I paid it. I steered a trip for Bart Bowen, of Keokuk, on the A. T. Lacy, and I was partner with Will Bowen

*Permission to publish from The Mark Twain House, Hartford, Connecticut.

on the A. B. Chambers (one trip), and with Sam Bowen a whole summer on a small Memphis packet.

The newspaper report you sent me is incorrect. Bixby is not 67: he is 97. I am 63 myself, and I couldn't talk plain and had just begun to walk when I apprenticed myself to Bixby who was then passing himself off for 57—and successfully too, for he always looked 60 or 70 years younger than he really was. At that time he was piloting the Mississippi on a Potomac commission granted him by George Washington who was a personal friend of his before the Revolution. He has piloted every important river in America on that commission, he has also used it as a passport in Russia. I have never revealed these facts before. I notice, too, that you are deceiving the people concerning *your* age. The printed portrait which you have enclosed is not a portrait of you, but a portrait of me when I was 19. I remember very well when it was common for people to mistake Bixby for your grandson. Is it spreading, I wonder—this disposition of pilots to renew their youth by doubtful methods? Beck Jolly and Joe Bryan—they probably go to Sunday school now—but it will not deceive.

Yes, it is as you say. All of the procession but a fraction has passed. It is time for us all to fall in.

Sincerely yours,

S. L. CLEMENS

From a letter to W. D. Howells, in New York:

HOTEL KRANTZ
WIEN I. NEUER MARKT 6
APRIL 2, '99.

DEAR HOWELLS,—I am waiting for the April Harper, which is about due now; waiting, and strongly interested. You are old enough to be a weary man, with paling interests, but you do not show it. You do your work in the same old delicate and delicious and forceful and searching and perfect way. I don't know how you can—but I suspect. I suspect that to you there is still dignity in human life, and that Man is not a joke—a poor joke—the poorest that was ever contrived. Since I wrote my Bible, (last year)—which Mrs. Clemens loathes, and shudders over, and will not listen to the last half nor allow me to print any part of it, Man is not to me the respect-worthy person he was before; and so I have lost my pride in him, and can't write gaily nor praisefully about him any more. And I don't intend to try. I mean to go on writing, for that is my best amusement, but I shan't print much. (for I don't wish to be scalped, any more than another.)

April 5. The Harper has come. I have been in Leipzig with your party, and then went on to Karlsbad and saw Mrs. Marsh's encounter with the swine with the toothpick and the other manners.—At this point Jean carried the magazine away.

Is it imagination, or—Anyway I seem to get furtive and fleeting glimpses which I take to be the weariness and condolence of age; indifference to sights and things once brisk with interest; tasteless stale stuff which used to be champagne; the boredom of travel: the secret sigh behind the public smile, the private What-in-hell-did-I-come-for!

But maybe that is your art. Maybe that is what you intend the reader to detect and think he has made a Columbus-discovery. Then it is well done, perfectly done. I wrote my last travel book—in hell; but I let on, the best I could, that it was an excursion through heaven. Some day I will read it, and if its lying cheerfulness fools me, then I shall believe it fooled the reader. How I did loathe that journey around the world!—except the sea-part and India. . . .

Sincerely yours,

S. L. CLEMENS

To Rev. J. H. Twichell, in Hartford:

RIVERDALE-ON-THE-HUDSON.

FEB. '02.

DEAR JOE,—"After compliments." From Bridgeport to New York; thence to home; and continuously until near midnight I wallowed and reeked with Jonathan [Edwards] in his insane debauch; rose immediately refreshed and fine at 10 this morning, but with a strange and haunting sense of having been on a three days' tear with a drunken lunatic. It is years since I have known these sensations. All through the book is the glare of a resplendent intellect gone mad—a marvelous spectacle. No, not *all* through the book—the drunk does not come on till the last third, where what I take to be Calvinism and its God begins to show up and shine red and hideous in the glow from the fires of hell, their only right and proper adornment. By God I was ashamed to be in such company.

Jonathan seems to hold (as against the Arminian position) that the Man (or his Soul or his Will) never creates an impulse itself, but is moved to action by an impulse back of it. That's sound!

Also, that of two or more things offered it, it infalliably chooses the one which for the moment is most pleasing to ITSELF. *Perfectly* correct! An immense admission for a man not otherwise sane.

Up to that point he could have written chapters III and IV of my suppressed "Gospel." But there we seem to separate. He seems to concede the indisputable and unshakable dominion of Motive and Necessity (call them what he may, these are *exterior* forces and not under the man's authority, guidance or even suggestion)—then he suddenly flies the logic track and (to all seeming) makes the *man* and not these exterior forces responsible to God for the man's thoughts, words and acts. It is frank insanity.

I think that when he conceded the autocratic dominion of Motive and Necessity he grants a *third* position of mine—that man's mind is a mere machine—an *automatic* machine—which is handled entirely from the *outside,* the man himself furnishing it absolutely nothing: not an ounce of its fuel, and not so much as a bare *suggestion* to that exterior engineer as to what the machine shall do, nor how it shall do it nor *when.*

After that concession, it was time for him to get alarmed and *shirk*—for he was pointing straight for the only rational and possible next-station on *that* piece of road: the irresponsibility of man to God.

And so he shirked. Shirked, and arrived at this handsome result:

Man is commanded to do so-and-so;

It has been ordained from the beginning of time that some men *shan't* and others *can't.*

These are to be blamed: let them be damned.

I enjoy the Colonel very much, and shall enjoy the rest of him with an obscene delight.

Joe, the whole tribe shout love to you and yours!

MARK

To Miss Picard, in St.-Dié, France:

RIVERDALE-ON-THE-HUDSON, FEBRUARY 22, 1902.

DEAR MISS HELENE,—If you will let me call you so, considering that my head is white and that I have grown-up daughters. Your beautiful letter has given me such deep pleasure! I will make bold to claim you for a friend and lock you up with the rest of my riches; for I am a miser who counts his spoil every day and hoards it secretly and adds to it when he can, and is grateful to see it grow.

Some of that gold comes, like yourself, in a sealed package, and I can't see it and may never have the happiness; but I know its value without that, and by what sum it increases my wealth.

I have a Club, a private Club, which is all my own. I appoint the Members myself, and they can't help themselves, because I don't allow them to vote on their own appointment and I don't allow them to resign! They are all friends whom I have never seen (save one), but who have written friendly letters to me.

By the laws of my Club there can be only one Member in each country, and there can be no male Member but myself. Some day I may admit males, but I don't know—they are capricious and inharmonious, and their ways provoke me a good deal. It is a matter which the Club shall decide.

I have made four appointments in the past three or four months: You as Member for France, a young Highland girl as Member for Scotland, a Mohammedan girl as Member for Bengal, and a dear and bright young niece of mine as Member for the United States—for I do not represent a country myself, but am merely Member at Large for the Human Race.

You must not try to resign, for the laws of the Club do not allow that. You must console yourself by remembering that you are in the best of company; that nobody knows of your membership except myself—that no Member knows another's name, but only her country; that no taxes are levied and no meetings held (but how dearly I should like to attend one!).

One of my Members is a Princess of a royal house, another is the daughter of a village book-seller on the continent of Europe. For the only qualification for Membership is intellect and the spirit of good will; other distinctions, hereditary or acquired, do not count.

May I send you the Constitution and Laws of the Club? I shall be so pleased if I may. It is a document which one of my daughters typewrites for me when I need one for a new Member, and she would give her eyebrows to know what it is all about, but I strangle her curiosity by saying: "There are much cheaper typewriters than you are, my dear, and if you try to pry into the sacred mysteries of this Club one of your prosperities will perish sure."

My favorite? It is "Joan of Arc." My next is "Huckleberry Finn," but the family's next is "The Prince and the Pauper." (Yes, you are right—I am a moralist in disguise; it gets me into heaps of trouble when I go thrashing around in political questions.)

I wish you every good fortune and happiness and I thank you so much for your letter.

Sincerely yours,

S. L. Clemens

To Robert Fulton, in Reno, Nevada:

In the Mountains,
May 24, 1905.

Dear Mr. Fulton,—I remember, as if it were yesterday, that when I disembarked from the overland stage in front of the Ormsby in Carson City in August, 1861, I was not expecting to be asked to come again. I was tired, discouraged, white with alkali dust, and did not know anybody; and if you had said then, "Cheer up, desolate stranger, don't be down-hearted—pass on, and come again in 1905," you cannot think how grateful I would have been and how gladly I would have closed the contract. Although I was not expecting to be invited, I was watching out for it, and was hurt and disappointed when you started to ask me and changed it to, "How soon are you going away?"

But you have made it all right, now, the wound is closed. And so I thank you sincerely for the invitation; and with you, all Reno, and if I were a few years younger I would accept it, and promptly. I would go. I would let somebody else do the oration, but, as for me, I would talk—just talk. I would renew my youth; and talk—and talk—and talk—and have the time of my life! I would march the unforgotten and unforgettable antiques by, and name their names, and give them reverent Hail-and-farewell as they passed: Goodman, McCarthy, Gillis, Curry, Baldwin, Winters, Howard, Nye, Stewart; Neely Johnson, Hal Clayton, North, Root,—and my brother, upon whom be peace!—and then the desperadoes, who make life a joy and the "Slaughter-house" a precious possession: Sam Brown, Farmer Pete, Bill Mayfield, Six-fingered Jake, Jack Williams and the rest of the crimson discipleship—and so on and so on. Believe me, I would start a resurrection it would do you more good to look at than the next one will, if you go on the way you are doing now.

Those were the days!—those old ones. They will come no more. Youth will come no more. They were so full to the brim with the wine of life; there have been no others like them. It chokes me up to think of them. Would you like me to come out there and cry? It would not beseem my white head.

Good-bye. I drink to you all. Have a good time—and take an old man's blessing.

MARK TWAIN

Biographical List of Correspondents

Burrough, Jacob H. (1825–1883). Clemens's friend from the time they roomed together in St. Louis, 1854–55. He was impressed by Burrough's wide reading and literary judgment. Burrough later became a lawyer and judge in Cape Girardeau, Missouri.

Clemens, Jane (1803–1890). Born Jane Lampton, she married John Marshall Clemens in 1823. Besides Samuel, she was the mother of six other children. After the death of her husband, she depended on the support of her three surviving children, and Samuel Clemens continued to provide for her financial welfare until her death.

Clemens, Orion (1825–1897). Oldest of Clemens's siblings, Orion was, among other things, an editor, farmer, lawyer, and the secretary for the Nevada Territory. Sam Clemens often became exasperated with his brother, for he was something of a dreamer who never quite succeeded at anything in life.

Crane, Susan (1836–1924). She was the oldest sister of Olivia Langdon Clemens. She had been adopted by the Langdons after the death of her parents. The Clemens family spent their summers from 1870 to 1903 with Susan and Theodore Crane at Quarry Farm, on a hill overlooking Elmira, New York.

Downing, Major "Jack" (1834–1914). Downing was a riverboat pilot for over twenty years. He was also an accomplished violinist. Clemens and Downing wrote one another from time to time after they left the River.

Fulton, Robert (no dates available). Fulton was involved in Republican politics and served as a Nevada delegate to the national convention in 1890. Apparently he was one of the organizers for some sort of pioneers' reunion to be held in California.

Gilder, Jeannette (1849–1916). Gilder was an editor and critic and the sister of Richard Watson Gilder, the editor of *Century Magazine*. Among other books, she coedited *Authors at Home: Personal and Biographical Sketches of Well-known American Writers,* which included a section on Twain.

Howells, William Dean (1837–1920). Prolific novelist and influential critic, Howells was the chief sponsor of the literary school known as American realism. He was the editor of the *Atlantic Monthly* for some fifteen years before moving from Boston to New York, where he began writing "The Editor's Study" columns for *Harper's Monthly Magazine*. From the time Howells and Clemens first met in 1869 until the latter's death in 1910, they were the closest of friends and maintained a more or less constant correspondence during those forty years. Howells had favorably reviewed many of Twain's books, urged him to write for the *Atlantic,* read his manuscripts, and otherwise helped and promoted Twain's career. After Twain's death, Howells published an affectionate and astute memoir of the man, *My Mark Twain* (1910).

Lang, Andrew (1844–1912). An influential English literary critic and respected man of letters, Lang shared with Twain an interest in Joan of Arc and other subjects. He published "The Art of Mark Twain" in the *Illustrated London News* and was otherwise helpful in promoting Twain's reputation abroad.

Moffett, Pamela Clemens (1827–1904). The only surviving daughter of the Clemens family, she was widowed in 1865. She shared a home with her mother in St. Louis, and later in Fredonia, New York.

Nichols, Frank (no dates available). Nichols was only the titular recipient of this letter. As Secretary of the Concord, Massachusetts, Free Trade Club, he had informed Twain that this club had just made the writer an honorary member. The timing was deliberate, for the Concord public library had just recently banned *Huckleberry Finn* and the gesture was meant as something of a counterstatement to that decision. Clemens's letter was intended to be made public, and it was released to the press soon after it was sent.

Picard, Helene (no dates available). Clemens apparently never met this young woman, but he "elected" her as the French representative of his "Aquarium Club," a club of his own making composed entirely of young girls he called "Angelfish." Nineteen letters from Twain to Picard are extant.

Twichell, Joseph H. (1838–1918). After W. D. Howells, probably Clemens's closest friend. He was a pastor of the Asylum Hill Congregational Church in Hartford, Connecticut, which the Clemens family attended regularly. Twichell had an earthy sense of humor and appreciated much, if not all, of Clemens's comedy and at least tolerated Clemens's supposed irreverence. Twichell was the model for the character "Harris" in *A Tramp Abroad.*

READ MORE MARK TWAIN IN PENGUIN CLASSICS

"All modern American literature comes from one book by Mark Twain called *Huckleberry Finn.*"—Ernest Hemingway

The Adventures of Huckleberry Finn
Introduction by John Seelye and Notes by Guy Cardwell
A novel of immeasurable richness, filled with adventures, ironies, and wonderfully drawn characters, all conveyed with Twain's mastery of humor and language, *The Adventures of Huckleberry Finn* is often regarded as the masterpiece of American literature. *ISBN 0-14-243717-4*

The Adventures of Tom Sawyer
Introduction by John Seelye
Evoking life in a small Mississippi River town, *The Adventures of Tom Sawyer* is Twain's hymn to the secure and fantastic world of boyhood and adventure. *ISBN 0-14-039083-9*

A Connecticut Yankee in King Arthur's Court
Edited with an Introduction by Justin Kaplan
This imaginary confrontation of a nineteenth-century American with life in sixth-century England is both a rich, extravagant comedy and an apocalyptic vision of terrifying violence and destruction. *ISBN 0-14-043064-4*

The Innocents Abroad
Introduction by Tom Quirk and Notes by Guy Cardwell
These irreverent writings on travel in Europe are a burlesque of the sentimental travel books popular in the mid-nineteenth century and launched Twain's career. Bringing his fresh and humorous perspective to bear on hallowed European landmarks, Twain ultimately concludes that, for better or worse, "human nature is very much the same all over the world."
ISBN 0-14-243708-5

Life on the Mississippi
Introduction by James M. Cox
Twain's firsthand portrait of the steamboat age and the science of riverboat piloting recalls the history of the Mississippi River, from its discovery by Europeans to the writer's own time. *ISBN 0-14-039050-2*

The Prince and the Pauper
Introduction by Jerry Griswold
This 1881 novel about a poor boy, Tom Canty, who exchanges identities with Edward Tudor, the prince of England, is at once an adventure story, a fantasy of timeless appeal, and an intriguing example of the author's abiding preoccupation with separating the true from the false, the genuine from the imposter. Included is the story "A Boy's Adventure," written as part of the novel but published separately. *ISBN 0-14-043669-3*

Pudd'nhead Wilson
Edited with an Introduction by Malcolm Bradbury
While it retains the comic exuberance of *The Adventures of Huckleberry Finn*, this is Twain's darker and more disturbing account of human nature under slavery. *ISBN 0-14-043040-7*

Roughing It
Edited with an Introduction by Hamlin Hill
A fascinating picture of the American frontier emerges from Twain's fictionalized recollections of his experiences prospecting for gold, speculating in timber, and writing for a succession of small Western newspapers during the 1860s. *ISBN 0-14-039010-3*

Tales, Speeches, Essays, and Sketches
Edited with an Introduction by Tom Quirk
Masterful short fiction and prose pieces display the variety of Twain's imaginative invention, his diverse talents, and his extraordinary emotional range. The volume includes "Jim Smiley and His Jumping Frog," "The Man That Corrupted Hadleyberg," "Fenimore Cooper's Literary Offenses," and the spectacularly scatological "Date, 1601." *ISBN 0-14-043417-8*

A Tramp Abroad
Introduction by Robert Gray Bruce and Hamlin Hill
Cast in the form of a walking tour through Germany, Switzerland, France, and Italy, *A Tramp Abroad* sparkles with the author's shrewd observations and highly opinionated comments on Old World culture, and showcases his unparalleled ability to integrate humorous sketches, autobiographical tidbits, and historical anecdotes in consistently entertaining narrative.
ISBN 0-14-043608-1

The Gilded Age with Charles Dudley Warner
Introduction and Notes by Louis J. Budd
With his characteristic wit and perception, Mark Twain and his collaborator, Charles Dudley Warner, attack the greed, lust, and naïveté of their own time in a work that endures as one of America's most important satirical novels.

"Our best political novel . . . To understand America, read Mark Twain."—Gary Wills

ISBN 0-14-043920-X